"This is thoughtful crime-thriller reading at its level best, told in typically sparse Box prose and packed with characters who excel at pursuing their own agendas at everyone else's expense. A tour de force."
—*The Providence Journal*

"One of Box's best." —*Kirkus Reviews*

"Outstanding . . . Vividly etched characters and a realistic plot lift this outing, and the well-done Montana setting is a plus."
—*Publishers Weekly* (starred review)

"Will render readers utterly immobilized until they've closed the book."
—*Booklist* (starred review)

"Box is in top form here, gilding his reputation for finely crafted suspense novels of the New West—a place you wouldn't necessarily want to live but that is endlessly intriguing to read about."
—*BookPage* (starred review)

Paradise Valley

"Reaches the same level of frightening realism that made *The Highway* so terrifying." —Associated Press

"Excellent . . . Box keeps *Paradise Valley* taut, with twists that are as suspenseful as they are believable." —*The Washington Post*

"[Box has] crafted fascinating characters and put them in riveting, challenging circumstances that test their mettle and threaten their worlds."
—*The Durango Herald*

BY C. J. BOX

THE CODY HOYT/CASSIE DEWELL NOVELS

The Bitterroots

Paradise Valley

Badlands

The Highway

Back of Beyond

THE JOE PICKETT NOVELS

Shadows Reel

Cold Wind

Dark Sky

Nowhere to Run

Long Range

Below Zero

Wolf Pack

Blood Trail

The Disappeared

Free Fire

Vicious Circle

In Plain Sight

Off the Grid

Out of Range

Endangered

Trophy Hunt

Stone Cold

Winterkill

Breaking Point

Savage Run

Force of Nature

Open Season

THE STAND-ALONE NOVELS

Three Weeks to Say Goodbye

Blue Heaven

SHORT FICTION

Shots Fired: Stories from Joe Pickett Country

BACK OF BEYOND

&

THE BITTERROOTS

C. J. BOX

MINOTAUR BOOKS
NEW YORK

Published in the United States by Minotaur Books, an imprint of St. Martin's Publishing Group

BACK OF BEYOND. Copyright © 2011, 2018 by C. J. Box. THE BITTERROOTS. Copyright © 2019 by C. J. Box. All rights reserved. Printed in the United States of America. For information, address St. Martin's Publishing Group, 120 Broadway, New York, NY 10271.

www.minotaurbooks.com

The Library of Congress Cataloging-in-Publication Data is available upon request.

ISBN 978-1-250-87940-0 (trade paperback)

Our books may be purchased in bulk for promotional, educational, or business use. Please contact your local bookseller or the Macmillan Corporate and Premium Sales Department at 1-800-221-7945, extension 5442, or by email at MacmillanSpecialMarkets@macmillan.com.

First Edition: 2022

10 9 8 7 6 5 4 3 2 1

BACK OF BEYOND

For T. Jefferson Parker, Brian Wiprud, and Ken Wilson (The Gauntlet)
...and Laurie, always

An Introduction from the Author

The initial idea for what later became *Back of Beyond* and led to the first book in the Highway Quartet came from a late-night conversation around a campfire deep in the heart of the Yellowstone wilderness.

I was on a multiday horse-pack trip in the early fall along with eleven other participants. We'd left the trailhead the day before after being partnered up with our trail horses. The expedition rode north in a fairly tight nose-to-trail configuration. The outfitter in charge of the trip led the string, and his wrangler followed it up, trailing mules packed with gear. In between were twelve people, including my three fishing buddies. Our reason for the backcountry trip was to access magnificent fishing waters filled with Yellowstone cutthroat trout. But we were the only dedicated fishermen on the trip. I had no idea why the other eight riders were there. We'd all met for the first time just that morning.

Yellowstone is still very, very wild. There is no cell phone service, no internet access, and few ranger patrols. The farther we rode from the northernmost trailhead, the deeper we got into pure, elemental, amoral nature. We rode past bison, and saw the remains of an elk eaten by bears. There were no other people on the trail and not even the spoor of a jet trail in the big blue sky. As I rode, I tried to imagine who the other people were on the trip—and why they were there.

The next night, after a big outdoor dinner and a few drinks, I found myself alone with the outfitter at the fire. He told me about past trips, about characters and personalities he'd encountered, how everybody on these kinds of adventures was searching for something. He said it was his job to find out what that something was and if possible, satisfy it. He said he was a "master of group dynamics" and he had the ability to manipulate and mold high-end type A personalities, bickering couples, loners, and agitators into a kind of cohesive platoon. Usually.

Think about it: twelve people from different places, with different incomes and social circles, with different agendas and philosophies, all thrown together for a week in a place where there was no turning back.

But what if you can't figure out what they're after, I asked.

His answer was simple. *Then you've got trouble.*

I thought a lot about that as the days went by and personalities emerged. Scenarios came to mind.

Cody Hoyt, a troubled cop who was introduced in my standalone *Three Weeks to Say Goodbye*, emerged as a perfect protagonist. This book is his showcase.

As dark as this novel is, things got even darker when the Lizard King, a long-haul trucker who is a serial killer, slithered onto the scene in the next book, *The Highway*. Cody Hoyt paved the way for Cassie Dewell in *The Highway* (2013), *Badlands* (2015), and *Paradise Valley* (2017).

Back of Beyond takes place in the most remote region still in existence in the lower forty-eight states. It's a place where wolves and bears are on the top of the food chain. And I thought it was the perfect location for what would turn out to be, in effect, a classic closed-room mystery where someone is picking off the members of the expedition one by one.

Welcome to *Back of Beyond*. Try to keep your wits about you. You'll need them for the first book in the Highway Quartet.

Who trusted God was love indeed
And love Creation's final law
Tho' Nature, red in tooth and claw
With ravine, shriek'd against his creed

—Canto 56, Alfred Lord Tennyson's
In Memoriam A. H. H., 1850

Part One
Montana

1

The night before Cody Hoyt shot the county coroner, he was driving without a purpose in his county Ford Expedition as he often did these days. He was agitated and restless, chain-smoking cigarettes until his throat was raw and sore. He drove right by the rural bars he used to frequent, not going in. Then the call came from dispatch on his cell phone: hikers claimed they found a burned-out cabin in the Big Belt Mountains to the northeast with maybe a dead body inside.

Even though it was the end of June the weather was unseasonably cold and it had rained in the valley for three straight days. That evening, before the clouds finally lifted and the sun died, he'd seen a dusting of snow on the tops of the Big Belts to the north and the Elkhorn Mountains to the south. *Snow.*

"Patrol has been sent up there," Edna the dispatcher said. He liked Edna even though she'd decided she was his surrogate mother and gave him pies and casseroles and tried to fix him up with Helena divorcees. She said, "My list says you're the one on call tonight."

"Yeah," he said. Cody was a Lewis and Clark County Sheriff's Department investigator. Detectives were automatically called to investigate any "unattended death," meaning accidents, suicides, or in the rare instance, homicides.

"Because you have nothing else to do," she said, mock joking.

"Not a damned thing," he said, deadly serious.

"Are you at home?"

"Yeah," he lied. "Watching the game on TV. Just a second, let me grab something to write on." He knew if Edna wanted to she could fire up the tracking screen in the dispatch center and find the location of his vehicle out in the county because of the GPS unit mounted under the front bumper. Or she could have at one time, before he dismantled it the month before because he didn't want anyone knowing where he'd been going or that he spent his other nights driving, driving, driving.

He pulled to the side of the road into the rough parking area in front of the Gem State Bar, the tires popping on the wet gravel. A single mercury vapor light on a pole threw dark shadows across the parking area. Pools of standing water from the recent rain reflected the light and the few stars that had appeared between night thunderheads. There were five other parked vehicles in front of the bar, all pickups. His pen was somewhere in the ashtray, which was spilling over with butts. As he pulled it out he noted the plastic barrel of the pen was rough with burn marks.

"Okay," he said.

"The cabin is located past Vigilante Campground on Highway 280, eight miles up Trout Creek on County Road 124. The map shows it's in the Helena National Forest, but maybe there's a private place up there."

He lowered the phone and sat back and closed his eyes without writing anything down. Outside his driver's side window, two men wearing dirty jeans and hoodies and ball caps pushed their way out the door of the bar. He recognized them as sapphire miners. Sapphire mining was a small industry in the county, and there were scores of one- and two-man claims that had been worked for years and still produced. The miner in the gray hoodie was practically as wide as he was tall. The one in the yellow hoodie was gaunt and skeletal with eyes sunk deep in their sockets. They were laughing and shoving each other. Yellow Hoodie had a twelve-pack of Coors Light under his arm for the road and he'd no doubt leave a trail of empties all the way up into the Big Belts to his little one-man mine. They looked up and saw him parked but didn't straighten up or try to act sober. He was just a guy in a muddy SUV to them because the vehicle was unmarked. Even the plates didn't give him away because they were skip plates. If anyone ran a check on them, they'd come back to a fictitious address and company name.

"Cody?" Edna asked.

"I'm here."

"Did you get that?"

"Yeah."

"The complainants called from the York Bar. They agreed to stay there until they met the officer so they could guide him to where the cabin is. Officer Dougherty was dispatched to the scene and he is there with them now taking their statement. Should I ask them to stay until you get there?"

"Not necessary," he said, "I know the cabin. Tell Dougherty to proceed—I'll meet him there. What did they say about a body?"

"Not much really. They said they thought it was an old place by the look of it and they poked around inside a little. They said that they think there's a body there because of the smell and what looked like a human hand, but they didn't actually see the body. They said it was raining hard and getting dark and they just wanted to get out of there."

"Male or female body?"

"They don't know. They said the hand might have been a glove or the arm from a dummy because it didn't look real."

He nodded to himself. Fire turned human bodies into sexless grotesques. He'd been on the scene where the fire was so hot the dead muscles of the arms and legs cooked and roasted and contracted the body into a fighter's stance: arms curled against the chest and knees bent, like a boxer in the ring. And the smell, like charred pork. . . .

Outside in the parking lot, the two miners put the twelve-pack on the hood of a pickup and pulled out two cans and opened them. The spray from a can hit Fat Gray Hoodie in the face and he bellowed a laugh as he took the beer.

"Okay," Cody said to Edna.

He said, "Edna, call Larry. Tell him I need him."

Larry Olson, the only other detective in the five-man Criminal Investigations Division whom Cody thought was worth a damn. Olson was short, solid, and shaved bald; a flesh-colored fire hydrant who entered a room like a quiet exclamation point. Larry Olson was a Montana legend. He'd solved crimes by careful observation and exhaustive investigation. He wore suspects down. He wore his fellow detectives down. When an unsolved crime went on too long anywhere in the state, the call went out to "borrow" Larry Olson. The word was the only reason he stayed in Helena instead of going state or federal was that he wanted to be there for his three boys who lived with their mother in town.

Edna said, "Larry's not on call tonight."

She waited for him to acknowledge, but he didn't.

Finally, she said, "Cody?"

He held the phone out away from him at arm's length and made a gargling sound in his throat that resembled static. He said, "I'm losing the signal right now. Call Larry. I'll call back when I get a better signal," and closed the phone and dropped it to the seat. Overwhelmed with a wave of nausea and needing air, he pushed open the door and stepped outside, his boots splashing in a deep puddle.

"Good one," Skinny Yellow Hoodie said, laughing. "Right in the hole."

Cody ignored them as he bent forward, grasping his knees with his hands. He breathed in the moist mountain air, filling his lungs with it. Mixing it with the smoke. His eyes watered and he stood and wiped at them. Cold water poured in over the top of his low boots, filling his socks. He wished he'd worn his cowboy boots instead.

"You okay?" Yellow Hoodie asked.

"Fine."

"Want another beer? You could probably use one now."

"No," he said. They assumed he'd been drinking. Or, he thought, they recognized him from when he haunted the bars.

"This fucking rain, eh? Day after day. My dad said never curse the rain in Montana, and I never have. But this is motherfucking *crazy*. El Niño or some such thing. I heard the weatherman call it 'The summer without a summer.' "

Cody grunted.

"Want a hit?" Fat Gray Hoodie asked in a voice indicating he was holding his breath in, and Cody realized the man was holding a joint between his fingers. Cody's face must have cracked the miner up because he coughed and expelled the marijuana smoke in a cloud.

"Jesus Christ," the skinny miner said to Cody. "Don't mind him."

"Just being friendly," the second miner said, bringing the joint back up to his mouth.

Cody Hoyt was thirty-eight years old but often mistaken for being in his late forties. He had unkempt sandy hair, a square jaw, high cheekbones, a broken nose, brown eyes flecked with either gold or red depending on the circumstances and often described as either "mean" or "dead," and a mouth that twisted naturally into a cop smirk even when he didn't want it to. He wore jeans, boots, and a loose long-sleeved fishing shirt. Detectives didn't wear uniforms and dressed to blend into the community. He reached down and pulled the hem of the shirt up so they could see the seven-point gold sheriff's department badge on his belt.

"I got a card for this," the smoking miner said quickly, nodding to the joint.

Practically every sapphire miner in the county had a card signed by a doctor for medical marijuana use, Cody had found. And many of them grew plants in quantities and potency well beyond simple home use. It wasn't a coincidence that the miners used most of the same instruments—scales, small tools, hundreds of small Ziploc bags—dope merchants used.

Cody raised his .40 Sig Sauer in a shooter's grip.

"Really," Fat Gray Hoodie said, stepping back and dropping the joint, which extinguished with a hiss between his feet in the mud, "really, I got a card. I'll show you. Shit, I know I'm not supposed to smoke in a public place, but damn, my back started hurting. . . ."

"Give me the rest of the beer," Cody said.

Both miners froze, then shot glances at each other.

"You want the beer? You can have it," Yellow Hoodie said. "Why the hell you want my beer? What kind of cop wants my fucking *beer*?"

"I don't," Cody said with a twisted smile. He holstered his weapon and climbed back into his Ford. He roared away, thinking he wanted that beer so goddamned bad right now he would have killed them both for it.

He'd heard a couple of maxims from Larry after they'd danced around each other for three months. Larry had stopped by his desk one afternoon when no one else was in the office, paused, leaned over until his mouth was an inch from Cody's ear, and said:

"I know you were a hotshot detective in Colorado and I also know your rep as a drunk and a screwup. I've heard about some of the things you used to do when you grew up here, and your crazy homicidal white-trash family. I've personally arrested two of your uncles and I sent one to Deer Lodge prison. I was shocked as hell when you moved back here, and even more shocked when the sheriff hired you on. I can only speculate that you've got something on him so big and nasty he didn't have a choice."

Cody said nothing, but locked in Larry with his best cop deadeye and refused to blink.

Said Larry, "If so, good for you. More power to you, brother. But since we have to work together, I called a couple of your old partners in Denver. They said you were crazy, violent, and unpredictable. They said you were a loose cannon and you were all over the place like a fart on a hot skillet. But they also said you were a fucking fantastic cop and you went at every case like a bulldog on steroids who wouldn't let go. That you nailed a child-porn king and a sitting Federal District judge in one fell swoop. But they said they didn't really want to ever work with you again because they wanted to keep their jobs and not spend half their fucking time defending themselves and you to Internal Affairs and the mayor's office.

"Me," Larry said, "I'll give you the benefit of the doubt. But don't ever screw me, and don't ever put me in a position I don't want to be in. Just do the job and show me what you've got, and you'll find out you can trust me. But you need to *earn* my trust because you brought a lot of baggage back with you to Montana."

Cody said nothing.

Larry continued, "There are four things you need to know about this place. One, we only get a homicide about once a year. But that's not good, it's bad. It's bad because most of these jamokes around here," he nodded toward the door to indicate the rest of the sheriff's department as well as the municipal police department across the hall, "never get enough experience to work a murder investigation smoothly. If the homicide is hinky and not a straightforward domestic or bar brawl, it's always the first time for most of 'em. They've grown up watching *CSI* and cop shows and they turn into actors they've seen on the screen instead of remembering their training.

"Second, the most important topic of every day is where to go to lunch. You'll find yourself discussing that particular dilemma more than anything else.

"Third, bad things always happen on a Friday, almost always after you're off duty. So if you're off duty but on call, you better not hit the bottle like I've heard you do.

"Fourth, and most important, take every possible fucking opportunity you can to eat and take a shit, because this county is thirty-five hundred square miles, a third of it roadless."

With that, Larry Olson stormed out of the room.

Cody thought of the third and fourth maxims as he drove up into the mountains. The rain had started again, and heavy-bellied drops smacked against the windshield as if they were committing suicide. The two-lane highway was dark and slick. Canyon Ferry Lake—so named because they'd built a dam to hold back the Missouri and submerge the historic river crossing—simmered like a stew on slow boil because of the rain. The dark wooded canyon wall rose to his left. He realized he was hungry because he hadn't had dinner. His vague plan had been to go to York and have a burger, but a burger without a beer seemed an impossible mission.

And he could use a toilet as well. There were outhouses at Two Camps Vista and another at Devil's Elbow. He hated outhouses because he could never not look down into the pit—sometimes using his flashlight—to see what was floating around down there. It reminded him of too many things.

The possible body in the cabin beyond Vigilante Campground made Cody's heart pound and his hands go cold on the steering wheel. His mind raced and scenarios formed. He immediately assumed the worst.

He dug out his cell phone and called Edna at dispatch.

"Is Larry coming?" he asked.

"He's not happy about it."

"I don't blame him."

"Quit pretending you're losing your cell phone signal when you aren't."

He sighed. "Okay."

After a beat, she said, "Should I call the Scooter?"

The county coroner, Sceeter Kerley, enjoyed his job a little too much and was considered a pain in the ass to work with ever since he found out he was the only elected official with the authority to arrest the sheriff. Plus, elections were five months away and he wanted to keep a high profile in the local press. Nothing could be done with a body until the coroner arrived. He owned all bodies in Lewis and Clark County and they couldn't be touched or removed without his authority.

"Naw, I'll call him if we have to," Cody said. "I'll confirm it's a body first. The hikers could have seen anything. Lots of things look like hands."

"And I should ignore the call I just got from a drunken miner saying a sheriff's department employee tried to steal his beer outside a bar?"

"Yeah, you should ignore that," Cody said.

He drove just under control, taking the switchbacks hard, crossing the faded double center line with each turn. There wasn't a light bar on the Ford so he'd toggled on the switch that turned his headlights into strobes that flashed psychedelically on the wet canyon walls and pine trees. And froze two cow elk in their progress across the highway.

Cody cursed and swerved to the left, his tires dropping off the pavement into the muddy ditch, but he wasn't fast enough. One of the elk inexplicably bounded in front of him and turned her head toward him and their eyes locked a split second before he hit her solidly in the shoulder with the right front fender of the truck. The impact made the Ford fishtail. If it weren't for the front right tire still gripping the pavement, he would have hurtled left into the bank of trees. He jerked the wheel and the Ford bounced up out of the ditch.

He stopped in the middle of the highway, breathing hard, knowing if his brakes hadn't bitten he would have gone straight off the edge of the mountain into Canyon Ferry Lake. Rain drummed on the roof. A single headlight pointed out into the dark, lighting only the rain that slashed through the beam. He checked his side mirrors. In the red glow of his taillights he could see the other elk bound up the canyon wall but the one he'd hit was down, its legs churning, head writhing.

"Shit!"

His boot eased off the brake and he began to roll forward again, making sure he could still go forward. The Ford went a few feet before it stopped again. He needed to assess the damage. And he couldn't leave her suffering like that.

Chanting *"Shit-shit-shit-shit-shit . . ."* he got out and walked back along the wet asphalt in the rain and drew his Sig Sauer and shot her in the head. Her thrashing went manic until it stopped altogether. He couldn't shed the afterimage of her eyes boring into him before he hit her, even when she closed them now. It took five minutes to pull her off the roadway. She was heavy, wet, and smelled of musk and hot blood.

He took a quick look at his bumper. His right headlight was out and thatches of elk hair were caught in the grille. There was a six-inch gap between the frame and the hood. He could smell the sharp odor of burning hair and meat on the hot surfaces of the motor. He had a couple of thousand dollars in damage and years of jokes from the county maintenance shop guys and fellow cops ahead of him. But the Ford still ran.

"Shit-shit-shit-shit-shit . . ."

For his next trick, he climbed into the cab of the Ford to locate a dead body in a burned-out cabin.

"Shit-shit-shit-shit-shit . . ."

A body that, in all probability, belonged to someone he knew and trusted and admired and who had kept him tethered to normalcy the past few months by a single fraying thread. And he could feel the thread unraveling.

2

The rain had turned to slush by the time Cody Hoyt drove through Vigilante Campground and continued up the sloppy road along Trout Creek. The patrol officer ahead of him was easy to follow because of the deep fresh troughs in the chocolate one-track. His single headlight seemed to light up and suspend the cold viscous rain in midair.

He could never enter the campground—which the U.S. Forest Service contracted with the L&C Sheriff's Department to patrol—without remembering the keggers he used to attend there when he was growing up in junior and senior high. That's when it started, he knew. When he learned that when he drank he could feel like a superman. His muscles and attitude swelled and his reticence and common sense stepped aside. He recalled a fight with baseball bats, remembered the hollow sickening sound his twenty-eight-inch maple bat made when it connected with Trevor McCamber's forehead. Remembered the creamy white belly and thighs of Jenny Thompson under the blue-green glow of his dashboard lights . . . before that belly swelled with his son and he married Jenny in a drunken and hasty ceremony at a ranch outside of town. His best men had been Jack McGuane and Brian Winters, fellow seniors and best friends at Helena High. Brian thought the wedding was hilarious. Jack tried to pretend it wasn't.

Jack's parents spent the ceremony shaking their heads and looking toward the road to see if Cody's father and uncle Jeter would show. They didn't.

After graduation from high school, Cody and Jenny moved from place to place until finally he was back in Montana without her or his boy.

Cody Hoyt drove under the towering knotty pine archway and over an ancient wooden bridge barely nosing above the foam and fury of Trout Creek filled with runoff. Around a wooded corner was the cabin, and suddenly there were lights in the pure darkness: the headlights of a patrol cruiser trained on the charred remains of the structure, and a single round Cyclopean eye of a departmental Maglite swinging his way and blinding him.

This was the crime scene, all right.

Cody pulled up next to the patrol SUV. Inside the next vehicle, illuminated by the interior lighting, were two citizens. A man in his forties and a woman who looked to be in her early twenties huddled in the backseat. They looked cold and tired, he thought. The man needed a shave. The woman needed a hot shower. He nodded at them through two sets of windows and they nodded back.

The patrol officer, Ryan Dougherty, appeared at his driver's window, and tapped on the glass with the flashlight. In the process of doing it, he blinded Cody again.

Cody powered down the window, and said, "Would you *quit* shining that fucking thing into my eyes?"

"Oh, sorry." The patrol officer, newer to the department than Cody, was blond and baby-faced with a trimmed bristly mustache that said, *Here comes a cop!* and eyes that had not seen enough. In fact, Cody thought, Dougherty looked flushed, despite the weather.

"What happened to your front end?" Dougherty asked.

"Hit an elk," Cody said.

"On the way up?"

"Yeah."

"Bull or cow?"

Cody hesitated. "Cow."

Cody knew what Dougherty would say next. "Got a cow permit?" he said, grinning.

"Ha ha," Cody said, deadpan.

"I bet you'll be hearing that one a lot."

"I bet I will," Cody said, nodding toward the patrol vehicle. "Those two the hikers who found the cabin?"

"Yeah. I met them at the York Bar and they showed me the way up here. Here, I got their names. . . ." Dougherty dug inside his raincoat for the notebook in his breast pocket. He was in uniform: brown shirt, tan pockets, and epaulets. The reason the dopers called them "L&C County Fascists."

"I don't need their names," Cody said. "Unless you think they did it."

"Oh, no. Not at all."

"Did they tromp all over the crime scene?"

"Just a little," Dougherty said. "It's hard to tell what they touched."

Cody said, "Why don't you ask them?"

"I can do that."

"Good. Put one of them in this vehicle and interview them separately. Walk them through their movements when they first saw the cabin. Find out which direction they came down, and what they did inside. Find out what they touched and if they took anything. It's amazing how many times citizens take souvenirs from a crime scene. If something sounds wrong or their stories don't match, come get me."

"Yes, sir," Dougherty said. The flush was gone from his cheeks. Cody could tell he was beating himself up for taking their story at face value.

"I'm gonna go take a look," Cody said.

"It's wetter than hell," Dougherty said. "The ash from the fire makes it all . . . soupy."

Cody glared at him. "Have *you* been in the crime scene?"

Dougherty looked away for a second, and when he turned his head back he said, "A little."

Cody's voice was ice. "How fucking little?"

"Enough to confirm there's a body. A big fat one."

Cody took a deep breath of wet air.

"You aren't gonna write me up, are you?" Dougherty asked. "I was thinking, Jesus, what if the person is still alive?"

"Don't lie." He repeated a sheriff's department bromide: "You lie, you die, Dougherty. You wanted to see a burned-up dead body. Everybody wants to see a dead body until they see one. Have you had your fill?"

"Christ, yes," Dougherty said, shaking his head. "I'll be seeing that *thing* in my dreams."

"Step aside so I can get my rain gear," Cody said.

It began to rain harder.

His foul weather gear was in a heavy plastic box in the back of his SUV and there was no way to reach it from the inside, so he grabbed his Colorado Rockies baseball cap, jammed it on, and opened the door. The cold rain stung when it hit his bare face and hands. He could remember only one other time when he got his rain gear out, the previous spring when he was called to a ranch because the foreman thought he saw Middle Eastern terrorists photographing a missile silo. Turned out the photographers were farmers from India on an agricultural mission sponsored by the State of Montana and their interest was wheat, not missile silos. But it rained so rarely in Montana, Cody thought, that packing rain gear was almost silly. He didn't know a single person who owned an umbrella, for instance.

He leaned into the back of the Expedition while he wrestled with the box. It was jammed against the backseat and he had to pull it over the top of the rest of his gear—his long-gun case, large evidence box, canvas duffel packed with two armored vests, a survival crate the sheriff insisted they carry with them filled with a sleeping bag, candles, food, and water. While he threw the boxes around and got the one with his crime-scene clothing, he could feel the rain soaking through the back of his shirt and jeans. His boots were already wet from the puddle in the parking lot.

Even though it was getting more pointless by the second, he pulled on rain pants and slipped Tyvek booties over his wet boots. Instead of a raincoat he pulled on a full-length Australian oilcloth duster. Rain immediately beaded on the fabric.

His cell phone burred and he dug it out and saw the call was from his son Justin. Justin was an anomaly to Cody—miraculously, the only genuinely good person he knew. Justin was kind, selfless, and admirable. Plus he was tall and nice-looking and had a sweet temperament. Cody had no idea how he could have spawned such a child, given his own foibles and his long lineage of white-trash relatives. Every time Cody saw his son he looked for signs of his own obsessions and bad traits and had yet to see them. Justin was a fucking miracle at seventeen years old, Cody thought.

"Hey," Cody said. "This is bad timing and my signal's weak."

"Hi, Dad. Sorry, but I wanted to ask you something."

"I'm on a crime scene," Cody said. "Can I call you back later?"

"Yeah, but do it quick. I'm gonna be gone for a while."

"Gone where?"

"Didn't Mom tell you?"

"I haven't talked to her."

"Oh."

"Look, Justin, this is a really bad time."

"You said that," his son said, not masking his disappointment well. "I wanted to ask you if I could borrow—"

"You can borrow anything you want of mine," Cody said. "Don't worry about it. I've got to go. Later."

He snapped the phone shut and crammed it in his pocket, feeling guilty and angry at himself for cutting off Justin.

———

Cody grabbed his digital camera and light setup and his favorite flashlight, a Maglite with an extension that held six batteries and could be swung like a heavy lead pipe—with the same results. It was better than that twenty-eight-inch maple bat. The long flashlights had been banned from most police departments, which Cody saw as a further sign of official wimpification. He turned toward the burned-up cabin.

As Dougherty escorted the female hiker into Cody's SUV, he said, "Look at you. You look like a gunfighter in that coat. I need to get me one of those. *Cool.*"

Cody sighed.

As he approached the cabin he tried to clear his mind of everything in it, including Justin's call, to make it a fresh whiteboard. He wanted to view the scene with absolute open-minded clarity. He knew this was his only chance to investigate the scene without anyone around. If there was a body, the place would be swarming with people within the hour. Skeeter would be there with his deputy coroner and perhaps a reporter from the Helena *Independent Record.* Skeeter would feign innocence as to why the reporter was there, but everybody would know he called her before he rolled. There might even be a team from one of two local television stations, although he knew they operated lean going into the weekends. And Sheriff Tub Tubman, also up for reelection, would no doubt arrive in his Suburban with Undersheriff Cliff Bodean just a few steps behind him. Mike Sanders, the other detective on call, might surprise him with his presence because the sheriff was there, no doubt bitching about the fact no one had called him. The forensics unit shared by the Helena PD would be present, as would the county evidence tech. So until the scene became chaotic, this was his opportunity to see it fresh. He couldn't do anything about the fact that the hikers had reported seeing a hand, but he tried to ignore that, also. He wanted to see the hand for himself as if he'd stumbled upon it. If there was a hand.

If there was a body.

Because if there was a body and it belonged to whom he thought and if the evidence pointed to a homicide, he'd personally go after who did it like a rabid dog until he took that person down. And he wasn't thinking Deer Lodge, Montana, where the state penitentiary was located. He was thinking Dirt Nap, Montana. Which was just about anywhere he wanted it to be.

Cody opened the beam on his Maglite as he approached on a flagstone footpath. He moved slowly, taking in not only the cabin itself but anything of note on the path, which was the only walkway to the place from a gravel parking area. Looking for anything out of place; a wrapper, a cigarette butt, a spent cartridge. He saw nothing unusual.

The cabin was originally built in the 1920s on the edge of a meadow that sloped down to Trout Creek. The twenty acres of wooded land that went with it was surrounded on three sides by the Helena National Forest. An agreement had been granted years before to the Forest Service for a public easement for access to the trails in the Big Belts. That's how the hikers stumbled on the scene.

The cabin was built of logs and had a deck overlooking the meadow in back and a covered porch in front. Tall spruce trees bordered it on three sides. Although it had fallen into disrepair in the 1970s, the structure had been expensively renovated and restored. At least before half of it burned down, that is.

The cabin was, quite simply, half the size it should have been. The left side was burned to the ground except for a black woodstove and chimney that leaned dangerously toward the creek. The right side was perfectly intact. He looked at the right side first, where the bedrooms and kitchen were. Rainwater coursed down bronze-colored logs, and there were lace curtains in the windows. A plaque near the front door read LEAVE YOUR TROUBLES OUTSIDE BEFORE ENTERING. He smiled bitterly at that.

He slowly circled the outside of the cabin, flashlight down, walking a perimeter he would later flag with yellow plastic CRIME SCENE tape to keep the press and public out. The ground was soaked and muddy. There was standing water in every depression. The grass was long and hadn't been mowed for a while. Long blades of it bent down as if depressed, heavy droplets on every point. He looked for footprints wherever the grass gave way to dirt. He saw none except for two sets of fresh hiking boot impressions. He shot photos of the footprints and checked to see if they were good shots on the display screen on the back of his camera. He knew where they came from, and glanced back toward the parking area. Dougherty had moved from interviewing the male in his Ford to the department vehicle where the female hiker had been asked to stay.

Then he carefully approached the burned-out part of the cabin, and twisted the lens of his Maglite to narrow and brighten his field of view.

The floor of the burned rooms consisted of black wet tarlike sludge; ash mixed with rainwater. It looked like wet black cement. Fallen timbers and collapsed framing stuck out from the soup. As did the woodstove, a charred black metal desk with a squared-off black box on top of it, and the metal frames of an easy chair, fold-out couch, and gun safe.

It all smelled of charcoal, smoke, rain, and damp. And something else: barbecued pork.

A tangle of wooden beams and wall joints had fallen on the metal skeleton of the couch. But protruding from the tangle was a swelled and waxy-looking arm. On the end of the arm was an outstretched human hand, the fingers splayed out as if to say *Stop!*, the hand so bloated he could barely see the glint of a gold wedding band on the third finger. The skin of the forearm looked crispy and black, like the burn on the side of a roasted marshmallow. Cody further narrowed the beam on the flashlight to a five-inch spot to peer further inside the load of burned wood. A naked thigh, the skin burned and split to reveal neon orange fat like a pig or a goose.

Cody closed his eyes and reached up and took his cap off and let the rain hit him in the face.

Larry Olson arrived a half hour later. By then, Cody had thoroughly photographed the scene. He'd placed plastic numbered tents near the body, the stove, the desk, and the couch. He'd set up his remote flashes on mounts that lit it up like daylight. The photos he saw on his display were sharp, focused, and thorough. He tried not to think about what he was shooting or who the body had belonged to. He shut off his mind from speculation, and made sure every possible angle and object was preserved digitally. He never once walked into the burned-out rooms, but did all of his shooting from outside. As he did, he found other objects of interest: a metal briefcase swimming in the black soup, the frame of a Winchester rifle with the stock and forestock burned off, a blackened bottle shape he recognized with such intimacy and disappointment that it was as if someone had punched him in the throat.

He looked up as Larry's flashlight bobbed along the flagstone path and eventually raised to take him in.

Larry said, "Nice raincoat. You headed to the OK Corral later tonight? You and the Earp brothers and Doc Holliday?"

"Yeah. I've got issues with Ike Clanton, that bastard."

Larry actually laughed. "Suicide? Tell me it's a suicide."

"I'm not going to tell you anything," Cody said. "I'm going to go back to my truck and burn one. I'll stay out of your way. Then I'm going to come back and listen to your initial theory. I've looked over the scene and I've got more than enough shots of it. And I've got a theory of my own, but I don't want to steer you one way or the other."

Because it was dark, Cody couldn't tell what Larry was thinking.

"Have you been in the unburned section?" Larry asked.

"Not yet."

"Good. Let's do that together."

"All right."

"Bad fucking night for this," Larry said. "You must really hate me to call me out on a night like this."

"I don't hate you, Larry. I want your opinion."

"Have you called the coroner?"

"Not yet."

"Jesus, Cody. You should have called him already."

Cody shrugged.

"I'll look things over and give you my opinion as long as you call Skeeter and the sheriff and we do this thing properly. Remember what I said. You remember, don't you?"

"Yeah, I do."

"A deal's a deal."

Cody nodded. He said, "Take as much time as you need. The scene is yours. I've got great photos, so you don't need to worry about that. Just look it over, tell me what you think. And I'll make the calls I need to."

Larry reached up and squeegeed the beads of rain off his shaved head with his hand. "I should have brought a hat."

"You can have mine," Cody said, handing him his cap as he passed. It was sodden and heavy with rain.

"Keep it," Larry said. Then: "Hey, what did you do to your unit? You've only got one headlight."

"Hit an elk on the way up."

"Yeah, I saw it on the side of the road. You must have been in a hell of a hurry."

Cody left Larry and walked toward his Ford. He looked up at the dark sky, hoping for an opening in the rain clouds. Nope.

"Hey, Cody," Larry called.

"What?"

"You got a cow permit?"

His cell signal had faded further, so Cody shooed Dougherty and the hiker out of his Ford. As Dougherty climbed out, Cody said, "Any discrepancies in their stories?"

"No, sir."

"Good work. Keep them here for a while in case we have more questions, then take them back to the York Bar or wherever they're headed. Just make sure we've got contact details on them if we need to get in touch later."

The patrol officer patted his notebook. "I've got all that."

"Okay then," Cody said.

Dougherty paused. "So you aren't going to write me up?"

"Go. Just go. But remember, never shut off an area of inquiry in any situation. Never assume anything. Always assume everybody is guilty as hell but act like they're innocent to their face. Remember that. Everybody is guilty of something, every single one of 'em. It may not be this," he said, chinning toward the cabin. "But it's something. No one is clean and pure and perfect."

Dougherty didn't say *Yes, sir.* He just stood there.

"What?" Cody said.

"I hope I never get like you," Dougherty said, and went back to his truck.

Cody said to no one in particular, "I hope you don't, either."

It was warm and dry in his Ford. The windows steamed on the inside of the cab due to his wet clothing. He called Edna on the radio. While he talked to her he watched Larry Olson retrace his own steps around the cabin, shooting his flashlight about, moving slow.

"Edna, please alert Skeeter and Tubby—"

"You mean Sheriff Tubman."

"Of course," Cody said, glad she pointed that out since there were plenty of locals who monitored the police band. "Sheriff Tubman."

"What should I tell them?" Edna asked.

"We've got a body," he said, signing off.

He gave Larry plenty of time. Dougherty and the hikers sat in Dougherty's vehicle waiting for the word to be given for clearance to leave. As Cody waited for Larry to finish up, he glanced into the backseat. The male hiker had left his daypack, the idiot. Cody thought he may need to call Dougherty, tell him to bring the guy over to get his property.

Before he reached for the radio, he slung the pack up to the front seat and unzipped it. He kept the interior light off and the pack below the window so the deputy or hikers couldn't see what he was doing. The contents smelled of woodsmoke. He felt sorry for the hikers, having to camp night after night in the rain. How fun could that be? Plus, the female wasn't exactly a looker with her matted hair, hairy legs and underarms (he'd noticed), and no makeup. A typical Missoula or Bozeman bark beetle type.

The pack was heavy and he rooted through the balled-up damp clothing. He found a Ziploc bag with residue of marijuana. *See*, he thought to himself, *everybody is guilty*. He wondered if they'd purchased it from a sapphire miner. He put it back, and dug further, thinking maybe he'd find matches and an accelerant and close the case like a supercop. Instead, he closed his fingers around the loving and familiar and understanding neck of a full bottle of Jim Beam.

He whispered, "Oh, no."

Then: *I've got to make another call.*

Then: *To whom? Especially now.*

Then: *This is not happenstance. This is fate. And Fate says, "You need to drink this. It's why I left it for you to find. You'll need it to get through this."*

Before he made the decision he knew he'd make, he looked up and saw Larry walking toward his Ford. And he shoved the bottle back into the daypack and pushed it aside.

"Well?" Cody asked, opening the door and sliding outside. His boots hit the mud with two *squish-plops*.

Larry's shaved head beaded with rain and a rivulet ran down between his eyebrow and pooled on his upper lip. "I'm thinking accidental death with an outside chance of suicide, so I'm happy."

Cody grunted. They'd discussed it before, how at every death scene they hoped like hell it was a natural or an accidental or a suicide, that they'd be done with it in a matter of hours after they turned it over to the coroner.

"Show me," Cody said, "show me what led to your thinking suicide."

"Which means you're not so sure," Larry said.

"Which means nothing at all."

"Is suicide on your mind?"

"Constantly."

"You know what I mean. So, did you call Skeeter?"

Cody sighed, "Yeah. But given the distance and the rain, I figure we've got an hour before he gets here."

"Sheriff coming?"

"Don't know."

The two of them slogged down the flagstone path toward the scene, when Larry suddenly stopped. "Hey," he said, "An hour for *what*?"

"To come to a consensus," Cody said, widening the beam on his light to encompass the burned half of the cabin. "Okay, walk me through it."

Larry pinched down the beam of his Mag to use as a pointer within the wide pool of light. He started with the blackened woodstove.

"First thing I noticed," Larry said, "is the door to the stove is open. I don't see that happening after the fire started, do you? The handle locks down from the top, so a falling beam wouldn't hit it and knock it open. So I conclude it was open before the fire started. So what likely happened was our victim had a fire going—it's sure as hell cold enough this summer—and left the door open for some reason. The logs inside shifted or sparks flew out or something. Thus starting the blaze."

Cody said, "Go on."

"It's speculation until the arson team comes and looks things over, of course," Larry said while he slowly moved the beam of his light from the open door of the stove to the black muck that was the former hardwood floor, "but it looks like the fire started here a few feet from the open door and spread outward. The floorboards are completely gone right here, burned completely through to ash."

He danced his light around the edges of the structure, where the floor butted up against the concrete foundation. "See, there's still some floor left up against the foundation. So I'm thinking the fire started in the middle of the room and took off from there in all directions. Probably caught some curtains or the walls and climbed up to the ceiling, and then spread across the inside top of the ceiling. With fire burning the floor and all four walls and the ceiling, it was like an incinerator in the room. A fire like that sucks all the oxygen out, so our vic could have died from smoke inhalation before he barbecued—but that's for the autopsy guys in Missoula to tell us. My guess from working a few of these fire cases is he was dead before he burned, and way dead before the roof came down on him."

"Okay," Cody said, "why'd the victim leave the stove door open and crash on the couch?"

"The question at hand," Larry said, playing it like a game, "the question we must answer in order to declare it a suicide and go home and climb into our dry beds with our hot mamas."

Cody snorted. He had no hot mama at home, and neither did Larry.

Larry stepped carefully over the exposed foundation and sank ankle deep into the black muck, cursing. He shuffled toward the couch frame and the body, the beam of his flashlight bouncing all over until it settled on a black stalk jutting up from the surface a few feet from the couch.

"You got pictures of this, right?" Larry asked, hesitating before he reached out.

"Yeah."

"Okay then," he said, leaning forward and grasping the black stalk and pulling it free. He held the bottle by the neck. "Here's our answer. Judging by the shape of it, I'd guess Wild Turkey. One hundred proof."

Cody concurred. He knew the bottle, even though the fire had puckered in the sides of it.

Said Larry, "No way to tell if it was empty, half full, or full. If there was any left when the fire burned this hot it would have boiled anything inside into vapor, which is a sad loss of pretty good bourbon. But it appears there wasn't a cap on it. Does Wild Turkey have a metal screw cap?"

"Nope," Cody said. "It has a cork plug kind of thing."

"Hmmm, then we'll have to get it analyzed to see if there's any cork or plastic residue inside the neck of the bottle. But I'd guess our victim opened this baby up and didn't cap it. Which means serious drinking to me. I mean, when a guy doesn't bother to put the cap back on between drinks, he's on a good toot. Right, Cody?"

Cody grunted with recognition.

"So the way I see it," Larry said, moving the flashlight to the blackened arm and hand sticking out from the couch and debris, "is our victim was feeding the fire and getting pounded at the same time. Except maybe toward the end of the toot he didn't latch the handle on the stove completely. He staggered back to the couch with his bottle of Wild Turkey and had another drink and likely fell asleep. When the logs in the stove shifted they pushed open the door.

"Of course," Larry said, raising his flashlight to illuminate his face so Cody could see Larry's index finger posing pensively alongside his cheek, "first impressions can be wrong, especially in these conditions, and I'm never one to jump to conclusions no matter how much I want to will them to be what I want them to be. For starters, this isn't an optimal crime scene. In fact, it's a fucking horrible crime scene, which is why I don't want it to be anything other than a suicide. The rain changes everything, as we know. There's both bad and good aspects of this scene because of this goddamned weather."

Cody could tell Larry was at his best and wanted to be prompted.

"Like what?" Cody said.

"Well, the bad aspects are legion. It's been two or three days since the fire occurred, for one, so the scene isn't fresh. Rainwater has contaminated it if we try and look for trace evidence of any kind. Animals have been in here."

"They have?" Cody said, genuinely surprised he'd missed it.

Larry squatted and trained his beam so it shone from a lower angle into the tangle of debris around the body, illuminating a swatch of dark red striped with white. Bone white: ribs.

"Yeah," Larry said. "A badger or something got in here and fed through the meat to the bone. So that's just gross."

He stood, and said, "Continuing, the slop of ash and water within this foundation is wet enough not to retain any prints or tracks. So we can't tell if anyone besides us and the hikers were in here. Not that it makes that much difference, since dead is dead. But if there was someone else here with the victim we have no evidence of that. No empty glasses, or cigarette butts, or anything like that. If there were tire tracks out in the parking area or footprints in the dirt they're gone. We've only got what we've got. And if anything was left in this part of the cabin before the place burned down it's literally in the soup now.

"If an accelerant was used as part of a suicide I doubt there would be any trace of it left. Of course, hundred-proof whiskey might have had the same effect."

Cody nodded.

"But there's some good things," Larry said.

"Which are?"

Larry shined his light on the unburned half of the cabin. "The rain put the fire out before it took the whole place down. We might find something in there. That's where the kitchen and dining room are, and a bedroom. There's a lot of smoke damage, but who knows? We might find something.

"And the rain and cold might work a little in our favor," he said. "If the rain hadn't come no doubt the body would have been subject to the wick effect, because our victim was big and had plenty of fuel."

The wick effect was when fat smoldered—sometimes for days—and rendered the carcass a mass of black gelatinous goo.

"So because we have a great deal of the body left, the autopsy boys might be able to determine cause of death."

Cody centered his light on the frame of a metal desk and the black melted hulk on top of it. "We might even be able to recover something from the hard drive of the computer, I just don't know. I don't know if data on a hard drive can survive that kind of heat and this damned rain. But we might be able to recover something, if it's even worth trying."

Larry said, "And there you have it, folks," bowing and sweeping his hand toward the body like a performer done with his act, "an accidental death in a remote mountain cabin."

Cody said nothing. The rain drummed.

"What?" Larry asked, finally. "Are you thinking something else?"

"Let's take a look inside the rest of the cabin," Cody said. "Let me grab my gear."

"You're thinking something else," Larry said, his disappointment palpable.

All the walls were black with smoke, but the kitchen was neat and uncluttered. The table was cleared except for salt and pepper shakers designed to look like rising trout. It felt good to get out of the rain.

There were no dishes in the sink. There were unopened packages of meat and vegetables still in the plastic bags from the store in the refrigerator.

"Looks like he'd just been shopping," Larry said. "There's no old stuff in here at all, like maybe he'd been gone and just came back with groceries. And there's plenty here—two big steaks, some potatoes, salad in a bag. Like he was expecting someone or maybe just eating for two. I bet these steaks are still okay, considering how cold it's been."

Cody opened the dishwasher, hoping there would be dirty glasses or dishes inside.

"Shit," Cody said. "He ran the dishwasher before the place burned down, so we won't pull any prints from the glasses or plates."

"He was a clean drunk," Larry said, rooting through cupboards. "I'll leave all these doors open so you can shoot 'em if you want. It might be better in the daylight, though."

Cody checked under the sink. Cleaning supplies, garbage bags, the usual. He shined his flashlight into the garbage can, which was lined with white plastic. Garbage cans often held good stuff, he knew.

There were a few items inside, and he took the can out and emptied it on the table. Crumpled paper Dixie drinking cups, wadded-up Kleenex, shreds of cellophane, and the missing cork cap to the Wild Turkey bottle. Cody photographed the contents.

Larry saw the cap in the flash of the camera and whistled. "So we can assume he was on a bender after all."

Cody pushed the cellophane strips around with the tip of his pen.

"What are they?" Larry asked.

"Cigar wrappers, I think."

"So maybe he was smoking a cigar as well," Larry said. "But I still think it was the open stove."

Cody bagged the cellophane and the Dixie cups and the bottle cap and marked them with evidence numbers.

"What's with that?" Larry asked, observing.

"You never know," Cody said. "Maybe a print can be pulled."

Larry nodded his head but eyed Cody with suspicion.

"Got something here," Larry called from the bedroom.

Cody entered. Because the door had been closed, there was little smoke seepage or damage. The room was pristine compared to the kitchen; i.e., white walls, made bed, a half-full closet. Larry had his flashlight trained on an open suitcase on a cedar chest. Clothes were folded neatly inside. "He just got back from somewhere and hadn't even unpacked yet."

"That's what it looks like."

"Either that, or he was one of those anal types who packs the night before. But that doesn't account for the fresh food in the refrigerator. Plus, the place just doesn't seem lived in. It seems like it was closed up for a while and he just got here and immediately decided to get hammered. That's kind of weird."

"Yeah," Cody said. Cody's beam slid off the suitcase and rested on a battered leather briefcase next to the cedar chest.

"And something else, I just realized," Larry said. "There weren't any other liquor bottles in the kitchen. None. So unless he kept his bar out in the den where he burned up and every trace of it melted into the mud, the only bottle here was the one he was drinking."

"Um-hmmm."

"Which kind of makes me think he picked it up on the way here."

"Um-hmmm," he said, taking several photos of the suitcase, the closet, the bed.

"Hold it," Larry said, moving farther into the room. He illuminated a dresser with several items on top; a comb, a Delta Air Lines envelope, a paperback, a pile of coins, and a wallet. "ID," he said.

"Wait a minute," Cody said. "Before you pick it up let me take some shots of the layout and the stuff on the dresser. Then I want to superglue the room. Then you can check it all out."

Larry stared at him and Cody could feel his eyes on him in the semidark.

"Cody," Larry said, "what the hell are you doing?"

"Investigating," Cody said. "We're investigators, remember?"

"Fuck you. I'm saying accident and you're not. You're treating this as a homicide."

"I'm crossing every *t* and dotting every *i*," Cody said. "You know, like they teach us."

"Bullshit," Larry said, his voice rising. "You're trying to show me up."

"Not at all," Cody said, opening his case and finding the extra-large can of superglue Fume-It. In a closed room, the aerosol glue would fog up the space and collect on any latent fingerprints on the surfaces of the walls, counters, or mirrors. Fingerprints would show on the flat surfaces like floral flocking on wallpaper.

"I'll wait for you in the kitchen, you . . . ," Larry said, not coming up with the foul name he wanted that fit the bill.

"Just be a minute," Cody said. "Close the door."

Larry slammed it shut so hard the rest of the house shuddered.

Before releasing the spray, Cody threw the briefcase on the bed and opened it.

Ten minutes later, Cody opened the door to the dining area. "Got some shots," he said. "The man was cleaner than hell. He must have scrubbed his walls. But I got some prints. Make sure we get the evidence tech to lift them."

Larry stood in the dark in the kitchen and said nothing. Then he shouldered past Cody into the bedroom. The dissipating fog of Fume-It made him cough. When he emerged, he pinched the flashlight between his jaw and shoulder so he could use both hands to hold the ticket jacket up and open it.

"Used tickets and a baggage claim check," Larry said. "Our man flew here on Delta from Salt Lake City three nights ago." He dropped the jacket on the table and opened up the wallet.

"His name was . . ."

"Hank Winters," Cody said.

"You knew him."

"Yeah. He was my sponsor."

3

"Sponsor?" Larry said. "Sponsor?"

As the realization dawned on Larry his face fell. "You mean, like Alcoholics Anonymous?"

"Yeah," Cody said. "He was my guy. I've been up here a couple of times. That's how I knew where it was and who he was."

Cody shined his flashlight to where the east wall of the room would have been. "That entire wall was covered with books. Hank was a collector and he had some really valuable first editions. He bought them all over the country when he traveled. Some of those books were really old and dried out. When the fire got to them I bet they went up like cordwood and probably made the fire even more destructive because of the heat of burning paper."

"But you didn't say anything. You were holding out on me."

"You mean knowing him? Or that I was in the program? Or that I think this wasn't an accident?"

"All of 'em, you son of a bitch. We work together. We talk to each other. No secrets. This is how you got in trouble down in Denver. This is why you're back in Montana. Damn you, remember when I told you never to put me into a position I didn't want to be in?"

Cody didn't shine his flashlight at Larry to see his face. He didn't need to. Larry was angry, and hurt.

"I wasn't holding out," Cody said. "I wanted your honest take on the scene. I wanted you to talk me out of what I was thinking. I hoped you would. You didn't."

Larry threw the wallet down on the tabletop. He started to say something but caught himself. Then, mocking, he said, "My name is Cody Hoyt. I'm an alcoholic *asshole*."

Cody couldn't help himself. He laughed.

Larry looked up, surprised. "That's funny?"

"Yeah, it is. Tonight when I got the call, I nearly double-tapped a doper outside a bar for his twelve-pack of beer."

Larry looked at him. "How long have you been in AA?"

"Two months. Just two months. Fifty-nine days, five hours to be exact. Hardest time of my life."

Larry chinned the direction of the body. "And he was your sponsor? I don't know exactly how this works, but this guy Henry—"

"Hank," Cody corrected.

"*Hank* was your sponsor. That means whenever you felt like taking a snort you called him and he talked you down? Like that?"

Cody said, "Like that. But there's a lot more to it. Nobody can talk a drunk out of a drink except a fellow drunk. He was good, too. He appealed to my best nature."

"I didn't think you had one."

"I don't," Cody said. "But I've got a kid. I don't see him much, but he looks up to me because he doesn't know any better."

Larry's face softened some. Not much.

Said Cody, "My dad was a drunk. My mom was a drunk. My uncle was a drunk. My kid could go down the same road. I don't want him to. So I want to clean myself up. Not give him a role model, you know?"

Larry looked away. "I hate this kind of sharing. Men *talk* to each other, they don't *share*. Sharing's for assholes."

"Yeah," Cody said, "believe me, I hate this Oprah bullshit. But it is what it is. I'm learning to find out what it's like to be clean and sober. I've been pretty much drunk for twenty years. And you know what?"

"What?"

"It *sucks*. I don't know how you people do it—too much reality. But Hank was good because he understood and didn't try to act superior. He knew where I am now. He went through it himself, and he was a tough bastard. Marine. Desert Storm, in fact. And he did it all on his own. His wife left him years ago and he had no brothers or sisters. His parents were dead. He did the Twelve Steps on his own."

Moments went by. The rain thrummed on the roof.

"Well, good for you," Larry said. "I didn't mean to give you a hard time. But it seemed you were holding out, like testing me or something."

"I told you it wasn't like that."

Larry took a deep breath and threw his shoulders back. "So can we get on with this now? Can we figure this stupid thing out?"

"Yeah," Cody said, grateful.

"So what did Hank Winters do? Was he coming back here from a trip?"

"Probably. He was on the road most of the time. A pharmaceutical rep. His territory was the whole mountain west, from what he told me. He didn't tell me the specifics, but he was gone three out of four weeks a month. He stayed sober even though he was surrounded by temptation—all those airports and hotel bars. Think about it. He once told me, 'Even if you're not at home you can always find a meeting.' And he did."

Larry nodded. "So how could he be your sponsor if he was gone all the time?"

"I thought we put that away," Cody said. "But since you asked, I called him on his cell. He'd answer me any time of the day or night, wherever he was. I pulled him out of some big meeting once with a hospital and he took the call and talked me down for forty-five minutes.

A couple of weeks later he said he got beat out of a commission for five thousand bucks. But he took my call. That's the kind of guy he was."

"A good guy," Larry said.

"Yes," Cody said, looking down at his sodden boots and feeling his chest contract. "A saint. My saint. And not the type of guy who would buy a liter of Wild Turkey and drink the whole bottle alone. He just wouldn't do that. No way. That's why I think this wasn't an accident."

"Who would kill him? Somebody local? Any ideas?" Larry asked. But it was obvious he wasn't convinced.

"No idea in the world," Cody said. "But AA is its own world. We share—I mean talk about—the most intimate things in the world with each other. But other than his job, I don't really know much about him. That's the way it works."

Larry took a couple of steps toward Cody. His voice was low. He said, "Cody, I know you want to believe that. And you may be right. But shit, man, isn't it 'once an alcoholic, always an alcoholic?' I mean, maybe something happened. Maybe he just fell off the wagon. You can't say it doesn't happen."

"Not Hank," Cody said. But a kernel of doubt had been planted.

"Maybe just this once he fucked up," Larry said. "It happens. You *know* it happens."

"*NOT HANK,*" Cody said.

"Okay," Larry said, putting his free hand up, palm out. "I'm just sayin'."

"There's something else," Cody said, suddenly feeling as if the floor was buckling under his feet. "I checked out his briefcase."

Larry said, "And . . . ?"

"His coins were gone. He always kept his coins in a plastic sleeve in his briefcase. He'd bring them out whenever we met face to face and show them to me. He was so proud of them."

Suddenly, the kitchen flooded with light. Cars had entered the parking area. Cody could see Larry without lifting up his flashlight. In the glare of the lights through the rain-streaked windows, the surface of Larry's face and head was patterned with shadowed rivulets that looked like channels in an ant farm.

"Skeeter," Larry said, chinning toward the window. "Maybe the sheriff, too. At least three units. A whole shitload of 'em."

Cody didn't look over.

"The coins," Larry said. "Were they gold coins or something? Valuable? So you're saying maybe it was a robbery and a murder?"

Cody shook his head. "The coins weren't worth shit."

"So what are you driving at?"

"They're AA coins," Cody said softly. "Twelve-step program coins. One for every year from the local chapter. They're probably worth twenty bucks each, if that. There's a goddamned elk on the Helena Chapter ones. Hank had nine of them. I'm ten months away from getting my first one and I've never wanted something so bad. And they're missing."

Larry shrugged. "So your point is what?"

"They're gone," Cody said.

Outside, he could hear the sound of doors slamming and loud voices.

Larry said, "We better go out and fill them in."

Back out in the rain, Larry said over his shoulder, "My cynical cop mind tells me Henry, I mean Hank, tossed the coins away when he decided to go on a bender. You know, like symbolic."

"Not Hank," Cody said.

4

Sheriff Edward "Tub" Tubman and Undersheriff Cliff Bodean arrived on the scene in identical beige GMC Yukons with LEWIS AND CLARK COUNTY SHERIFF'S DEPARTMENT decals on the front doors. They parked side by side next to Larry's rig. Dougherty jumped out of his car to greet them. Both hikers remained inside his vehicle. As Larry and Cody approached, Tubman was unfolding his rain suit. His new gray Stetson rancher—an affectation that appeared the day after he declared he was running for reelection—was on the wet hood of his Yukon, the top of it already darkened from the rain. Cody was annoyed the sheriff didn't know enough to rest a good hat like that crown-down on a surface like real ranchers did.

Bodean was still in his vehicle and talking to dispatch over the radio.

The sheriff shot his arms through the sleeves of the suit but it got bunched around his head and he struggled. Cody was reminded of a turtle.

"Let me help you with that," Dougherty said, giving the back hem of the coat a yank. When he did, Tubman's head popped through the material and he came up sputtering.

"Damn thing anyway," he said, reaching for his hat. "So what have we got, boys?"

Tubman was short and doughy with a gunfighter's mustache and a tuft of hair that circled his round head like a smudge.

Larry and Cody exchanged looks, waiting for the other to start.

"A body, right?" Tubman said, annoyed. "You've got a body?"

"We've got that," Larry said. "Likely three days old. Male. Burned up in the fire."

Larry briefed the sheriff on the crime scene and what they'd found. He offered no opinions or speculation, just a solid accounting of the facts as they'd found them. He did it with such authority, Cody thought, that on the facts alone there was only one conclusion. He appreciated that Larry didn't even hint at their earlier discussion.

"Accidental death then," Tubman said with some relief. "Or what we like to call 'death by misadventure,' if you add in the empty bottle. Is Skeeter on the way?"

"As far as I know," Larry said. "Cody had him called."

"Let's hope he shows up alone without his fan club," Tubman said, shaking his head.

The sheriff nodded toward the hikers in Dougherty's truck. "Those folks the people who called it in?"

"Yes, sir," Dougherty said. "I questioned them separately."

"Did they check out?"

"Yes, sir."

"Are they county residents?"

Cody heard, *Are they voters?*

"No, sir," Dougherty said. "The man's a college professor from MSU. The woman's his student, apparently. They really don't want their names out, if you catch my drift."

Tubman smiled. "Too bad. Their names will be in the report. So tell the professor he better start doing some damage control with his wife."

Dougherty laughed.

"And get them out of here," Tubman said. "Take them back to their car so they can go home."

"Yes, sir."

Cody watched Dougherty get into his vehicle and start it up. He waited for the professor to remember his backpack in Cody's Ford, but the professor looked distraught. The woman stared out the window, as if contemplating what the rest of the semester would be like now. As they left the two of them appeared to be engaged in an angry exchange, based on the waving of hands.

Cody thought: *They left the backpack.*

Then he thought: *Fate.*

The bad blood between the sheriff and the coroner had recently come to a boil when Tubman was quoted in the *Independent Record* declaring that the cause of death of a twenty-five-year-old drifter found in Lincoln was due to an overdose of meth. He used the opportunity to make a case for increased drug-enforcement funding for the sheriff's department. The next day, Skeeter held a press conference for the newspaper and the two television stations and made a point of saying they were awaiting autopsy results and, "Maybe our local sheriff should just stop by my office to learn how we actually do our job, since he seems to somehow know things that haven't yet been determined scientifically."

Although the victim *was* later declared to have died due to an overdose, the war had begun over which one of the two would be the official spokesman for law enforcement in the county when it came to dead bodies. Because both men were running again and wanted as much authoritative face time in the press as possible, it was often an ugly race to the cameras for both of them.

Bodean opened his door and leaned out. "We've nailed down the owner of this place," he said. "Local man name of Henry Winters, age fifty-nine. No record."

"We found his ID," Larry confirmed.

"It didn't burn up?" the sheriff asked Larry.

"The wallet was in his bedroom in the side of the cabin that's still standing."

"I don't know him," Tubman said dismissively. Meaning Winters wasn't influential with the city council or a campaign contributor.

I did, Cody thought. He was angry with the sheriff's gut reaction.

Tubman took his wet hat off and looked at it in his headlights. "I gotta get me one of those plastic hat condom things so the felt doesn't get stained."

Another set of headlights strobed through the lodgepole pine trees.

"Who smashed up the unit?" Tubman asked, turning his attention to Cody's dented Ford.

"I hit an elk on the way up."

"I hope you've got good insurance," Tubman said, not kindly.

"I hope you've got a cow permit," Bodean laughed.

Cody cleared his throat. "I think it's a homicide."

Even in the diffused light from the headlights, Cody could see the sheriff's face darken.

"Larry thinks it could be accidental, but I don't. I think somebody killed Hank and tried to cover the crime by burning the place down. If it wasn't for the rain, he would have completely gotten away with it."

Tubman spat between his feet. "It *sounds* accidental, Cody."

"I'll give you that. But I knew the man. It wasn't an accident."

The sheriff turned on Larry: "Why didn't you say so in the first place?"

Larry shrugged. "We're still working it out," he said.

"Before Skeeter gets here," Tubman said to Cody, "tell me why you don't think this is what it appears to be."

Cody told him, leaving out the part about him being in AA. Leaving out the part about the missing coins. Saying he knew Hank Winters never drank alcohol.

"*That's* your reasoning?"

"Yes." Cody could feel Larry glaring at him but didn't look over. Hearing in his head, *Don't ever screw me, and don't ever put me in a position I don't want to be in.*

Tubman crossed his arms and shook his head. "So what do I tell the press? What do I tell that fucking Skeeter?"

"Whatever you want," Cody said. "I'm investigating it as a homicide."

The sheriff set his jaw. "I know you sometimes forget this, Hoyt, but you work for *me*. And from what I've heard, it's an accidental death. Do you dispute anything Olson told me?"

"No."

"Then keep your theories to yourself until you've got something a hell of a lot better than what you've got. The last thing I need right now is an unsolved murder leading up to the primary. Do you understand? It's an accidental death until you can prove to me it isn't. Like if the autopsy boys in Missoula find a bullet hole in his skull or a knife in his gut. Then we've got something that changes the situation. Got that?"

Cody felt a familiar rage building up in him. But he managed not to lash out.

"Got that?" Tubman said again.

"I hear you," Cody mumbled.

Deep in the trees from the direction of the main road he could hear the sound of a vehicle approaching.

"Oh no," Bodean said, zipping up his long yellow raincoat and turning toward the road. "Skeeter's coming."

"Shit," Tubman said, turning away from Cody, dismissing him. "Skeeter's been showing up places wearing a sidearm lately. He's trying to hammer home the fact that he's law enforcement. Let's see if the joker is packing."

Skeeter was called Skeeter, Cody'd been told, because he didn't like his first name, which was Leslie. SKEETER was stenciled on his vehicle doors. He pulled his four-wheel-drive behind Cody's Ford, blocking him, and jumped out quickly, already dressed for the weather. Before he zipped his rain jacket, Cody saw Skeeter was wearing a holster.

Skeeter Caldwell was tall, slim, and gaunt with deep-set eyes and a long bladelike nose and he'd recently had his teeth capped so he wouldn't look quite so much like a ghoul. But, Cody thought, he *still* looked like a ghoul.

"Sheriff," Skeeter said in greeting, nodding toward Tubman.

"Skeeter," the sheriff said, unenthusiastic.

"Where's the body?"

Four vehicles were lined up shoulder to shoulder with all of their headlights aimed at the burned cabin. Tubman said, "Guess."

"Can we be professional here?" Skeeter asked.

"Absolutely."

"Then please have your men show me the victim."

Tubman turned to Larry. "Perhaps you could escort the county coroner to the scene."

Larry grunted.

"So what is your first impression?" Skeeter asked.

"Accident."

"We shall see."

Tubman rolled his eyes.

"I hope you don't mind if a reporter from the *Independent Record* comes along," Skeeter said. "Carrie Lowry. I guess she heard the report over the radio."

"I bet," Tubman said sourly. "And I *do* mind. We haven't even secured the scene yet." He turned to Cody. "Put up some crime tape. Make her keep her distance. I don't want her at the cabin taking pictures or getting in the way. Tell her we'll talk to her when we've got something to say."

Cody saluted and said, "Yes, sir!"

Before Tubman turned to follow Skeeter, Bodean, and Larry toward the cabin, he said to Cody, "That'll be more than enough of that shit, mister."

Another set of headlights fanned through the lodgepole pine trunks. Unlike Skeeter, the driver was going slowly, picking through the forest, as if unsure that the road was the correct one. Cody had a six-inch roll of yellow plastic tape that read DO NOT CROSS DO NOT CROSS. He'd tied one end to a tree trunk near the entrance to the parking area and was letting it unwind as he walked toward the other side. He shot glances over his shoulder at the cabin as he unwound the tape. Skeeter was bending over the body while Larry provided the light. Tubman and Bodean stood behind them in the rain looking useless.

The vehicle made the last turn and headlights blinded him. Again. He held up his free forearm to block the light and the vehicle braked to a stop with a squeal.

A woman's voice said, "Oh, come on. You're telling me I can't get any closer than *that*?"

"Sheriff's orders," Cody said.

"You've gotta let me through."

"Sorry."

"Cody," she said, "you are such an asshole."

"Hi, Carrie," he said. "How are you tonight?"

"I thought I was lost," she said. "Then I finally find it and . . . it's *you*."

He shrugged. "Did you bring a poncho or something? It's raining."

"Oh, really?"

He nodded, then continued stripping the tape across the road. She killed the engine and he heard a door slam. He looked over and saw her raise the tape up over her head and start to stride toward the cabin.

"Whoa," he said. "I don't want to have to arrest you and/or torture you until you confess."

She turned toward him, hands on hips. She wore a battered raincoat that bulged near her waistline and a slouch cap that looked like it had been in her trunk for ten years. Her red hair fell on the shoulders of the raincoat and stuck to the wet fabric.

"Nice look," he said. "I hope you didn't dress up just for me."

"Fuck you, Cody," she said.

"Language," he said. "God is listening."

"*Fuck You,* Cody." Then added, "And the horse you rode in on. Skeeter told me I'd have access."

"I'm sure you will," he said, "once the scene is released to him. But that hasn't happened yet. Right now, this is a crime scene under investigation by the sheriff's department. When it gets turned over to the coroner, you'll be the first to know, I'm sure."

She huffed, "What am I supposed to do in the meanwhile?"

"You could help me string this crime-scene tape," he said. "I could use a hand."

"You are *such* an asshole."

"Get back before I shoot you," he said, shining his flashlight on her face so she flinched. But before she did, he got a glimpse of her green eyes, the constellation of freckles across her cheeks and nose, that nice mouth.

"Bastard," she said, wheeling around and stomping back toward her fifteen-year-old Subaru. She climbed back in and slammed the door and he watched her fume until the interior light went out.

He'd met Carrie the year before, shortly after he returned to Montana from Denver. He'd been with the department less than a month, and he sidled up to her bar stool at the Windbag Bar and Grill. He'd watched her fend off rural legislators in town for the session like swatting flies and told her he admired her high opinion of herself. When she didn't swat him away, he bought her another Jack and Coke, even though he explained that by drinking the concoction she was ruining two good drinks.

Over the next three hours he bought her four more. He kept up with her. She told him about growing up in Havre, going to J-school, marrying twice to losers, landing at the *Independent Record.* She covered the police beat, she said. She asked him if he'd be a source. He said sure, if she'd quit talking shop and go home with him.

Somehow, he drove her to his apartment without being picked up by the Helena police, even though he cruised through at least two red lights, maybe more. She never noticed because she was pawing at his belt, fumbling at it, pulling the wrong way on the tongue of his belt but with surprising strength. When he threw her over his shoulder and carried her into his place, she laughed and hit at him until he tossed her on his bed. She was a crazy back-scratching wildcat for ten minutes before he, or she, passed out the first time. He recalled little after that, but he had a vague memory involving him trying to connect the dots of her freckles with a felt-tipped pen, which they both found hilarious at the time.

When she came by the station a week later to interview the sheriff after a Marysville outfitter who had shot his wife twelve times (pausing twice to reload) with a .30-06, their eyes locked for a moment and she tossed her red hair, said, "It was hell getting that ink off of my face," and turned on her heel and clicked away down the hallway.

He knew he wasn't wanted or needed at the cabin so he returned to his Ford and climbed in. The windows steamed again, but it was good to be somewhere dry.

Through the fogged windshield he saw flashlights dancing in the dark at the cabin and figures moving slowly through the black muck. He thought about Hank and something gripped him hard inside like a talon and suddenly he was tearing up. He couldn't believe it. Cody hadn't cried since his dog died when he was twelve. Funerals for his father and mother had been uneventful. But Hank was different. Hank was a tough old bird who wanted to help him solely because he was a kind and good man. Hank was willing to help a fucked-up stranger and show him goodness existed. And Hank was gone.

Cody's hand, as if on its own, crab-walked across the bench seat until it paused near the day pack of the hiker. Cody didn't look over. His hand had a mind of its own. It was out of his control. Then it grabbed the neck of the bottle of Jim Beam.

His other hand, also thinking independently, reached across his body and unscrewed the cap. He took two big gulps, as if it were water and he was thirsty, then he jammed the bottle between his thighs. Something inside him said, *Stop now, while you still can.*

He shrugged the voice away. That had never been difficult, he always won that contest. At first, his belly clutched painfully, as if it were shutting down and rejecting the alcohol. He grunted and leaned forward, doubling up, his forehead on the top of the steering wheel. Then the pain stopped and, as if he were welcoming an old friend, he could feel the familiar warmth radiate through him starting with his chest and spreading out to his arms and legs and head. It was as if he was filling his tank up with rocket fuel.

He sat back and the blackened image of the arm and bloated hand flickered on the inside of the windshield like the screen of a drive-in movie, and he said, "Hank, is this what happened to you? Is this what you did? You opened a bottle again? Tell me I'm wrong because buddy, I believed in you."

He thought about it. He had another drink.

Then: "Hank, I'm going to find whoever did this to you."

Cody drank fast on an empty stomach. When he put the cap back on the bottle half of it was gone. He wiped his mouth with the back of his hand, turned on the interior light, and looked at himself in the rearview mirror. He remembered that flushed face from scarred mirrors in bar restrooms and from his own bathroom when he got home after closing time.

He said, "Helloooo, handsome. And welcome back."

And he suddenly had a plan.

Then he unwrapped and crammed three sticks of Stride Winterblue gum (every drunk's secret gum) into his mouth and lit a cigarette. The combination would disguise his breath. He knew this from experience. And he opened the SUV door and once again was pelted by rain. If it weren't for the furnace raging through him, he thought, it might feel cold outside.

———

Cody walked toward the plastic barrier and wriggled his fingers at Carrie as he pushed the crime-scene tape over his head and approached her car on the driver's side. She didn't respond so he leaned his butt against the front fender and drew in deep on his cigarette. He listened to the rain coursing through the pines and heavy drops plunking into surface puddles. Raindrops smacked his cigarette and he felt it important to smoke it to a nub before a lucky drop hit the cherry and drowned it out.

Finally, she rolled her window down. "Yes? Are you here to tell me I can go in?"

"Nope."

"Then get off my car."

He wouldn't tell her he needed to lean against her car for a moment so he wouldn't fall down. Instead, he laughed. "I don't think I can make it look any worse than it does now."

"Jesus," she said. "You are such an—"

"Sticks and stones," he said in a way that even charmed *him*. And he noted she hadn't rolled her window back up.

"Carrie, do you remember when you asked me to be a source? Remember? It was in the Windbag."

She was quiet. Cautious. "Yes."

"I'm ready," he said.

"Are you jerking me around?" Her voice was attractive, kind of husky.

"No, ma'am."

"Are there conditions?" she asked. Her voice had become business-like. Which for some reason made him want to take her home again, but he'd settle for another cigarette. He slapped his raincoat until he found the pack and matches.

"Those things will kill you," she said.

"Bring it on," he laughed. "Bring it on."

"Cody."

He got the cigarette lit and turned and dropped to his haunches so he was eye-level with her in the car. She didn't draw back away from him, he noticed. He wished he could see her face better.

"Promise me what I tell you will be confidential," he said. "My name can't be in the story and you have to promise you won't even hint at where this comes from."

She hesitated, then said, "Okay. But it's got to be of substance."

"It's of substance. And you can't do one of those 'an unnamed source in the sheriff's department' kinds of things. Or I'll make your life so miserable you'll have to leave Montana."

That made her wince, and she sat back. "Don't threaten me like that."

"No threat," he said. "Just what it is. Are we clear?"

"We're clear."

He looked around. Although he couldn't see everyone at the cabin, he did see flashlight beams bouncing around.

"This isn't an accident, whatever the sheriff or Skeeter tells you. It's a murder."

"Jesus."

"And whoever did it tried to cover his tracks by burning the place down. The victim was a great man named Hank Winters, and we're gonna find who did it."

She shook her head. "Why would the sheriff or Skeeter want to cover that up? I don't understand."

He whispered conspiratorially, "Because it's important to them not to call it a murder. It's political, and it's big. Bigger than hell. This could be the story that gets you on the map if you play it right."

"Oh, Cody," she said, reaching out of her window and touching his arm. Her eyes glistened in the reflection of the flashlights at the scene.

"Look," he said. "The murderer left a clue to his identity. I can't tell you what it was but we're going to follow it to the killer once we get some outside experts up here with some special equipment. And we *will* get him. He's on borrowed time until the analysis comes back."

"What kind of analysis?"

"That I can't tell you yet."

With that, Cody stood and patted her hand back. "Remember," he said, "you didn't hear this from me."

After a beat, she said, "Thank you, Cody. I owe you."

"Just no scratching this time," he said as he turned to walk away.

As he passed under the crime-scene tape he nearly ran into Larry, who stood in the dark with his flashlight off. Cody felt the familiar grip of guilt that came with secret drinking.

"What in the hell are you doing?" Larry said in an urgent whisper. "I heard what you told her, you son of a bitch."

Cody reached out for Larry but Larry backed away. Cody said, "I'm baiting the trap."

"What the fuck are you talking about? What was that about special equipment and analysis?"

Cody found himself grinning maniacally, and couldn't douse it out. He held out his hand to Larry, and said, "I'm pretty sure she bought it."

Larry stared at him, unmoving. They faced off for over a minute with no words.

Finally, Larry said, "You found a bottle, didn't you?"

"Yup."

"And now you're going to self-destruct and try to take me with you."

Cody shrugged. "You don't have to come, Larry."

"You asshole. You stupid jerk."

"I've been hearing that a lot tonight."

Larry said, "What am I going to do with you?"

Cody suddenly felt sober. It happened at the weirdest times, he thought. He said, "Help me find the guy who killed Hank. I'll take it from there."

Larry moaned.

Cody stepped close to Larry and said, "Larry, I'm a drunk but I'm not a joke. You've never seen me unleashed before and believe me, it's a sight to behold. I'll go after this guy like nothing you've ever experienced. And when I find him I'll kill his ass a million times over."

Larry stepped back. "Man, are you okay?"

Cody said, "I've never been okay. But now I've got a *purpose.*" He spat the last word.

Larry's eyes got wide and he shook his head slowly. "You're out of control," Larry whispered.

"Maybe." Cody winked and walked back to his Ford for the bottle. The rest of the night he functioned in a blackout. And he woke up the next morning in his apartment covered with blood. Not his.

5

On the night he shot the coroner, Cody Hoyt was back at Hank Winters's cabin, hiding in a copse of pine trees in the dark. Waiting.

The last twenty hours had been a dense, almost impenetrable fog. He'd called on his reserves to simply stay upright for most of it. As he sipped from the pint bottle of Evan Williams bourbon he'd brought with him to Vigilante Campground, certain disconnected scenes came up to the surface as if for air and he recalled them before they sunk again to be replaced by another. *Whack-a-mole memories!* he thought. Just like the bad old days.

He tried to put them in order.

Driving down from the mountains following Larry's car, Larry pulling over twice to get out and curse at him, saying Cody nearly gave himself away when he was slurring his words to the evidence tech and EMTs as they bagged the body and collected all the evidence they'd tagged. Telling Cody that luckily, the sheriff and undersheriff were back in their vehicles at that point, bitching about Skeeter and not thinking about why one of their lead investigators had to lean on trees or the cabin to keep upright. Noting that Carrie Lowry was long gone, and Skeeter was annoyed about that. Not objecting when Larry pushed him away from the cabin in the dark so no one could hear him talk or see him trying to maintain his balance;

Cutting up the dead cow elk with Larry on their way down the mountain, quartering it with a bone saw Larry had in his gear box, all so Cody could take the meat to the battered women's shelter even though he could barely stand and the huge chunks of raw, still-warm meat had covered his clothes with blood. Ignoring Larry as he bitched and moaned about it, saying those women had plenty to eat as it was and they'd think Cody was crazy;

Hauling the quarters into the walk-in freezer of the shelter after waking up the manager, winking at Larry when she cried and said how grateful she was, how the women and kids staying there would love the meat, offering to clean him up and make some coffee because there was something wrong with his eyes;

Climbing back into the Ford ten minutes after Larry dropped him off at his building, his promises to his partner that he'd go straight to bed and stay off the bottle ringing in his ears, then coming right back out the door when Larry was gone and starting the engine and driving away;

Pounding on the door of a man who ran a roadside liquor store, waking him up because it was four hours past closing, demanding a case of beer and two pints of bourbon, paying for them with a hundred-dollar bill and a pat on the grip of his .40 Sig Sauer to remind the owner to keep quiet about the intrusion;

Calling Jenny, his ex-wife, waking her and making her angry, asking to talk to his son Justin to tell him he could borrow anything he wanted to borrow and to stay away from alcohol and parties, but Justin wasn't there. He was already gone, with Jenny's new rich fiancé, on a goddamned male bonding adventure in the wilderness. Jenny calling him an asshole which made him laugh because he'd been called that so many times that night that *it just might be true,* and her slamming down the phone and refusing to pick up when he called her number three more times until he passed out in his lounge chair with the receiver stuck to his hand by congealing blood;

Waking up covered in stiff brown blood, his pants, shirt, and hands caked with it, dried flakes spackling his hand like cracks in a dry lake bed. Swirls of it in the shower, rich and red and revolting. Kicking at the pink swirls and flakes with bare feet, trying to get them to go down the drain;

Swallowing six ibuprofens to blunt the savage pounding in his head, throwing them up in the kitchen sink, taking six more, finally drinking a beer and a raw egg for breakfast which eased him back into the slipstream and stopped his hands from shaking and made it possible for him to brush his teeth and shave without mutilating himself;

Showing up for the eight thirty staff briefing with the town cops from across the hall, Undersheriff Bodean outlining the circumstances of the death of Hank Winters, sleeping through it with his eyes wide open until the sheriff stormed into the room waving the morning's *Independent Record,* cursing Carrie Lowry and especially that damned Skeeter, who must have been the one who fed her full of lies about the accident being a murder and a lead left at the crime scene that would identify the killer, ordering all of his cops to boycott the local paper until they apologized and ran a front-page retraction;

Feeling Larry's absolutely chilling glare from across the room while Tubman ranted;

Cutting out early after the briefing because he couldn't concentrate and he needed a beer, taking his notes and camera with him;

Spending the afternoon at the Windbag and the Jester, seeing his old friends, laughing at their stories and telling some of his own, feeling like it was a family reunion of sorts for the men and women who drank in the daylight, *his people!*;

Taking the Ford back up the mountain as dusk came, shotgun in the rack and pistol in his holster, hoping to avoid hitting another elk, hoping against hope that whoever did this to Hank would read the paper and be puzzled as hell and return to the scene to try and retrieve whatever it was the cops found;

Knowing it was nuttier than hell but somehow made complete sense;

Parking the vehicle on a road a half mile from Hank's place so it couldn't be seen and hiking through the dark forest still dripping with rain from the storm that afternoon, carrying the shotgun, packing his pistol, and swinging a six-pack of beer by the plastic holder.

He didn't know how long he'd been passed out when the sound of a motor woke him up. Cody moaned and opened his eyes. His head throbbed. He found himself sitting on the damp ground, leaning back against a tree trunk. The cold wet had soaked through his jeans and underwear, and his butt was freezing.

Since it took a few moments to figure out where he was and why he was there, the sound of the tires on gravel and the motor confused him. Then he realized his plan had worked, that the killer had returned to the scene.

He stood up and the waves of dizziness and nausea nearly buckled his knees. He kept his head down, waiting it out, trying to listen to what was going on through the roaring. He heard a man's voice say, "Here it is," and he thought: *There's more than one of them.*

Unless the guy was talking to himself, which was doubtful.

"Here?" A woman's voice.

"There, on that frame that was once a couch. His body was there."

Cody took a deep breath of cold mountain air and it cleared the clouds from his mind a little. The night and his situation started to come into focus. He wished he'd been lucid when they drove up so that he could have seen them before they got out of their car. But that moment had passed.

He left the three full beers and the empty bottle of bourbon in the grass, and took a step toward the back of the cabin. His legs were rubbery, and he lurched to the side, about to fall. Luckily, the trees were close together and his shoulder thumped into a trunk and kept him upright. He inhaled and held the cold air in his lungs, hoping it would sober him up.

"So what are we looking for?" the woman asked.

"I really don't know," the man said. "Whatever was left. If anything."

The unburned part of the cabin was between Cody and the visitors, so he couldn't see them. A shaft of light sliced through the air—a flashlight being turned on—then quickly descended out of view. They were looking for something in the black muck.

He thought, *I have you now, you scumbags.*

"This is sick," she said. "I wished I knew what we were looking for."

"Probably nothing," he said. "It might be the sheriff's idea of a stupid trick to make him look like he's doing something. He may drag this out past the election, is my guess."

The back of the cabin was suddenly in front of him. Cody reached out with his left hand and touched the rounded logs. All he'd need to do was slip along the lengths of the logs until it opened up on the burned section, and they'd be there in the open.

Then he realized he'd left his shotgun back where he'd passed out. Hesitating, he considered feeling his way back to retrieve it. But he'd gotten this far in silence without slipping or stepping on a dead branch to reveal himself. Doing it twice more without making a sound was unlikely at best. He cursed himself and reached up and pinched his cheek so hard he winced. But it helped wake him up. Then he reached down and slowly unsnapped the plastic restraint on his holster and drew his Sig Sauer. As always, there was no safety to worry about and one in the chamber so there'd be no need to rack the slide.

He'd had Trijicon self-luminous sights put on his weapon back in Denver, and he raised it and fitted the front green dot between the twin dots of the back sight. Although he'd never fired at anyone at night on the job, he'd put in hours at the range. He knew if he squeezed the trigger when the three dots were horizontal he should be able to hit what he was pointing at. His only issue was whether or not he'd take out the both of them without warning, or identify himself first. Of course, however it went, in his after-action report he'd say he ordered them to freeze and they didn't, so he had no choice.

Kill the man first, he thought. A double-tap into the thickest part of his torso as fast as he could squeeze the trigger, then swing on the woman and do the same. Then, if necessary, killshots to the head.

Could he kill a woman? The idea sickened him. "There," the man said, his voice rising. "Right *there.* Look."

Had they found it? he wondered.

He saw the pool of their flashlight before he saw them. There was a glint of gold in the muck of the floor.

"It looks like a coin," she said.

"Yes, it does," he said, distressed. "I don't know how I could have missed it."

Because, Cody thought, *I put it there two hours ago.* Gold-foil-wrapped chocolate coins went for $1.89 at Walgreens these days.

And he cleared the edge of the logs and barked, "FREEZE, YOU FUCKERS!"

She screamed and threw her flashlight into the air with the same motion that she covered her mouth.

He blinded Cody with his light but before he did Cody saw a hand reach down and grip a pistol and raise it and there was a star-shaped explosion of fire tinged with blue and a deafening crack. And something white-hot and angry slapped the side of his face.

And that's when Cody shot the county coroner. Double-tap, two loud snaps and two yellow-green tongues of flame. Skeeter went down like a puppet with its strings clipped.

Cody lowered his weapon, the sharp smell of gunpowder and his own blood biting at his nose, and said, "Oh, shit."

Carrie Lowry didn't stop screaming until her sobs and admonitions took over.

6

Cody sat back in an uncomfortable chair across from Sheriff Tubman in his cramped little office. The door was closed, and had been for an hour. There had been no eight thirty briefing that morning. Undersheriff Bodean perched on the corner of Tubman's desk, looking almost straight down at him. On the credenza behind the sheriff was his hat, brim-down, and the morning's *Independent Record* with EYE-WITNESS ACCOUNT: CORONER SHOT BY SHERIFF'S DEPARTMENT blaring across all four columns of the front page. Cody thought, *Carrie got that big story I promised her after all.*

"You really ought to put your hat crown-down when you're not wearing it," Cody said. "You'll ruin the brim that way."

Tubman closed his eyes, to keep from exploding, Cody guessed.

"How you can joke at a time like this is beyond me," Bodean said, shaking his head.

"Really," Cody said, "it'll flatten the brim. Trust me on this."

"Look at my phone," Tubman said. "All the lights are blinking. Everybody wants a statement and they're willing to stay on hold until they get it."

"Sorry," Cody said.

"Yes," Tubman said, "you are."

Bodean cleared his throat and stuck his chin out. "In case you don't know the procedure, Detective Hoyt, this is an officer-involved shooting, so give me your badge and your gun."

Cody shifted in his chair and unclipped the badge and slid it across the desk to Tubman. He pulled his Sig Sauer and handed it grip-first to Bodean. "Careful," he said, "it's loaded."

Bodean walked the weapon over and put it gingerly on top of a metal filing cabinet. He said, "You are officially on administrative leave with pay. We've got a call in to the state to send an outside team to investigate the incident. They're likely to be here tomorrow, so stay in touch with us at all times."

Cody nodded.

"Don't go anywhere for seventy-two hours. That's when we'll take your statement and based on what the state criminal investigation team says, you might be placed under arrest."

Even though he knew it could happen, Cody felt a chill crawl through his scalp.

Said Bodean, "It's my duty to advise you to keep your mouth shut until you give your official statement. At that time, you should be aware that under *Garrity versus New Jersey*, you may be disciplined if you refuse to answer questions about your conduct on the job. You have no Fifth Amendment rights as a cop. In the meantime, the only person you should talk to is a peer counselor we'll assign. Do you understand what I just said?"

"Yeah, but I don't mind talking. And if you send a social worker to my place I'll mace him," Cody growled. "It went down exactly like Carrie Lowry wrote in the paper. Skeeter drew first and fired after I told him to freeze. I shot him in self-defense."

Tubman continued to shake his head, as if he were watching his career slink away.

Bodean said, "She wrote that you didn't identify yourself."

"I didn't get the chance. Skeeter was fast for a ghoul."

"You refused to take a breathalyzer test."

"It's my right. I don't trust those portable things. I took one later here at the station."

"*Hours* later," Bodean said, "after the alcohol in your system had a chance to metabolize. And you still came in a .88. That's barely sober and it was four hours after the shooting. And the officer on the scene said you smelled like a still."

"Dougherty wouldn't know a still if he tripped over it," Cody said.

"You're lucky Skeeter was wearing a vest. Your first slug hit him here," Bodean gestured toward his heart. "The second one was above the armor and really messed up his shoulder. But he should be okay and giving press conferences any time now."

Instinctively, Cody reached up and touched the compress taped over his right ear where Skeeter's round had clipped him. The bullet had taken a half inch of his earlobe and the wound bled like crazy until they got it stopped.

After the emergency room docs had bandaged and released him, he'd tried to talk to the coroner, who was upstairs in the same hospital. He wasn't sure if he wanted to yell at Skeeter or apologize or shoot him again. He didn't get an opportunity to make the choice because a hospital security officer wouldn't let him past his desk until visiting hours.

"Why in God's name was Skeeter wearing a vest and carrying a weapon in the first place?" Cody asked. "He's the *coroner.* And he shouldn't have snuck a reporter into a crime scene just so she could get some photos. That's not right. He was acting suspiciously."

"We'd all like to know that and it'll come out in the investigation," Tubman said. "He might be in as much trouble as you are or more. But in this instance I'm glad he had the vest or we'd have a homicide investigation going and you'd be in our jail."

Cody shrugged. "Speaking of homicide," he said, "I'd still like to help on the Hank Winters murder investigation."

"It wasn't a homicide," Tubman said with force.

"It was," Cody said.

"Stay away from it," Tubman said. "Stay away from this office. Stay away from Larry." He leaned forward on his desk and balled his fists. "And stay the hell away from *me.*"

The door opened and Edna stuck her head in. "Sheriff, the governor is on the line. He wants a briefing."

Tubman moaned and sat back. To Cody, he said, "Go away. Go straight out the door and go home. Don't even talk to anyone. And stay by your phone."

Before Cody left the room, he ducked behind the sheriff and turned the offending hat over.

Larry was alone in the detective room, scrolling through digital images of the crime scene Cody had shot two nights before. Although his shoulders tensed when Cody entered the room, he didn't greet him. And when Cody shut the door behind him, Larry seemed to be studying the screen even more intently than before.

"I'll be out of here in a minute," Cody said.

He went to his desk and started filling an empty box he'd grabbed outside the evidence room with his papers, gear, and the nascent murder book he'd begun.

"Next time," Larry said finally, "go for a head shot."

"*Ha.*"

"Man, when you dive in you go *deep.* I'll give that to you."

Cody grunted.

"A gold-wrapped chocolate coin?" Larry laughed.

"It worked, sort of," Cody said. "If the killer thought he'd left one behind . . ."

"You know what's going to happen," Larry said. "Skeeter knows he's in trouble, too. So he's going to try and get out ahead of it with the press and the voters. He's going to start yapping and paint you in the worst light possible and try to taint the investigation."

Cody shrugged.

"So, what happened with the sheriff?"

"I'm suspended until they clear me."

"You are so fucking lucky, Cody. You could have killed the coroner or gotten killed yourself. And I don't doubt for a second that you were hammered at the time."

"I was blitzed," Cody said. "But when I pulled the trigger I felt completely sober. Strange how that happens. Adrenaline trumps alcohol: remember that."

"Are you over it? The binge, I mean?"

Cody said, "I think so. I'm not promising anything, though."

"Yeah," Larry said, finally swiveling around in his chair to face him, "I found out how solid your promises are."

"I'm really sorry about that," Cody said, looking out the window at the lawn in front of the Law Enforcement Center. "And I want to thank you again for covering for me."

"The last time," Larry said. "Ever."

"That's reasonable."

Larry let a beat pass. Then, "I'm rethinking the Winters death."

"You are?" For the first time in forty-eight hours, he felt a little nudge of hope.

"Yeah. While you were partying with your old pals yesterday, I was doing police work."

"And?"

"The preliminary autopsy shows blunt head trauma. Of course, they don't know yet whether is was pre- or postmortem. I mean, the guy was covered with the beams from his roof that fell on his noggin. But there wasn't any smoke in his lungs. Meaning he was likely dead before the fire got out of hand. As you know, it's never the fire that kills 'em. It's the smoke."

"Interesting there was no inhalation."

"And there's another thing good about all that rain and cold weather," Larry said. "According to the lab, there had been too much time between the death and the discovery of the body to find out if there was any alcohol in his bloodstream. Plus, the heat of the fire could have literally burned it out. But because the body was kept fairly cool, they're going to cut his eyes out and test 'em."

Cody winced. "His *eyes*?"

Larry read from his notes. "The vitreous humor can be tested. This is the jellylike substance within the eyeball. Alcohol can be detected there and it lags behind the blood level. That is, it reflects the blood level about two hours prior to death. If it is elevated, the ME can say that the victim was likely intoxicated. They can't get a blood alcohol level, but they can *possibly* say it was there at the time of death."

"When will they call you back?"

Larry shrugged. "Soon, I hope. It's not definitive, but if there's no smoke in the lungs and no sign of alcohol consumption, it will pretty much kill my accident or suicide theory. Because that means somebody opened a bottle and left it to be found with the body, and somebody opened the door of the stove."

Nodding, Cody said, "So our killer bashed him in the head, drank or poured out the bottle, and set the place on fire."

"You're jumping to conclusions," Larry said.

"Well," Cody said, "here's another jump. Whoever did it knew Hank once had problems with alcohol. Since Hank hadn't had a drop in five years, they'd have to know Hank's history. A stranger wouldn't likely know that, would he?"

Larry started to argue but the edges of his mouth turned down and he nodded. "I see where you're going. But who would know, besides you?"

Cody didn't answer. He let Larry figure it out.

"Every other person in your AA group," Larry said. "You people confess everything to each other. *They* would know."

Cody said, "Exactly."

Larry said, "So we need to establish the whereabouts of all of the Helena AA members between the hours of eight and midnight three nights ago."

Cody paused. "How'd you determine the time of death? The ME?"

"Naw. The receipt from when Winters bought the steaks had the exact time on it: 6:03 P.M. It takes almost an hour to drive from the store to his cabin, so let's say he was there by seven. Montana Power and Light said the cabin had a power outage at midnight, which I attribute to the fire. So there's our window."

Cody was impressed. Larry *was* good.

"Back to the alcoholics," Larry said. "Do you know them all?"

Cody nodded.

"Do you have a list?"

"At home," Cody said. "There's thirteen in our little group. Of course, there are groups all over and a hell of a lot more alcoholics in Helena than you'd imagine. But our group is small because of when and where we meet. I can e-mail it to you. I can't officially work on the case, but I can feed *you*."

"Cool," Larry said. Cody could see a light behind his eyes. They were getting somewhere.

"I hate this, though," Cody said. "I'm betraying their trust. This is really a shitty thing to do to them. I mean, you'll be surprised. We're talking doctors, lawyers, a couple politicians. Even somebody in our office."

Larry *was* surprised.

"Edna," Cody said. "But you don't need to question her. She was working dispatch here every night this week."

"Don't worry," Larry said. "I won't even hint at how I got their names. I'll say we're simply following up on everyone we could find who might have known him. I might even fudge it a little and say we recovered an address book and we're just calling all the names in it. I won't mention AA and I won't bring up your name."

"Thank you, Larry. Really."

"But you've got to understand something, you asshole," Larry said. "I'm not being your pal here. I want you to go back. You *need* to go back to AA, or I'll never work with you again. And I'm not blowing smoke."

"I know you're not."

"Oh," Larry said, slapping the tops of his thighs, "I forgot to tell you something else. I sent the hard drive of that fried computer down to some IT guys at MSU. They think they may be able to retrieve the data off it. That surprised the hell out of me because I thought data would, you know, *melt*."

"No shit."

"They're looking at it now. I'll let you know what they come up with."

Cody stroked his chin. "See if they can find any letters or documents he had stored away. That and e-mails, of course. There might be an e-mail exchange with whomever he invited to dinner that night. That would be a hell of a stroke of luck. And the history on his Web browser. Maybe we'll know what he's been looking at lately."

Larry rolled his eyes. "Gee, I hadn't thought of any of that before, Cody. Good thing you're here to straighten me out."

Cody grinned.

The office door opened without a knock. Bodean filled the doorframe, hands on hips. His face was dark.

"I thought I heard your voice," he said to Cody. "Why in the hell are you still here?"

"Larry got all emotional when he heard I'd been suspended," Cody said. "I came in to comfort him and talk him off the ledge."

Larry snorted.

"Get the hell out of here or I'll have you arrested," Bodean said. "You have no authorization to be here. And give me your key card so you can't come back."

Cody handed it over and picked up his box to leave.

"And the keys to your Ford. It's a county vehicle."

Cody said, "I'll leave 'em at the shop when I turn the Ford over to the maintenance guys. Remember—it's kind of wrecked."

Bodean considered that a moment, and nodded. "Sort of like you," he said.

"Wow," Cody said, "that was a good one, Bodean. Clever."

Cody picked up his box to leave.

"It stays," Bodean said. "That's county property, too."

Cody shrugged. Larry simply watched, and raised his eyebrows.

"Go home and stay by your phone," Bodean said.

"Bye, Larry."

"Cody."

"Try not to weep."

"I'll try," Larry said.

The morning was warm and sunny and the sky was achingly blue. Cody shuffled across the lawn toward his vehicle in the parking lot. As he reached it he turned back and looked at the buildings he'd left and wondered when and if he'd be back.

The county courthouse next to the modern brick and glass Law Enforcement Center was a regal old Victorian building built of stone blocks. He saw the DA and his assistant come out holding files. When they saw him they stopped and the DA pointed. He could read his lips even though he couldn't hear him at that distance. The DA said, "There he is."

"Here I am," Cody mumbled.

He patted the keys in his pocket. He was glad Bodean let him keep the vehicle for the time being. His personal pickup hadn't run for months; he needed the Ford to get around.

As he pulled out of the lot onto the corner of Breckenridge and Ewing, he noted faded lettering on the side of an old brick building he'd never even noticed before. BOARDING STABLES was still legible in paint.

He hesitated on the corner. If he turned left he would drive by the Jester Bar. He breathed deeply and closed his eyes. He could use an ice-cold beer. Just one, though. To calm his nerves and maybe take the edge off the nasty jagged edges in his brain. He would leave after just one.

His cell phone burred. Larry.

"The ME called. They sliced his eyeballs open. Winters had *no* alcohol they could detect in his system. You were right."

"We're just getting started," Cody said.

"Wait until I walk down the hall and tell Tubman we might have a homicide after all. With the day he's having, this won't exactly brighten it up much."

"Keep me in the loop," Cody said, turning right toward his place. "I've got a lot to think about. I'll keep feeding you."

7

Even though he was exhausted and stabs of pain pulsed through his ear, Cody refused to take the medication they'd given him because he knew, he just *knew*, that if he let his defenses down even a little he'd start drinking. He knew himself. He'd find a justification to start off on another bender.

His ear hurt;

He was suspended;

Precious hours for finding the killer had been wasted and he'd never get them back;

His dog had died (granted, it was twenty years before, but it was still dead);

He missed his son;

His 401(k) wasn't worth crap anymore.

And that was just off the top of his head. He had to stay as sharp and determined as possible, despite the pain and bone-weariness, so he drank strong coffee and chain-smoked cigarettes and paced and thought.

He lived in a rented duplex with a decent view of Mount Helena from the backyard deck. But the structure was getting tired—old carpets, scarred molding, torn screens, windows that didn't shut tight. It had three bedrooms and two bathrooms, which was too many of each. One bedroom sat completely empty, the other was full of junk and empty moving boxes from a year before, and he had a bed he rarely used except for sex because he always fell asleep on the couch. Books were stacked from floor to ceiling in the living room but he'd never bought a bookcase since his divorce. He kept the downstairs bathroom door closed because it stank of duck. Bringing that wounded mallard drake home and letting it paddle around in the bathtub for weeks had left a stench that wouldn't go away. Stupid duck, he thought. He was glad when it finally flew away.

He went into his basement office and fired up his computer and sent the list of names to Larry. Within seconds, Larry thanked him in a terse e-mail. Then Cody started pacing.

Every time he passed one of his two phones he stared at it, willing it to ring. On the hour, he checked for messages from the sheriff or Larry or anyone. His hands shook and his skin felt twitchy.

He ran through the scenario that best fit the facts and his own speculation. Hank flew back from Salt Lake City and stopped at the supermarket on the way from the airport, buying food for two. He rushed home to cook it.

Cody stopped and smacked his forehead with the palm of his hand. Maybe it was a *woman*. Maybe Hank had a *date*. He hadn't even considered a woman before, but now it made even more sense than a man. But big steaks? That was man food. He shook his head and started pacing again.

So the guest arrived not long after Hank. They hadn't even started the grill yet, so they must have been catching up (man) or who-knows-what (woman). Then, for some reason, the visitor clocked Hank in the head. He didn't even eat first, which said to Cody the attack was likely quick and premeditated and not a crime of passion that arose from whatever transpired in the cabin that night. When Hank was incapacitated, he (she?) took Hank's AA coins and maybe something else—cash?

Drug samples? Gold? A treasure map?—opened a bottle of alcohol, and left it close to the body. The visitor opened the door to the wood-stove, filled it with lengths of pine until it was roaring, and then started the curtains or rug, and left the scene. And it all could have been just about perfect if it hadn't started raining and not stopped for three days.

God, how he hated coming down. It hurt. If he could just have one beer. . . .

As the sultry afternoon melded into dusk he went out on the deck with his handset and began his round of telephone calls. This was one of the things he hated most about coming off a bender: apologizing to everyone he'd offended. Sometimes, it went on for hours. Sometimes, he found out friends and relatives never wanted to talk to him again, and he prepared to lose a couple more.

He started with Carrie Lowry, who listened with impatient silence until she interrupted and said she was busy. That her boyfriend Jim didn't like getting awakened like that and blamed it on *her.* Then Skeeter, who refused to take his call. Then Skeeter's wife Mayjean, who was cold and distant and irritatingly formal. The guy from the liquor store, who said, "No problem, come again any old time and throw hundred-dollar bills at me." Finally, Jenny.

"You were drunk, weren't you?" she said.

"Yes."

"Do you remember denying it? You always deny it and act like you're offended I even asked. That's how I know."

"Yeah, yeah." Cody lit a cigarette off the one he'd been smoking so he wouldn't miss a second of nicotine. He pictured her: long dark hair, blue eyes, pug nose, lush mouth, nice curves. She had a good sense of humor, too, *once,* before he separated her from it. He'd always love her, always want her, and she knew it. She just couldn't live with him the way he was then, and the way he was the last two nights. He didn't hold it against her.

"So this is the apology tour," she said. "Am I the first stop?"

"No, I saved the most important one for last."

"Ahhh," she said, mocking.

He told her about what had happened. She broke in when he mentioned Alcoholics Anonymous.

"I'm so proud of you for going," she said, her voice softening. "Why didn't you tell me?"

"Because if I fell off the wagon I didn't want you to think I was a failure at that, too. Which, by the way, I did. Fall, I mean."

"Then climb back on," she said. "There's no rule against that, is there?"

He thought about the group, how supportive they were. How he was rewarding them for their confidentiality and support by having his partner interview them one by one to determine if any of them might be guilty of murder. Man . . .

"My sponsor was murdered," he said. "That kind of triggered things."

"You're kidding," she said.

"I wish I was." Then: "Oh—did I tell you I shot the county coroner last night?"

Silence.

"He's not dead. And he shot at me first. I'm suspended but it's just procedure. What's killing me is I want to go after the bad guy and take him down—"

"Cody," she interrupted. "You *shot* the coroner?"

He laughed. It sounded funny coming from her. Then he had to tell her how it happened.

It took a while for her to be able to change the subject. He glanced at the sun sliding behind Mount Helena and realized this was the longest conversation they'd had in two and a half years. Then he remembered something from two nights before about her new rich fiancé being gone.

"Where did you say they went? His Richness and Justin?"

"Stop calling him that. I told you all this the other night but you don't remember. He took Justin on a week-long wilderness pack trip. They don't even have cell service, so it's driving me crazy. It's Walt's idea because he wants to get closer to Justin if he can. He feels sort of distant, and . . ."

Cody tuned out. The thought of His Richness and *his* son spending that much time together made him instantly morose. He sort of listened. Something about horses, fly-fishing, all in Wyoming. What a fortune that must cost, he thought.

"Justin called me the other night," Cody said. "He needed to borrow something. I barely talked to him. In fact, I cut him off. I feel bad about that."

His phone clicked—another call coming in.

"I have to go now," he said.

"Call again," she said, surprising him. "Just don't make it part of your next tour."

Larry said, "Dry hole with your fellow alcoholics. Everybody has a decent alibi. That doesn't mean none of them are lying, but three of them were out of town and the other eight gave me names of people who'd vouch for them. Everybody heard about Winters, but since they didn't put any of the info about that bottle we found in the paper, no one connected the dots as to why I was calling."

"That's only eleven," Cody said. "Who couldn't you find?"

"Duh. Hank Winters and Cody Hoyt."

"Oh."

"You need to get some sleep."

"I don't know whether I'm relieved or pissed," Cody said. "Because our best angle just got shut down."

"Yeah, it sucks. My cop radar never went off once talking with any of them. They all were helpful and they sounded sincere."

"Maybe it was Edna," Cody said, his voice dropping into his conspiratorial rhythm. "Maybe she was banging Hank and something went wrong."

"Or maybe it was you," Larry said. "Can you account for your whereabouts that night?"

This is what they did, Cody thought. Cop-talk. But maybe there was a hint of curiosity in Larry's question. In fact, he thought, he had no alibi. He'd been out driving, driving, driving. There was no one to confirm where he'd been.

"Tying flies," Cody said, thinking of what his son was doing.

"You're lying. You need steady hands for that."

"Come and get me, flatfoot," Cody said. Actually, he did tie flies. He'd tied two hundred—caddis, hoppers, Adams, stimulators, tricos, nymphs—in the last two months when he wasn't driving aimlessly around the county. "Did you hear anything from your IT folks?"

"As a matter of fact, yes. They were able to access part of the hard drive but not all of it. The bad news is no e-mails were found. None. So we're screwed on that front. But remember you asked me about the history in his browser? Which Web sites he'd been on?"

Cody said yes. He was starting to feel a tingle just by the way Larry was setting it up.

"They're faxing me printouts and I don't have them yet, but they said most of the sites he visited were from a week before, apparently before he went on his trip to Salt Lake. News, weather, Drudge, ESPN, no porno or weird shit. But the most recent site he visited was at nine on the night he died."

Cody waited. Finally: "Was your guy an outdoorsman?"

"Not really," Cody said. "I remember him talking about hunting, but my impression was it was way back. He didn't fish because I offered to tie him some flies and he didn't want any. Why are you asking?"

"Because the last site he visited was for an outfitter."

Cody heard Larry shuffling papers. "Okay, got it. It was for something called Jed McCarthy's Wilderness Adventures. I don't know what the hell they do, but I'd guess hunting trips. I'm in the cruiser right now going back to the office after dinner so I haven't been able to look it up."

Cody scribbled down the name. "Thanks, man. I'll check 'em out, too."

"Hey, did you hear Skeeter held a press conference from his bed in the hospital?"

"No."

"Called you a 'rogue cop.'" Larry laughed. "The spin has already begun."

"Great."

"In his version, a shadowy creep jumped around the side of the crime scene brandishing a weapon and he fired instinctively to protect himself and the reporter. He said he wants you fired."

Cody said, "You're right. I should have gone for a head shot."

"Next time," Larry said.

The Google search took two seconds and Cody brought the site up: *Jed McCarthy's Wilderness Adventures.* "Wilderness Adventures" was in a bold frontier font and the name of the owner/outfitter was in script across the top at an angle, indicating to Cody the name of the company was a well-established brand if Jed himself was not.

The site was clean and well organized, unlike many of the local productions he'd seen where a fishing guide, dude ranch, or lodge owner hired his granddaughter to throw something up on the Web. The Wilderness Adventures site had a menu including Day Rides, Pack Trips, Multi-Day Adventures, Photos, Fly-Fishing, Rates, Booking, Maps, Virtual Tour, on and on. Even an online booking form. He clicked on "Pack Trips" and read through pages of text accompanied by stunning photos of Yellowstone Park. It turned out Jed McCarthy was one of the few outfitters licensed by the National Park Service to provide long excursions into Yellowstone, and McCarthy took every available opportunity to point it out.

He accessed the calendar page. There were a dozen or so different trips, leaving on different dates. He wished Larry would have told him if the IT guys had isolated Hank's browsing history to a specific trip, or whether Hank was simply looking at the home page.

But it just didn't seem right.

Cody recalled the hours he had spent talking with Hank. They had discussed their failures and their dreams together. He couldn't recall Hank ever saying he wanted to ride a horse into the backcountry, or go on a long wilderness trip, or anything similar. Although Hank obviously liked the mountains—that's why he bought his cabin there—he recalled Hank once saying he'd already spent more than enough time roughing it when he was a marine.

Which led to a new possibility in the murder scenario Cody had put together earlier.

Maybe it wasn't Hank who was going on the trip, he thought. *Maybe it was his guest.* Maybe the guest was showing Hank where he was headed next after leaving Helena. And as Hank read the screen, the visitor slipped behind him and hit him in the head with something. . . .

"Shit," Cody said, his mind swimming. Thinking, which trip? There were so many of them. . . .

He flashed through them. Snake River. Geysers and Explorers. Slough Creek. Hoodoo Basin Progressive Pack Trip. Lower Falls Adventure. Lamar River. Electric Peak and Beyond.

Then he brought up the calendar again.

"Ah," he said, and it all became clear. Cody had assumed Jed McCarthy had an army of guides and employees and trips going everywhere at once. But the calendar showed only June, July, August, and September. Within those months, three-, four-, five-, and seven-day blocks were marked out and color-coded by which trip was scheduled then. The trips didn't overlap. So what appeared to be the deal was McCarthy and his people took a group out for three or four days and returned to the base camp. A few days later, he led another trip. One after the other from the last week of May through mid-September, the trips bookended by melting snow on one end and flying snow on the other.

He clicked on the link that said "Meet Our Guides." There were two of them. Jed McCarthy wore a big cowboy hat and a silk scarf and in the photo he was striking a manly pose. There was also a nice-looking woman named Dakota Hill, who was pictured with a horse. She looked young enough to be Jed McCarthy's daughter.

His phone rang and he snatched it up. Larry.

"I'm looking at that Web site . . ."

"So am I," Cody said. "I've got a question—did the IT folks fax you the specific page he was looking at? I mean, was it a specific trip?"

"It was the home page," Larry said. "But Hank had been looking at a bunch of the pages previous to that in the last ten minutes before. 'What to Bring,' 'Menus,' 'Interactive Maps.' He was really scoping out this Web site. Which makes me think Hank was either doing some research or planning to go on a trip."

"That doesn't sound right to me," Cody said. "It could be a side of Hank I never saw, but it doesn't ring true. If this was the kind of thing he was into we should have found camping gear, saddles, a sleeping bag, that sort of thing. I don't remember any outdoor gear at all, do you?"

"It could have burned up in the fire," Larry said, but not with much conviction. "And besides, how do we know he wasn't just checking out the site? Maybe thinking about it for some other year? There's nothing we've got that suggests he was planning a trip *this* summer."

Cody shook his head. "I'm not buying. Think about it. He buys dinner to cook, rushes home to greet his guest. He's been gone for days. But instead of unpacking completely or getting dinner ready, he sits in his den and bounces around on the Internet? Does that make sense to you?"

"No."

"But what if it was his guest?" Cody said. "What if the killer was showing Hank where he was going next?"

Silence. "I hadn't thought about that," Larry said.

"Just a second," Cody said, clicking again on the calendar. "What is it, the thirtieth of June today?"

Larry chuckled. "Yes."

"Well, according to the calendar, the biggest and longest trip of the year is this one called 'Back of Beyond: The Ultimate Yellowstone Backcountry Adventure.' A whole bunch of nights in the middle of nowhere." Cody paused. "It leaves tomorrow, July 1."

Said Larry, "So if our man was headed south to Yellowstone to go on a trip with Jed McCarthy, even five nights ago, this would be the only one he could go on now."

"Yeah," Cody said, "because according to this calendar, Jed was finishing up the Hoodoo Basin Trip then. He couldn't have been on that."

"Boy," Larry said, "we're taking a mighty leap here. Just because Hank was looking at a Web site on the night he died, we're saying the killer was headed to Yellowstone. I'm not sure I can buy that one without some kind of corroboration."

Cody groaned his assent. Then: "I wish that damned trip didn't leave tomorrow morning. I wonder if it's possible to get ahold of Jed and find out who's on it? See if Hank's name is on his guest list? Jed probably has a pretty complete manifest or whatever you call it. We can run all the names and see if any of them came from this direction, or if anyone has a record, or if we can link him up with Hank in any way."

"And how do you propose to do *that*?" Larry asked.

"Police work," Cody said.

"Ha ha."

"Don't go anywhere," Cody said, "I'll call you right back."

He punched in the telephone number for Wilderness Adventures. They were based in Bozeman, meaning their headquarters was well outside the northern border of the park. If Jed was leading the trip the next morning, it was unlikely he'd be in Bozeman, but . . .

Cody got a voice mail. An erudite man's voice with a touch of country twang: "You've reached the voice mail of Jed McCarthy's Wilderness Adventures, the home of the only licensed multinight outfitter in Yellowstone National Park. We're on a pack trip right now so we're unable to take your call. And because of the nature of the trip, I won't be able to check messages for a week. Please go to our Web site and—"

He hung up and called Larry back.

"No one is there," Cody said.

"It's ten at night, Cody. What did you expect? I'm sure there'll be an office manager or somebody there tomorrow."

"Don't be so sure," Cody said. "These outfitter types are generally mom-and-pop operations. Believe me, I know. I grew up with them. My uncle Jeter used to manage his whole outfitting operation from scraps of paper he carried around in his shirt pocket. Jed is probably more sophisticated than that, but what if there isn't anyone to check the files tomorrow and see who is on the trip? We can't wait a week to find out who went. What if our killer is on this backcountry trip?"

"Then he'll still be there when they come back," Larry said. "If any of this pans out we can be waiting for them wherever Jed's base camp is located. That'll give us time to run this all down, see if any of it makes sense. Then we'll need to bring in the state boys and the Park Service rangers. We can't just go charging down there."

"Hmmpf."

"You know we need more time and a hell of a lot more corroboration," Larry said. "We start in Bozeman, at his office. He's got to have someone there answering phones and keeping the business running while he's out on a trip. Probably a receptionist or bookkeeper. We can call down and ask the sheriff or PD in Bozeman to be there when they open tomorrow morning."

Cody moaned. *Tomorrow morning . . .*

Larry said, "This is quite a leap, Cody. Just because that page was on his computer doesn't mean the killer is on the trip."

"I *know* that," Cody said. "But it's the only thing we've got that might indicate where he's going. We have to rule it out first."

Larry said, "If somebody, say Dougherty, brought to you what we've got so far I can hear you laughing your head off."

Cody snorted. "I hate it when you're right."

"I know."

Cody suddenly wanted a tall triple bourbon and water. He said, "If this killer is on the trip, though, how do we know he won't be a danger to everyone else on it? This Web site says the trip is full. So we're talking maybe a dozen people. It would be horrible if this guy is some kind of psycho—like the kind of person who would kill the most gentle man in the world and burn his place down around him. If we don't go at this angle hard we may be putting innocent people in harm's way."

"There's that," Larry said. "But still ... I mean, I can't spend all night on this and you got yourself suspended."

"I know," Cody said gruffly. "Jeez, I hate being in my house now. Can I ask you a favor?"

Larry sighed. "Man, I'm doing overtime *now*. Bodean put out that memo about no more overtime without his authorization. I mean—"

"We need to play catch-up," Cody said, ignoring him. "Call RMIN and ViCAP, see if there are any other crimes similar to the Winters murder."

RMIN (pronounced "Rimin") was the Rocky Mountain Information Network, a regional clearinghouse of incidents recorded in Idaho, Montana, Wyoming, Colorado, Utah, Nevada, and New Mexico. Vi-CAP was the Violent Criminal Apprehension Program of the FBI. Both organizations had analysts on staff who could research similar crimes. ViCAP had profilers available as well as a password-protected Web site that could be accessed by law enforcement agencies after hours.

"You're grasping at straws," Larry said. "We can't do much more until tomorrow, Cody. Once we talk to the receptionist and hear back from RMIN and ViCAP, *then* maybe we'll have something to go on."

"I know. But that trip leaves tomorrow morning. Call those guys, Larry. Get things going."

"You owe me so many dinners," Larry said, and slammed down his phone.

While he waited, he did another Google search on the outfitting company, hoping he could find another contact, maybe an after-hours number. He assumed Jed and his people and horses were already in Yellowstone at their base camp, likely out of cell phone range. But surely he would have a way to communicate with his office, Cody thought. Like to check on clients who were late or didn't show up? Although he couldn't find any way to make contact other than the office number, e-mail address, and Web site, he did find an old online article from the Bozeman *Chronicle*: SALE OF PARK OUTFITTING BUSINESS PENDING NPS APPROVAL.

Even though he couldn't see how it would be of much help, Cody read it. It was from February, five years before.

> Bozeman newcomer Jedediah McCarthy announced on Wednesday that he was awaiting National Park Service approval to acquire the assets of Wilderness Adventures, the longtime outfitting operation specializing in Yellowstone Park pack trips. McCarthy said he intended to continue the legacy established by Frank "Bull" Mitchell, who ran the company for the past 32 years.
>
> McCarthy stated he planned to maintain the quality of the company and perhaps—with NPS approval—expand the available multiday excursions into the most remote reaches of Yellowstone Park.
>
> "It's time," Mitchell told the *Chronicle*, "Somebody else can put up with all that Park Service BS . . ."
>
> McCarthy aims to emphasize low-impact camping with a

greater emphasis on the unique properties of the Greater
Yellowstone Ecosystem, he said. . . .

Cody read the rest of the article but found it boring: Jed McCarthy
extolling the virtues of his trip and the excellent and professional
methodology of the National Park Service. *Stroking bureaucrats in the
paper while they considered your application,* Cody thought. *No wonder he got the concession.*

He smiled and jotted down the name "Frank 'Bull' Mitchell."

Then it hit him and he called Jenny again as panic rose inside.

She sounded groggy. "When I said call again, I didn't mean midnight."

"I'm sorry, but I just thought of something. It's nuts, but I have to
make sure I'm wrong."

"About what?"

"Justin and His Richness. Where did you say they went?"

"Wyoming. I told you—"

"I know. But where specifically did they go? And did they go on
their own? Is His Richness driving them around, or what?"

"Well, he drove them there. But they're going on some kind of long
wilderness trip in Yellowstone Park. With some outfitter on horses—"

"Jesus," Cody said.

"What? You're scaring me, Cody."

"Don't be scared," he said to her as well as to himself. "Just find the
name of the outfit they're using."

"I think I have a brochure," she said. "But I can't call them. Justin
said they'd be out of cell phone range . . ."

"Jenny," he said, "we might have a big problem."

Cody had the Ford backed up to his open garage door and was throwing
gear into it—sleeping bag, tent, pad, cooking set, Uncle Jeter's old
saddle—when Larry pulled his SUV into the driveway and blocked
him.

Larry kept his motor running and his headlights on and swung out. "You didn't answer your phone."

"I was out here," Cody said.

"You can't leave. You know that. You'll give the sheriff a damned good reason to fire you."

Cody said, "Let him."

Larry spun Cody around so they were face to face. "Have you been drinking?" Larry asked.

"Not yet."

Larry leaned forward on the balls of his feet and stared into Cody's eyes. Cody didn't flinch, and said, "Get any closer and I'll clock you."

Larry relaxed a little, apparently content that Cody was sober. "You need to slow down. It's two thirty in the morning. You can't just run away in the middle of the night."

"I'm not running," Cody said. "I'm pursuing a lead."

"You're not a cop right now."

Cody shrugged. "I'm *always* a fucking cop."

"I was afraid you were going to do this," Larry said. "All I can say is it's stupid, and useless, and you're doing more harm than good."

"Sounds like me," Cody said. "Hey, why don't you give me a hand. I was looking for an old pack saddle of my uncle's in that mess of a garage. Maybe you can find it."

"To hell with that," Larry said, squinting past Cody toward the garage. It was piled with junk Cody had never bothered to unpack or organize. His disabled pickup truck took up most of the space.

"Look," Larry said. "I left messages at RMIN and ViCAP, but nobody is working tonight. We should hear back from them first thing in the morning. There's no reason for you to leave tonight and risk your job. And risk *my* job, because if you take off now they'll ask me if I knew you went."

Said Cody, "Tell them the truth, Larry. Tell them you tried to talk me out of it but you couldn't."

Larry shook his head, and his eyes flashed with anger. "Cody, damn you, I can't risk this job. I've got child support payments and no one is hiring. I have to stay in this town to be near my kids. You can't put me in this position. You're such an asshole."

"Yeah, yeah," Cody said, flicking a cigarette butt into the street where it exploded in a shower of little sparks. He lit another. "I know," he said, drawing deep, "but—"

"I found something," Larry cut in. "On the ViCAP Web site."

Cody went silent, squinting at Larry's face through the smoke.

"We won't know for sure if we've got anything until I can talk to an analyst or profiler tomorrow. But since they're on eastern time, I should hear back from them early tomorrow."

"What did you find?" Cody asked.

"I used the national crime database they've got," Larry said, dragging it out like he always did. "I used the keywords *murder, arson, single victim, head injury,* I don't remember what else. Just trying to find out if there were any hits. It isn't an exact science . . ."

Cody felt something red and hot pop behind his eyes and reached out as if he were going to grab Larry's throat. Larry anticipated the move and ducked to the side.

"*What did you find, goddamn you?*" Cody hissed.

"Four of 'em," Larry said.

Cody's mouth dropped. "Four?"

"One in Virginia a month ago. One in Minnesota two weeks ago. Hank Winters. And another one in Jackson Hole, Wyoming, two nights ago. Three men, one woman. All professional, middle-aged. Alone at the time. No suspects in any of them, and as far as I could tell no one has linked them up yet. They're all classified as still under investigation, although they read like accidents. Just like ours."

"Four?"

Larry nodded. "Of course, we won't know until—"

Cody said, "Justin is on that trip."

Larry rubbed his eyes. "Oh no, man."

"You need to move your rig," Cody said. "I need to get the hell out of here to Bozeman."

Larry sighed and his shoulders slumped.

"Larry, move your truck."

Cody roared down down U.S. 287 toward Townsend, the flat south end of Canyon Ferry Lake shimmering with moonlight. The night was warm and he kept his windows open so the rush of air would keep him awake. Synapses in his brain seemed to be firing with the crackling machine-gun rhythm of a spark plug. He shot by the sleeping ranch houses and barns, past the faded wooden archway to the ranch his friend Jack Mc-Guane's parents still ran.

The sight of the ranch brought back a flood of memories both painful and euphoric. A year and a half before, he'd laid it all out there for his friends Jack and Melissa McGuane. In the end he'd lost his boyhood friend Brian Eastman, gutted his own reputation, and lost his stripes in the Denver PD, but it all still felt right to him. Even with the high body count of scumbags, he'd gleefully do it all over again.

That was the thing, he thought. Throughout his life his friends, lovers, and colleagues wondered aloud what made him tick. As if he were like Churchill's description of Russia, a "riddle wrapped in a mystery inside an enigma," when really it was so damned simple. So damned simple. Cody was born damaged. His Maker had flinched when soldering his hard wires together, and they would always short out or overheat at the wrong time. He could probably blame his white-trash family for his criminal tendencies and penchant for self-delusion and self-medication, but he didn't believe in justifying bad behavior with that kind of touchy-feely crap. Cody was not good and he was incapable of being good, but that didn't mean he didn't recognize and revere goodness, and he'd do anything—*anything*—to protect those blessed with clean, unimpeded wiring. Like his friends the McGuanes, whom he'd helped. Like Hank Winters, whom he'd failed. Like Justin, his miracle son, whom he *had* to save.

He slowed through Townsend, glancing over his shoulder at a yelp that came from two drunks stumbling out of the Commercial Bar into the street. Thought maybe he might even know them, and smiled bitterly.

Two miles south of Townsend, the inside of the Ford exploded with red and blue light. He glanced into his rearview mirror and squinted at the intensity of the wig-wags on the light bar of the Highway Patrol car.

"Shit," he hissed, noting he was only five miles over the speed limit.

Fuming, he pulled over. He reached for his badge which was no longer there and sat back and closed his eyes. He hoped like hell he knew the trooper and could manage to talk his way out of a ticket so he could get back on the highway as soon as possible. For a second he considered flooring the Ford once the trooper got out of his vehicle, but he knew that wouldn't work for long. No doubt, his plates had already been called in, and there wouldn't be a record of them.

He was caught, unless he could talk his way out of it and get the plate search canceled.

A flashlight blinded him through the driver's window and he looked away.

The trooper, an unfamiliar beefy youngster who looked six months out of the training center, said, "You were aware you only have one operating headlight, mister?"

Cody said, "I'm an investigator for the sheriff's department. I'm in a hurry."

The trooper grinned, his teeth glinting in the secondary light of his flashlight's reflection.

"Well, you'll just have to show me a badge and get the sheriff on the horn," the trooper said. "And in the meanwhile you can follow me back to town until we can get that headlight fixed. What happened, anyway? It looks like you hit something."

"A fucking elk," Cody said, not able to keep the anger out of his voice.

"Yeah," the trooper said, shining his beam on the damage. "I can see some hair and blood. Male or female?"

Cody sighed and covered his face with his hands. "Female," he said.

"Got your cow permit?" The trooper chuckled.

Part Two

Yellowstone National Park

8

Sixteen-year-old Danielle Sullivan was furiously texting her on-again off-again boyfriend Riley as fourteen-year-old Gracie Sullivan looked on. Their father drove the rental car and pointed out bison far below in the valley and two distant elk crossing a river in the early morning sun. Danielle and Gracie were in the backseat.

"I'm surprised he's even up this early," Gracie said to Danielle. She marveled at her sister and the desperate fire in her eyes as she tapped out messages with a blur of her thumbs.

"He's got to get up early for work," Danielle said, not looking over. "Remember—he's got that stupid job with the grounds crew with the schools. They make him show up every morning at eight. They're evil." Gracie nodded and snapped her phone open. She didn't expect any messages although she'd be ridiculously thrilled if there were any. There weren't, so as she often did in the presence of her beautiful, popular, constantly in-demand sister, she tapped out a message to her own phone via her e-mail account:

How are you this morning?

When it came through, she wrote:

Crappy start, but thanks for asking.
I'm sorry.
Don't be. Things are looking up. WE'RE IN YELLOWSTONE
PARK.

Even though Danielle thought Gracie pathetic for spelling out all the words in her texts rather than using text-speak or shorthand, Gracie thought there was no harm done since she was, in effect, talking to herself. It was a scheme she'd come up with to make Danielle think she had admirers in constant contact as well.

You're up early.
I couldn't sleep. I kept thinking I forgot something.
Like what?
Toothbrush. Glasses. I got up at 2:30 to make sure I packed
underwear. I had a nightmare I didn't bring underwear and
I had to borrow a f**king thong from Danielle.

She lowered the phone to her lap with the screen facing away from her sister and looked through the window. There were no buildings, no roads, no power lines. To the south was a vast river valley with tall grass that rippled in the cold morning breeze. A ribbon of river that looked like sheet metal serpentined through the valley floor. To the north the terrain seemed to swell and rise to meet tendrils of pine trees, and above them a dark wall of forest.

"Oh my God," her dad said as the car slowed suddenly. "Look, girls: *wolves.*"

Gracie snapped her phone shut and hurled herself forward. All her life she'd wanted to see a wolf.

Her dad pulled over to the side of the two-lane blacktop and rolled down his window. The small of pine, sage, and cool fresh air wafted in. He pointed toward the river.

"See them, at that bend? Near those big rocks the sun is starting to hit?"

Gracie threw her arms over the front seat and squinted where her father was pointing. Far below, she saw movement.

"They look like dots," she said. "Two little dots."

"They're wolves," her dad said. "Aren't they magnificent?"

Magnificent *dots,* she thought. She wished she could see them closer or figure out what they were doing to make them seem magnificent to her father, who tended toward hyperbole.

"Here," her father said, handing her a pair of binoculars that still had the price tag on them. "You focus using that little wheel in the middle."

While Gracie tried to manipulate the binoculars and frantically rolled the wheel all the way to the left and then to the right and finally realized she was bringing the hood ornament into sharp relief, she heard her dad say to Danielle, "Don't you want to see these fantastic animals, Danny?"

"Maybe in a minute," Danielle said, still texting.

"They may be gone in a minute," he said, trying to disguise the disappointment in his voice.

Gracie finally figured out where to point, and started bringing the animals into focus.

"Dad, it's not like we won't have a chance to see wolves," Danielle said, not looking up from her phone. "Aren't we going to be in the middle of nowhere for five friggin' days? We'll be *sleeping* with wolves. Like that movie."

Gracie mumbled, "*Dancing* with wolves, not sleeping with them," as she brought the animals into sharp detail.

"Whatever," Danielle said sharply.

"I think there's a difference," Gracie whispered, and not too loudly, wishing she'd never said anything at all. To confirm her thought, Danielle drove a sharp fingernail into her ribs that made her jump and lose the animals. She recovered and refocused.

Then she sighed, sat back, and handed the binoculars to her father. "Those are coyotes, not wolves."

"Oh, come on," he said, taking the glasses back.

She waited. She could tell he wanted to turn them into wolves.

Finally, he said, "I'll be damned. I thought they were wolves." He was disappointed they were coyotes and seemed disappointed in Gracie for pointing it out.

Gracie said, "Dad, I *read* those books you sent us. You know, *The Wildlife of Yellowstone, Yellowstone Flora and Fauna, Death in Yellowstone, The Geysers of Yellowstone.* I read them. I studied them," she said, hoping for a grunt of appreciation. "You know," she said, "so Danny wouldn't have to."

That got a smile out of him.

"You suck," Danielle mumbled. "Some of us have lives."

"You read those books?" her dad asked, nodding.

"Some of them more than once," Gracie confessed, and wished she hadn't. She sounded so . . . *without a life.* But the fact was she was captivated with the books about a place on earth that could hold so many fascinating things that weren't made or constructed by man. It had never occurred to her before she read those books that there was an amazing natural location not designed or driven by people. It made her think about how small she was. How small everybody was.

"Don't drive off, Dad," Danielle said.

"Do you want to take a look, then?" her dad asked eagerly, handing the binoculars over his shoulder so Danielle could grab them.

"Naw. I've got a good signal here," she said, deadpan.

"It's gonna get worse," Gracie said. "In fact, we'll lose it for good in a minute."

Danielle looked up, horrified. "Shut *up*," she said to Gracie. There was terror in her eyes. Then: "Dad, tell me that's not true."

When he realized Danielle didn't want the glasses he lowered them to his seat as if he'd not held them out to her in the first place. Like he was embarrassed, Gracie thought. He said, "I thought I told you,

Danny. There's no cell service where we're going. It's the wilderness. It's the most remote part of the whole country. At least the lower forty-eight states, to be exact. That's the whole *point*."

Gracie watched Danielle do a slow burn with a whiff of absolute panic.

"*Are you telling me I can't use my phone?*" she said.

"Honey," her dad said, turning around, making his face soft and sympathetic, "it'll be great. You'll forget you even have it. I know I told you all this about how remote it would be."

Danielle's tone was icy. "You didn't say I couldn't use my phone."

"I think I did."

Gracie nodded. "I think he did."

Danielle turned on her. "I don't know why you'd even care, Gracie. Nobody even knows your number."

Gracie looked away, instant tears stinging in her eyes. She should be used to how quickly and ruthlessly Danielle could humiliate her and learn not to tear up. She hated when she let her sister get to her.

"This isn't Yellowstone," Danielle said to her dad, "It's friggin' *hell*."

"Honey . . . ," her Dad said, turning in his seat so he could plead with her.

"My friends go to Europe, or Disneyland, or Hawaii, or Mexico for summer vacation," Danielle said. "But no, my dad takes me to friggin' hell."

"Darling . . . ," her dad said.

"I should have stayed home," Danielle said, twisting the knife. "I should have stayed with Mom. At least there was civilization and broadband. And my friends. And friggin' cell service."

Her dad turned back around in silence and engaged the transmission and the car eased forward into the lane.

Gracie said, "We can call it Hell-o-stone!"

"Shut the fuck up," Danielle spat.

"Don't say that," Gracie said. "It's against the law to say *fuck* in a national park."

Danielle looked at her suspiciously. "It is?"

Her dad sighed, "Girls, please . . ."

It had been their dad's idea, this trip to Yellowstone National Park. He'd come up with it the previous summer—they stayed with him summers—and he'd announced it suddenly when the sisters returned from an afternoon at the swimming pool at his condo village on the outskirts of St. Paul. Danielle, who'd just broken up with her then-local boyfriend at the pool an hour before and never wanted to see him—or Minnesota—again, said she was all over it.

Anything to get away from Alex and his stupid friends, she'd said, wiping her hands on her pool towel as if rubbing off his disgusting germs.

Gracie, who could never get used to the heat or humidity of the long green summer months compared to where they lived the rest of the year in dry, high-altitude Denver, was thrilled with the idea. Gracie loved animals, hiking, nature, and the idea of a great adventure. But most of all, she wanted to make her dad happy.

It had been obvious for the ten years since the divorce that her dad wasn't really comfortable with them, maybe because they were girls. He'd never outright said he wanted boys instead, but it was clear that at least he'd know what to do with them: take them to baseball games or something. He really wasn't an outdoorsman of any kind even though he'd grown up in Colorado, but Gracie guessed he'd take quicker to learning to hike, fish, or hunt for the sake of his sons than he did ferrying his daughters to movies, the Mall of America, restaurants, or waiting for them to return from the pool. He was dutiful, but there was always something sad about him, she thought. Like he liked the *idea* of having his daughters for the summer more than he actually liked having them there taking over the bathroom or hanging their wet bathing suits from the shower rod to dry.

But this trip really did seem to excite him in a way she'd never seen before. Once he cleared it with their mother—who thought he, and they, were crazy as ticks but acquiesced in the end—he could talk of nothing else for the rest of the year. His eyes sparkled, and his movements seemed more rapid. He fired off e-mails and links about Yellowstone and horses and camping and wildlife. For Christmas he sent them both sleeping bags, flashlights, headlamps, travel fishing rods and reels, new digital cameras, rain ponchos, and *National Geographic* maps of the park.

Gracie read everything he sent, and obsessed over the "What to Bring" list forwarded from the outfitter. Danielle rolled her eyes and said, "What—does he think we're his *boys,* now?"

Gracie suspected there was an ulterior motive to his enthusiasm, but she didn't know yet what it was. She suspected through comments her mother had made over the years that her dad wasn't very happy growing up, that his intensity (he was a software engineer who traveled a lot all over the country and the world) prevented him from ever being loose or carefree. He thought in terms of circuit boards and digital switches, and when the level of drama was high—which it often was with Danielle and sometimes Gracie—that he was "better at hardware than software," as if that explained everything. She thought maybe he was hoping he could go on this wilderness cowboy pack trip and . . . be a *boy* again. She wasn't sure that was something she really wanted to see.

The trip the day before had begun on a jarring note, Gracie thought. It was taking her a while to process what had happened and why it bothered her, other than her natural and annoying propensity to simply worry too much about everything.

They'd kissed their mother good-bye at Denver International Airport in the morning and boarded the United/Frontier flight to Bozeman. Although they'd planned to carry on their luggage—which was ridiculously slight given the weight restrictions Jed McCarthy imposed—but because of all the metal and equipment in their duffel bags, they'd had to check the bags through. Gracie thought her mom looked forlorn and vulnerable, as if she wondered if she'd ever see her daughters again. *That* wasn't a good way to start the trip.

Their arrival was slightly delayed—the airplane had to circle Bozeman while early summer thundershowers lashed the airport. Gracie had the window seat and looked out at the mountains in all directions and the black thunderheads on the northern horizon.

"Which way is Yellowstone?" she'd asked her sister.

"Like *I* would know?" Danielle said in a way that was both incredulous and offended.

"That's right," Gracie had said, "how dare I assume you know anything."

Which was met with a hard twist on her ear.

She'd looked out expectantly for their dad in the luggage area because he was scheduled to arrive an hour before from Minneapolis, but he wasn't there.

"His plane must be late," Danielle told her. "I'll check in a minute."

When their bags arrived and the rest of the passengers cleared out, Gracie waited near the outside doors. She knew there was a problem by Danielle's worried face as she came back from the Northwest counter.

"The plane arrived on time but he wasn't on it, they said."

Gracie fought panic. She looked up at the mounted animal heads and stuffed trout on the walls and out at the cold blue mountains to the south. She thought of how miserable it would be to be stuck in Bozeman, Montana, with her sister until they could figure out a way to get back home. And she was worried about what might have happened to their dad. Was he sick? Did he get in a car crash on the way to the airport? She flipped open her phone and powered it up, hoping there would be a message.

"I'm calling Mom," Danielle said, having already opened her cell phone.

That's when their dad bounded into the airport. Not from the area where the planes landed, but from outside on the street.

"*Girls!*" he shouted. His grin and his open arms made Gracie's black dread melt away as if he had touched a flame to a spider's web. He seemed almost too exuberant, she thought. As if he was happy but with a bit of desperation thrown in.

"Come on, the car's out front," he'd said. "Let me help you with your stuff."

Danielle told him they were starting to worry, and what the people at the airline counter had said.

He waved it off, saying, "That's ridiculous. Obviously, I was on the plane. I'm here, aren't I?"

They turned onto a dirt road by a brown National Park Service sign indicating the campsite and trailhead. Her father once again closed his window to prevent the roll of dust from filling the car. Gracie turned off her phone and put it in a side pocket of the door and made a mental note not to forget it when they returned. She watched as Danielle seethed—*no signal at all*—and finally snapped her phone shut.

"Great," her sister said, "I'm completely alone in the world."

"Except for your sister and your father," her dad said with caution.

"Alone in Hell-o-stone," Gracie mocked gently, "Hell-o-stone alone . . ."

Danielle mouthed *Shut the fuck up, Gracie.*

"That's your second offense," Gracie said, deadpan. "We may need to turn you in to the rangers."

"We're here," her dad said with an epic flourish.

Gracie once again bounded forward and hung her arms over the front seat. They'd rounded a corner and could now see that at the end of the road was a very long horse trailer in a parking lot. People stood around the trailer in the sun; a couple were already on horseback. Gracie counted ten or eleven milling about. When she saw the horses her heart seemed to swell to twice its size.

"We're really going to do this, aren't we?" she said, reaching up and putting her hand on her dad's shoulder. He reached across his body and put his hand on hers.

"It'll be the greatest adventure of our lives," he said.

"I'm taking my phone," Danielle said as if talking to herself. "Maybe we'll find a place with a signal somewhere." Then: "Oh my God. Look at all the people! We're going to be stuck for a week with *them*?"

9

Outfitter Jed McCarthy pulled back and tightened the cinch on a mare named Strawberry—she was a strawberry roan—and squinted over the top of a saddle at the car that had just rounded the corner on the side of the hill. It was a blue American-made four-door sedan. Nobody normal drove those, he thought, meaning it must be a rental and therefore the last of his clients to arrive.

"That better be the Sullivans," he said under his breath to Dakota Hill, his wrangler. She was in the process of saddling a stout sorrel a few feet away.

"Is that the party of three?" she asked. "The father and two teenage daughters?"

"Yup."

Dakota blew a strand of hair out of her face. "You know what I think about teenage girls on these trips."

"I know."

"I may have to kill one someday. Push her off a cliff. Damn prima donnas, anyhow."

"I know."

"Or feed her to some bears."

"Keep your voice down," McCarthy said. "Their money's as good as anyone's. And we've got a full boat of paying customers for this one. This keeps up, I can get that new truck. Life is good."

"For you," she said, tight-lipped. "Me, I get the same damned wages no matter what."

"At least you did before you started getting under my skin," he said, smiling his smile that he knew could be interpreted as cruel. "Besides, you got perks. You get to sleep with the boss." He waggled his eyebrows when he said it.

"Some perk," she grumbled.

"I ain't heard any complaints."

"You ain't listening."

Almost twenty-five, she'd grown up on ranches in Montana and drove her father's pickup at eight years old and was breaking horses by the time she was twelve. She had a round open face, thick lips that curved quickly into an unabashed and purely authentic smile, naturally blushed cheeks, and dancing brown eyes. She'd attended a couple of years at MSU, but quit to barrel race and never went back. He'd met her when she delivered some horses to him two summers before. Her barrel horse had come up seriously lame just that day at the local rodeo. The horse would never run again and never earn any more money. She needed a job. He needed a wrangler.

He stepped closer to Strawberry so none of his clients could see him draw a laminated three-by-five index card out of his breast pocket. On it were the names of each of his customers for the trip as well as vital information they'd sent him regarding weight (to match them with a horse), age, riding experience, food allergies, dietary needs, and what they most wanted out of the trip, from fly-fishing opportunities to horseback riding to wildlife viewing to "being one with nature." He made it a point of pride to know the names of everyone on his excursions from the initial introduction, and to constantly surprise his clients with probing questions about their personal needs and to ask them about their lives based on a short questionnaire he'd required them all to fill out and send along with their booking form. People liked that kind of personal attention, he'd found, and he was rewarded for it at the end of the week by the size of the tip. Sometimes they'd rebook a trip because of it. And despite Dakota's grumbling, he knew it was vital to hook the teenage girls early. Usually, it was to match them up with a horse they'd fall in love with. He'd feed the girl some kind of backstory on the horse they were riding—sometimes it was even true—about how the animal was particular and only responded to people who were gentle and special. Then, a few miles up the trail, he'd remark how well-behaved the horse was and compliment the teenage rider for her prowess. Generally, that would do it: the girl would fall in love and never even consider how many other girls before her—and after—would have the same passionate relationship with the same horse.

He'd make sure to send a Christmas card to the girl from the *horse,* telling her how much her horse missed her and that she was the animal's favorite human. Often, it resulted in a customer for life, because he'd found today's parents did not deny their children *anything.* At two thousand dollars a client, it was important to know that.

This particular trip was full. There'd been no cancelations and everybody showed up at the appointed place at the agreed-upon time. With the arrival of the Sullivans, he had everybody.

Before gathering them together for an orientation, he walked along the length of his long horse trailer and looked at a reflection of himself in the passenger window of his pickup. He liked what he saw.

Jed McCarthy was a short, solid fireplug of a man with a gunfighter mustache, trimmed short beard, and blue eyes so pale they were practically opaque. He was a year shy of forty and he'd been running horse pack trips into the Yellowstone wilderness for eight years, one of only two licensed outfitters deemed worthy and compliant by the authorities at the National Park Service. He wore snug Wranglers and lace-up outfitter boots with heels for riding, a sterling silver rancher set for a buckle, and a leather vest with plenty of pockets to hold all the tools and small gear he needed. Around his neck was a red silk kerchief folded over and knotted in the cowboy style. His hair was thinning on top so he rarely took off his droopy brown Resistol hat. He knew from experience his clients spent a lot of time studying him. The women did it because he was interesting and exotic and a damned good-looking cowboy who was also sensitive, manly, humble, and mysterious. They'd likely read on his Web site he was a poet and painter as well as an experienced horseman and man of nature: a wilderness Renaissance man! The men studied him not only as a leader but as a rival. Some of them sucked up to him, trying to get his approval. Others shut up and conceded Jed was the boss because he was a man's man and he was in charge of the outfit.

And he *was* in charge. It didn't matter if his clients were CEOs or actors or millionaire lawyers or doctors or whatever. Once they mounted up and fell in behind his black gelding and his string of three pack mules (Dakota followed up on her horse with a string as well) he was the trail boss. He was the boss of everything. And with the exception of Dakota, he was the only one on the trip who knew where they were going, what to expect, what to watch out for, where they'd camp, what they'd eat, where they'd sleep and relieve themselves. This was his company, his stock, his equipment, his plan, and his permit.

Behind him in the reflection, he saw Dakota slump by. He wished her posture was better as well as her attitude. But she was a hell of a hand, and she was unabashed and enthusiastic in a way that only country girls could be when they zipped their sleeping bags together. Country girls who'd grown up around life and death and sex and birth on the farm or ranch had few inhibitions, he'd found. Plus, she was a quick learner and eager to please. He liked horses and women with that quality. What he didn't like was the way she kept her own counsel at times and the way she vanished for a week here and a week there without telling him where she was going or when she'd be back. He'd have fired her long ago if he could have found a replacement. But it wasn't easy to locate a nice-looking girl twenty years his junior who was not only an experienced wrangler with horses and mules but good in the sack as well. But he never told her that. Sometimes, he hinted there was a long line of eager replacements out there ready to step in if she left. As long as she believed that, he thought, he'd have the advantage.

He pocketed the index card and closed his eyes and repeated their names over and over like a mantra before he turned around, put on his kind but competent expression, and said to the clients milling around near their piles of clothing and gear, "Let's gather here for a few minutes, folks, so we can get to know each other."

He took a few steps into the clearing and stopped. He stuck his thumbs into his jeans pockets and rocked back a little on his boot heels. He'd not go to them. He'd make them come to *him*. This was the all-important first impression, perhaps the single most important half hour of the entire week. He'd learned it could sometimes take days to undo a bad first meeting if he came across as soft, confusing, or incoherent. It was imperative everyone understood the rules, the procedures, and who was who. It started with them all coming to *him*.

And dutifully, in singles and loose groups, they did. Dakota took her place to his right about ten feet away. She led a saddled horse over to use for demonstration purposes.

He waited for the Sullivans to join them. The father looked pale and nervous and had a weak chin and darting eyes. Obviously a desk jockey of some sort, Jed thought. Those types tended to remind him of mice, like this guy did. Whatever Sullivan did for a living—he'd need to check his records but he knew "automation" and "digital" were in the title and he was vice president of development of something—it paid well. Treating his daughters to a trip like this, plus the transportation, was pricey.

The taller girl was striking, Jed thought. Jet-black hair, bangs, blue eyes, nice mouth and figure. Plus, she was looking right at him. That showed attitude and confidence. When he looked back she didn't drop her eyes. He thought: *Arrogant, too.* Then: *Dakota's going to love this one.*

The younger girl was skinny, flat chested, freckle faced, and looked serious and bookish. Freckles *and* braces. His eyes slid right over her and his brain said, *Nothing to see here folks, move along.*

But he'd have to get to know that tall one. . . .

"Folks, I'm Jed McCarthy and this is Dakota Hill. We're your guides, and we're about to embark on the longest, most scenic, and most remote horse packing expedition into the Yellowstone backcountry wilderness available. It's the best trip we do all summer and it's the one we enjoy the most. This is the first and only time we'll do this trip this season, and because the snows last winter were so heavy and have just recently melted away, we're likely to be the *only* people going where we're going. For you, all I can say is I envy you for what you're going to see and experience for the first time. It truly is the trip of a lifetime into the farthest reaches of America's first and best national park.

"I know you all got the materials I sent you and read up on our itinerary and the other info on the Web site, but in a nutshell, we're going to match you up with a horse that will be your horse for the next six days and ninety miles," he said, letting that sink in amidst titters.

Jed continued, "We'll be leaving from here within the hour, so I'd urge you to make sure you've got all your gear out and piled up so we can load it on the mules. This is a progressive trip, meaning we'll be at a new camp every night. Camp One is fifteen miles away along the shore of Yellowstone Lake. Tomorrow, we go into the Thorofare along the river and we follow it upstream to Camp Two. Camp Three is a hell of a climb from the river valley toward the top of the Continental Divide and Two Ocean Pass. We'll ride a few thousand feet up into the mountains, and some of you may experience shortness of breath or maybe a touch of altitude sickness. The best way to ward that off is to keep hydrated. Keep drinking water, folks—it's magic. If you're doing it right, you'll drink two or three times the water you usually drink. That's what we want.

"It's called Two Ocean Pass because the water on the east side of the mountains begins its flow to the Atlantic, and on the west side it's headed for the Pacific. It's high mountain country, and the most remote location in the lower forty-eight in terms of its distance from any road or structure. It is true primitive wilderness, but that's what you signed up for, isn't it?

"Keep this in mind, folks: only two percent of Yellowstone's 3,468 square miles is developed in any way. It's the largest remaining nearly intact ecosystem in the Earth's northern temperate zone. What you see around you right now—a road, cars, a parking lot—are the last items of modern civilization you'll see for the next week."

He scanned his clients as he spoke, already putting them into categories. Rarely anymore did anyone truly surprise him. Everyone was a type, and he'd been with all types on his trips. As he looked his clients over he fitted them into slots.

Jed said, "We've all heard the term 'beyond civilization' without really thinking much about it because for most of you, being out of range of cell-phone towers or Wi-Fi isn't something you've thought real hard about. But that's where we're going: the most remote wilderness left in our country. We like to call it *Back of Beyond*."

As always, the phrase produced a nice murmur of trepidation.

He'd briefly talked to the lone married couple on the trip, Tristan and Donna Glode. Although in their sixties, they were fit and vigorous. He was a CEO of a manufacturing company in St. Louis and he spoke as if used to being listened to. Tristan seemed clear-eyed if hard-assed— even with that unfortunate name—Jed thought. A guy he could depend on if he didn't cross him or fill him full of bullshit—which he wouldn't. His wife, Donna, was arch and cold. She was one of those fine-boned skeleton women who no doubt did Pilates and had her plastic surgeon's number on her speed dial. She was a horsewoman of a type—the type who stabled her expensive horses and rarely rode them but enjoyed long lunches with the girls and society functions. Jed guessed the two didn't get along all that well with each other anymore. They wouldn't be the first longtime married couple to come on one of his trips with the purpose—either stated or most likely implied—of trying to rekindle a failing or already dead marriage. But when he looked at them, the way they stood apart from each other, he guessed the rekindling would turn out to be unsuccessful. He just hoped neither of them drew any of his other clients into the dispute.

As individuals, these types always wanted to gain sympathetic ears, and gather allies to be on their side. The women were worse than the men in that regard. Already, Jed had noted Donna shooting brief side-long glances toward the only single woman on the trip, Rachel Mina. She'd already no doubt targeted her as her first and most likely coconspirator.

Jed said to everyone, "We have a method to our madness on the trail, and we'd appreciate your cooperation. First, nobody brought any bear spray, did they?"

No one said yes.

"Good. I know the Park Service advises everyone to have bear spray because we will absolutely see bears, both black and grizzly. But bear spray does the same thing to horses as it does to bears. If there was an accidental discharge while we were riding along, it could set off a panic and a stampede. So I always ask my clients not to bring bear spray. Of course, I won't even ask about firearms because it's illegal to have a gun in a national park. Everybody knows that, right?"

There was general assent.

"Nobody has a gun with them, right?"

Vigorous "Oh, no's" and head shakes all around, except for one man. The single, Wilson. Jed noted it and tucked the impression into his mental "To Do" basket.

He continued, "You may have heard Congress passed a law that it was now legal for individuals to carry firearms in national parks, but that's only half the story. It means if you have a valid concealed-carry permit in the state where the park is located—Wyoming, in our case— you can legally have a gun. It doesn't mean anyone can just show up packing iron. And the releases you signed with us clearly state *no firearms*. Everybody clear on that point?"

General assent. Except for Wilson, who didn't respond either way.

To the left of the Glodes were Walt Franck and his stepson Justin from Denver. Walt had salt-and-pepper hair, he was short, and he looked soft. He had a kindly unimpressive face and a bulbous nose spiderwebbed with veins, suggesting he was a drinker. He wore a fishing shirt and zip-off pants, and there was a rod tube poking out of his pile of gear. Justin was in his late teens. He was tall, chiseled, and athletic looking. He had long unkempt hair and smoldering dark eyes. As Jed spoke, Justin's eyes were on the dark-haired Sullivan girl who'd just arrived. Jed thought, *This will be interesting.*

As he did with all of his clients, Jed tried to guess the motivation for Walt and Justin to come on the trip. By their age disparity, he guessed Walt was much older than Justin's mother. That fact alone suggested Walt was bringing the stepson along to forge a bond that had been missing between them. Or was it Justin's idea? While Justin looked fit and able, Jed thought, the kid didn't look like an outdoorsman. He was missing all the telltale high-tech outdoor clothing and attitude. No, Jed decided, this was Walt's deal. Take the boy on an adventure, show him how to camp and fish. Show the boy Walt had some skills besides his interest in his mother, after all. Plus, it showed the boy that Walt had serious money that he was willing to spend on *him*.

"I see we have some fishermen with us but according to the registration forms, we also have some wildlife enthusiasts," he said, nodding toward Tristan Glode and the younger Sullivan girl (he couldn't remember her name), "And I can tell you right now you won't be disappointed. I'd suggest you take the strap of your camera and loop it through a button hole and put the camera in a shirt pocket so you can get to it real quick. You don't want to drop your camera or lose it along the trail, that's for sure. The Yellowstone Thorofare is home to all of the major species in the park. We'll see bison, wolves, grizzlies, mountain sheep, mule deer, antelope, black bear, and moose. We'll see smaller species along the way as well—coyotes, beavers, marmots, and dozens of species of birds including bald eagles. We'll see critters in their natural habitat doing things critters do—like kill and eat each other. We won't interfere with them and they won't interfere with us. In all my years of guiding these trips and all the bears we've seen, I've only lost a couple of clients and it was their own fault because they ran slow."

That always got a decent nervous laugh. He glanced over to see Dakota roll her eyes. She'd heard him say that *so* many times.

"Just remember," he said, grinning to show he was kidding, "you don't have to outrun the bear. Bears are fast. You just have to outrun the guy or gal next to you.

"I'm joshing, of course," he said. "Nobody yet has been killed and eaten by a bear." He paused dramatically. "Of course, attacks by wolf packs is another matter."

He soaked in the dark laughter, and clinically noted the exchanges of looks between the father and daughters, between Walt and Justin, between the group of three men, and the absence of sharing between Tristan and Jennifer Glode. Yup, he thought, he had *that* one figured out.

The group of three men in their thirties were the easiest to peg, Jed thought. He knew what they were about when they opened the doors of their rental car and empty beer cans fell out. They were still squinting from high-altitude hangovers. James Knox, Tony D'Amato, and Drey Russell were three gregarious buddies who worked at different firms on Wall Street who went on an annual male-bonding adventure.

They were the cut-ups, the goofballs. Knox, a light-haired man with a long thin nose and brusque East Coast go-get-'em manner, was the organizer. He was maybe a few years older than the other two.

Of all the clients, Jed had been most concerned about the three Wall Streeters. Three men like that could take over a trip and pose a challenge to him if they had the wrong attitude or expectations. But after seeing them emerge from the car and watching them josh with each other and laugh, he was relieved. They were there for the adventure.

Drey Russell—short for André, according to his booking form— was a light-skinned black man with dark kind eyes and a quick smile. Jed didn't get many people of color on his trips, and welcomed Drey so he could get some photos of him in the group to use on his Web site. The National Park Service loved that diversity crap, he knew.

Tony D'Amato looked as dark and Italian as his name, and had a heavy New Jersey accent. He played the part of the perpetually flummoxed big-city boy stuck out in the country, the man who "don't know nothin' about horses except the ones on the carousel," who was the butt of Knox's and Drey's jibes. These three would be no trouble, Jed thought. They were into themselves and their group, and they were there to fill up a sackful of memories to laugh about later when they met after work at the bar. So for them, the tougher, the crazier, the more primitive the trip the better because it would make for better tales to tell. A little high maintenance, maybe, Jed thought, even though they didn't intend to be. Folks raised entirely in cities didn't have perspective when it came to so many outdoor adventures. But they'd try to get along. No doubt they were all used to snappy service at resorts and lodges and probably not the grind of the trail, despite what they might think. He remembered seeing the previous male-bonding trips listed on their applications, including Mexico, Europe, and Scandinavia. Of course, that was before the economic meltdown, back when these guys pulled down seven figures or close to that. Now, as Knox had made it clear on his initial call, the circumstances were

such that the group agreed to keep doing their annual adventure together, even if "they had to slum it for a couple of years." Although Jed
took silent offense to that, he also decided upon seeing them that they
seemed almost normal. Jed would just play to Knox and Drey to get
them on board. They'd keep Tony D'Amato in line. These three could
be Jed's allies, if he played it right. It was always good to establish allies early on.

"You see we have mules as well as horses," Jed said, gesturing behind him to where the animals stood tied abreast along the length of
the horse trailer. "The mules are our pack animals."

Jed paused and smiled slyly. "For our friends from New York City,
the mules are the goofy-looking ones with long ears who are fast
asleep right now."

That got a bit of a laugh and the Wall Streeters enjoyed being highlighted. Yup, Jed thought, they'd be all right.

Said Jed, "I'll lead a string of three and Dakota here will follow up
the rest of you with a string of three as well. In those canvas boxes on
the sides of the mules will be all our equipment—tents, food, first-aid
kits, cookstove and kitchen setup, plates and silverware, feedbags,
everything we'll need. That's why I asked all of you to keep your personal gear down to no more than twenty pounds each. We just don't
have the space or animals to take any more. I know it's tough to get all
your possessions down to twenty pounds, but for the sake of the animals and the weight on them, that's what we have to do. You'll learn to
live with and maybe even enjoy not having too many choices of what
to wear each day.

"Even though I sent you a checklist, let me just make sure you all
have what you need, starting with a good sleeping bag. . . ."

As he went through the list: sleeping bag, sleeping pad, rain gear, on and
on, he picked out the two remaining clients on the trip, the two singles.
Singles were often a pain in the butt to Jed, since they tended to try to
pal around with him or Dakota if they didn't fit in with any of the

other clients, which was often the case. Singles could sometimes be broody and standoffish, and create dissension. Jed was always relieved when other clients took in the strays so he wouldn't have to.

The singles were a man and a woman. They stood as far away from each other as possible while still being within the group of clients, meaning they had no immediate intention of forming an alliance. The man was named K. W. Wilson. Ken. He was dark and pinched and had provided the least amount of personal information on his registration form of anyone. The only thing Jed knew about him was Ken was from Utah, wanted to fish, and that he couldn't eat cheese. Jed would try to figure the guy out at Camp One so he'd know how to handle him and integrate him into the larger group. If K.W. wouldn't talk, Jed would ask Dakota to sidle up to him. Men liked to talk to Dakota, even if she didn't particularly like talking with them.

Wilson had his camera out and was taking digital photos of everybody and everything. What was odd about it was the man never asked anyone to smile or even permission to click away.

The other single was a woman, Rachel Mina. Aside from the dark-haired Sullivan girl, Mina was the best-looking woman on the trip. She had high cheekbones, white skin, and long auburn hair tied back into a ponytail. She filled out her jeans nicely, Jed thought. And he knew her type the minute the booking form had come through his fax machine: midforties, well-to-do, and recently divorced. The last of the children out of the home, probably, and finally able to do the things she'd never been able to do before, ready for anything, game for anything. Jed could tell Dakota had picked up the same impression right off by the way she glared at her.

It was interesting, Jed thought, that the booking forms for Ted Sullivan and Rachel Mina arrived within days of each other back in November the year before. He assumed they might be together. But Sullivan and Mina hadn't greeted each other or even shared a glance that he'd seen. He chalked the close arrival of the forms to coincidence. Which meant she may be in play after all.

———

"Any questions?" Jed asked.

Tony D'Amato raised his hand. As he did, Drey and Knox coughed into their hands.

"What do we do if we can't get along with our horse? You know, like we've *never even friggin' ridden one before?*"

Jed said, "Walk." Deadpan. Then he grinned. "You shouldn't have to worry. We'll match you up with the easiest and gentlest horse we've got. The horse knows to follow the horse in front of it. All you'll have to do is keep balanced. The less steering you do the better. These horses know where we're going and who's in charge. They'll fall right into line. We don't allow any cowboy stuff, folks. You're all riding trail horses along a trail. No breaking off from the line, no riding fast. We're into safety and not rodeos. So just sit back and relax. And once we get going, Dakota and I will help you out and give you some tips."

"Maybe you can ride a mule," Drey said to Tony, and both he and Knox broke out laughing.

"I've got a question," said Tristan Glode. His voice was stentorian and without humor.

"Yes, sir?" Jed said. He knew instantly Glode was the kind of man who would expect and appreciate deference and would reward it with a big tip.

"I've been following the weather and the conditions in Yellowstone for the past six months since we signed up for this adventure," he said. Jed noted the Wall Streeters looking at each other and rolling their eyes at his out-front arrogance but looked away before Glode saw him. "It's been unseasonably cold and wet. More rainfall than usual by a large degree. My question is if we'll need to deviate from your established routing because of the high water."

Jed answered quickly, so as not to concern the rest of his clients. "You're absolutely right about the rain, sir," he said. "We've had a hell of a wet spring and early summer. In fact, I had to cancel my first two trips because of it. I didn't want to risk taking folks or these horses through swelled-up creeks and rivers. But the rains finally let up, as you can see. The water levels are going down, and the Park Service gave me the okay. So I don't think there's anything you need to worry about. We can be a little flexible if we need to. If the camp we plan to stay at is washed out, there are plenty of others to choose from. This is a big damned place."

As he said the last part, Jed felt Dakota's probing eyes on the side of his head. He ignored her.

Glode stood perfectly still, absorbing the answer. For a moment, Jed anticipated Glode would say something disastrous, like, "Maybe we should come back another year."

Instead, Glode said, "As long as we get the experience we're paying for, I'm okay with that. I don't want some cheap route because of conditions. I want to take the trip into the back of beyond I paid for."

"That you'll get, sir," Jed said, grinning with relief. "But keep in mind what I said about flexibility."

"What do you think?" Jed whispered to Dakota when they were back at the trailer saddling up the last of the horses.

"Not a bad group overall. Maybe a couple of minor problems."

"Which ones?"

"The older teenage girl looks like trouble but nothing we can't handle," she said, keeping her voice down. "The older couple look like they're spoiling for a knock-down-drag-out with each other any minute. The three Wall Streeters seem okay, but I'd bet they've got more than twenty pounds of gear each on them and most of that is liquor."

Jed nodded. She was getting good at this.

"I like the younger of the two sisters."

"I didn't even notice her."

"You wouldn't," Dakota said. Then: "What was that about using other campsites? You know what the Park Service says about *that*. Why'd you say we might change up the route?"

He shrugged. "You never know. Conditions might dictate a change."

"I thought it was kind of a strange thing to say," she said, trying without success to get him to look back at her.

He changed the subject. "What about the single man? Wilson?"

She looked over. "He's the one who gives me a bad vibe."

He nodded, agreeing. "Maybe you can get him to talk to you a little. Find out what his deal is."

"I knew you were going to ask me to do that."

"He's likely to talk to you before me," Jed said.

Jed finished up on the saddle and leaned into her. He whispered, "If the situation presents itself I may take a look in his duffel to make sure he don't have no gun."

Dakota arched her eyebrows. "And if he does?"

"I'll figure out a way to make it a nonissue."

He could tell his turn of phrase puzzled her but he didn't say more. He liked to leave her hanging, make himself a little mysterious. That was good for a relationship, he thought. Plus, he didn't want her thinking this was their last trip together.

Which it was. Because, Jed thought but didn't say, it was likely to be his last trip back of beyond. And if everything fell into place the way he'd planned it over the long and dark winter, he'd be set for life. Smart-ass girl wranglers like Dakota Hill—and needy clients like the ones who milled around before him—would be things in his past.

Hell, he thought, if things worked out like he planned them, *he'd* be the one getting catered to.

10

Gracie got Strawberry, a light red roan mare with dapples of white on her sides and haunches that had the effect of making her look like a pink horse. After sitting on Strawberry's back for fifteen minutes as the long train of riders wound up out of the parking lot into the trees on the rocky trail, Gracie knew one thing for sure: she was in love.

Already she liked the sounds and rhythm of the ride; the heavy footfalls of the animals, their snorts, the rocking motion, even the smell of them. And she was thrilled with that big-eyed look Strawberry gave her when the old mare turned her head back and seemed to assess Gracie with a practiced eye, apparently satisfied with what she saw.

"I like you, too," Gracie whispered, leaning forward in her saddle to pat Strawberry on the neck. "I like you, too. We're a good team, I think."

"What—are you talking to your horse?" Danielle said over her shoulder as she rode ahead. "Don't be kissing him, now."

"It's a her," Gracie said. "And you *should* talk to your horse. That's one way to get her to like you."

"What's mine?" Danielle said. "I forgot. I know the name is Peanut."

Said Gracie, "You're riding a gelding." She'd overheard Jed the outfitter and Dakota Hill brief her sister on Peanut and his particular tendencies, the worst of which was to take every opportunity available to grab a bite of grass from the side of the trail. "You know what a gelding is, don't you?"

"Of course," Danielle said. "He's a unit."

"A *eunuch*," Gracie corrected.

"Right," Danielle said, "a horse with no balls. A Peanut with a limp penis. Just great."

"You wouldn't want a stallion," Gracie said. "They have only one thing on their minds."

"I'm used to boys like that."

"I know you are."

"*Shut up*," Danielle said. "Just because you took some lessons you act like you're an expert."

"I'm not," Gracie said. "But I wish you would have gone to those lessons with me like I asked you. I learned a lot, and you would have, too. If nothing else, you could have listened to Jed and Dakota tell you about him. I don't know how you get by never listening to anyone."

"Yet somehow I do," Danielle said, looking over her shoulder, smiling seductively, and batting her eyelashes.

Gracie rolled her eyes.

From behind her, Gracie heard Dakota Hill say, "S'cuse me while I puke."

Gracie giggled and looked around. Dakota was leading her three mules and mumbling to herself, and acted embarrassed that Gracie had heard her. Gracie winked. Dakota grinned and winked back, obviously relieved they had something in common.

Gracie wondered what the deal was with Jed and Dakota, if they were an item. She'd seen how they talked with each other at the horse trailer.

Yes, she decided. They were a couple, even if Jed was too old for her. Maybe, Gracie thought, there weren't many choices of men in Montana.

The order of the riders, horses, and mules was established in the parking lot by Jed. Once everyone was mounted, he'd explained that the reason for the order of riders was not based on merit or preference, but by how the horses behaved with each other.

"If you want to change the order," he said, "we can maybe work it out at some point. We may find we want to change things up as well to keep the peace. But right now, just memorize the look of the rider's butt and the horse's butt ahead of you and follow those butts. Horses have an established pecking order. They also have friends and enemies. We know these horses better than we know you folks at this point, so trust us on this. Safety first, folks. If you change up the order you increase the chance of a wreck."

Gracie rode next to last on Strawberry. When Jed handed her the reins of the pink horse, he told Gracie the animal was a sweetheart and "Don't have an ounce of mean in her anymore if she ever did." Strawberry was older than Gracie, he said, and this may be her last trip before she was retired to be a brood mare. All Strawberry required, Jed said, was kindness and she'd pay Gracie back with loyalty and predictability. "You look like a nice girl," Jed had said.

"Most of the time," Gracie answered.

"You've ridden a little?"

"Quite a bit, actually," she said.

He gave her a paternalistic smile. "We'll see," he said.

11

Cody Hoyt said, "So, do you have a headlight that will work?"

It was ten thirty in the morning and the mechanic leaned against a rolling, red-metal standing tool chest and drank a cup of coffee. Above his head was a Snap-On Tools calendar featuring a blonde winking while holding a wrench. The little garage was dark and close and smelled of oil and gasoline. Dust motes floated through the shafts of light from the cloudy windows. The mechanic wore gray coveralls and a Rocky Mountain Elk Foundation cap. He was short and wiry with deep-set eyes and short-cropped salt-and-pepper hair. He'd shaved but had missed a triangle of whiskers above his Adam's apple. Cody had waited for him outside the shop for an hour while the mechanic had leisurely morning coffee with other locals at the diner next door.

"I might have one," the mechanic said, "depending on your attitude."

Cody nearly launched himself across the floor at the guy, but managed to take a deep breath and look away. Orange spangles danced around the edges of his vision. He wanted to flash his badge or show his gun. He wanted to put the mechanic in a sleeper hold and threaten his eyes with pepper spray—anything to get the guy moving. He *hated* being a civilian. And he hated the fact that he had to operate below the radar and on his own. If he'd told the trooper the night before where he was going and why, the patrolman would have been duty bound to call it in and check the story. Cody couldn't afford to have the sheriff know he was gone, and Townsend was close enough to Helena that Bodean might send someone to get him and bring him back. So, gritting his teeth against his nature, he'd followed the trooper back to town and nodded meekly when ordered to "Park it."

If he leaned on the mechanic the trooper would come back and he might never get out of Townsend, Montana, population 1,898.

"Look," Cody said, "just please put your other jobs aside long enough to wire in a new headlight."

The mechanic eyed Cody with a squint, sizing him up. Waiting for more groveling, Cody imagined.

"I've been here all night," Cody said. "The trooper said you're the only mechanic in town right now. I'm really desperate to get on the road and he won't let me go until I've got a headlight that works."

Finally, the mechanic said, "I doubt I can match the headlight. I might have to order one out of Helena or White Sulpher Springs—"

Cody broke in, "It doesn't have to look pretty. It doesn't even have to *fit*. It just has to light up."

The morning was cool and sunny and there were no pedestrians on the street. The Commercial Bar across the road was open, as it always was. Cody watched as a ranch truck parked at the curb and a beat-up old cowboy got out and went in for his breakfast beer. He wore irrigation boots and a sweat-stained straw hat. *Jesus*, he thought, *a breakfast beer.*

As he walked he thought of Justin, and his stomach turned sour. Therefore, he *had* to keep it going. He *had* to find his son and keep that going. He owed the world the favor.

He pulled out his cell and speed-dialed Larry's extension.

"Olson."

"Larry, it's me."

There was a beat before Larry cleared his throat and said, "Excuse me, what did you say your name was?"

"Come on, Larry."

"And you're with what company again?"

"Ah," Cody said, "Bodean's in the room. Got it."

"Yes," Larry said, clipped.

"Can't talk?"

"No. How did you get this number?"

"I'll call back on your cell, then."

Larry said, "I don't purchase toner or anything else for the office, lady. I'm a detective for the sheriff's department, for crying out loud. I've got important work to do." And slammed his phone down.

Cody called back three minutes later to find out Larry's cell phone had been turned off.

Cody closed his phone, puzzled. Larry *never* turned off his phone. So either Bodean was still in the room or something else was going on. What?

Cody's phone went off. He looked at the display. It was an unknown number but had the Montana 406 area code.

"Yes," Cody said.

"Me," Larry said. By the background traffic noises from Larry's cell, Cody guessed his partner had taken a walk outside.

"Don't call me on my cell or the office number again," Larry said. "They don't know you're gone. There can't be a record of calls between us on either phone. And if they ask me if I've heard from you, I'll tell them the truth. I can't lie for you, Cody."

"I understand. So what is this phone you're using?"

"You know, it's one I borrowed," Larry stammered.

"You're learning." Cody smiled to himself. He remembered the afternoon when he showed Larry how many phones there were in the evidence room, each tagged for specific cases. Some still had a battery charge left. He'd told Larry how, down in Denver, he'd used confiscated phones to make calls that couldn't be traced back to him and sometimes, to aggravate a criminal, he'd call random numbers in Bolivia and Ecuador just to run up astronomical phone charges.

"So, where are you?" Larry asked.

Cody sighed. "I made it as far as Townsend and an HP trooper picked me up and marched me back to town for that fucking missing headlight."

Larry laughed. "Townsend? That's all the further you got? You're *kidding*."

"So I spent the night bouncing off the walls of the Lariat Motor Lodge. I'd recommend it only because it's probably the last place in America that still has black-and-white TVs in the rooms and bed-spreads that remind you of your grandmother's house."

"You should have stayed home," Larry said.

Cody grunted, "No way. I'll be back on the road in a few min-utes."

Larry sighed.

"Have you heard anything back from ViCAP or RMIN?"

"Sort of," Larry said. "RMIN is running the police reports from the most recent victim in Jackson Hole and they'll be getting back to me. The case was classified as an accident but it sounds, well, real familiar. A woman named Karen Anthony, forty-six, divorced and living alone, was found dead in her home outside of Wilson. Same deal, Cody. Her place was burned down around her and she was found the next day underneath the debris. Head injuries the likely cause of death."

Cody said, "Anything like what we've got in terms of an open stove, or the bottle?"

"Nope. The evidence so far doesn't match up to ours. But the cir-cumstances of the death ring true."

Cody walked down the empty sidewalk, pacing. He noticed a face watching him from the window of the Commercial Bar. It was the cow-boy he'd seen enter earlier. The man tipped his hat and took a deep drink from a beer mug as if to taunt him. The cowboy was drinking a red beer—spiced tomato juice and Bud Light. Cody used to start the day with one. Its properties were magical.

"Bastard," Cody said.

"What?" Larry asked.

"Not you. What did Karen Anthony do? What was her job?"

"Let's see," Larry said. "Okay, here. She was an independent hospital consultant. Had her own firm, and apparently a pretty successful one. She had an office in Jackson and one in Denver, Minneapolis, and Omaha."

Cody rubbed his face. "One of the victims was from Minnesota, right? Is there a connection there?"

"I don't know. We're too early in this thing. I've got a telephone meeting scheduled with an analyst at ViCAP later today so maybe we'll be able to establish a link of some kind. The only thing I can figure, obviously, is Winters was a pharma guy and Karen Anthony was a hospital consultant. So maybe they worked together somehow or knew each other. But it'll take a hell of a lot more digging."

"Yeah," Cody said. "We still don't know anything about the Minnesota and Virginia deaths. They could be connected to these two or not. ViCAP might be able to help with that."

Larry said, "And Cody, nothing really connects Winters and Anthony yet except for the burned-down houses and the proximity of the dates. This thread is so thin. . . ."

"I know," Cody said. "Keep me posted, okay? My cell should work all day until I get to Yellowstone."

"So you're still going," Larry said.

"Damn right. Hey—did you get in touch with Jed McCarthy's office yet?"

Larry paused while a diesel vehicle passed him, the engine hammering away. Then: "I've left two more messages to call me."

Cody stopped. "You haven't asked the Bozeman PD to roust it? Come on, Larry!"

Silence. Then it dawned on Cody but Larry spoke before he had a chance to apologize.

"You asshole," Larry said. "You were supposed to be at that office when it opened. You weren't supposed to be playing with yourself in fucking Townsend, Montana. And how would it have been for you if you showed up at Wilderness Adventures at the same time as the local cops? Don't you think they'd ask questions? Don't you think they'd figure out real damned quick you were a suspended detective and call up here and talk to Tub?"

"I know," Cody said, "I'm sorry. You're thinking clearly and I'm not. Thank you, Larry."

"I'm tired of doing you favors," Larry said.

"I know. I don't blame you."

"You are an unthinking prick sometimes," Larry said.

"*Okay*," Cody hissed, "I've got the point."

"Good," Larry said with finality.

Cody heard the rolling-thunder sound of the garage door being opened up. He turned to see the mechanic backing out his SUV. There was a headlight there, all right. It didn't fit into the damaged fender but was wired and taped around the dented hole. It looked like a detached eyeball.

"I'm ready to roll," Cody said. "Keep me posted on what you find out from ViCAP and RMIN."

Larry sighed.

"You call me, I won't call you," Cody said, "but keep that burner phone handy and hidden, okay? In case I find something out from the office in Bozeman."

"Gotcha," Larry said.

"Thanks, buddy."

Cody waved and took a deep breath as he drove by the highway patrol car pulled over on the side of the highway a mile out of Townsend. The trooper whooped on his siren and gestured for him to pull over.

Cody sat seething while the trooper slowly got out of his car and slowly walked up along the driver's side. He powered the window down.

"Now what?" Cody said.

"I see you got a headlight. It doesn't look so good, though," the trooper said. "I hope you'll get that front end fixed and get a new light as soon as you can."

"I will."

"I've got a question for you," the trooper said, tipping his hat back and watching Cody's face carefully for tics or tells. Cody knew the drill. He was about to be asked a question he wouldn't want to answer, and the trooper hoped to catch him in a lie. "I ran your plates. According to the Department of Motor Vehicles, this vehicle doesn't exist. Your number doesn't correspond with a name, in other words."

"That doesn't surprise me," Cody said quickly. "I bought it at a county auction up in Helena. They used to use it for undercover surveillance, the auctioneer told me. He said the sheriff's department uses some dummy plates so the bad guys don't know who they are. I guess they just kept the plates on."

The trooper rubbed his chin, thinking that over.

"I'll get some new plates as soon as I get home to Bozeman," Cody said. "I promise you. I'll send you the receipt to prove it."

At that moment, the trooper's handheld squawked. Cody heard the dispatcher reporting a one-car rollover five miles north of Townsend.

"Guess you better go," Cody said.

The trooper hesitated for a moment, then said, "Send me that receipt. But something about that story of yours is fishy."

"Check it out," Cody said. "You'll see."

The trooper waved at him dismissively and started back to his car. Cody silently thanked whomever had lost control of their car north of town, and eased back out onto the road.

The headquarters for Wilderness Adventures was located south of Bozeman on U.S. 191 near the Gallatin Gateway Inn on the road to West Yellowstone and Yellowstone Park. Cody arrived at 1:30 P.M., cursing himself yet again for the debacle in Townsend that put him twelve hours behind where he wanted to be.

The office was a converted old home shaded by ancient cottonwoods and surrounded by rolling pasture and outbuildings and corrals in decent repair. Six or seven horses grazed and twitched their tails against the flies and didn't look up to greet him. It wasn't the kind of office guests were likely to visit, he thought, but no doubt it made for a good staging area for large-scale horse operations. The pasture fed the horses when they weren't on a pack trip. The sign for Wilderness Adventures was homemade; a modern swooping logo painted on a frame made of old barnwood. There was an older blue sedan parked on the side of the building.

He killed the engine, vaulted up the wooden steps to the porch, and banged on the frame of the screen door.

"Yes?" A woman's voice. She sounded startled.

"My name's Cody Hoyt," he said. "I need to talk to someone who knows something about the pack trip in Yellowstone."

"Oh my," said a plump older woman who suddenly came into view through the screen. "You weren't booked on the trip, were you? Because it left this morning."

Her name was Margaret Cooper and she was the sole office employee of Wilderness Adventures and had been for twenty-five years, she said. She wore thick glasses and her hair was tightly curled and looked like steel wool. She wore jeans, a white shirt that bulged in the middle, and a Western pattern vest embroidered with cowgirls and lariats. The lobby of the office was filled with large cardboard boxes reading DELL.

"We're in the process of computerizing," she said, shaking her head sadly. "Jed is making me learn how to run one of those things. He says it will make us more efficient, but I think it's, you know, a *fad*. This old dog doesn't need new tricks. I've been running the business part of the company all these years and I don't need a machine. I've got everything I need in there," she said, and gestured toward a bank of old metal filing cabinets. "I'm supposed to put all that information back there into the machine, and Jed says he wants me to update the Web site so he doesn't have to do it from home. Can you imagine that? The World Wide Web? I want no part of it."

Cody nodded curtly. He noticed the telephone on her desk was blinking with messages.

"Don't you answer your phone?" he asked. "My colleague was calling you all morning."

"Of course I answer the phone," she said, her eyes flashing behind those thick lenses. "But it's a little hard to do when you're sitting in a computer class the entire morning learning how to work a program called Excella."

"Excel," Cody said. "So you haven't been in until now?"

"I just got here a half hour ago," she said, still miffed at him. "I was working. I just wasn't here. Jed insisted I take that class once a week and today is the day."

Cody said, "Do you have the list of clients on the current trip? I need to look at it."

"Of course I have it," she said. "But can you tell me why you want to see who is on it? Isn't this kind of an invasion of privacy?"

Cody caught himself before he rolled his eyes. "I don't see how it could be," he said. "Look, I need to know if my son is on this trip. It's important. There's an emergency in the family."

"You won't be able to contact him," she said, shaking her head. "There's no way to communicate with a pack trip once they've left into the park. There are no cell things."

"Towers," he said. "Look, I know that. But if he's on it I need to know. I'll figure the rest out."

She squinted at him and pursed her lips. "Your manner is very brusque."

"Sorry," he said, stepping toward her. "But show me the *list*."

She made a show of sighing dramatically, then turned around and approached the filing cabinets. "I know where everything is," she said. "I have my own filing system. Apparently, it aggravates Jed that he can't find anything, even though I've tried to explain to him how it works. Let's see, today is July first, so 07/01. Seven corresponds with G in the alphabet, the seventh letter. One corresponds with A. . . ." She reached for a middle drawer and pulled it out and started fingering through tabs marked by handwritten letters.

Cody tried to remain calm.

"Here it is," she said, pulling a file. "All the applications and signed releases of liability. And here," she said, slipping a single handwritten sheet out of the file, "is the complete list in alphabetical order."

He snatched it out of her hand and read down the list.

1. Anthony D'Amato
2. Walt Frank

"His Richness," Cody mumbled. "Damn it."

3. Justin Hoyt

"*Damn it,*" Cody whispered. "He's on it."
Cody scanned the rest of the list:

4. James Knox
5. Rachel Mina
6. Tristan Glode
7. Donna Glode
8. André Russell
9. Ted Sullivan
10. Gracie Sullivan
11. Danielle Sullivan
12. K. W. Wilson

None of the other names rang a bell. But he thought one of them might produce a ViCAP hit.

"I'll need that back," she said.

"In a minute," he said, shuffling through the applications. Here, in the folder he held in his hand, were the names, addresses, physical descriptions, and details of each client on the trip. He was ecstatic. "Where's your fax machine?"

"Is it long distance?" she asked. "You know, each fax is just like a long-distance phone call."

Cody dug in his pocket and threw her a twenty-dollar bill. "That should cover it."

"Where are you faxing the pages?" she asked.

"Just tell me where the goddamn machine is," he said.

"No need to be like that," she said, pointing to a supply room behind her.

While Cody fed in each page and transmitted it to Larry, he turned on the copy machine next to the fax. After each application was sent he made a copy for himself. Margaret Cooper was at her desk retrieving telephone messages, and had left him alone. He hoped she wouldn't object to him making copies but it didn't matter—he was taking the applications with him. Because one of these people, he thought, killed Hank Winters and was near his son.

When he was through he returned all the original documents to the folder and stuffed the copies in under his shirt.

He handed the folder to her at her desk.

"Why do you suppose a detective is calling me?" she asked him. "Is this your colleague? Are you a policeman?"

He nodded.

"Why didn't you tell me?" she said, suddenly sitting up straighter.

"Undercover," he said. "And this matter is confidential. Please tell no one I was here. Do you understand?"

She nodded furiously.

"Now I need you to think for a minute," he said. "What is the best way to catch up to the pack trip? Don't tell me the outfitter doesn't have a satellite phone or some way to get in touch with the outside world."

She shook her head. "I'm sorry, but he doesn't."

"How can that be in this day and age?" Cody spat. "What if the Park Service needs to contact him? What if he's got an emergency, like a client has a heart attack or something?"

She smiled sympathetically. "Then he's to locate a park ranger and the park ranger places the call. You don't understand how they can be. The Park Service, I mean. Such bureaucracy! They're the reason Bull Mitchell finally sold the business. I wish he never had. I know *he* wouldn't be making me learn how to work a computer."

Cody took a deep breath. "Okay, so I can't call them. So how would I find them? Is there a designated route? Doesn't the Web site indicate they stay at a specific camp every night of the trip?"

She nodded her head. "Unless they camp somewhere else," she said. "Things happen out there. Sometimes they'll camp in other places, or even on a different trail if the trail is washed out or trees fall over it or something. All I ever know is where they start and where they end. The middle is kind of . . . random."

He slapped the desk in frustration. Then he said, "Where can I find Bull Mitchell?" Thinking: *Does he even live in Bozeman? Is he alive?*

She looked at her watch.

"It's nearly two," she said. "That means he'll be at the library."

"The *library*?"

A misty look came over her eyes. "You'll see," she said.

12

Gracie didn't mind being so far back in the string at all. She liked being able to observe the riders ahead of her, something she couldn't have done if her horse was higher in the pecking order.

Jed was first, trailing three mules strapped with massive pack-boxes of gear and food. He constantly turned in his saddle to make sure everyone was behind him and in the order he'd set for them.

Behind the mules was the older couple, Tristan and Donna Glode. Gracie hadn't heard Tristan say much so far on the trip, but he had a kind of serious and businesslike bearing, she thought. His wife seemed cold and aloof, but Gracie noted how gracefully she'd climbed on the saddle and how elegantly she rode. She was the only guest wearing honest-to-God English riding boots. Gracie tried to model her riding style—relaxed, not slumping, head up, reins loose in her left hand—after Donna Glode. But that's the only thing about Donna Glode Gracie wanted to learn.

Walt and Justin were next. Gracie noted how often Walt turned in his saddle and sized up his soon-to-be stepson and then nodded approvingly at what he saw. She wondered what it was Justin was doing that was worthy of the head nods since it seemed to her the only thing Justin wanted to do was bump along and steal looks at Danielle. Justin rode well, Gracie thought, the way a natural athlete would ride. He wasn't smooth but he looked strong and well balanced. He had a certain style about him, an attitude: confident, cocky, maybe a little full of himself. He knew he was the only young buck on the trip. He apparently saw no reason to put his feet in the stirrups, for example, and they dangled on the sides of his horse.

Rachel, the divorcée or widow or whatever she was, rode behind Justin on a slick jet-black gelding. Gracie thought the horse, named Midnight, was by far the best-looking of the herd. Midnight's coat was so black it shined dark blue, like Superman's hair, Gracie thought. And Rachel Mina looked good on him. She wasn't as self-consciously slick as Donna Glode, but she'd obviously ridden before. Her posture was good, Gracie thought, as she found herself sitting more upright in Strawberry's saddle. Gracie thought it would be interesting to talk to Rachel Mina to find out why she'd come alone on a trip like this. She had a feeling the woman was interesting, or had a good story, at least. And was she mistaken, or did Rachel Mina smile at her earlier in an almost familiar way? Like they'd met before, which Gracie was certain hadn't happened.

The three Wall Streeters rode behind Rachel Mina; James Knox, Drey Russell, and Tony D'Amato. Gracie guessed that *maybe* Knox had been on a horse before, and possibly Drey. But certainly not Tony, who kept saying things like, "Where is the brake on this thing?" and "What good is a saddle horn that doesn't honk?" Tony kept the other two laughing with his stupid asides and observations, and Gracie guessed it was kind of an act. Tony pointed out each time Knox's gelding's long penis unfurled and swung loose from side to side as the horse walked, saying, "Look who's relaxed," or "He reminds me of *me* when he does that." The three men together were interesting, she thought. She'd seen very few male friendships up close in her life and the way they chided and insulted each other was a way of showing affection, she guessed. If women talked like that to each other there would soon be scratching and blood. She also thought how quickly boring it would become if every other statement was about their sexual organs, as it was with the male Wall Streeters. Despite their goofiness, though, Gracie liked having the three men around. They seemed solid and anchored. Better than three women, she thought. Especially on a trip like this.

The strange man, K. W. Wilson, rode behind them on a pale gray gelding. Although he wasn't wearing a black hat or shirt, there was something dark about him. Brooding but at times kind of smiling to himself. Like he had a secret or found his thoughts amusing. The ghostly pallor of his horse only added to the image. He was thin and his face was made of sharp planes shoved together, as if he'd once had a normal face but somebody crumpled it in from the sides where it bent like sheet metal. His eyes were mounted close over the sharp bridge of a hatchetlike nose. He needed a shave and the trip had barely even started. He didn't seem to laugh at the jokes of the Wall Streeters, not at all. Gracie was wary of him, and unlike Rachel Mina, had zero desire to get to know him at all.

Her dad rode behind Wilson, and Danielle was just ahead. Danielle rode well even though she didn't have a clue as to what she was doing. Gracie wished *she* filled her saddle as well as Danielle, and wondered if and when her own butt wouldn't be skinny and bony like a boy's. Already it hurt. She could use some of Danielle's padding, she thought.

"How's that horse ridin'?" Dakota Hill asked in a tone Gracie could hear but low enough the others couldn't.

"Good," Gracie said. "I really like her."

"Strawberry's a good little horse. You can depend on her. Just don't get her too close to those horses up front if you can help it, especially that black one, Midnight. Midnight don't like Strawberry."

"That's too bad," Gracie said, again leaning forward and patting Strawberry's neck, " 'cause she's such a sweet girl."

"Yup."

Gracie thought Dakota Hill looked like a natural cowgirl in a way that Jed didn't look like a natural cowboy. She was the type of woman, Gracie thought, who would be almost beautiful if she wore makeup. But Dakota seemed determined to fight against type by playing at being gruff and no-nonsense. What kind of woman wanted to be known as a "mule-skinner"? Gracie was puzzled by her but oddly fascinated at the same time.

When she turned back around in the saddle with the smile still on her face, she was jarred by two sets of eyes directly on her. From the front, Jed McCarthy looked on in what seemed like disapproval. And from a few horses away, K. W. Wilson smirked.

They were walking their mounts through the middle of a large green saddle slope rimmed by trees on all four sides. The air smelled slightly of sulfur. Jed had walked his string off the trail and let the others pass by. Gracie could see him talking to each rider in turn as they rode past him.

As she rode up next to him he asked, "You and that horse getting along?"

"Yes."

"You sit a nice horse," he said, nudging his horse into a walk until they rode side by side.

"I've been telling everyone to make sure to stay on the trail," he said. "It's more important here in Yellowstone than anywhere else." He gestured toward a large white patch of ground to their right about a hundred feet away. "See that there?"

"Yes."

"See anything unusual about it?"

"There's no grass on it, I guess."

"Look closer. Look at it about an inch above the ground."

She squinted and noticed how the air seemed to undulate slightly, as if it were underwater. In the center of the white patch, a slight wisp of steam or smoke curled out of a hole the size of a quarter.

"What is it?"

"This is the thing about this place," he said. "That's a fumarole, or steam vent. The white is a dried mineral crust that's covering a place where superheated water comes up out of the ground. The hole there releases some of the steam. Otherwise, it might build up too much pressure and erupt."

"Wow," she said, shaking her head.

"The crust is brittle," he said. "If you walked over the top of it or took your horse over there you'd break right through. The water underneath would scald the hell out of you or your horse. Might even kill you if you got bucked off in it."

"Really?"

"Really. It's the reason we have to stay together on the trail and not ride off. Those things are everywhere, and some are much worse," he said. "There's a little canyon in the park where so much methane gas is produced naturally out of the ground that any living thing that wanders into it will die within minutes. The floor of the canyon is covered in elk and bison bones, and maybe even some old Indian bones."

He'd softened his voice and she found it oddly rhythmic. She felt a chill ripple through her.

"But when you look at that white patch," he said, "I want you to imagine something else. Imagine most of Yellowstone Park itself is that white patch. There's a real thin crust covering hell itself, which is trying to boil over. That *wants* to boil over. And someday, it will. It's known as the Yellowstone Caldera. In fact, darlin', when it blows it'll take two million people with it. It's blown a few times through history, and we're sixty thousand years overdue."

"Why are you telling me this?" she asked.

"To heighten your awareness," he said. "I want every one of my clients to be awake."

"I'm awake," she said.

13

Although it once seemed like he lived in one, Cody Hoyt had not been in a public library for years. And as soon as he entered the Bozeman Public Library on East Main Street, he felt like he was being hurled back in time to when he rode his bike to the Helena library after telling his buddies he was going home. He loved the library, although he kept it in absolute confidence. Only the librarians knew, and they gave him his space and not-so-secretly delighted in the fact that a Hoyt of the violent and rough-hewn Hoyts was actually in their sanctuary of civilization. Often, a librarian would give him a sandwich because he was obviously missing dinner and he'd eat it at his own private table in the back.

He read everything; newspapers, magazines, hunting and fishing books, crime novels, biographies of American presidents, anything he could find on World War Two. He read reference books and *Ripley's Believe It or Not* and sex manuals that got him all worked up. Not once did he check out a book and take it with him, because he didn't dare take a chance that his dad would see it and tease him. And as far as his father knew, he wasn't home because he was at football or wrestling practice. Since his dad never went to any games anyway, he never found out Cody didn't participate in the sports he claimed he did.

Lying to his friends about going home and lying to his dad about staying at school started a prominent pattern in his life, he realized later. Leading parallel lives and telling serial lies helped prepare him for the trials and rigors of full-blown alcoholism, which, in itself, was like a second full-time—although secret—career. He'd learned early how to multitask.

Cody learned nothing in school and everything he knew in the library. He still read widely and constantly, and was never without a book in his glove compartment (along with a pint of bourbon). For the past year, he'd been alternating among Jim Harrison's novels, John McPhee's nonfiction, Flannery O'Connor's short stories, and the crime novels of John Sandford, Ken Bruen, and T. Jefferson Parker. His books were stacked like Greek columns in his living room and basement. Once he finally built those bookshelves, he could showcase an impressive collection. But he never got around to it.

He was mildly surprised by the banks of computers and the teens and twenty-somethings at each terminal. As he walked past, he noted a familiarity in what they were doing—updating their Facebook pages. He thought, *Some people used to go to libraries to gather information. Now they come to write about themselves.*

He approached the information counter and a slim girl with bangs and a nose ring swiveled his direction and arched her eyebrows as if to say *Yes?*

"Someone told me Bull Mitchell would be here," he said. "Do you have any idea where to find him?"

She pointed across her body past the reference book aisle. There was an archway painted with Mother Goose and Dr. Seuss characters and a sign that read *children's room.*

"No," Cody said, "I'm looking for an old guy named Bull Mitchell." She said, "Yes, and I'm telling you where to find him."

Cody checked his wristwatch as he entered the children's section, wondering how much time he was wasting when he should be coursing down the highway toward Yellowstone. But since he was here, he entered the room and walked toward the back where he could hear a gruff deep voice.

It's me again, Hank the Cowdog.

I just got some terrible news. There's been a murder on the ranch. . . .

"Jesus Christ," Cody grumbled.

Two young mothers were standing in the aisle and they turned when they heard him, and one of them lifted a finger to her lips to shush him. She was wearing a track suit and her blond hair was pulled back in a ponytail. She was vaguely attractive but already angry with him, so he looked to the other one. She was tall and slim with auburn hair and kind brown eyes and a nice mouth. Her face was wide open. She was pretty in a natural, athletic way.

He shrugged his apology and sidled up to them. He noted other mothers gathered along the windows on the side of the room.

"I'm looking for Bull Mitchell," he said. "Do you know him?"

"Of course," the tall woman whispered. "That's him reading."

Well, you know me. I'm no dummy. There's a thin line between heroism and stupidity, and I try to stay on the south side of it. . . .

"That's Bull Mitchell?" Cody asked. "I can't see him."

"Here," the tall woman said, stepping aside.

Cody nodded his thanks.

There, in the middle of twelve or thirteen kids gathered on the floor, was a big man sitting in a comically undersized chair wearing a heavy wool work shirt, jeans, and cowboy boots. His head was a cinder block mounted on wide powerful shoulders and his huge hands held *The Original Adventures of Hank the Cowdog* indelicately, like a grizzly cradling a candy cane. He had silver-white hair but jet-black crazy eyebrows that looked like smudges of soot. He was an unpracticed and halting reader, Cody thought, but when his voice boomed for exclamations like *Good dog!* and *Will you please shut up?* the walls seemed to shake and he likely scared the bejesus out of the kids.

That's when he noticed a tiny white-haired woman in a wheelchair next to the seated children. She had a wool Pendleton trapper's blanket over her lap and she leaned forward to listen with a gauzy smile of pure enchantment.

"What's with the old lady?" Cody asked the tall woman. "What's she doing here?"

She reacted as if he'd slapped her. The blond woman rolled her eyes and snorted in contempt.

"What?" Cody said, genuinely surprised and puzzled.

Oh Hank, there's been a killing right here on the ranch and we slept through it! . . .

The tall woman said, "He's my father and 'the old lady' is my mother. She's in the advanced stages of Alzheimer's, and this is the only way he can connect with her these days, by reading children's stories."

Cody slumped and sighed. "I'm such an asshole," he said.

"Yes, you are," the tall woman said. "But I can see you didn't know."

The blond mother shushed them both.

Cody said to the tall woman, "When he's done will you introduce me to him?"

She almost smiled. "How can I introduce you when I don't know your name?"

"Cody Hoyt," he said. "I'm a cop."

She eyed him suspiciously. "Is this official business? You don't seem to have a badge."

Cody said, "It's more important than that. Give me a few minutes and I'll lay it out."

"Angela Mitchell," she said, extending her hand. "I'm the proud daughter."

Cody thought, *In other circumstances I would like to get to know this woman.*

The blond mother leaned toward them hissing, *"Shhhhhh."*

And Bull Mitchell read:

> *. . . Being Head of Ranch Security is learning to ignore that kind of emotion. I mean, to hold down this job, you have to be cold and hard. . . .*

Cody hovered behind Angela and Bull Mitchell as Bull pushed his wife through the aisles in her wheelchair to the van to return her to the nursing home. The children had joined up with their mothers or nannies and dispersed. Bull said to Angela in a flat, declaratory tone not unlike his reading, "So who's the guy?"

"He says his name is Cody Hoyt. He wants to meet you."

"Hoyt?" Bull barked.

"Yes."

"I knew a couple guys named Hoyt. One was a drunk and the other one was a criminal. Why does he want to meet me?"

"Hey," Cody said, "I'm right here. I can speak for myself."

Bull paused and twisted slightly to a quarter profile, as if he wasn't sure turning around to talk to Cody was worth more than that. He looked Cody up and down, said nothing, and said to his daughter, "Tell him not to interrupt my stories, goddammit."

"I apologize," Cody said. "I just wasn't expecting a guy named Bull in the children's room."

Bull kept his back to him and guided his wife's wheelchair out the front doors of the library. The attendant in the van climbed out to help position her chair on the lift. Cody saw she was still smiling and her eyes were wistful. She was small and reed thin and her body seemed to be drawing inward as if to fold up on itself. Her back was hunched, which made her head stick out forward rather than up. A baby bird, Cody thought, she's turning into a baby bird in the nest, stretching out on a long neck. He felt sorry for her, for Bull, for Angela, and for him being there at that moment.

In a wavery voice as light as mist she said to her husband, "That was a wonderful story, Mr. Bull. One of my favorites. I wish I could have read it to my daughter Angela, you know."

"I know," he said softly.

Cody noted how Angela flinched when she heard what her mother said. She didn't say *I'm right here, Mom.* No point.

Bull dropped to his haunches so he was eye level with his wife. She smiled at him with big teeth stained by decades of coffee.

"Good-bye honey," he said, and bent forward and kissed her on the forehead. "I'll read to you in a week."

Her waxen face flushed pink and she giggled and batted her eyes, admonishing him, "Mr. *Bull* . . ."

He leaned forward and whispered something in her ear and she blushed further and windmilled her tiny hands as if naughtily delighted by the words. Cody looked away.

The van driver activated the hydraulic lift and secured her in the van and drove away.

Angela said, "She was happy."

Bull grunted.

"I think she's falling for you," Angela said.

"Who wouldn't?" Bull said. Then he focused on Cody. His tone was gruff. "Now what do you want?"

Cody said, "Can I buy you and Angela a cup of coffee? I need your help."

"You can buy me a beer," Bull said. "Come on, I know a place a few blocks down."

In the gloom of the Crystal Bar, the kind of old dive Cody loved with its dim lighting and the midafternoon musical clicking of pool balls from a table in back, Bull said to the waitress, "I'll have a PBR."

Cody hesitated a moment, then ordered a tonic water. Angela asked for coffee.

Bull eyed him across the table for an uncomfortable length of time, then said, "You don't like Pabst Blue Ribbon or are you an alky?"

"Why do you ask?"

"Because only alkies drink tonic water. It kind of reminds 'em of a real drink. Or so I've been told."

"Guilty," Cody said.

"Thought so," Bull said. "You have that look about you. Believe me, in this country I see that look you got a lot."

Cody looked to Angela for help. She shrugged back with a *that's-the-way-he-is* kind of look.

"So," Bull Mitchell said, "why are we here?"

Cody shot a quick glance to Angela, then told the entire story, leaving nothing out. Hank Winters, his binge, the coroner, his suspension. Bull listened wordlessly. Angela squirmed toward the end, getting more and more alarmed.

"So that's the deal," Cody said. "I need to find that pack trip as fast as I can but I don't know the park well enough and I've got to keep quiet about it or I'll lose my job at the very least. You're the only guy I can think of who is familiar with Jed McCarthy and 'Back of Beyond: the Ultimate Yellowstone Backcountry Adventure.'"

Bull scowled, "I didn't name it that. That was Jed's deal. He thinks he's a wizard with words."

"And women," Angela added acidly.

Cody waited for more but it didn't come and she obviously wished she'd said nothing by the way she shifted her weight in the booth.

To Bull, Cody said, "You've done it, this trip I'm talking about, right?"

"Dozens of times," Bull said. "I blazed the trail in the first place after the park rangers at the time said there was no realistic way to take packhorses where I told them I wanted to go. So I had to prove them wrong. I goddamn *invented* that trip."

Cody tried to keep himself low-key and persuasive when what he really wanted to do was get going. He said, "Can you tell me how to find them? Where they left from, which trail they took? Where they'd likely be right now as we're talking?"

Bull nodded. "Pretty close. But what are you going to do? *Hike* after them?" he said with sarcasm.

"Dad," Angela said with alarm, "he wants you to guide him."

Cody kept quiet.

Bull said, "I don't do that kind of stuff anymore. I haven't in years."

"I'll pay you," Cody said, trying not to let Angela's glare penetrate him.

"How much?" Bull said, gesturing to the waitress for another beer. "Jed McCarthy charges more than two grand a head."

"I'll pay you four," Cody said, thinking he had barely eighteen hundred dollars between his checking and savings accounts and he could maybe get another thousand if he got his pickup running and sold it. Maybe he could get a thousand from Jenny, who could dip into the bottomless coffers of His Richness. . . .

Bull scratched his chin, thinking about it.

"Dad," Angela said, "this is crazy. It could be really dangerous. You said yourself horse packing like that is a young man's game—that's why you sold the business, remember?"

"I sold it because I couldn't take dealing with the Feds anymore," Bull said, flashing a look at Cody to gauge his reaction.

Angela put her hand on her father's arm. "Dad, if you find them you're finding a potential killer. Think of Mom."

He just looked at her. His voice dropped. "Your mother is all I think about and you should know that by now. Do you have any idea how much that facility she's in costs? Thirty-five hundred a *month*. A *month*. I'm burning through the savings."

Angela didn't back down. "Dad—if you'd get some help . . ."

"I don't want any goddamn help," he said flatly. "I never asked for it and I don't want it now."

She said as an aside to Cody, "We've had this discussion many times before. There are federal programs my parents qualify for but he won't take the money. In fact, he sends it back with mean notes attached. I've read some of them and they'd curl your hair."

Bull nodded. "If everybody did that we wouldn't be in the shit-house like we are now."

She said, "And you won't let me help you, either."

"Nope," he said. "Taking charity from my daughter is the last thing I'd ever do. Might as well just shoot me in the head and leave me there if it comes to that."

Angela said to him, "But you wouldn't have to be seriously thinking about going back to the park right now. Like I said, think of Mom."

"Your mother," Bull said to her, "she don't know me from week to week, Angela."

"Then think of *me*."

Bull placed his own massive hand on top of hers.

Cody said, "Five thousand just for trying. And two thousand bonus for finding them." He'd get His Richness to kick in more. "That's more than two months of care."

Angela shot him a look that was designed to freeze him into silence.

Bull took the second beer and drank half of it in two long pulls.

Angela said to Cody, "With all due respect, you should be talking to the park rangers, not my dad. It's their job to do this kind of thing in Yellowstone. And if you didn't get yourself in trouble, you could be doing this all legitimate."

Bull said, "Talk to the bureaucrats? The time it would take you to lay this all out to the Park Service and for them to have meetings and come up with a budget . . . hell, you don't have that kind of time. And I doubt any of 'em really know the backcountry well enough to find that trip. They'd probably have to hire me anyway, as much as they'd hate that."

"Exactly," Cody said.

Bull leaned forward and his daughter's hand dropped away from his arm. He said to Cody, "It'll take me some time to put everything together. I haven't used any of my equipment for a while."

Cody nodded.

Bull said, "And we need to go in and get back within a week. One week, because I can't miss the storytime. You got me? I can't miss it. And I'll tag a three-thousand-dollar-a-day penalty on you if we do."

"Okay," Cody said, refusing to even consider the ramifications. He could tell by Bull Mitchell's eyes that it was a deal kill should Cody balk or want to negotiate further.

"I don't suppose Margaret will mind us taking some of Jed's horses and panniers," Bull said to himself.

"Dad, you can't be really thinking about this," Angela said. "Just do the smart thing—both of you—and call the park rangers."

"They'll fuck it up," Bull said, growling. "We can't risk lives while they screw around."

Angela left the booth and stomped toward the bathroom.

"She's upset," Bull Mitchell said. "In her mind, I've been out of the game for a long time."

Cody said, "What you do at the library, man. It's, you know, pretty dedicated."

Bull shook the compliment off. "Gotta do something. She was there for me for forty-five years and believe it or not, being with me ain't a sweet picnic all the time."

"Somehow," Cody said, "I can believe that."

Bull stifled a smile.

Cody said, "You knew my dad and my uncle Jeter, then?"

"Yeah," Bull said, his face contorting as if he'd bitten into something sour. "I turned in your uncle for poaching elk in Yellowstone, and he threatened to kill me for it. I said, 'Come on down to Bozeman, Jeter Hoyt.' I think he was on his way when the judge sent him to Deer Lodge the first time. I've been kind of looking out for him ever since. Is he still around?"

Cody looked away. "We can talk about it later." Then: "Why are you called Bull?"

" 'Cause I'm hung like one," he said, and finished his beer.

As Angela came back to the booth, Bull said to Cody, "I'll meet you at Jed's place at four thirty tomorrow morning. Get some good boots and clothes and put your personal crap together in a duffel bag weighing no more than twenty pounds."

Cody nodded. He was seeing Bull Mitchell the outfitter reemerge. "Any way we could get going sooner?" Cody asked. "I mean, I've already wasted a day."

"That's your problem, not mine," Bull said. "I got things to get ready and business to put in order."

Angela said, "I guess there's no point in talking about it anymore."

Bull said, "Nope. Sorry, sweetie. We've got to go get this young man's boy."

She said to her dad, "This has nothing to do with his boy. This has to do with you acting like one."

Bull clapped his hand over his breast, and said, "Straight to the heart."

Cody was outside the door of the Crystal Bar when Angela chased him down and grabbed his shoulder.

Her face was set. She said, "If my dad gets hurt on this trip, I'll be your worst nightmare."

Cody said, "I understand."

"I don't think you do," she said. "I think you're just focused on your son. But if my dad gets hurt or doesn't come back—it's on you.

And if you think getting suspended from the sheriff's department is a big deal, just wait to find out what it's like to find me on the other side of the table."

Cody said, fingering her card, which read ANGELA MITCHELL, ATTORNEY AT LAW, "I was kind of hoping we could be friends. But I've never gotten along real well with lawyers."

"I'm shocked," she said, her eyes flashing. She said, "I'm going to open a case file this afternoon with a tab that reads 'Cody Hoyt.' By the time I see you next I'll know everything there is to know about you. And I have the feeling it'll be a real thick file."

He nodded. "You're probably right."

She said, "The only way you're going to skate is if you bring him back better than he left and you do it within a week. Otherwise, I'm calling your sheriff and every cop I can find to come after you."

"Got it," he said, sliding the card in his pocket.

"Good," she said. "Now if you'll excuse me, I've got to go help my dad get ready."

He watched her storm back into the bar. He thought she looked pretty good doing that. He tried to imagine what her face would look like when she started researching his record.

"Another reason to get the hell out of here," he said aloud to himself.

14

After Jed the outfitter peeled off the trail into the trees and called out "Welcome to Camp One, folks!" the long line of horses followed his lead, glad to be done working for the day. It was almost comical, Gracie thought, the way the animals just turned off the trail and at the same time they broke the psychic connection with their riders. They *knew* their shifts were done. Jed and Dakota led the mounts one by one to a makeshift corral designated by a single strand of white electric fence wire Jed had strung through the trees.

"Hey Jed," D'Amato called out. "What—are these union horses?"

Which made most of the riders smile or laugh.

Gracie waited her turn to dismount behind Danielle, who was squirming in her saddle.

Gracie said, "What's the problem?"

Danielle turned to Gracie. In an urgent whisper, said, "I have to pee. Where do I *do* that? In the woods like an animal?"

Gracie shrugged. That's what *she'd* done earlier when nobody was looking.

It was late afternoon and to the east the sun shimmered across the surface of the southeast arm of Yellowstone Lake. Small lazy waves lapped against pink football-sized rocks on the shoreline, making background music like a cool jazz soundtrack. Far across the lake, dark timbered mountains plunged sharply into the water. The sultry warm afternoon was being penetrated by slight currents of colder air washing down through the trees from the mountains to the west.

Gracie was tired, sore, hungry, and mentally overwhelmed with the sights, sounds, and smells of the trip so far. She'd not only fallen in love with Strawberry, she was falling in love with the park itself. They'd seen a bull and a cow moose in the willows, five bison grazing on a treeless sagebrush hillside, and a bald eagle feeding on a fish. The national symbol stood on the bank of the river, tearing bloodred fillets off the sides of the trout and eying the riders as they passed. When they rode over the ridge, the Yellowstone River valley sprawled out before them. The vista was made up of endless mountains, lakes, clouds, and trees as far as she could see. All of it was lit in golden afternoon sunlight. The vastness and altitude made her slightly out of breath, and exhausted her.

It was another world and she'd willingly given herself up to it, holding back little.

"How's it going?" Jed asked Gracie gruffly, taking the reins from her and guiding her horse toward the others.

"I'm blown away," she whispered. "Dad told me it would be beautiful, but this is amazing."

He smiled in a perfunctory way—his eyes were elsewhere as Danielle walked past after dismounting—and said, "It'll get better tomorrow."

"Better than blown away?" she said, realizing he hadn't heard a word she'd said.

She waited with Danielle for their dad. Danielle shifted from foot to foot and grimaced. Most seemed to hurt already from the ride, Gracie observed. The Wall Streeters were moaning comically, with D'Amato flopping on his back in the grass and stretching out as if making snow angels. Walt had already broken out his fly rod near the water and was stringing line on it while Justin stood by him and watched and asked quiet fishing questions. She looked at her wristwatch: only five hours from the parking lot, but it was a completely different planet.

Gracie watched as Jed and Dakota led each unsaddled horse from the makeshift corral out through the trees to a sunlit grassy meadow. Strawberry, like the others, had a wet square of sweat on her back from where the saddle blanket had been. Dakota buckled some kind of straps on Strawberry's fetlocks and returned for the next horse.

"Those must be hobbles," Gracie said. "So the horses can move and graze but so they can't run off. I've read about them."

"So, are you going to find out?" Danielle asked Gracie impatiently.

"You're the one who officially has to pee."

"You'll have to eventually. You can't hold it in for five days."

"I can," Gracie said, deadpan, "I've been practicing."

"You are so full of shit sometimes, girlie."

Gracie shot a glance at her sister to see if she was making an intentional pun. Nope.

"Maybe we can get Dad to ask them," Danielle said. "It's sort of embarrassing. It's like we're just supposed to know everything even though none of us have been out here before."

Their dad was obviously feeling the effects of the first day of riding as well, the way he limped toward them. Despite the apparent pain, though, he was beaming.

"Look at him," Gracie said. "Look at his face."

"What about it?"

"I've never seen him look so happy," she said. "Look at that smile."

Danielle studied him as he approached. "My God, you're right. Who took our dad and switched him with this guy? He looks friggin' *goofy.*"

Gracie giggled at that.

"What did I tell you, girls?" her dad said, shaking his head with pleasure. "Didn't I tell you it would be great? I mean, look at this! It's like we're the first explorers in the Garden of Eden or something.

Look," he said, squeezing between them and pointing across the lake toward the trees. "You can see steam from a fumarole coming out from the trees over there."

"A what?" Danielle asked.

"A fumarole. A steam vent. There are four kinds of thermal features in the world and all of them are in Yellowstone: geysers, mudpots, hot springs and fumaroles. That's a fumarole. So we not only have this spectacular wilderness around us, we are also in one of the world's most active thermal areas. Jed said there were over ten thousand thermal features in the park. It's just amazing." As he talked, he reached out and pulled both girls in to him. He said, "And there's nobody on earth I'd rather share this with than my two girls." Gracie smiled and felt a tiny sting of tears in the corners of her eyes.

"I have to pee," Danielle said. "Do you know where the bathroom is, or do we just wander off into the trees like cavewomen?"

Gracie watched her dad flush. He said, "There aren't any *bathrooms.*"

"It's just an expression, dad," Danielle said, rolling her eyes and hopping from foot to foot. "Could you go ask them?"

Her dad made a face, but he said, "Sure," and started off for Dakota and Jed, who were carrying stacks of rolled-up tents toward a grassy shelf that overlooked the lake. Gracie glared at her sister.

"I'm sorry," Danielle said, her eyes flashing. "I know it was a lovely family moment, but . . ."

While their dad talked with Jed, Gracie surveyed the group. Walt and Justin were still rigging up to fish. James Knox, Tony D'Amato, and Drey Russell stretched out on rocks and downed logs near them, listening to Walt explain the parts of his fly rod and the line to Justin, who stood by, feigning patience. It was obvious he was ready to take the rod from his stepfather and start casting. Tristan Glode stood quietly farther down the shoreline smoking a cigar and looking out over the water as if he owned it. Donna Glode had stripped to tight bicycle shorts and a tank top and was doing some kind of yoga or exercises in

BACK OF BEYOND 153

the middle of a clearing in the trees where Gracie guessed the cooking stove and eating area would be set up. Although the woman was isolated from the others, Gracie had the impression Donna wanted to be watched as she stretched her long limbs and bent over so her chiseled butt was in the air.

Over on the grassy bench where their dad had walked, Rachel Mina hovered near Jed and Dakota holding her duffel bag, looking like she couldn't wait to get into her tent when it was set up.

Gracie narrowed her eyes and swept the area a second time. K. W. Wilson was nowhere to be seen. Maybe, she thought, he didn't need instructions from Jed and Dakota where to relieve himself.

"You're not going to like this very much," her dad said to Danielle as he walked back to them. Gracie could tell he was suppressing a smile.

Said Danielle, "What?"

"There's a little portable toilet up the mountain," he said, pointing into the trees away from the lakefront. "Dakota said the trail goes up from the eating area over there where that lady is making a spectacle of herself. It's about a quarter mile up the mountain, Dakota said."

"A *quarter mile*?" Danielle cried.

"Park Service regulations, is what they told me," her dad said, still controlling the grin. "Anyway, Dakota said she set it up first thing so you're the inaugural user. There's a roll of toilet paper in a Ziploc bag near the firepit."

Danielle nodded and started for the trees.

"One more thing," he said, winking at Gracie so Danielle couldn't see him. "The Park Service has a regulation about the paper. After you're done with it you need to bring it back down and throw it in the firepit. It has to be burned so there's no trace."

"What?" She was outraged. "I have to wipe myself and bring the paper back down? In my *hand*?"

He shrugged. "It's the rules."

Danielle turned to Gracie. "You're coming with me."

"I don't have to go."

Danielle narrowed her eyes. "You need to help me find it."

"I don't have to go."

Her dad said, "Gracie, it would be nice if you went with her."

"Let's go *now*," Danielle hissed.

Gracie said, "Ugh."

"I'll wait for you here," their dad said. "I'll figure out which tents we get in case you girls want to take a rest or change clothes or anything."

It was striking, Gracie thought, how cool the temperature was in the shadows of the trees away from the lake and the clearings near the shore. She trudged along behind her sister's long strides beneath the high canopy of the trees. They pushed their way up the hillside through knee-high ferns. At one point, Gracie turned and could see the sun-fused lake through an opening of branches and a glimpse of a yellow dome tent being set up on the grassy bench. Her dad stood near the yellow tent talking to Rachel Mina. Their conversation looked comfortable—even animated. Gracie was fascinated because she so rarely saw her father in the context of other people. Especially single women around his own age. She wondered if her dad was different with Rachel Mina. Maybe not so uptight and stiff as he was with them. And she wondered what Rachel Mina thought of him.

"Hmmm," Gracie said.

"Come on," Danielle said, "quit stopping." Then: "My God—we have to have hiked a quarter of a mile so far. I wonder if we passed it?"

"We didn't pass it," Gracie said. "Keep going."

"I might just drop my jeans and go right here."

"Go ahead," Gracie said, "I'm not stopping you."

"Maybe a little farther," Danielle said. "But if they think I'm carrying down the paper in my hands they're out of their fucking minds. Jed can come up here and *get* it."

"Sure, okay," Gracie said, "let's piss off the outfitter the very first night of the trip. That's good thinking, Danielle."

Her sister pushed her way through pine boughs and suddenly came to an abrupt stop before a small portable toilet with four metal legs and a square of plywood with a hole in the middle of it. A dark plastic bag hung down beneath the seat, the bottom of the bag inches from the pine-needle carpet. There were stunted pines near the apparatus, but basically it was in the open.

"*Oh. My. God,*" Danielle said, looking around as if trying to find the missing walls of the outhouse.

"Not a lot of privacy, is there?" Gracie said, needling her sister. "It's like anybody could be hiding in the trees out there watching you. Or like a bear could come out of the woods and bite you on your naked white butt.

"Or ravens," Gracie said, reveling in it, recalling when Danielle had once confessed her fear of the black birds. "Maybe ravens will fly down while you're squatting and take a big old chunk out of your right cheek! You'll be scarred! You'll need surgery. You can never wear bikini bottoms again without people pointing and laughing at the girl with one ugly cheek!"

"Sometimes," Danielle said, lowering her pants and shooting dagger eyes at her little sister while she squatted over the seat, "I could just kill you."

Gracie turned away. It would be funnier, she thought, if *she* wouldn't have to use the little toilet later.

And if she hadn't just heard the muffled crack of a branch from someone coming up the trail toward them.

"What was that?" Danielle whispered. "I heard a sound. And don't tell me it was bears or ravens."

Gracie held her finger up to her lips to indicate to Danielle to be quiet, that she'd heard it too. Danielle's eyes got wide and she mouthed, *Who is it?*

Gracie shrugged and stared into the forest below them. It was so green, wet, and dark up there, so different from the camp and the lake. So much foliage. So many places for a man or animal to hide.

"Keep them from coming up here until I'm through," Danielle said.

Gracie put her hands on her hips and shouted, "Hey—whoever you are—give us a minute. We're up here right now. Wait your turn, please."

There was no response, which was disconcerting. Behind her, she could hear a hard stream of liquid strumming against the inside of the plastic toilet bag. Danielle was hurrying the best she could.

Then, after a beat, there was the sharp crack of a twig. Only this time, it wasn't from below on the trail but to the side of them on the slope of the mountain. Whoever—or whatever—it was had deliberately left the trail and bushwhacked into the wet brush. For what reason, Gracie wondered—a better view?

"Hey," Gracie called, "who's out there?"

No response. She wished she had bear spray with her. Or a knife or club or some kind of weapon. She looked around and saw nothing she could really arm herself with. There was an old dry stick a couple of inches thick on the ground near her feet and she bent over to grab it, but it was rotten and broke apart as she lifted it.

Finally, Danielle was done. It had been only a few seconds but it seemed like forever to Gracie. Danielle cursed as she stood and fumbled for her thong and long pants. While she cinched her belt, she yelled, "This isn't funny, pervert. Not funny at all. Hear me? *Not funny.*"

"Always the diplomat," Gracie said under her breath.

Then there was a deep cough from the brush. It sounded closer than Gracie would have thought possible since she still couldn't see anyone.

The cough did it. Gracie and Danielle exchanged terrified glances, then broke for the trail, their boots thumping the ground. Gracie thought about screaming, but didn't.

Danielle passed her on the way down as Gracie paused to look over her shoulder to see if anyone was coming after them. She could see no one, although she thought she might have heard a chuckle.

"Did you hear that?" Gracie said to her sister as Danielle went by.

"What?"

"Somebody laughed."

"Fucking pervert!" Danielle said over her shoulder before continuing down the switchback trail. Gracie followed. They ran down the trail for twenty feet before Danielle veered off, choosing to cut the corner for a more direct route through the brush. Danielle shoved branches aside that whipped back and hit Gracie in the face until she learned to duck under them.

Danielle led them into an impassible tangle of downed logs. The logs were old and gray, and blue-green lichen clung in clawlike pods in the elbows of branches. Something small, long, and dark scuttled out of the tangle away from them, rustling through the tall grass. Gracie couldn't see what kind of animal it was.

"Shit," Danielle said. "I don't know if we can climb over this. It's like we're trapped here."

"*You* trapped us," Gracie said, letting her annoyance come through. "I thought you knew where you were going."

Danielle turned on her and said with perfect logic, "So when have I *ever* known that?"

"You're right. You're off the hook."

Danielle nodded triumphantly.

Said Gracie, "We'll need to go back and find the trail. Then we can get back to camp. Whoever isn't down *there* was up *here*. We'll know who it was spying on you."

Danielle said, "Which one of them do you think is the pervert?"

Gracie shrugged and led the way back until she broke through the foliage and found herself back on the trail. At least, she thought it was the right trail. For a second, she was confused which way to turn.

"Go right," Danielle said, and Gracie did, even though she wasn't any more confident of Danielle's sense of direction than she was of her own. She made a promise to herself right then to wake up and pay more attention to her surroundings. She couldn't just blindly follow Danielle, or Jed or Dakota or even her dad. She never wanted to feel lost like this again. Her stride lengthened and she picked up speed. The slope and the trees started to look familiar again. She almost ran through a mud bog but managed to skirt around it. The bog was the result of a thin trickle of water that came down from a spring somewhere higher on the mountain. She remembered the spot from the way up and felt a warm wave of relief because now she was sure they were going the right direction. But as she ran past it she noticed something different and stopped. Danielle practically ran over her.

"What?" her sister asked.

Gracie pointed toward the mud. "Look."

There was half of a large fresh boot print on the edge of the mud, as if whomever had made it had tried to avoid stepping into the mud at the last second and almost succeeded.

Gracie wished she knew more about men's boot sizes. But she could tell it was maybe a size ten or twelve since her dad wore size eight and these were bigger. The print had sharp lugs pressed into the dirt, a deep heel imprint, and a little diamond brand where the wearer's arch was. The print was pointed up the trail.

"I don't remember seeing that on the way, do you?" she said.

"No, but I didn't look."

Gracie nodded. "Memorize it. We may see who wears that boot later."

When they broke through the trees into the sunshine Danielle passed Gracie again and they ran toward their dad. He was still standing next to Rachel Mina. All the tents were up and Dakota was shoving the last of the tent stakes into the soft ground. Gracie noticed an amused look on her father's face as they approached.

"That go all right?" he asked.

Danielle answered with a rush of words. "Somebody up there was *spying* on me. He scared the *shit* out of us."

Rather than concern, her dad suppressed a grin. "Come on, girls," he said. "Who would do something like that?"

Gracie ignored him and concentrated on doing inventory of the camp. Not a lot had changed, although she noticed there were four men missing: Wilson, Tony, Knox, and Jed.

Her dad said, "Don't let your imaginations get the best of you. Do you know how many animals there are up here?" It was obvious he didn't want to believe them, didn't want the trip to take this kind of unpleasant detour on the first day. Her dad didn't like detours, or surprises, or events wrought with emotion. No matter what the situation or the crisis, his first words were generally *I wish I would have known about this sooner,* as if it were possible to know everything in advance and avert every problem if he just had the foreknowledge. It was a trait that annoyed Gracie because it always put the burden on *her.* Danielle was never expected to know anything in advance.

Her dad looked at both of them. Neither budged.

Gracie said, "Animals don't wear boots."

He sighed, said, "Okay, let's go take a look."

Gracie nodded and turned to lead the way.

"Mind if I come along?" Rachel Mina said to them as they started toward the trailhead up the mountain. "I overheard and I don't like the idea of being spied on, either."

Her dad said, "We're not exactly sure what happened." To Danielle, he asked, "Did the guy say anything at all?"

"No. He just coughed and laughed."

"He *laughed*?"

Gracie and Danielle exchanged guilty looks.

"Gracie thought he did," Danielle said.

"Did you feel threatened?" Rachel Mina asked them both.

"Pretty much, yeah," Danielle said.

Said Gracie, "They should let us carry bear spray."

"Or they should build a real fucking toilet," Danielle mumbled.

"Language," their dad said, and Gracie caught him shooting a quick glance to Rachel Mina to see her reaction to the profanity.

"Sorry."

Her dad said, "Did you consider maybe he was as embarrassed to find you girls as you were? I mean, I've stumbled into a bathroom before and found somebody in it. It's always a shock and I've been embarrassed. I remember opening the door on a stall once in a gas station and seeing this fat guy on the toilet looking at me. We were both kind of horrified."

Rachel Mina laughed politely.

Her dad continued, "I remember I didn't say anything—I was too red-faced. I just shut the door and went outside the station. When the guy finally came out neither one of us looked at each other. He went on his way, I went on mine. We both sort of pretended it didn't happen, you know?"

Gracie hadn't thought about it that way and she felt a needle of doubt creep in. Maybe they *had* overreacted with their shouting and Danielle calling him a pervert and all. Who would want to respond after being called a pervert? And much of the panic she'd felt earlier was more as a result of thinking she was lost in the forest than anything anyone did.

Still . . .

As they entered the trees Gracie did a 360-degree pivot to see if anyone was watching them carefully. Dakota waved from near the firepit where she was breaking sticks into kindling. No one else met her eyes.

Within five minutes she found the bog. The footprint was gone, obscured in the mud by a gnarled knot of pitchwood that had been dropped on top of it. Whoever had left the print had crushed it out of existence.

"It was here," she said to her dad and Rachel.

"I'm sure it was," he said, waggling his eyebrows in a way of saying maybe they'd been mistaken.

"It was," Gracie said with less assurance.

"Who knows what we thought we saw?" Danielle said. "You know how you get. Remember when you used to say there was a werewolf under your bed?"

Her dad stifled a smile. Rachel looked away.

Gracie hated her sister at that moment.

When they returned to the camp. Jed was setting up the aluminum cooking station—a series of interconnected boxes that became a counter, sink, and chuck box—and Dakota set a coffeepot over the fire. James Knox, Drey Russell, and K. W. Wilson sat on separate logs watching the fire burn. All of them looked up as the Sullivans and Rachel entered the camp from the trees.

"Everything all right?" Jed asked.

"Fine," Gracie's dad said quickly. He wanted to preempt either of his daughters. To say something now, Gracie thought, would seem silly. She collapsed on a log bench to watch the fire across from her dad and Danielle, who chose another log. Rachel sat next to Gracie, saying nothing but sitting close enough that Gracie felt the woman was sympathizing with her. That was nice.

"You folks might want to get your stuff all laid out in your tents," Dakota said. "We'll have dinner ready in about an hour and it'll get dark fast. This way, you won't have to try to unpack everything by flashlight."

Her dad slapped his knees and stood up. "Makes sense."

As Gracie rose she noticed Wilson had changed into moccasins. Maybe, she thought, so they wouldn't see that his boots had been muddy.

15

Cody chain-smoked cigarettes in his room at the Gallatin Gateway Inn, breaking the filters off each stick and lighting the new one from the cherry stub of the old one. It had only taken him two minutes to dismantle the smoke detector on the ceiling by unscrewing the faceplate and disconnecting the white and red wires. He hoped he'd remember to put it all right before he checked out in the morning.

He paced and surveyed his new gear piled on the bed. Before the stores closed, he'd found Ariat cowboy boots that didn't hurt his feet at Powder Horn Sportsman's Supply on Main as well as a straw cowboy hat, chaps, jeans, two sets of nylon saddlebags, and denim jacket. He'd felt foolish buying Western wear, but Bull Mitchell had insisted. Everything else he needed—sleeping bag, pad, water filter, daypack, .40 caliber Smith & Wesson cartridges, .223 rounds for his scoped departmental AR-15, a saddle sheath for the rifle, Steiner binoculars—he found at Bob Ward Sporting Goods on Max Avenue. Rounding out his purchases was a plastic grocery bag packed with two cartons of cigarettes, a long sleeve of Stride gum packets, plastic bottles of tonic water, and instant coffee. He'd spent five agonizing minutes staring at a pint of Wild Turkey behind the clerk's head—*Just one pint, just one, what could it hurt?* Hell, he thought, he'd save it until he had Justin with him and the killer in cuffs or in the ground. It would be his *reward*.

While he argued with himself he tried to conjure up the image of Hank Winters saying, "Once you start you cannot stop. That is our curse." Instead, the image of Hank was of a roasted and bloated arm reaching up from the black muck in the rain. And when the eager young clerk behind the counter asked, "May I help you?" Cody snapped, "Go to hell," and stomped out of the place.

He felt guilty for that now.

He was pleased to find out they had available rooms at the Gallatin Gateway Inn—a restored grand hotel from the early railroad days—because it was less than a half mile from the headquarters of Wilderness Adventures. The female receptionist wore a crisp white shirt and sniffed at him, saying, "Please keep in mind we have a strict no-smoking policy here."

"I thought this was a railroad hotel," Cody said. "Railroaders *smoked*."

"At one time," the clerk said. "Many many years ago. And there aren't any railroaders around here anymore, if you noticed."

"So this is a snooty place," he said.

"Not at all," she said crisply.

He winked at her and gave her his credit card. After she took the imprint, he hauled all his gear to his room to unwrap his purchases, clip off the price tags, and fill two new nylon saddlebags. To hell with Bull Mitchell's twenty-pound limit, he thought.

It was dark by the time he had everything packed. He'd made several trips to and from his Ford. There were things in the tool box and investigations lockers he wanted to take with him, including his rain gear. He was pleased he remembered to bring the Motorola Iridium

9505A handheld satellite phone. He'd stashed it in his SUV a few months ago after he stole it from the evidence room. Drug runners had used the phone so they wouldn't be tracked via their cell phone calls by law enforcement, and the case was a slam dunk because the bad guys turned on each other so the phone was never introduced in court. The phone was small for a sat phone, less than a pound, and cost sixteen hundred dollars retail. It had three and a half hours of talk time without recharging and thirty-eight hours of stand-by time. He stuffed it in a saddlebag.

Then he sat at the small desk in the room, turned on the ancient banker's lamp, and placed his cell phone within reach, waiting for Larry to call. It had been way too long not to have heard from him since he faxed the material, he thought. His partner must know something by now—he'd had the sheets all afternoon. Cody vowed to himself that if Larry didn't call him by midnight he'd break his pledge and track Larry down like a dog.

He poured a glass of tonic over ice and lit yet another cigarette, and opened the file he'd taken from Margaret Cooper. He looked at his list of suspects:

1. Anthony D'Amato
2. Walt Franck
3. Justin Hoyt
4. James Knox
5. Rachel Mina
6. Tristan Glode
7. Donna Glode
8. André Russell
9. Ted Sullivan
10. Gracie Sullivan
11. Danielle Sullivan
12. K. W. Wilson

On the bottom of the page he scrawled,

13. Jed McCarthy
14. Dakota Hill

He thought, *Everyone on the list could be the killer.* Except Justin, of course.

The applications had arrived in Jed McCarthy's office throughout the past year. They were designed to elicit information Jed needed to know to plan the trip and to match up horses with riders. There was a short questionnaire about dietary restrictions, riding ability, allergies, medical issues, and emergency contact information. The last item on the application was "What do you hope to gain from this backcountry wilderness experience?" Cody wished there were more questions and information but he was grateful he had what he had. He hoped Larry was running the whole lot of them through every criminal background database he could access.

Anthony D'Amato, thirty-four, was from Brooklyn, New York, and worked for Goldman Sachs. He was married, no children. He weighed 185 pounds and listed his wife Lisa as his emergency contact. He'd ridden a horse once, at the Iowa State Fair when he was visiting relatives as a teenager. He answered the last question, "To not be eaten by a wild animal."

Walt Franck, fifty-four, listed his home locations as Aspen and Fort Collins, Colorado, as well as Omaha. He was a commercial Realtor and developer of strip malls in the Mountain West and Midwest. He was soon to be married to Jenny, Cody's ex, and listed her as his emergency contact. Cody snorted derisively when he saw His Richness listed his weight as 220 pounds, and he planned hereafter to refer to him as "His Fat Richness." Walt was a novice rider, and he hoped the trip would "provide unique fly-fishing locations and bonding opportunities for me and my future stepson." Cody snorted again.

Justin Hoyt, seventeen, Fort Collins, 165 pounds, stepson of His Fat Richness, was next. Cody recognized the handwriting on the application as Jenny's, and it elicited a sudden desire for her again that had been rekindled the night before. He shook it off and continued reading. She said Justin wanted to experience "nature and outdoor skills."

"Shit," Cody said. "Send him to me in Montana. I could do *that.*" But he doubted Justin had even seen the application, much less discussed it with his mother.

James Knox, thirty-seven, Manhattan. Not married but had a partner named Martha, who was also his emergency contact. Worked as an executive with Millennium Capital Advisors and weighed 180 pounds. He had no experience with horses, and wrote that he and his two friends wanted to experience "the nature and diversity of Yellowstone while waiting for the market to come back."

Cody smiled at that, and skipped ahead in the stack to find the third of the buddies.

André Russell, thirty-nine, of Manhattan. Married, two children, a boy and a girl, ages twelve and nine. Wife and emergency contact was named Danika. A VP with J. P. Morgan and had ridden horses at stables in Central Park to prepare for the trip. Cody was impressed by that. For his ambition for the trip he wrote, "To try and keep Tony D'Amato from being eaten by wild animals."

Cut-ups, Cody thought. Or liars. A three-man team of killers from the East? He shook his head. The idea didn't grab him, and seemed much too cinematic and far-fetched. He moved on.

Rachel Mina was single. She didn't indicate whether she was divorced, widowed, or never married. A hospital administrator on leave from Chicago. She was thirty-seven and weighed 115 pounds. In Cody's experience, that meant he should add a few years and at least ten pounds, so he scratched in "40" and "125" on the page. Mina indicated she was a vegetarian (fish was okay) and intermediate rider. She wrote: "Discovery tour."

He wondered what "on leave" meant. His first thought was she seemed to be the only one of the clients thus far who might have had the free time—and means—to visit homes in four states and leave bodies and ashes behind. But a woman, and a single one at that?

Discovery tour, Cody mouthed, squinting through smoke at the page. It sounded phony and new-agey, he thought. Or facetious. And an interaction between a hospital administrator and Hank Winters seemed possible.

He placed her application aside from the others into what he thought of as the hot stack.

Tristan Glode was the president and CEO of The Glode Company of St. Louis. Cody didn't know what the company did but planned to find out. Glode was sixty-one and claimed to be an expert rider. He'd indicated he weighed 211 pounds and had written in the margin that he had bad knees and would prefer a Tennessee walker for a horse. In the margin, someone (Jed?) had scribbled, "Call Pat." Cody guessed Pat, whomever he or she was, knew of a walker that could be leased for the trip.

In the space for what Tristan was seeking, he wrote, "TBD." To be determined.

"What the hell does that mean?" Cody grumbled, thinking the man sounded arrogant. Asking for a specifically gaited horse, claiming to be an expert rider, listing his weight at 211 pounds. Anyone normal would write "210," Cody thought.

He put Glode's application in the hot stack with Mina's. Now he had two prime suspects.

Then he read the next application: Donna Glode, sixty, St. Louis, 130 pounds. Another expert rider. For what she was seeking she wrote, "Yellowstone by horseback. A peaceful journey."

So, husband and wife. Cody reached over and pulled Tristan's application and put it on the cold pile along with his wife's.

Ted Sullivan, forty-five, was divorced and lived in Minneapolis. He was a 185-pound software engineer with a firm called Anderson/Sullivan/Hart. He'd scratched an "X" between beginner and intermediate, slightly closer to beginner. Very precise and engineerlike, Cody thought. And in carefully printed handwriting, Sullivan said, "I hope to gain a closer and more intimate relationship with my daughters, Gracie and Danielle. I hope it will be the greatest shared experience of our lives." He listed his emergency contact as his ex-wife.

Nice, Cody thought. Heartfelt. He skimmed over the applications for Sullivan's daughters, ruling them out immediately.

He started to toss the three documents on the cold pile, then stopped himself. He retained Ted's app and looked it over again. At first, he'd thought there would be no way for the father to have done the crimes with teenage girls around, and based out of Minneapolis. But because the man was divorced, that meant it was possible the girls hadn't been with him until recently. Cody had never heard of Anderson/Sullivan/Hart but the fact that it was simply a string of surnames and that they apparently felt no need to add "software" or "consulting" or "business solutions" to the end of it indicated that they either wanted to be thought of highly or they *were* prestigious. Meaning it was a good likelihood Sullivan traveled. Cody often saw men like Sullivan in airports; road warriors who were constantly on their Bluetooth cell phones and computers, those things hanging out of their ears, talking to clients all over the country and checking in with their colleagues to form strategies and solutions.

But would a cold-blooded killer pause to take his daughters on a wilderness pack trip? Cody asked himself. His answer was, not likely. Still, though, he couldn't rule him out and he put the application between the hot and cold stacks.

Cody looked at the last application and whistled. As he read over it he started to nod. Jesus:

K. W. Wilson, fifty-eight, Salt Lake City, Utah. No marital status indicated. No occupation listed except "transportation." One hundred seventy pounds and an intermediate rider. Under dietary restrictions Wilson had scrawled, "No cheese." For what he was seeking, Wilson had written, "Fishing and adventure."

Cody said to the application, "Congratulations, you're now number one," and placed it on the hot stack.

Doubts remained, however, if he was even on the right track.

Cody remembered seeing a business center in the lobby with two computers for guests. He gathered the applications back into the file to take them downstairs. He'd find more about all of the names, as well as get some background on The Glode Company, Anderson/Sullivan/Hart, Rachel Mina's hospital, and anything he could locate on K. W. Wilson.

His cell went off and danced across the surface of the desk since he'd set it to ring and vibrate.

He checked the display: Larry.

"About time," he said.

"Are you sitting down?" Larry asked.

16

―――――

Gracie wished she'd unpacked her heavier jacket because when the sun doused behind the mountains the temperature dropped a quick twenty degrees or more within minutes, as if the thin mountain air was incapable of retaining the afternoon heat. She thought about going back to her tent to dig out her hoodie, but the instant darkness didn't encourage a trip and the warmth and light of the campfire held her in place as if it had strong gravitational pull.

She was sitting on a smooth downed log with Danielle and Justin. She couldn't stop staring into the fire, which was mesmerizing. The meal had been huge and consisted of things she normally didn't like that much: steak, baked potatoes, baked beans, half a cob of corn dripping with butter. She'd wolfed most of it down, leaving only a quarter of the steak. She had no idea why she'd felt so hungry, or how the food possibly tasted so good. The apple cobbler baked in a jet-black Dutch oven was one of the best things she'd ever eaten, and she'd had two helpings of it. Her mouth still tasted of cinnamon from the cobbler and hot fat from the meat. Now, the entire meal sat in her stomach as heavy as a rock, and it made her sleepy and uncomfortable.

Normally, Gracie hated it when portions of food touched each other on her plate. This time, though, she didn't care that the steak tasted of bean juice and the potato turned pink because it sat in pooled grease. It was all so wonderful she'd nearly forgotten about what had happened earlier. But not completely.

Earlier, when Dakota had twirled an iron bar around on the inside of a battered metal triangle to signal dinner, they'd all stopped whatever it was they were doing and lined up at the portable aluminum kitchen station holding empty tin plates. One by one, they presented their plates so Jed McCarthy and Dakota could serve the slabs of meat and plop down the sides. The line was interrupted once when Tony D'Amato whooped—and jumped back—when he saw a snake slither through the grass between his feet.

"Damn," he shouted, his voice high-pitched. "It went over my *boot*."

Dakota reacted quickly and tossed her spoon aside and chased down the snake. She grabbed it behind its head and held it up, asking if anyone wanted it for dinner. D'Amato and his friends laughed at that, and he seemed embarrassed by his outcry. Danielle, who was standing in line in front of Gracie, had turned and said, "Great. Snakes, too. This place *sucks*."

"It's harmless," Gracie said. "It's just a snake. Maybe we should try it."

"Just a snake," Danielle said. "Jesus, you're weird."

Gracie sat quietly while Justin and Danielle talked. She eavesdropped halfheartedly, absorbed with re-creating the incident up at the latrine that Danielle seemed to have already forgotten. Something had happened up there that bothered her, because it suggested someone on the trip had an agenda besides the adventure itself. It reminded her that people could be evil, something she believed more and more the older she got.

Danielle, however, was at her charming best. Subjects ranged from their schools to Facebook pages to sports, television shows, and bands. Gracie found herself rolling her eyes each time Danielle and Justin discovered more and more common bonds. When Danielle mentioned their parents were divorced, Justin said, "Shit, mine too."

Justin was handsome and well built but shallow, Gracie thought. Exactly Danielle's type. Gracie wanted to warn him now, before it was too late. But she didn't think he wanted to know what her sister could be like, how she collected and discarded boys like him. And, Gracie thought, maybe he wouldn't even care. It wasn't like he was on the trip to establish a meaningful relationship, was it?

The more Gracie stared at the fire, the more interesting it was. Unlike her sister and Justin.

"So your dad has you for the summer?" Justin asked Danielle.

"Sort of," her sister said, keeping her voice low so only Justin—and Gracie, unfortunately—could hear her. "My dad's had a bug up his butt about this trip for a year. It's like a father-daughter bonding thing, I guess."

Justin said, "Same here, only Walt is my stepdad. He thinks we'll become lifelong buds after this or something. He thinks fly-fishing is, you know, *religious* or something. And it's all right, I like it and all, but Walt is kind of old and everything. So I don't know."

"What's your real dad like?" Danielle asked, leaning closer to him. "Is he around, I mean?"

Justin hesitated, then shook his head. "He's okay. He's a cop. He's tough to figure out. Sometimes he's a great guy, and sometimes he's just an asshole."

Danielle acted like that was the funniest thing she'd ever heard, and covered her mouth while she leaned back and laughed, making sure to grasp Justin's thigh to keep her balance.

"He's in Montana," Justin said, "but he calls me and stuff. He never knows what to say and neither do I. He sends me stuff—fishing rods, computer games, CDs, things he thinks I'll like. But," he said, leaning even closer to her and lowering his voice, "sometimes he forgets to take the evidence tags off. I mean, I'll get a set of walkie-talkies with a piece of tape on 'em that says 'Exhibit A' or some damned thing."

Which made Danielle squeal with laughter. Gracie tried to tune her out.

After a few minutes, Danielle shoved her and nearly knocked her off the log. Justin chuckled.

"*What?*" Gracie said.

"I was talking to you," her sister said softly, not wanting the others to overhear.

"I thought you were talking to Jason."

"Justin," she corrected. "And I was. I was telling him about what happened earlier up on the mountain and I said you were there as my witness."

Gracie looked over. Their faces were lit with firelight. Justin *was* good-looking, but the way his eyes reflected the fire made him look kind of creepy. And, she wondered, was it him? Then she dismissed it because he'd been fishing with Walt at the time.

Justin leaned toward her, resting his hand on Danielle's knee. Her sister didn't seem to mind.

"So you think it was that Wilson guy?" Justin whispered.

"I don't know," Gracie said. "But I noticed he's wearing moccasins tonight so we can't see his boots."

Justin started to turn his head to confirm it but Danielle clasped her hands on both sides of his face and said, "Don't look, silly. He'll know we're onto him."

Then she stood up. "Now just keep an eye on him. I've got to go pee."

"Again?" Gracie said.

Danielle narrowed her eyes at her sister and said, "This time I'm not going up to that stupid toilet. I'll be back in a second. Don't try to steal Justin away, as if you could."

After she was gone, Gracie and Justin sat together uncomfortably. Or at least Gracie did.

Justin said, "Your sister seems nice."

"She isn't."

Justin chuckled. "I guess what I mean is she could be nice, if she tried."

"Don't count on it," Gracie said, warming to him. "I know her."

"There's good in everybody, Gracie."

She looked over to see if he was serious. He was. He said, "I always expect the best out of people. I think when you do that, you get the best most of the time. I just kind of bump along, expecting the best, and good things just happen. That's my secret."

She said, "Why are you telling me your secret?" She was flattered. She thought a strapping, good-looking guy like Justin would be unapproachable in every instance. He was too handsome, too confident, and too cool.

"I'll tell anyone who will listen," he said softly. "What I can't figure out is why everybody doesn't do it. Look for the best, I mean. It's easy, and it makes life go easier."

Gracie just stared. He was too good to be true, she thought. Her instincts were not to trust him.

"That's a nice thing, I guess," she said to her shoes.

"Sure it is. Just accept yourself and look for the good in others. It's not complicated."

"Do you see good in me?" Gracie asked.

He smiled. He even had a nice smile. "Of course. You watch out for your sister and your dad, I think."

"So who watches out for me?"

"I will, if you want," he said sincerely.

Gracie shook her head. She'd never met someone so comfortable in their own skin. It weirded her out. There must be more to him, she thought. A dark side. But when she looked into his open face and that impossible smile, she couldn't see it. No one was that good. Maybe he was a *sociopath*. And she felt immediately guilty for thinking it.

"See how it works?" he said, as if reading her mind.

Gracie was grateful when Danielle suddenly reappeared and grasped Justin's face between her hands before sitting back down.

Justin didn't pull his face away, and smiled at Danielle sloppily. He liked it. Gracie rolled her eyes again and looked back to the fire. "Hey, look," Justin said to Danielle, "out on the lake. Can you see what's going on?"

"What?" her sister asked.

"The fish are rising."

Gracie followed his outstretched arm. The moon lit the still surface of the lake in light blue and sure enough, ringlets were appearing everywhere, as if it were raining upside down.

Justin said, "Want to go down to the shore with me and see if we can catch one?"

Danielle was up like a shot. She stood in front of Gracie and blocked the light and heat, and Gracie felt as if she'd been plunged into cold. She started to stand but Danielle reached back and put a hand on her shoulder, preventing her from rising. Danielle turned and bent over close to her ear, and said, "Not you."

Justin winked and asked Gracie, "Do you want to come along?"

"No," Danielle said. "She doesn't."

And Gracie thought, *She doesn't deserve him.*

After they'd left, Gracie considered asking Dakota to help her find that snake so she could put it into the bottom of her sister's sleeping bag.

She hugged herself against the chill, now that her sister had abandoned her. It seemed very late but it wasn't even ten yet. The sky was a bright smear of stars she'd never known existed before, and the busy sky above and the absolute darkness of everything beyond the fire made her feel smaller than she'd ever felt.

The campfire was the hub that held everyone in place. When it started to die Dakota or Jeb would leave their place behind the cooking station where they were washing dishes and toss another piece of wood on it.

She observed the others without staring at them.

The Glodes kept to themselves. They were the farthest away from Gracie, on the opposite side of the fire. Tristan Glode smoked a big black cigar, and the glow danced in the darkness. Donna stared into the fire as if she were comatose. Gracie thought that although they were by themselves they weren't really with each other. It was as if there were a wall between them even though they were a couple of feet apart. How sad, she thought.

Two of the three Wall Streeters, Tony D'Amato and Drey Russell, were whittling on sticks and joking about it. Everything, it seemed, was a joke to them. Little light-colored piles of shavings gathered on their boots, and the blades from their pocketknives flashed in the firelight.

"A year ago," D'Amato said in a singsong, bluesy cadence, "I was looking out over the Sea of Cortez from my air-conditioned bungalow in Baja. Now here I am in the freezing mountains, sittin' on a log. Whittlin'."

"You a whittlin' man," Russell sang along.

"I'm a whittlin' man," D'Amato sang back. "Whittlin' 'til I ain't got no stick left."

"You a whittlin' man . . ."

"Think I'll whittle me a boat and float on out of here back to Baja. . . ."

"He a whittlin' man who ain't a-scared of no snakes!" Russell laughed, and the two of them collapsed in on each other. Luckily, they held their knives out to the side.

"You guys are embarrassing me," James Knox said from the cooking station.

Gracie found herself staring at them with more than a little awe. Knox caught her, smiled, and said, "Do you find us strange?"

Embarrassed, she said, "I've never met any New Yorkers before. I've heard about you and read about you and you're on all the television shows, but . . ."

D'Amato laughed. "But you've never met any of us in real life. You make me feel like a zoo animal or something."

"Sorry," she said, and looked down. It was just that they were exactly how they were portrayed, and she'd always thought they couldn't possibly really be like that: fast-talking, ethnic, animated. Like they were playing the roles of New Yorkers according to the script. Just like TV. But she didn't say it.

To the right, Gracie's dad was perched on a large rock next to Rachel Mina, who sat in the grass with her plate in her lap, finishing her dinner. Gracie had noted how Rachel had waited patiently for everyone else to be served steaks before getting her dinner—panfried fish and the last of the beans and corn. She admired the fact that Rachel hadn't made a fuss but simply waited for her nonmeat meal. Too many of Gracie's vegetarian friends went on and on about their preferences in the lunchroom, she thought. On and on about what they could eat and what they wouldn't. They could learn something from Rachel Mina. The clicking of her utensils on the tin plate was rhythmic and delicate and Gracie hoped that someday she could be as graceful and feminine when she ate.

Then, obviously thinking no one was paying attention, her dad reached down and snatched a small piece of fish off Rachel's plate and popped it in his mouth. She looked back but rather than object, she smiled at him. Her dad raised his eyebrows in an *It's actually good* gesture. Rachel turned back around and finished her plate.

It had happened quickly, and without a sound. But Gracie sat transfixed as if a thunderbolt had hit her in the chest.

They knew each other, she thought. The scene had a kind of sweet intimacy about it, like it had happened often before and had become a shared joke.

They knew each other. Really well.

She felt bushwhacked. Her eyes misted and she looked away.

When she opened them she saw Wilson, who'd suddenly appeared from the direction of the tents. Standing there, staring at her, his face lit orange with firelight.

"What do *you* want?" she asked, too loudly.

The others around the campfire stopped talking or doing what they were doing. Jed and Dakota peered over the top of the cooking station, washcloths poised and still.

"Goodness, little girl," Wilson said. "What is *your* problem?" He looked at the others with his palms open and held up. "All I did was walk up here to get warm. I didn't do anything."

No one said a word. A beat passed, and she was glad no one could see her face flush red. She wiped angrily at the tears in her eyes with the back of her sleeve.

From the right, her dad said, "Gracie, are you okay?"

She stood up and refused to look at him. "I'm going to bed," she said, and started for the tents.

She was gone before her eyes could adjust from the fire to the total darkness, and she tripped over a root or rock and she sprawled forward. She landed spread-eagle, grass in her mouth.

Somebody—D'Amato or Russell or Jed—barked a laugh. Someone else said, "Cool it, that's rude."

"Sorry."

She scrambled to her feet spitting grass and dried weed buds and stomped toward the tents. D'Amato called out to her, "Sorry, darlin', I didn't mean to laugh at you. Come on back and join us."

And her dad followed her, saying, "Gracie, what's going on? Are you all right, Gracie?"

She kept going until she approached the collection of tents. She wasn't sure at first which was hers—they all looked alike. Nine lightweight dome tents, looking in the soft moonlight like plump pillows.

"Gracie," her dad said, finally grasping her hand.

She pulled away. The third one, she thought. Her stuff was in the third one from the top.

He grabbed her again, said, "Honey . . ."

She wheeled on him. "When were you going to tell us?" she asked, her voice catching like ratchets on sobs. "Is this why you brought us with you? So you could be with your secret *girlfriend*?"

Her dad just stood there. She could see his stupid face in the moonlight. His mouth was moving but nothing was coming out. He finally said, "Gracie . . . really . . ."

But what she heard was his lack of denial.

"Stay away from me!" she said, and she dove into the opening of her tent. It was small inside but the sleeping bags cushioned her dive. She spun and zipped the opening closed. As she did, her last glimpse of her dad was of him standing there like an idiot with a swarm of stars around his head, trying to come up with the right words—as if there were any. She said, "Go away. This is the worst fucking trip of my life."

Inside, she could hear him. For five minutes, he stood there, breathing shallow breaths. Then he moaned and said, "I was waiting for the right time to talk with you girls. Really, honey."

She didn't respond.

Finally, he turned and trudged away back toward the fire.

An hour later, Gracie heard footfalls approaching the tent and she opened her eyes. She hoped it wasn't her dad coming back, and if so she planned to feign sleep.

The door zipper hummed and she sat up, alert.

Danielle said, "Oh my God, I *love* him."

Gracie flopped back down.

"He's so damned cute I want to eat him up," Danielle said. "He tried to help me cast to the fish but I couldn't get past how he put his arms around me. Damn, he's hot and I love him."

Gracie said, "Did you think for a second I might be asleep?"

Danielle hesitated, said, "No." Then went on, "Before I came back here he gave me just a little kiss—nothing major—and said, 'To be continued.' Is that classy and cool, or what? Is that awesome, or what?"

Gracie rolled away from her.

"What's your problem?" Danielle asked.

Gracie told her sister about their dad and Rachel Mina.

"You're kidding," Danielle said, finally.

"I'm not."

Danielle shook her head back and forth. "That just doesn't seem right," she said.

Before Gracie could agree, Danielle said, "She's much too awesome for *him*. What does she see in the guy?"

In the dark, Gracie covered her face with her hands and moaned.

"They're all still out there," Danielle said, regaining her stride, pushing the news aside. "Except for Justin, I mean. He went to his tent, too. Gee, I wonder what he's doing in there all alone?" she giggled.

Gracie said nothing.

"I saw one of the Wall Streeters open a bottle," she said. "I think they're all going to pass it around and tell stories or something. I hope they don't stay up too late or get too loud, 'cause we need to get some sleep."

"You think?" Gracie said.

"Yeah, there's a big day tomorrow," Danielle said, slipping out of her clothing to her sports bra and wriggling into a pair of light sweatpants. "At least it'll be a big day for *me*."

"That's what's important," Gracie mumbled.

"Are you being sarcastic?"

"Never."

"Well, don't," Danielle said, sliding into her sleeping bag and pulling the zipper up. "It's boring."

"Justin is too good to be true," Gracie said.

"He is, isn't he?"

Gracie thought any more conversation would lead to an argument. "Good night."

"Good night, Gracie."

———

She lay brooding in the dark for hours. Occasionally, she could hear a whoop or laugh from the direction of the campfire. Danielle's breathing got deeper and she slept the sleep of the dead and Gracie wished she'd gotten that snake from Dakota.

She'd never hated her father before.

17

Larry said to Cody. "A pattern is emerging in these cases."

Cody felt his scalp tighten. He stood. "You mean besides the method of death, right?"

"Yeah."

"Where are you now?"

"At the office. Unauthorized overtime, as usual."

"Good," Cody said, standing and gathering his files under an arm while holding the phone with the other. He snuffed out his cigarette, pocketed the keycard, and pushed his way out into the hallway. "I'm at a hotel and I saw a business center downstairs. I'll go down there and fire up one of the computers so we can both be online."

"Want me to call you back?"

"No way," Cody said. "I've been waiting all night to hear from you. Don't worry, I can walk and talk at the same time."

The hallway was shadowed and cavernous and he padded down the carpeting toward a curving staircase at the end. As he approached he could hear a swell of conversation and laughter from the lounge on the first floor.

Cody descended the stairs. Across the lobby the receptionist saw him and nodded. He nodded back, gestured toward the closed door of

BACK OF BEYOND   183

the business center, and the receptionist indicated it was open for use. He sat at a PC beneath a window that looked out into the lobby. The doorway to the lounge was straight ahead, and he could make out bodies inside lining a bar. The men and women were well dressed with the women in dresses and men in suit jackets with no ties, about as formal as Montanans were likely to get. The crowd looked young and elite; professionals out after a concert or fundraiser. The kind he usually made a point to avoid.

"So what's the connection?" Cody asked Larry as he placed the files on the counter next to the computer.

Larry said, "Before I spill it, let me say this is pure speculation at this point."

Cody sighed. "Of course."

"And it's just me right now. I don't have anyone else on the case to confirm what I'm saying or poke holes in it."

"Yes, Larry," Cody said impatiently.

"Let me walk you through it," Larry said. "Got a pen?"

"Sure," Cody said, firing up the PC and waiting for it to boot. He opened one of the files to take notes on the front inside cover.

"First," Larry said, "we've got nothing new on our end. The arson tech is still sifting through the burned-out cabin and they've confirmed everything we thought. I talked to one of them today and he said there was no sign of accelerants, which tilts it toward an accident rather than a homicide, but in my mind it isn't convincing. The place was old and dry to begin with and built with logs. Those kinds of buildings go up like a box of matches, especially when there is spilled alcohol on the floor to help it along. The guy said the fire spread normally from right in front of the open woodstove throughout the room."

Cody said, "Has anything else been found by the crime-scene techs? Hair, fiber, anything like that?"

"Nope. It looks like whoever did it literally left no fingerprints. But more likely, he spent the whole evening in the living area and didn't venture into the kitchen. There are some latents in the bedroom, as you know, but we don't have any hits on them yet."

"Damn," Cody said. "Call me if anything comes of that."

"Yeah," Larry said. "I'm thinking the bad guy knew the best way to cover his tracks was to burn everything down around him when he was through."

Cody nodded. "I agree. It accomplishes a couple of things. The fire not only destroyed any latent evidence, the fire itself points us away from homicide."

"Speaking of," Larry said, "the three victims other than Hank Winters I found through ViCAP all died within the last month. There might be more and there could be other methods of death, but for now that's our universe, okay?"

Cody nodded as if Larry could see him. He could hear Larry shuffling papers.

"The first was a William Geraghty, sixty-three, of Falls Church, Virginia. The police report on him says he was a midlevel Democratic political consultant. He was found at his beach house three and a half weeks ago. His cottage was burned down and his body was found in the wreckage. The police there initially called it an accident but a few days later a witness said they saw a vehicle coming from the place in the dark shortly after it was established the blaze took off. No good description of the vehicle or driver, but because the cottage was located on a dead-end road and it was the middle of the night, the car was considered suspicious. The autopsy of Geraghty sounds real similar: blunt-force head injuries and lack of smoke in his lungs. The cops there list it as a possible homicide and the case is open. I spoke to the lead detective in Falls Church and he basically said there has been no progress in the case; no further leads at all."

"Sounds familiar," Cody said.

"Yes. But in this case the fire damage was total. They didn't have rain to stop it. Which means no hair or fiber, and no DNA to run."

While Larry talked, Cody Googled the name "William Geraghty" and found items including his death notice in the local paper and older references to his involvement in political campaigns throughout the country. He would study the items later, when Larry was done.

"What do we know about him besides his job and his death?" Cody asked.

"I'm getting to that, but let me do this in my own way."

Cody knew better than to try and get Larry to cut to the chase.

Larry said, "The second victim identified by ViCAP is Gary Shulze, fifty-nine, Minneapolis. This was two weeks ago. He was a professor of literature at the University of Minnesota in Minneapolis. His body was found at his cabin near a place called Deer River in the northeast corner of the state on Lake Winnibigoshish. Same thing we're getting used to: burned cabin, body inside, head injuries. The difference here is it appears there was a deep puncture wound into his brain as opposed to bludgeoning. The wound was initially explained away as a postmortem injury caused by glass shards driven into his body by falling timbers, but the coroner doesn't rule out the possibility it was caused by a knife blade driven into his skull and withdrawn. Obviously, the locals initially thought it was a suicide or accident, but Shulze's wife Pat convinced them her husband had recently cleaned up his act and had undergone some kind of conversion. She said he was loving life. There was no way he'd do himself in, she said. Of course, we've heard that kind of thing before from loved ones, but the detective told me she was so convincing that they listed the case as open even though they have their doubts."

Cody opened another window on the browser and Googled the name "Gary Shulze." In addition to his participation on various literature councils and a personnel listing for the U of M faculty, there were death notices in both the Minneapolis *Star Tribune* and the *Western Itasca Review*.

"Same total crime scene devastation as Geraghty," Larry said. "No traces of evidence have been found that point to anything other than an accident involving a single victim."

Larry sighed. "The last one before Hank Winters is the one we know about, the close one in terms of time and mileage."

Cody said, "Karen Anthony."

"Yeah, her," Larry said. "Forty-six-year-old hospital consultant living in Jackson Hole and Boise. She's a little different because her place in Jackson—actually Wilson, Wyoming, outside of town—was some kind of historic home she'd refurbished. Like Geraghty's, the place is pretty remote and only accessible by a two-track through the trees. A neighbor saw a vehicle come down their shared road about a half hour before he noticed the flames up on the hill and called the fire department. The Teton County Sheriff told me they got a partial on the vehicle: dark blue or black SUV, single driver, light-colored license plates, which apparently means out-of-state but the witness couldn't tell which."

"That's no help," Cody said. "Finding an SUV in Wyoming is like looking for a fly at the dump—they're everywhere."

"I know," Larry said.

"So," Cody said, opening another window and typing in Karen Anthony's name, "we've got three victims who basically died the same way, burned in their homes long before the fire could be put out. And the victims are all roughly middle-aged and professional. And alone. That's a string of similarities but really not much to build on."

"Exactly," Larry said. "I spent half the day reading and rereading all of the police reports, trying to find something that linked them beyond the obvious and trying to find a connection to Hank Winters."

"And?" Cody said.

"Nada," Larry said. "The cops I talked to couldn't come up with anything either. When I told them about the other cases, they were surprised there were similar incidents. So nobody has been looking into this as a pattern, including the FBI."

"So," Larry said, "I took a flyer and called Geraghty's wife in Falls Church. I told her who I was and what I was investigating, and you know how that goes. She was falling all over herself trying to help. My guess is she hadn't heard from the locals since shortly after the fire because they didn't have anything to tell her. So she was excited I was working it."

Cody nodded, then said, "Hmmm," so Larry would know he was listening.

"I asked the usual. Any enemies, ex-wives, business problems or rivals, financial problems, et cetera."

"Hmmm."

Larry said, "What she told me was almost too good to be true. She said they'd had some real rough patches in their marriage but that Geraghty had straightened up in the last few years and everything was fucking wonderful. She said that was the worst part about it all—that things were going so well when it happened."

Cody felt a jangle in his chest. He said, "Didn't Shulze's wife say kind of the same thing?"

"That hit me, too," Larry said. "So I kept asking Mrs. Geraghty questions. She was a little reluctant at first, but she finally spilled the beans. Geraghty was a big drinker for a long time. A good-time-Charlie type who spent a lot of time on the road with other political types. Between the lines, I got the vibe he was abusive to her when he was on a toot. But she said after he got a DUI he finally entered a twelve-step program and cleaned up his act. She said he's been stone-cold sober for the last two and a half years.

"So I called Pat Shulze," Larry said. "After a while, I got the same story. Shulze had checked himself into rehab three years before because the university made him, and it took. She said it was like having the guy she married back. He was writing a book about his recovery and doing speaking engagements at faculty association meetings around the country, I guess. He even had a Web site on recovery where he answered questions and such."

"Damn," Cody said. "So what about Karen Anthony?"

Larry said, "I called her sister in Omaha. Same deal. She said Anthony was a hard partier all her life until the last five years, when she found Jesus and AA. So it looks like our guy is targeting ex-alcoholics."

"Christ," Cody said, thinking of Hank. "That's just *wrong*." Then: "For the record, there's no such thing. But we can talk about that later."

"Yeah, yeah," Larry said.

Cody paused. "I'm trying to wrap my mind around this. So we've got a guy traveling the country and setting up rendezvous with recovering alcoholics, then bushwhacking them in their homes. I see a pattern but not a motive."

"Me neither," Larry said. "I've been racking my brain. Who would want to go after people who'd straightened out their lives? What's the point of that?"

Cody grumbled that he didn't know, then thought of something. "Larry, did any of the locals in Virginia, Minnesota, or Wyoming find any AA coins at the scenes?"

He could hear Larry shuffling through papers. "No mention of them anywhere," he said. "But that doesn't mean anything for sure. They didn't catalog every item they found at the scene. No reason to."

"Unless," Cody said, "the bad guy is taking the coins with him like he did with Hank. That way the locals wouldn't even have a reason to bring the AA angle into the picture. Hell, we wouldn't have gone down that road if I didn't know Hank took his coins with him everywhere he went."

"I didn't think of that, dammit," Larry said. "Or I would have asked the detectives."

"Find out," Cody said.

"I will tomorrow," Larry said. "But we still don't know why our bad guy even knew them at all."

"I don't know," Cody said, "unless maybe the victims did something to the guy before they sobered up. Maybe, I don't know," he said. "I can't come up with a scenario that makes any sense. Not without knowing if the victims even knew each other or were ever in the same place."

Larry agreed. "We've got four different locations thousands of miles apart. Four different lines of work. I can't see where they possibly intersect."

"This is going to take some fine police work," Cody said. "Can you pull in the cops in all those states to help?"

"Some," Larry said, his voice dropping. "But you know how it goes. They're all up to their asses in alligators. They'll probably all agree to help, but no one is going to make this top priority. I can't blame them. I'd do the same thing if one of them asked me. I'd put it on the back burner and concentrate on my local caseload. I wouldn't drop everything to go investigate this based on my speculation."

"What about the Feds?" Cody asked.

"I've got a call in to them," Larry said. "Which means I had to clear it with the sheriff and Bodean. Luckily, I asked Tubman in the middle of another blowup with the coroner who, by the way, announced his intention to run for sheriff next year."

"Did Tubman ask about me?" Cody asked.

"Not yet. But Bodean hit the roof. I walked him through what I had so far thinking he'd ease off, but he came unglued. He said if I heard from you I was to tell you to get your ass back here ASAP."

Cody exhaled deeply. "Duly noted."

"I wouldn't be surprised to see Bodean throw his hat in the ring for sheriff," Larry said. "He seems to suddenly be doing damage control."

Cody's mind was elsewhere. He said, "Larry, this seems like the right track, but I can't see things coming together fast. I need them to come together fast."

"I need a lot of things I can't get," Larry huffed. "Like a raise and some hair."

"Sorry," Cody said. "I've got to think about all this. We have to be able to connect the victims with somebody or someplace. Then we can get the other agencies and departments moving, once we've done that."

"Agreed. But it's that first part that seems impossible," Larry said, gloomy.

"You can do it," Cody said. "If anyone can."

"Yeah," Larry said, "I know."

"I'm still going after Justin tomorrow," Cody said. "I'll turn on that satellite phone. Call me with anything else, and I'll do the same."

After a beat, Larry said, "Are you going to alert the Park Service that you're entering their sacred domain?"

"Hell no."

"Cody . . ."

"They'll just muck it up. I don't have the time for them to have a bunch of meetings and go up the chain of command. I have to find my boy and put this bad guy on ice."

Larry was exasperated. "How many violations are you going to break on this deal? I can't even keep track."

Cody shrugged. "I don't care," he said.

"Look," Larry said, "you may not care but I'm complicit in every stupid thing you do. So I'm going to cover my ass a little. I've already figured out that the sheriff is so distracted by Skeeter I can claim I told him everything at some point and he'll probably believe me. He won't know the difference. Of course, Bodean is a different animal. I'll have to figure out how to bypass him."

Cody agreed.

Larry said, "And tomorrow I'm going to call a buddy of mine named Rick Doerring with the Park Service. He's the ranger I met last year."

Cody shook his head, not liking where this was headed. "Last year?"

"Yeah, remember when someone from Bozeman called in that they saw a small plane headed toward Yellowstone? Remember, the citizen said the plane looked damaged and it was flying real low toward the park."

Cody vaguely remembered the incident. From what he could recall, the FAA had no record of the aircraft and there were no reports of a missing plane. Since Larry and Bodean were the departmental assignees to an interagency Homeland Security Task Force, they'd had to scramble because unknown airplanes headed for federal land were a big deal these days. Rick Doerring was on the task force as well. The plane was never found, and no one ever reported it missing. The incident faded away quickly.

"Rick is a good guy," Larry said. "Almost normal, for a Fed. I may run this by him on the sly and see what he says."

"I can't stop you," Cody said. "But at least give it until the afternoon. By then, I should be deep into the park where he—or you—can never find me. I don't want their help with this unless it's on my terms."

Larry didn't agree, but he didn't argue.

"Look at the bright side," Larry said. "Your son is likely not a recovering alcoholic." It was meant to be funny.

"No," Cody said, "but why is our guy on this particular trip? What is he after, or is it his way of hiding out after his spree? No matter how you cut it, the guy must be a little desperate after all he's done. I wouldn't think anyone around him would be very safe," he said, tapping the file of Jed McCarthy's clients.

"We still don't know if he's on the trip," Larry said.

"I *know*," Cody replied. "Don't remind me how much of a leap this is."

"So where are you now?" Larry asked.

Cody said, "Close to the park."

There was a beat of silence. Larry said, "You're not going to say, then?"

"Nope."

"Don't you trust me?"

Cody said, "Larry, you're the only guy I trust. But the less you know, the better for both of us. As you said, you're complicit in every stupid thing I do."

Larry snorted. "I see your point. But answer me this, cowboy. How in the hell are you going to find this pack trip in the middle of the wilderness?"

Cody said, "I've got a plan."

"I hope it's a good one."

Cody said, "Me, too."

He showered and left his clothes in a pile on the bathroom floor, and slipped into bed naked. He set his alarm for 3:30 A.M. and called the front desk and requested a wake-up call for the same time.

He knew he wouldn't sleep. Couldn't. The things Larry had told him swirled around the dark ceiling, darting in and out of his consciousness. He hoped strands of what he knew would somehow miraculously connect and he'd sit bolt upright with an epiphany and suddenly know the connections as well as the answers.

Didn't happen.

What did happen, two hours later, was the slight creak of old flooring outside in the hallway. He turned his head in bed and glanced at the digital clock that showed 2:23 A.M. glowing in red.

When he smelled a sharp odor he thought it must be his breath. Then he recognized it as lighter fluid.

Cody propped up on an elbow and stared at the yellow bar of light beneath the door to his room. He rubbed his eyes and tried to convince himself what was happening was not his imagination. Two shadows of feet were evenly spaced within the bar. Someone was standing just outside. And there was a growing pool of liquid that streamed from under it across the tile floor, rivulets reaching out toward his bed like grasping fingers.

Then the distinct sound of a match being struck.

18

Jed McCarthy liked the way the situation was shaping up. He considered himself a kind of master of managing group dynamics, and he had once again proved himself right. He tried not to act too smug or vainglorious about it, although it wasn't easy.

It had started out with an hour or so of stories after dinner, after Ted Sullivan had come back from the tents. After he'd had some kind of scene with the youngest daughter. Sullivan had settled back on the log next to Rachel Mina and they shared a long, sad look that told Jed as much as he needed to know about them. Sullivan sat with his head down and his arms hanging between his legs, as if he'd received a slip of paper in a game of charades that said *Dejected.* Jed had left his place with Dakota behind the cooking station and conspicuously walked around the fire. All the voices quieted and faces turned toward him. He handed Sullivan a bottle of Jim Beam. Sullivan took it, both surprised and grateful for the gesture, and took a long drink that made his eyes water and sparkle from the fire. Sullivan offered the bottle to Rachel, who said, "No thanks." The man tried to give the bottle back, and Jed said, "Keep it. Have another drink, then pass it around."

From that moment on, Jed knew he had Sullivan on his side. A gesture was all it took with weak men like Sullivan who weren't used to them from men who weren't weak, like Jed. It elevated Sullivan in the eyes of the others that Jed had sought him out like that. The only person who didn't appear impressed was Rachel Mina, who eyed Jed with caution. Jed pretended not to notice.

He returned to the cooking station and monitored the progress of the bottle as it made its way around the campfire, and soon there were other bottles as well.

Inhibitions lowered as voices rose, and Jed made it a point to keep the fire going but not too brightly. Just bright enough he could see their faces and expressions and confirm they were all on the tracks he wanted them to be on.

He felt Dakota's eyes on him. She was standing beside him at the cooking station, washing dishes and the pots and pans.

Finally, he glanced over at her and mouthed, *What*?

She whispered, "What in the hell are you thinking?"

He grinned and looked away.

"Why are you doing this?" she asked. "You've always told me to keep our alcohol packed away for later, in the tent. You've never brought it out before, and you sure as hell haven't passed it around."

He thought her whisper was getting loud enough to be overheard, so he did a quick survey of his guests to see if anyone was looking up. Nope.

"I know what I'm doing," he said. "Don't question me with the guests present."

She grunted her assent.

He said, sotto voce, "And don't forget you've got a mission tonight."

"Which tent is his?" she asked softly. That meant she was still with him, even though she was angry. But she still wouldn't meet his eyes.

"The blue and green Mountain Hardwear."

"The one with the stain on the side of it?"

"That's the one."

She nodded that she understood.

He again reached out for her and she jerked away again and he left her there fuming.

"Hope you don't mind if I join you," Jed said to his guests, taking the sitting log used earlier by the Sullivan girls and Walt's soon-to-be stepson.

"Cool," James Knox said, "please do."

"And to what do we owe this pleasure?" Tristan Glode asked.

"I've got a proposition for you folks a little later," Jed said. "But first I'd like to have a drink."

"Try this," Walt Franck said, offering the single malt.

Jed raised his eyebrows in false trepidation, getting a couple of laughs, then sipped the smooth liquor. It burned nicely on the way down. He said, "It's not Jim Beam, but it's pretty good," to more laughs.

Jed let them ask him to expound about Yellowstone, wildlife, horses, and outfitting. He did, but not at great length. He wanted them wanting more.

He did a quick inventory. The Sullivan girls and Walt's stepson Justin had gone to their tents. Perfect, he thought. He didn't want the young ones to weigh in. Sullivan Senior sat by Rachel, Sullivan still moping over whatever it was his daughter was worked up about, but coming out of it. The alcohol helped. Rachel looked on at Sullivan as if sizing him up, as if unsure of her conclusion. Women only *thought* they liked weak men, Jed surmised. Jed wondered what she'd be like with a strong one. Probably a pain in the ass, he thought.

The three Wall Streeters sat on the ground on a tarp with their backs to a downed log and their feet splayed before the fire. They passed their bottles back and forth. They were tired and getting pleasantly drunk. He doubted they'd make a late night of it, but he didn't want things to get too wild before he made his proposition. Drey Russell had been quiet a long time and wasn't as boisterous as Knox or D'Amato. Jed wondered if Russell was having a good time, or doing his best to pretend he was. Russell seemed introspective. Jed wondered if Russell had camped much in his youth, or been in the mountains in such a raw state before.

Tristan and Donna Glode sat on separate stumps to the left of the Wall Streeters. Tristan did take a sip of the single malt but declined the Jim Beam, which didn't surprise Jed. Donna gulped both, to hoots from D'Amato and Knox, and Jed stifled a smile. This woman was a *drinker*. And a looker, in her day. Too bad her day had passed. Jed had a feeling Donna was grinning a bit too much at D'Amato and Russell. D'Amato seemed to respond, but Russell had none of it. When he saw her lean over and touch D'Amato on the knee to ask for a sip of his tequila, he saw potential trouble brewing for Tristan.

Jed focused on Tristan, and thought he had the man figured out. He seemed uncomfortable, but not because of Donna. Jed got the impression Tristan was a man used to being catered to and he fancied himself an outdoorsman but he didn't necessarily enjoy being with other clients not in his social stratum. The joshing and passing of the bottles didn't amuse him but he knew enough about human nature to know if he got up and left he'd be talked about and made the butt of jokes. So he stayed and endured and simply hoped the night would break up early. Tristan had made it clear to Jed he'd studied their route in advance and was as familiar with it as anyone could be.

For that reason, Jed saw Tristan as a challenge. He hoped he'd be able to turn him. And now that he saw Donna flirting with D'Amato, he knew he had leverage he hadn't before.

K. W. Wilson sat alone. He was dark and quiet. When Walt Franck offered him a sip of Scotch, he started to reach out for it, then declined. Jed found that interesting, and wondered why Wilson wasn't drinking. He *looked* like a drinker. His haunted eyes and hollow cheeks practically told drinking stories of their own. But he didn't take a sip, meaning he was choosing to be antisocial or he had a problem. Or an agenda, something he wanted to keep sharp for. Jed shot a quick look over his shoulder. Dakota was gone. He smiled to himself. It wouldn't be long before he knew a lot more about K. W. Wilson. Not that it would matter all that much in his strategy, which was to use Wilson's sour personality as a tool to isolate him and to make his opinion irrelevant, whatever it would turn out to be.

Walt Franck was simply affable. He was slightly younger than Tristan, Donna, and Wilson, but older than the rest. He laughed politely at jokes but told none of his own. Jed thought he might be concerned that his son Justin had suddenly found a new interest—Danielle Sullivan—that might change the purpose of the trip from stepfather/stepson bonding to the blind pursuit of a hot little chick. Surely, Walt wouldn't really welcome that development, even though there was next to nothing he could do about it. Jed knew that trying to stand between a hormone-fueled teenager and his love interest was akin to walking between a grizzly sow and her cubs, and Walt didn't look dumb enough to do either. Walt's distraction would help Jed, though, and that's all that mattered.

After a few minutes, Rachel Mina stood up and announced she was going to her tent for the night. She said it in a way that made it obvious she expected Ted Sullivan to go with her. Obvious, that is, for everyone except Ted Sullivan, who took a bottle from Knox and took another swig.

"Before you go," Jed said, "I wanted to float a proposition. I'll go with whatever you all decide. This is a simple majority rule deal, and I'll go with the majority because it's your trip."

She still eyed him with doubt and put her hands on her hips, waiting. He decided right then he'd need to either win her over or isolate her if she didn't fall in line. It would be her choice either way it went.

Jed gathered himself to his feet and cleared his throat. "What I'm wondering about," he said, "is how married everyone is to the route and the trail we talked about this morning to get to our next camp tomorrow night."

He let that settle in a moment before continuing. "Here's what I'm thinking. We've had a boatload of rain up here this summer, much more than usual. I mentioned it this morning to Tristan," he said, nodding toward Glode. "See, the trail down along the Yellowstone River is pretty swampy, even in a good year. As I mentioned before we left, the snowpack took a long time to melt this year because there was so much of it and the temperatures have been so cool, plus all the rain we've had. I'm concerned if we go down there the regular way we might be walking our horses through miles and miles of gunk. That's no fun and it slows us way down. It's hard going for the animals, plus it means mosquitoes. There's also the possibility the trail is washed out enough that we might lose quite a bit of time finding workarounds."

Jed presented his left palm to the group and pointed to it with his right index finger.

"If my palm here is a map, think of the lifeline as the Yellowstone River," he said, tracing it from top to bottom. "The trail parallels the river pretty much, going north to south. Normally when we get almost to the southern border of the park," he jabbed the heel of his hand with his finger, "we take the fork by South Boundary Creek and leave the river valley and cut due west into the mountains up toward the Continental Divide and Two Ocean Pass. That's where we've got our camp for tomorrow night, up on Two Ocean."

He looked up to make sure everyone was paying attention. They were, although only Tristan Glode and K. W. Wilson seemed rapt. The rest looked pliable.

He continued, moving his finger up an inch on his palm. "So what I'm proposing we do tomorrow is leave the trail earlier than we'd normally turn west. That means cutting to the west between Phlox Creek and Chipmunk Creek. I've been studying my topo map and it looks doable. We still have to climb up into the mountains and we should still be able to get to our camp, it's just that we're arriving an unconventional way through country that probably hasn't seen ten people in a hundred years."

Somebody, likely D'Amato, whistled.

"Excuse me," Tristan cut in, "but I remember asking you about the trail this morning. You didn't indicate then we may have trouble."

Jed said patiently, "Mr. Glode, I believe I did. I said it was possible the trail might be washed out in places. This is the first time I've been up this way this year, so there was no way to know for sure. Even the Park Service doesn't send many rangers down where we're going until hunting season when they try to guard against poachers coming up from Wyoming. There were really heavy snows last winter and big runoff this spring and the rain this summer. I don't think there's been anyone down that direction yet this season to provide a report."

"So what changed your mind?" Tristan asked. There was an edge to his voice.

19

The ignition of the lighter fluid had been instant, less than a second after Cody heard the match strike. There was a *whump* that sucked most of the air out of the room and his lungs, which left him gasping. Bitter smoke lit hellishly with the orange and blue tongues of flame. His eyes filled with water and his lungs screamed from smoke he inhaled rather than air and he thought he knew how Hank Winters and the others must have felt if they were conscious in their last moments.

Outside the door, he heard footfalls thumping down the hallway so quickly he knew he'd never be able to catch who did it.

The flame seemed to burn away his sense of time as well. He had no idea if it was seconds or minutes before he scrambled out of the bed and stood naked. Since it was pushed against the wall, the only way he could get out was toward the fire. It had likely been a few seconds since the *whump*; he felt sluggish and cloudy-headed and blind due to the thick smoke. He felt around his feet for the saddlebags because he needed to save them. As he reached toward one of them it ignited, the fire eating up the nylon exterior as if starving for it. He managed to snatch the other one off the floor before it went up, too, and he backed around the foot of the bed into the bathroom. He stood trembling, his back against the sink, gasping, looking through the doorframe at the violent orange glow in the bedroom. He squatted to his haunches and he was able to get below the roiling bank of black smoke. He sucked in the superheated air and was thankful his lungs didn't explode. The fire had consumed the rug near the door and was curling the flooring. It spread to the sheets and comforter of his bed. He gathered his discarded clothes in his arms.

Then he remembered why the smoke detector didn't trigger an alarm or activate the sprinkler system, and thought, *Shit!*

He reached behind him into the bank of smoke for the sink. When he found it he turned on both taps, then stood and jammed down the stopper with the heel of his hand so the sink filled. While the fire in the bedroom was snapping angrily, he grabbed two towels off the rack and plunged them into the water to soak it up.

His riding boots were within reach in the bedroom near the bed and he found them and pulled them on. The soles were hot. He shoved his arms into a hotel bathrobe that was hanging from a hook behind the door and cinched the tie. Then he dropped down toward the floor again to get a gulp of air. Retrieving the wet towels from the sink, he wrapped one around his head and the other around his hands and ran toward the door using the bag out in front to help block the heat. As he bolted through the flames he felt the hairs on his legs and forearms burn down to the skin and the soles of his boots melt into gel. He could smell the awful acrid smell of his own burning hair.

Cody prayed that whomever had set the fire hadn't blocked the door so he couldn't get out, then remembered it was unlikely since the door opened in. In the time it took him to run from the bathroom across the bedroom the heavy water in the towels heated up.

He hit the door hard with the saddlebag out in front of him to cushion the impact. He couldn't see through the smoke but he reached around the bag for the handle. When he turned it the deadbolt rescinded and he threw himself out into the hallway. The rush of fresh air flowed into the room and fed the fire and the heat from it on his back and neck was instant and intense. Particularly, he felt it on his buttocks.

The hallway was empty except for the round bland face of a disoriented woman who'd just opened her door to peek out. Her eyes fixed above him at the roll of dark brown and yellow smoke that was advancing across the ceiling.

"Get out," he said to her, "there's a fire."

"My things!" she said, her eyes welling with tears.

"Buy new ones," he said, grasping her hand and pulling her out her door. "Is there anyone in there with you?"

"Sam!" she cried, and turned and tried to wrench her hand free.

Cody shouldered her aside and thumped into the room. Sam, who, like her, was in his midseventies, was sitting up in bed in a pair of boxers and a threadbare wife-beater, rubbing his face.

"Who are you?" Sam asked.

Cody didn't take the time to answer, but jerked Sam to his feet and pushed him toward the door.

"Let's get out of here," he said, herding Sam and Mrs. Sam out ahead of him like stubborn steers. As they went down the hallway he slammed his fist on every door and wished he knew which ones were occupied and which ones were empty, but at each one he yelled, "Get the hell out now! The place is on fire!"

The three of them descended the stairs and were suddenly joined by guests from the other wing and Cody realized that the ringing in his head was from the fire alarms. The alarms bleated and emergency lights flashed in staccato everywhere. Overhead sprinklers suddenly hissed to life making flower-shaped showers that streamed down the walls and pattered on the carpets. The guests covered their heads against the water, and one woman said she was going back for her umbrella but her husband put a quick stop to *that*.

Cody was impressed by the lack of shouting or panic as barely clothed people of all ages streamed across the lobby. There were several sharp shouted curses, but most delivered by him.

As the people were herded toward the massive front doors, the hotel staff shouted and gestured for them to keep moving. From outside, sirens were whooping and Cody thought, *Man, that was fast.* Too fast. And he guessed whoever had lit up his room had called it in so there would be only one fatality.

In the river of guests headed toward the doors, under the interior lights that strobed in rhythm with the honking fire alarms, he searched for anyone who looked out of place. He didn't remember kicking or seeing an empty can of lighter fluid in the hallway, so he searched the throng for anyone who might be holding a can or trying to hide one or someone fully clothed booking it toward a side exit. He saw no one that made *his* alarm bells go off.

He was outside in the instant chill before he thought to check out the hotel staff and emergency responders to see if one of them might be the guy who did it. There was already a fire truck in front of the hotel with firefighters pouring off it, and another coming down the drive.

When he turned to go back inside, a firefighter in heavy gear blocked his path and shooed him away. He dumped his pile of clothing and the remaining saddlebag.

"Let me back in," Cody shouted at him, "I can help get people out."

The firefighter, who had a wispy blond mustache and pale blue eyes under his helmet, said, "Now why would you want to do that? Now turn back around and go with the others. You're blocking the door."

"Let me by," Cody said.

The firefighter shook his head. "Get back, sir. We've got this under control."

Cody thought about guests who might have slept through the alarms who were now unable or unwilling to get out, and he thought of the burning bag of gear in his room.

"Let me in," he said, trying to squeeze by the fireman in the doorway. "Look, I'm a cop. I can help in there."

"Get with the others, now," the fireman barked, inadvertently whacking Cody on his injured ear. The blow stunned him, froze him, the pain sharp and furious. His eyes teared again.

"Sorry," the fireman said, "but I mean it. Get back with the others."

The door filled with two other firefighters and a staggering night manager. Cody assumed they'd entered through the rear entrance, meaning there was another truck back there. The firemen were quizzing the manager: "Is that everyone? We need a count. We need to know if anyone's still inside."

The manager said, "I think so, I think so . . ."

"You better be right," one of the firemen said.

The man who'd hit Cody gestured toward him, telling his colleagues, "This guy is a problem. He says he wants back in."

Cody backed off.

He'd fought against his instinct to badge the guy and demand his way back in, but he remembered it had been taken away. And now that he was outside, he knew why his butt had felt the heat so much when he reached back and found the basketball-sized burned hole in his robe. He melded into the crowd, sidling around them so they wouldn't look at his singed butt, and the more he thought about it the more he realized he was glad he hadn't had access to his badge. He retrieved his clothing and the saddlebag and melded into the night.

20

"The water levels," Jed said quickly in response to Tristan's question. "I've been noticing every stream we've crossed is quite a bit higher than normal, almost like May or early June flows. The lake is higher than I've ever seen it this time of year as well. So if the water is high where we're at, it'll be a hell of a lot higher lower down in the Thorofare valley."

Rachel Mina said, "Have you ever taken this new route before, Jed?"

Jed shook his head. "No, ma'am. We'll be seeing and riding through country very few people have ever seen, including me. But according to my topo maps, the elevation rise isn't much more severe than what we were going to do anyway, so I'm not worried about *that*. What I can't guarantee is that we won't have to stop from time to time and scout out ahead, which is something we haven't had to do today. We'll want to avoid black timber that may have trees down in it our horses can't navigate through. And I'll want to ride ahead from time to time to make sure we don't get into a situation where we get rim-rocked."

"Rim-rocked?" she asked.

"It means riding or climbing up into rocks and boulders but not being able to get back down," he said.

"Great," D'Amato said.

"But there's an upside," Jed said. "We may discover some thermal activity and see vistas and wildlife we'd never experience any other way. There are over ten thousand thermal features up here in this park, and who knows what we might find in the kind of virgin territory I'm talking about."

"I'm from Brooklyn," D'Amato said. "I do not know of this virgin territory."

Which got a laugh out of Donna Glode, if no one else.

"The other thing," Jed said, "is we're likely to get to our next camp even earlier than the normal route, since we're kind of cutting the corner. We might even discover a shortcut.

"Of course," he said, "we don't have to try this new route at all. We can stay on our trail and give it our best shot despite the mud and the potential of washouts. I just want you all to know there is an option available."

He stopped talking. Jed knew one sure way of killing a sale was to oversell it. He wanted the group to come to their own consensus without him appearing to force it.

No one, it seemed, wanted to speak first.

Then Russell said, "We'd be like the Lewis and Clark Expedition. We'd be going through a part of Yellowstone Park practically no one has ever been through. That appeals to me, at least. I like being an explorer."

D'Amato cracked in a bad pirate voice, *"Beware, there be monsters."*

Knox said, " 'Back of back of beyond,' we'll call it. I like the sound of that."

"Me too," Donna Glode said. "Bring on the adventure!" She rubbed her hands together in what Jed thought was an overplay designed to show the Wall Streeters—D'Amato in particular—she was with them.

Walt said, "Is there still good fishing this new route?"

Jed said, "It looks like it, anyway. Those creeks I mentioned earlier,

Phlox and Chipmunk, plus Badger Creek. One thing for sure, they haven't been fished much. So you and Justin might be in for a rare treat—native cutthroat trout that've never seen an artificial fly."

Walt nodded and smiled. "I like that idea," he said.

"I think I'm in," Sullivan said. "I think my girls would like the idea of seeing country no one has seen for a long time. I know I would. Go big or go home, I say."

Jed noticed that Rachel Mina shot Sullivan an approving look.

Tristan stood up, and turned away from Jed to address the group. "I feel it's my obligation to bring something up," he said, the back of his shoulder to Jed. "What Jed is suggesting is kind of radical. We don't have radios or cell phones. The only thing the Park Service knows about us—or our families at home—is where we're *supposed* to be from day to day. So if we don't show up at the end they know where to look. If we deviate from the trail and get lost or 'rim-rocked,' no one will know where to find us."

Tristan said, "I've had a lot of success in my life by determining where I want to get to and staying the course. It's when my partners convinced me to deviate from the plan that I failed. What Jed is suggesting here is trading in a sure thing—even though it might be unpleasant for a while—for a flier filled with unknown variables. I'd rather stay the course. It's what I—and all of you—paid for."

Even Jed conceded to himself Tristan was persuasive.

"Oh for Christ's sake, Tristan," Donna said, "didn't you just hear him? You are *such* a tight-ass. This isn't a product launch. I thought the purpose of this trip was for us to experience high adventure. Isn't that what you said?"

Tristan didn't answer her, but even in the firelight Jed could tell his face flushed red. She had embarrassed him, cut his feet out from under him. And his argument. Jed felt the momentum shift back.

"I'm in," Knox said. "The worst that could happen is I never make it back to the firm to be at my desk when I get laid off."

"Damn right," Russell said. "Me, too."

D'Amato covered his face with his hands as if horrified, then squeaked, "Me, three."

Jed looked around. All in favor, one opposed, one not heard from.

"Mr. Wilson?" he asked, expecting it to go five–two.

Wilson said nothing, but his glare was intense.

Jed tried to read Wilson's eyes, and what he saw was genuine surprise. As if *he'd* had his feet cut out from him, too. Finally, because all the attention had turned toward him, Wilson said, "That's fine. I'll go with the majority."

Tristan looked around, and said, "I'll have to decide tomorrow if we'll even stay with this expedition."

His words fell heavily, until Donna said, "Speak for yourself, kemosabe."

Humiliated again, Tristan Glode stormed past Jed, headed for the tents. Over his shoulder, he said, "Democracy is no way to run a business, Jed. You'll need to learn that."

After a beat, Knox said, "I don't think he likes losing arguments."

"You think?" D'Amato said. "Man, what a buzz kill."

"Welcome to my life," Donna said, sliding across the ground toward D'Amato and taking the bottle of tequila from his hands.

Rachel Mina was curt: "Good night, everyone." She strode away from the fire, followed by Sullivan.

"Okay then," Jed said, taking the rest of his bottle from Walt, who'd gotten stuck with it. "We've got a decision. That means it's going to be a real interesting day tomorrow, and we'll be getting up early."

"Interesting," D'Amato said, repeating the word and getting up. "As if today was boring."

"That's what I like to hear," Jed said, smiling.

Jed turned to the sound of Rachel and Sullivan arguing in the dark near the tents. He saw Dakota standing there, glaring at him. He wondered how much she'd heard.

That question was answered when she slowly shook her head, as if she couldn't believe what was happening.

21

Framed by the pulsing wig-wag lights that painted the stone walls and arched windows of the front of the Gallatin Gateway Inn in vivid reds and blues, Cody Hoyt tossed the duffel he'd saved into the back of his Ford. He had trouble breathing due to the smoke inhalation and he coughed violently and spattered the back windows with globules of black sputum.

Behind him, guests gathered in knots in the front yard. The staff who'd helped evacuate them formed a perimeter with several firemen and now a few deputies who'd just arrived. Cody had slipped away while they all watched a bucket truck back across the lawn toward the hotel. He paused to take it all in before entering the Ford. His room on the second floor was easy to spot because of the bright orange glow of flames from inside. Several firefighters had climbed into the bucket and were now being raised toward the second level. When they were even with the orange window, the bucket paused and swayed a bit while a horizontal column of water blasted through the window. When the glass broke a ball of flame shot out of the frame accompanied by gasps from the guests on the lawn.

He noted the fire seemed to have stayed within his room and not spread to any others, no doubt due to the sprinkler system. Cody guessed it would be short work now to put it out and gain control of the building. It wouldn't be long before the investigators figured out who had been staying in the room and would want to question him.

He swung inside the Ford and it was immediately filled with the acrid smell of the smoke from his clothes and hair. His bare skin stung from exposure to the fire, and when he brushed his forearm with his other hand the singed hair on it broke and fell off.

Thumping the steering wheel with the heel of his hand hard enough to crack the plastic, he cursed and spat and started the engine and rolled away.

The lights and sirens faded as he turned from the inn grounds onto U.S. 191 South. It didn't take long before he was engulfed in darkness and safely away from the scene. He wheeled the Ford into a pullout and killed the engine.

Someone had found him and tried to burn him alive.

He found a half-full pack of cigarettes in the console and lit one. He inhaled deeply—smoke on smoke—then coughed. Jesus, he thought, it was like he was trying to burn *himself* up from the inside out. He tossed the cigarette out onto the gravel.

There was a bright side to the fire, he thought. Now he knew he was on the right track, because someone was trying to kill him.

The more he thought about what had happened and what had almost happened, the more his skewed world tilted even farther off plumb.

He was glad he hadn't gone cop on the fireman or spoken to anyone on his way out, even though possibly they could have found whoever did it through the process of elimination. But his story would sound preposterous at first, he realized. The firefighters would quickly discover he'd dismantled his smoke detector and they'd find the small mountain of cigarette butts in his room. The conclusion they'd reach immediately was he was smoking in bed and started the fire and had come up with a story about lighter fluid to cover himself. Or they'd accuse him of accidentally—or intentionally—spilling the accelerant on the floor and it went up. Hell, he thought, given the facts on the ground he'd come to the same conclusion. Within minutes they'd have his ID and call it in, discover who he was and where he was supposed to be, and he'd likely spend the rest of the night in the Bozeman jail waiting for a Helena deputy to come get him and take him back. No doubt the damage to the hotel caused by the fire and water would cost millions to repair. He thanked God all the guests had been accounted for, or there would be a murder charge as well.

He couldn't risk *that*.

Since the attempted method of getting rid of him had been fire, he wondered if the murderer he was tracking wasn't on the pack trip after all, but had stayed around Bozeman. But how would the killer know he was in town, or what he was up to? And how could he possibly know he was spending the night at the Gallatin Gateway Inn, or which room? It made no sense.

Did this mean he was next on the killer's list? Cody dismissed it, since the other victims had been clean and sober for years and he hadn't. Unless, of course, the killer knew Cody was getting close and had decided to try a preemptive strike.

In many ways, Cody thought, the crime could have been almost perfect. The flames had moved so fast that if he hadn't been awake at the time the match was struck, he might have been incinerated in the bed. A little digging would bring forth stories of the recent incident with the coroner in Helena, his suspension from the Denver Police Department a year ago, and his infamous alcohol-related binges.

Which meant that whoever had done it knew him well enough to know they might get away with it.

He thought about the few people he'd been in contact with who knew where he was or what he was doing. Larry, obviously, but he'd withheld crucial info from him, like his location.

Cody retraced his steps that day. Other than Cooper and the Mitchells, he'd encountered a half-dozen sales people and the hotel staff.

There had also been the state trooper and the mechanic in Townsend. While each may have known a very small piece of what he was up to, no one could have realistically put it all together, he thought.

This was the kind of puzzle he liked to bounce off his partner, because the two of them could usually brainstorm their way to a plausible answer.

His cell phone had a good signal and he scrolled through his contacts until he found Larry's home phone, but something stopped him before he speed-dialed. He sat in silence, staring at the lit screen, then closed the phone and turned it off. He opened the driver's door and let the phone drop to the gravel, then smashed it into pieces with the heel of his boot.

Whether they'd followed him from Helena or called ahead he wasn't sure. If they were keeping tabs on him through the GPS embedded in his cell, that would be the end of that.

Then it hit him with a force that took his breath away.

The stop in Townsend, the overnight there that slowed him down. The long delay that held him in place until tonight. Had the trooper been tipped to keep an eye out for him?

He climbed back into the Ford and covered his face with his hands. Only two people could possibly know the entire story, every part of it. Only two people knew where he was going, why he was going there, and what he planned to do.

One of them was the killer. The other . . .

He said aloud, "Larry, you treacherous son of a bitch. Why?"

22

By the light of a headlamp, Jed McCarthy stripped down to his T-shirt and underwear in his tent and jammed his outside clothing into a stuff sack he'd use for a pillow, then checked his watch. Getting late. Dakota should be back any second.

He'd left some clients at the fire. Two of the three Wall Streeters were still there, Knox and D'Amato. So was Donna Glode. And K. W. Wilson. Ted Sullivan had left a half hour after he had words with Rachel Mina, saying, "Better go try to patch things up." Walt Franck had also gone to his tent.

His tooled leather business backpack was stored where it always was, near the head of the tent. He retrieved it and unzipped the front flap, then reached down through his files, canisters of bear spray, the new portable GPS unit, and his loaded .44 Magnum secured in an Uncle Mike's Cordura holster by an interior zipper that was hidden by design. The light from his headlamp bobbed around while he did it. He kept his ears open for Dakota's boots swishing through the tall grass toward the tent.

He withdrew a thin brown envelope made stiff by the eight-and-a-half-by-twelve-inch piece of cardboard inside and dumped the contents on the top of his sleeping bag. Newspaper clippings, GPS coordinates, and most important, the Google Earth maps he'd printed off on high-grade photographic paper while Margaret Cooper was choking back tears out in the reception area as she read (out loud) the instructions on how to operate Windows Vista. She'd had no idea what he was doing.

The photographic images were precise. He found the location of Camp One, where they were now, and traced the trail south along the shoreline of the lake with the tip of his finger. He reviewed the place he'd marked with an X at the natural junction where they'd cut west toward Two Ocean Plateau as he described it to his clients around the campfire. Although the terrain and the creeks were burned into his memory from endless hours with the maps, he wanted to reassure himself for the hundredth time that it looked passable, that he could lead the group up and away from the Thorofare on terrain they could handle, that the horses and mules could navigate.

He hoped the new route from the Thorofare to Two Ocean was as clear and unencumbered as the photographs showed. He wished he knew how old the images Google had posted were. If they were a couple of years old, he prayed there'd been no severe timber blowdowns or microbursts in the meanwhile. In the back of his mind was his memory of seeing an entire mountainside in Yellowstone leveled by a nighttime weather phenomenon that scattered hundreds of acres of lodgepole pines like so many pick-up sticks. No one had seen it happen, and the Park Service, being the Park Service, refused to acknowledge that it did. But Yellowstone was a world of its own, as Jed knew better than anyone, and the physical landscape could change literally overnight as geysers shot through the thin crust or earthquakes rattled the ground or unspeakably violent storms blew through. Fires would be okay because they'd help open up the undergrowth, and he knew there had been a dozen lightning-caused blazes in the area the previous fall.

But he knew that no matter how carefully he'd planned things they'd never go exactly right in Yellowstone. The place seemed designed to foil human plans and aspirations. Conditions within the Yellowstone ecosystem were ramped up and exaggerated compared to the world around it. Every natural phenomenon—storms, fires, temperatures, thermal activity, wildlife, geography, weather in general—always seemed pushed to extremes. The more time he spent in the park the smaller he felt, and the less in control of the world around him. All he could do at times was point himself in the general direction of where he wanted to go—both figuratively and literally—and hope he'd get there. He remembered Bull Mitchell telling him something like that when he bought his company, but Jed discounted the statement and credited Bull's advancing age. Now he knew it to be true.

He jumped when Dakota suddenly entered the tent. He hadn't heard her coming, and she hadn't signaled him in any way like she sometimes did with a whistle or a finger-drum on the taut tent wall. It was simple camp etiquette to do so and he'd taught her that. She'd disregarded it, though, and he scrambled to stuff the maps back into the envelope before she saw what he was doing.

She winced when he looked up at her and shined his headlamp directly into her eyes, pretending it was inadvertent.

"Jeez, Jed," she said, waving her hand at him, "you're blinding me."

"Sorry."

"I bet."

Once the papers were back in the envelope and the envelope slipped under his sleeping bag, he turned his head and the beam of light. *That was too close,* he thought.

She didn't unzip her jacket or remove her boots, but sat Indian style on the foot of her sleeping bag.

He pulled the headlamp off and hung it from a loop so the light hit the inside tent wall and was diffused. "Horses okay?" he asked.

"Yup."

"Food hung up?"

She nodded.

"Kitchen wiped down and locked up?"

"Like always," she said.

"Anyone left at the camp?"

Dakota said, "Donna Glode is still there with Tony D'Amato and James Knox. Knox is trying to protect his friend from her, I guess."

"Donna will be easy to track if she gets lost," Jed said. "We'll just have to follow the cougar tracks."

Dakota didn't even smile as she fixed her eyes on him. "Jed, what the *fuck* is going on?"

"Keep your voice down," Jed said. Even though their tent was two hundred yards from the other tents and closer to the horses than the camp itself, he always worried about being overheard by any guests, since the topic of conversation was generally them.

Her eyes blazed in the semidarkness. "You're breaking every damn rule you've ever told me about," she said. "You've got something going on here or else you've just lost your damn mind."

He started to speak but she cut him off.

"*Never* leave the guests to tend the fire at night," she said. She lowered her voice and added a low drawl to mimic his cadence as much as possible. "Gently encourage the guests to take their socializing to the tents and wait them out if necessary so you can secure the camp and make sure there's no food or anything around to draw animals in, then put the fire out with water. Then do a walk-around to double-check the night checklist. Last, make sure the animals are fine."

He hated when she mocked him.

Which didn't stop her. She said, "*Never* encourage alcohol consumption. We may want a nightcap of our own in the tent before we turn in, Dakota, but *never* drink in front of the clients or encourage them to do so.

"*Never* antagonize a paying guest and promote rancor among the group, Dakota," she said. "Be the facilitator to smooth out any disagreements. Be on everyone's side, or lead them to think you are. Be a benevolent dictator, but more the former than the latter. The whole experience gets poisoned if resentment is left to linger."

He held up a hand to interrupt her but she was on a roll.

"*Never* fraternize with the guests until the last night, Dakota. Keep a professional distance so they respect you. You are the captain of the ship. Maintain a little mystery about you, so they'll listen when you tell them something. Be professional at all times. Don't become one of them, Dakota. Never let your guard down to the clients, Dakota," she said, angry.

Then she leaned forward and backhanded him on his shoulder. Before he could react, she said, "So what do you do, you hand them a bottle! Then you sit with them and get them all stirred up about taking a new route. And what is this about water levels bein' up so we can't stay on the trail, Jed? Where in the *hell* did *that* come from?"

He sat back and glared at her although he was a little taken aback. "Keep your voice down," he said through clenched teeth. "And where do you get off talking to me like that?"

"I'm using your own words," she said.

He said, "This is my trip and my company. I've been keeping a close eye on the creeks we crossed and the level of the lake all day while you emptied your head and tugged your mules along. You would have seen the same thing I did if you'd been looking. And keep the hell in mind I don't need to clear every decision with you. Keep the hell in mind this is my outfit and my risk and you're the hired help."

She reacted as if he'd slapped her. She said in her own voice, "Is that all I am to you?"

He was sorry he said it because he still needed her. But he didn't take it back. He could tell she was trying not to tear up. No matter how tough she talked or acted, he thought, she was still just a damned girl.

He knew what her next move would be. Furiously, she started clawing at her sleeping bag, gathering it into a ball she could carry away.

This wasn't their first fight, but he sensed the cold edge of finality creeping in unless he headed it off.

"You can still sleep here," he said calmly.

"Bullshit," she hissed, backing away on her hands and knees toward the door of the tent. "You can sleep alone. I don't even want to breathe the same air as you tonight."

It was the word *tonight* that made his shoulders relax and his stomach unclench. *Tonight* meant she didn't consider the rift permanent.

He chuckled, then said, "Do whatever you have to do, darlin'. Just don't let any of the guests see you."

"Fuck you, Jed."

He quickly sat up and reached over and cupped her chin in his palm, forcing her to stop and look at him. "Don't escalate things out of proportion," he said. "I know what I'm doing. Trust me a little bit."

"Why should I?" she said, but he knew she was softening.

"Have I steered us wrong before?"

She paused, then said, "Not much up to now."

He laughed, and felt the tension in her dissipate a little. He said, "Before you go, did you complete your job tonight?"

He knew her slavish obligation to her duties would further override her anger. She was like that.

Dakota jerked her face away from his hand, sat back on her haunches, and dug into her coat pocket. He figured she was as angry now at her own caving in as she was at him.

She threw a handful of cartridges in his lap. They landed heavily and he picked one up. He said, "Three-fifty-seven Magnum. Did you find any more? A box of shells?"

She shook her head.

"And you left the gun, of course," he said. "So he might not even know you unloaded it."

She just glared at him.

Wilson would be in a dilemma, now, Jed knew. If the man asked who took the bullets, he'd be admitting he brought a firearm on the trip. It had happened before, and in every case the guest never said a word afterward.

"You don't have to leave," Jed said. "It's cold out there."

But she'd committed herself and although there was a hint of doubt on her face, he knew she'd go.

"Come back in if you get cold," he said.

She grunted the curse at him again as she backed out through the door trailing her sleeping bag and pad. Before disappearing into the night, though, she paused and looked in.

"I nearly forgot," she said. "He also has a satellite phone."

Jed's eyes widened. "He does?"

Her mouth curled into a sneer. "And he's got a file folder filled with aerial photos," she said, "just like those ones you tried to hide from me when I came in."

And she was gone.

Oh shit, Jed thought. *This I didn't expect.*

Gracie didn't know what time it was during the night when she snapped awake at the sound of blows or thumping footfalls outside the tent, or heard what she thought must be the grunting of a bear. Or a man or woman being wordlessly beaten.

Part Three

Back of Beyond

23

Gracie was late to breakfast. She'd barely slept until the last few hours as the tent walls fused with morning sun, and when she finally awoke she was sweating in her sleeping bag and Danielle was already gone.

She stood and stretched and yawned. Her face felt dirty and her hair was matted to the side and took furious brushing to set right. Danielle's sleeping bag was crumpled and puffy on the pad. She vaguely remembered her sister cursing and grunting as she pulled her clothes on earlier.

Outside the tent, it was cold, still, clear, and breathtakingly beautiful. Bright white sun danced on the ripples of Yellowstone Lake and electrified the dew in the grass. A bald eagle cruised along the surface of the water, talons dropped, fishing. Far across the water was the smudge of an island in the lake. Boils of steam rose from vents and dissipated in the clear morning air. She smelled woodsmoke from the fire and heard subdued voices from the kitchen camp.

Her father stood on the path between her and the morning fire, hands in the pockets of his jacket, head down, feet set on opposite sides of the path as if blocking it.

She thought, *Ambush.*

As she walked out into the wet grass to go around him, he said, "Gracie, please. We have to talk."

"Nothing to talk about."

"I didn't like how things developed last night," he said. "I don't like to see you go to bed angry with me."

She snorted and rolled her eyes and passed him. He fell in behind her, speaking low so he wouldn't draw the attention of the group already eating breakfast.

"I wanted you and Danielle to get to know her, get to like her," he said. "I wanted you two to get comfortable with the idea of us together. I wanted you to *want* us to be together, for me to be happy and for us to be happy. I guess what I'm saying, Gracie, is I want your blessing."

She stopped and turned around. He was right behind her. She said, "You use words girls use when they talk to each other. If I want to talk to girls I'll talk to girls, not my dad. If you want to be with Rachel then tell me and be with her. I'm fourteen years old. I don't give blessings. You're the dad, be the dad," she said. "And man up. That's all I ask."

She left him there with his mouth open but no sound coming out.

She expected chiding for being late but no one said a thing and she realized the moment she stepped into the campfire ring that something was seriously wrong. All she received were brief and furtive glances. She felt as though she'd just blundered into the middle of an argument and stopped it cold.

Danielle sat with Justin on the same log they'd occupied the night before. Walt sat near them, as did Rachel Mina, who eyed her coolly. The Wall Streeters stood and held their plates aloft, as if they had an appointment to keep. The menu was scrambled eggs, bacon, hash browns, toast, and coffee. Although the food looked and smelled good, no one appeared to be really eating it. Donna Glode sat alone. She looked pale and sick. Strands of her hair fell into her face and the food on her plate was untouched. She stared at the fire although the flames were hard to see in the morning light.

Who was missing?

Jed, who was behind the kitchen station, said, "Hey, girl, come over here and get some breakfast. Get your dad to come eat, too."

She looked around for Dakota but couldn't locate her.

Dumbly, Gracie started to go get her dad but he'd joined her. He looked under his brow at her, as if trying to transmit a message.

They got tin plates and eating utensils. She glanced over her shoulder at the others.

She said, "Where is Mr. Glode and that guy Wilson? Where's Dakota?"

Her dad said, "I think that's what everyone was discussing when you walked up."

Jed gave her a scoop of eggs and three strips of bacon. He said, "I sent Dakota back on the trail to find a couple of strays."

Gracie waited for a further explanation, but Jed ignored her. He was studying the others around the campfire with an almost scary intensity, she thought.

Gracie sat by Danielle and her sister reached over and patted her on the shoulder, as if touching base. It was an unusual and warm gesture, Gracie thought.

She listened in. Tristan Glode and K. W. Wilson hadn't come to breakfast because they were gone. Their things had been cleared out of their tents and both of their horses were missing.

"No," Jed said to answer a question from James Knox, "I can't say it's ever happened before. I've had the few rare unhappy customers, but I've never had any who up and went home. Especially on my horses."

"I don't see them sneaking away together," Walt said, to snickers from Knox and Drey Russell.

Jed said, "I wish they would have talked to me about it. Being on your own in Yellowstone is dangerous."

Gracie found herself watching Donna Glode, seeing what kind of impact the speculation was having on her. After all, her husband had left her. But she didn't look distraught, Gracie thought. She looked *guilty*.

This was confirmed when Danielle leaned over and whispered in her ear, *"She didn't spend the night in her tent with him."*

Gracie nodded slightly to indicate she'd heard but didn't give her sister away by looking at her or responding. Gracie noted how Donna glanced repeatedly at D'Amato, hoping, no doubt, he'd share a wink back. As far as she could tell, D'Amato pointedly didn't turn his head toward Donna. And he seemed much more inhibited than he'd been so far. In fact, he looked ashamed, like a little boy. His two friends shot glances at him while they ate as if seeing him in a new light.

Walt said, "Do you think Dakota will find them and talk them into coming back?"

Jed said he hoped so. He looked stricken as well, Gracie thought. Maybe a little unsure of himself, for the first time. Like he had too much swirling around in his head. "I wish we knew when they left," Jed said.

That's when Gracie said, "I heard something last night. Am I the only one who did?"

She was. With Rachel observing her very carefully, her dad asked what she'd heard.

"It's hard to describe," she said. "I heard some feet thumping around outside and a kind of grunt, like someone got the wind knocked out of them. I didn't recognize anyone or hear any voices, just the thumping and the grunt. I thought it might have been an animal in the camp."

Her dad said, "Why didn't you wake me up and tell me?"

Gracie looked over, her eyes dead. "I wasn't sure whose tent you were in."

"Meow," Danielle whispered.

Her dad turned red and looked quickly away. Gracie felt both good and ashamed at the same time. She expected a glare from Rachel, but the woman eyed her stoically. As if assessing her for later.

"What time did you hear it?" Jed asked, ignoring the others.

Gracie shrugged, and chewed on a piece of bacon.

"I mean," Jed said, "was it right after you went to bed or was it closer to this morning?"

"A few hours after I went to bed," she said. "After midnight, I'm sure. I didn't look at my watch, but I'd guess two or three in the morning."

Jed nodded to himself, as if fitting this new information into a narrative.

"So they could have five or so hours on us," Knox said. "I don't see the point in going after them, then. By the time we caught up to them they'd be at the parking lot."

"Maybe," Jed said, worried. "But they might not have gotten that far while it was dark."

"I still don't see the two of them together," Walt said. "I'd guess they're traveling separately in the same direction."

Russell said, "Fools. On their own they might get lost."

D'Amato cleared his throat. "I volunteer to go after them. After all, it's my fault . . ." He didn't finish the sentence.

"You're not going anywhere on your own," Knox said flatly.

"They'll be okay," Russell said. "It's their deal, not ours. It was their choice to leave."

Jed nodded and addressed his comments to Donna. "I don't think they'll get lost or anything. Hell, the trail just parallels the shore of the lake nearly all the way back. There are a few side trails, but they'd follow our tracks from yesterday. I'm sure Dakota will find them. That girl can *ride*."

Walt said, "It just doesn't make sense to me. Just because there was a disagreement on which trail to take—it just doesn't make sense."

Gracie's dad agreed. Rachel said nothing.

Donna Glode said to the fire, "You don't understand. Tristan is all about control. And last night he lost it." She looked over at D'Amato. "You're not the reason he left. *I'm* the reason he left."

D'Amato stared at his boots, still pointedly ignoring her. No one followed up with a request to Donna for clarification.

"But why Wilson?" Rachel Mina asked. "Why did he leave? He didn't seem that concerned about the vote or which trail we are going to take."

"Who knows about that guy," Walt said. "He was a hard guy to read."

Knox agreed. "It doesn't break me up too damn much that guy's gone. He seemed kind of strange from the start, I thought."

"Hear, hear," Russell said.

"Tristan is another matter," D'Amato said, as much to himself as anyone. "I think maybe it would be a good effort on my part to go try and get him. I want to do this. I want to make things right."

"Forget it," Donna said, ending the discussion. "He won't listen to you, of all people. And he's never listened to me."

She stood and turned to Jed. "I know exactly what he'll do, so you might as well prepare for it. He'll go straight to the top, to the superintendent of the park, and demand that your license be taken away for deviating from the scheduled trip. And I would be surprised if he didn't get his way. That's the way he is."

It was only for a second, but Gracie thought she saw real fear in Jed's eyes.

"Dakota will find him," Jed said, assuring no one.

Gracie found the whole scene fascinating and a little sickening. There was no filtering of words or emotions for the sake of Danielle, Justin, or her. She felt suddenly older and more mature but she didn't like the feeling.

Jed said to Gracie, "What you probably heard last night was one or both of them clearing out their tents to leave. Maybe one of them tripped on a tent stake or something."

Gracie shook her head. "I don't think it was that."

"Then what was it?" her dad asked, suddenly perturbed. "If you can't say what you heard, maybe you shouldn't say anything at all."

Gracie felt her face flush. She knew his anger had more to do with her snub of him than anything else. She said softly, "It sounded more like a fight."

No one said anything. The silence around the fire became oppressive.

Finally, Jed said, "I don't see much sense in discussing this any further. It's time to eat up, pack up, and mount up. We're burning daylight, folks."

The sound of hoofbeats filled the awkward silence, and everyone turned toward the sound.

Dakota rode up and reined to a stop. She was alone.

"I couldn't catch them," she said.

Gracie looked up to see Jed glaring at Dakota, his hands knotted into fists at his side.

Dakota didn't meet his eyes.

Gracie walked with Danielle back toward the tents. When they were far enough away from the adults, Danielle said, "Fuck this. This trip sucks. Why couldn't we go to Mexico or a beach or something?"

Gracie shrugged.

Danielle said, "Who cares if those two guys are gone or what trail we take? It's just stupid. I'm glad that creep Wilson is gone anyway, so he won't be sneaking around trying to look at me when I go to the so-called toilet. And I want to take a hot shower."

"What do you think about Dad and Rachel?"

"I guess I would have liked to have known about it before we did this," her sister said. "But Dad needs to get a life. This might help. Maybe he won't be so clueless and intense all the time."

"That's all you think about it?"

Danielle shrugged. "She seems kind of cool. I don't have anything against her."

"I don't know her well enough to say," Gracie said.

Danielle said, "What I think is if the rules of this trip are everybody sleeps around with everybody else, then they ought to just say so and I'll stay with Justin. He can rub my back and tell me how beautiful I am and we'll see what develops."

Gracie sighed and unzipped their tent so they could repack their things for the day's ride. As she did she saw Rachel Mina come out of a green and blue tent with her sleeping bag bundled in her arms. Gracie thought she looked angry and puzzled, as if trying to struggle through a difficult problem. Then their eyes locked for a moment and Rachel's face softened and changed. Rachel took a deep breath, blew a strand of hair out of her face as if she'd just made a momentous decision, and let her sleeping bag drop to a pile at her feet.

"Uh-oh," Gracie said.

"What?"

"She's coming over."

"Who?" Danielle asked, then saw Rachel working her way through the other tents toward them. "Oh, her."

Gracie looked around. There was nowhere to run.

"Hello, Danielle," Rachel said. "Hello, Gracie."

"Hi," Danielle said. Gracie stood and nodded.

"We haven't officially met," Rachel said, looking from one sister to the other and extending her hand. "I'm Rachel."

They shook her hand.

Rachel said, "I wanted to take this opportunity, since we're away from everyone, to set the record straight regarding your dad and me."

Gracie braced for it.

"I want you to know something," Rachel said, talking mainly to her. "I don't want to be your stepmother. I don't necessarily want to be your best friend. But I want to get along with you and I hope you'll give it a shot to get along with me. We all know the situation, even though the truth came out much more awkwardly than I wanted it to.

"I'm very, very fond of your father. I know he feels the same about me. We're both lonely, and there's a very good possibility we'll be together in the future. That's where you two come in."

"Hey," Danielle said, "as long as you don't try to run my life, I'm okay with it."

Rachel still spoke primarily to Gracie. "I've been around the block. I don't try to pretend your father is young, single, and carefree. I know he's got a family. And I know he absolutely adores you two girls. This isn't an either/or situation unless we make it such," she said. "Do you understand what I'm saying?"

Gracie said, "I'm not sure I do."

Rachel said, "You two are the most important people in his life. I recognize that fact and I admire it and I'd never try to change it. If we can't accept each other and get along, I'll step aside. I won't force him to make a choice and he doesn't need to. Most men are trying to do the right thing but they don't know how. That I've learned. They don't understand what we want and need and expect. They assume we think love is a zero-sum game—either he goes with you or he goes with me— which it isn't. I know he's attracted to me, and I to him. I could draw a line in the sand. But I won't, because then I'd be with a man I don't respect and you'd have a dad you resented. What I'm saying," she continued, "is we're not rivals. Not either/or. You've already got a mother and from what I understand she's a wonderful woman. I look forward to meeting her as well. I don't plan on disliking her or resenting her."

Gracie said, "You talk to us like we're adults."

Rachel said, "And I plan to continue to do that. I'm too old to start playing games, and this . . ." she waved her hand over her head to indicate the situation they were in that morning, "is an incredible distraction. If we don't talk now and talk bluntly, who knows when we'll get the chance?"

Danielle said, "Hey, I'm here, too," attempting to break up the two-way conversation.

"You are," Rachel said. "And I'm sorry. I just had the impression you weren't the one I'd need to convince."

Danielle started to argue, then rolled her eyes and said, "I'm not, I guess."

Rachel turned back to Gracie. "And what about you?"

Gracie hesitated and felt her sister and Rachel Mina looking at her. She said, "I need to think about it."

"*Gawd,*" Danielle sighed. "Gracie, you are such a little—"

"No," Rachel said, holding up her hand to silence Danielle, which impressed Gracie because it actually *worked,* "that's perfectly fair. I'd probably say the same thing."

And with that, she turned and went back to her tent to pack up.

Gracie and Danielle watched her in silence until she was out of earshot.

Danielle said, "I have to admit, that was pretty cool. I like her, even though I still don't see what she sees in Dad. I mean, I could live with her around, I think."

Gracie nodded, although she wasn't yet ready to agree. She didn't want Danielle to think Rachel had won her over so quickly, even though she nearly conceded to herself she had.

Danielle giggled. "I was kind of hoping she would have said she *did* want to be our best friend, though. That's the way you get stuff, you know? There's nothing better for a girl than to have two sets of parents competing for your affection, and buying you things to make you like them more, you know?"

Gracie looked at her sister with disgust. "What planet are you *from,* anyway?"

"Planet Danielle," her sister said with a lilt. "It's a good and happy place. And it has hot showers and cell phone service."

Jed waited until everyone had dispersed before tracking down Dakota, who was picketing her horse with the others. His voice was tight and low. He said, "Why in the hell didn't you keep going until you found them? Do you know what this might mean?"

She slid the saddle and pad off, leaving a sweaty matted square on her horse's back. "No, what does it mean?"

He reached out and grasped her shoulder, preventing her from turning away from him. "It means he'll go to the Park Service, that's what it means. I could lose my contract, is what it means. Why didn't you track him down? Why did you quit on me before you found him?"

She broke eye contact and let her gaze slip to his hand on her shoulder. She wouldn't speak until he let go, so he did.

Dakota said, "I lost them, Jed. I followed their tracks for two miles and then the tracks just vanished. I can't figure out why they left the trail or where they went. I rode another half mile to see if they got back on the trail, but they didn't. I don't know where they are, but I didn't want to say that in front of our clients."

Jed shook his head. "They just disappeared?"

She nodded defiantly.

Jed felt a weight lift. If Tristan and Wilson had wandered away from the route they might never get back to the trailhead.

"Should we notify Search and Rescue?" Dakota asked.

"No," Jed said. "Not yet. Those two might realize the error of their ways and come back yet."

He ignored the puzzlement in her face.

While they were packing, Gracie asked, "Did you hear anything last night?"

"No. I had a bad dream about something, but I forget now what it was about."

"So maybe you heard what I heard."

"I don't know," Danielle said. "Maybe. But who cares? He's great, isn't he? Justin, I mean."

"You think they're all great at first. This one is, but I'm sure you'll screw it up somehow."

"*Shut up.*"

Gracie cinched her sleeping bag stuff sack and started to carry it and her duffel toward the horses. On the way, she stepped off the path into the moist grass and bent down. The sod was churned up in several places exposing soft black soil. She looked up at her tent, which was twenty yards away. "This is where it happened," she said to Danielle.

"This is where the noises came from. Nobody tripped on a tent stake. It's too far away from the tents."

Danielle stayed on the path. She looked from Gracie back toward the camp. The adults were still milling around.

"So what are you saying?" she asked.

Gracie said, "I'm not sure. But there's something really wrong going on. Something evil. Two grown men supposedly just left us in the middle of the night without a word to anyone. We're supposed to believe that two guys who've known each other for a day get together and make a plan like that? Why didn't anyone hear them or notice they were taking two horses? And did you see the way Jed and Dakota were treating each other? Or how Donna Glode and Tony D'Amato are acting?"

"I didn't notice."

"I know you didn't. And why the big deal about taking another trail?" Gracie said. "We wouldn't know what trail we're on, anyway. Why does that matter?"

24

Cody Hoyt rode a tall gelding paint named Gipper behind Bull Mitchell's black horse through a dark stand of lodgepole pine trees that seemed to have no end, on a trail that was so overgrown it barely existed anymore, and he called to Mitchell, "Are you sure you know where we're going?"

It was mid-morning and up beyond the interlaced canopy of trees the sun was out and the sky was intense blue and cloudless. They'd been riding for four hours straight without a break and Cody felt quarter-sized spots on both inner thighs burn through his jeans into his flesh from leather ridges on the saddle. He knew little about horses except he'd never much liked them and he had the distinct impression Gipper thought the same about him, evidenced by the way the horse would drift off the path toward overhanging branches that, if Cody wasn't alert, would have knocked him backwards out of the saddle to the ground.

It was still moist in the trees from a brief rain shower that came at dawn as they set out, and raindrops clung like tears to the tips of pine needles. Occasionally, there was a break in the canopy and light streamed through like jail bars. But mostly they'd been in the shadows on a trail that barely was and Bull Mitchell hadn't said three words to Cody although the old man mumbled plenty to his horse.

Mitchell trailed a packhorse with full canvas panniers and Cody rode his gelding behind them both.

Cody inventoried their weapons. Both he and Mitchell had rifle scabbards lashed onto their saddles. The scarred and faded wooden butt of a scoped .30-06 stuck out of Mitchell's scabbard and a black polymer adjustable butt stock for a departmental AR-15 poked out of Cody's. Mitchell's rifle looked substantial and serious, Cody thought, while his high-tech semiautomatic rifle resembled a kind of toy. He'd switched out the thirty-round for a ten-round magazine so the rifle would slip into the creaky leather sleeve that simply wasn't designed for it. Cody's .40 Sig Sauer was clipped high on his belt, making the weapon difficult to get at but at least it didn't rub along the saddle. Mitchell had strapped on a long-barreled .44 Magnum single-action Ruger Super Blackhawk revolver. Like his rifle, Mitchell's handgun was rubbed nearly clean of blueing and the wooden handgrip was worn and scratched. He wore the .44 Magnum in a holster that covered most of his thigh. It was a bear weapon.

"I said," Cody repeated, "are you sure you know where we're going?" Mitchell pulled his horse to an abrupt stop, which caused the packhorse to do the same. Gipper used the occasion to stop, dip his head, and eat grass.

"I heard you the first time," Mitchell growled. His voice was so deep it seemed to vibrate through the ground. He sounded annoyed.

"Well?"

"What do you think?" Mitchell said.

"I think we've been riding in these trees for a long time and even I can see we're the first people to use this trail in years," Cody said. "So it's a little hard for me to believe we're going to catch them on it."

Mitchell shook his head as he looked away, as if deeply disappointed.

"What?" Cody asked.

"I got a question for you," Mitchell said, turning his horse around so he could glare at Cody and leaning forward in his saddle with both of his huge hands on the horn. Cody had learned from his Montana outfitter uncles that true horsemen—unlike himself—would rather turn their mounts around than turn their heads. "Why the hell did you hire me if you're going to question every damn thing I do?"

Cody shifted his weight, trying to find a position in the saddle that eased the burns. "It's just this trail we're on. It's obvious it hasn't been used in years and there are places I can't even tell it's there. So naturally I—"

"Naturally you start yapping at me," Mitchell said basso profundo, "when you should be keeping quiet."

"I want to know what's going on. You can't expect me to just sit here for hours wondering where we're going."

Mitchell reached up and tilted his cowboy hat back and rubbed his forehead. "I thought you wanted to catch them," he said.

"I do."

"Then the only way we're going to do it in a timely fashion is to ride cross-country and cut all the corners. We should intercept the main trail by early this afternoon. They'll still have about half a day on us but with all those rookie riders and trail horses, we'll make up plenty of time."

Cody nodded. "Thank you for that. All you needed to tell me was you knew where you were going and you had a plan."

Mitchell shook his head again.

Cody said, "All you had to tell me was you were familiar with this sort-of trail we're on and that it will eventually run into the main trail where Jed is."

Mitchell said, "I ain't never been on this trail in my life."

With that, he grinned crookedly and turned his horse back around and clicked his tongue to get him moving again.

Cody moaned and patted his shirt for his cigarettes.

Cody and Bull Mitchell had approached Yellowstone Park from the north-west in the dark pulling a beat-up horse trailer. They'd hidden Cody's

Ford in an empty outbuilding at Jed McCarthy's compound and transferred his gear to Bull Mitchell's rig. Mitchell drove a dented F-250 pickup and sipped from a plastic go cup of coffee, and Cody tried to get some sleep since he hadn't gotten any the night before. Every time he closed his eyes his mind swirled with Technicolor visions of cabins burning down, hotels burning up, conspiracy, and betrayal.

He'd finally dozed for a few minutes when he was jolted awake by a violent pitching of the truck. When he opened his eyes and reached out for the dashboard to find out what had happened, he saw they'd turned off the highway onto an ancient two-track that skirted a dark river and vanished ahead in a bank of dark timber.

"What's this?" he'd asked, groggy.

"Old Indian trick," Mitchell said.

"What the hell does that mean?"

"Means we sure as hell can't drive through the gate at the park and explain to the ranger who you are and why we're bringing horses in without taillights, so we're sneaking in through a back door."

Mitchell gestured vaguely ahead in the dark. "This is an old fire and service road nobody's supposed to know about. It's from the old days when the Park Service actually provided service and put out fires, so we're talking a really long time ago. We can get pretty deep into the park without anyone knowing we're here."

Then Mitchell added, "I hope. They might have blocked it off."

Cody asked, "How long has it been since you were on it?"

Mitchell shrugged and sipped at his coffee. "Seven, eight years," he said. "Maybe more."

"Jesus," Cody said. "What if it's blocked?"

"We'll figure something out," Mitchell said, and shrugged. "Always do. I got a chain saw in the back in case we need to cut trees and a winch on the front in case we get stuck. Of course, I haven't tested either one out in a few years, so let's just hope they work if we need 'em. I got shovels and a handsaw if they don't. At least I think I do."

When Cody just stared, Mitchell said, "Keep in mind this is Yellowstone. Anything can happen here and plans always go wrong. It's just the nature of the place."

The road was passable, although Cody and Mitchell twice had to get out of the truck and cut a path through fallen trees.

"This just seems wrong," Cody said, lifting green branches out of the way of the idling F-250.

"It is wrong," Bull Mitchell said, revving the motor on his chain saw to keep it running. He was haloed by oily blue smoke.

"Breaking into a national park seems like breaking into a church," Cody said.

Mitchell snorted and said, "That's a result of too much indoctrination in public school and too many Disney shows. It's great country— you'll see—but it isn't all sweetness and light. Charlie the Lonesome Cougar would happily take a chunk out of Bambi's tender throat. This place will eat you up and spit you out if you're ever off your guard. Especially where we're going."

Dawn rose pink and cold and sudden waves of rain lashed at the trees and drummed on the hood of the truck but went away as suddenly as they'd come.

Cody told Mitchell about the fire in his room at the Gallatin Gateway Inn as Mitchell eyed him warily but didn't utter a word.

Cody let the story trail off without sharing his suspicions about Larry.

"Got a question," Mitchell said, minutes afterward.

"What?"

"Why are your hands shaking like that?"

Cody had held up his right hand. Mitchell was right.

"DTs?" Mitchell said.

"I guess."

"Let's hope you don't have to aim your gun at anything," Mitchell said.

"Mind if I smoke?"

"Damned right I mind."

As they saddled up in a treeless alcove at the end of the service road, Cody admired Mitchell's experience and abilities. Although the old man moved slowly, there wasn't a wasted step or gesture. Mitchell had obviously spent his life around horses and outfitting, and he saddled the horses, filled and balanced the panniers, and tied a series of intricate outfitter knots over the cargo practically in the dark.

When Mitchell pointed toward the paint horse and grunted, Cody asked why he was called Gipper.

"Last good president," Mitchell said, as if the answer had been obvious.

"Don't cross him neither," Mitchell warned. "He ain't as affable as he looks. Just like his namesake, and his owner: *me*."

After five straight hours of riding Cody noticed a subtle increase in hue within the forest and more bars of sunlight. Soon there were large enough openings in the canopy he could see blue sky and distant strings of high-altitude cirrus clouds and finally the trees fell away and the horses broke through over a ridge and the whole bright green world, it seemed, was laid out in front of them. The day had warmed considerably and the wind was so slight it barely rippled through the grass. The sun was straight over their heads and the air was thin and smelled of pine and sage from the valley below and it smelled so fresh he was afraid it would unclog his lungs and slough off the tar and nicotine and give him a coughing fit.

Bull Mitchell paused his mount. Cody wrestled with Gipper until the gelding finally understood he was to keep walking alongside the packhorse, and Cody pulled his horse to a stop abreast of Mitchell.

When Cody looked out over the vista of green carpeted saddle slopes with tree-choked river valleys, massive red-veined geological upthrusts that bordered the eastern horizon until they gave up and became mountains, and the vast sprawling tableau of Yellowstone Lake miles ahead and below them, he said, "What big country."

Mitchell grunted and reached back into a saddlebag for his binoculars. "Don't fall in love with it," Mitchell said. "It's guaranteed to break your heart."

Cody used the pause to dismount. His legs were stiff and his knees felt as if they'd been tortured on a rack to bend them inward. He hobbled toward the packhorse and began to unbuckle one of the panniers where he'd seen Mitchell pack his duffel bag.

"See anything?" Cody asked Mitchell.

After a long pause, Mitchell said, "I see a herd of elk, a couple of coyotes, and an eagle. And a whole meadow filled with buffalo chips. Must have been a hundred of them critters there not long ago."

"I meant the pack trip," Cody said, irritated.

"Nope."

Cody withdrew his duffel and dropped it on the ground. It hurt to squat. As soon as he opened it his stomach clenched. Manically, he rooted through the clothing and the gear.

"Shit!"

Mitchell didn't look down from his glasses, but asked what the problem was.

"My cigarettes," Cody said. "I bought a carton of them for the trip. I know I bought a carton and I remember packing them."

Mitchell was silent.

Cody stood up and felt a wave of pure panic. Then he kicked the bag. "Shit. They must have been in the duffel bag that burned up. *Shit.*"

Mitchell said, "It's a long way to the nearest convenience store."

Cody stanched an impulse to pull his Sig Sauer out of his holster and shoot the outfitter right there.

Mitchell shrugged. "Now's as good a time as any to quit, I suppose. I did it years ago. Just stopped. No big deal."

Cody rubbed his face. It felt as if there were tendrils of sinew inside his body tightening up, waiting for the familiar shot of nicotine to relax them. The sky began to spin and the earth itself seemed to undulate, like slow waves across a pool. He patted his pockets, hoping he'd find a spare pack. He rooted through his coat and his saddlebag. In the bottom of a saddlebag he located a cellophane pack that contained . . . *two* cigarettes. Cody felt as if he'd won the lottery.

Mitchell said, "Might as well save 'em."

Cody said, "Bullshit," and lit one up. He'd figure out later when he'd have the last one.

As he sucked in the smoke his body relaxed and seemed to moan with delight. The sky stopped spinning and the valley below stilled.

Cody asked, "Does Jed smoke?"

"Not that I remember."

"I bet somebody in that group does," Cody said, swinging himself painfully back into the saddle. The sores on his thighs burned instantly. "Which is another reason to find 'em fast."

Mitchell clucked his tongue and his horse stepped out. He said, "I'm not sure I'm getting paid enough money to come out here into the wilderness with a desperate man withdrawing from alcohol *and* cigarettes."

"Please shut up," Cody said.

Mitchell laughed. "First you chew my ass for not talking, and now it's *shut up*," he said. "Make up your damned mind."

"I know one thing," Cody said twenty minutes later, as they descended toward the valley floor. "If I can't find some cigarettes pretty soon I'm likely to rip the heart out of the guy we're chasing with my bare hands and feed it to him."

Mitchell said, "So who are we chasing, anyway?"

"Hell if I know."

Cody rode in silence, consumed by the maelstrom in his head. He recounted the conversations he'd had with Larry and the information Larry had conveyed. The pieces of the puzzle had been laid out on the table by Larry, along with a few more he'd added himself, so the logical sequence should have been for the two of them to start assembly and come up with a viable theory or conclusion or at least to be able to discard unworkable scenarios. But if Larry had been working against him, could he count on *anything* his ex-partner had said? Were there even other victims at all? Was Larry the puppet master pulling his strings, leading him to where Larry wanted him to go? Or was it simply a matter of Larry getting Cody out of the picture and out of the way? There was no place in the country more isolated than where he was right now, Cody thought. If Larry's plan had been to get him out of the way, he couldn't have succeeded better.

So was there any validity at all to Larry's information? Was it even true that the last Web site Hank Winters had looked at was the one for Jed McCarthy's pack trip? Or was that all part of Larry's misdirection, too?

He weighed the possibility of turning around and going back. That way, he could wring Larry's neck and blow up whatever game Larry was playing.

They were in the middle of Camp One before Cody even realized it. Only when Bull Mitchell stopped his horse and swung down to the ground did Cody notice there were rough squares of flattened grass on the plateau where tents had been and an alcove in the trees with a fire pit.

"Jed's doing a good job," Mitchell said, with a lilt of admiration. "He's running a low-impact outfit. You wouldn't even know they were here last night except if you knew the exact location. No garbage or human sign except where they flattened the grass."

Cody dismounted as well. He thought he knew why real cowboys liked to sit their horses so long: it hurt too much to get off.

He leaned against Gipper while the blood flowed into his legs and the pain receded. He watched Mitchell roam the campsite and thrust his hand into the fire pit. When he came back wiping the ash on his jeans, he said, "Yup, they were here this morning. The rocks are still warm and the ash is moist from when they put the fire out."

"Any idea how long they've been gone?"

Mitchell said, "It's hard to get everybody up, fed, and get an entire camp packed up. My guess is that they were probably on the trail by nine. So four or five hours is all."

Cody swallowed. He tried to imagine his son in the camp just hours before. He hadn't seen him since last Christmas. He wondered how tall he was now, and how long his hair was.

Cody started to ask Mitchell how long it would take for them to catch them when he noticed Mitchell looking down toward the shore of the lake and squinting.

Cody turned, and said, "What are you seeing?"

Mitchell said, "I thought I caught a glimpse of something down by the water. Something moved. You see it?"

Cody couldn't see well enough through the trees so he shifted to his left. Branches were parted enough for him to get an unimpeded view all the way down the slope to the shore of the lake.

"Wolves," Cody said. "At least three of them."

One wolf was jet-black, another was silver, and the third was mottled gray. Cody could see they were feeding at the water's edge.

25

Gracie lagged behind her sister on the trail, putting distance between Strawberry and Danielle's horse. It seemed odd to her there were four fewer riders ahead on the second day.

Despite his friend James Knox's disapproval and Jed's pleading, Tony D'Amato had decided the only way he could live with himself was to track down Tristan Glode and try to persuade him to come back. Drey Russell thought D'Amato was on a fool's mission, but agreed to ride with him. Their plan, they said, was to rejoin the group at Camp Two. Grudgingly, Jed had given the two his maps and told them to look for a marker on which trail to follow when they came back.

Gracie noticed how Dakota watched the exchange in silence, shaking her head.

It had warmed up enough that Gracie had stripped off her hoodie to her T-shirt. Although she could still see Yellowstone Lake to her left, the path had climbed away from it and they'd gained hundreds of feet of elevation. The rhythmic *clop-clop-clop* of the horses soothed her and reminded her she was in a beautiful, wild place on a perfect summer day and that not everything was horrible. That Rachel Mina had smiled at her with a hint of sympathetic understanding while they were saddling up had buoyed her more than she would have thought.

But all of the questions remained unanswered.

"Everything all right up there?" Dakota asked from behind her. "You need to keep up, girl."

Instead of goosing Strawberry into a faster walk, Gracie reined her horse off to the side of the trail so Dakota could catch up. The trail was not so narrow or the trees so close as they climbed that they couldn't ride side by side for a while.

When Dakota caught up Gracie fell in beside her.

"Nice day," Gracie said.

"Yes it is." Dakota looked over with a hint of suspicion.

"You do this a lot, right?" Gracie asked.

"This is my third summer. So yeah, a lot of pack trips. Most of them are quite a bit shorter than this one, though. This is the big one of the year."

"How'd you meet Jed?" Gracie asked. "Are you two a couple?"

Dakota smiled slyly. "Right to the point."

Gracie tried to smile back innocently.

"I met him in Bozeman," she said. "I was in my third year at the university and I was helping pay the bills by barrel-racing and riding horses for rich folks. There are quite a lot of rich people who've moved to Montana and they like the idea of owning horses but hardly any of 'em know a thing about them. But horses need to be ridden, and I put an ad in the *Chronicle.* Pretty soon, I was getting paid for going out to ranchettes and riding their horses for them to keep the animals in shape and to keep them well trained. Getting paid to ride horses is just about the coolest thing in the world, you know."

"That sounds pretty fun," Gracie said.

"So one of the ladies I worked for got divorced and decided to sell out and move back to L.A.," Dakota said. "Jed bought all three of her horses. In fact, Strawberry there was one of them. So I delivered the horses to Jed at his place and we started talking and he offered me a job as wrangler. Seems his last guy wasn't dependable. I started off as his wrangler and, well, you know. We were already spending a couple of months together day and night, so pretty soon we figured we might as well share the same tent, I guess."

"I sort of know what that's like," Gracie said. "I mean, Danielle is my sister."

Dakota laughed. "Yeah, even I can see how pretty she is."

"So do you love him?"

"Jesus, girl," Dakota said, actually blushing.

"It just seems . . ."

"It seems like what?"

"You seem really different from each other."

"You mean because he's older?"

"That," Gracie said, "and he's your boss. But you don't seem to be the kind of person who needs a boss. And he's not like you at all, you know?"

Dakota went silent for a few moments and Gracie feared she'd offended her. "I'm sorry."

"It's okay," Dakota said. "I'm just trying to figure out how to answer.

"I guess," she said, "it's kind of an unusual situation. I never knew my dad except that he worked in the oil fields in Wyoming, and when I grew up the only thing I could do well was hang around horses. I trust horses more than people, even though they can be knuckleheads. At least they're innocent knuckleheads, though. They never do anything because they're mean, only because they're scared or spooked or trying to get away. But they aren't mean, like people are. When I talked to Jed he pretty much said the same thing. Plus, do you know how hard it is for a girl like me to find a partner my age who isn't an idiot? So many of the guys my age are slackers who are just plain scared of girls in general and me in particular. I get tired of waiting for them to grow up, you know? I don't think I can wait forever. I tried to find someone to take me as I am, but pickings are slim, girl."

Gracie nodded. "So what's he like? I mean, when he isn't being the boss?"

"I can't believe you're asking me these questions," she said. "And I especially can't believe I'm answering them."

"He seems mysterious," Gracie prompted.

"Oh, he is that. He's always got something going," she said. "Did you know he was a poet? He's published a couple of books of poetry. Can you believe that?"

"Is it good poetry?"

"I can't tell," she laughed. "It's beyond me. I mean, I get parts of it, but it's really difficult to understand. He's even won a couple of awards for it, I guess. And there have been times when he reads it to me. It sounds beautiful when he reads it out loud because he has so much passion, but it's not like I understand most of it. I pretend I do, but I don't. I think he's kind of frustrated more people don't recognize his genius."

Gracie peered ahead, trying to see Jed McCarthy in a different light.

"Is he nice to you?" she asked Dakota.

"Much of the time," Dakota said.

"But not always."

"No," she said. "He can be the most obtuse son of a bitch I've ever met sometimes. Worse than a mule. And when he gets a new idea in his head, like a new poem or a new way to make more money, he gets pretty full of himself. I think he prefers his own company to anyone else because he's the only one smart enough to stand himself, if you know what I mean. That's when I feel like throwing in the towel and just hitting the road."

"Are you feeling that way now?"

Dakota looked over and gave Gracie a long searching look. "How did you know that?"

"I watched you two earlier."

"Sometimes I just can't figure out what's going on under his hat," she said. "And this is one of those times."

"Why do you think Mr. Glode left?"

Dakota sighed. "Mrs. Glode," she said.

"Simple as that?"

"It's a hell of a lot more complicated," Dakota said. "I think the two of them were hoping they'd find something out here they didn't find. There have been other couples on these trips looking for the same thing. So at least I can sort of understand that."

"What else?" Gracie said.

"Wilson," Dakota said.

"You mean you don't know why he left, too?"

Dakota nodded. "I'm going to tell you something nobody knows," she said. "I didn't stay with Jed last night. We had a fight and I slept outside by the fire. At one point I had to get up to pee and I walked up above the tents into the trees. In the moonlight, I could see somebody lurking around. Kind of moving real slow and deliberate—walking back and forth from the tents to the lake. I sort of snuck down there and I saw it was Wilson. I don't know what the hell he was doing, but he gave me the creeps. He was just out walking around."

"Did you tell Jed?"

"Not yet. His head is too far up his butt to listen to anyone."

"What do you think Wilson was doing?"

She shrugged. "I don't know. But it looked like he was planning something, or waiting for someone. Maybe it was Tristan Glode, but that doesn't make much sense to me."

Gracie thought about that.

"Maybe it was Wilson and Mr. Glode who had a fight?" she said.

"Maybe. But you're the only one who said they heard anything."

"Don't you believe me?"

Dakota said, "Let me put it this way. I believe you think you heard something."

Gracie said, "But why would they leave together after that? And what would they fight about? I mean, if it was Tony and Mr. Glode at least they'd have a reason."

"I know. It beats me."

"I didn't hear an argument," Gracie said.

Dakota shrugged. "I don't know what the hell is going on, but something is. You look ahead of us at all those people on horses in this setting, and you think, what a perfect thing. But what you don't know is what's going on in everyone's head, and what they might be thinking about everyone else.

"That," she said, "is the reason I prefer horses."

Jed had pulled his horse and mules off to the side of the trail to let his clients ride past. When Gracie and Dakota reached him, Jed said, "Dakota, you take lead for a while. I'll tail up."

Gracie saw that Dakota wanted to argue but clamped her mouth closed, pulled her hat tight, and urged her horse and mules on. Jed fell into place where Dakota had been but he didn't stay there long.

He said, "So, you enjoying the trip so far?"

There was something disconcerting in the way he asked, she thought. Like he couldn't wait to get past the formalities. Like he kind of enjoyed playing with her, enjoyed reeling her in with his soft voice.

"I guess."

"What about your sister? She seems like maybe this isn't her dream vacation."

Gracie had to smile at that.

"Thought so," he said.

"I wanted to ask you something," he said. "I saw you talking away with Dakota. What on earth were you girls chatting about for so many miles?"

"Nothing in particular," she lied.

"Really?" A hint of sarcasm.

"Girls do that," she said. "We just talk about nothing for hours. You know, clothes, nails, shoes. Girly things. That's just how we girls are."

He chuckled. "You are a pistol," he said. "Now really, what were you two talking about for so long?"

Gracie squirmed in her saddle. She wondered why it felt like it had gotten warm, like those car seat heaters did in her mother's Volvo. She said, "I asked her how she liked her job. Since I like horses and all."

"Ah," Jed said. "And she told you what?"

"She said it was pretty good most of the time."

"My name come up?"

"Of course," Gracie said. "You're her boss."

Up until that moment, she hadn't noticed the sheath knife on his belt that lay across the top of his thigh. She guessed it had always been there amidst the things he wore, but she'd just not focused on it before.

He said, "Females always talk too much."

She didn't know if he meant her or Dakota. Or both. He had looked away from her but there seemed to be a lot going on in his head.

"Are we going to find those two guys?" she asked.

"Oh," he said, almost vacant, "we'll find 'em."

26

Bull Mitchell roared and fired his .44 Magnum over the backs of the wolves. The concussion in the epic stillness was tremendous and Cody flinched and came back up with his ears ringing. The big slug slapped the surface of the water twenty feet out and all three wolves wheeled toward them on their back haunches.

Cody could look into their black eyes and see their long red teeth and pink-tinged snouts and he instinctively reached for his Sig Sauer. He'd bought bear spray the day before in Bozeman but it had been in the duffel with his carton of cigarettes so therefore he didn't have any. He couldn't get over how doglike they were, yet they weren't dogs. They had the eyes of dogs and the fur of dogs, but they were wild, big, and menacing. The black one had yellow-rimmed eyes that seemed to burn in their sockets.

"Hold on," Mitchell said. "Stand tall and tough. They want to protect their food but we've got to face 'em down and show no fear."

To the wolves, Mitchell barked, "Get the hell into the woods where you belong. Now get . . ."

To emphasize his point, he ratcheted back the hammer on his Ruger and fired again, this time exploding a plume of swamp mud from a depression five feet in front of the wolves.

The black alpha male—Cody guessed he'd weigh 175 pounds—
woofed and exhaled and loped away along the shoreline to the south.
The silver female followed and Cody caught a glimpse of something
long and blue that reminded him of sausage swinging from her jaws as
she ran. The mottled wolf, likely also a male, Cody thought, followed
her without conviction, as if he'd wanted to fight. He couldn't believe
how fast they ran or how powerful they looked, like ghosts with teeth.

"They might not have gone far," Mitchell said, "so keep your eyes
open."

"My God," Cody said, and lifted his hand. "Look at this. I was so
scared my hand *stopped* shaking."

Mitchell chuckled while he withdrew the empty brass cartridges
out of the revolver and replaced them with fresh hollow-point shells.

"I'll keep this out and cover us," Mitchell said, chinning toward the
shoreline where the wolves had been. "You might as well keep that
little popgun of yours in your holster. It'll just make 'em mad if they
decide to come back."

The first thing Cody noticed as they approached the shoreline was the
smell. Mingling with the thin warm air and algae-tinged odor from
the lake was a primal whiff of musk from the thick hides of the wolves
and the dank metallic smell of viscera.

A tangle of partially submerged driftwood stretched from the shore
into the lake for twenty feet. A scum of algae sucked in and out of the
water-worn branches of the structure as if being inhaled and exhaled
by the structure itself. There was a deep shadowed undercut beneath
the driftwood.

The body was half in and half out of the water with the head on the
beach, face to the side. Its legs were submerged in the water and pointed
down toward the undercut at such an angle that the feet could hardly
be seen in the murk. The body appeared to have no arms.

Male, thin, pale, middle-aged, the waterlogged skin alabaster white
except for the jagged gaping holes between its ribs and between the

legs. All the soft internal parts had been torn away and eaten by the
wolves. The clothing on the victim—a lightweight long-sleeved shirt,
baggy cargo pants, cowboy boots—had been flayed into ribbons by
the teeth of the wolves. The dark sand beach was trampled with canine
paw prints, some slowly filling with chocolate-milk-colored swirls of
water. The deep indentations of their claws looked like small-caliber
bullet holes in the sand.

"Oh man," Mitchell said.

It wasn't Justin. As soon as Cody was assured of that, he felt his
cop blinders descending like the shield of a motorcycle helmet. The
shield would help him disengage from making a personal connection
with the dead body and treat it for what it was: meat whose soul and
life spark had long since left it. The wolves had certainly understood
that.

Cody turned the body over to find that the arms weren't missing
after all. The wrists had been bound with wire behind its back.

He bent down and found handholds beneath the arms and tried to
pull the body fully out of the water but it wouldn't budge. He frowned.

"Are you going to give me a hand?" Cody asked Mitchell.

"Nope," the outfitter said. "This is your department."

Cody looked up for clarification.

Mitchell chinned toward the dark timber to the south as they both
heard the muffled crack of a branch. "We interrupted those wolves,"
he said. "They like to eat their fill, then drag what's left into the trees
and cache it for later. I'm sure they're watching us and they probably
think we're stealing it from them. Keep in mind some of these wolves
don't have much fear of man anymore, if they ever did. All these wolves
have known for the last couple of decades is that every time they encounter any humans, the Park Service rangers rush in and cordon off
the area to keep the people away from them. These critters have learned
they have nothing to fear since it's obvious they've been put on the top
of the food chain. That's fine for the wolf population, but the ramifications aren't so pretty for us two-legged creatures.

"So if they decide to come back, I want to be ready."

Cody said, "Okay."

He tugged again but the body was held tight by something under the water that gave only slightly. Then he saw the cord wrapped around the ankles that vanished into the hole beneath the driftwood structure. He waded to his thighs in the water. It was startlingly cold for midsummer, so cold it stung. He followed the cord down with his fingers until he could get a good grip with both hands, and he grunted and leaned back, putting his back into it. Whatever the cord was attached to gave and Cody grunted again and walked backwards toward the sand until he was on dry land. His effort spun the body around as well as revealed the large round rock intricately tied to the other end of the cord. He kept yanking until both the body and the rock were out of the water.

For the first time he noticed another length of cord around the victim's neck, so deeply imbedded into the flesh he'd missed it earlier. A two-inch length stuck out from a tight knot, with the loose end slightly frayed. Cody recognized it as nylon parachute cord—a staple of hunters, hikers, and trekkers everywhere.

Cody said, "Whoever did this tied rocks to his feet and neck and dropped them under the driftwood, dragging the body beneath the surface. Whoever did it probably thought no one would ever find the body. They didn't count on the wolves fishing him out and biting through one of the cords."

Mitchell grunted. He looked pale and a little gaunt, and he did his best to scour the trees for signs of the wolves and avoid looking at the body.

Cody dropped to his hands and knees and crawled around the body, looking over every inch of it. He guessed the victim was in his late fifties or sixties and had been in pretty good shape. Unfortunately, his eyes, throat, belly, and genitals had been eaten away.

"Ah," Cody said, bending in close to the victim's head and turning it so the grotesque features no longer faced him, "Here we go."

There was a one-and-a-half-inch cut under the man's right ear. It was J shaped, with a jagged entry at its wide end tapering to a narrow slice slightly above the jawbone.

"Knife wound," Cody said. "The puncture looks deep enough the blade likely went all the way into his brain. An instant kill. Since the thick part of the blade points toward the back, I'd guess the killer came at him from behind, probably grabbed the man's hair and pulled back, then shoved the knife in hard. Perfect placement, too. The killer could have stabbed the guy in the back or reached around and slit his throat. But he went for the single-thrust kill."

Mitchell grunted.

Cody recalled Larry's findings: *Gary Shulze. . . . The difference here is it appears there was a deep puncture wound into his brain . . . caused by a knife blade driven into his skull and withdrawn.*

"Let me get my camera and my file," Cody said. "We'll treat this as a crime scene, as low-tech as it is."

"You're the cop."

"I'm going to get my file of the applications for the pack trip," Cody said.

Mitchell said, "I'll go with you to cover you and I'll bring the horses down here with us. Wolves like to eat horses, too."

While Cody photographed the body, the scene, the rope, the rock, and the wounds with his digital camera using his camera case in the shots for perspective, Mitchell ate lunch. The outfitter sat on a large rock with his back toward the lake and his .30-06 across his lap and gnawed on pieces of jerky and washed them down with water. His eyes swept the timber from side to side.

Cody knew he'd fouled the scene. He'd moved the body and walked and crawled all over the sand next to it.

"If it wasn't for that knife wound," Mitchell said, "I might have thought the poor son of a bitch could have been mauled by wolves and then sunk in the water to hide him away from more mutilation."

Cody nodded. He'd been replaying scenario after scenario in his mind for the past half hour.

"It's happened before," Mitchell said. "In the deep backcountry like this, folks leave a dead body so they and the Park Service can come after it once they get out. Packing a body along just invites bears and mountain lions and such. It's like trolling for predators. It's not a good idea."

Cody didn't respond. He pulled his duffel out of the panniers and withdrew the file folder.

It didn't take long. He said, "My guess is this is Tristan Glode, president and CEO of The Glode Company of St. Louis. He look sixty-one to you?"

Mitchell grimaced when he looked over. "Yup. Could be."

"He fits the physical description here in the applications," Cody said. "There's only two other older men on the pack trip. One is named K. W. Wilson and there isn't much background on him. The other is Walt Franck, His Richness, and I know that son of a bitch and this isn't him. Which is kind of a shame."

"Want some jerky?"

"No," Cody said. "I want a cigarette."

"Sorry."

"I wonder what he did to deserve this," Cody said. "Knifing a sixty-one-year-old man. His wife's on the trip, it looks like. I wonder if she's involved or if we'll find her body up ahead. I can't see her just going along after her husband's been killed. And how many in the group saw it happen? And what kind of hell are they going through now?"

Mitchell shrugged.

"Do you have a GPS?" Cody asked. "Mine got burned up in the fire. I'd like to get the exact coordinates here so we can let the rangers know to come get the body."

Mitchell said, "I know the exact location of Camp One. I'll tell 'em."

"There may be more forensic evidence around here," Cody said, looking up toward where the tents were pitched on the grassy shelf. "A crime-scene crew could find something if they got here before too long. Maybe where the killing took place, or footprints, or pieces of parachute cord. Or blood. It's not unusual to find the blood of the killer at the scene of a knifing. It's amazing how often the assailant cuts himself with his own knife during a struggle. Lots of times they don't even know it until later."

"Yeah," Mitchell said with a slow smile building, "I watch them shows on television. The CSI folks would get here and we'd know the whole story and catch the bad guy in forty-eight minutes flat."

"It doesn't work like that," Cody said.

"And it sure as hell wouldn't work here," Mitchell said. "I promise you that. It'll likely rain this afternoon and wash evidence away, or the wolves will come back and clean things up. Nothing works here like normal, like I told you earlier."

Cody sat down heavily on a rock next to Mitchell.

He said, "I've never been on a crime scene before when it was just me. Usually we've got evidence techs and forensic guys on the way, not to mention all my own equipment. I can't even communicate with anyone except you. I feel so goddamned helpless."

"So maybe we better get on our horses and find the rest of 'em," Mitchell said. "That's the only way we're going to know what's happened here."

"Yeah. So you said earlier we have to leave the body?"

Mitchell nodded. "We ain't takin' it with us, that's for sure."

"Then what do we do with it? Sink it back into the lake? Bury it?"

"Wolves'll come back," Mitchell said, shaking his head. "There won't be nothin' left. There's only one thing we can do."

Cody said, "Hang it up?"

"I know where the food pole is," Mitchell said, struggling to his feet, his back popping. "A hundred yards up the mountain away from the camp. Unless Jed moved it. We can run the body up the pole until the rangers get here."

"Man."

"Unless you've got a better idea."

"I wish I did."

It wasn't easy. Cody got kicked in the face with Glode's boots as the body was pulled up into the air. Mitchell had dallied the rope around his saddle horn and walked his horse toward the north until the body was raised twenty feet into the air. Cody looked up. Glode's arms were splayed straight out to the sides from the rope looped under his arms. His head was cocked to the side and his legs hung straight down. The body turned slowly as they tied the rope off after wrapping it around the sap-heavy trunk of a lodgepole pine.

"Birds'll get at it," Mitchell said, "but there isn't much we can do about that. This is about as dignified as we can get for now."

Mitchell tied the rope off. "Things have changed around here in more ways than one," he said, as much to himself as to Cody. "If anything, they've gotten a hell of a lot wilder and more dangerous than they used to be. The grizzly bear population is *way* up, and there's nothing going to keep it down. And the reintroduction of wolves has changed the whole ecosystem. I've heard old-timers compare this wolf deal to introducing street gangs back into inner cities where the gangs had long since been wiped out. I'm not sure I'd go that far," Mitchell said, "but it sure has changed things. There are a hell of a lot more critters around that can eat us than there used to be."

"Great," Cody said.

As they rode away from Camp One the trail was instantly recognizable. It was churned up by the hooves of multiple horses and mules.

"One thing I'm sure you noticed, being the detective and all," Mitchell said over his shoulder as he rode, "was that rock holding the body underwater."

Puzzled, Cody said, "What about the rock?"

"I guess I mean the knots on it."

"What about the knots?" Cody asked, annoyed.

"You didn't recognize the style of knots used to secure that rock to the line?"

Cody sighed. "I'm getting tired of being strung along here."

"Diamond hitches," Mitchell said. "Damned near perfect ones. Not the easiest thing to tie in the world, but probably the best damned knot in an outfitter's arsenal."

Cody felt his face go slack.

"Think about it," Mitchell said again.

Cody reached back into his saddlebag as he rode and found the satellite phone. After staring at it in his hand for a few minutes, he powered it on.

It took two minutes to boot up, find the satellite, and come back with full reception.

He had five messages. All from Larry.

27

As Gracie and Dakota topped the hill they found the others. Jed had ridden ahead and gathered everyone off to the side of the trail and they sat their horses and looked back at the stragglers.

Dakota said, "Oops, looks like we let them get too far ahead of us."

"Are you in trouble?"

"Naw, I can handle it."

Gracie saw where Jed had tied a red bandana on a sapling to indicate to D'Amato and Russell—and possibly Tristan Glode and Wilson—where to turn off.

Jed said to Dakota, "You need to keep the hell up."

Dakota lied, "Gracie was having a little trouble with Strawberry. We got it all worked out."

Jed narrowed his eyes and looked from Dakota to Gracie and back. Gracie could tell he wasn't sure he was buying the explanation.

Her dad rode over to her. "Everything okay, honey?"

"Fine," Gracie said.

He rode close alongside and reached out and touched her cheek. "I'm sorry about earlier."

"Me too," she said.

She could see the relief in his face. He said, "We still do need to talk."

"I know."

"Danielle, too. We all need to talk. I thought it would be easier on this trip but we're constantly with everyone else."

Gracie nodded, and he touched her again and walked his horse back to his place in line.

She said, "Dad?"

When he turned, his face filled with concern, she said, "Danielle and I talked with her. She seems nice."

He beamed, and said, "She is."

"Okay," Jed barked, gesturing toward a thick copse of trees at the edge of the meadow, "this is where the trail breaks off. And if everyone will keep in line and follow me and not wander too far behind," he glared at Dakota, "we should all be okay."

And with that he turned his horse and gathered his mules and set off across the meadow. To Gracie, it didn't even look like a trail.

Where are we going?

She turned and looked over her shoulder at Dakota. Dakota shrugged and extended her arms palms up in a *who knows?* gesture.

28

Cody wanted to hurt someone, break something, unleash holy hell. He'd chewed up two packages of Stride gum and drained his Nalgene bottle, pretending the warm plastic-tasting water was 100-proof alcohol, but it wasn't. His cravings for nicotine and booze pulled at him from the inside like talons and he thought, *One cold beer, one cigarette, that's all I fucking ask. That, and my son.*

The single cigarette he had remaining was in his breast pocket, but he'd sworn to himself to save it for when everything was over and Justin was safe. As he rode past pine trees he wondered what their bark would taste like if he stripped it, crumbled it into powder, and inhaled. When he rode Gipper over small streams of water he looked down and wished it came from a brewery.

His head swam and he couldn't concentrate, but there was one thing he knew and he finally said it to Bull Mitchell.

"You need to turn around and go home."

Mitchell acted as if he hadn't heard him. He rode ahead, comfortable in his saddle, his shoulders wide as if telling him to shut up and go away.

They were an hour from Camp One, an hour from where they'd found the body. They hadn't talked, but Cody recognized that Mitchell had picked up the pace and made his horse and the packhorse work harder than before.

"I said, you need to turn around now and go home," Cody said again.

Mitchell didn't turn his head. He drawled, "And why is that?"

"Because I promised your daughter I wouldn't put you into a bad situation. But we're in one. We've got a dead body and who knows what we're riding into. The deal was you'd guide me. I figured we'd find them and you could hang back and let me do my job. But we've got a dead man hanging from a tree and this isn't what the deal was."

Mitchell rode along.

Cody said, "This trail we're on is all churned up by Jed's horses. An idiot could follow this, it's like a highway. I don't need you anymore and your daughter does. Your wife does. I'll return the horses when I'm through."

Mitchell chuckled drily, and said, "Will you now?"

"Yes. Go back to the truck and trailer and I'll meet you there when this is through."

Mitchell rode along.

"I'm not kidding. It's not a negotiation. I'll pay you what I promised because you delivered. You got me here and pointed me where I need to go. Like I said, any idiot could follow their trail now that we're on it."

"And you're the idiot?"

Cody said, "Pretty much, goddamn it. I've got it covered. Go back to the truck, relax, and I'll see you tomorrow or whenever."

"You're sure?"

He said it in a way that led Cody to believe he might have been thinking the same thing.

"I'm absolutely sure."

Mitchell conceded, "There is a pretty obvious trail."

"Yes, there is."

"An idiot could follow it."

"Yes."

"If I get back to the truck, you want me to call the Park Service? Tell them about the dead man?"

Cody hesitated a moment, thinking about the ramifications. He knew the Park Service would respond but probably not quickly. The logistics of ordering up rangers or a helicopter would take hours, and maybe more time than that. He should be on Justin by then. He said, "Yes, call 'em."

Mitchell seemed to be thinking about it. He said, "You think I'm too old and feeble to finish this job?"

Cody said, "Jesus, no. But I made a promise to your daughter. I want to keep it."

"Damn her."

"She's just looking out for her dad. I'd like to think Justin would someday do the same for me," he said, wondering if that would ever happen.

Mitchell clicked his tongue and turned his horse around. Cody saw disappointment in his face. As he rode by headed the opposite direction he handed Cody the reins to the packhorse.

"Dally the rope around your saddle horn once and keep it loose," Mitchell said. "That way, if she gets spooked she won't take you with her or take you down. But don't forget she's there."

"Okay," Cody said, taking the rope.

"There's four days' worth of food in the panniers and some oats for the horses tonight. Feed them before you feed yourself and hobble them up. Make sure they get to water and brush 'em good. They haven't been out much."

"All right."

"Take care of yourself," Mitchell said, looking into Cody's eyes. "And take this," he said, pulling his .44 Magnum from his holster and handing it over butt first. "For bears."

"I don't need—"

"The hell you don't," Mitchell said. And rode away.

———

Cody was sad to see him go, and more than a little scared being completely and totally alone. Not that he didn't do his best work by himself, but Bull Mitchell had a sense of confidence and purpose in the wilderness Cody could never match, or try to. It was as if the last of his confidence was riding away. He kept glancing back at the packhorse, willing her to behave. Willing her to pretend he knew what he was doing.

He slid the long barrel of the .44 Magnum beneath his belt on the left side of his body so he could pull it—if necessary—with a sidearm draw. It was heavy and ungainly. But if the wolves came back or a grizzly blocked him on the trail he wouldn't hesitate to fire. Mitchell's observation about the many animals who could eat him had resonated.

29

Jed McCarthy led his clients west through dark and close stands of timber broken up by lush mountain meadows humming with insects. The alternate trail they had taken was faint, no more than an unpopular game trail at times, but he was sure he was on the right one and he didn't dare stop and check his materials because he didn't want anyone behind him to doubt he knew where he was taking them. Leaders, if they were true leaders, led. They didn't dither, they didn't doubt themselves. They led. He'd made that point to Dakota numerous times, back when she chose to listen to him. He didn't know what her deal was now, which was her loss, not his. And he really didn't care.

His stomach growled with tension and his hands were cold. He didn't slow his pace or turn around, but he raised his right hand to his face and used his teeth, one finger at a time, to loosen his leather glove. Then he tucked it between the saddle and his Wranglers. Still looking ahead, he let his bare right hand creep back to the right nylon saddlebag, where his briefcase was. He worked his fingers inside and probed for the handgrip of his weapon, found it, and squeezed. The weight and texture of it reassured him. He was glad it was in easy reach.

They emerged into another grassy meadow and he clucked his

tongue and led the mules off the trail over to the side against the wall of trees to make room for the rest of the riders.

When they were gathered he smiled at them because they looked apprehensive and they didn't know why he'd stopped or what kind of news he might have for them. Dakota squinted at him, trying to guess the reason for the pause, as she rode past the group and over to the side. Everyone dismounted.

"I'm gettin' a little concerned about Tony and Drey," Jed said. "I thought they would have caught back up with us by now. Least I hoped they would."

Knox, their friend, said, "Me, too." He seemed alone and uncomfortable without his buddies to bounce his comments off.

Jed shot a glance over at Donna. She looked back with no reaction at all even though he'd not mentioned her husband.

Jed said, "I'm thinking it's possible they might have ridden past my red bandana back there and not gotten on the right trail. That's the only place I think they could have gotten confused, even though these horses leave sign like we're an army on the march or something."

He let the implications of that settle in, before he said, "So I'm thinkin' I might ride back there and find those guys before they get too far down the wrong trail."

He could tell by the dark looks on three faces in particular—Ted Sullivan, Rachel Mina, and Walt Franck—they didn't like his idea at all. He didn't even look over at Dakota because he could feel her eyes burning twin holes in his neck.

Walt said, "You're gonna *leave* us?"

"Just for an hour or so," Jed said, keeping it light. "I'll ride hard down where we were, find those guys, and ride hard to get back. We should meet back up with you about the time you folks get close to Camp Two."

He nodded toward Dakota and said, "Dakota knows our camps as good as I do or better. You don't need to worry about her guiding you at all."

Dakota's voice was tight. "What about your mules?"

"I'll leave them with you," Jed said, looking over at her and showing his teeth. She glared at him but said nothing back. He knew she'd hold her fire until later, when the clients couldn't hear her. Which is why he'd set up the whole scene to take place in the open.

Ted Sullivan cleared his throat. He said, "I'm not worried about Dakota leading us to the next camp, not at all. But I'm kind of wondering if it's the best idea for you to go back for them and leave the group."

Jed laughed drily. "Hell," he said, "I always leave the group when I need to on any given trip. It ain't unusual. Sometimes I need to go back for something—like a camera—that somebody left in camp, or sometimes I have to ride ahead and check trail conditions. Luckily," he said, again tipping his hat toward Dakota, "we have this fine hand here to take over the outfit when that happens."

Sullivan nodded conspicuously, as if to convince Jed and the others he had no further objection.

But Rachel Mina had fire in her eyes. She said, "We started this trip with fourteen people. Then last night we lost two. Today we lost two more. And now *you're* leaving?"

Jed said, "Think of it as more food at dinnertime for everybody else."

Walt chuckled, but that was it.

"Sorry," Jed said. "I shouldn't joke. But really, wouldn't you rather get two and possibly three of the group back before dinner? That may not happen unless I go after them."

"Still," she said, "what if something happens to you? What if you get injured? This is *your* trip. How are we going to know what to do or where to go? We're in the middle of nowhere and you gave your maps away to Tony and Drey, so we won't even have those to go by."

Walt nodded as she talked.

Donna Glode put her arms up, palms out, as if to quiet the crowd. Everyone turned toward her. She said, "Given what's happened, I would suggest we abort the trip. There's no reason to continue on as far as I'm concerned. I suggest tomorrow we go back to the vehicles and consider this trip the disaster it's turned out to be."

Silence. Gracie looked from face to face to see if anyone agreed.

Jed kicked at the dirt with obvious anger, but said softly, "I've never quit a trip before. But it's up to everyone else. Any takers on Donna's idea?"

No one spoke. Knox finally said, "I'm not in favor of going back until my friends find us or we know what happened to them."

Walt jumped in, "Mrs. Glode, some of us don't have the, uh, emotional investment you have in quitting. We paid good money for this. I'm not in support of going back yet."

No one else spoke until Jed said, "Okay, it's settled. We'll find our strays and revisit this topic if necessary. But please keep in mind if you decide to quit you'll be missing out on some great scenery and experiences. And now that we've agreed, I'm going to go find those missing boys."

"I'm going with you," Knox said. "They're my friends."

"Not a good idea," Jed said flatly. "I'm going to ride all out to go get them. I'm talking balls-to-the-wall, if you ladies will excuse my French. Unless you can guarantee me you can keep up, it's not a good idea."

Knox flushed and said, "You know I can't. This is my second day on a horse."

"Then with all due respect, fall in behind Dakota and I'll deliver your buddies to you.

"See you at Camp Two or before!" he said, climbing up and spurring his mount. He loved the feeling of his horse digging in and taking off, the hundreds of pounds of bunched muscle between his legs. Of being untethered from this slow gaggle of city-bred dudes who looked on at him with dumb eyes and stupid faces.

As he rocketed through the meadow he tipped his hat at each and every client, and most of them grinned back.

He knew he looked pretty damned dashing.

Gracie had to relieve herself but was not interested in locating any far-off portable toilet so she stepped into a thick copse of pine trees to find James Knox there zipping up. He was as startled as she was.

"You don't want to go all the way up the hill either, I take it," he said. "Sorry."

"No, I'm sorry," she said. "I didn't know you were here."

He waved her concern away. He said, "When you were looking at us last night, what were you thinking?"

She was surprised how direct he was. She stammered, "I don't know. I've just never met anyone from New York City before, I guess."

Knox flashed a quick grin. "We probably disappointed you."

"Not really."

He put his hands in his jeans pockets and leaned against the trunk of a tree. He was looking at her but he seemed distracted. "It would probably surprise you to know in real life the three of us are pretty serious people. People think we're just a crew of cutups, but that's just one week a year. We're hard workers and we don't screw around. What happened with Tony and—that woman, Donna—that was unusual. I'm sorry it happened, and I know Tony is busted up about it."

She nodded. He seemed to be talking to himself as much as to her. His skin looked waxy and drawn as if it had been drained of blood. He looked older than she'd thought before.

"We've been good buddies for almost fifteen years," he said. "The three of us. We all started together on the Street. We've been in each other's weddings, helped each other out. Tony was supposed to have been in the World Trade Center that morning on 9/11 to meet a client, but he didn't make it because he was hungover from my bachelor party the night before. That just goes to show you how fate works, you know? You're young, but you know about 9/11, right?"

"Yes."

He nodded. "Our wives always say be careful on these trips. They say don't do anything stupid. We tell them we don't. This kind of stuff never happened before. That's not why we go on these adventures, to screw around. Now my friends aren't here and I get this sick feeling," he said as he gestured toward his heart. "I get this sick feeling . . ."

Then it was as if he woke up. He looked at her, shook his head, and flashed his smile again. "Why am I telling you this?"

"I don't know."

"What I'm trying to say, I guess, is friends are important. You've got to stick by them, even when they screw up."

As he left the copse he reached out and patted her on the shoulder.

30

After a half hour of lone riding, Cody pulled up at a clean small stream that crossed the trail and painfully climbed down to let his horses drink. He hated depending on two animals he neither knew nor trusted, but he had no choice and his thought was to treat them well and maybe they'd reciprocate.

As both horses lowered their heads to suck up the cold water, he went a few feet upstream to fill his own bottle. He'd purchased a water filter kit, but it, like his cigarettes, had been in the duffel that burned up. Giardia contamination was the least of his worries. He thought if he got it, it would at least take his mind off no cigarettes or alcohol. To drive the point home, he drained a quarter of the icy unfiltered water and topped his Nalgene bottle and sealed it.

While the horses rested—oh, how he admired their dumb animal ability to grab a nap whenever they could—he sidled up to Gipper and withdrew the satellite phone again.

The first of Larry's messages was blunt:

"Cody, where the hell are you? You said you'd turn your phone on. Call me back on this number as soon as you get this, partner."

"Partner" was said with heavy sarcasm.

Cody said, "You'd like me to do that, wouldn't you, *partner.*"

Then the second message:

"Hey, I don't know what's going on. I tried your cell and they said it wasn't a working number. Which means you turned it off—stupid move—or your phone fucked up. Either way, you need to call me as soon as you can. Things are happening here. I'm on it. I'm starting to connect the dots and it's getting real fucking interesting. Call me."

His voice was urgent and elevated. Cody fought his instincts to return the call. Larry sounded excited. Cody said, "You'd like that, wouldn't you?"

But he retrieved the third message:

"Cody, goddamn you. I know about the fire. I had a hunch and called the Gallatin Gateway when I heard about it and found out you registered there. And I talked to the Bozeman PD and Gallatin County Sheriff's Department and found out you couldn't be located but the fire started in your room. By the way, there's an APB out for you. They want you for questioning and they suspect you of arson.

"What, are you on the bottle again? Are you flushing your life down the toilet and taking me with you? I can't believe I lied. I hope you understand what I'm saying. I lied for you—again. Why am I doing this? What kind of dumb shit am I, anyway? I lie for you and you won't even call me back.

"Then I start thinking: I know you. I know how you think. You're a conspiracy-minded bastard and you probably suspect somebody fingered you. Assuming you didn't set the fire yourself by getting hammered and passing out in bed with a cig hanging out of your mouth, of course. But only you know if that's the case. And if it wasn't, you're wondering who fingered you and sent the arsonist. Right? Am I right, you jerk? Did you think it was me, the guy who is covering for you every step of the way and keeping you in the loop? You son of a bitch, I know how you think. And I'm disappointed in you to the point where I'm done with you. I'm over you. I heard you were never any good to begin with but I didn't listen. You're a half-breed white-trash asshole who doesn't know enough to trust the only friend he's got—"

Cody felt his ears go hot as the message timed out with Larry yelling at him. He staggered back until his shoulder blades thumped a tree trunk. He lowered the phone and thought about it. Usually, when someone attacked him personally—like Jenny—he agreed with them, he deserved it. But this was . . . confounding. Either Larry was the most evil manipulator he'd ever run across—and so many of the scumbags he encountered were able to justify anything they'd done with a straight face—or he'd misread completely what had happened and why.

Larry was good, Cody thought. He'd rattled him. As intended, he thought. Because nobody but another cop would think as many moves ahead.

Cody raised the satellite phone and retrieved message number four.

"*Okay, you ingrate. That's the best word I can think of for you. Either that, or you forgot the sat phone and your cell and in that case you're just a fucking idiot, which seems more and more possible. I wouldn't be surprised anymore if we found you in some drunk tank in Livingston or Ennis or maybe back where you belong in Denver. I've pretty much given up on you, I want you to know that.*

"*But if you ever get this and actually listen to it, I want you to know something. You need to find them—the pack trip your son is on—and call in the location. I've got the Park Service and the Feds alerted. They know what I know, and that this thing is bigger and worse than either of us thought. I've almost got it dialed in. And man, you're not going to believe it. You're in the middle of a shitstorm neither one of us anticipated. It goes back to the dead alcoholics, and I'm honing in on the explanation. But I'm sure as hell not going to leave it on your fucking message mailbox. So call me. I can't say all is forgiven, but you don't know what you're getting into. It's worse than—*"

The message time ran out. Cody felt the hairs stand up on the back of his scalp. He took in a long quivering breath and punched the buttons on the phone for the last message. Larry whispered.

"*I don't know where you are or even if you're getting this, Cody.*

But the shit has hit the fan. They know you're gone and where you are. You're fucked, and so am I. I never thought it would come to this. Call me."

There were no more messages from Larry on his satellite phone.

Cody withdrew the last cigarette from his pack and lit it and inhaled it as if it were angel's breath. Either Larry was the best actor in the world, or his messages were genuine. He leaned slightly toward the latter.

31

It had been thirty minutes since Cody thought he'd heard gunshots. Two of them, two distant heavy *booms,* far up ahead of him. If the wind had not died to a whisper a few minutes before, he thought, he might not have heard them at all.

They'd come just seconds apart. He'd reined in his gelding and cocked his head and listened further but there was silence. And slowly, with the sound of water pouring over smooth river rocks, the breeze picked back up in the treetops and returned with a whispery white noise just loud enough to swallow up any more distant sounds.

Since then, he'd questioned himself as to what he'd actually heard. The forest was full of creatures and sounds. Having grown up around hunting and guiding with his father and uncle in Montana, he'd never put any stock into the old saw, "If a tree falls in the forest and there's no one to hear it . . ." Because in his experience, nature could be raucous, sloppy, and loud. Especially in a place like Yellowstone that teemed with large-bodied ungulates and bizarre natural phenomena. Although gunshots were the most likely, the faraway sounds could have been trees falling, branches snapping, rocks being dislodged, or thunderclaps. He'd heard that big grizzlies searching for grubs to eat were known to knock over big rotten trees and uproot small ones, and moose sometimes scratched themselves so vigorously on trunks and outcroppings that they knocked them over. Plus there was the internal pounding coming from his own body.

He wished his head was clear and his guts and muscles weren't screaming for nicotine to bring them back to level. Blood that seemed thin and panicked and needy coursed through his ears and whumped at his temples, trying to burst out of his veins as if they were a ruptured hydraulic hose. His vision had constricted and he saw black curtains closing and cutting down his peripheral vision. He knew he was capable, right then, of doing just about anything for a cigarette or a shot of bourbon or both. He cursed his dependency and his weakness while at the same time justifying it to himself because of the situation he was in.

At the time that he'd heard the sounds he'd withdrawn the AR-15 from his saddle scabbard and jacked in a .223 cartridge and laid it over his pommel. He kept riding while the churned-up trail of hoofprints turned deliberately off the main trail toward a copse of trees to his right.

That's where he saw the red bandana tied to a branch and wondered why Jed McCarthy had left the trail and where he was taking his clients. And why someone had left a marker.

At times the new trail was so narrow Cody had to brace the rifle butt on his thigh with the muzzle pointed up so it wouldn't get caught in a tree branch or overgrown foliage on the sides of the trail that seemed to reach out to grasp at his arms and knees. Gipper walked deliberately and haltingly as Cody pushed forward, and he had to keep nudging and kicking him to keep moving. He knew sometimes horses could sense danger ahead, but he also knew horses were sometimes simply overly cautious and tentative. He found that his mouth had become dry as his heart raced.

The lodgepole pine trees had closed in around him. They weren't tall but they were dense and so closely packed it would be difficult for a man to walk through them without turning to the side. It had been so long since the trail had been used, long silky remnants of spiders' webs, broken by Jed's party ahead of him, fluttered like ghosts from boughs over his head. It was as if he were riding through a shroud.

He heard a grunt, and he thought: *Bear.*

Gipper heard it, too, and the horse planted his feet and leaned backwards with his heavy haunches. Gipper's ears cocked forward and his nostrils opened and he snorted either a warning or a cry of alarm. Cody brought the rifle up to his shoulder one-handed, aiming it vaguely ahead of him, keeping a hold on the reins with his left hand. The packhorse, oblivious to what was going on, walked into Gipper's hindquarters and jostled Cody's shaky aim.

There was another grunt, this time closer, and a heavy footfall. It was coming toward him, whatever it was.

Cody didn't know whether to dismount or stay in the saddle. He longed for solid footing, but knew he couldn't slip gracefully to the ground and not risk losing control of the horses. If he was on the ground and they decided to panic and run off, he was stuck. The rifle just seemed to be in the way.

There was a flash of color through the thin trunks ahead. Beige and red.

A low moan, *"Naugh."*

"Who's there?" Cody called out. His mouth was so dry his voice cracked. "Who is it? Identify yourself. I'm a cop."

A man on foot lurched into view, startling Gipper further and the gelding crow-hopped, fouling Cody's aim. As he tried to gain his balance in the saddle, he dropped the reins to the ground. The only thing that stopped Gipper from turning completely around was the wall of thin trees on both sides of the trail.

"Easy," Cody said, as much to himself as to Gipper, "Easy . . ."

The man, an African American wearing jeans, a once-beige shirt soaked almost entirely in glossy red blood, and a look of horror and anguish, cried out again and pitched forward onto his knees on the trail.

Clumsily, with both of his horses stutter-stepping, Cody dismounted and managed to gather up Gipper's reins. While he was tying his horse to the trunk of a thick aspen tree, the packhorse jerked back and the lead rope unraveled from Gipper's saddle horn. Cody reached out for it as it pulled away, missed it, and he stood seething and confused for a few seconds, watching the packhorse gallop away back down the trail. He could see chunks of dirt flying from the horse's hooves and the panniers flapping hard, spooking the horse further.

The drumbeat of the hooves and occasional snap of dry twigs faded away. Cody spat out a string of curses and kicked at the ground.

Then he turned toward the injured man.

Never in his career had Cody confronted a dying man. In nearly every case, the victim was already dead—in many cases for days—and Cody could observe with clinical detachment and dark humor. Bodies were no more than heavy wet bags of organs, muscle, tissue, fat, and bone bound together by a taut wrapping of skin. He studied those bags for likely offered evidence of what method was used to douse the flame of a soul inside.

Cody sat on the trail. He'd never cradled a stranger's head in his lap before while the man cried real tears and choked on pints of his own blood when he tried to speak.

"Jesus," Cody said, elevating the man's head by raising his own leg, trying to find a position where the victim wouldn't have to make the gargling sound. "I don't want to hurt you."

The man shook his head quickly but couldn't form words yet. He was still lucid despite appearances. But, Cody knew, he wouldn't be for long. The victim was bleeding out before his eyes and there wasn't a single thing either of them could do about it. Bull Mitchell's field first-aid kit had been in the panniers of the packhorse. But even if the horse hadn't run away, Cody wasn't sure he could have done anything to save this man's life.

He'd known the end of this story as he approached him minutes

ago. There was a hole the size of a fist in the man's back, the exit
wound. It was inches deep and pulsating. Cody dropped down to the
trail and turned the man over. The victim had watched, his eyes clear
and sharp. The entry wound was the size of a nickel and it was framed
by a hole in the fabric of his shirt. The hole in the cloth, just below the
breast pocket on the left side of the victim's chest, was burned black on
the edges in an outline that resembled a blooming flower. The reason
for the pattern was powder burns—meaning that the shot had been
made practically point-blank. The weapon had been of large caliber.
Cody saw no other bullet wounds but there didn't have to be any.

Cody said, "I'm not going to lie and tell you you'll be okay."

The man closed and reopened his eyes. Not out of disappointment,
but a means of signaling Cody that he understood.

Cody could feel blood from the exit wound soaking into the denim
of his trousers. It was warm.

"Can you hear me?" Cody said.

Again, the man blinked.

"Are you with the pack trip led by Jed McCarthy?"

Blink. *Yes.*

"Is there an older boy on the trip? Named Justin? Seventeen, eighteen?"

Yes.

"Is he okay?"

Yes.

"Man, I don't know what to do. There's no way to stop the bleeding."

Yes.

"Did you see who shot you?"

Yes.

"Can you try to talk? Can you please try to tell me what happened
and who did it?"

Yes.

The man closed his eyes and swallowed painfully. Cody looked skyward for a fresh thought or a signal that would give him—and the gunshot victim—some kind of hope. Or something he could do to make this poor man more comfortable.

He felt the man die. It wasn't a sound or a movement, but a sudden absence of firmness in his lap. Cody looked down. "Not now," Cody pleaded. "Not before you tell me what happened."

The man's eyes were still open but there was nothing behind them. His mouth was slightly open and red inside, the color of candied cherries. Cody reached up and closed the eyes, pulling the lids and hoping they'd stay that way. They did.

Cody rolled the body off his legs. In death, it seemed twice as heavy as before. He stood unsteadily. His muscles ached from riding and he was covered with a man's sacred lifeblood; his jeans were black and sticky and orange half-moon-shaped pine needles stuck to the denim. He bent over and dug through the victim's clothing and found a wallet and flipped it open. André Alan Russell, resident of Manhattan. Cody remembered the name from the file he took from Jed's office.

As he'd done earlier in the day, he photographed Russell's body and wounds, knowing while he did it that the shooting had happened someplace else and this wasn't the crime scene. He wondered how far Russell had come from where he'd been shot. He dragged Russell's body off the trail. Before tucking it in beneath a massive fallen tree and covering it the best he could with heavy logs and branches, Cody looked skyward for a moment, then looted all of Russell's pockets looking for a package of cigarettes that wasn't there. Cursing, Cody then covered the body. The cover wouldn't prevent predators from finding it—probably nothing would—but he hoped he could return with help to get the body out before it was torn up.

He kept Russell's New York driver's license but cached the wallet and the contents of the man's pockets in the crook of the aspen tree he'd used to keep Gipper around.

Since Mitchell's GPS was gone and he couldn't get a reading of coordinates, Cody found a T-shirt in his saddlebag and ripped it up and tied one strip to the cover where the body was and another on a low overhanging branch at the trail to mark the location. He scribbled in his spiral notebook what he'd found and what he'd done with the body and Russell's possessions.

When he was through he stood and wiped sweat from his face and took off his hat to cool the top of his head. He could see no trace of Russell's body beneath the cover he'd put on it, but he knew it was there. And the image of Russell's last attempt to speak would be with him forever.

Back on Gipper, Cody contemplated turning around to try and retrieve the packhorse, but he feared the animal was still running and was miles away. He couldn't afford to let more time elapse between him and Justin.

He nudged his horse and Gipper reluctantly stepped back on the trail. As he walked his mount, Cody reached behind him into his saddlebag for the satellite phone. He'd thought long and hard about the situation he was in and had decided he couldn't take any more chances on his own.

Because now there were two bodies, and he had no reason to think there wouldn't be more.

He turned on the phone and watched the display screen. It was working, but there was no signal. He looked up; the tree cover was too thick. He'd need to wait until he rode into a clearing where the phone could hook up with a satellite. Clipping the phone to his belt next to the Sig Sauer, he cautiously rode on. He could smell Russell's blood on his clothing and it mixed with the odor of his own fear.

Things were happening ahead of him. He was hours and miles behind the pack trip, but closing in. He couldn't wrap his mind around the motivation for the murders but it was obvious whomever was behind it was entering a new stage. The killings leading up to the pack trip departure had been meticulously planned to resemble accidents or suicides. A good deal of thought had gone into them.

Tristan Glode's body had been well hidden. It was possible, Cody thought, the murder had taken place out of view of the others on the trip and they may not even know it had occurred. But Russell was different. He'd somehow managed to get away and he'd not been pursued, probably because the killer knew his victim would bleed out. But unlike the murders preceding Russell's, there was no indication of careful planning or execution. Russell had not been chased down and disposed of to hide the crime.

Which meant, for one reason or another, that the situation had grown desperate. Desperate men, Cody knew, were capable of anything.

As was he.

A few minutes went by and Cody checked the phone to see if he'd acquired a signal yet so he could call Larry. He looked up ahead of him and saw a pair of splayed boots that belonged to a third victim.

Gipper woofed and started to backtrack furiously.

Filtered sun shimmered on their coats and he could see at least one massive round head and the humps on their backs and the bulge of heavy muscles beneath the fur.

He'd have to fight off a feeding grizzly sow and her two cubs to identify the body.

32

With Gipper in a panic—backtracking blindly, woofing, eyes white and almond-shaped, ears pinned back—Cody jerked on the reins and tried to stay in the saddle. He knew his reaction was as out-of-control as his horse's and he wasn't helping the situation, but he didn't know what to do. The big brown grizzly sow looked up with a mouthful of red meat. The two cubs—one auburn, the other brown like his mother—scrambled back over the body and fell in behind her giant haunches, peering out at him with black eyes.

Cody managed to crank Gipper's head to the side and stop him from scrambling long enough to slide his right boot out of the stirrup and swing down to the ground with his rifle. Gipper pranced as if he was electrically charged and pinned Cody to a tree trunk, crushing the wind out of him, then crow-hopped back toward the trail. Cody slipped off the side of the horse, stunned and gasping for breath, and felt the reins being pulled away through his fingers.

Gipper was gone, crashing through the timber straight away from him, bouncing through the tight grouping of trees, leaving behind showers of broken branches and pine needles. He could hear his horse grunting and feel the hammering of his hooves on the forest floor through the soles of his boots.

Cody swung the muzzle of the AR-15 toward the body and the bears. The cubs had turned their heads away to the right, transfixed by the panicked run of the horse as it crashed through the trees. The sow, though, locked her eyes with Cody and stretched out, guarding the body with her baseball-mitt-sized paws. The long red strip of flesh swung back and forth in her jaws.

"*Get away,*" Cody hollered, fitting the butt plate of his rifle to his shoulder, aiming down the peep sights and fitting the front sight on her arched left eyebrow. "*Get the hell away from there.*"

The auburn cub switched his attention to Cody and stood up. He was only three and a half feet tall, a nascent miniature of his mother. His front paws curled down and rested almost comically on his bulging belly. Although he wanted to, he didn't look formidable except for the blood on his snout.

The brown cub mewled and shot out from behind his mother on all fours, scrambling over the body, straight toward Cody.

"*Get back, little guy,*" Cody bellowed, stepping toward the charging cub and stomping his lead foot while fixing his sights on him. "*GET BACK!*"

The cub came within ten feet before stopping abruptly. It was a deliberate false charge, a bluff move apparently hardwired into grizzly bears that often worked, but Cody refused to run and wouldn't fire and reveal himself unless he had to. Because he knew if he harmed the cub the sow would be all over him before the ejected brass hit the ground. The .223 rounds from his rifle might slow her, but they wouldn't likely stop her.

Standoff.

He couldn't run because the grizzlies could chase him down. Even the cubs had flashing claws and teeth.

Gesturing with the rifle, he advanced several steps as aggressively as he could manage. He screamed at them and bellowed for them to leave and ended up coughing raggedly in what ended as a series of rough barks.

The brown cub wheeled and ran back to his mother. As soon as he reached her, the sow snorted and jumped back from the body, then spun and crashed away into the timber, followed inches away by the brown cub. The auburn cub remained standing on his hind legs.

"You better go, too," Cody growled.

The auburn cub seemed to suddenly realize he was alone, and he fell to all fours, yelped, and scampered into the woods.

Cody lowered the rifle, closed his eyes, and let out a long chattering breath. He looked down to see if he'd fouled himself and he was relieved to find out he hadn't. Over the next minute, he felt his heartbeat slow down. He propped the rifle against a tree trunk and rubbed his face with clammy hands, thinking that the sensation of receding adrenaline was not unlike the first stages of a hangover.

He sensed the bears had not gone far. As he approached the body he held the rifle out in front of him and swept the timber on both sides with his eyes. He could still feel his heart beating hard, and the tips of his fingers and toes ached for nicotine to stop the nerve ends from jangling.

He winced. The smell of fresh blood and exposed stomach contents was acrid. Shards of flesh were ripped from clean white bones and the pile reminded him of the aftermath of a Thanksgiving turkey.

Trying not to look at the mutilation directly, he kept his head to the side while he rolled the body over. The underside was not as torn up. In the back pocket of the trousers he found a wallet. Inside was an EasyPayXpress Unlimited MetroCard for the New York subway system, $480 in cash, assorted credit and business cards, family photos of a very large and dark-haired clan, and a New York State driver's license identifying the victim as Anthony Joseph D'Amato.

D'Amato's clothes had largely been torn away and they'd bunched beneath his back. Cody rooted through the shredded clothing and felt something crackle. It was the familiar and fantastically welcome sound of crinkling cellophane, and Cody dropped manically to his knees and ripped at the bundle with both hands.

Within a slit and blood-spattered double Ziploc bag was a crushed, half-empty pack of Marlboro Lights.

"D'Amato," Cody said, "bless you for being a secret smoker."

It was obvious one of the grizzlies had swiped the plastic bag with claws that sliced through the cigarettes to the skin below. Cody rooted through the pack, breathing in the sweet smell of powdered tobacco, and found three intact cigarettes. The longest one had a small smear of red on the side of it.

He looked at it for a second and conceded that yes, he was smoking a dead man's last bloodstained cigarettes.

He lit up and sat back and inhaled, looking around for the bears, half expecting them to come barreling out of the forest like demons to rip his throat out while his defenses were down.

And he wasn't sure it would be the worst way to go because at least it would be epic and quick.

He left the body of D'Amato on the trail until he could figure out what to do with it. He had no rope to hang it, and it would be a matter of time before the bears came back. His camera was gone with Gipper.

Cody bushwhacked through the brush in the general direction his horse had run. As he shouldered through tree trunks and stepped over downed timber while smoking his cigarette, he felt it was getting lighter. He walked toward the light and within ten minutes stepped out of the trees into a small grassy clearing.

The satellite phone had a signal. He punched the number for the cell phone Larry had said to call. Reception was clear and he heard it ring on the other end. Four, five, six rings. No voice mail prompt. Cody let it ring, figuring Larry would eventually hear it and pick up.

While he waited he slowly pivoted in the meadow so he could keep his eyes out in every direction. He held the AR-15 muzzle down in his right hand. The safety was off. There were no signs of bears, or wolves, or his horse, or whomever had killed Tristan Glode, Russell, and

D'Amato. And before them, the string of recovering alcoholics including Hank Winters.

Two minutes later, Cody was surprised when he heard a click through his earpiece. Someone was on the other end.

"Larry?" Cody said.

Breathing.

"Larry, is that you?"

No other background sound. Just rhythmic breathing. Cody checked the display on his phone to make sure he dialed the correct number. He had. A phone rang somewhere in the background. It was a familiar ring.

"Who is this? Can you hear me?"

The breathing quieted and there was silence but the line was still open. Cody recognized the action as when someone places their hand over the microphone to muffle sound.

"Speak to me," Cody said. "Say something. I'm calling on official police business. *This is an emergency.*"

After a beat, the line was disconnected.

Battling doubts and tendrils of cold fear rising up from his lower stomach, he punched in the numbers again. He did it deliberately, making sure he didn't misdial.

The recorded message said the number was no longer available.

Cody lowered his handset and stared into the sky. It hadn't been Larry, he was sure of it. And it hadn't been a stranger answering an unfamiliar phone, like if Larry had inadvertently left the phone unattended on his desk or at a restaurant.

Whoever answered kept quiet until Cody identified himself. Until Cody had spoken, revealing himself. As if he'd been waiting for the call for quite some time.

And the ring in the background—before it was muffled—was as familiar to him as the sound of his alarm clock. He knew it because it was how the obsolete phones rang in the Lewis and Clark County Sheriff's Department headquarters.

Deep in the timber, in the direction of the trail, he heard a branch snap.

Cody kept the satellite phone on and clipped it back on his belt. He squinted toward the wall of trees to the east where the sound had come from.

There was the click of steel on rock, a distinctive sound. Then the snort of a horse.

Gipper?

Wrong direction, Cody said to himself while raising the AR-15. He wished he had his gear because he very much wanted to replace the short magazine in his rifle with a thirty-rounder.

He heard the squeak of leather and another footfall. His mouth went dry.

A horse was coming. Maybe more than one. It was approaching in a deliberate manner that meant someone was in the saddle.

He lowered himself into a shooter's stance and took a deep breath.

33

As Jed approached Camp Two walking his horse behind him, the conversations stopped abruptly.

"My horse went lame," he said. "I didn't get very far on him before he pulled up hurt."

"So you didn't find them?" Knox asked, distressed.

"Didn't get that far," Jed said.

"Jesus," Knox cried to the others, "is anything going to go right at some point?"

Jed knew he had to extricate himself and turn their attention to other matters. He thought, *Get out ahead of the situation and take over in the lead again.*

He was heartened that no one actually confronted him as he entered the camp. Although Dakota, Rachel Mina, and the girl Gracie seemed to view him with challenge and fear—fear was okay, challenge wasn't—none of them said a word. Which meant they were ceding control of the situation to him, at least a little. He shot a glance at the dad. Angry fathers could be a force to themselves. He hadn't expected Ted Sullivan to take him on and the man didn't.

Whatever they'd been saying about him was suddenly off-limits now that he'd shown up. It used to bother him a little when he'd overhear his clients criticizing him or the decisions he made, but it didn't anymore as long as it didn't evolve into open revolt, which it never had. Jed understood how groups worked. A bunch of strangers thrown together sought common ground, and that common ground was often the outfitter who'd brought them together. He was the common denominator among clients of different social strata and interests. So in order to converse, they'd have to find something to either celebrate or bitch about, and that usually turned out to be him, one way or another.

Jed said to everyone, "Look, folks, I know you're all worried about what's going on. It's crazy to have lost those people, and I'm damned sorry it happened. I'm also damned sorry I took off after them on a horse with a bad wheel." He gestured toward his bay.

"What I need to ask you folks," he said, "is to remain calm. Please remain calm. I can kind of tell there are all sorts of conspiracy tales flying around and all sorts of speculation. That's natural. But you're here in this fine camp with plenty of food and comfort. There's no reason to be worried about anything."

Knox stepped out from behind the kitchen setup. "Jed, I'm worried as hell about my friends. I wish I would have gone with you to find them."

He said to Knox, "I'm going back after them but I've got to switch horses. I need a better mount."

Suddenly, Rachel Mina asked, "What did you do to them?"

It felt as though a shard of glass had been shoved under his skin.

"Excuse me?" he said, still maintaining his smile.

Her eyes flashed. "I said what did you do to them? Tristan, Wilson, Drey, and Tony? Did you hurt them and leave them back there?"

Jed slowly removed his hat and stared at the inside of it. He ran his fingertips along the leather sweatband inside, as if testing for irregularities. He felt his stomach contract and it hurt a little to breathe.

All eyes were on him.

"Ma'am," he said after a beat, "I don't have any idea at all what you're talking about or what you're asking me."

From across the camp, Ted Sullivan said, "Jeez, Rachel . . ." He was aghast.

"You heard me," she said to Jed. "You're picking us off one by one. I want to know why. I want to know what your game is and what you're after. I mean, look at us. We're no threat to you—"

"Jesus, Rachel," Ted Sullivan said to her. Then to Jed, "Man, I'm really sorry. I don't know what got into her." He strode across the camp with his arms out toward her.

Sullivan said, "Rachel, really, I've never known you to jump to conclusions like this." As he approached her she turned, said, "Ted, stay away. Don't touch me."

Sullivan's two daughters watched the scene open-mouthed. Jed couldn't tell which side they were on.

"This is getting out of hand," Walt Franck said, slapping his thighs from where he sat on a log and using his hands to push himself to a standing position. "This isn't helpful in any way." He gestured toward Jed and said to Rachel, "This man has spent the best part of a day trying to track down a couple of his clients who left voluntarily in the middle of the night.

"If I can fault him for anything, it's for letting Drey and Tony take off on their own this morning to try and make things right. But given the circumstances," Walt nodded toward Donna Glode, who looked back nonplussed, "I would have probably done the same thing. But no one threw them out, or pressured them to leave. To accuse him of . . ." He couldn't say it. He shook his head as if ridding his thoughts of the unpleasant words. "It's just crazy," he said.

"He's right, Rachel," Sullivan told her. "You're not being helpful or positive. Please, let's take a breath and calm down." He grasped her by the arm and tried to spin her away, but she shrugged him off.

"She might be right," Gracie said, looking straight at her dad. Ted Sullivan dismissed his daughter with an angry wave. The girl's face turned crimson.

Jed said bluntly to Rachel, "I ain't going to lose my temper here, lady. I know it's a stressful situation. But making accusations with no proof at all isn't helping anything."

He looked around the camp for assurance.

And he got it from everybody, he thought. The only people who wouldn't meet his gaze were Gracie and Rachel Mina. Dakota looked back, but she did so with an upward tilt of her chin and slitted eyes. Like she was making some kind of decision about him.

A beat of silence, then two. Rachel Mina was being led away by Ted Sullivan. Jed watched them go, and noticed that after they'd cleared the camp and were in the trees Sullivan tried to hug her and reason with her, but she pulled away and stomped off alone. After she left, Sullivan stood in the trees with his head down and his shoulders slumped, a sad portrait of a weak but useful man, Jed thought. In a moment, Sullivan turned on his heel and walked the opposite way from where Rachel Mina had gone. Probably to break down and cry, Jed figured.

Jed turned his attention to Dakota. "Please take this bay down to the corral and pick me out the best horse to ride and get it saddled up so I can go after our wayward boys. I've got to gather some more gear because I may be back pretty late. I'm not coming back without those strays."

"Thank you, Jed," Knox said.

Jed nodded, in his best friendly-like reaction.

He walked the bay to Dakota, who still eyed him coolly. She took the reins, as instructed. That's all he needed from her at the moment.

Gracie, Danielle, and Justin walked side by side toward the collection of tents on the grass. Justin and Danielle were holding hands, but Danielle seemed distracted and vacant.

"Those people are just making me crazy," Justin said, "They're turning on each other instead of pulling together. I wish we could all go home now."

He seemed to be waiting for agreement from Danielle, which didn't come.

Danielle said to Gracie, "I can't believe Dad acted like that. He really dissed you, didn't he?"

"Mmmm," Gracie said. "He dissed Rachel, too."

Danielle said, "I thought he might take Rachel's side and yours, too. I mean, he's our *dad*. You don't want your own dad to side with the other guy."

"Mmmm."

"I guess that's one thing," Justin said. "My dad probably would stand with me. He's like that. I guess I never really thought about it before."

"Lucky you," Gracie said.

"You know what?" Danielle said, letting go of Justin's hand and stepping in front of him next to Gracie.

Gracie said, "What?"

"I'm not sure we can trust him."

"Mmmm."

"I don't," Danielle said. "Not anymore."

Dakota led Jed's bay to the temporary electric corral. As she walked the horse the voices from the camp faded behind her. Jed was holding court; explaining to Knox, Walt, and Donna how he was going to go back down the trail and come back with Drey and Tony, at least. Saying he couldn't promise Tristan and frankly didn't care all that much about Wilson although he'd like to get all his horses back. That he'd likely be back deep into the night or early next morning at the latest. Explaining to Knox, once again, that he didn't need his help.

As Dakota turned off the electric fence charger and parted the string, she glanced up the hill toward the camp. Knox, Donna, and Walt were still there. Jed had apparently gone to his tent to retrieve gear or clothing he would need for a longer trip. Rachel and Ted were off quarrelling—or avoiding each other—somewhere.

Her eyes swept the trees and the tents. The three teenagers were by themselves, walking away. No one was watching her from the camp.

She picked up her pace and practically dragged the bay along behind her. The horse limped badly but she couldn't care about that now. The grass was teeming with grasshoppers and they shot away like sparks through the air as she crossed the meadow. A plump one landed on her left breast and she brushed it away. There was a thick spruce in the middle of the makeshift corral and she led the horse behind it, so the trunk was between her and the people in the camp.

Before opening Jed's saddle panniers, she looked around again. She was in the clear.

She fumbled with the straps of the dual panniers and loosened the top flap. Stretching on the toes of her boots, she pulled the lip of the bags down and peered inside. Jed's handgun was on top. She thought she got a whiff of gunpowder.

She pushed his rain gear aside and found his briefcase on the bottom of the pannier. Grasping it by the worn handle, she pulled it up and out. Jed's rolled yellow raincoat came out with it and fell to her feet.

Using the back of the bay like the surface of a desk, she placed the briefcase on it and unsnapped the hasps. They sprung up with two solid clicks.

The manila folder she'd glimpsed the night before in their tent was on top of his other materials and she could see the corners of the printouts peeking beyond the stiff file cover.

She took a deep breath and centered the file folder and reached for the smudged tab to open it.

The white flash in front of her eyes was not another grasshopper, but the blade of a knife wielded by someone who pressed into her back, pinning her to the side of the bay. It sliced so deeply through the flesh of her throat she felt the steel scrape on bone.

34

The sounds in the trees became more pronounced; twigs cracking, the click of hooves against rock, the squeak of leather on leather, the nickering of horses. He felt more than saw the presence of heavy-bodied beings approaching en masse. Cody thought, *How many of them are there?*

He glanced down at his rifle. Likely not enough bullets. And if they were armed? He might need to pull his Sig Sauer when the rifle was empty.

Then a deep-throated shout: "Cody?" The voice carried through the trees.

Cody closed his eyes and took a deep breath and stood up. "Bull?"

"Where the hell are you?" Mitchell grumbled.

"Here. Ahead of you, I think. In a clearing."

"Gotcha," Mitchell said, "so don't shoot me. I'm coming toward your voice."

"I won't," Cody said. "Who is with you? How many of you are there?"

"Just one," Mitchell said.

Cody didn't know if that meant just Mitchell or another. Nevertheless, he could feel heavy weights release from the tops of his shoulders. "I've got to say I'm glad you came back."

"It's taking me a while," Mitchell grumbled, "seeing I've been gathering up loose horses for miles."

Cody lowered his rifle and waited. He could hear Mitchell and the horses coming, picking their way through the timber and brush, but he couldn't see them yet.

Finally, a horse head with a white star blaze on its forehead pushed through the brush. Mitchell's horse.

"There you are," Mitchell said, and Cody could see him. He was a big man but he sat the horse as if they were conjoined, and Cody had trouble discerning where the horse stopped and Bull Mitchell began.

"Damn, I'm glad to see you," Cody said. "Why'd you come back?"

"Hell, I don't know," Mitchell said. "As Hank the Cowdog says, there's a thin line between heroism and stupidity."

Cody found himself grinning at the answer. "Then you'll probably want your gun back."

"Yup."

Mitchell was leading Gipper and the packhorse that had run away. Behind them, tied with a series of lead ropes, were four more horses. The first three had empty saddles.

The last one, a gray, had a rider. Cody was surprised and instinctively raised the rifle again. A dark man, hatless, glowered back at him. So there *was* another. The man rode oddly, shifting around subtly as if he were trying to maintain his balance, as if he were simply cargo. That's when Cody noticed the man's hands were cuffed behind him and he'd been lashed by the waist and legs to the saddle with rope he'd last seen looped on Mitchell's saddle.

"Says his name is Wilson," Mitchell said. "I don't care if you shoot him because he's been nothing but trouble. But I was thinking you might want to talk with him, first."

"K. W. Wilson," Cody said, "fifty-eight, Salt Lake City. Or, as I like to call you, Suspect Number One."

Wilson didn't react. Cody noticed the contusion under Wilson's left eye and his bloody and fattened lower lip.

"Doesn't like cheese," Cody said, remembering Wilson's trip registration.

"I had to thump him a couple times," Mitchell said, patting the butt of his rifle. "He didn't want to work with me very much."

Cody thought Wilson didn't give off any indication of fear—or innocence. Like so many criminals he'd encountered in lockup over the years, Wilson's bearing was a dismissive mix of arrogance and regret. Not regret at what he'd been picked up for, but regret he'd been caught.

Cody nodded. He wondered if he was meeting the killer of Hank Winters and the others.

"I found a couple of things on him you might find interesting," Mitchell said, leaning back and digging into his saddlebag. He produced a six-inch Buck knife in a sheath and a stubby handgun. He handed them both butt-first to Cody.

Cody inspected the revolver, a snub-nosed .38 Special. It was a double-action Taurus six-shot revolver made of stainless steel with rubber grips. It had a two-inch barrel. He sniffed the muzzle and cracked open the cylinder.

"Two rounds have been fired recently," Cody said to Mitchell, who nodded.

Cody snapped the cylinder home, spun it, and pointed the gun at Wilson. Wilson didn't flinch. Cody said, "This is an odd choice of weapon to bring up here. It's not big enough for bears and hard to hit anything at a distance because of the short barrel and fixed sights. I used to carry one of these as a backup in an ankle holster in Denver, but I knew this kind of piece is strictly for self-defense and it's only good for close-in work. Meaning," he said to Mitchell without taking his eyes off Wilson, "he was right on top of D'Amato and Russell when he shot them. Probably a couple of feet away, max. They knew him well enough to get close. I doubt it was an ambush. He probably looked right into their eyes before he pulled the trigger."

He slid the gun into his belt and drew the knife out of the sheath. The blade had been wiped clean but there was dark gummy residue where the fixed blade met the brass guard. Cody dug some out with his fingernail and tasted it. "Blood," Cody said, then spat it out. To Wilson, "This is what you used on Tristan Glode, then. More close-in work."

He circled around Wilson and came up from behind him. He could sense the man start to stiffen, possibly anticipating the stab of the knife. Cody reached up and pressed the point of the blade to Wilson's spinal column just to make him jump. But what he was interested in was an intimate view of Wilson's bound hands.

"You've got blood under the fingernails of your right hand," Cody said. "Looks just like the blood on this knife. There's blood spatter on your cuff, too, it looks like."

"Oh," Mitchell said, digging something silver and square out of the front snap pocket of his shirt and flipping it through the air to Cody. "Something else. Check *this* out."

Cody fumbled the catch and reached down in the grass for the object. "I was hoping it was a pack of cigarettes," Cody said.

"Nope," Mitchell said, "Wilson's camera. You might want to take a look at some of the shots in there to see if there's anyone you recognize. While you do that I'm gonna tie these horses up and get Wilson down."

"I'll help you," Cody said, doing the math. He assumed the three riderless horses had belonged to Tristan Glode, D'Amato, and Russell.

Mitchell swung off and put his hand up to Cody. "Stay there, if you don't mind, pard. The only thing you seem to know about horses is how to lose them."

Cody shrugged. "True enough." He pushed buttons and flicked toggles on the digital camera until the display came alive. The first dozen shots were obviously from the departure area. People milled around eyeing horses, their faces mixes of excitement and anticipation as they got ready to get under way. There were vehicles in the background and glimpses of a long horse trailer with JED MCCARTHY'S WILDERNESS ADVENTURES painted along the side.

As he advanced through the photos he tried to match up faces with the names and descriptions he'd memorized from the file he'd borrowed.

The cowboy with the mustache was obviously Jed himself, shadowed by a younger woman in a floppy sweat-stained hat. He recalled her name: Dakota Hill.

The older stiff couple were the Glodes. Cody recognized Tristan and winced. He'd been a regal man in bearing with striking silver hair, cool blue eyes, and a prominent chin.

The father and his two teenage daughters were the Sullivans; Ted, Danielle, and Gracie. The youngest girl appeared to be much more animated than the older girl, who looked bored.

A single woman, open face, attractive, looking away from the camera as if she was furious about being photographed by him. Rachel Mina. Her face reminded him of the glare Jenny had once given him when he photographed her as she stepped out of the shower. It was the last time he ever did anything like *that* again. Cody wondered why Suspect Number Two was so angry at Wilson.

Three men posed on their horses like the characters from the movie *Three Amigos*. The shot would have been amusing, Cody thought, if he hadn't seen D'Amato's and Russell's mangled remains a couple of hours before.

And there were Walt and Justin, sitting side by side on horseback. Cody felt his heart race. Justin looked older and more mature than when he'd seen him last. He had a weariness in his eyes and an easy smile as he looked over at Walt in the photo.

Cody whispered, *"Yes."* Until that second, he hadn't been absolutely sure Justin was on the trip.

The last three shots were taken in deep timber. Although not focused well, Cody could see they were of the two Sullivan girls. One was using a camp latrine.

He looked up as Mitchell untied Wilson from the saddle. Wilson stared straight ahead.

Mitchell said, "I found this guy about a mile from where I left you. Apparently, he'd gotten off his horse to pee and the horse ran off. I seem to be surrounded by goddamned amateurs. I heard him yelling obscenities and I sneaked into the trees. I finally found him chasing his horse around a meadow with that pistol in his hand, like the horse was gonna be threatened by him. He's as good a horseman as you."

Cody studied Wilson's face while Mitchell talked. It was inscrutable.

"I watched him for a while. His horse finally stopped trotting at the edge of the meadow and Wilson here walked right up to it from behind. He didn't know that when a horse pins its ears back and positions his butt toward you you need to get ready for a kick," Mitchell said, and chuckled.

Mitchell said, "Laid Wilson out. Caught him right in the chest. I rode out there to see if he was okay and he woke up going for his popgun. So I had to thump him a couple times. I took the liberty of borrowing a set of handcuffs from your gear. I hope you have a key somewhere."

"Maybe," Cody said.

Wilson reacted with a jerk of his mouth to the side when he heard that. Mitchell dismounted and tied his horse to the trunk of a tree with a lead rope. Now that he'd climbed down from his mount he looked old and he moved like a stiff old man, Cody thought. Mitchell limped down the line of horses he'd gathered to the gray. When Mitchell got the ropes untied he slid Wilson off by grasping the back of his belt and pulling. Wilson's boots thumped onto solid ground.

Mitchell said, "I'm officially turning him over to you now while I get these critters some grain and water them."

Mitchell put his big hand in the middle of Wilson's back and shoved. Wilson stumbled toward Cody but managed not to trip and fall.

Cody said to him, "Is my son okay? His name is Justin. He's seventeen."

Wilson stared back, noncommittal.

Cody studied Wilson's face for any kind of tell, but the man's eyes were black, still, and unyielding. He took it as an encouraging sign, assuming there would have been at least a flinch or glimmer of reaction if something had happened to Justin.

"So that's the way you want to play it," Cody said. He noted the twin horseshoe impressions on the front of Wilson's shirt where he'd been kicked. As Cody walked up to him he imagined Wilson's chest must be badly bruised. Although the man was two inches taller, Cody was thicker. "I heard the shots and found Russell and D'Amato," Cody said. "We located Tristan Glode's body earlier. You've left a hell of a mess."

Wilson looked back through heavy-lidded eyes.

Cody gestured toward a pedestal-like rock that jutted out of the grass. "Sit."

Wilson didn't move until Cody prodded him with the muzzle of the rifle, then he did so grudgingly. Wilson grunted and settled on the rock and looked at Cody with bored contempt.

Before speaking, Cody made sure Mitchell was out of earshot. He said to Wilson, "Do you know who I am?"

No response.

Cody felt himself smile as his demons took over. He said, "Do you know who I am?"

Wilson didn't even blink.

"Let me tell you who I am, then. I'm Cody, and I'm an alcoholic."

Wilson twitched. At last, a chord was struck.

"Thought so," Cody said, and swung the butt of the rifle into Wilson's face. He could hear the muffled snap as the man's nose broke and feel the cartilage flatten through the stock of the rifle. Wilson cried out and tumbled over backwards off the rock into the grass.

Cody bounded forward and straddled the rock and pressed the muzzle of his AR-15 into the flesh between Wilson's eyes, which had misted from the pain. Blood coursed down the sides of Wilson's face from the twin spouts of his nostrils. Cody growled, "Let me tell you who I am. I'm the scariest fucking cop you'll ever meet. My son is on that trip and you murdered the best man I ever knew. We've been finding the bodies you left behind all fucking morning. I haven't had a drink in days and I smoked my last cigarette two hours ago. All I want is an excuse to kill you five times over and piss on your remains. Do you understand me?"

Wilson's eyes were open wide. He looked bloody and scared.

Cody said, "What, you expected to hear your Miranda rights?"

He moved the muzzle a few inches to the right and fired into the ground so close to Wilson's head it creased his scalp and furrowed through his hair above the temple. The concussion was deafening in the quiet woods, and when Cody's ears stopped ringing all he could hear were Wilson's terrified curses.

"Jesus Christ, you shot me. You son of a bitch. You can't do this to me. *You're a cop.*"

Cody said, "Yada-yada-yada. Tell me something I don't know."

"Cody," Mitchell called from the timber, "everything all right?"

Cody didn't look up. "Everything's fine," he said.

He moved the muzzle back over where it belonged between Wilson's eyes, said, "Now tell me, is my son okay?"

"He was fine when I saw him last," Wilson said. Then: "You busted my nose." He pronounced the last word *node.* "And I can't hear out of my right ear." *Cadt.*

"I'm just getting started," Cody said softly. "Now what I'm going to do is ask you a series of questions. Your job is to answer each and every one of them with absolute truth and clarity. I've interviewed hundreds of dirtbags like you in my life and I know when I hear a lie. If I hear one it's the last thing you're ever going to say. Do you hear *that*?"

Wilson nodded.

"Good. Tell me why you killed Hank Winters."

"I didn't kill him, I swear."

"You're an idiot," Cody said, feeling his face get hot. "We've got bodies all over Yellowstone Park. I've got the gun you used and the knife. Now you're going to tell me you're innocent?"

"I said I didn't kill *Winters,* whoever the hell he is," Wilson hissed. "I've never heard of the guy. It wasn't me who did that. It wasn't me, I swear it."

Cody paused. "Are you going to try and tell me you didn't kill D'Amato, Russell, or Glode, too?"

"No, I ain't going to tell you that."

"But you know who killed Hank Winters?"

Wilson nodded so slightly Cody almost mistook it for a tremble.

"Do you know why?"

Another barely perceptible nod.

"So what in the hell is going on?" Cody said, pressing the muzzle and front sight against Wilson's forehead hard enough to draw blood.

35

"Is he gone?" Danielle asked Gracie.

"I think so."

They were in their tent, waiting for Jed McCarthy to leave camp. Gracie had unzipped the front flap wide enough to see. She could see the aluminum cooking station and James Knox pacing but her field of vision was blocked in back of her. The trail was beyond the camp over a rise. If Jed was indeed gone she hadn't seen him ride away. But the sounds of the adults talking was muted and random, the sounds of nervous small talk. If Jed was still there she would have heard his voice, which seemed to cut through the air like a saw.

The afternoon sun lit the nylon walls and it was hot inside and Gracie could smell the dirt and perspiration on her body and Danielle's. She couldn't remember ever going two days without a shower, much less two days outside being coated by dust, wood smoke, horse, sweat, and a new smell: fear.

"So we're agreed?" Gracie said, sitting back on her sleeping bag. "We'll gather up Dakota and Rachel and get out of here."

"Don't forget Justin," Danielle said.

"He'll want to bring Walt," Gracie said, a hint of a whine in her tone. "Walt will be the good politician and he'll probably tell everyone what we're doing and want them to come, too. Then it'll be all of us and we're back to where we started."

"With this pack of losers," Danielle said. "But as long as we go home, I don't care. And I can't just leave Justin." She'd brought a file along as well as red polish and she was methodically grooming herself finger by finger. "By the way, I saw where Dad hid the keys to the rental car. He put them by the gas cap and closed that little door. So when we get back we can drive right on out of here." Then, "Man, I want to take a shower and clean this trip off of me. Except for Justin."

Gracie put her head in her hands.

"You don't understand love," Danielle said solemnly.

"You've known him for *two days*," Gracie said.

"Like I said. You don't understand love. I hope someday you will," Danielle said, studying her nails. "But you'll need to lose the attitude."

Gracie flopped back on her sleeping bag and kept one hand over her face.

The silence went on for a while, Danielle working on her nails and Gracie sweltering and miserable. Finally, Gracie said, "What about Dad?"

"I thought you said you didn't care about him, the way he treated you."

"I said that," Gracie said, "but I was mad at him. We can't just leave him here."

"Why not?" She sounded half miffed and half bored. Danielle seemed more than amenable to let Gracie make all the profound decisions, and didn't seem to like the idea of her waffling because that required her to once again become involved in the discussion.

Gracie said, "Because he paid for this trip and everything's gone wrong. I feel sorry for him, you know? I'm not sure Rachel even likes him anymore, and that was the whole point. I mean, besides us bonding with him in the wilderness and all of that. He's going with us."

"I like Rachel," Danielle said. "She's cool. She treats us like adults. Like we matter."

"Yeah.

"Unlike Dad, I mean."

"Yeah."

"I think he doesn't know whether we're little girls or young adults, so he goes with what's most comfortable to him—meaning we're his little girls. He can't think of us as real people. That's why he doesn't believe me when I say someone is spying on us or believe you when you say you heard something happen in the dark outside the tents."

Gracie spread her fingers apart on her face so she could look at her sister with wonder. Rarely did Danielle say something that made her think.

"What?" Danielle asked, defensive.

"Nothing."

"Anyway, wouldn't it be weird if Rachel turned out to be our friend even after she dumps Dad?"

"I hadn't thought of that."

Danielle said, "That's the kind of thing I think about all the time. You know how so many of our friends say they wish their parents could get back together? Well, I never think that. I think Mom is better off without him. I think he's kind of embarrassing, to be honest. He'd rather make that idiot Jed like him than show respect for his own daughters."

Gracie sat up and shook her head at her sister. "You're talking about our dad."

Danielle shrugged. "Really, basically, he's just another dude. He's got to show me something to get me to think otherwise, and I haven't seen it."

"Danielle!"

"Hey," she said, sliding her nail file back into its plastic holder like a sword into a sheath, "that's what I feel. So why shouldn't I say it?"

"Maybe you should think rather than just feel," Gracie said. "It's possible, you know."

Danielle shrugged. "Yeah, if you're a pathetic loser, I guess."

Gracie flopped back down on her back. "This is the worst trip I've ever been on."

Danielle said, "Welcome to Hell-o-stone Park, sister. Maybe we'll see some wolves and bears and birdies and other stupid animals on the way out."

Gracie moaned.

Danielle leaned over on her and put her lips to Gracie's ear. "Now let's go find Dakota and Rachel and my boy and Dad and get the friggin' hell out of here."

They avoided the camp and skirted along the edge of the trees toward where the horses were picketed.

"We'll ask Dakota to get our horses ready," Gracie said. "I can help her. Then we'll find Rachel."

Danielle nodded.

Shadows lengthened across the open ground as the sun sank beneath the tops of the trees. The temperature dropped a quick ten degrees in the shade.

"Leaving in the dark might be a problem for us," Gracie said.

"I don't care when we leave as long as we leave," Danielle said.

"There's Rachel," Gracie said, seeing her coming up from where the horses were. Their dad wasn't with her. And something was off about the way she walked; arms crossed around her like she was hugging herself, head down. She appeared deep in thought.

"Rachel," Gracie called.

Rachel's head snapped up. Her face was drawn and white.

"What's wrong?"

Rachel took a deep breath, as if trying to gain control of herself. She said, "Oh, girls, it's horrible. I just found Dakota down there. Somebody slit her throat and killed her. It just happened. Her body . . ."

Gracie gasped and Danielle froze beside her.

"This isn't a joke, is it?" Danielle asked.

Rachel shook her head and gestured behind her. Her eyes were rimmed with red and she looked like she could collapse. "There's so much blood," she said, and opened her arms so they could see it on the front of her shirt. Rachel said, "I turned her over to see if she was still alive, but . . ." She couldn't finish again. She was trembling.

Gracie gasped. "Could it possibly have been an accident?" she asked, her voice trembling.

"No."

"Did you see anyone?"

Rachel turned away, deflecting the question.

"Rachel," Gracie said, "who did you see down there?"

"She saw Jed," Danielle said. "Jed did it."

Rachel nodded her head and tears streamed down her cheeks, making them glisten in a shaft of sunlight.

"Oh my God," Gracie said, reaching out for Danielle so her legs wouldn't collapse. "She saw Jed kill Dakota."

Rachel nodded, apparently unable to speak.

"We've got to get out of here," Danielle said. "*Now.*"

Gracie watched as Rachel's horror transformed into anger. She reached out and grasped both sisters and leaned into them.

"Your dad and I were down by the horses. We heard them arguing and we hid. That's when Jed did it. And he just left her there and took his horse. He just left her there in the grass."

Danielle covered her mouth with her hand.

"Your dad asked me to get you out of here. He said he'd stay in the camp with the others and try to keep Jed under control until we're gone. Get your horses," she said. "I'm going to lead us out of here."

Gracie felt a flood of relief. Then: "What about everyone else?"

Rachel's eyes flashed. "I don't care about them and I don't know if we can trust anyone but each other anymore. It's time to take care of ourselves now. The rest can be on their own."

Gracie swallowed, "Even Dad?"

"I know," Rachel said, gripping her arm harder, "but it's what he asked me. He's going to quietly tell the others what we saw and get them to help him jump Jed and tie him up until we can get help. He doesn't want you two in the camp in case things go bad."

"Justin's coming with us," Danielle said, pulling away from Rachel and folding her arms over her breasts. "I won't leave him behind."

Rachel grimaced, but she seemed to realize she'd come up against an immovable object.

"Get him," she said. "We leave in five minutes."

Gracie and Danielle walked up the hill into the camp. They tried to not betray their anxiety or their plan. Gracie noted that Danielle was better at deception than she was, and she could only imagine how she looked so she covered her head with her hood and kept her eyes down. Jed wasn't there, and neither was her dad.

What was going on?

She followed her sister to where Justin was sitting on a rock. Danielle approached him, held out her hand, and Justin took it with a quizzical but amused look on his face. She led him away.

Walt didn't say a word.

As they led Justin back toward the horses, Gracie chanced a look over her shoulder. Donna Glode, Knox, and Walt stared at the fire, absorbed in their own thoughts.

36

From the edge of the clearing where he was resting the horses, Mitchell called, "Hey, Hoyt. When you get a minute you may want to come look what this guy has in his saddlebags."

Cody didn't ease up on the pressure he was applying with the muzzle of the rifle. He said, "In a minute, Bull."

But he noticed something pass across Wilson's bloody face.

"Christ," Wilson said. "You're Cody *Hoyt*?"

"That's right."

"Shit, I should have figured it out. I knew your uncle Jeter. We used to drink together at the Commercial Bar in Townsend."

Cody let up a bit simply because he was trying to process what Wilson said.

"You're a damned Hoyt," the man said. "A damned *Hoyt*." As if it meant something.

"Then who the hell are you?" Cody asked. "I've never heard of anyone named K. W. Wilson."

Wilson clammed up, and Cody stepped back and kicked him hard in the ribs. When the man grunted and curled away, Cody dropped on him with a knee in his back and snatched his wallet out of his jeans pocket.

The Montana auto license was in the front sleeve. "Jim Gannon," Cody said. "Shit, I know that name."

Gannon, like his uncle Jeter, was an outfitter who used to work out of Lincoln. Cody had never met him, but he'd heard stories. Gannon was a hard-drinking, hard-charging fourth-generation Montanan. He had a reputation as a poacher and a wild man, and Cody remembered hearing he'd been brought up on charges and had his outfitting license revoked and his hunting lodge shut down.

Cody said to Mitchell, "Bull, you know who we've got here?"

"Jim Gannon," Mitchell said, ambling over. "That's what I was going to show you. He's got a bunch of personal crap in his saddlebag with his name all over: 'Property of Jim Gannon.' I told you we were dealing with an outfitter. Hell, I thought he looked familiar. I guess I must have seen his picture in the paper once when they brought him up on charges."

Cody swung his rifle back over. "Why'd you register for this trip as someone named Wilson?"

Wilson/Gannon rasped, "Why d'you think?"

Cody said, "So Jed or anyone else in his office wouldn't recognize the name. It would have seemed kind of suspicious for a bent guide like yourself to pay all that money to go on a trip with dudes."

Gannon nodded, still trying to get his breath back from the kick.

"I think you should just shoot him now," Mitchell said, leaning against a tree. "He gives outfitters a bad name. I never knew him because he wasn't in the Montana Outfitters and Guides Association. Hell, he doesn't even know how to handle horses worth a damn."

"So I ask again," Cody said, "what the hell is going on?"

Gannon gathered himself and sat up with a moan. "Every inch of me hurts," he said.

"More is about to," Cody said, and shot him in the knee.

"Jesus!" Mitchell said, jumping back. "Why'd you do that?" The spent casing landed between his boots.

Cody said to Mitchell, "I've seen this particular method of inter-rogation work pretty well before." Thinking about the year before in Denver. It had certainly worked then, to a point.

Gannon howled and grabbed his mangled leg with both hands. Cody hoped he wouldn't pass out from shock before he started talk-ing. Nevertheless, he took careful aim at Gannon's other knee.

"Please, no, no . . . ," Gannon begged.

"Hoyt, I don't know about this," Mitchell said, shaking his head.

"Tell me why you're on this trip," Cody said to Gannon.

"We're trying to find that plane," Gannon shouted, fighting through the pain. "That goddamned plane that went down."

"What plane?" Cody asked, but as he said it he recalled something Larry had said. Something about a disabled private airplane flying south toward Yellowstone that was spotted by citizens in Bozeman but never reported missing by anyone. The incident had caused the assembling of the interagency Homeland Security search and rescue team and that was when Larry said he met Rick Doerring of the Park Service.

"That goddamned plane that went down last winter," Gannon said through clenched teeth. Black blood seeped through his fingers, which were laced around his shattered kneecap.

"What's in the plane?"

"Jesus. Money. Jesus. Drug money."

"Why go with Jed? Why didn't you just come up here on your own and go get it? Why involve all these people?"

Gannon was starting to shake. His teeth chattered. "It wasn't my fucking idea. Jesus, I'm going to bleed out and die."

"Let's hope," Cody said. "So whose idea was it? You said 'we.' "

"My partner. All my partner's idea. All of it."

Cody took a deep breath, fighting back the urge to shoot again. Mitchell hovered, shaking his head.

Cody said, "So your idea was to what? Come up here with Jed's clients and break off and find this damned plane? Use him so he could lead you here?"

Gannon nodded his head. "Yeah, that. We wanted to come on our own but with the snowpack and the flooding, this was the first time we could get to where we think the plane crashed. When we found out Jed was leading his clients where we wanted to go—and would be the first to get there anyway—we signed on. Believe me, there wasn't supposed to be all this trouble."

Cody gestured with the rifle, urging Gannon to keep talking.

"None of this other stuff—those three stupid guys back there—was supposed to happen. But that idiot Jed decided to take a different trail, and one of 'em—Glode—got mad about it. That and his wife going down with D'Amato. So he said he was going back on his own. We couldn't risk him getting back to the vehicles and telling the Park Service where we were going. What if they sent rangers after us? They might locate the plane before we did."

Cody thought the likelihood of the Park Service sending rangers to tell Jed McCarthy to get back on the established route was crazy and unlikely, but he didn't want Gannon to stop talking, so he urged him on.

"So I went with Glode. I tried to talk him into going back with the others, but he was stubborn and had a bug up his ass and he wouldn't turn around. And you know what happened. I had to stop him."

Cody took a step toward Gannon, still aiming down the sights at his other knee. "Why take out D'Amato and Russell, then?"

Gannon closed his eyes. His chin shook. "They wouldn't have found Glode or me and they might have gone all the way to the parking lot looking for us. There was a good chance they'd call the Park Service and report a couple of missing men. It was a worse situation than what happened with Glode, because at least that guy deserved it."

"So you shot them both point-blank when they found you," Cody said. "And left them to bleed out or wait for animals to find them. Thinking they'd be mauled beyond recognition if their bodies were ever found and maybe not even point to you."

Gannon rocked back on his haunches holding his knee. He said, "This whole damned thing is a clusterfuck. Everything's gone wrong."

Cody said, "So why did Jed take the other trail?"

"I don't know, I don't know . . . it's all his fault this happened."

"He didn't kill three people," Cody said, "or put my son in danger."

Gannon writhed in pain. "Worse," he said. *"Worse."* As if that somehow lessened his own guilt.

"So your partner is still with the others on the pack trip?" Cody said.

Gannon nodded, his eyes closed, his mouth contorted.

"Which one is he? Jed?"

Gannon either couldn't speak or refused to say.

"I said—"

"Damn you!" Gannon bellowed as his eyes shot open. He glared at Cody with unbridled hate. "You're a cop. I know you're playing rough and you'll think of some story to cover you later. I know you won't kill me. But I damned sure know she will."

Cody felt the hairs on his neck stand up. *"What* did you just say?"

37

Jed McCarthy was angry and anxious and almost missed the game trail he was seeking to go up the mountain. That Dakota was miffed at him was one thing. But to blatantly disregard his instruction to bring him another horse, to vanish like that leaving only his saddle on a stump, was another. And why did she take the lame horse with her? Where in the hell did she go when she should have been getting dinner ready for his clients?

So he'd gotten another damned horse from the herd and put his saddle on it and ridden out of there.

"Women," he said, as if it were a curse word.

He wondered if she'd be there when he got back to camp. He wondered whether—hoped—Tristan Glode, Tony D'Amato, and Drey Russell had returned as well. He didn't care about Wilson, never had.

If they were all back his world would be in order again, even if Dakota had split the blanket for good. He could cope for the rest of the trip without a petulant Dakota dragging him down.

He'd make sure that future didn't have any women like Dakota in it, he thought with a crooked grin.

As he wound his way up the mountain directly west away from the trail he caught a glimpse through the trees of a J-shaped glacier on the side of a mountain face. He recognized it and nodded to himself, then reached back and undid his saddlebag to compare it against the Google map printouts in his file. The file was missing, and he bellowed, "Dakota! *You bitch!*"

He thanked God she hadn't dug deeper and found the satellite phone. He'd never even told her it existed, or that he brought it along on every pack trip just in case he got into some kind of trouble. He was afraid she'd make a casual reference to it and a client would hear her and want to use it. Pretty soon, he'd have clients lined up wanting to call home, check on their kids, call the office, and so on. He was a purist about the wilderness and about the experience he wanted to impart on his trips, and that experience had very much to do with isolation and forcing his guests to not keep in contact with home.

But this was different. This was about *him.* He punched in the number he was told not to call under any circumstances until he was done with the trip and it rang three times before it was picked up.

"What?"

"This is Jed. I've got a problem."

"I know who the hell it is. It's not a good time."

"I said I have a problem. I need your help."

"You've got more problems than you know, Jed. I've been trying to reach you for two fucking days. Don't you ever turn that thing on?"

"No," Jed said. "I told you. I don't even tell anyone I have it. If someone heard me talking on it—"

"I know, I know, you already told me, for Christ's sake. But given the circumstances, I thought you'd at least *check* it."

Jed said, "Someone took the map."

Silence.

"I said—"

"I heard you! How in the hell did that happen? Who took it?"

"Don't worry," Jed said. "I know who it is and I'll deal with her later. She works for me. Correction: *worked* for me. I don't think she's smart enough to figure out what we're even looking for. But right now I'm practically there. I can see the glacier. I need you to send me that map again as an attachment. You can do that, can't you?"

"If she's got the map she might figure it out."

Jed took a deep breath and looked up at the sky. "She won't figure it out. I'll make sure she doesn't. I'll make up a story about something—don't worry about it. Right now, I need another copy of that map. Can you send it or not?"

A long sigh. "I told you it wasn't a good time. I'm on the way somewhere now. I've got to deal with a problem of my own."

"Are you on duty?"

"Yeah. But what I'm doing is off the books."

"Can you send it to me when you get back to your office?"

"Yeah." He was distracted. "Yeah, I can do that."

"How long before I can expect it, then?"

"I don't know. Forty-five minutes at the latest. Providing there's no one around."

Jed nodded. "Okay then. Good. So what's the other problem you referred to?"

"There's a cop after you."

Jed felt his insides contract. "*What?*"

"There's a cop after you. His name is Cody Hoyt, and he's completely fucking nuts. His son is on your trip, I guess. Jed, he somehow thinks there's a connection between some murders and someone on your trip. That's why he's after you."

Jed shook his head. "I don't understand. What murders?"

"The last one happened up here a week ago. He thinks whoever killed this guy—his name was Winters—is on your pack trip. He wants to find him."

"So what are you telling me?"

"To watch out. I lost track of him two nights ago in Bozeman, but he was definitely headed your direction."

"Are you saying he's in the park?"

"I don't know. I'm going to find out. That's where I'm headed right now. I know a guy who probably knows where he is."

"He's in the park?" Jed said again.

"I told you, I don't know."

"And what do you mean he thinks there's a killer on my trip? Who in the hell is that supposed to be?" Thinking: *If anyone, it's Wilson.*

"I don't have a name. I don't even have a description. I'm not sure *he* knows."

"The boy must be Justin because he's the only boy on the trip."

"Okay."

"Why in the hell would a killer book a pack trip? This makes no sense."

"I know, I know. I'm just telling you what I know."

"Look," Jed said, trying to keep his anger at bay, "You told me you'd take care of the back end. You told me all I'd need to worry about was finding that wreckage and you'd handle your end and make sure nobody put things together. You fucking told me you'd use all your . . . influence . . . to make sure I was the only one looking for that plane."

"I know all that. You think I don't?"

"I don't know anything," Jed said, shouting into the mouthpiece, "except you assured me you'd handle your end. What the hell is going on here? Can't you control a single fucking cop?"

A long sigh. "He's gone rogue. Nobody can control this guy. Believe me, I thought I'd put him out of the picture, but somehow he got away."

Jed said, "So what do you want me to do? Do you want me to just turn around and forget everything? Do you want me to quit? Well, I can't do that because I'm here. I see the glacier. This whole trip has fallen apart and I've got clients gone and angry and I'll probably lose my business if any of 'em tells the Park Service."

"Just calm down, Jed. I'll handle my end."

"You've fucked up your end, if you ask me."

"Look, I'm here. I'm ten minutes away from his house. I've got to go inside and get some answers. I'll call you back as soon as I know where Hoyt is. And I'll send you that map and the GPS coordinates the minute I get back to the office. Just don't fucking panic."

Jed said, "You'd better make this right. The rest of my damned life depends on it."

"I will. Don't worry. Now keep your phone on."

38

At the same time, two and a half miles away, Cody and Bull Mitchell hoisted Jim Gannon up over a high branch. They'd decided based on what Gannon had told them they had to move as quickly as they could to overtake the pack trip, and bringing along the wounded Gannon and four extra horses would slow them down. Using tape and bandages from Mitchell's first-aid kit, they'd bound up Gannon's knee the best they could and tied his hands and feet together. Mitchell had fashioned a seat harness out of rope they could use to lift him.

"Give me a couple of minutes," Mitchell said, breathing hard from the labor of pulling on the rope with Cody. "I need to get these spare horses picketed so they'll be okay."

Cody nodded and unhooked the satellite phone and powered it up. He had a good clear signal and no messages. He started to key in the number for Larry's secret cell phone, thought better of it, and called Larry's ex-wife's cell. She was a real estate agent and was never without it day or night.

"Cindy Olson."

"Cindy, this is Cody Hoyt. I'm out of town and I need to reach Larry."

"Oh, it's you. The man who shot our coroner."

It seemed like ages ago, Cody thought. "Yes, well, there's a good story that goes along with that but I'll need to tell you at a better time. Right now, it's urgent I get ahold of Larry."

"Ah," she said, "you probably tried his office and his cell but he didn't pick up."

"Sort of."

"Then you probably didn't hear. I'm surprised you didn't, since you two have such a deep bromance. Larry's been suspended. You can reach him at home, I suspect. Suggest to him that he spend some of his downtime looking for work because he's got a child support payment coming up."

"Why was he suspended?"

"Guess, Cody." And she hung up.

He called Larry's house. He lived outside of Helena near Marysville on U.S. Highway 279.

"Larry," Cody said.

There was a beat. Then, "It's you, you son of a bitch. Where *are* you? Did you get my messages?"

"I got 'em."

"Then why in the hell didn't you call me back?"

Cody said, "I don't have time to explain, but in a nutshell I got paranoid. I didn't want you to know where I was because of that fire in Bozeman."

"What are you saying?" Larry sounded hurt. "You thought I had something to do with that? Is that what you're saying?"

"I don't know what I was thinking," Cody lied. "Blame it on the DTs. I'm fucking miserable, but we got the bad guy. Or at least one of them."

"Who is it? And who the hell is 'we'?"

Cody outlined hiring Mitchell, and the trail of bodies leading them to Gannon. "He's here now," Cody said. "We hung him up in a tree so the bears and wolves won't eat him. The Park Service can cut him down and take him to a clinic. Not that I really care about that, but we'll need his testimony to nail his partner, who is also on the pack trip."

"His partner?" Larry sounded genuinely baffled. That made Cody feel better toward him.

"A woman."

"Ah, Rachel Mina," Larry said. Cody leaned into the phone, shocked Larry knew the name. "Although that's not her married name, which is Rachel Chavez."

"How do you know that?" Cody asked.

"You dumb shit, it was what I was trying to tell you when I called. I didn't know about Gannon, but I did know about Rachel Mina Chavez. It's called police work, and I think I connected all the dots. Of course, that's before they suspended me for withholding what I knew about *you*."

Cody felt his head begin to spin. "Tell me what you know," he said.

Larry sighed. Cody could anticipate from that sound Larry was going to roll it out in the only way he could. He glanced up to see if Mitchell was still taking care of the horses and saw he was. And Jim Gannon swung slowly in a circle over his head, passed out. The late evening sun made a long shadow across the meadow of Gannon's figure, and in silhouette it looked like the outfitter was hanging from the tree by the neck.

"We were looking at the wrong angle with those murders," Larry said. "At least I was. All I could think of was alcoholics. So how do we get a connection between all these alkies in four different parts of the country? The thing I was trying to figure out was if it were possible they were all in the same place at the same time, like we talked about. Like an ex-alcoholic convention or something. And if not that, something to do with their jobs. But their professions didn't lend that any hope. They might all travel from time to time, but not to the same places or for the same reasons. I couldn't figure out how to put them in the same place at the same time, or to have something in common to link them besides drinking. To all be exposed somehow to whatever would later cause them to be murdered."

Cody said, "You've got to get to it, Larry. We need to get going."

"I know, I know. But do you remember when you told me Winters said no matter what, you can find a meeting?"

"Yeah."

"So I got together with the brains at ViCAP and they were able to access his travel records. Winters flew exclusively on Delta out of Helena, so it wasn't difficult. Man, that guy was all over the west but nothing jumped out at us. But one of the FBI boys thought to pull the records from Shulze as well, thinking if we could cross-reference just one flight or destination between them—put the two of them in the same place at the same time—we'd have something to go on."

Cody started to pace back and forth through the grass. Adrenaline rushed through him.

Larry said, "October 27 of last year, both Winters and Shulze were on the same flight bound for L.A. They probably didn't even know the other was on the plane. Shulze was going to some academic conference at UCLA and Winters was connecting through LAX to Sacramento. But here's where it gets interesting: the flight didn't make it to LAX for two days because it got diverted to San Diego."

"Diverted?" Cody asked. "Why?"

"Wild fires," Larry said. "October 27 last year was the worst of the fires out there. They closed LAX for two days because of the smoke, and all the inbound flights were diverted to other airports. Winters and Shulze found themselves in San Diego October 27 and 28 with nothing to do.

"So we kept digging. William Geraghty was diverted to San Diego on a United flight for the same two days, and Karen Anthony was there visiting her sister."

Larry said, "So imagine the situation. Four alkies away from home. Three killing time at the airport hanging out, just waiting for an announcement so they could get back on their schedules, surrounded by airport lounges and bars and high tension all around. Karen Anthony is there with family, but keeps getting those old urges. So in that circumstance, where would they go?"

Cody said, "To an AA meeting."

"Bingo," Larry said. "So I find a detective in San Diego and run this theory by him and he buys it. So he starts doing the research and calls me back within an hour. An hour! And he tells me the specific AA meeting they all went to at a church. He even says he has photos of them going into and coming out of the meeting. He sends them to me and goddamn it if he isn't exactly right. I've got entrance and exit photos of Hank Winters, William Garaghty, Gary Shulze, and Karen Anthony."

"Hold it," Cody said. "Since when do the police run surveillance on who goes to AA?"

"Never," Larry said. "Unless they've got heavy surveillance going on somebody else who happened to go to the meeting. Like Luis Chavez, the now deceased head of the Chavez drug cartel based out of Tijuana. Seems he saw the light like all of these folks and would cross the border once a week to attend the AA meeting."

"Chavez," Cody repeated.

"Rachel Mina's ex-husband."

"I'm getting lost," Cody said, pacing faster.

Larry said, "It's no secret the cartels are at war. We know that. But what this San Diego cop tells me suddenly clears things up. Seems Chavez had a daughter named Gabriella who was a junior at the University of Colorado in Boulder. Gabriella was apparently the apple of his eye. She was from his first marriage, before he married Rachel Mina. The cartel fighting Chavez sent some guys north to kidnap Gabriella from the house Chavez had bought for her, and held her for ransom. They wanted Chavez to give them Tijuana and pay them millions in exchange for her. They knew he'd do anything—*anything*—to get her back. Apparently there was bad blood between Rachel and this girl, but that didn't matter to Chavez. So Chavez literally cashed out. We're talking *tens of millions* of dollars here, Cody. They agreed on a drop location in our country on neutral ground. The speculation was they took Gabriella to Jackson Hole, but nobody can confirm it. But that's where Chavez's plane was headed when it apparently had engine trouble and made it. So the bad guys assumed they'd been stiffed. They didn't believe Chavez's claims that the plane went down with their money inside, and it was beside the point because whatever happened they wouldn't get the loot. So those bastards took Gabriella with them to Laredo, Texas."

Cody felt his scalp crawl. He said, "Now I remember what happened to her."

"That's right," Larry said. "They murdered her and beheaded the body. After that, from what my San Diego guy said, it took just days for the bad guys to move in on Chavez's territory and take over. There was a bloodbath involving his holdouts, and Rachel wanted to fight, but Chavez was a broken man and let it all happen. When he started showing up at the meetings in San Diego the cops thought he was planning his comeback or something, but they didn't know at the time he'd lost his will to live or fight. But that's why they were watching the meetings. And shortly after that meeting," Larry said, "Chavez was found with a bullet in his brain down in Mexico."

Cody's head was spinning with all the information when suddenly it clicked. "Chavez told the story in the AA meeting," Cody said. "He told it to Geraghty, Shulze, Anthony, and Hank. He was confessing his sins, preparing to kill himself or be killed. But because everything that's said in those meetings is confidential and a lot of the time it's pure bullshit, nobody told."

Larry said, "But Rachel never knew that, and she wanted her money back and didn't want anyone else getting bright ideas. The San Diego detective said the Chavez cartel owned enough Mexican cops who were privy to what the San Diego cops were doing that they probably had copies of the photos. So Rachel knew who was in the meeting and who she had to shut up. By the way, Rachel was suspected of being involved in her husband's death, but the Mexican police never arrested her before she vanished. Now we know what she's been doing."

"Jesus," Cody said, glancing up at Gannon, slowly turning in the rope harness. "So she traveled across the country to find everyone who'd been at that meeting. She wanted them all out of the picture before she came here. She must have contacted Gannon thinking: he's an outfitter from Montana, he'd know his way around the park, where the plane with the money crashed."

Larry said, "Gannon probably came pretty cheap."

Cody said, "But how could an airplane crash in a national park and nobody know about it?"

"It's simpler than you think," Larry said. "You know about all the reports we get about aircraft taking off and landing on private strips. Those drug guys disable the tracking beacons and they don't exactly file flight plans. The plane might not even have been registered. If it was flying north to south to Jackson Hole instead of the other way, it wouldn't have attracted any undue attention. And the big thing is no one reported it missing. Our task force was assembled because a couple old folks thought they saw a plane that didn't look healthy flying toward Yellowstone. If it crashed somewhere close to where you are there sure as hell wasn't anyone around to see it come down."

Cody nodded. "So the only people who knew what was in the plane or where it likely crashed were Chavez's inside guys. Not even the bad guys knew where the plane was coming from. Rachel got her info from her husband's inner circle, but she had no way of getting here on her own. Except for Jed McCarthy's pack trip."

Bull Mitchell mounted his horse and signaled to Cody. He was ready to go. Cody waved a *just a second* wave.

"This Rachel," Cody said. "She must be a hell of a looker or a hell of a charmer."

"Both," Larry said. "A stone-cold manipulator with an ice cube for a heart."

Cody said, "She managed to get acquainted with all the victims. I wonder if she played her Rachel Chavez card on them? Maybe she called Hank and said, 'You met my husband in San Diego. He thought you were a wonderful man and he wanted me to give something to you for maintaining his confidence.' Knowing Hank and the importance he placed in mentoring and trust, he'd buy it. Especially coming from a woman."

"That's what I figured, too," Larry said. "She used their bond of confidentiality against them. Shulze and Garaghty, for example, never even told their wives who they were meeting. And she cleaned up her tracks by burning down the homes she killed them in and took things like AA coins—anything that would prevent us from connecting the dots."

Cody paused. Gannon's shadow now stretched all the way across the meadow into the bank of trees. He said, "You said you called the Feds. So they're on their way?"

"Should be. I haven't talked to them since this morning, when I got suspended. I didn't tell them about you because I didn't know where the hell you were. I kind of thought you might be in a drunk tank in Ennis, so they don't know you're there."

"I'll watch for helicopters," Cody said. "I haven't seen anyone but killers and dead bodies all day."

"I'd be surprised if they show up tonight," Larry said. "I can't see them trying to find you guys or the pack trip in the dark."

"Shit."

"Yeah."

"I'm going to kill her, Larry."

"Don't tell me that."

"She's dead," Cody said. "She just doesn't know it yet. For what she did to Hank and the others, for putting Justin in this situation, she's going to die."

"Ah, man . . ."

He glanced up. "We've got Gannon for testimony. We don't need her to make the case."

"Cuff her," Larry said. "Bring her in. Hell, I want to meet this dame and look into her eyes. I want to see for myself what's there."

Cody walked toward his horse. Mitchell was clearly getting impatient. Cody said, "Larry, one more thing. I called that cell number you gave me earlier today. Somebody picked up but wouldn't say anything. What was that about?"

A long pause. "Shit, Cody, I don't know. When did you call?"

"Around ten."

"That's when I was in Tubman's office getting my skin peeled off for not telling him you'd left Helena."

"Where was the phone?"

"In my briefcase. Next to my desk. Oh shit," Larry said.

"Somebody answered your phone," Cody said. "Somebody listened to me. Somehow they know I'm here."

"I can't imagine who . . . ," Larry said. Then: "Hold on a second. Somebody's banging on my door. I'll be right back."

Cody said, "Somebody's been tracking me, Larry. Someone tried to burn me alive on the way here."

He realized Larry had stepped away.

Cody heard the receiver thunk on Larry's kitchen table. He heard a greeting, a shout, and a gunshot. Then someone picked up the phone. Cody heard breathing. Like before.

"Larry?" Cody asked.

The connection ended.

39

Gracie asked Rachel, "How did you and my dad meet?" She couldn't get him, or what Rachel had told them, out of her mind.

They were riding down the trail Jed had taken, following his hoof-prints. Rachel, Gracie, Danielle, and Justin. They'd left the camp under Rachel's direction, and they'd moved quickly and quietly. Rachel made a quick trip to her tent to retrieve a backpack that was now lashed to the skirt of her saddle and hung low like there was something heavy in it.

The last moments of the evening sun reached through the trees and lit the snowcapped peaks of the eastern mountains, fusing them with a good-bye wink of neon orange and pink. Gracie had barely had enough time to retrieve her hoodie before they left and she was glad she had. It seemed cooler than it had the night before and she was grateful for the warmth from Strawberry between her thighs.

"I said—"

"I heard you," Rachel replied. There was a cool businesslike edge to her voice, and Gracie recoiled.

"Probably the wrong time to ask," Gracie said. "I'm sorry."

Rachel rode ahead, her face set into the mask Gracie had seen earlier. Gracie thought, *She's distracted. She's leading three teenagers through the back of beyond and she's unsure she can do it. She's distracted.*

"It seems awful to just leave him like that," Gracie said, as much to herself as to Rachel.

"It's what he wanted. Would you rather go back?" Rachel said with the same edge in her voice as before. "You can go back there if you want to. I told you what happened."

"No," Gracie said softly.

"I just had a human being die in my arms," Rachel said, not looking over her shoulder at Gracie or trying to soften her tone. "And I saw the man who did it."

Gracie felt sick.

"We've got to find help," Rachel said. "We've got to get out of here."

From behind, Justin said, "Excuse me, Miss Mina?"

Rachel jerked around in the saddle and looked past Gracie to Justin. "Yes?"

"I'm wondering why we're on this trail? If we're headed back to the trailhead this is the wrong direction, I'm pretty sure."

"It's the trail we're taking," Rachel said.

"I don't get it," Justin said, undeterred. "Seems like we're going the wrong way."

Gracie looked ahead for the first time at the trail itself. It was unmarked except for a single set of horse tracks. She was confused.

"What's going on?" Danielle asked from behind them.

"Nothing," Rachel said sharply. "Just please keep quiet, all of you."

Danielle rode up beside Gracie and leaned in to her. "I've been thinking," she said.

Gracie refrained from expressing surprise.

"Remember when we got to the airport in Bozeman? Dad wasn't there."

"I remember."

"Where do you suppose he was?"

Gracie shrugged. "I don't know."

"I don't know either. But he's the one who made such a big deal out of this trip. Knowing him, he should have been there three hours early pacing around and getting all worried about us."

Gracie nodded. "That does sound more like him."

"There's been something going on since the beginning," Danielle said. "He's been up to something. And why wasn't he in camp like he was supposed to be?"

"There has to be an explanation," Gracie said, unsure of her own words.

"Tell me when you come up with one," Danielle said, and slipped back into line.

Ten minutes later, Rachel said, "Here he goes," and turned her horse from the trail onto a faint game route that went west into the trees. She looked back to make sure everyone was with her. Gracie refused to meet her eyes and kept her head down. She couldn't stop thinking of what Rachel said she saw, and the fuel Danielle had added to the fire.

"This way," Rachel said, spurring her horse onto the new trail.

"Now I'm sure we're headed the wrong way," Justin said.

Gracie watched Rachel carefully. How her chest swelled with a big intake of breath, how her mouth was set, how her eyes looked like slits because the skin on her face was pulled back tight. She turned her head and glared at Justin and seemed to be holding back her words.

"Stay in line," Rachel said to Justin. "And stop talking. I'm trying to save us all."

"It just doesn't make sense to me," Justin said. "I mean, we want to go back to the vehicles and we're heading up into the trees on the side of a mountain. I just don't get it."

"No," Rachel Mina said, "you don't."

"Danielle?" Justin said.

"Don't ask me," Danielle said.

Gracie wondered exactly who was leading them and who Rachel

had become. She felt sick to her stomach and wished she'd talked to her father and at least said good-bye.

And as she watched Rachel ride ahead, she noticed the bulge on her right calf where the top of her boot was. Something pushed out against the fabric of her jeans. Gracie leaned over to her left to confirm Rachel's left calf didn't look like that. It was as if something was protruding out of Rachel's boot top. Like a stick.

Or, Gracie thought with sudden realization, like the handle of a knife.

"I met your father in Minneapolis," Rachel said to Gracie. The tone of her voice was warm, like it had been until recently. Like she was trying to reestablish their friendship. "I was there on business and I was staying at the Grand Hotel. My laptop was acting up and I was frustrated I couldn't get it to work so I went down to the bar. He was at the hotel meeting a client, he said. I told him about my computer and he offered to take a look at it. I brought it down to the bar and he fiddled with it and had it working again in no time flat. Then we started talking."

Gracie said nothing. She felt uncomfortable thinking of her dad in any situation where she wasn't with him. She knew he was a man, and he likely had wants and needs. But she was sorry she'd asked Rachel the question in the first place, and wasn't sure she wanted to hear the answer. And she didn't want to set her off again.

Rachel said, "I told him I'd lost my husband recently as well as my stepdaughter. He said he was divorced but he had two daughters he was devoted to. That's when I first heard about you and Danielle and how much you meant to him. I was touched."

"That's nice," Gracie mumbled.

"Then he told me about you two and this trip. He was so excited and passionate that I just fell for him. We kept in touch and he suggested I come along so I could meet you two. So he could introduce us. I'd always wanted to see Yellowstone Park and he seemed to have it all organized and planned, so I came along. I had no idea . . ." Her sentence trailed off.

Gracie said, "Rachel, he wasn't in the camp back there. Jed was gone and Dad wasn't there."

Rachel nodded in a sympathetic way. Then: "It must be hard to think of your father as a coward," Rachel said. "I can't even imagine what's going through your head right now, so tell me. Maybe I can help."

Gracie didn't want to answer. Something about the way Rachel was asking, in such an intimate way, put her off. The swing from warm to cold back to warm made Gracie feel unbalanced, as if the ground beneath her feet was buckling. Finally, Gracie said, "I don't know what I think."

"That's understandable," Rachel said. "It's the worst when someone you love does something beyond comprehension. It's as if you never knew that person at all. As if your entire life together was based on a set of false assumptions. When it happens, it's like everything you ever thought or knew turns out to be based on clouds and lies. You start to wonder, am I the fool here? Am I the gullible idiot who let a *man* ruin me because he was weak and tainted? It's just so hard when it happens, and it eats at the very marrow of your soul until you either give in or decide to get out there and make your own way. You need to take back what you deserve, what belongs to you."

Gracie said, "I don't understand what you're saying."

Rachel shot a puzzled look at Gracie over her shoulder, then shook her head and shrugged. Gracie got the impression Rachel had said things she didn't mean to say.

"Never mind me," Rachel said. "Sometimes I just get going. You know how it is."

No, Gracie thought. She looked again at the backpack Rachel had strapped to her saddle. Something heavy in it. And Gracie thought about the fact that she hadn't seen Dakota's body. No one had, except Rachel. Just like she hadn't seen her father. She took it on Rachel's word he was there with her when they saw Jed murder Dakota.

As she rode she found herself looking hard at Rachel in a different light. Justin was wrong. There might be good in everybody, but there could also be evil.

Gracie continued to stare while her stomach knotted. There was a bulge next to Rachel's calf that could be the handle of a long knife. Rachel said Dakota had her throat cut.

Gracie couldn't help herself. She lurched to the left and got sick, emptying her stomach on the grass.

Rachel looked back with suspicion masquerading as concern, and said, "Are you okay, darling? Is this whole thing getting to you, poor girl?"

Dusk gave way to darkness.

40

Jed McCarthy dug his headlamp out of his jacket and strapped it on the crown of his cowboy hat. He wasn't ready to turn it on yet because there was still enough light to see, but that wouldn't last much longer.

Even after years of wilderness pack trips, he was still slightly awed by twilight in the mountains when for a short period of time a natural transition unfolded as the wind stopped and the hidden animals became still and quiet and the nocturnal predators began to stir awake. It was immensely quiet and he could hear each footfall of his horse and his own nervous breathing.

Ahead of him, when the trees parted, he could see the massive J shape of the glacier in the bald side of the mountain. The glacier glowed light blue in the afterlight and it looked clean and pure and it seemed to beckon him.

His horse labored up the trail, climbing with a rocking motion. Jed sat forward in the saddle, urging him on. They continued to rise, switching back on sharp corners, but always going up. The pitch of the mountainside was getting so sharp he could reach out and touch the wall to his right at times. As it got darker he prayed the trail was passable and had not been blocked over the winter by rockslides or deadfall.

Finally, the sky opened up and although it wasn't pitch-dark yet he could see the sudsy wash of stars in the cloudless sky. The full moon was rising and would soon take over the sky and keep the mountain illuminated.

His senses were on full alert. He was looking for anomalies. He noted a smudge of pale color in the shadowed branches of a pine tree and it caught his attention because it was out of place. He rode over and leaned and reached deep into the needles to retrieve it. It had some heft but was pliable and he pulled it out. A perfect little bird's nest. Empty. The materials used to build it seemed unnatural, a blending of paper and fabric. He shook it and noted how spongy it was.

Birds and mice made nests of whatever material was available. It seemed to Jed much too far from anywhere for the birds to use man-made fabric, but there it was. What had they found?

He dropped the nest to the ground and rode on.

He was almost unaware of it at first, the dusting of snow on the ground in his peripheral vision. It was scattered and mixed in with the mat of pine needles.

Then he thought, *Snow?* In July?

He looked up. It wasn't snowing, and it certainly wasn't cold enough. Could it have snowed earlier in the day?

"This makes no sense," he mumbled to himself while he pushed his horse farther, up the trail and finally to the top and he emerged on a long flat bench of rock.

He reined to a stop to take it all in. The glacier loomed above him like a dimly lit billboard. The bench was solid rock but puckered in places where shallow pools of water gathered from recent rains. Straight ahead of him, toward the face of the mountain, full-grown pine trees that had found purchase in cracks of the rock were knocked down. He could see where they'd been snapped off because the jagged trunks stood like a line of fence poles.

Snow was everywhere on the ground but it wasn't cold, and he dismounted. His boots thumped on the solid rock, and he led his horse to the side where the snow was thickest, where it was caught in short grass.

He clicked on his headlamp and squatted down. The headlamp pointed wherever he looked, and he reached out to touch the snow.

Scraps of paper. Thousands of them. None bigger than a square inch. It was the same material that had been used to construct the bird's nest. He grasped the largest scrap he could find and lifted it into the pool of light. A pair of hooded and wise eyes stared back from the scrap. He recognized the eyes, and said, "Ben Franklin."

He stood, still holding the scrap between his thumb and forefinger. With his other hand, he reached up and twisted the lens of his headlamp to make the beam sharper.

At the far end of the bench, beyond the sheared-off trees, looking like the last glimpse of a whale sounding off the coast, the V-shaped tail of the airplane stuck straight up out of a crevice where it had fallen after crashing the winter before.

41

"What is that out there in that field?" Mitchell grumbled. "An elk? It's almost gettin' too dark to see."

Cody looked up and squinted. Ahead of them, to the left of the trail in a moon-splashed clearing, was a horizontal dark form elevated above the grass. The form had been still as they approached but now it moved a few feet to the right. The figure was hard to make out because it was dark against a green-black wall of pine trees.

"Damn if it isn't another stray horse," Mitchell said. The string of docile horses was behind him. "But it looks like there's something on it."

Cody held his satellite phone up to his ear and was talking with Edna at dispatch in Helena. He was glad she was on duty and he'd ignored her pleas to tell her where he was and what had happened since she'd seen him last. When she took a breath, he said, "Edna, send a car up to Larry's house in Marysville. I was talking to him ten minutes ago and I got cut off. I think something happened to him."

She repeated, "Something happened to him? What?"

"I don't know. But I've called back four times since and he won't pick up. Edna, send whoever you can as fast as you can and warn them there may be someone else in Larry's house. Tell them to nail the guy and hold him. Go!"

"Cody—"

"*Go!*" Cody barked, and punched off.

Mitchell and Cody rode up to the stray horse. Mitchell said, "Be calm, Hoyt. Don't rush it or charge it or you'll make it panic and run away. Don't bark out *Go!* anymore."

Cody hung slightly back and let Mitchell walk his gelding to the horse.

There *was* something on its back. Cody's first thought was it was a roll of carpet or a set of slim panniers the way it hung over on both sides of the horse. He could see the horse didn't have a halter or bridle.

"Easy now," Mitchell cooed to the horse.

It was a bay and it took a few unsteady steps forward as Mitchell approached. Cody said, "He's lame."

"Yup," Mitchell said, slipping off his mount and walking patiently toward the bay. With a movement as quick as it was gentle, he slipped a rope over the bay's neck to keep it in place. The horse seemed docile but Cody could see white on the edges of its eyes. It wouldn't take much to set it off.

"Oh, no," Mitchell said with what sounded like genuine sadness. "We've got a woman this time."

With that, he turned the bay and walked it a few steps into the moonlight.

Her body was draped over the back of the horse facedown. Long brown hair hung limply, obscuring her face and ears. Her hands had been tied under the belly of the bay to her boots to keep the body secure.

Cody gritted his teeth, and said, "Shit."

"Look at this," Mitchell said, pointing to a thin gash on the bay's haunch that glistened with fresh blood. "They tied the body on and gave the horse a prod to get it running away."

Mitchell looked up. "Do you know who she is?"

"I think so."

"Want to make sure?"

Cody tried to swallow, but couldn't. He nodded.

Mitchell gently grasped her hair with one hand and cupped her chin in the other and lifted her face up into the light.

Cody could see the gaping wound across her throat and he tasted bile in his mouth.

"Her name was Dakota Hill," Cody said, his voice dry. "And we're going to go find who killed her before there's no one left."

They approached the camp cautiously, even though Cody's inclination was to storm it like Vikings. He could see a fire going, but only four people around it. Justin wasn't one of them. Rachel Mina and Jed were gone as well.

There were four adults huddling around the fire. The firelight on their faces made them look gaunt and shell-shocked.

Mitchell had agreed to stay back in the trees to cover him with his hunting rifle as Cody walked his horse up. He kept looking for others in the camp. After all, there were nine tents pitched neatly in a meadow to the north of the camp. No one seemed to be in them.

Cody had his rifle out and across the pommel as he rode up. He was locked and loaded. He'd checked his .40 to make sure there was one in the chamber with a full twelve-rounds in the magazine.

Before they even knew he was there, before anyone looked up to see a strange rider approaching from the dark, Cody could feel a palpable sense of doom from the people sitting around the fire. Like they'd given in, defeated.

He recognized Walt immediately. His Richness sat there with his hands hung between his knees, his head down. The skeletal woman must be Donna Glode. The younger, slim man who looked out of place had to be James Knox. And the nervous man, the one who sat by the others but didn't seem to be with them, must be Ted Sullivan.

Cody said, "Everybody stay where they are, I'm a cop."

Walt said, "Cody? Is that you?"

"Yeah, Walt. Where the hell is my son?"

Walt gathered himself to his feet and swallowed. "He's gone, Cody. I don't know where."

"Jesus," Cody hissed, "what do you mean you don't know?"

Donna Glode looked up from the fire. "Four more horses are missing. We think Justin is with the two Sullivan girls and Rachel Mina. They sneaked out of here without a word to anyone."

Cody turned to Ted Sullivan: "Where are your girls?"

"I don't know," Sullivan said, standing with closed fists, "but I want to find them. I'm coming with you."

Cody snorted. "Can you ride?"

"Not really."

"Cody," Mitchell said as he approached from the shadows, "I hate to break it to you like this, but you can't ride worth a damn either."

Cody said to Mitchell, "You'll stay here with these three?"

Mitchell nodded.

Cody said to Walt, "Do you want to come, too?"

Walt sighed and looked away. "I'll stay," he said softly.

Cody shook his head, disgusted. To Ted Sullivan, Cody said, "Come on, then."

42

Gracie noticed how Rachel Mina's shoulders tensed as she spurred her horse from the trail up into the open. Then Strawberry nickered and a horse up ahead nickered back. Rachel didn't turn around in her saddle but Gracie saw the woman's hand move back and untie the string bow on the top of the pack she'd retrieved from her tent.

Gracie was beside herself. She had nothing but speculation to go on but with every foot they rode higher up the trail she became more convinced that everything they'd believed an hour before back at Camp Two was a fantasy. She hurt deeply and wanted to cry out for her dad and for herself.

But there was little she could do. Rachel rode ahead on the trail and both Danielle and Justin were behind Gracie. The steep wall of the mountain hemmed her in on her right and the ground dropped off to the left. She couldn't turn and run, or even turn to talk to her sister to convey her fears. It was getting dark and cold. She had no weapon.

Rachel's horse stepped up and over a solid lip of granite and Gracie could hear hoofbeats clatter on solid rock. In a moment Strawberry was on top as well. Danielle and Justin were right behind her.

Rachel had reined to a stop next to a riderless horse tied to the trunk of a tree. She turned in her saddle and whispered, "I'm going to protect you. Do you understand?"

Justin said, "Protect us? All I see is Jed's horse."

Rachel ignored him. "Everybody get off. We're going to walk the rest of the way. I need you all to keep completely silent, and I mean that."

Gracie looked to the others. Danielle looked miffed. She hated to be told what to do, especially if it involved silence. Justin was confused, and he scowled at the older woman.

Reading the same reaction Gracie had seen, Rachel reached back into the open pack and came out with a large handgun. She waved it toward them.

"Get off," she said. "Now."

"Where'd you get that?" Justin asked, swinging off his horse. "I thought nobody was supposed to—"

"Justin," Danielle said sharply, cutting him off. She slid off her horse as well.

Gracie felt fear grip her insides and seem to clamp her legs to Strawberry. She wasn't sure she could move.

"You too," Rachel said to her. "*Especially* you."

Gracie found the will somewhere and stiffly climbed down.

"Listen," Rachel said to them, dismounting herself. "I don't want you to be alarmed. I brought this for self-protection and I'm glad I did."

She moved closer to them as she talked so she wouldn't have to raise her voice. Gracie noticed Rachel kept the revolver down by her side, but not exactly pointed away from them. And she also noticed that when Rachel climbed down from her horse her pant leg had ridden up and the knobby end of the knife handle in her boot was now out in the open. Gracie shot a glance at her sister and Justin to see if they'd picked up on the same thing. They hadn't.

"Look," Rachel said, leaning closer. "That's Jed's horse but obviously he isn't here. I don't know where he is but we can't be too cautious. We need to walk along here until we can find him. I hope nothing's happened to him or anyone else is up here. But," she said, gesturing toward the gun, "I want to be ready if there are any surprises."

Justin and Danielle nodded. They probably didn't fully grasp what Rachel was saying, Gracie thought, because Rachel made no sense. But she'd said it urgently and with gravity and it had worked on them.

Gracie said, "This isn't about getting out of here, is it?"

Rachel looked over at her with icy contempt. She said, "We can talk later, Gracie. Right now I need you to stay with me here and keep quiet. Do you understand?"

"She does," Danielle said, and elbowed Gracie in the back.

"Good," Rachel said, giving Gracie another glance for good measure. "Follow me."

Gracie couldn't really feel her legs, although they seemed to move okay. She led Strawberry through the darkness behind Rachel, followed by the others. *Protect them from whom?* she thought.

She scarcely registered the snowlike substance gathered wherever there were tufts of grass.

But when she looked up over Rachel's shoulder she saw a shaft of yellow light flash across the tops of the trees to the right, then to the left. The effect reminded her of Hollywood floodlights coursing through the sky from the ground. Then she heard a muffled thump and clank up ahead.

She was about to speak when Rachel snapped on her headlamp and illuminated the white metal tail of the airplane.

An airplane?

"What the hell is *that*?" Justin said.

"Shhhh," Rachel cautioned him, holding a finger to his lips. Then, whispering, "All of you come up beside me. Bring your horses. Stand by me on both sides."

Gracie hesitated. What were they doing?

"Come on," Rachel said, heat in her voice. She was addressing Gracie directly.

Reluctantly, Gracie walked up and stopped on Rachel's right. Danielle and Justin stood abreast on Rachel's left. All of their horses milled and sighed behind them. The thumping and banging continued from the opening of the crevice, out of view.

Rachel raised her pistol toward the tail of the plane, and called, "Jed, you can come out now."

The sounds stopped.

"Jed," Rachel said, "we're here. We know what you've found. You need to come out now."

Gracie held her breath. The night was still except for the gentle shuffling of the horses behind them, nosing along the rock surface for blades of grass.

Suddenly, Jed McCarthy's hat appeared above the rim of the crevice, followed by his face. Rachel's headlamp light lit his features. His brow was furrowed in confusion and his mouth, as always, was hidden by his heavy mustache. He had a headlamp on as well, and the beam bobbed from Justin across to Gracie. That's what she'd seen, Gracie thought, the beam of Jed's headlamp escaping from within the crevice as he moved around down there.

"You found it," Rachel said, "but it's still my money. Now Jed, we need to see your hands. Pull your hands out and put them out in front of you on the rock."

Then Gracie realized what Rachel had done. She'd gathered them around her in case Jed came out shooting. Not only would Jed think he was outnumbered, but a bad shot would kill a kid. They were standing, unaware hostages, she thought. And she knew at that moment every suspicion she'd had toward Rachel was true.

Jed said, "Yours?" But he pulled his hands out and put them on the rock. He had nothing in them, but the backs of his knuckles were smudged with dirt or soot.

Rachel said, "Mine. I guess I should be surprised someone else was after it, but I'm not."

Jed raised one of his hands to shadow his eyes from the glare of

Rachel's headlamp. He said, "I see you got Justin and Danielle with you. Gracie, too. What, are they part of your *gang*?" When he said the word he grinned. He shook his head and said, "That goddamned Dakota. She just can't keep her mouth shut, can she?"

Gracie thought there must be something wrong with him. Rachel held a gun on him and he was making jokes? Then she realized Jed assumed Dakota had not only told them about the printouts she'd found, but that he thought she was still alive.

Which meant . . .

"Look," Jed said, chinning behind him toward the hidden fuselage of the plane, "I've been down there and it ain't pretty. The pilot and copilot are long dead. They're suspended from their seatbelts and the scavengers have been working on them for months. Worse," he said, looking directly at either the muzzle of the gun or Rachel's eyes or both, "the birds and mice have shredded whatever money is left. I haven't been able to find a single bill that isn't chewed up. That isn't to say maybe if I keep digging I might find a bundle of cash somewhere the rodents haven't chewed through, but I've been at this twenty minutes and I'm discouraged as hell."

Gracie glanced over at Rachel. Her face was frozen into a porcelain mask of rage. Her lips looked almost blue. Her voice was tight and threatening when she said, *"I don't believe you."*

43

Cody spurred his horse wildly up the mountainside on the well-trod trail in the dark. He felt out of control because he was; he'd lost his balance once and slipped down the side of Gipper and nearly tumbled to the ground under his hooves but managed to pull himself upright. A few minutes after, he'd been swept out of the saddle backwards by riding under a low-hanging branch he couldn't see in the dark. Cody's shoulders and back ached where he'd hit the ground and the branch left a gash across his nose that oozed blood. He felt his ear burning where he'd been injured and realized he'd probably left the scab from it back on the branch. Ted Sullivan had done no better, and he'd fallen straight off the back of his horse and said he was pretty sure his tailbone was broken.

Cody relied on his horse to find the rest of the herd up ahead. That, and there was nowhere to go but up.

It was full dark in the trees now except for the perfectly blue-white orb of the full moon that winked down through openings. Cody was astonished how bright it was in the clearings now that the moon was up, and how the stars lit the ground as well, like an upside-down city illuminating overhead clouds. Without electric lights around for dozens of miles, the forest was capable of lighting itself, he thought. *Who knew?*

He was starting to question himself if they were on the right path when he saw a gold splash of light up ahead on the side of a tree. The top of the J-shaped glacier came into view and Cody heard a sharp voice, then another.

Cody pulled to a stop on Gipper and Sullivan's horse slammed into him and both horses crow-hopped away from each other. He held on to the saddle horn and kept his head down but heard Sullivan fall heavily behind him with a grunt. Gipper calmed down, and he looked back, making sure Sullivan's horse was in its proper place and not crowding him again. "Horses, Jesus," Cody said under his breath. "They're worse than kids."

When he dismounted after clearing his rifle from the sheath, he heard rather than saw the thundering of Sullivan's horse running away back down the mountain. Sullivan lay in a heap, writhing. Cody tied off Gipper to a tree trunk and crab-walked up the last twenty feet of the trail before it leveled. As he neared the top the voices got louder.

Painfully, he straightened his legs and rose up until he could see over the lip of the flat rocky bench. Horses blocked his view, but between their legs he could see four people standing side by side with their backs to him. Beyond them was the tail of an airplane and Jed McCarthy's hands waving around in a beam of light as he talked. He appeared to be mostly underground, with only his head and shoulders visible. The dented white metal of the tail stood out in bizarre juxtaposition to the rock and trees that overwhelmed the area, but Cody instantly could see why it hadn't been spotted from the air.

Justin was there. He recognized him because his son towered over the others. Justin held hands with a girl with long dark hair. He could tell by their rigid grip that the situation they were in was tense. A woman he couldn't yet identify but guessed was Rachel Mina was next to them pointing a handgun toward the aircraft. Next to Mina/Chavez on her right was a slim younger girl shifting her weight nervously from foot to foot.

Cody spun and ducked back down and jogged down the trail to

where Sullivan was. The man had managed to sit up and rest his back against a trunk. His face was contorted with pain.

Cody leaned in to him and whispered, "They're up above. All of them. I'm not sure what's going on yet, but I need you to stay here and not make a sound."

"Are my daughters there?"

"I'm pretty sure. There are two girls, but I can't see their faces. But it looks right. My son's there, too."

"Don't let anyone hurt them."

Cody reached out and squeezed Sullivan's shoulder. He noticed how the man was positioned by, in effect, holding his buttocks in the air by digging in his bootheels and flexing his legs to avoid contact between his tailbone and the ground.

"Must hurt," Cody said.

Sullivan nodded frantically.

"Don't yell," Cody said, and left him there. "Let me do my work here."

Jed tried to stifle the grin that pulled on the sides of his mouth. Rachel Mina didn't respond. In fact, the glint in her eyes and the set of her face said *trouble*.

He ignored the teenagers even though he wasn't sure why they were there. They didn't seem to know what was going on, the way their eyes shot back and forth from Rachel to him as if watching a tennis volley. Still, he felt responsible for them. They were his clients.

"Rachel," Jed said, "there's been a big misunderstanding, obviously. We can work this out. A couple of nights ago Dakota handed me some printouts she said she found in Wilson's tent, but she must have been in the wrong damned tent. She must have been in *your* tent.

"I got curious as hell and wanted to see what he was looking for, so I rode up here tonight. How could I know there was a plane crash, or what was in the plane? Come on."

Gracie thought, *He's lying.*

Dakota had said Jed had some kind of scheme going. This was it.

Jed had fed them a story to convince them all to take an alternate route that would get him closer to the location.

He'd left Camp Two to try and find his missing clients, he'd said. So why was he up here on the side of a mountain, at least a mile off the trail?

She stole a look at Rachel Mina. She didn't buy it, either.

So why did he keep smiling?

Cody's sight lines were blocked by the horses and he couldn't get a bead on Mina. He could clearly see her forearm and hand gripping the pistol, but the heavy front shoulders of a horse blocked the rest of her. Shooting guns out of hands was reserved for old Western movies. He needed a bigger and better target.

Feeling his way, he shinnied along the lip to his right. As he did so he got brief vignettes of Justin, Mina, and the girls through the horses' legs, like viewing a set piece through the blades of a slowly spinning fan. He could see Jed clearly now, lit up in Mina's headlamp. Jed seemed surprisingly relaxed, smiling even. Cody had a thought: were Jed and Mina in it together? Was this a falling out among conspirators?

But when he got a quick glimpse at Rachel Mina's face and posture, he concluded it didn't matter. The woman was cold as ice, and determined.

Jed said, "You need to let me crawl on up out of here, Rachel. I've got one foot on a ledge of the crevice and the other on a piece of metal. Either one might give the way I'm balancing myself. If you want, you can come over here and shine your light down this hole. You'll see what I saw: dead guys, and a whole shitload of shredded cash. Below that, it drops down farther than hell. I couldn't even see the bottom of this crevice, even before it got full dark."

Mina didn't budge. He couldn't tell what she was thinking. He was getting tired of looking straight into the wide O of the muzzle of her revolver.

Finally, he said, "Rachel, there's something you've got to know because this is getting old. When Dakota went to the wrong tent the other night she found that gun. Here, let me show you something. Don't worry, I'm not armed."

He slipped his right hand along the rock and cautiously dropped it down out of view, never taking his eyes off her. Wondering if she'd pull the trigger before he could show her.

Gracie braced for an explosion while Jed took one of his hands out of view. The man, she thought, was incredibly brave or foolish. Or he knew something no one else did.

Then she thought she heard something—a grunt or moan—from back beyond the horses and broken trees where the trail came up to the rock ledge. Had someone followed them?

She looked at Rachel out of the corner of her eye to see if she'd heard it as well. If she had, Gracie concluded, she showed no reaction. Gracie guessed Rachel was so focused on Jed and what he was doing she'd blocked everything else out.

Cody wanted to holler to Ted Sullivan to get the hell back. The man had crawled up the trail and was at the lip, peering across the rock toward the scene. He'd grunted in pain as he hefted himself to see.

Cody tried to get Sullivan's attention by waving at him. But Sullivan couldn't or wouldn't look over.

Instead, Cody turned his attention to the plane. One of the horses had shifted slightly to the left and he could see the side of Mina's face clearly. The background was good; the teenagers were to the sides and wouldn't be hit by an exiting bullet or a possible miss.

Cody lowered himself to the rock and pulled the rifle butt to his shoulder and leaned in to the peep sight. Forty yards. An easy shot if his sight lines were clear.

The side of Rachel Mina's face filled the tiny metal ring hole of the back peep sight. He noted her high cheekbones and attractive profile, her smooth skin, the glint of her eye.

His insides churned. He'd never in his life pointed a gun at a woman, much less shot one in the face. The realization and revulsion came out of nowhere.

Jed brought his hand back up as slowly as he dropped it. His eyebrows were arched in a way that suggested he was about to reveal a magic trick. He could sense Mina's trepidation, he thought, and feel it from the others. Not that he was worried.

He laid his fist out on the rock knuckles down and opened his hand. Six bronze-colored .357 Magnum bullets winked in the light of their headlamps. Jed said, "Dakota took these, also."

Gracie turned for Rachel's reaction, hoping it was over.

Rachel shook her head at Jed. She said, "You must think I'm stupid. You have no idea what I've had to do to get here. You actually thought I'd bring only six bullets?"

Jed's mouth opened and Rachel shot him between the eyes. The bark of the gun was sharp and Gracie saw the big tongue of flame. Jed's head jerked back, his hat flew off, and he dropped out of view.

Despite the ringing in her ears, she could hear Jed's body dropping down the crevice, smashing on the sides of the walls, until it landed with a thump several seconds later.

"*Girls! Run!*" Ted Sullivan bellowed.

Cody cursed and tried to keep track of the sudden activity through his sights.

Justin and Danielle let go of their horses and bolted for the far wall of trees. Mina spun on her heels with her smoking pistol in firing position. The horses, startled by the gunshot and the yelling, backpedaled away from them, then joined together and ran the opposite way from

Justin and Danielle, crossing Cody's view and blocking everything out for a moment as they passed by. The horses plunged over the lip of rock to Cody's right a few feet away and crashed down through the timber.

And when they were gone Cody saw that Mina had grasped the younger girl around her throat and held her in front of her like a shield. The gun was pressed against the girl's temple.

The girl, Gracie, was terrified. But she was taller than Cody thought, and blocked most of Mina's body. When he peered down his sights he could see Mina's flashing eyes, but barely over the top of Gracie's head. He couldn't take the shot and regretted he hadn't fired moments before.

"It's my dad," Gracie said to Rachel, her voice altered by the pressure across her throat. "Don't hurt him, please."

"That's up to him," Rachel said. Then to her dad, "Ted, turn the fuck around and walk back down that trail or you'll get your girls killed. Is that what you want?"

From the darkness, Gracie heard her dad say with a choke in his voice, "No, Rachel."

Rachel said, "Are you here alone? Is anyone with you?"

Cody thought, *That son of a bitch will say the wrong thing.*

He prayed for Mina to shift her position. To move. Even if she'd turn to the right a little he might be able to see the back of her head and put one there.

Thinking, *If only I'd fired earlier. . . .*

Gracie said again, "Don't hurt him, please, Rachel. He does his best."

Rachel snorted bitterly. "And we both know that isn't much, don't we?" Then lowering her voice, she said to Gracie, "I don't want to hurt him. I don't want to ever see his face again, but I don't want to hurt him. And I don't want to hurt you. But I want what's mine, and I want to get out of here with it. My life is in that plane. I'm not leaving without it."

Gracie didn't think it was wise to mention Jed said all the money was shredded.

"Ted," Rachel called out, "you never answered me. Is anyone else with you?"

Suddenly, Gracie realized someone *was*. Because although her dad could never communicate well, he'd never *lied*. He wasn't capable of telling a lie, even now. He was probably beside himself, she thought, trying to figure out what he could say. And the fact that he'd said nothing meant yes, someone else was out there.

"Ted?"

Gracie glanced down. Rachel stood with her legs braced behind her. She could see the top of the knife handle poking out of Rachel's right boot.

The pressure of the muzzle eased slightly on her temple as Rachel yelled for Ted to answer her. Gracie took that moment to slump back and let her legs buckle, as if she'd suddenly passed out from the tension. She felt herself slide down Rachel's body. Rachel braced herself and reset her grip on Gracie's neck, but in the moment she did so Gracie felt the muzzle of the gun lift up and away.

She touched the handle of the knife with her fingertips then closed her hand around it and drew it out fast. Before Rachel realized what was happening, Gracie jerked the knife out and away from her, then back as hard as she could in a chopping motion, plunging it nearly to the hilt in Rachel's right thigh.

The whimper that came from Rachel was wholly unexpected and a sound Gracie would never be able to forget. But the pressure on her neck eased and she was able to pull herself away and tumble to the rock.

Cody shot Rachel Mina in the heart twice with a furious double-tap. The woman was likely dead before she hit the ground.

Gracie saw the cloud of bright red mist balloon from the back of Rachel's jacket, and felt the heavy gun drop on her leg. She heard the dull crack of Rachel's head as it slammed down against the rock as she fell.

Cody was up and scrambling. He approached Mina's body with his sights set on her head, hoping he wouldn't need to pull the trigger again. He was struck by how small she looked now, like a broken doll. Rivulets of blood streamed from her body and filled cracks in the rock like a spring flash flood hitting the plains.

Gracie was sitting up covering her mouth with her hands.

He said, "You all right?"

She nodded.

"Damn, that was brave what you did," he said. "Gutsy as hell, Grace."

"It's Gracie."

"Gutsy as hell, Gracie."

She nodded and he liked that she knew she'd been tough.

Gracie nodded toward Mina's body. "She's just so . . . *dead*."

"That's how it goes," he said. Then to the others, "You can all come out now." He almost said, *Even you, Ted, you stupid moronic son of a bitch who just about got your daughter killed.* But he didn't.

Cody looked up to see two figures coming out of the woods. One of them had a flashlight.

"Justin?"

"It's me."

His son shined his flashlight beam up so his face was illuminated. Although the shadows should have looked monsterlike, Cody saw a huge smile and an expression he could only think of as awed.

And for the first time in at least ten years, Justin walked straight up to him and threw his arms around him. Justin said, "My God, Dad. I just knew you'd come. As soon as things went bad, I knew you'd be here."

Cody said, "You *did*?"

"I had faith in you," Justin said.

Stunned, Cody said, "Hell, I didn't."

"I did," Justin said, squeezing harder. "I can't believe you. I just can't frigging believe you."

Cody grunted but hugged him back for a moment.

Gracie ran to her dad, Danielle behind her. He was crying with joy, tears on his face. She helped him walk up over the lip of rock, and wrapped her arms around his waist.

"Careful," he said, sobbing, "I think I broke my tailbone."

"Jeez, Dad," Danielle said, and Gracie could almost feel her sister rolling her eyes in the dark.

Cody said to Justin, "Can you build a fire?"

Justin stepped away. His face was still lit with wonder, and he shook his head as if trying to wrap his mind around what had just happened. Cody felt the same way as his adrenaline crash started to take hold. He noticed his hands were trembling.

"Yeah, I can make a fire. We've had a lot of practice the last couple of days."

Cody nodded. "Then please gather some wood. Maybe you can get your girlfriend to help you."

"Her name's Danielle," Justin said. "I don't know if she's my girl-friend."

"Can she help gather wood?"

"I guess."

"Good enough," Cody said. "I'm going to make a couple of calls and get us out of here."

An hour later, Cody peered down the crevice. The beam of his Maglite wouldn't reach the bottom where Jed's body had ended up. He could see bits of clothing and blood on the walls where Jed's body had pin-balled his way down.

From what he could discern, Jed had been telling the truth. The fuselage of the airplane had been ripped open by the trees and peeled back like the lid of a soup can. One wing had come off and likely fallen to the bottom and the other was mangled and parallel to the crack in the opening.

Two partially clothed skeletons hung from the cockpit by seat re-straints. Inside the plane, Cody could see mounds of shredded money as well as a few skittering field mice. It was possible, he thought, there could be some intact bundles of cash buried deep or even down on the floor of the crevice. That would be for the investigators to determine.

He heard a bass thumping in the night sky and turned around. Jus-tin and Danielle had built a massive bonfire that crackled and lit up the rock walls and the trees and threw off so much light the stars had retreated into urban mode. Ted Sullivan lay across two downed logs, suspending his injured tailbone.

Cody said, "Helicopters coming."

In the distance he could see approaching lights in the sky. Two sets of them. He hoped the pilot of one of them would see the fire from Camp Two and swoop down for the others, as he'd instructed the dis-patcher.

He hadn't noticed Gracie approach him until he looked down. She was a slip of a girl.

"I want to thank you," she said.

He nodded.

"Justin's really proud."

"That means a lot. Your dad should be proud of *you*."

"Yeah." She shrugged.

"Don't be too hard on him," Cody said. "He came up here even though he couldn't ride. He obviously cares about you and your sister."

Gracie nodded, looking over at her father on the downed trees. "He does, in his way," she said. "I feel bad that Danielle and I thought he'd run. Rachel pretty much convinced us. You see, he told us why he showed up late at the airport to get us. It turns out he was late because he was booking a weekend at a spa for us in Billings when we were done with this trip. He'd arrived the day before to meet Rachel and he wanted us to feel all girly again when we went back home. And the reason he wasn't in the camp was because he was feeling sick and resting in his tent. He had no idea Rachel told us that story."

Cody had nothing to say.

"Rachel had me completely fooled," Gracie said.

"She fooled a lot of people."

"Even though she's dead and I wanted her to be, I feel kind of bad. Jed, too."

Cody squeezed her on the shoulder. "You should feel that way," he said. "It's the difference between you and them."

She nodded, not sure.

"I hope you don't mind if I smoke," he said, digging the last of D'Amato's cigarettes out of his breast pocket.

She looked up, said, "Justin said you'd quit."

"Nope," he said, lighting and inhaling as deeply as he could without falling back into the crevice.

Epilogue

MONTANA

Three days later, Cody Hoyt slumped in the uncomfortable chair across from Sheriff Tub Tubman's desk, but Tubman wasn't there yet. Under-sheriff Cliff Bodean perched as he usually did on the corner of Tubman's desk, looking down at him. Cody had brought a small briefcase with him filled with statements and his files and another object and had placed it near his feet.

"He said be here at eleven to discuss my situation," Cody said. "So I'm here."

"I don't know where he is," Bodean said, shooting a cuff to look at his watch. He gestured toward the credenza in back of the sheriff's chair. "His hat is here."

"Goddamn it," Cody said, standing with difficulty and walking around the desk to turn the hat crown-down, "the man doesn't *listen*."

Cody sat back down in the chair and moaned. It seemed like every inch of his body still hurt. The gash on his face across his nose was stitched closed and there was a fresh bandage on his ear. His body was a mass of bruises. His knees still hurt from riding the horses.

"Frankly," Bodean said, "I'm surprised he's taking you back."

Cody snorted in response.

"The coroner is likely to use it as a campaign issue against him,"

Bodean said, shaking his head. "You're coming out pretty damned good on this. I don't know how you do it. Larry used to joke about you having illicit photos of him. Is that the case?"

Cody looked up and grimaced. "I'll never tell."

Bodean looked at his watch again. Then: "I hear there have never been as many Feds in Yellowstone for an investigation before. They're practically tripping over each other. They've got FBI, DEA, Park Service, Homeland Security, not to mention detectives from Minnesota, Utah, California, Wyoming, and our state guys. You must have given a lot of statements."

Cody grunted.

Bodean said, "I read your initial one. I noticed you didn't say anything about being suspended while you were there."

"It wasn't relevant."

Bodean raised his eyebrows. "Oh really?"

Cody said, "I could have told them, I guess. But then I'd have to tell them the reason I was there was because I was freelancing on a murder investigation prohibited by my superiors. How do you think that would play in the press?"

Bodean didn't respond.

Cody said, "I've got requests from *USA Today*, *The New York Times*, *The Wall Street Journal*, AP, and five cable news shows. I haven't called any of them back. Would you like me to amend my statement before I call them so they know why I was in the park on my own?"

"You can be such an asshole," Bodean said.

Cody shrugged.

"Following up on your statement," Bodean said, "are the other survivors back home?"

"Far as I know. Bull Mitchell is back with his daughter and his wife in Bozeman. I guess he's quite the local celebrity. I owe him a lot of money but he's graciously set up a long-term payment plan. Knox is doing a lot of interviews for the New York press. I've seen a couple of them. As you can imagine, it's quite a story there. Donna Glode isn't talking. Walt went home with his tail between his legs."

"What about the Sullivan family?"

Cody nodded. "They're okay. My son Justin is constantly texting the older daughter. They're scheming something but I don't know what. I plan to keep in touch with the younger one, Gracie. She's a smart little lady." When he said her name he smiled. He couldn't help it.

Cody said, "They found Gannon where we hung him up. He's singing like a bird, from what I understand. Telling the Feds everything he knows. Pieces are falling into place."

"Speaking of," Bodean said, "I understand he's accusing you of torturing him. Of shooting him in the ear and the knee to get him to talk."

Cody shook his head. "That guy. I shot in self-defense. You can check it out with Bull Mitchell. He'll corroborate my story."

Bodean smiled bitterly. "I don't know how you keep getting away with it."

"I chalk it up to clean living," Cody said. "Mind if I smoke?"

Bodean looked at the ceiling tile and took a deep breath.

Cody withdrew a packet of cigarettes from his jacket and tapped one out and lit it. He tossed the spent match on the little placard on Tubman's desk that said NO SMOKING.

Bodean said, "So you say the Feds are putting it all together, connecting the dots. I assume you mean they're getting evidence linking up Mina, Gannon, Jed, and maybe an outside accomplice working with Mina."

Cody studied Bodean's face, letting him go on, but saying nothing.

"That Rachel Mina or Chavez, or whatever," Bodean whistled, "she must have been something. I read all of Larry's files, the stuff he got from the San Diego PD and DEA. He traced her all over the country, to every one of those murders. She operated completely under the radar. I saw photos of her. She was a looker, but not a knockout. She must have been something," he repeated. "A stone-cold killer who looks like the cute girl next door."

"She knew she had to get to Yellowstone," Cody said. "When she met that poor schmuck Ted Sullivan she planted the seed. Of course, he accommodated her. She knew a single woman on a trip like that would draw suspicion, so Ted was her cover."

Bodean nodded. "So as far as you're concerned, she was working with Wilson—I mean Gannon—and no one else?"

He seemed to be prying, Cody thought. He refused to play.

"When's the funeral?" Cody asked.

"Larry?"

"Who the hell else?"

"Tomorrow. I'm surprised you didn't get the e-mail. Wear your Class A's." That was department-speak for dress blues.

"I didn't get the e-mail because I was giving statement after statement in the park," Cody said, annoyed, "and I was still officially suspended, remember? I didn't have fucking *access* to my e-mails."

"Oh, yeah."

Cody felt like standing up and decking him, but he fought back his rage.

"As soon as we've buried Larry," Bodean said, "we're ramping up our effort on going after his killer. Everything gets shoved aside. Finding the bastard who did it is Job One."

"It's about time," Cody said, gripping the arm of the chair so hard he was surprised he didn't leave dents in the wood.

"Jesus," Bodean said, looking at his watch again. "Where the hell is the sheriff?"

Cody shrugged. Then he changed the subject. "Larry always used to lay things out for me in the most methodical way. It used to drive me crazy, but he wouldn't let me rush him. He told me things his way, which was deliberate as all hell and very linear. I used to beg him to get to the bottom line but he'd never get there until he was good and ready after he had the storyline laid out."

Bodean looked puzzled. "So?"

"So pretend I'm Larry," Cody said, "and listen. You might want to sit down until the sheriff gets here. This won't be as good as if Larry were telling it, but I'll do my best."

Bodean started to object, but bit his lip. His eyes showed concern. But he moved around the desk and sat in Tubman's chair and leaned forward holding his hands together, fingers loosely laced.

"The assumption here with the Feds," Cody said, "is it's all connected, as you said. Mina, Gannon, Jed, maybe even Dakota Hill. And given that assumption, there's the assumption Mina's net spread farther out, that she had an accomplice on the outside. Whoever it was tried to burn me alive at Gallatin Gateway and was more successful with Larry. And that suspect is still out there."

Bodean broke in: "I'm confident the Feds will find him with all the cooperation they've got. They can do a nationwide investigation. We're limited to the county—"

"I know all that, Bodean," Cody said impatiently. "Now please shut up and listen. We're doing this Larry's way."

Bodean took a deep breath and held it, then leaned forward. "Go ahead," he said.

"Okay. Things started to go bad for me in Townsend when I left here. I got pulled over by the local cop and spent the night there, putting me a day behind I'll never get back. Who knows how many lives might have been saved if I'd been able to get into Yellowstone and break up the pack trip before they left? I will always be haunted by that.

"It seemed odd to be picked up like I was," he said. "I thought at the time the local cop might have received a tip of some kind, likely anonymous, to watch for my car. That's when I first got the inkling maybe Larry was playing a double game with me. That for some reason—maybe for my own damned good—Larry wanted to slow me down. Save me from doing something stupid."

Bodean nodded for him to continue.

"After that fire in my room in the hotel, I was even more sure it was

Larry. It could have been the perfect death. Whoever did it knew me pretty well. Out of control, suspended, drunk alcoholic, disabled smoke alarm, smoking in bed. It would have been a slam-dunk accidental death. But for some reason I saw the fire and got out in time. No one saw who did it, and I never really thought it was Larry but maybe someone he sent."

Cody noted the small beads of perspiration forming on Bodean's upper lip. It wasn't warm in the office.

"I realized in Bozeman someone was tracking my cell, so I smashed it. Of course, not just anybody can get the phone company to track a cell phone. Only law enforcement can do that, so again, it pointed to Larry—the only guy who knew where the hell I was or why I was going. I've since confirmed that the phone company had a request to track my cell phone and the request came from this office."

Bodean's voice cracked when he said, "That son of a bitch."

Cody raised his eyebrows this time. "Yeah, that Larry," he said with sarcasm. Then: "Later, in the park, I turned on my phone. There were five messages from Larry on it. I listened to them. They're still on the phone, by the way. I could tell from what he was saying and his tone he was working on something big, that he'd found something huge. Now, if his intent was to steer me away from the pack trip, why would he keep investigating? Unless, of course, he was trying to completely mislead me. But that didn't jibe with his tone. He was excited, and angry with me. He wanted to help me. Larry was my partner. I believed him.

"So I called back," Cody said. "Someone picked up his cell phone from the briefcase sitting next to his desk. Larry said it wasn't him because he was getting reamed out by the sheriff at the time right here in this chair. But you know what? He didn't mention anyone else being in the room. And knowing Larry, he wouldn't have left a detail like that out, because Larry didn't leave out details.

"So someone heard my voice and knew I was alive and probably in the park. Any idea who that might have been?"

Bodean's gaze was hard and steady. "It could have been anyone who picked up that phone. You're on thin ice, Hoyt."

Cody conceded that. "But it wasn't just anyone, I don't think, because what would just anyone have learned from my call? Only that I was calling Larry. Nothing else. Supposedly at that time no one knew about my trip south, or the fire."

"I'm confused," Bodean said.

"Sure you are," Cody said. "So whoever picked up Larry's phone knew that I was trying to reach him. And they knew if I was trying to reach him Larry would tell me what he'd discovered. That he'd spoken to the San Diego PD and so on. If someone was involved in the whole mess in Yellowstone, that wouldn't be a good thing.

"I'm guessing Sheriff Tubman didn't decide to suspend Larry on his own. I'm guessing maybe his undersheriff convinced him Larry was going rogue and withholding information about me, as well as what he was learning in his unauthorized investigation. It went right by me when Larry told me you became unhinged when you found out our investigation was pointing toward Yellowstone Park and Jed McCarthy's outfit."

Cody noticed Bodean's hands were now two fists on the desk.

"When I gave my statement to the Park Service, I met Larry's buddy Rick Doerring. Rick confirmed that Jed McCarthy had been around doing some kind of concession business when the interagency team assembled in Mammoth about that report of the disabled plane. Rick said the rumor mill was really cranking along, as usual. Then I remembered something Larry said to me in passing, and I'd almost completely forgotten about it."

"What?" Bodean said.

"The sheriff sent *two* members of the department down to Yellowstone. Larry and you."

Bodean swallowed hard but said nothing.

Cody said, "That's where you met Jed McCarthy for the first time and learned about his pack trips. I'm sure Jed told you all about them

because he was a yapper. I'm sure he told you all about his big Back of
Beyond itinerary, since that was his pride and joy, not to mention his
cash cow.

"But that isn't the only task force Undersheriff Cliff Bodean belongs to, is it?" Cody asked. "You're also our official liaison to the
DEA. So later, after you got back from the park and everyone forgot
about the airplane since no one reported it missing, you heard the rumors and read the reports about the Chavez cartel and the kidnapping. You put the dates of the kidnapping and the plane disappearance
together and found they were days apart. There was a rumor the exchange was to have taken place in Jackson Hole, but it never did. So
you got out a map and drew a line between Bozeman, where the plane
was last seen, and Jackson, where the plane was supposed to land. I did
it myself last night. That line goes straight through the Thorofare country of Yellowstone. Practically on top of Jed's route."

Bodean tried to laugh it off, but it sounded like he was barking,
Cody thought.

"So you contacted Jed," he said. "I guess you probably met with
him a few times and laid it all out. You shared your information and
made him maps. You agreed to cover his back on the law enforcement
side—make sure nobody decided to suddenly look for that plane—if
he'd actually retrieve the cash."

"This is insane," Bodean said.

"No, sorry, it isn't."

Bodean said, "You're trying to connect me with Rachel Mina. I
never knew Hank Winters from Adam. I swear."

Cody said, "I believe you. Nice try. But this is where everyone investigating this has it wrong. The thing is, there is no connection between you and Mina and Gannon, is there? The key to this mystery is
that it *wasn't* connected. It was two completely independent schemes
both working to find that plane, but unaware of the other. There was
Mina and Gannon on one team, and you and Jed on the other. Two

schemes, one trip, one destination. I don't think even Jed and Mina figured that out until the very end."

Bodean wiped the sweat from his lip. His face was drained of color. He said, "You've got nothing."

"I didn't until this morning," Cody said. He leaned forward in his chair. "Until the FAA investigators pulled Jed's body out of that hole. He had a satellite phone, too, Bodean. He'd made one call on it and it was to your private cell number."

"It must be a mistake," Bodean said.

"And something else," Cody said, reaching for the briefcase he'd brought. "I had Edna look over the logs the night Larry was killed. You know those GPS units we all have under our cars? Well, I disabled mine, but you never did. It shows your midnight trip to Bozeman to try and burn me up. And Edna found you took a trip up to Marysville twenty minutes *before* I called her to send a car. Either you're real fucking prescient, or you killed Larry."

Bodean said softly, "Do you realize what you're saying?"

"Yup," Cody said. "I'm saying up in Deer Lodge those convicts are gonna *looove* you. A former undersheriff? Man, you'll have plenty of dates, I'd guess. And if you think the prison guards are going to protect a cop killer, well think again."

Cody opened his briefcase and took out the bird's nest he'd found near the crevice and spun it across the desk so it landed between Bodean's fists.

"Look," Cody said, "it's made of money. A nest made of money. You thought you'd have one of your own and now you do. Pretty cool, if you think about it."

Then he reached into his pocket and plucked out the microphone. Said, "Heard enough? If you guys don't come in here in the next five seconds I'm going to rip his throat out for killing my best friend."

Cody stood aside as the FBI agents rushed in the room, followed by a hang-dog Sheriff Tubman.

As they stood Bodean face-first against the wall and cuffed him, and before they could read him his rights, Cody said, "I wanted to shoot you in the head, myself. But the sheriff said no, that would hurt his reelection campaign, so he made me go through all this."

One of the FBI agents gave Cody a withering glance. As did Tubman.

"I'd start with his knees," Cody said. "That makes 'em talk, believe me."

He turned to Tubman. "Look at it this way, sheriff. You've eliminated a rival."

Cody trudged across the lawn toward Jenny's van. Justin sat in the back, no doubt texting Danielle Sullivan. Justin looked up and nodded.

"Tell her to say hello to Gracie for me," Cody said.

He swung in beside Jenny and gave her a quick kiss. She didn't seem affected by the sudden breaking of her engagement to Walt. "I hope you've picked a smoking restaurant," he said.

"I was thinking Chubby's in Clancy," she said, pulling away from the curb. "The sign out front says 'Greatest Food You'll Ever Eat.'"

"Sounds promising," Cody said.

"Cody," she said, "it has a lounge. I know you'll probably want to toast Larry's memory . . ."

"I know," he said. "But I can't do that kind of thing anymore. I made a promise to Larry."

Acknowledgments

The author would like to sincerely thank the many friends, relatives, and colleagues who assisted in the research, reading, editing, and publication of this novel, starting with Investigator Cory Olson of the Lewis and Clark Sheriff's Department in Helena, Montana, and including Investigator Larry Platts, Sheriff Leo Dutton, my friend Pam Gosink, and forensics guru D. P. Lyle, MD.

Thanks always to my first readers: Becky Box Reif, Molly Box, and Laurie Box.

Thanks also to John R. Erickson for the use of the lines from *The Original Adventures of Hank the Cowdog,* Puffin Books, 1983.

Thanks to Don Hajicek for cjbox.net and Jennifer Fonnesbeck for the rest of the on-line presence.

It's an absolute honor and privilege to work with the excellent and enthusiastic team at St. Martins Minotaur, including Sally Richardson, Andy Martin, Matthew Shear, Matthew Baldacci, Hector DeJean, and the absolutely peerless Jennifer Enderlin.

For Ann Rittenberg: You. Are. The. Greatest.

THE BITTERROOTS

For Laurie, always

Part I

The root of the kingdom is in the state. The root of the state is in the family. The root of the family is in the person of its head. —Mencius (Meng-tzu), *Works*

Going home must be like going to render an account.

—Joseph Conrad, *Lord Jim*

one

⊷═◉═⊷

The Crazy Mountains were on fire and Cassie Dewell sat alone in her car at night on McLeod Street across from the Grand Hotel in Big Timber, Montana, looking for a twenty-four-year-old reprobate known as Antlerhead.

That's when the call she'd been dreading came on her cell phone.

It was from Rachel Mitchell, the primary defense attorney in the firm of Mitchell-Estrella in Bozeman. It was from Rachel's personal cell phone rather than from her office, which was unusual in itself. The attorney was working late and it meant a chit had come due.

The call created a stab of cold dread in Cassie's gut. She didn't need the distraction of a call from Rachel Mitchell at that moment. A call from her meant Cassie's life could be altered one way or another. She declined to answer and let it go to voice mail so she could return it later.

She brushed crumbs from a half-dozen chocolate-covered mini-donuts from her lap and lifted her gaze from the empty sidewalk that led to the front door of the hotel to the fire on the distant mountain. It was mesmerizing and officially out of control.

The long fire line extended across the entire southern face of the range like an orange zipper. It dipped into canyons and emerged on the other side. It raced down over meadows and plateaus in spots but never broke contact with the extended fire line itself.

Because it was dark, there was no delineation between the fresh fuel in front of the blaze and the smoking cinders behind it. The fire seemed like a living thing, a snake, a nocturnal beast more alive at night than during the day. It burned bright enough that it stained the bellies of low-hanging clouds with pink hues. When Cassie closed her eyes, the fire lingered as if imprinted inside her eyelids.

She could imagine the line of fire eating its way down through the timber and eventually consuming the grassland of the prairie all the way to I-90 and Big Timber itself unless the wind turned it west or south.

Like most of the summer, the September air was thick with smoke. It haloed the few downtown streetlights and she could smell it on her clothing. She had a sore throat from breathing it in all day. On some mornings, she brushed a thin film of white ash from the hood and windshield of her Jeep Cherokee as if it were snow in the winter.

It had been the Summer of Fire in Montana, and it wasn't over yet.

She thought about how many fires there were—seventeen at last count throughout the state—and how they'd likely keep burning until the snow finally put them out. They could be seen from space. Both the state and federal budget for fighting them had run out of funds in mid-August.

Hundreds of thousands of acres of timber had burned. So much that the numbers no longer had meaning. Several hundred mountain cabins and homes were destroyed and dozens of towns had been evacuated more than once.

Against the backdrop of the Summer of Fire the case for finding Antlerhead seemed very small in the grand scheme of things. She felt small as well.

The phone in her lap chimed and lit up again and Cassie was afraid it was Rachel again. Instead, it was a text message from her fourteen-year-old son Ben, who was home in Bozeman, sixty-one miles to the west.

> When R U home?

She replied that it would be a few hours, that he needed to do his homework and go to bed and to not wait up for her.

> She's feeding me brown rice again.

She meaning Cassie's mother, Isabel, a free spirit and self-proclaimed progressive who had recently returned from North Dakota where she'd been participating in protests against an oil pipeline opposed by indigenous people. Since getting back she'd refused to cook or serve anything white.

Cassie pondered her response. At least Ben was getting dinner when his own mother wasn't home to prepare a meal. There was that.

Before she could tap something out Ben asked,

> Can I ride my bike to McD's?

It was warm enough outside and Bozeman was safe enough to say yes. McDonald's was three blocks away. But giving Ben permission to skip Isabel's meal would undermine her mother's authority. It would fan the flames on the tension between them that was already smoldering like one of the fires in the mountains.

Cassie texted:

> We'll go there tomorrow.

Ben replied with:

> Like U'll be home for once.

It was followed by an angry face emoji.

> Good night. I love you.

The words "I love you too, Mom, and I realize you have to

work late so we have a nice home to live in and food on the table"
didn't appear on her phone.

In fact, Ben didn't text back at all and Cassie sighed and
swallowed a lump in her throat. She could stare at the screen and
wish for those words to appear but this was Ben's way when he was
angry with her. He knew that the meanest thing he could do to
her was to withhold his affection. That it would hurt her more
than anything he said.

When she looked up, she saw a rail-thin form emerge from the
alley behind the Grand and dart back into the shadows to avoid
being seen by a passing car.

Antlerhead.

She'd guessed right.

Antlerhead's given name was Jerry Allen. He'd received his nickname several years before while on work release from the Montana State Prison in Deer Lodge after his conviction for a series of
house and cabin burglaries. Allen was assigned part-time at a wild
game processing facility outside of Anaconda during hunting season. That's where he hefted the newly delivered severed head and
the set of six-by-six antlers onto his shoulders and said to his co-
workers and fellow inmates, "Look at me—I'm an *elk*!" seconds
before he slipped on a smear of blood and his strength and balance
gave out. A hundred and twenty pounds of antlers crashed down
on top of him and laid him out on the loading dock. One of
the sharp tines entered his skull just above his right eyebrow and
another halved his clavicle and punctured a lung.

His next job, once he was released from the hospital after a two-
month stay and ten months of physical rehab courtesy of Montana
taxpayers, was in the prison laundry.

Antlerhead later went on to become one of the most inept heroin dealers in Gallatin County. He'd been arrested along with
two others for selling heroin laced with fentanyl to three male

Montana State University students in Bozeman. All three Bobcats were rushed to the emergency room at Bozeman Health Deaconess. While two recovered, the third went into a coma and lingered for months before regaining consciousness.

That the third student survived meant Allen avoided additional homicide charges to those already levied against him: felony charges of criminal possession of dangerous drugs, criminal manufacture of dangerous drugs, criminal possession with intent to distribute dangerous drugs, and conspiracy.

The recent arrest photos of him showed a rail-thin, gaunt-faced man with a mop of brown hair, a long crooked nose, and dull feral eyes. Above his right eyebrow was a sunken red dent of a scar that was no doubt the spot where the antler tine had penetrated his skull that resulted in his nickname.

Cassie was reminded that in just about every instance losers *looked* like losers. Allen was a poster child for losers.

Antlerhead Allen was going to go back to prison in Deer Lodge for a very long time, which was fine with Cassie. That's where he belonged.

Except that following his arraignment hearing two days before, after his parents scraped together the $150,000 bond that allowed him to walk out of the county jail until his criminal trial, Antlerhead had vanished.

And his parents were on the hook for the money.

Cassie shifted her weight on the seat and winced. She'd been sitting in her car so long that her right butt cheek had gone numb. Her stomach rumbled from her dinner that consisted of a box of Hostess chocolate-covered donuts and an energy drink from a convenience store. She'd vowed to stop eating like that until she dropped twenty pounds. Unlike Ben, who wore slim-fit jeans and didn't have an ounce of fat on him, Cassie *should* be eating Isabel's brown rice.

Like always when she was on the job, she wore her unofficial

Montana PI uniform: jeans with enough play in them that she wasn't uncomfortable sitting in a car for long hours, a roomy blouse, and a tunic or jacket. She always wore her tooled cowboy boots for a couple of reasons. One was a nod to her state and her upbringing. The other was that she could tuck a backup weapon into the shaft of her right boot. Plus, she *never* stood out in Montana because of her clothing.

She'd kept a close eye on the alley behind the Grand Hotel for another glimpse of Antlerhead. She didn't want to try and go after him if he was there in the dark. Instead, she wanted him to appear on the illuminated sidewalk and his identification could be confirmed before she took any kind of action.

Several people had left the Grand, climbed into their vehicles, and driven away. There were now five autos parked diagonally at the front of the hotel—a sedan, a crossover, and three pickups. All had Montana plates. She knew from walking around the block before dark that employee parking was next to the building on a gravel lot. There were four cars in the lot. From where Cassie had strategically parked her Jeep, she could see the front and side doors of the hotel as well as the employee lot.

If Antlerhead was lurking in the alley as Cassie suspected he was, he would be blocked from viewing any activity from the front and side doors. But he'd have a clear angle on the employee parking from the back corner of the building.

Which, if her working theory was correct, would be what Antlerhead cared about most.

Nayna Byers. The waitress Cassie had met who worked at the Grand.

To find Antlerhead, Cassie had placed a call to the administration office of the Montana State Prison and asked for Johnny Ortiz. She'd worked with him when they were both deputies at the Lewis and Clark County Sheriff's Office in Helena. Since then, she'd moved to North Dakota and Ortiz had taken a job with the Department of Corrections.

Ortiz had provided background and unofficial intel to her before, and in turn Cassie always left a dozen cinnamon rolls from Wheat Montana at the front desk for him every time she passed through Deer Lodge.

After small talk about the fires, Ortiz tapped on his keyboard and told Cassie that during Antlerhead's incarceration he had only four names on his approved visitor list: his parents Buford and Nadine Allen, his defense attorney, and Nayna Byers of Big Timber.

Cassie wrote down the name and thanked Johnny for his help. She could tell from his hearty, "You bet, Cassie," that he was grateful she hadn't asked him for anything dubious or untoward. Visitor lists for prisoners were public records.

It took less than two minutes on the internet to find her.

Apprehending Antlerhead and delivering him back to his parents' house could get tricky. Cassie couldn't legally arrest him or detain him without cause and Antlerhead hadn't actually broken any laws that she was aware of.

She'd notified the Big Timber PD via email from her phone of her presence there earlier in the afternoon but she hadn't said what she was doing other than "investigating a case." She'd done it as a courtesy. There was no requirement to alert the locals but it was good policy if things went haywire or if she was questioned by the police as to why she was in their town with an array of equipment and weapons.

She didn't want to call them now. A police car might spook Antlerhead and she might lose him. Or the cops might provoke him into doing something stupid like resisting arrest that would result in another charge and another bail for his parents.

★ ★ ★

Her strategy was simple: confront him and firmly persuade him to go back to his home with her. She would tell him about the financial consequences his parents faced if he refused to come with her and she hoped he'd feel some guilt about that. Additionally, she'd let him know that she was duty-bound to inform the court that he'd disregarded the judge's instructions to stay home. Which meant he'd go back to lockup.

She knew Antlerhead was not a smart person. She could only hope he was smart enough to realize that the best thing he could do for himself was to let her take him back.

Nevertheless, Cassie patted herself down to check her gear and weapons. Her .40 Glock 27 was on her hip and her five-shot .38 snub-nosed Smith & Wesson was in an ankle holster. There was a Taser in her large handbag on the passenger seat as well a canister of pepper spray, a Vipertek mini stun gun, and several pairs of zip ties.

Since she'd opened her agency she'd never once been in a situation where it was necessary to draw any of her lethal or nonlethal weapons. She hoped the streak would continue.

The most important tool she had on her person was the most innocuous—her cell phone. She'd activate the recording app before leaving her Jeep and keep it running during her confrontation and conversation with Allen. Digital audio records had come in handy dozens of times in her career when it came to proving what had actually transpired. If nothing else, she could play it back for the Allens to prove that she'd earned her fee if Antlerhead didn't bite.

Cassie caught a glimpse of yellow light from the shadowed side of the Grand as a side door opened and someone exited. It wasn't one of the public doors and Cassie assumed it accessed the kitchen. When it closed she couldn't see the figure well.

Cassie had a night vision scope in the back of the Jeep but she didn't want to call attention to herself by climbing out to get it. So she waited, narrowing her eyes and hoping they'd adjust to the dark or that the person would move into the light.

It wasn't necessary, though, because Nayna Beyers thumbed a lighter and raised it to the tip of a cigarette in her mouth. Cassie could identify her clearly.

The flame went out and was replaced by the lone red cherry of Nayna's smoke.

The cherry on the end of Nayna's cigarette was suddenly bobbing up and down and advancing down the sidewalk. Then Nayna appeared in a pool of yellow from the streetlight near the front of the Grand. She was walking quickly and looking over her shoulder toward the back.

Antlerhead was right behind her, loping from the alley. Apparently, he'd seen her come out for her smoke break as well and when he caught up with her, he grabbed her by her arms and spun her around to face him. Her cigarette dropped into the gutter with a display of sparks.

Cassie cursed herself for not seeing it coming and she opened the door of the Jeep and pushed herself out. The call from Rachel had thrown off her concentration. She fumbled for the recording app on her phone as she walked quickly across the street toward Nayna and Antlerhead. Nayna struggled to break his grip.

Cassie took a deep breath to calm herself. She hadn't expected Antlerhead to escalate the situation so quickly.

"I just want to talk to you," Antlerhead said.

"Let me go, you asshole."

"Nayna, please. I just want to talk."

"There's nothing to say. Let me go or I'll call the cops. I'll start *screaming*."

He prevented that by wheeling her around again so he could clamp her in a headlock with his left arm across her throat.

Cassie heard a muffled yell, and Antlerhead said, "Stop it, Nayna, goddamn you. I don't want to hurt you. *I fucking love you.*"

Nayna's eyes were wide open and panicked but they locked on Cassie's approach. Antlerhead hadn't seen her yet because he was so focused on getting Nayna to stop struggling.

Cassie gave up on turning on the recording app—too many wasted seconds, too many stupid swipes of the screen—and she thumbed the icon for her camera. A red dot appeared and she punched it. She was now recording video and she raised her phone to chest level and aimed it at Antlerhead and Nayna with her left hand while reaching back for the grip of her Glock with her right.

"Jerry, let her go."

Antlerhead's head bobbled at the sound of his name and he glared at Cassie. He kept Nayna in the chokehold. Cassie hoped the waitress could get enough air to stay conscious.

"Who in the hell are you? This is a private conversation."

He even sounded dumb.

"It's not a conversation, it's an assault," Cassie said. "Let her go right now or I'll blow your stupid head off."

She drew her gun as she said it and leveled it at Antlerhead. The front sight was aimed squarely at the dent above his eyebrow.

"Shit, man," he said. He sounded offended. "Put that down and turn that camera off."

Cassie steadied the weapon and hoped her hand wouldn't tremble.

Then he relaxed his grip on Nayna and she twisted away. As soon as she got her balance she coughed, then turned on her heel and kicked Antlerhead so hard between his legs it lifted him off the ground. He wheezed—it was a pathetic sound—and he dropped to his knees.

Nayna cocked her leg back for another kick and Cassie said, "Back off, Nayna. It's over."

"It ain't over," Nayna said as she kicked him in his sternum. "He was choking me."

Antlerhead moaned and fell over in slow motion.

"I'm not kidding," Cassie said to her. "That's *enough* or I'll call the cops on both of you."

"He's supposed to be in jail anyway," Nayna said. "He won't leave me alone."

"I get that."

"Who are you anyway?" Nayna asked. Then: "Oh, I remember you from earlier. Are you some kind of cop?"

"I'm a licensed private investigator. My name is Cassie Dewell. I'm here to take our friend back to his parents' house."

"He ain't my friend."

"He used to be."

"Well, he ain't no more. He's an asshole."

"I'll give you that."

Cassie neared Antlerhead and holstered her weapon. He writhed on the asphalt with both of his hands clamped between his thighs. His clothing was white from the film of ash on the ground.

"Did you hear that, Jerry? It's time to go home. We can do this without getting the police involved. How does that sound?"

"Just get him out of here," Nayna said. "I don't ever want to see his stupid fucking face again for the rest of my life."

From Antlerhead, a childlike sob. His body shook as he cried.

"Come on, Jerry," Cassie said. "Let's go over to that Jeep across the street."

"Nayna," he cried. "*Nayna.*"

Cassie could see that Nayna was positioning herself for another kick so she stepped between them. The waitress backed away.

"Please get back to work," Cassie told her.

Arm in arm, they staggered across the street toward her Jeep. Antlerhead was unsteady on his feet and he hadn't stopped sobbing.

Cassie saw the Big Timber PD unit turn the corner and drive slowly down McLeod Street toward them.

"Straighten up," Cassie said sharply. "Act like a man."

She guided him into the passenger seat and closed the door. Antlerhead slumped forward and put his head in his hands. Cassie would have preferred to cuff him and stow him in the back for the drive to Laurel but she didn't want to draw attention from the local cop who passed by.

"That was close," she said as she climbed in and turned the key to the ignition.

"*Nayna.*"

"Oh, please," Cassie said as she drove cautiously out of town toward I-90. "You're not the victim here."

"The hell I ain't," he said. "She told me she loved me once and now she *kicks me* in the *nuts.*"

That struck Cassie as funny and she looked away so he couldn't see the expression on her face. The release of tension from the situation and Antlerhead's perceived victimhood made her want to laugh out loud.

After a few minutes, she said, "Let me know when you stop crying and can hold it together long enough for me to return a phone call."

two

━━◦◦◦━━

The law offices of Mitchell-Estrella were on the second floor of a newish office building on Main Street on the western flank of downtown Bozeman. It was a cool sunny morning tainted by the brackish odor of smoke from the forest fires in the mountains. Not until the temperature climbed to forty-five degrees would the inversion layer open up and allow the smoke to disperse into the atmosphere.

Cassie parked in the first visitor space in the lot and fished a notebook out of her handbag. She left the tools and weapons and stuffed the bag under the passenger seat so it couldn't be seen from the outside.

Before getting out, she paused and sighed heavily. She was tired and it wasn't even nine in the morning. She'd not arrived home until one thirty after delivering Antlerhead to Buford and Nadine Allen, and she'd been up at six forty-five to make breakfast for Ben and spend some time with him before he went to school and Isabel got up.

Of course, her son had barely spoken, and when she asked him about school, wrestling practice, and his friends he'd said all were "fine."

"Just fine?"

He rolled his eyes, exasperated with her. "What do you want me to say, Mom?"

Fourteen-year-old boys were a challenge.

And so was making the effort to see Rachel Mitchell, even though Cassie had known this day would come.

Climbing the stairs to Rachel's office, she fought the feeling that she was crossing a line that she didn't want to cross.

Everything that happened in western Montana happened in one of the valleys between mountain ranges. The towns, the roads, the rivers, and the railroads were all funneled into the valleys between the Absaroka and Beartooth Range to the southeast, the Gallatins and Crazies to the southwest, the Bridger, Big Belt, and Elkhorn ranges to the north, and the Bitterroots to the northwest.

Cassie worked those valleys on a daily basis, and it wasn't unusual for her to drive three hundred miles in a day as a private investigator working several different cases at once. She was the owner and principal of Dewell Investigations, LLC. She was a fully licensed private investigator and her services included skip tracing, asset searches, background checks, fraud, criminal defense investigations, domestic cases, and surveillance. Her Montana PI license number was number 7775.

After years of existing in the backstabbing bureaucracy of local law enforcement, she'd decided to strike out on her own. She thought it would be a good move for her and a good thing for Ben. Cassie liked the ideas of setting her own hours, choosing her own cases, and being her own boss.

Her career in law enforcement had been intense and tumultuous. She'd pursued and taken down Ronald Pergram, the infamous Lizard King, who was a serial rapist and murderer who operated as a long-haul trucker. He'd also become her obsession.

She'd also shot and killed Montana state trooper Rick Legerski who was a coconspirator of Pergram's and the murderer of Cassie's mentor, Cody Hoyt.

Her work as chief investigator in North Dakota both saved the life of a then fourteen-year-old boy with fetal alcohol syndrome and dismantled a violent MS-13-financed drug ring.

But instead of kudos and promotions, Cassie had been made the scapegoat by a politically ambitious county attorney for a sting operation that went horribly wrong and resulted in the deaths of several fellow deputies including her fiancé at the time. She'd eventually been cleared and offered her job back, but she couldn't make herself put on a badge again.

Although her sense of justice and respect for the law remained intact, her enthusiasm to "ride for the brand" had been crushed. There had been too many self-aggrandizing officials, too much misanthropy among the good old boys in the system, and too much politicization instead of investigation. She still wanted to put bad guys away and protect innocent people, but she could no longer fight the bureaucracy in order to do that.

It had all worked, sort of. Her idea of setting her own hours and not being beholden to a departmental superior had resulted in longer days, fewer vacations, and serving the toughest boss of all—herself.

Setting up shop had been more difficult than she thought it would be. She hadn't given enough thought about how tough it was to deal with landlords or the city administration when it came to leasing space and setting up shop. There were so many taxes and fees it was as if the system was set up to make her fail.

The hardest part, though, was overcoming her aversion to private investigators due to her years in local law enforcement in Montana and most recently North Dakota. Jon Kirkbride, the sheriff of Bakken County and her boss in NoDak, once told her, "TSA agents are folks who were too dumb to pass the test for a job at the post office, and private investigators are folks too dumb to qualify for the TSA."

Nevertheless, she met the minimum license requirements in Montana and passed a background investigation and fingerprint check, she had the requisite experience in spades, and she could afford the two-hundred-fifty-dollar application fee and the premiums for a half-million-dollar commercial liability policy. Her references included cops she'd worked with in her native Montana as well as Kirkbride, who wished her well. She'd passed the examination for private investigators with the highest score ever recorded, according to the clerk who'd administered it. And for another fifty-dollar fee, she'd automatically received a firearms endorsement because of her previous qualification certificates on the range in both states.

She was a neophyte when it came to hiring competent clerical and administrative help. In the two years since she'd launched Dewell Investigations, she'd been through five administrative assistants. Two had left on their own and three had been fired for incompetence.

If it wasn't for Isabel filling in—her mother justified the hours as "assisting the downtrodden of society"—Cassie might have given up or gone to work for someone else. Or even put aside her revulsion and applied with the local sheriff's department or police department.

Income hadn't been an issue after the first four months of her new enterprise. Word got around that she was professional, efficient, and honest. She had more work than she could handle and she had the luxury of not taking unsavory cases—usually.

She'd been told more times than she cared to be told that she "didn't look like a private investigator" and she was never sure how to take the comment. Cassie was in her mid-thirties, five foot four, ten to fifteen pounds overweight, and her hair was thick and unruly. She didn't have the commanding presence that would instantly bring a room to order, and she was more of a listener than a talker. Since she no longer wore a uniform, she was rarely taken for a cop.

The only person in her life who thought otherwise was Ben, who said she had "cop eyes." Whatever that meant.

Cassie had quickly become the PI of choice for several bail

bondsmen, a half-dozen insurance companies, two car dealerships, the county realtors' group, and one criminal defense firm: Mitchell-Estrella.

Mitchell-Estrella was gaining both prominence and notoriety in Montana legal circles. Although partners Rachel Mitchell and Jessica Estrella were Cassie's age and the firm was less than ten years old and the majority of their clients were still lowlifes looking for plea deals, Mitchell-Estrella had recently won acquittals in several high-profile criminal trials. The most lurid case involved Monte Schreiner, the ex-governor of the state who'd been accused of hiring a transient to murder his mistress near his vacation cabin by hitting her over the head with an oar, loading her unconscious body in a drift boat, and pushing it out onto Flathead Lake where she was later found dead of exposure. Cassie had carefully followed the trial in the *Bozeman Daily Chronicle*.

The blustery Schreiner, who was known for his frequent appearances on cable television news shows wearing a bolo tie and who brought his dog along to every event, came across in news reports as likely guilty to most Montanans, Cassie included. In a state where nearly everyone had met the governor and seen him in action on a personal basis, it just seemed like the kind of thing he would do. Cassie had once seen the governor work a room and put his hands on every person in it, lingering just a little too long with the younger and attractive women whether they were married or not.

The transient, who admitted to the crime and agreed to turn state's witness against Governor Schreiner, was shredded on the stand and caught in a half-dozen lies by attorney Rachel Mitchell. Mrs. Schreiner, who eagerly wanted to see her husband sent to prison and had agreed to testify against him, was forced to admit under Rachel's cross-examination that she had conducted multiple affairs in the past and that she'd exchanged text messages with a fly-fishing guide promising to be with him if "she could just get rid of Monte."

Monte Schreiner was found not guilty and Mrs. Schreiner had moved to Seattle.

After the verdict, Rachel gave a press conference on the courthouse steps declaring that justice had been done.

Cassie saw the clip on the news and thought that a guilty man with a sharp and aggressive lawyer had beaten the system. Although the prosecution's case had some holes in it—didn't they all?—this was the kind of thing that had soured her about the criminal justice system in the first place. She'd vowed not to ever be a part of it.

But Cassie and Rachel Mitchell had history. Rachel's father, Bull, had been a cantankerous outfitter who had guided both Cassie and her mentor Cody Hoyt into the Yellowstone wilderness. Cody had been in pursuit of a client on a multiday horse pack trip who was also a multiple murderer. Cassie had later hired Bull to go after the Lizard King.

Rachel had been in the middle of both situations, both trying to look out for her father's welfare and providing local legal counsel.

Against her better judgment as well as Rachel's admonitions, Cassie had persuaded Bull to come out of retirement one more time and even though he was excited to go and at the time was rejuvenated by the adventure, his physical and mental health deteriorated rapidly upon his return. Although still in Rachel's home in his own special wing, Bull rarely ventured out of his recliner and frequently forgot the names of his daughter, son-in-law, and grandchildren. He only came to life during prime time on Fox News, when he awoke to rail and shake his fist at liberals.

Although Rachel didn't blame Cassie outright for Bull's rapid decline, Cassie felt tremendous guilt for her direct role in it and she knew her requests of him had accelerated his physical and mental decline.

She felt she owed Bull and Rachel, but she'd also made it clear to Rachel that she didn't like the idea of helping to exonerate Rachel's criminal clients no matter who they were. Rachel had assured Cassie that she'd never ask her to do work that would "offend her sensibilities." She'd said it in a wry and irritating way, Cassie thought.

Shortly after that conversation, the firm of Mitchell-Estrella sent the first monthly retainer check to Dewell Investigations. Cassie weighed the decision but cashed it. She needed the money to get started. By doing so she acknowledged her obligation.

Which was why the phone call the night before had thrown Cassie off her game. She knew at the time that Rachel was calling to collect.

Rachel Mitchell stood up from behind her desk as Cassie entered her office. Rachel was slim, stylish, and graceful—everything Cassie was not. The attorney had auburn hair, a sly smile, and green eyes. The credenza behind her desk was filled with framed photos of her teenage boys white-water rafting, fishing, and skiing at the local mountain called Bridger Bowl. There was a large shot of Rachel and her handsome husband waving from the basket of a hot air balloon taken somewhere tropical. A black-and-white still showed a much-younger Bull Mitchell astride a horse guiding a long string of pack horses into the Yellowstone Park wilderness.

"Cassie, you look tired," Rachel said after grasping both of Cassie's hands in hers in a firm greeting. Right to the point.

"You don't," Cassie replied. She knew Rachel either ran or swam every morning before coming to work to stay healthy and fit.

"I was up late on a case," Cassie said as she sat down in one of two leather-bound chairs across from Rachel's desk. She dropped her handbag on the surface of the other.

"Anything I should know about?"

"I don't think so. A skip trace in Big Timber. He's back home with his family for the moment awaiting trial."

"Sounds like one of our clients," Rachel said with a smile.

"I can't say." Cassie knew that Antlerhead's attorney had been assigned through the public defender's office for his new trial and that Rachel took fewer and fewer of those kind of charity cases. Either way, it was unprofessional for Cassie to discuss her clients.

"Well, I'm glad you're in one piece," Rachel said. "It can't be fun going after desperate people."

"It isn't. But it's part of the job."

"You're doing well for yourself," Rachel said as she glided into her chair. "I'm very pleased to see how well you've done here."

"Thank you."

"I think it's important that we stick together as much as we can, you know?"

Cassie nodded her agreement. They'd had this conversation before. Like her own small private investigations firm, Mitchell-Estrella was owned solely by women. Rachel seemed to be more concerned about the fact than Cassie ever was, but it was certainly a bond between them and something Rachel often brought up. This was Montana, after all—the land of big skies, Gary Cooper, ranches the size of small countries, and barely a million people. Cassie had grown up there and was pleased to be back. But there was no doubt that prejudice and misogyny lingered in backwards pockets.

A criminal defense firm run by women was a rarity. Rachel had once told Cassie that when she got together with Jessica Estrella to form their partnership, they were both known by their middle name of Angela. Angela Estrella and Angela Mitchell. They'd agreed to change their professional names to avoid being marginalized and lumped together in the legal community and law enforcement as "the Angelas."

"And how is Ben?"

"He seems to be doing all right," Cassie said. "It's hard for a teenager to fit into a new place and a new school but he seems to be doing fine."

Rachel nodded her approval. She'd remembered Ben's name and Cassie couldn't recall any of the names of Rachel's boys. She felt her neck flush red. Rachel had a way—whether intentional or not—of making Cassie feel inadequate. Cassie thought it might be one of Rachel's techniques for getting what she wanted out of people, and it likely served her well with witnesses in the courtroom.

"Jake, Van, and Andrew are doing well," Rachel said breezily as if to bail her out. "They grow up so quickly, but I'd be lying if I said I wanted all my little boys back. Jake and Van have discovered girls and I'm lucky to see them at all. Andrew, though, is like a young Bull. All he wants to do is go up into the mountains to fish and kill animals. He's been hardwired like that since he was a baby."

"Ben's a wrestler," Cassie said. "He's not very good but he's trying."

In fact, he'd lost every match thus far in the season. She hoped he'd stick with it. Isabel disliked sports and encouraged Ben to "find his passion," whatever that was. It was one of several items of contention between Cassie and her mother in regard to raising Ben.

Cassie contemplated trying to get Ben together with Andrew Mitchell because Ben complained about never having the opportunity to go fishing. Cassie felt guilty about that but she didn't know how to teach him and at the moment there wasn't a man around who could. She wondered if Andrew would take Ben under his wing or if that was a disaster of an idea cooked up by a sometimes desperate single mother.

There was a pause and Rachel said, "We've got a new client and I'd like you to investigate the circumstances of his arrest."

There it was.

Cassie raised her eyebrows. "The circumstances of his arrest?"

"Everything about it. From the charge to the investigation to the arrest. I'm very interested to hear what an experienced investigator like yourself thinks of everything that has happened to date."

"Who are we talking about?"

"Our client is Blake Kleinsasser."

Cassie jumped in her chair as if poked from behind. "*No way.*"

"Hear me out," Rachel said without a smile.

Cassie had read about the case and heard officers gossip about it. Blake Kleinsasser was the oldest son of a very prominent ranch family that owned a huge cattle and hay operation in the shadows of the Bitterroot Range up north in Lochsa County. Kleinsasser had been away for years under a black cloud but had recently returned under mysterious circumstances. He'd been accused of molesting and sexually assaulting the fifteen-year-old daughter of his younger sister—his own niece—at a distant outbuilding on the ranch and leaving her there when he was through. The victim had come forward and named her uncle as her assailant. His arrest had created a great deal of attention because of the Kleinsasser name and their influence in the area.

Fifteen years old, Cassie thought. Just a year older than Ben.

"No way," Cassie repeated as she shook her head back and forth. "I won't help you defend a child rapist. I put bad guys like him away, Rachel. I don't get them off. We talked about this. You agreed."

"We talked about finding justice," Rachel said evenly. "Everyone deserves that."

Then she asked, "Why are you so sure I'm asking you to help

a guilty man go free? Are you saying the cops and overzealous prosecutors don't make mistakes?"

Cassie paused. "What mistakes?"

"I don't know and neither do you," Rachel said. "This arrest
took place up in Lochsa County, and I wasn't there to see it go
down. Until I talked to him and reviewed the charges and the
evidence—or lack of it—I knew as much about this case as you
do right now and it all comes from newspapers and gossip.

"Up until a week ago he wasn't on my radar at all and I probably had the same view of him as you do," she said. "This was all
a Lochsa County crime and I don't know my way around up there.
Blake Kleinsasser hired a local attorney named Andrew Johnson
for the arraignment and preliminary hearing and he wasn't my client. We didn't get involved until a week ago when the trial was
moved here and Blake's counsel removed himself from the case for
health reasons."

Cassie smirked. In her experience the only time defense attorneys resigned or stepped aside was because their client was either
supremely difficult to work with or so obviously guilty that they
didn't want to be associated with the accused. It happened more
often in rural communities than urban environments, Cassie knew.
Small-town attorneys had to live there after the trial.

"Why was the trial moved?" she asked.

"There are some highly unusual circumstances in this case but
they're not all bad. My client was arraigned up there and entered
a not guilty plea and bail was denied because Kleinsasser is considered a flight risk. During the pretrial hearing, the judge did a loop-
de-loop and agreed with the defense that it was unlikely my client
would get a fair hearing in Lochsa because the Kleinsasser family
is an institution of some kind up there. I agree with that decision.

"Then after the case was assigned to here, my client's lawyer
withdrew from the case for health reasons."

"What health reasons? That sounds hinky."

"I agree but I can only guess because my client won't share

much with me," Rachel said. "But after looking at the charging documents and the evidence I think the attorney made the right decision for whatever reason. Let's just say that in my opinion there were a lot of things his previous counsel *didn't* do, and a lot of evidence he didn't challenge for some reason. Maybe he was just out of his depth with these kinds of serious criminal felony charges. I'll leave it at that because I'm hesitant to disparage another defense attorney."

"You people do stick together," Cassie observed.

"It's a small community. Too small to burn bridges, Cassie. Blake Kleinsasser's ex-lawyer may turn out to be the judge I'm trying a case for one of these days. You never know.

"Have you been to Lochsa County before?" Rachel asked.

"A million years ago. Not since our girls' basketball team played there in high school."

What Cassie could remember was murky. She recalled a bus ride on narrow country two-lane roads through miles of dark timber, the emergence of the snow-capped Bitterroots through the windshield as they neared the rural high school, and a foreboding sense of claustrophobia within the town of Lochsa Springs itself. It had been so unlike the rest of the state with its open vistas and wide skies that it stuck in her memory.

The game itself had also left a bad taste in her mouth. It was played in a tiny and ancient gymnasium and the stands were packed with local fans who booed the interlopers from Helena with a vehemence that rattled all the players. The Lochsa Springs girls were rough and nasty, and Cassie's team got killed.

"Lochsa County is an odd place," Rachel said as if reading Cassie's thoughts. "Some people might say it's about as backwards and inbred as you can find in this state. It's like the twenty-first century passed it by. Maybe even the twentieth."

She continued, "We can be grateful that the judge up there agreed to change the venue of the trial and we don't have to go up there for it. Did you know that there has never been a murder conviction in Lochsa County if the accused is from there? I've heard from prosecutors that if you're a local and you shoot someone in that county it's probably because they deserved it. Seriously. But if an out-of-stater is on trial for doing something to a local you can be pretty much assured that they're going to end up in Deer Lodge. So, we dodged a bullet there."

Cassie squirmed in her chair. "So, you think he's innocent?"

"I didn't say that. But I think he's entitled to a fair trial. Don't you agree?"

"A fifteen-year-old girl said he did it," Cassie said. "I don't want to be in the position of impeaching the testimony of a scared fifteen-year-old girl."

"It may not come to that."

Cassie sat back in her chair and grimaced. She wanted no part of this.

"We're waiting for all the prosecution discovery evidence to arrive," Rachel said. "In my opinion they're slow-walking everything, which unfortunately isn't that unusual. We're also waiting for the files from my client's ex-attorney that he prepared for the case before he withdrew. But I *can* tell you what the prosecution's case consists of because we have the transcripts from the preliminary hearing."

Cassie nodded for her to go on. Although Cassie knew it was lawyer-speak, she found Rachel's constant use of the term "my client" interesting. Cassie guessed that if she used "Kleinsasser" it would be confusing because the case was filled with Kleinsassers. If she said "Blake Kleinsasser" each time it would sound stiff. And simply "Blake" would convey familiarity that could come across as unprofessional.

Rachel consulted no notes and she met Cassie's defiant glare with a no-nonsense look of her own.

"According to the prosecution, my client arrived back in Lochsa

County three months ago—in June. For years he's been on the East Coast working in the financial industry. I don't know the details of what he did except I take it he made a small fortune for himself and apparently didn't keep in contact with his immediate family. It's well known up there that he's the black sheep of the Kleinsasser clan and apparently no one was very happy to see him come back."

"Why?"

"My client's problems with his parents and siblings go way back," Rachel said. "I don't have many details but I think it boils down to the fact that he's seen as a turncoat—a climber—who abandoned his multigenerational family legacy as well as the area. He's the oldest and firstborn son. You know how that goes."

Cassie was well aware of the phenomenon known throughout the Mountain West as "the curse of the third generation," wherein the founders of the ranch passed it on to their children, who later passed it on to *their* children. But it was that third generation where the situation sometimes went nuclear: family members who either did or didn't want to carry on the tradition, members who wanted to sell the whole place to get out and avoid taxes, members who went to war with brothers and sisters for what they saw as their rightful inheritance.

Lawyers and accountants had made their careers representing different factions of the third generation because the legal battles often went on for decades. It was the nastiest kind of war: brother versus brother, brother versus sister, sister versus sister.

"So, your client came back to reclaim his inheritance?" Cassie asked. "Sort of a backwards prodigal son thing?"

"Unclear, but that's the assumption. Look, I'll cut to the chase," Rachel said. "The prosecution alleges that on the night in question, July second, Blake got in a big fight with his younger brothers and ended up drunk at a local bar. From there, he left in his rental car and picked up the fifteen-year-old victim—his niece—after a church event and drove her to a remote outbuilding on the property where he assaulted and raped her and left her to fend for herself. Her name is Franny Porché."

"That's exotic," Cassie said. "Not Kleinsasser?"

"She's from my client's sister's third marriage. The sister, named Cheyenne, is divorced from what I understand."

"Okay," Cassie said. She already knew that if she went forward one of her first tasks would be to sketch a family tree. Not that she intended to go forward though.

Rachel said, "The other side claims they have a mountain of evidence and the Lochsa County prosecutor agreed with them. So did the judge, obviously. They say they can place Blake in the bar that night and later at the church. They say they have witnesses who will testify they saw the niece get into his rental car and drive away. They say the niece gave a statement that led to his arrest at a motel in Horston the next day.

"Of course," Rachel said, "They're throwing the book at my client and overcharging him as usual. We're talking felony sexual assault, kidnapping, criminal endangerment—the gamut."

Before Cassie could ask about the credibility of Franny, Rachel held up her hand palm-out to quash the question.

"The charges go well beyond he said, she said if that's what you were wondering."

"I was."

"According to the charging documents, the Lochsa County sheriff's department have four pieces of physical evidence to bolster their case. One is a whiskey glass found in the cabin where the girl was raped that's covered with my client's fingerprints. Two, they've got tire tracks from his rental car on the dirt road from the highway to the cabin. Three, they say they have semen residue and DNA on her underwear that matches up with my client. And four, they say they processed a conclusive rape kit with hair, fiber, and DNA evidence pointing to my client."

Cassie snorted and said, "Is that all?"

"I don't appreciate the sarcasm," Rachel said quickly.

"He's guilty," Cassie said. "Every box has been ticked. There's motive: a dispute with his family. There's opportunity: he was there. And there's both direct *and* circumstantial evidence that he did it."

"He says he doesn't think he did it," Rachel said. But her tone was tentative, not strident.

"You mean he says he doesn't know?" Cassie asked.

"He says he remembers getting in the argument with his brothers and later getting hammered at the Hayloft Saloon in Lolo. I've been there—it's a classic dive.

"My client recalls drinking shot after shot and then apparently blacking out. He didn't come to until the Lochsa County deputies were banging on his motel room door the next morning."

Cassie whistled. Open and shut.

Rachel sighed. "He insists on pleading not guilty, despite my advice."

"Of course he does. Ninety-five percent of criminals think of themselves as victims, not perpetrators. He's no different."

Rachel leaned forward and steepled her fingers. She said, "I know how it sounds. It sounds that way to me, too. But you yourself just said there's a five percent chance."

"I was pulling that number out of my butt," Cassie said. "I've spent my life around these scumbags. They blame everyone but themselves for the things they do. Of course he's not going to admit it."

Rachel lowered her hands to the desktop as if showing a hand of cards. "I'm not asking you to compromise yourself. I don't want that. I don't want you to set out to free a child rapist."

"Then what do you want from me?"

"I want you to step back a couple of years in time. You're once again the chief investigator for Bakkan County and this horrific crime is presented to you. I want you to do the same things you'd do if you wanted to put this guy away for the rest of his life, which you probably do. Interview the witnesses," Rachel said, tapping the tip of one manicured finger with her other hand to indicate *one-two-three*. "Examine the evidence. Go through the arrest warrants and the police reports. Look twice at everything you find to see if there are inconsistencies or holes. Do it not from the standpoint that you're trying to help a defense attorney blow holes in the prosecution case against her client. Do it as if you want to assure the prosecutor that every step you've taken as lead investigator is by the book and one hundred percent legit."

Cassie blinked.

"When you're through I want you to brief me on what you've found," Rachel said. "I want it straight, warts and all. If I learn from you that the prosecution's case is as bombproof as it sounds, well, I'll try a different tactic like a plea deal if I can convince my client that's the only way he can go. I need an airtight argument to convince him.

"But if mistakes were made—I need to know that, too. And if you discover new evidence or inconsistencies, well, I need you to share them with me as well."

Cassie thought about it. Rachel seemed sincere. It was almost as if she didn't know what she was asking.

"Based on what you've told me I think he's guilty as charged and he needs to go down for it," Cassie said. "I can't imagine a scenario where I'd change my mind."

"There might not be one," Rachel said with a sigh. "But I need to know that before the trial starts and we have to give our plea. That way I'll know how best to proceed."

Cassie hesitated. She weighed the likelihood of confirming the prosecutor's case and sending a scumbag to prison against the very dubious possibility of discovering gaping holes in the case.

"He's going to spend the rest of his life in Deer Lodge," Cassie said.

"Probably."

"That's where he belongs."

"Probably."

"This will all be an expensive waste of my time and your client's money."

"So it's a yes. Good."

Cassie nodded.

"How does your schedule look for the next couple of weeks?" Rachel asked.

Cassie didn't need to consult the appointment app on her phone. "I've got several jobs in the works right now—two insurance fraud investigations and a whole stack of background checks. Most of that work can be done from my computer in the office, although I do need to do a little surveillance of an insurance claimant up in Missoula."

"Is anything urgent?"

"Not really. Of course, I can't anticipate when someone will walk through the door like my skip trace job last night."

"You might have to turn them away."

Cassie squinted, trying to discern the reason for the rush.

Rachel said, "Please clear your calendar starting today. We came late to this case and we're behind the eight ball. I need the intel you can get as soon as I can get it."

Then it came to her. Cassie said, "If I find something to derail the prosecution's case you want to be able to use that information at pretrial motions. Before jury selection."

Rachel sat back. "When did you get your law degree?"

"I didn't. But I've been fighting people like you—overaggressive defense attorneys—for a long time. I know some of your tricks."

"I'd call it a legitimate legal procedure. Not a trick."

"Whatever."

Rachel stood up and handed an inch-thick file to Cassie. The meeting was apparently over.

"If I do this, we're square," Cassie said, accepting the file. "No more obligation to you and your dad."

Rachel hesitated a moment and then nodded in agreement. "You might want to get reading," she said. "We're scheduled to meet with my client at ten in county lockup."

Cassie looked at her watch. She had forty-five minutes.

three

⊷≡◉═⊷

Blake Kleinsasser was led into the interview room adjacent to A Pod of the Gallatin County Detention Center by a uniformed county correctional officer with a buzz cut and a wad of chewing tobacco in his lower lip. Kleinsasser had to shuffle from the door to the chair across from Cassie and Rachel because of the shackles and chains on his ankles. He held his hands out in front of him as if he were making an offering—but that was due to the handcuffs.

As he approached, Cassie had a severe hot flash that made her gasp for breath. Kleinsasser's entrance had immediately taken her back to a similar room in a similar jail in Wilson, North Carolina, when the Lizard King was in custody and she was sent there to identify and interrogate him. The man responsible for perhaps hundreds of rapes, murders, and mutilations of truck stop prostitutes and other innocent victims had loomed over her as he approached and had assessed her with dead shark eyes. He was operating under a new name and he'd added glasses and a beard to change his features, but there was no doubt it was him.

A few minutes later, after Cassie baited him, the Lizard King tried to crush her windpipe.

The scene in that room came back to her. She took a breath and felt her eyes flutter. She could feel the prick of perspiration under the collar of her blouse and she hoped her face hadn't flushed red.

Even though she knew the Lizard King was dead on this earth, he was still very much alive in her everyday thoughts and night-mares. He might always be. He was partially to blame for the fact that she could never go back to North Dakota, why she didn't want to be rehired by a law enforcement agency, and why she shuddered every time an eighteen-wheeler roared by her on the highway.

Cassie tried to shake it off and observe Kleinsasser carefully. He was fairly tall and slim, six foot even, with longish sandy hair and hooded blue eyes. He had wide shoulders and he looked at them both with a kind of self-aware, self-satisfied smirk. His orange jumpsuit was several sizes too large so that the short sleeves of his top extended past his elbows and the fabric bunched around his jail-issued slip-on boat shoes. The effect made him look younger than his forty-three years, Cassie thought. He looked like an adolescent forced to wear adult clothing.

Jailers liked to humiliate prisoners in subtle ways, she knew. Especially high-profile inmates who arrived with attitude. They were issued clothing that was laughably too small for them or, in this case, much too large.

"Will you please unlock him for our meeting?" Rachel asked the CO.

"I can unlock his wrists but not his ankles."

"Then please unlock his wrists."

Kleinsasser nodded his appreciation as he sat down. The CO leaned over his shoulder with the cuff key and Kleinsasser held up his hands but didn't look over at the officer. Cassie noted the arrogance of the gesture, like holding up an empty glass at a passing waitress but not making eye contact.

When his wrists were unshackled, he rubbed them with his opposite hands before dropping his arms to his sides.

"I'll be right outside the door," the CO said to Rachel.

"I know you will. Please respect our privacy."

"Sure, ma'am," the CO said with a roll of his eyes.

Rachel waited for the *clunk* of the door lock before speaking. She turned in her chair and addressed the closed-circuit camera that was mounted in the top west corner of the room behind them.

"If this camera is live and somebody is watching this feed, now is the time to shut down your system. Observing an interview between the accused and his counsel is illegal and provides a basis to vacate the charges. Not only that, but I'll go after anyone snooping with everything I've got in a court of law."

Cassie couldn't swear to it, but she thought she heard a barely audible *click* from the direction of the camera.

Rachel turned to face Kleinsasser, who seemed amused by what was taking place.

"This is Cassie Dewell of Dewell Investigations," she said. "She's my investigator on this case."

Kleinsasser nodded his head slightly to Cassie, but didn't give her the focus she was giving him at the same time.

He didn't *look* like a rapist, Cassie thought. But that meant nothing. Some criminals, like Antlerhead, looked the part. Others simply didn't. The Lizard King looked like an overweight midwestern blue-collar worker, but he'd exuded menace despite his outward appearance. Kleinsasser gave off an air of bemused resignation.

After reading the file on the case, Cassie had Googled his name and looked for images. The disparity between what she found was striking. The most recent shots of him were of a gaunt and disheveled man being led across a motel parking lot to a sheriff's cruiser the morning he was arrested. In those photos, he looked confused and lost. His hair was pasted to the side of his head and he had a three- or four-day growth of silver-flecked whiskers. His eyes were dull.

Prior to that string of images, though, were many from what appeared to be New York City. In those, he wore stylish suits and ties and his hair was groomed. He was pictured with other hedge fund executives and bankers at social events, IPO launches, and financial instrument rollouts. He looked brash and above-it-all, a man almost too comfortable in his own skin. He looked smug and confident—a man used to winning, a fast-talker. There wasn't even a hint of Montana in his bearing.

He looked smug and confident, kind of like he looked today.

Before he opened his mouth and judging solely on his presence, she put herself into the role of a jurist in his upcoming trial and asked herself, *Is this man before me capable of raping his fifteen-year-old niece?*

As if reading her mind, his eyes darted toward her and then back to his lawyer in a dismissive way that set her on edge.

And she thought, *Yes. He's capable of that.*

"I'm fucked, aren't I?" he said and almost smiled.

"Let me answer your question this way," Rachel said as she dug into her briefcase for the file Cassie had read and a fresh legal pad to take notes, "you're charged with a half dozen Class A felonies. If you're convicted of even a couple of them, say kidnapping and forcible rape—you could be sentenced to two hundred years. But the bright side is you're going to get the best defense possible."

"Anywhere?" he asked with a sarcastic grin. "The best defense anywhere? Or the best defense in Podunk, Montana?"

Rachel froze for a moment and then her eyes narrowed into slits. Cassie felt the tension and fought the urge to slide her chair away from Rachel.

Rachel said, "Podunk, Montana, is where you've been arrested and charged for kidnapping, conspiracy, and the assault of your own niece. If you want to reach out to one of your high-priced New York criminal law firms and pay for them to fly out here and save your ass, I'll gladly step aside like your last lawyer and leave this hot steaming piece of shit case to them."

She set her jaw and said, "If you think a Montana jury would be impressed with the thousand-dollar-an-hour fast-talking New York lawyers, you're sadly mistaken."

Kleinsasser didn't flinch, as Cassie had. It said something about him, she thought. He was used to that kind of hyperbole. She wasn't.

"Color me impressed with that little speech," he said to Rachel. "People talk around here. I heard you were a bulldog."

He had a flat and fast New York accent that he must have picked up in the years since he left the ranch.

Rachel opened the file. "To answer your question: yes, based only on the prosecution's evidence and the charging documents, I think we're fucked. But that's why we're here today. So, try to keep your attitude in check long enough that maybe I can figure out a way to mitigate your situation."

Kleinsasser cocked an eyebrow.

"As usual, the prosecution has overcharged in this case," Rachel said. "As I think you know, you're looking at conspiracy, kidnapping, sexual assault, and rape. In Montana, section 45-5-503 of the criminal code for rape allows the judge to put you away for a hundred years if the victim is less than sixteen years old."

Kleinsasser snorted. "That ought to do it. Why all the other charges?"

"They always do that because it makes better headlines and they hope that if the judge or jury doesn't buy some of the charges, they'll find guilt with at least one major crime.

"I'll be blunt," Rachel told him. "It doesn't look good. There's nothing I've seen or nothing you've told me that even gives a whiff of hope for an acquittal. So, what we need to establish is whether or not we can base our defense not on your innocence, but somehow mitigating the worst of the charges so it'll result in fewer years in prison."

Kleinsasser tapped his fingertips on the tabletop. "You mean so I'll only go away for ninety years instead of a hundred."

"Ninety would be generous, Mr. Kleinsasser."

"Like I said, I'm fucked."

"Have you given any thought to changing your plea?"

Kleinsasser sat back and blinked. "Changing my plea?"

"That's what I asked."

"Why would I do that?"

"To avoid a trial. The county attorney *might* be willing to drop a couple of the charges and you *might* face less time in prison if they'll offer a plea bargain."

Kleinsasser glared at her. "No thanks to that."

"I had to ask," Rachel said, breaking their stare down. "If at any point you change your mind please ask the administration here to get in contact with me."

"Yeah, I'll sure do that if I change my mind." He rolled his eyes as he said it. "Don't ask me that again, Counselor."

Rachel took a deep breath, obviously trying to stanch her annoyance with him. "Look, Cassie here has reviewed your case and she has some questions for you. Please take your time and answer them in full. That way, when she goes up to Lochsa County she'll be better informed."

For the first time, Kleinsasser turned his full attention on Cassie. His eyes did a full assessment of her and Cassie could tell he found her less than impressive.

"You're going up to the ranch?"

"Probably."

He slowly shook his head. The grin that formed on his mouth was terrifying.

"Do you believe in God?"

"Yes, I do."

"Then may God have mercy on your soul. You have no idea what kind of fucking snake pit you're going to fall into."

Shaking off the implications of the statement as best she could, Cassie reviewed her notes. It was a way to avoid Kleinsasser's

withering instant negative impression of her appearance and abilities. "Let's get some background to start. Why did you come home,
Mr. Kleinsasser?"

He narrowed his eyes and shook his head. "I didn't come *home*.
I came *back*. There's a big fucking difference."

Cassie said, "Look, we don't have to make this difficult. I can
do without the sarcasm, attitude, and profanity. Just answer the
questions so I have some kind of basis on which to operate."

Kleinsasser briefly closed his eyes as if trying not to snap. Then
he opened them and spoke in a lower, more modulated voice.

"I guess I forgot you're on my side," he said.

"I'm not on your side. I'm doing investigative work for your
attorney. There's a big fucking difference."

"Gotcha," he said with an approving nod. "Using my own
words against me."

"Get used to it," she said. "It's likely to happen in a courtroom,
too."

Rachel nodded her agreement.

"So again, why did you come back?"

"My parents are old. They're on their last legs and even though
they're truly awful people all hell will break out when they're gone.
As you probably know, I have experience in finance and I thought
maybe I could broker a deal among everyone because whatever
they think of me, I'm still the oldest son. I guess I foolishly thought
I could help out with transition within the family. Obviously, I've
been away too many years and I wasn't thinking clearly. If I had it
all to do over again, I would have stayed in New York."

Cassie shook her head. "Broker what?"

"The inheritance. I thought I might be able to figure out a way
to divide up the assets of the ranch and all of their enterprises in a
way that would make everybody happy. I guess I figured I was the
only one who could pull it off since it was obvious I had no interest in getting anything myself."

"Why is it obvious?"

He started to roll his eyes again but caught himself. "It's obvious because I left as soon as I could get out of that place. That isn't done in the Kleinsasser family. No one ever leaves. It doesn't matter if you make your own way in the world and don't ask them for anything. The problem is you left in the first place. That's considered the ultimate act of disloyalty. With them, if you leave or strike out on your own it means you look down on them and they resent you for it. Like I said, it's a snake pit."

Cassie glanced down at her notes. "I assume you're referring to your sister Cheyenne and your brothers John Wayne and Rand."

Cheyenne was the next oldest in the Kleinsasser family at thirty-nine. John Wayne was thirty-five and the youngest brother, Rand, was thirty-two. All still lived in Lochsa County.

"That would be them," Kleinsasser said through gritted teeth. "They all want the ranch for their own twisted reasons. They're so wrapped up in the legacy of the place that they think it's worth something—which it's not. I tried to tell them that."

"But how can that be?" Cassie interrupted. "The Kleinsasser Ranch is nearly eighty thousand acres."

"Over half of that is mountains," Kleinsasser said. "No good for anything besides scenery. Cows can't eat scenery, and the area is too remote to develop. There's no oil or gas on the property and not even enough wind for a damned wind farm. If you split that place up everybody would go broke separately.

"I tried to reason with them that it made the most sense to prepare to put the whole place on the market and we could split up the proceeds. Sell it to some billionaire land collector and forget about trying to make it work as a cattle ranch. I told them I didn't want any part of the payout but my share, that I'd sign any document they wanted attesting to the fact that I didn't want more.

"That just made them even more suspicious of me," he said. "My brothers, especially. They knew that because I was the oldest, I was entitled to the lion's share and they couldn't believe that I was willing to lower my inheritance to twenty-five percent. They figured I must be involved in some kind of big scheme to screw them or freeze them out. They figured I must know something they didn't—that it was a money grab by me because I don't love the place the way they do, which I don't.

"That's what you need to know about my family," Kleinsasser said. "It's all about two things: legacy and resentment. If you know that going in everything will be clear to you. It'll start to make some kind of sense."

"Since you claim to be wealthy, why do you even want twenty-five percent?" Cassie asked. "Why not just stay away and let them fight it out?"

"If only it was that easy," he said. "I wish it could work that way. But as I said—I'm the oldest son. They'd suck me in so they could pick the meat off my bones. I could see being involved in litigation for the rest of my life with people I never want to see again. I wanted to head off the coming war.

"Besides," he said, "Twenty-five percent isn't as much as you might think it might be once you go through all of the legal crap, all of the taxes, paying all the creditors—everybody with their hands out. In the end I figured I'd get a couple of hundred grand. That's chump change in my world, and it sure as hell doesn't compensate me for the years I spent growing up around those people."

Cassie tapped the tip of her pen on her notes. "Okay, there are a lot of family issues. I'm not sure us knowing them helps your case."

"It explains everything," he said defensively. "I haven't even told you about the Kleinsasser Family Trust."

Cassie cocked her head and Rachel leaned forward.

"The Kleinsasser Family Trust?" Rachel asked.

"It was established by my grandfather, Horst Kleinsasser. He was the so-called leader of a breakaway Hutterite cult who established the ranch in 1916 after being shunned by the rest of his colony. He was a strange and twisted dude, which maybe accounts for why my family is the way it is. But yes, he wrote a long document and deed establishing how the ranch would be passed down through the generations. My dad has it memorized and so do my idiot brothers."

Cassie wrote down the words *Kleinsasser Family Trust* for later research.

"Going by the Kleinsasser Family Trust, I should get everything," he said. "I'm the oldest son. It's all mine if I want it. It's up to my discretion whether my siblings get a piece of it or not. But there's a catch. The only way the heir can be expelled from the trust is by denouncing the family name or committing 'moral turpitude.'"

Rachel sat back. "Like rape."

"That's correct. Like rape."

Cassie was intrigued but suspicious. "Are you saying they conspired against you in some way to establish moral turpitude?"

"I guess that's up to you to prove," he said. "But they already tried to get me kicked off the trust. They said that by leaving the ranch I'd denounced the family name. They hired attorneys and everything, but the judge concluded that going to work some place other than Lochsa County, Montana, isn't the same as formally denouncing the family, even though to my fucked-up family it was. So this is the next best thing."

"Again," Cassie said forcefully, "you're trying to convince us that they hate you so much that they *forced you to assault your underage niece*?"

With that, she dropped her pen on her notes and sat back with her arms crossed across her breasts. She wasn't buying it.

"I'm telling you what I know and what I suspect," Kleinsasser said. For the first time, there was a hint of desperation in his tone.

"Did you pick up Franny Porché from church that night?"

He nodded. "I did. I thought she was innocent. I thought she might be redeemable because she's of the fourth generation and that the magical hold the ranch has on the rest of them might not be as strong with her. I guess I thought that she might be able to talk some sense into J. W. and Rand."

Cassie switched her glare from Kleinsasser to Rachel. Rachel responded by looking away.

"You took a fifteen-year-old girl to an old outbuilding on the ranch because you wanted to talk with her?" Cassie asked. She couldn't keep the incredulity out of her voice.

"I know how it looks," he said, "but that cabin is where I spent the only good years of my life growing up on that place. I guess I wanted to show her that I did have a connection to the family after all these years despite what her mom and her uncles told her."

"You guess?"

"I'd been drinking for three days," he said looking down at his hands. "I can only remember bits and pieces of those seventy-two hours. I remember picking her up and I remember waking up when the deputies pulled me out of my bed at the motel."

Cassie shook her head. She disliked Blake Kleinsasser and she thought he was pathetic.

"How do you explain the whiskey glass they found at the cabin with your fingerprints on it?"

He shrugged.

"How do you explain your semen found on her underwear?"

To his small credit, he cringed. But he shrugged again.

"You're not going to claim that the sexual intercourse was consensual, are you?" Cassie challenged. Because if he did, she thought, she'd walk out of the room.

"There was no sexual intercourse," Kleinsasser said. "It didn't happen. Believe me, if it happened, I'd remember it. That's something even a drunk remembers."

There was no reason to ask him about the tire tracks from his rental car. He'd already admitted picking Franny up and taking her out there.

"Have you been accused of assaulting underage victims before this incident?"

"God, no."

"So, when we dig into your past there won't be similar incidents? I ask because for sure the prosecution is looking."

"I'm not a monster," he said. "I'm just a stupid drunk uncle who
thought he was doing the right thing."

Cassie bit her tongue. The sudden shift to victimhood in his
tone rankled her. Like Antlerhead, like most criminals, nothing
was ever their fault.

"Why did your lawyer quit?" Cassie asked. Out of the corner
of her eye she could see Rachel tense up at the question. It was
likely out-of-bounds. Cassie didn't care.

"You'll have to ask him," Kleinsasser said. "But as you'll find
out, everybody in Lochsa County is connected to my family in
some way. Maybe he figured that if he wanted to continue his practice into the future he needed to step aside."

"Cassie," Rachel cautioned, "do you have any more questions
about the facts of this case?"

Cassie slumped in her chair. Her disgust with Kleinsasser and
her role in his defense made the bile rise in her throat.

She asked him, "Can you give me the names of people who
might have witnessed you during the time you started drinking to
when you were rousted out of your bed at the hotel?"

He squinted as if trying to remember. "There's a man I met at
the Corvallis Tavern."

"What is his name?"

"I think it's Frank."

"Anyone else?"

"I met a woman there. Lindy. Blond, late twenties, nice . . .
figure. We spent a lot of time together before I blacked out."

"Last name for Lindy?"

"You think I got her last name?"

Cassie sighed. "Anyone else?"

This time, he closed his eyes while apparently trying to recall
more details.

"There was a goofy old cowboy—a ranch hand. He was the foreman back when I was a kid but apparently he got let go. Named Hawk. He was nice to me. I remember sitting next to him at the Corvallis Tavern. He seemed to know me from my youth but I couldn't remember him as well as he remembered me. One of those old-timers, you know? He had a hard-on for my dad and my brothers. We talked about what assholes they are."

"Was this the first night of your bender?"

"No, the second, I think. But don't hold me to that."

"Did you spend time with Lindy that night?"

"Yeah."

"Anyone else?"

"Probably, but I can't think of anyone right now. It's all kind of a blur, like I said."

In her notes, Cassie wrote down: *Hayloft Saloon / Lolo / Lindy. Corvallis Tavern / Hamilton / Hawk.*

"You're less than helpful," Cassie said. "Can you help me with a time line from the hour you entered the Hayloft Saloon to when you were arrested?"

"Not anything other than what I told you. I was blotto."

Cassie sat back. "How often does this happen—these blackout periods when you're drinking?"

He shrugged. "Back when I was a young big swinging dick on Wall Street it was every couple of years, but it hasn't happened in a long time. This place isn't good for me, I guess.

"I don't know what it is about coming back to Montana," Kleinsasser mused. "But whatever it is—the big sky or the bad memories—it makes me want to find a bar stool as fast as I can."

Cassie looked over at Rachel again. The attorney looked as exasperated with Kleinsasser as Cassie felt.

He said, "They used to tell me when I went on a bender that the people I talked to didn't even know I was drunk," he said. "They described me as 'lucid.' But afterwards, I couldn't remember a damned thing."

"Let's say there was a scheme against you," Cassie said to him. "Who would likely be the prime mover in it?"

"J. W.," Kleinsasser said quickly. "Absolutely John Wayne. He thinks of himself as the keeper of the family name. Rand is unstable and he worships J. W., so I wouldn't be surprised if he were in on it."

"What about your sister?"

He shook his head. "Cheyenne and I have the same problem. We tend to go on benders where we can't remember what we did. Except when Cheyenne goes on one she comes back pregnant."

"Your parents?"

"I wouldn't put anything past them."

"And why would Franny lie?"

"I wish I could tell you. I *liked* her. She's a little off in the head but anyone would be growing up in that family."

"So, in conclusion," Cassie said, "everyone in your family is poison, twisted, and paranoid except for you. Your role is to show up and try and help everyone out of the goodness of your heart after twenty-five years of being away. Did I get that right?"

Kleinsasser started to talk but caught himself. Then he turned to Rachel. "I don't have to listen to this bullshit."

Rachel said, "This is nothing compared to what you'll hear in the courtroom."

"I'm not copping a plea," he said. "There's no way I did this."

"I thought you said you couldn't remember what happened," Cassie said.

Cassie waited on a worn bench in the jailhouse hallway for Rachel to finish her meeting with Blake Kleinsasser. She couldn't spend another minute with him.

When Rachel came out she flashed her palms up. "Don't say it, Cassie. I know."

Cassie nodded.

"If you go up there and come back with corroboration maybe, just maybe, I'll be able to convince him to change his plea and we can move past this."

"How do you do it?" Cassie asked. "How do you look at yourself in the mirror?"

"I don't."

"We're on the wrong side here," Cassie said.

Rachel didn't disagree. She looked out the smudged jailhouse window and said, "The fires are bad this morning. My throat feels like I smoked a pack of cigarettes."

"I'll go tomorrow," Cassie said as she stood up.

They walked down the hallway together but didn't say another word until they parted for their separate cars in the parking lot.

"Sometimes, they're not guilty," Rachel said over her shoulder.

But most of the time they are, Cassie thought to herself.

Like Blake Kleinsasser.

four

The dining room still smelled of soy and MSG as Cassie gathered the dishes after dinner that night with Isabel and Ben. She'd stopped at Chinatown Restaurant on West Main on her way home and picked up cartons of sweet and sour pork, cashew chicken, fried rice, and hot and sour soup. Chinese was a compromise of sorts: Ben liked it because it was still exotic to him after living in North Dakota, and Isabel tolerated it because in her mind it was the product of struggling indigenous immigrants in a Caucasian world even though Chinese had built the railroads and had been established in Montana for generations.

Dinner had been quiet: Cassie with her thoughts, Ben with his, and Isabel scrolling through her iPad. But they'd all eaten together and not argued about anything, so it was a win. Often, lack of tension was all she could ask for.

While she scraped off the dishes and placed the half-full containers in the refrigerator for future meals, she tried to fend off feeling dirty for what she'd taken on. It had hung with her throughout the afternoon after meeting with Blake Kleinsasser. She hadn't mentioned a word of it to either her son or her mother because she wasn't sure she could defend herself against their questions.

Cassie, Ben, and Isabel lived in a three-bedroom ranch-style home on West Kagy Avenue in Bozeman that was south of Montana State

University and within sight of the Museum of the Rockies. The
neighborhood was old and established, and the homes in it ranged
from well-appointed to worn-out. Cassie's thirty-year-old house
was closer to the latter. She knew she needed to get it painted and
reshingled, replace the carpets and drapes, and update the kitchen.

Someday.

It wasn't her dream home by any means but it was good enough
to be a placeholder until she could afford a rural property with
some space around it. Maybe even a horse or two. The idea of
grooming a horse seemed restful. Riding one at dusk and letting
the tension of the day melt away . . .

After dinner, Ben had gone straight to his room without a word
and Isabel had moved into the family room and turned on the television. The only three channels she watched were CNN, PBS,
and MSNBC.

Her mother stood near the bookcase shaking her head at whatever the president had said or tweeted that day. As usual, Isabel
wore a flowing full-length dress and her long white-gray hair was
bound in a ponytail. The bare nubs of her toes stuck out from the
sandals she wore most of the year. For as long as Cassie could remember, she'd never seen her mother wear makeup.

Isabel, who refused to answer to "Mom," or "Grandma" in
Ben's case, was a stubborn caricature of what a sixties radical should
look like two decades into the twenty-first century and she knew
it and it didn't bother her. Once, after several glasses of wine, she'd
mused about "changing her look" but she never had. Cassie was
so used to it she was only reminded when strangers gaped at her
mother when they saw her for the first time. It must be, Cassie
thought, like suddenly meeting an actual cartoon character in the
flesh.

"Don't let yourself get worked up," Cassie said as she entered
the room drying her hands on a hand towel.

"It's impossible not to," Isabel said. "Just look at that orange clown. Just *look* at him. What is wrong with you people?"

It was a mantra. The current president had won Montana by nearly twenty percent. It was a source of apoplexy for Isabel and her small circle of like-minded friends.

"Has your life changed in any way?" Cassie asked, despite herself. "Mine hasn't. Is there something in your life that has gotten worse since he got elected?"

Isabel didn't look away from the screen. "I'm waiting for the internment camps. I'm waiting for the armies of intolerance to take over the streets and round up the gays and brown-skinned immigrants."

She was only partially kidding.

"In Bozeman?"

Cassie regretted even bringing up politics. She knew better. Plus, she had a favor to ask.

"Isabel, I might need to be away for a few days. Are you able to look after Ben?"

That got her attention. "How many days?"

"I'm not sure. It's for work. I may have to be gone a week at most."

"A week?"

"It may not be that long."

"Where are you going?"

"North," Cassie said. "I've got to do an investigation in Lochsa County."

Isabel's eyes left the television and narrowed on Cassie. "Have you ever been there?"

"In high school but I'm sure you don't remember."

Isabel didn't. She'd never paid any attention to high school sports or attended any of Cassie's games. That wasn't Isabel.

Cassie added, "Since then I've only driven through."

"Let me tell you about that place. I went there once with your father and it was horrible."

Cassie's dad had been a long-haul truck driver who was away weeks at a time, leaving her and Isabel, his common-law wife, in Helena at the time. That arrangement seemed to work for the both of them because they were such different people that absence served to keep their marriage alive far longer than if they'd lived together in the same house. In the middle was Cassie.

"When were you there?" Cassie asked.

"Years ago. I let your father convince me to go on a run with him and I regretfully said yes. I remember rolling into Victor in time to see a mob shaving the hair off a Native American outside a bar. They held him down and shaved off his long black hair and let it fall into the street. I told your father to keep driving and I've never been back."

Cassie pursed her lips. "I've never heard that story before." She couldn't imagine that at one time in her parents' union that they'd been close enough that Isabel would actually agree to accompany her dad on the road.

"It was horrible," Isabel said. "I swore I'd never go back."

"Was this the sixties, then?"

"No—early seventies. How old do you think I am?"

Cassie didn't take the bait. "That's a long time ago and a whole different world."

"And I seriously doubt those people have changed." Isabel sniffed.

Then her face softened. "Of course, I'll be here for Ben, but he's getting more difficult. We used to have such a wonderful time together, but now I see how he looks at me."

"He's at that age," Cassie said.

She didn't add, *He looks at me that way, too.*

"I'll leave cash for groceries and I'll call every night," she said. "Maybe you can figure out separate dinners while I'm away so there isn't so much drama."

"He needs to eat healthy foods for his own good," Isabel said.

Cassie smiled. "Did you see him tonight? He ate twice as much as you and I. Wrestling practice after school makes him ravenous when he gets home, and he hasn't gained an ounce of fat. I wish I could eat like that."

"You could, once," Isabel said, taking in Cassie in a way that Cassie didn't like. "It's that cop diet. You cops eat garbage all day."

Cassie didn't want to argue. She recalled a piece of advice once given to her by her then-mentor Cody Hoyt of the Lewis and Clark County Sheriff's Office, who said of day-to-day law enforcement routine, *Take every possible opportunity you can to eat and take a shit, because this county is 3,500 square miles, a third of it roadless.*

"So, you'll work it out with Ben?" Cassie said as if they'd agreed on something.

"I'll do my best if he will," Isabel said as she looked back to the television. Within seconds, she was shaking her fist at the screen.

Cassie tapped on Ben's closed bedroom door and waited a beat.

"Yeah?"

She was still not used to the deep croak of his adolescent voice.

"Can I come in?"

"I guess."

He lay fully clothed on his bed and as she entered the room and closed the door behind her, Ben shoved his phone under a pillow to obviously hide what was on the screen. To cover the move, he reached out and pulled an open history book closer to him.

He was still wearing his shoes and she fought the urge to tell him to remove them from the coverlet. It was one of those small battles she no longer needed to win because of the overall consternation it would cause.

"Doing some homework?" she asked, knowing he hadn't been.

"I've got a couple of chapters to read."

She sat on the end of his bed. "Then maybe a little more reading and a little less texting."

He rolled his eyes and sighed, but Cassie smiled. She was

encouraged by the fact that he *had* been texting with someone. She could only imagine how tough it had been for him to start the ninth grade at Bozeman High School having recently moved there and without knowing anyone. He was at a tough age to be a freshman *anywhere*. And she could only imagine it because Ben didn't talk to her about it.

She glanced around his room because she didn't enter it very much anymore. There were dirty plates on his desk from midnight snacks, a new poster with the MSU Bobcats football schedule, clothes piled on his chair, and an overflowing trash can.

"I know, I know," he said. "I'll clean it up."

She nodded.

Ben's father and Cassie's husband, Army Sergeant Jim Dewell, had died in combat in Afghanistan. Ben had never met him but he'd hung a photo of him in the camo uniform and helmet on his wall back in North Dakota and it was on his bedroom wall now. With every month, Ben resembled his father more and more: dark-haired, wide-spaced eyes, a slouched and ambling gait, a little more of a passive-aggressive attitude than necessary. In Ben's mind, his father had been a hero and Cassie encouraged his perception.

So many years had lapsed that she no longer dwelled on the fact that Jim had enlisted in the military shortly after he learned she was pregnant. If Ben had ever done the math himself, comparing his age and his dad's enlistment date, he'd never brought it up.

"I'm going to be gone for a few days for work," she said.

He moaned and threw his head back.

"It won't be so bad," she said. "I'm asking for you to try and find a way to get along with Isabel."

"She's such an old hippie, Mom. And the stuff she tries to make me eat . . ."

"She's your grandmother and she loves you."

"I'm trying to gain weight and that brown rice crap she feeds me doesn't help at all."

"Why are you trying to gain weight?"

"So, I can move up a wrestling class. There's this guy, Jason—I can't beat him. He owns the hundred-and-thirteen-pound weight class and as long as he's there I'll never be able to travel with the freshman team. I need to get to one twenty."

"I'm sure you will," she said, trying to remember what it was like when she didn't have to worry about putting on more weight. "Or maybe you'll beat him."

He shook his head as if to say it simply wasn't possible. "Maybe if he died or something."

"Ben."

He shrugged. "Mom, I've really been thinking about the sport of wrestling lately."

She arched her eyebrows but she had an inkling what was coming.

He said, "What would you think if I quit? I don't think I'll ever beat Jason. It's like he's a superhuman monkey or something. And I'm not sure I really love it, you know?"

"I understand what you're saying but you're a Dewell. Dewells don't just quit when things get hard."

"Isabel says I should follow my passion."

"And since when did you listen to Isabel?"

He moaned and rolled his eyes.

"Your dad never quit," she said. "He didn't like quitters. *I* don't quit. Just because something is difficult is not a good reason to run away."

He seemed to be thinking about it. "Did Dad really say that? That he didn't like quitters?"

Although Cassie couldn't actually recall Jim using the words, Cassie nodded in the affirmative.

"I'll tell you what," Cassie said. "Finish out the season. Do your best. If you absolutely don't want to sign up for wrestling next year, we can talk about it then. But you made a commitment and you have to see it through. It wasn't a commitment to me or your coaches—it was a commitment to yourself.

"If you start letting yourself off easy every time things get tough, you'll regret it," she said.

He sighed. "Okay. I'll stick with it this year. But if they kill me or cripple me that's on you."

"I'll take that chance." She smiled.

"Don't forget me here while you're on your trip," he said. "Isabel might try to poison me with that health food crap."

"I'll leave enough money that you can eat out a couple of times if you must."

He moaned again but it wasn't as forceful as the first time.

She caught herself from wondering out loud if maybe he could stay with a friend for a night. It might give him something to look forward to. But she wasn't sure he had any close friends. Back in North Dakota, it would have been Kyle Westergaard.

She patted him on the leg and said, "So how are things going? You don't talk much about school."

"They're fine." Deadpan.

"Are you meeting some people? Making some new friends?"

"Please," he said squirming, "I told you everything is *fine*."

"You can still talk to me about things, you know," Cassie said.

"Yeah, I know."

"So maybe you should."

"Don't say you worry about me, Mom. Okay?"

She knew there was no point going on. She pursed her lips and patted his leg with finality and stood up.

"You can always call or text while I'm gone," she said.

"I know."

"By the way," she asked, trying to make the question sound simply conversational, "You were chatting with someone on your phone when I came in. Do you mind if I ask who it was?"

"Ah, it was nobody," he said but his face flushed. "Just someone I met in English class. She's kind of weird."

"*She?*"

"That's why I didn't tell you," he said adamantly. "I knew you'd blow it up into something I didn't want to talk about."

"I'm not blowing anything up."

"She just moved here, too. That's all."

"Okay, Ben."

"Really," he said, "*That's all*. Jesus, Mom."

Cassie closed the door behind her. In the hallway, she hugged herself and smiled.

Then it was time to get to work.

five

◆━━◯━━◆

With her laptop open on the kitchen table and glass of Syrah within reach, Cassie flipped to a fresh sheet on her legal pad.

She'd decided to start at thirty thousand feet and zoom in.

Hutterites were communal Anabaptists who traced their roots, like the Amish and Mennonites, to the Radical Reformation of the sixteenth century in Germany. They faced religious persecution in Europe and fled to Russia, which welcomed them to establish farm colonies to help feed the local populace—until the Russians threw them out as well. The Hutterites did what so many persecuted religious sects did: migrated to either Canada or America in the 1870s. Shortly after establishing themselves on the prairies of western Canada and the Rockies, the group branched out into three distinct congregations, called *Leuts*, known as *Schmiedeleut, Dariusleut,* and *Lehrerleut.* All three factions lived in colonies, practiced pacifism and socialism (which they described as "the sharing of goods"), dressed in traditional clothing, and spoke English as well as an off-brand Bavarian dialect.

There were nearly fifty thousand Hutterites still in Montana, most of them members of the *Lehrerleut* branch, named after their leader who was a teacher, or *Lehrer* in German.

Hutterites believed in six guiding principles:
Baptism was for adults, not children;

Members should not wield the sword;

The Lord's Supper is symbolic of the suffering of Jesus and
should be done in remembrance of Him;

Pastors in the church are responsible for teaching, disciplining,
and other duties;

Oaths are not to be taken;

and the ban should be applied to those baptized members who
fall into sin repeatedly.

It was the ban Cassie was most interested in, because that was
the reason the Kleinsassers had ended up leaving the colony and
founding their ranch in Lochsa County in the first place. They'd
been banned from the *Lehrerleut*.

She could find no additional information online why Horst
Kleinsasser and his wife, Pauline, had been thrown out of the *Lehrerleut* sect. She wasn't really surprised, since the Hutterites online
presence seemed to be limited to anodyne website documents and
a few video clips from documentaries done on the colonies in Montana. It was obvious that the sects didn't like to speak to the press
or issue statements of any kind.

If there were other families banned from the sect, Cassie
couldn't find any mention of them. Only the Kleinsassers, and no
reason was given. Was it some kind of religious offense, she wondered, or did the grandfather commit other sins, like assaulting
young women? Maybe it ran in the family.

On her pad, Cassie sketched the family tree from what little
information she could find on Hutterite websites and Lochsa
County records and made notes next to each name.

Horst (deceased). *Born 1892, Russia. Patriarch of the family,
banned from his sect. Founded the Kleinsasser ranch south of the town of
Lolo in 1916 in Lochsa County. Supplied beef to U.S. Government
during WWI. Established the Kleinsasser Trust. Married to Pauline.
Died 1981.*

Pauline (deceased). *Matriarch. Married to Horst. No info. Died 1983.*

Jakob (deceased). *Firstborn son (1925), inherited and expanded the ranch to 60,000 acres. Officer, Montana Stockgrowers Association. Republican. Ran and lost a bid as lone Montana congressman in 1952. Married to Rita. Died 1972 on the ranch.*

Rita (deceased). *Born 1928. Three children: Horst II, Wilhelmina, Susanna. Married to Jakob. No info. Died 1980 in Great Falls.*

Cassie searched in vain on the internet for any records for Wilhelmina or Susanna and gave up after fifteen minutes. It was as if they'd vanished. Horst II, however, had plenty of hits.

Horst II (67). *Born 1952. Inherited and expanded the ranch to present 80,000 acres. Served in U.S. Navy during Vietnam War. Established a small chain of livestock feed stores in western Montana. Found not guilty of second-degree murder of a ranch hand. Named Montana Stockgrower of the Year, 1992. Lochsa County Commissioner, 1984–2004. Chairman, Montana Republican Party Central Committee. Montana delegate to 1980 and 1984 Republican National Convention. Married to Margaret. Still on ranch.*

Margaret (64). *Born 1955 in Victor. Four children: Blake, Cheyenne, John Wayne, Rand. Married to Horst II. Still on ranch.*

Blake (43). *Born 1976. Left Montana in 1995, age 18. Graduated Columbia University 1999. Employed Bridgewater Associates (1999–2002), JPMorgan Asset Management (2002–2005), D. E. Shaw & Co. (2005–2009), Kleinsasser & Associates (2009–present). Divorced, no children. Residence: NYC and Gallatin County Jail.*

Cassie snorted at that. His resumé was . . . discordant.

Next, there was: Cheyenne (39). *Born 1980. Lolo High School graduate. Two years, Montana State University. Married and divorced (three times). Currently single. Daughter Franny Porché, age fifteen. Lives on ranch.*

John Wayne (35). *Born 1984. Graduated University of Montana 2006, Agribusiness Degree. Married to Rochelle. Currently CEO of Kleinsasser Ranch. (Suspected by Blake to be behind it all.) Two sons, John Wayne Junior, and Tristan. (Ages?)*

Rand (32). *Born 1987. Entered U.S. Army in 2005, dishonorably discharged 2006. Divorced, no children. Convicted of assault—eighteen months in Deer Lodge. Currently working on Kleinsasser Ranch. (Said by Blake to worship John Wayne.)*

Cassie sat back and noted a few things that might be of significance.

The Kleinsasser women, from Pauline through the present time, seemed to make no mark. This was unusual in Cassie's experience. On the Montana ranches she grew up around, the women were the heart and soul of the enterprise. While their husbands worked and catted around, the women maintained the family enterprise. The Kleinsasser clan appeared to be an aberration from that.

Second, the journey of the family seemed to follow the pattern she'd discussed with Rachel earlier when it came to so many private ranch holdings. The multigenerational Kleinsassers were an illustration of "the curse of the third generation." Horst and Pauline founded the place, Jakob and Rita expanded it, Horst II and Margaret grew it further, and the third generation of Blake, Cheyenne, John Wayne, and Rand were blowing it all to hell.

The third generation also appeared to be an aberration from the past, which appeared to Cassie to have been fairly stable. The oldest, Blake, had run away at his first opportunity to make a life elsewhere. Cheyenne remained but had multiple husbands and at least one child. John Wayne was married, but Rand seemed to exist in his own dysfunctional world.

What *happened* to them?

She thought of a quote she'd once read by Samuel Butler in *The Way of All Flesh*: "If there are one or two good ones in a very large family it is as much as can be expected."

Yet the Kleinsassers appeared to have missed even that meager benchmark.

Also, John Wayne seemed to have been the first manager of the ranch not to expand it or create additional enterprises.

Lastly, she thought it was odd that there were only three grandchildren: Franny Porché, John Wayne, Jr., and Tristan. How could that be? Hutterites were known around Montana for large families. The Kleinsassers seemed to be an odd exception to that.

Then Cassie thought about what Blake had told her about the trust and the moral turpitude clause.

With Blake out of the picture, would fifteen-year-old Franny as the oldest grandchild eventually inherit everything?

Cassie made a note to ask Rachel her legal opinion on that the next time she talked with her.

She turned to the discovery evidence that the prosecution in Lochsa County had turned over to Blake's original attorney and that had since been forwarded to Rachel.

Cassie confirmed that Blake's first lawyer was named Andrew Thomas Johnson. Cassie underlined that name because he was a man she wanted to talk to. Whether Johnson would talk to her remained to be seen.

The arrest report file for Blake Kleinsasser contained a document that was entitled "Statement of Franny Porché."

Cassie read it over.

STATE OF MONTANA
COUNTY OF LOCHSA

The undersigned, FRANNY PORCHÉ, being duly sworn hereby deposes and says:

1. I am under the age of 18 and am a resident of Montana. I have personal knowledge of the facts herein, and, if called as a witness could testify completely thereto.
2. I suffer no legal disabilities and have personal knowledge of the facts set forth below.
3. I'm accompanied by my mother Cheyenne (Kleinsasser) Porché and my uncle John Wayne Kleinsasser, both of legal age.

Executed this third day of July, 2019.

The statement was signed in a loopy, childish script by Franny as well as by her mother and her uncle.

On the evening of July 2 I participated in my church youth group at the First Congregational Church in Lolo. When the youth group concluded I went outside the church to wait for a ride from my mother back to the ranch. I was alone.

I was surprised when instead of my mother waiting for me in the parking lot it was my uncle Blake. He opened the passenger door of his car, which was a blue four-door sedan, I believe. He said he'd drive me home.

I asked him about my mother and he said my mom had given him permission to pick me up. I didn't have any reason not to believe him even though I didn't really know him all that well. Uncle Blake had not been around when I was growing up and I'd heard things about him from my uncles but I'm not one to judge.

I got in the car and we drove out of town in the direction of the ranch. Even though the windows were open (it was a hot evening), I thought I could smell alcohol on his breath when he spoke. His eyes were red and he looked flushed.

Uncle Blake asked me if he could borrow my phone so I gave it to him thinking he was going to call my mother and let her know we were on our way home. But he didn't use the phone and instead placed it in the center console and closed the lid.

He said it was hard to talk to anyone these days because they were always on their phone—especially kids my age.

Then he said he wanted us to get to know each other better so that we could trust each other. He said he really wanted me to get to know him better. I know how that sounds, but it wasn't creepy at the time. I was kind of flattered that he thought of me that way.

He said he wanted to show me where he spent most of his time when he was growing up on the ranch. He said he wanted me to know that even though my uncles told me different, Uncle Blake had spent a lot of years there and he had a real connection to the ranch that I probably wasn't aware of.

I thought that was weird, but most adults are weird. I didn't feel threatened at that time and I was curious to see where he was taking me. I've spent the last few years on the ranch when my mom moved back but I don't know it all that well. I didn't grow up on the ranch like everyone else. I knew there were old buildings scattered around but because I can't drive yet I've never been to them.

We went down a kind of rough dirt road up into the trees. It was in a part of the ranch I've never seen before. Uncle Blake said it used to belong to some neighbors before my grandfather bought it from them. He seemed to know where he was going but it was farther from the ranch headquarters than I thought it would be.

We arrived at a two-story old house on the side of a

meadow. The house was kind of dumpy, I thought. Some of the windows were broken out and the cattle had been on the porch and collapsed it. There was old cow manure everywhere. It was outside the house and inside the front door. The place smelled like cows. I'm not fond of cows. I'm a vegan, you know.

I thought we'd look at the place and then go home, but Uncle Blake said he wanted to show the inside of it to me. He said he used to spend so much time there and he was curious what it looked like now.

I asked him if he used to live in the old house and he said no, that ranch hands used to live there. He said the ranch hands were friendly to him and let him hang around.

We stopped the car in front of the porch and Uncle Blake got out and asked me to follow him. The door to the house was unlocked and he went in first. It wasn't dark outside yet because it was summer but it was dark inside the house.

I know you aren't supposed to go somewhere with a stranger. But Uncle Blake wasn't a stranger. He was my uncle.

Uncle Blake lit a candle thing called a kerosene lamp and put it on the table. He said he wanted me to see all the old rooms but I said I was kind of scared. I was afraid the floor would collapse and there were all kinds of rat turds and stuff all over it. Uncle Blake took my hand and sort of gave me a tour. He knew who used to stay in which room. He showed me a room with bunk beds in it where ranch hands used to stay together.

When we were done with the tour, he poured two glasses of whiskey from a bottle he must have brought from the car. We were back at the table in the dining room. I'm not a drinking girl like some of my friends at school and church, and I told him I didn't want any. He said it was a special occasion and I should try it. I took one sip and thought I was going to throw up. He drank his whole glass and poured another one. I recognized the smell from inside the car.

He did a "toast" to me and we clinked glasses and he made me drink. I didn't really like it but I did like the way he was treating me, like an adult. Then he started to tell me how my uncles had him all wrong and that he'd come back to try and reconnect with all of us. He said he wanted to talk to me because I hadn't been around long enough to be poisoned against him.

I guess at that point I was getting drunk, which is something I never want to do again. My head was really fuzzy.

Then Uncle Blake came around to my side of the table and lifted me up. He was strong. He sat me on top of the table and started kissing me. He has really fast hands and he was touching me everywhere. He stood there between my legs and held me in place.

I told him I didn't want to do anything with him. He said not to think of it that way, but to think of it as a way to get closer to each other. He said he really liked my eyes, which is weird because I don't think they're anything special.

I didn't scream because I didn't know what to do and there was no one to hear me. I thought if I fought him with my fists, he might beat me up.

It happened really fast. He pushed me back and pulled my panties down and put his penis inside me. I'm not a virgin but it really hurt.

I didn't know what to do so I just let him finish. When he was done, he said, "That's what I think of this family," and he just walked out. He said it really mean.

I stayed inside and cried because I didn't want to go anywhere with him. He drove away just as it got dark, and I realized he still had my phone so I couldn't call anyone for help.

I walked down the road in the moonlight until I could see lights in the distance.

That's when I knocked on my uncle J. W.'s door and I told him what happened and he brought me here.

"You bastard," Cassie said aloud. "I hope you rot in Deer Lodge."

Before Cassie could reread Franny's statement and start a fresh page with her observations, her phone lit up on the table with an incoming call.

The screen read BRYAN. She snatched it up and punched the icon to refuse the call.

"Another bastard," she whispered while she reached for her glass of wine. "This place is full of them."

Bryan Pederson was the sheriff of Park County and she'd known him—and known of him—for years. He'd been there for her after the shooting of the trooper and he'd been there for the final act of the Lizard King. She'd noted that some time between the two encounters that he no longer wore his wedding band.

He was a good man, an honest cop as far as sheriffs went, and she let herself start to feel comfortable around him off the job. And he was certainly attractive in a laconic cowboy kind of way.

Cassie became suspicious of him after the first night she stayed over at his house. She'd opened a closet door by mistake instead of the bathroom door and saw that it was filled with his ex-wife's clothing. When she brought it up to Pederson he explained it away by saying his ex-wife had never come to retrieve her clothes and he'd forgotten about them since he never used that closet. He bolstered his case by saying she was such a spendthrift that she'd likely already replaced her old wardrobe. Bryan said by the next time Cassie came to stay for the night the closet would be cleaned out and all of the clothes donated to charity.

Cassie had let herself believe that, but there was a kernel of doubt in the back of her mind that remained there for months, waiting for another shoe to drop.

It dropped on that afternoon in June when she opened his office door and saw Bryan and his ex-wife grunting on the carpet behind his desk. He looked over his naked shoulder at the sound of the intrusion and their eyes locked. There was panic in his face but Cassie didn't say a word. She had stepped back, closed the door, and walked straight out of the building to her car without looking back.

And she still hadn't.

There was nothing that needed to be said after that, and Bryan hadn't even attempted to make contact with her.

Until tonight.

Cassie muted her phone and placed it screen down on the table in case he called back. She didn't even want to see his name again.

He was out of her life, whatever the reason for the call. It was likely, she speculated, that his ex had thrown him out again so he was reaching out to her to try and mend fences. Men thought that way. Cassie didn't. Betrayal was betrayal.

She was grateful she'd not brought him to her house to meet Ben last summer. Ben would have likely been in awe of Bryan, and that would have made the split even more bitter and complicated.

Her instincts had been right on that count, even if they'd been a little skewed when it came to going out with Bryan in the first place. But she'd been lonely, and she still was. It had almost been worth it—at least for a few months.

She refilled her wineglass and tried to shove Bryan and his call out of her mind while she turned back to the affidavit and her observations about it.

On the evening of July 2 wasn't something a fifteen-year-old would lead with, Cassie observed. It was legal language, and likely prompted by the prosecutor in the room. Neither was Franny's description of the "blue four-door sedan." What teenager used a phrase like that? It was cop language, not teenager talk.

Those phrases weren't disqualifying at all, but they indicated to Cassie that at least some of the language in the document wasn't as free and natural as it could have been. The heavy hand of the prosecutor was present in the affidavit. Cassie was sure Rachel had picked up on that as well and she'd likely use it in court to taint the evidence.

Cassie knew from her years in law enforcement that of course prosecutors "improved" witness statements. A literal transcript of witness recollections was filled with unclear sentences, incomplete thoughts, and dozens of "ums" and "you knows." A literal transcript was often a mess. Editing was necessary for clarity.

At the same time, editing allowed for a prosecutor to create a document more damning to the accused than what was actually said. It wasn't supposed to be done, but Cassie knew it happened all the time.

Cody Hoyt had once told her, *You'll find, Cassie, that it's us against the world. We do our damnedest to put away degenerates and douchebags so innocent people won't be hurt by them, but all the forces out there are set up to make us fail. We've got county attorneys that won't take on a case unless it's airtight, judges who want to invent the law instead of enforce what's there, defense attorneys who want to show publicly how fucking incompetent we are, and juries who want to stick it to the man. So, when we've figured out that someone is guilty as sin, sometimes we need to stack the deck a little. You know what I'm saying?*

She did.

Cassie read further and scrawled more notes.

Cheyenne gave permission to her brother Blake to pick up Franny at church? Why would she do that if Blake was a non-person within the family? There was more to that story.

I'm not one to judge also struck Cassie as a phrase unlikely to be used by a fifteen-year-old. It sounded paraphrased or coerced, unless Franny was exceptionally mature. But the rest of the document didn't indicate that. There was a flippant undercurrent in the statement Cassie thought odd and misplaced for a traumatized girl, including the lines about not liking cows and being a vegan. But Cassie also knew that victims sometimes focused on strange recollections.

Where was Franny's phone now? Back with her or missing? The phone wasn't listed on the impound sheet, which could be a clerical error or possible proof that the prosecution was withholding evidence. Cassie knew that *everything* was on a teenager's phone: photos, texts, contacts, and call records. Having the phone in custody was like having Franny's brain in custody. Would the prosecution withhold an item so vital and important, and if so, why?

That's what I think of this family also didn't ring true to Cassie as something Blake Kleinsasser would say. It came across to her as too melodramatic for the man she'd met that day. It seemed more like something Franny thought he might have said due to his heinous crime and demeanor. Maybe she'd misheard him, or it was a line fed to her by her mother, her uncle, or the prosecutor taking the affidavit.

Finally, Cassie found it interesting that Franny went first to her uncle John Wayne's house and not her own. Of course, there could be a simple explanation. Maybe John Wayne's house was closer. Or was there another reason?

For the second time that day, Cassie felt dirty. She didn't like finding questions and inconsistencies in the statement of a girl who was likely traumatized and emotional at the time she gave it. Cassie knew that's what defense lawyers had to do, but it bothered her once again that she was on the wrong side of the crime.

She reviewed the arrest report ("subject appeared inebriated and disoriented"), the witness list made up primarily of youth group participants as well as the youth pastor of the Congregational church who would all vouch that Blake picked her up that night.

There were printouts of digital photos: the interior and exterior photos of the old ranch house that looked as described by Franny, and shots of Blake's tire tracks on the dirt road that led to the abandoned home next to comparison photos of the tire tread marks on his rental car.

The statement from the medical examiner from Ravalli County confirming a match of the semen found on Franny's underwear with Blake Kleinsasser's DNA was the killer, though, as far as Cassie was concerned. Ravalli County bordered Lochsa County, and Cassie assumed that law enforcement in the region shared resources, including the medical examiner himself. Even without the affidavit and all of the other available evidence, the DNA match was enough to put Blake away.

Seeing the additional documentation tamped down the doubts Cassie had from the affidavit. No case was ever perfect. There were always nits to pick, which is what defense lawyers did as a matter of course.

Overall, though, she thought it was a pretty clean and straightforward case. All of the history she'd read earlier about Hutterites in Montana and the Kleinsasser family tree was irrelevant when it came to the cold hard facts of the arrest. She'd taken much weaker cases to county attorneys that had resulted in guilty verdicts.

Blake Kleinsasser was going to prison and he deserved it. His trip home to Montana had turned out much different than he'd thought.

She was so focused on her thoughts that it took a moment to realize that her house was shaking. Her first thought was, *It's a mild earthquake.*

The wine in her glass rippled and she could feel a low rumbling through the soles of her slippers from the floor. She pushed back from the table and looked around. She could hear the tinkling of glasses from inside her kitchen cupboards.

Cassie pushed back from the table. The source of the disturbance, she realized, wasn't from beneath her. It was coming from outside on the street.

She retrieved her Glock from where she stashed it every evening on the top of the refrigerator and she gripped it muzzle-down as she padded through the living room toward the front door. The vibration and rumbling increased in volume the closer she got to the front of the house.

The gun was out of view along her right leg when she opened the door and stepped out onto her porch.

What she saw chilled her to the bone.

A massive eighteen-wheel tractor-trailer idled right in front of her taking up the entire suburban street. It was a black Peterbilt tractor: the boxy shape of the cab and long nose were unmistakable. There was no reflection from chrome that had apparently been removed or from the exhaust stacks, which were blacked out. The cab was high and she couldn't see who was behind the wheel due to her angle and the dark tinted windows. Dim amber lights ran down the length of the trailer and their glow reflected on the windshields of parked cars as far as three houses away.

The semi was so huge, so dark, and so out of place in her neighborhood. It was a replica of the Lizard King's unit or the truck itself.

She was frozen in place. Her heart raced. She couldn't walk toward the truck or back up into her house. She could feel the rumbling of the diesel engine not only through the concrete but from within her chest.

When the driver released the air brake and there was a sharp hydraulic squeal she gasped for a moment and couldn't get air.

Then it slowly rumbled forward. She stood on the porch trembling, unable to move or act until it was gone. She'd tried to get a license plate number from the rear of the trailer but the light back there was broken—or disabled. She couldn't even see the state of origin.

Cassie peered at the houses on the block on both sides of the street, expecting to see her neighbors with their faces pressed to their windows to determine the cause of the disturbance.

There were a few lights on, but most of the curtains and blinds remained closed. It was as if they'd heard nothing at all.

Finally back inside, Cassie closed and locked her front door. She couldn't stop trembling.

She *knew* it couldn't have been the Lizard King. She *knew* he was dead.

Was it a sick copycat driver who knew where she lived?

Or was there a more innocent explanation, like a confused freight driver lost within the circuitous labyrinth of Bozeman's suburban streets?

Isabel opened her bedroom door and stumbled out toward the bathroom with her sleep mask pushed up on her forehead. When she saw Cassie, she stopped.

"What are you doing standing there with your gun?" her mother asked.

"Didn't you hear that?"

"Hear what?"

"The truck outside our house?"

Isabel gestured to the earplugs she wore, shook her head, and went into the bathroom and closed the door.

Cassie quietly opened the door to Ben's room. He was asleep with his phone next to his head on the pillow.

He'd obviously slept through it as well.

She placed her Glock in the nightstand next to her bed and climbed under the covers. Her mind was swirling: an unholy mix of Kleinsassers, Franny's statement, what she'd need to pack for her trip to Lochsa County in the morning, and that eighteen-wheeler parked outside her home in the middle of the night with its engine running.

And there *had* been a truck out there.

Right?

six

--=○=--

A few blocks away, the driver parked his truck on a side street near the high school and turned his engine off.

He sat and waited, rotating his head from the windshield and side windows to the mirrors outside his doors. There was no one out on the sidewalks and no headlights in front or behind him. Nevertheless, he gave it fifteen minutes. For cover, he opened a map across his lap. If a patrolman knocked on his door he would say that he had gotten lost and was trying to find his way back to the highway. He'd have the map handy to bolster his argument.

Plus, there was no law against parking on a public street, even in the People's Republic of Bozeman.

The driver leaned back in his seat. With the heat off he could feel a few small tendrils of fall cold enter the cab, but it wasn't uncomfortable. Winter was still a couple of months away, even though there could be a cold front or even snow at any time in Montana.

There was very little wind in the air, and smoke from the distant forest fires seemed to catch and hold on the streetlights. Each one looked as if it had its own halo. The back of his throat was scratchy from breathing smoke all that day and when his eyes raised above the profile of the school building he could see the jagged line of the flames from distant mountains. And there were no stars. The smoke blocked them out.

* * *

The school was as big as he remembered it although it looked like there were a few add-ons near the old brick gym. The grounds were grass turning yellow, cottonwoods shedding leaves, and dark spruce trees standing like sentinels. Hanging wisps of smoke gave it an eerie feel. The light blue glow from overhead lights cast shadows and made the campus look far more serious and formidable than he knew it to be.

Seeing the building again—peaked roof, brick and glass construction, everything unimaginative and institutional—brought back a flood of memories that made him stir in his seat. They weren't good memories.

If it was possible to hate a building, he hated the building in front of him. He hated every brick, every bland tile in the hallways, every locker, every teacher, every administrator, every classroom but one—auto shop.

And he despised nearly every kid that went to the school back then. He doubted they were any different today and they were probably worse.

From what he'd observed, the coming generation was just a bunch of pussies. Coddled, softheaded narcissists, all of them. They were all heroes in their own minds and in the minds of their parents and the school administration. They all had a shelf stacked with participation trophies.

They were so into their own feelings. Their heads were on swivels to constantly look for offense so that they could be righteously outraged by something. He'd read where the senior class of the school in front of him had gone on strike the previous year because of something a gym teacher said that was construed as racist and homophobic. The students were portrayed in the press as champions of tolerance. The gym teacher was suspended and later let go.

Pussies.

These little snowflakes had no idea what they were going to face when they got out into the real world. They should all have to spend thirty days in prison to find out what the law of the jungle was truly like. They should be assigned to a cell in D Pod with no television, no cell phones, no social media, and no Wi-Fi. They should have to bunk with a Crow Indian from the res who was in there for murdering a seventy-year-old Good Samaritan couple from Missouri who stopped on the highway to help him and his broken-down pickup.

That thought made him smile.

He'd promised to himself to stay clean for the night. No alcohol, no weed, no meth. He'd kept his promise, although he couldn't stop his left leg from bouncing up and down as he sat.

The driver painted the whole of the school with his eyes. He picked out individual classrooms where he'd once been trapped. He recalled that his only solace was staring out the window toward the mountains and waiting for the final bell of the day.

He was surprised how vivid his memories were and how much they affected him now. He hadn't expected it.

Few knew what it was like to go to a high school in the wake of a legacy—his siblings—and come up short. To be judged not on your own accomplishments or attributes but solely in comparison to those who had gone before. You could see it in the eyes of his teachers once they established his lineage. Sometimes they told him stories about those before him as if that somehow would make him feel better about himself. Instead, though, it drove home the fact time and time again how he paled in comparison. Every damned time.

And he hated the factions: the stoners, the cowkids, the hipsters, the socials, the athletes, the emos, the nerds, the elites. He never belonged to any of them. He was an outcast and he hung around with other outcasts, most of whom he couldn't stand.

He would forever be an outcast.

But it was different now. He was an outcast with a plan.

A plan and a gun.

With the weapon tucked into his waistband and his jacket pulled over it, the driver climbed out of his truck and shut the door behind him and walked toward the high school.

He crossed the teacher's parking lot quickly because it was wide open and illuminated by overhead lights, pausing only when he was in the deep shadow of a campus spruce. He looked around again, checked the streets, checked the sidewalk.

He turned his back on the front doors of the school where he knew there were closed-circuit cameras. There had been cameras even when *he* went there, although he wasn't sure they'd actually worked.

The truck driver knew about the cameras from a clip he'd watched on YouTube depicting an act of student bullying that took place inside the entrance vestibule. The cameras clearly identified the perpetrators—they pummeled a kid who looked like he deserved pummeling—and the offending students were later suspended. He didn't care about that. What interested him was the range and quality of the video cameras. It was like a fucking television studio inside the vestibule.

No one could enter the front doors of the school without being clearly seen, and it was a long way inside—past the principal's office, past the guidance counselors, past the school security room—to where the classrooms were located.

There was no need to take that gamble.

From tree to tree, shadow to shadow, he progressed the length of the long building toward the back. He paused at the gym building and stood tall to look through a window into the interior. The gym was lit by widely spaced emergency lights but from what he could see it still looked the same. The uncomfortable stands, the gym floor, the stupid paintings of the mascot on the walls under each basket. Looking inside brought back a flood of feelings he didn't like.

He could smell the sour sweat and piss from the locker room and hear the reverberation of sharp sounds inside the gym itself. That place was a special kind of hell and he fought an involuntary shiver when he took it in.

He stayed close to the exterior brick walls because the angle of the moonlight kept them in complete shadow. The grass ended as he got closer to the farthest building from the front of the school, the auto shop. They didn't bother to keep the grass groomed back there because it couldn't be seen from the street and the students who hung out there were losers anyway.

His boots crunched on gravel mixed with cigarette butts and it nearly made him smile. He used to smoke there, right there in the same place. He was glad the tradition had been upheld.

At the corner of the end of the building the driver paused and reached for his pistol. It was a Browning Buck Mark .22 semi-auto with a homemade suppressor and a ten-round magazine filled with hollow-point rounds. It felt balanced and substantial in his hand.

Then he leaned around the corner and aimed up. Under the high eave was a glass bulge that looked like an upside-down bowl. That's where the closed-circuit camera was housed.

He racked a cartridge into the pistol and caught a glimpse of brass before it was seated. Then he raised the weapon again and steadied it by leaning against the brick. He thumbed the safety off and squeezed the trigger.

Snap-snap-snap-snap-snap-snap.

Shattered glass and pieces of the surveillance camera fell to the driveway. What remained of the camera itself stuck out of the housing like the tongue of a dead animal.

The sound of the shots were high-pitched and, he thought, not loud enough to draw attention.

He targeted what was left of the camera.

Snap-snap-snap-snap.

The unit dropped out of the housing and hung there, held up by a single electric wire. It twisted in the moonlight like a dead rabbit caught in a snare.

The driver gathered up all the spent casings and counted them twice to make sure he had them all. They'd all been kicked out the same direction and most of them had been nestled in a crack in the concrete driveway. He dropped them into his pocket along with the empty magazine and shoved an extra ten-shot magazine into the grip.

With the pistol tucked back into his waistband—the barrel was surprisingly hot—he walked around the corner and tried to turn the knob of the outside door. Locked, as he thought it would be.

Then he bent and grasped the handle of the big garage door. If the students were like the ones he'd gone to class with, they sometimes forgot to lock the overhead garage door. He pulled up on it. Locked.

But he knew a trick that used to work.

He grasped the garage door handle with both hands and set his feet. The latch that anchored the folding garage door to the track used to not line up to the locking slot correctly. It had been installed poorly when the building was built.

In the driver's view, maintenance people working for the school system, like the teachers and administrators, did the absolute minimum possible. They did their day-to-day chores, enough to keep them employed. But they rarely took the initiative to fix a fundamental problem like a misaligned garage door unless it was an immediate problem.

Then he jerked the door hard left, putting his weight into it. The latch gave with a *click*.

He thumbed the green button next to the doorjamb and he heard the opener inside growl to life. The door rumbled and began to raise.

He paused it after two feet, just enough to see the shiny concrete floor on the inside and to get a whiff of motor oil and transmission fluid. Then he closed it and rocked the door to the right until the latch reseated.

From the auto shop there was an annex that led to the main classroom building. There were no doors or barriers in between.

He knew there were probably cameras in the hallways but he wasn't concerned with them. They might capture his image, but by the time they did he'd be well inside moving to his destination. It would be too late to stop him.

The driver knew he could get into the school any time he wanted to.

He also knew it might take weeks for the repair order on the outside camera to work its way up through the administration and back down again to a breathing maintenance man, who would then have to order a whole new closed-circuit video assembly and wait for it to get shipped before he could even think about installing it.

The driver stayed in the pools of shadow as he made his way back to his truck.

He climbed inside the cab, closed the door, and returned the Browning to the center console.

After checking the streets to ensure that no one was watching, he started the engine and rumbled away. His target, he thought, would never see him coming.

Part II

Envy slays itself by its own arrows.

—*The Greek Anthology, X 111*

You shall not hate your brother in your heart.

—Leviticus 19:17

seven

As Cassie drove to Lochsa County the next day, she was
still unnerved from the encounter the night before with the tractor-
trailer outside her house. It had been so unexpected and it had
awakened in her a feeling of dread and doom that she thought she
had left behind.

Maybe she should see someone, she thought, a counselor of
some kind. If simply seeing a semi-truck in a state filled with them
on every highway brought out this kind of dread . . .

She tried to push it aside. Cassie had always thought herself
smart and strong enough to deal with her issues and she had secret
contempt for people who ran to psychologists as a matter of course
to dissect their feelings. But maybe when things slowed down she
would see someone, she thought.

The last thing she needed, though, would be for word to leak
out that she was undergoing psych treatment. That might discourage current and future clients. She knew from experience how fast
rumors could travel within law enforcement and legal circles even
among the more enlightened. She knew she'd have to discreetly
ask around for a name or two of counselors who could keep their
mouths shut.

But first, she had work to do.

Blake Kleinsasser, rapist and moral reprobate that he was, deserved a competent defense. And if he was as guilty as he seemed,
Rachel needed to know it so she could negotiate with him on solid
ground to cop a plea.

That would be the best route, Cassie knew. Blake would go to prison and Franny would be spared reliving the crime in front of jurors and press coverage.

Smoke hung in every valley and it distorted the view of the mountains in every direction, as if someone had smeared Vaseline on the interior windows of her Jeep. It was so thick she could taste it.

She glimpsed makeshift camps of temporary firefighters as she drove west as well as distant helicopters and aircraft carrying loads of water and fire retardant. The fires were everywhere there was timber, and that meant there were fires throughout the Northern Rockies.

Cassie chose to leave Interstate Highway 90 after Butte and she cut south and west on two-lane state roads. There was no direct route because the Sapphire Range ran north to south between the interstate and Lochsa County. There was one unpaved road that switchbacked over Skalkaho Pass, but she'd seen digital roadside warnings reporting that there was an active fire on top and long delays were likely.

So she took Highway 43 to Wisdom, Montana, with the Pioneer Mountains on her left, the Sapphires and Continental Divide on her right, and the Big Hole River coursing through the stunning empty valley. She encountered less than a half-dozen cars along the route, although she glimpsed drift boats and fly fishermen at times on the river.

Cassie recalled from her Montana history that the Big Hole Battlefield was where Chief Joseph and his Nez Perce engaged the U.S. Seventh Infantry in a day and a half battle in 1873. It was a sad and depressing story, as well as a typical one.

The American government renounced a treaty they'd signed with the Nez Perce to allow settlers and white miners into their lands, and Chief Joseph—betrayed too many times already—had decided to lead the entire tribe through the mountains to Canada where he hoped to team up with Sitting Bull and his relocated Lakota. The army intercepted them along the Big Hole River and attacked, killing almost a hundred Nez Perce men, women, and children.

With the survivors, Chief Joseph fled east through what was now Yellowstone Park, then cut to the north hoping he could elude the army. Forty miles short of the border and starving, he surrendered.

The valley might be breathtakingly beautiful, she thought, but it cloaked one of the worst episodes from the settling of the state and the country.

She was slowed twice by farm machinery inching along the blacktop and at one point by a large herd of black Angus being driven by mounted cowboys. The pavement was covered with wet green manure and the inside of her Jeep smelled of it for fifteen miles. Then she began to climb into the mountains.

Finally, she descended via a sharp set of switchbacks into the Bitterroot Valley on U.S. Highway 93. The route would take her north parallel to the Idaho border into the series of communities and counties in far western Montana.

As she drew closer to Lochsa County, she was reminded of observations she'd made in her high school sports days when the bus she was in ventured to that part of the state. While Montana was made up of mountains, valleys, rivers, and plains, it was as if those massive formations and vistas were pushed together and jammed against a wall the farther one traveled west. Mountain ranges seemed taller and closer together, meadows and hayfields were smaller and steeper. It was as if the terrain of the state was pinched together from the sides up against the sawtooth border of Idaho—which ran along the top of the Continental Divide all the way to Canada—and it was all extreme and mildly claustrophobic.

Because she hadn't been able to sleep after her encounter with the curbside trucker, Cassie had researched Lochsa County itself and its odd origins.

With Missoula County to the north and Ravalli County to the south, Lochsa was small by Montana standards. It stretched east to west, sandwiched between the two and without a town with more than two thousand residents. The county seat was Horston, population eighteen hundred. She found it striking to study the map and see that between Hamilton and Lolo it was almost a void. And in the center of Lochsa County, hard against the Bitterroot Mountains to the west and the Bitterroot River to the east, was the vast Kleinsasser ranch.

After reviewing Blake Kleinsasser's arrest report and all of the documents Rachel had provided for a second time, Cassie had turned to a fresh page on her legal pad and made a list of what she hoped to accomplish on her trip to Lochsa County: interview Sheriff Ben Wagy and review evidence and charging documents; try to interview Blake's former defense attorney, Andrew Thomas Johnson; find Hawk; find Lindy; Kleinsasser Ranch; try to walk through building where assault took place; write report with conclusions for Rachel.

Of those, the only item she felt good about was talking with the local sheriff. The others could be stymied by noncooperation (Johnson) or pure shots in the dark (Hawk, Lindy, getting permission to view the crime scene).

Cassie found the website for Lochsa County and composed a brief email introduction of herself and made the request to speak to Sheriff Wagy the next day. She knew that being the sheriff of a rural county was equal parts political, social, and law enforcement. If the sheriff was cooperative with her—and most in her experience were—it was by far the best way to start an investigation and build a time line.

She also did a deeper dive into the founding of the county itself, and the name "Kleinsasser" popped up everywhere. Horst I, Jakob, and Horst II were involved in everything: local politics, county politics, planning commissions, joint powers boards, school boards, weed and pest control boards, on and on. John Wayne and Rand were mentioned on a much smaller scale. Blake's name was nonexistent.

Horston, of course, was named after Horst I.

She also found it interesting that the Kleinsasser Ranch had another name. It was officially registered as the Iron Cross Ranch, and its brand was the German Empire symbol:

As the late afternoon heated up into the seventies, the heat and dry air fueled the many fires and Cassie had to slow down as visibility decreased. She turned right at Chief Joseph Pass and dropped into the Bitterroot Valley on a steep highway featured with S-curves.

The sharp outline of Trapper Peak, at 10,157 feet, dominated the western wall of mountains, but Cassie had to remind herself that there were 199 peaks in the state that were higher.

Like everywhere in Montana, small white crosses designated highway deaths on the side of the road. Some were decorated with plastic flowers, ribbons, and totems from their loved ones. Others weren't. Cassie always felt sorry for those souls that were bare of remembrance.

Both sides of the road were heavily timbered with ponderosa and spruce. The mountains and the trees kept the highway heavily shadowed, and *this* is what she remembered about the area: that instead of the infinite views and big Montana sky she'd grown up with, it seemed as if the rough villages were linked by narrow tunnels through the forest.

A dead cow elk, freshly killed and abandoned by a motorist, lay sprawled across the northbound lane of the highway. Shards from broken headlights sparkled around the carcass as well as pieces from a shattered front grille.

Cassie winced and drove around it.

Hamilton, like so many small towns in Montana, was in the process of being gentrified. There were espresso bars, clothing stores, brewpubs, hipsters, and more stoplights than she recalled. The timber, hunting, and ranching culture of the valley was being transformed.

As she sat at one traffic light, she noted several men emerge from one of the brewpubs and approach an SUV with California plates. To a man, they wore colorful fly-fishing shirts with lots of pockets, zip-off trousers, floppy hats, and river sandals. It used to be, she thought, that these tourists would no doubt be dedicated fly fishermen. These days, though, it could just as easily mean they were parishioners from the Church of Trout, a religion coined by her mentor, Cody Hoyt.

The Church of Trout, Cody claimed facetiously, was made up of hundreds of thousands of members who looked the part, dressed the part, and never went near a river. Montana was now filled with them.

She drove past a series of custom log home building companies north out of Hamilton, and within several miles she noted that commercial buildings and private homes along the roadside became fewer.

Cassie filled her Jeep with gasoline in Stevensville ("Home of the Fighting Yellowjackets") and breathed in thin mountain air colored by the fragrances of pine and woodsmoke. The border of Lochsa County was ten miles away.

It was after five when she took the highway exit into Horston and she cursed under her breath. She'd hoped to get there at least an hour earlier so she could meet the sheriff of Lochsa County before the close of the county building. She checked her email on her phone to see if he'd replied to her inquiry. He hadn't. She hoped he hadn't been put off by the 3:47 A.M. time stamp on her message and concluded that she was a crazy woman to be avoided.

Downtown Horston consisted of three blocks on Main Street. Unlike Hamilton, the cool people hadn't yet discovered it. The storefronts looked almost deliberately retrograde and there were few people out on the sidewalks. The town, she thought, could serve as the location for a movie set in the 1950s or '60s and she got the distinct feeling that the place was barely hanging on despite the growth north and south of it.

Horston was what Hamilton used to be, she thought. Before the Church of Trout discovered it.

It was notable, she thought, that the only retail businesses that appeared to be open were three saloons that stood shoulder to shoulder. Two other saloons were spaced out on the other side of the street.

She recalled something she'd learned when she visited the tiny town of Ekalaka in eastern Montana, which was six hundred miles and ten and a half hours away: *any location in Montana is a good place for a bar.*

Although there were two ubiquitous brand-name chain motels on the outskirts of Horston, Cassie had made online reservations at an aging motel called the Whispering Pines in the middle of town. It was located on the next block from the small herd of saloons.

The neon tubing on the motel sign out front quivered with electric light but formed three tall pine trees. A red VACANCY notice hummed beneath it. The lot was shaded with mature ponderosas that gave the facility the appearance of a mountain oasis right off Main Street.

For investigative work, Cassie opted for older motels rather than modern facilities. In newer hotels, it was always necessary to enter and exit through the lobby and encounter the employees behind the front desk. Older motels like the Whispering Pines had individual units at street level with no central hallway and separate doors opening out into the parking lot. That way, she could come and go at odd hours and no one could inquire where she was going or why.

She pulled under an overhang next to an attached structure with a sign outside that read OFFICE. There was something familiar about it, she thought. She wondered if perhaps her high school team had stayed there, but she didn't think so.

Cassie was still trying to recall if and when she'd been there before as a bell sounded when she opened the door to the office and went inside. She was immediately greeted by the smell of cooking meat emanating from an open door behind the worn front desk. The office obviously served as living quarters for the manager as well.

"Coming," a deep male voice said from beyond the door.

"No worries," Cassie replied.

She looked around while she waited. The lobby was dark and close. Faded Charles M. Russell prints were hung on the walls as well as a framed notice that spelled out WE LOVE OUR GUESTS in what she first thought were small white seashells but on closer inspection turned out to be ivory elk teeth. Since every elk had only two ivory teeth—called "whistlers" or "buglers"—that meant eight animals had died to make the greeting.

"How nice," she grumbled to herself. Cassie had no issue with hunting and she'd grown up with it. But removing the ivory teeth with pliers and displaying them this way repulsed her. Always had.

The manager was a large bald man with a full beard. He wore a flowing open flannel shirt over a green T-shirt that stretched across his belly. He dabbed at the corners of his mouth with a napkin as he approached the counter.

"Sorry," he said. "You caught me at dinnertime."

"Smells good. I'm Cassie Dewell. I have a reservation."

The manager nodded with recognition and lit up the monitor of his ancient computer. He stabbed at the screen with a stubby finger.

"Four nights, right?"

"It may be less than that. I'll keep you posted."

"Not a problem," the man said. "We're between tourists and hunting season. I don't guess there will be a big run on the rooms."

She anticipated his next request and slid her driver's license and credit card across the counter.

While he punched in the numbers on his keyboard, it hit her. She thought she knew why the motel seemed familiar.

From the photos she'd reviewed the night before she recognized the mature trees in the parking lot and the layout of the individual units in the background. It was the same motel Blake Kleinsasser had been in when he was arrested.

The manager stopped typing. When he looked up his expression was inscrutable.

"Unit number eleven," the man said. "That's the one on the far end. It's a little larger than the other units and very comfortable."

In fact, she thought, it was the same room Blake had been in. The photos had clearly shown that it was the last unit in the complex.

She hesitated. Staying in the same room as a rapist repelled her at first. She didn't want to say why that was to the manager. Then she thought staying in Blake's room might turn out to be an advantage in her investigation. Being in the same space might give an insight to his state of mind. There could possibly still be evidence of him in it as well.

"Yes, that's fine," she said.

He hesitated for a moment before giving back her company credit card. "Dewell Investigations," he said. "Are you here on business or pleasure?"

"Business."

"Are you investigating something?"

"Nothing you need to worry about," she said, wishing she'd lied.

"And you're from Bozeman?"

She nodded.

"Bozeman ain't how I remember it anymore," he said. "Too many newcomers. It's hardly Montana in my mind anymore. No offense."

"None taken."

"Well, welcome to God's country. I like to think of this place as what Montana used to be before the folks from California moved here to ruin it."

Cassie had heard similar sentiments from Bull Mitchell, Rachel's crusty father.

He said, "Let me know if there's anything I can help you with while you're here."

"I'd like to get a good steak and glass of wine. Is there someplace you'd recommend?"

"France." Then he guffawed. "I'm just kidding. I don't know

anything about wine, but if a place doesn't serve good steak it doesn't last around here. I'd suggest the Hayloft up in Lolo."

"Is there any place within walking distance? I've been in my car all day."

"Stumpy's," the manager said. "Right at the end of the block. Tell 'em I sent you."

"And you are?"

"Glen Steele," the man said. "I own this place. It's been in my family for years."

"Nice to meet you, Mr. Steele."

He did a well-rehearsed oration on the location of the ice machine, the Wi-Fi password, and where the bell was outside the office in case she came in late and forgot her key.

As she turned to leave he said, "This doesn't have anything to do with that Kleinsasser thing, does it?"

"Nothing you need to worry about," she said again. She thought Glen Steele asked too many questions for a motel owner.

Room number eleven was the corner room, the last one of the wings. She parked in front of the door and noted that there was only one other vehicle in the lot in front of room number three. It was a green Subaru wagon with Oregon plates.

She threw her duffel and gear bag on the bed inside. The room was dark, clean, and stuffy. On the walls were the same Russell prints as in the office. Steele must have bought them in bulk, she thought.

The room was paneled with knotty pine and the heater and air-conditioning unit was mounted under the front window. She turned it on and set the thermostat at sixty-eight degrees. It awoke and filled the room with cool air.

She closed the door and noticed that the wall shook when she did. The room was cheaply constructed, she observed. Thin walls, cheap carpeting, exposed plumbing under the sink counter. She looked around. There was no telling—although Steele could probably figure it out—how many guests had stayed in the room since Blake Kleinsasser had been hauled out of it by the cops. She looked at the bed and envisioned him passed out on it, and she looked at the plastic garbage can under the sink and imagined it overflowing with empty liquor bottles.

Although the room had been cleaned and disinfected, she thought she could even smell him.

Before unpacking, Cassie dropped to her hands and knees and looked under the bed. There were dust balls, a lone balled-up sock, and an empty condom packet. There was no telling how long any of the detritus had been there, and she made a note to herself to tell Steele his housekeeper needed to do a better job as a courtesy for future guests. But she'd save that advice until she was checking out, she decided. No need to antagonize the man.

Because he had offered her that particular unit, she was a little suspicious of him. As she'd done countless times before, Cassie did a thorough sweep of the room for cameras or listening devices. She unscrewed the light fixtures and heating vents using the screwdriver tool on her Swiss army knife, and checked out the table lamps and hardwired phone near the bed. The single overhead light was out of reach and the desk chair looked too rickety to hold her weight, so she made a note to herself to borrow or buy a small stepladder to check it out later.

Cassie keyed the Wi-Fi password into her phone and laptop and sent Rachel a quick message.

She wrote, Made it to Horston and will start tomorrow. I'm staying in Blake's motel room.

A balloon filled with pulsing dots appeared on the screen. Rachel was responding right away.

Rachel: That's interesting and a little creepy. Have you connected with Sheriff Wagy?

Cassie: Tomorrow, I hope.

Rachel: Please ask for a copy of the DNA report and a sample we can test ourselves.

Cassie: Will do.

Then she checked in by text with Ben and Isabel. She did so separately.

Ben replied that he was fine but completely bored.

Isabel reported that she was already feeling stifled and she looked forward to having her liberty back.

For Cassie, it was good news. They weren't at each other's throats yet.

eight

At a small table in the corner at Stumpy's, Cassie placed a Denise Mina novel on the table and sat down. The novel, although interesting and well-written, was also a prop she kept handy for work. It meant: *yes, I'm a single woman traveling alone. But I'm busy.*

A young blond waitress with floral tattoos on her neck and forearms seated her and slid a laminated one-page menu on the tabletop.

"Would you like to start with a cocktail?"

"Absolutely."

She ordered a glass of red wine and put her handbag on an empty chair at the table. It clunked as she lowered it due to the weight of the .40 Glock she'd slipped into it before she left Whispering Pines.

Stumpy's was decorated with a Church of Trout motif: fly rods and nets attached to the walls, fly-fishing prints, framed posters with sayings including TIE ONE ON; IF AT FIRST YOU DON'T SUCCEED, TRY ANOTHER FLY; A TROUT IS A MOMENT OF BEAUTY KNOWN ONLY TO THOSE WHO SEEK IT; and MANY MEN GO FISHING ALL OF THEIR LIVES WITHOUT KNOWING THAT IT IS NOT FISH THEY ARE AFTER——HENRY DAVID THOREAU.

There was a small bar and lounge adjacent to the dining room where several loud men drank craft beers and chided each other about the fish they'd failed to catch that day on the Bitterroot River.

The only other customers in the restaurant itself was an older couple obviously passing through. The man had an aluminum-colored flattop haircut and he wore cargo shorts, a baggy Detroit Lions T-shirt, and sandals with black socks. He was talking loudly on his cell phone.

"Yellowstone's on fire, Glacier's on fire," he complained to someone. "The whole damned place is on fire. It's ridiculous. I'm not sure where the hell we're going to go."

His wife was a tiny woman wearing a surgical mask. Cassie guessed it was because of the smoke in the air. The woman tugged the mask down for each dainty forkful of meat loaf.

Cassie ordered a second glass of wine when her steak arrived. She was cutting into it when she heard a disturbance in the lounge.

A door banged open and an angry male voice said, "Somebody in here blocked my truck outside. That means somebody driving a GMC with Colorado plates has to get off their ass and move their fucking car."

Cassie leaned over in her chair to get a better angle to see into the bar. The three fishermen had gone quiet and had swiveled on their stools toward the angry man.

"I think that's my Yukon," the middle man said.

"Then I'd suggest you move it," the angry man said. "Like right now."

He was wiry and compact and he exuded menace. He wore tight jeans, cowboy boots, and a big hat with the brim folded up tight to the crown. His arms were pressed to his sides and his fists were clenched. His face was flushed red and he reminded Cassie of an aggravated rodent.

"I'll take care of it," the fisherman said.

"Goddamn right you will. Or I'll smash the hell out of it getting out."

"Just calm down, mister."

"Goddamn out-of-state fishermen," the cowboy said, his voice rising. "You come up here and act like you own the goddamn place. Can't you see when you park and block a vehicle from getting out of the goddamn lot?"

"I said I'd take care of it," the fisherman said.

"Calm down, buddy," one of the other fishermen said.

"I am calm," the cowboy said with a bloodless smile. "You should see me when I'm pissed, you asshole."

Cassie flinched. The older man in the dining room threw cash on the table and helped his wife up. They quickly exited Stumpy's.

"You're *all* assholes," the cowboy added.

She noted that rather than intervene, the bartender busied himself looking down and cleaning beer glasses.

The middle fisherman slid off his stool and walked tentatively toward the saloon doorway where the cowboy stood. He was a head taller and broader at the shoulders than the cowboy, but he seemed smaller.

"Excuse me," the fisherman said.

After a beat, the cowboy stepped aside so the man could go out. As the fisherman passed beside him, the cowboy wheeled and kicked the man in the buttocks with enough force to send him flying through the door.

At that moment, the waitress emerged from the kitchen with Cassie's wine. She paused near Cassie's table and shook her head at the scene in the saloon.

"*Oh, no,*" she whispered.

"Do any of you other assholes want to make a statement?" the cowboy asked the two remaining fishermen.

"I don't think he meant anything bad," one of them said. "We just parked and got out."

"And you failed to notice a Ford F-250 sitting in the corner of the parking lot?" the cowboy asked. "That's a big damned rig to not even see."

"Sorry," the third fisherman said. "We didn't mean anything by it. We were just ready for a beer after a long day."

"What are you drinking?" the cowboy asked.

Cassie took a deep breath, presuming the confrontation was just about over. She noticed that she'd instinctively placed her hand on her bag with the gun in it just in case.

"I'm having a Bitter Root IPA," the fisherman said. "Tad here's having a Huckleberry Honey. They're both local, I believe."

"Let me try 'em," the cowboy said.

Cassie noticed how the two remaining fishermen drew back a little when the cowboy walked up between them to the bar.

The cowboy took their beer glasses, one in each hand. He tasted the IPA, then the Huckleberry Honey. He seemed to be considering which one to order for a moment, then he turned both mugs upside down and emptied them on the floor.

"Fucking swill," he said. "Fucking hipster beer."

"Hey," the third fisherman said, "that was completely unnecessary."

The cowboy slammed the empty mugs on the counter so hard it sounded like gunshots.

"Get the fuck out of here," the cowboy said. "Go back to Missoula or wherever the hell it is you're staying. Go back to your goddamned little bubbles."

The two fishermen exchanged looks. It was obvious they didn't know what to do.

"We can take this outside if you want," the cowboy said. "I'd like nothing better than to fuck up some Colorado fly fishermen."

Cassie beheld the three men. The cowboy was much smaller than both of them, but he seemed tightly coiled and ready to explode. The body language of the two larger fishermen was of defeat: slumped shoulders, awkward movements, no attempts to engage the cowboy.

One turned toward the door, then the other followed. The

cowboy stood at the bar until they were gone. Then he dug a roll of cash out of his jeans pocket and threw several bills on the bar.

The bartender didn't reach for the money until the cowboy was gone. As he did he glanced into the dining room and his eyes locked with Cassie's for a moment. Then he quickly looked away.

Cassie sat back when the waitress placed her bill on the table.

"Sorry about that," the waitress said as much to Cassie as to herself. "That's one of the reasons I just want to get the hell out of this town."

"Who was that?" Cassie asked.

"Ah, he's a pain in the ass," she said. "Rand's always spoiling for a fight."

"Rand?" Cassie asked. "Rand Kleinsasser?"

The waitress looked surprised. "You know him?"

"Not really. But Rand is an odd name."

"Rand is a hothead as you can see. His family has been here since forever. I went to high school with him before he got expelled for fighting. Now I just sort of see him around."

Cassie dug out her credit card. Before she handed it over she asked, "What's your impression of the family?"

The waitress drew back as if stung. "Oh, no," she said. "Honey, I don't know you well enough to say anything. I'm not going there."

She took Cassie's card and spun away on her heel.

Cassie could see narrow yellow lines of fire on the sides of the mountains in three directions as she walked back to the Whispering Pines from Stumpy's. Illuminated smoke formed wispy orbs around the streetlights.

She considered what she'd witnessed at the restaurant. She also kept a look out for Rand Kleinsasser's F-250 and wondered if she'd see it on the street.

"Spoiling for a fight," as the waitress had put it in regard to Rand's behavior only partially described what she'd seen. There were also equal parts entitlement and recklessness. Rand was a loose cannon, and he didn't seem to fear any kind of law enforcement intervention. And certainly not from the bartender, who cowardly stayed out of the situation while Rand chased his customers out the door.

The waitress sold her a bottle of wine to go but didn't speak beyond saying, "Thank you for coming in."

She walked past the Lochsa County Sheriff's Department. It was a modest concrete structure set back from the curb. Next to it was an ancient jail constructed of heavy logs. The plaque on the exterior wall said it was the original jail that had been constructed in 1864 and that it was still in use today. Notorious local outlaws Henry Plummer and Kid Curry had spent time there. Rough iron bars covered the windows.

So that's where Blake had been held, she thought. What a journey—from Wall Street to a historic jail cell in a structure older than the state itself.

As she rounded the corner and walked through the motel parking lot she stopped cold.

The lights were on in room number eleven and the drapes had been pulled back. The front door was wide open.

Cassie paused and reached into her bag for her handgun. She kept it there as she closed the distance to the open door.

That's when she noticed the utility cart parked to the left of the door frame and Glen Steele's hulking frame inside with his back to her. He was unmistakable.

She sidled up to the side of the door and peered inside keeping her bag and weapon out of his view.

"What's going on?" she asked.

He jumped, obviously startled. When he turned around she

observed a heavy white cloth in one of his hands and a spray bottle of cleaner in the other.

"You scared me," he said. "I thought you were out for the night."

"I'm back."

"I see that," he said. Then he explained, "I got to thinking after you checked in that it's been a while since I inspected this room. The cops had it sealed off for a long time after Blake's arrest because his stuff was still in it, and we just recently put it back on line. I've been having trouble keeping reliable housekeepers because nobody wants to work around here anymore. So I thought since you're staying here a few nights that I'd make sure it was clean for you and there were fresh towels."

That was a lot of information, she thought. She looked around and saw that the dingy towels on the rods near the bathroom had been replaced with higher quality versions. The floor gleamed from the mopping he'd obviously just done.

She glanced at her gear bag on the dresser. It was packed with weapons, electronics, and other tools of the trade. It didn't look disturbed. Her clothes were where she'd hung them in the closet, and her overnight bag was still on the side of the basin.

"Well," she said, "it's just that you startled me."

"You startled *me*," he said with a heavy laugh.

"Do you want me to come back?" she asked.

"Oh, no. I'm done. But I hope you let me know if there's anything else I can do to make your stay a pleasant one."

"Thank you," she said.

She stepped aside as he lumbered out.

"Good night," he said.

"Good night."

When he was gone and she could hear the utility cart being pushed down the sidewalk toward the office, she closed the drapes again and bolted the door. Cassie also attached the chain lock. The room smelled sharply of disinfectant.

She double-checked to make sure nothing had been moved or taken from her belongings. Everything seemed to be exactly how she'd left it. Her briefcase with the Blake Kleinsasser file was still locked on the small worktable.

She wanted to believe that Steele was sincere, that he was in her room to ensure its cleanliness.

Cassie opened the bottle and poured wine into a plastic water cup. She wished she would have thought to bring a proper glass.

Then, before changing into the oversized T-shirt she wore for sleeping, she once again got on her hands and knees and looked under the bed. The dust, the sock, and the condom wrapper were gone.

She placed the Glock on her bedside table and opened up the novel.

She wasn't tired although it had been a long day and she'd been awake most of the night before. She poured another cup of wine with the hope that it would relax her. She hoped sleep would come.

It didn't for a long time.

Several hours later, Cassie sat up straight in bed and tried to catch her breath. Her heart raced and there was a sheen of sweat across her breasts.

It took her a few panic-filled moments to figure out what had happened.

She'd had a dream. An extremely vivid dream.

In it, she was in her Jeep along the side of the state highway in heavy timber. An afternoon shadow from the timber cast a dark pall. Her location was somewhere along the road south of Horston— the road she'd taken to get there. Apparently, her vehicle had broken down and she'd just pulled over.

It was hot out and the evening cool had yet to enter the forest. She wished she knew more about cars so she could attempt to fix the problem. Nevertheless, she prepared to pop the hood, open the door, and check the engine to see if she could discern why it had quit on her.

As she reached for the door handle, a massive tractor-trailer rounded the bend behind her and filled her rearview mirror. The semi was matte black, and every bit of chrome on it except the front grille was blacked out as well.

The truck slowed and inched over onto her side of the road with the shrill whistle of pneumatic brakes. The grille filled her back window. It stopped behind her so close that she could see the red Peterbilt logo on the snout in her rearview mirror. Its rumbling diesel engine shook the ground itself. Even the steering wheel of her Jeep vibrated with it.

She tried in vain to start her Jeep, hoping against hope that the engine would start.

No response.

Cassie checked her side mirrors and saw both the driver's-side and passenger door open on the truck. Two men swung out and dropped to the gravel.

For some reason, her gear bag and weapons weren't on the passenger seat where they should be. Her Glock wasn't in her handbag, either. She couldn't explain why her shoes and socks were missing. She *never* drove barefoot.

Two men approached her Jeep from either side and she froze. She dismissed the idea of leaping outside and running away because she had no shoes.

Where were her shoes? Her weapons?

The driver was the Lizard King, Ronald Pergram himself, although he looked different. His hair was wispy and white, and rolls of skin hung down from his jaws. There were gaping holes where his eyes should have been. He looked partially decomposed.

But his gait was strong and he strode toward her.

On the other side was a young rooster of a man wearing a curled-up cowboy hat. She recognized him as Rand Kleinsasser.

He was grinning. He had a stiff coil of rope in his right hand and he thumped it against his thigh in a jaunty way.

That's when she woke up in a sweat.

But all was quiet and dark in her room. There was no rumbling semi outside, and the only light was a dim beige frame of it on the borders of her drawn curtains from the streetlight in the parking lot.

She realized in her panic she'd reached for her weapon but had mishandled it and knocked it to the floor. Cassie was grateful it hadn't gone off.

When she stopped shaking, she slipped out from under the covers and padded to the window. There was nothing to see.

She counted out four ibuprofens from her travel kit and swallowed them with a cup of brackish water from the tap. She hoped they would relax her back to sleep.

Cassie ran her fingers through her hair and looked around the dark room. She tried to analyze the nightmare for clues but she gave up.

It was four thirty. Her alarm was set for six.

She stared at the ceiling and memorized the pattern of the ceiling tile. There was still a half a bottle of wine but she knew drinking more would be a bad idea.

It was nights like this when she longed for a man in bed beside her. Even if he was a knucklehead she met at a bar, his presence would be welcome. It would be easier and less messy to make that scenario happen in a strange town away from Ben and Isabel, she thought.

She tried to conjure up men who'd been in her life and will them beside her. The first was Jim, her dead husband and Ben's father. Jim was young, taut and firm, the age he'd been when he went to war. She could smell beer and chewing tobacco on his breath.

The second was Ian, her ex-fiancé from North Dakota. Poor Ian. He lay on his back and his breathing whistled softly through his nose. He had long eyelashes and his profile in the dark was delicate.

The third was Bryan Pederson. He lay on his side with his naked back to her. His skin was white and there was a wash of freckles across the top on his shoulders. He was no doubt dreaming about his ex-wife.

She fell back asleep fifteen minutes before she had to get up.

nine

When Cassie saw Lochsa County Sheriff Ben Wagy arrive at the county building the next morning she threw down the last of her bitterly bad motel-room coffee and tossed the cup to the floorboard. She identified Wagy by where he parked his county SUV: under a sign that said the space was reserved for him.

She caught up with him as he reached for the door handle on the side of the building next to a COUNTY EMPLOYEES ONLY header stenciled on the exterior block wall.

"Sheriff Wagy?"

He paused and turned and his eyes narrowed. He was short but broad-shouldered and his beige and brown uniform was already rumpled. He had wide-set blue eyes, a heavy jaw, and a thick auburn mustache that bristled over his top lip.

"That's me," he said without warmth. Cassie recognized the instant protective shell that went up around him. It was a shield that hardened with every year in law enforcement to fend off attacks from defense lawyers, county commissioners, potential rivals, the press . . . and private investigators.

Cassie held out her hand. "I'm Cassie Dewell. I'm doing some work on behalf of the law firm hired to defend Blake Kleinsasser. I was hoping I could ask you a few questions about the investigation."

"Blake?" Wagy said, arching his eyebrows. "You're working for Blake?"

"Kind of," she said. She did so in a way that suggested she wasn't very enthusiastic about it, and she hoped he picked up on that.

"Do you have an appointment?"

"No, sir. I tried to make one but I didn't receive a reply."

"You did?"

"I sent your office an email from Bozeman," she said.

"I've got about four hundred emails on my computer. I can't get to them all."

She smiled. "I worked for a sheriff over in Bakkan County, North Dakota, who was the same way. He had over two thousand unanswered emails in his inbox. He told me he was shooting for three thousand by the time he retired."

"Did he make it?" Wagy asked, amused.

"I believe he did, sir."

"Man after my own heart. Do I know him?"

"His name was Sheriff Jon Kirkbride. He was my mentor."

Wagy nodded his head and his eyes softened. "I remember Jon. He was one of the good ones."

"I agree."

"Those bastards forced him out, if I recall correctly."

"Something like that. It was very nasty and political."

"It always is."

"So . . ."

Wagy shot out his sleeve and checked his wristwatch. "I've got a meeting with the county commissioners at eight thirty. I'll give you a half hour so I hope you're prepared."

"I am."

"Follow me," Wagy said while punching in a code on a keypad near the steel door frame. "I hope you like bad coffee."

"I'm used to it," she said.

"So you're a private investigator?" he asked over his shoulder as he led her down a dark hallway.

"I am. Dewell Investigations."

"I have to admit I don't think a whole lot of PIs," Wagy said.

She sensed that his shield, which had been down for a minute due to his acquaintance with Sheriff Kirkbride, was now back up in full.

"I'm used to that, too," she said.

On the way to his office, Wagy nodded good morning to an administrative assistant about Cassie's age. She was seated behind the front counter. A plaque on the counter said her name was Linda Sue Murdock.

He asked, "Any urgent messages?"

Murdock shook her head. "No, but I wanted to remind you about that county commission meeting at ten."

"I didn't forget," Wagy said. "Bring us a couple of coffees when you get a minute."

"Yes, sir," Murdock said after shooting Cassie a sidelong glance.

Cassie got the message. Murdock didn't like being treated like a secretary in the 1960s asked to bring coffee to the boss in the morning. Cassie didn't blame her.

Plus, she noted that Murdock said the meeting was two hours away. Either Sheriff Wagy had been confused about the time or he'd lied to Cassie so their interview would be short.

"Have a seat," Wagy said when they entered his office. He didn't acknowledge or address the time discrepancy. Cassie took a hard chair across from the sheriff's desk and placed a file on her lap.

His office was spartan. There were pronghorn antlers, a dusty mounted rainbow trout, and a few photos of the sheriff posing with Governor Monte Schreiner and other politicians.

He said nothing until Murdock brought the two coffees and placed them on his desk.

"Will that be all?" she asked.

"For now," Wagy said to her. "Please close the door on your way out."

Murdock turned and shared another burning look with Cassie.

"Thank you," Cassie said to her as she reached for her cup.

"You're welcome," Murdock said.

No thank-you from the sheriff.

Oblivious to the exchange, Wagy said, "I'll tell you straight out. I'm not in the business of undermining my team, our investigation, or my office. If you're here to screw with me you'll find your time in Lochsa County pretty unpleasant."

Cassie ignored the threat and tried to get in front of the conversation.

"Sheriff Wagy, I'm not your adversary. I approach every case I take from the side of law enforcement. I'm not here to punch holes in your case in regard to Blake Kleinsasser. I'm here to confirm all of the facts so that my employer can make a convincing argument to the accused that he should take a plea deal if one is offered."

Wagy took a sip of his coffee, cringed, and raised his eyebrows. "Forgive me if I'm a little skeptical about that."

"I understand," Cassie said. "I've been where you are many times. I know how defense attorneys can be and I can't guarantee you my employer won't try some of those tactics if this case goes to trial. I can't speak for her.

"But what I can promise," Cassie said, "is that my report on the evidence and investigation will be truthful and honest even if it doesn't help Mr. Kleinsasser's defense. My job here is to cross the t's and dot the i's of the record. I'd like nothing more than to report back to my client that the investigation was sound and by the book and that the evidence is rock-solid."

Wagy looked skeptical. "Can you tell me with a straight face that you're not starting this thing from the standpoint that Blake is innocent?"

"I'm not."

"Good," Wagy said. "Because he's guilty as hell. And he's also an asshole."

"I'm aware of that."

"Your employer—what is her name?"

"Rachel Mitchell of Mitchell-Estrella."

"Ah," Wagy said with a knowing smirk. "The crusading Bozeman female activists. I've heard of them."

Cassie ignored Wagy again. She wondered if he was trying to provoke her into saying something that would prove to him that she wasn't playing it straight.

"I've read the arrest report and it looks very cut-and-dried," she said. "Were there ever any credible suspects in the assault besides Blake Kleinsasser?"

"Nada," Wagy said. "And not because we were out to get him. I know the history of that family in this valley—everybody does. I know there was bad blood between Blake and the rest of the family. But I don't work for the Kleinsassers. I work for the people of Lochsa County, even those who didn't vote for me.

"When Franny was brought in here with her story we didn't jump to conclusions even though she clearly named Blake as the perp. We got her statement and went through proper procedure. Are you familiar with a Christmas tree test?"

"Yes."

It was a fairly simple and accurate DNA test that could be done on-site by law enforcement personnel. Acid phosphatase applied to an alleged semen sample under a microscope made the heads of sperm appear red and the tails green.

"Of course," Wagy said, "the Christmas tree test just confirmed that there was semen in her panties. It doesn't identify who put it there. That came later after we arrested Blake and swabbed him. We drove the samples to the crime lab in Missoula and they came back with a perfect match."

"Did Blake deny it to you?" Cassie asked.

"He sure did. But every part of Franny's story was corroborated. From the witnesses at the church who saw Blake pick her up to the old cabin out on the ranch. If you've read the charging documents you already know all of this."

Cassie nodded. "I don't remember reading who brought Franny in to you. I'm not sure that was in the file."

"Her mother and her uncle brought her in that night," Wagy said. "Franny had to walk all the way back to the ranch headquarters in the dark after being assaulted. She told them what happened and they brought her here."

"Which uncle?"

"John Wayne."

"Thank you."

Cassie entered the new detail into her notebook.

"Was her statement taken that night?" she asked.

"Nah, just a preliminary statement. The official statement was taken the next day. That's the one that you read, I'll guess."

Cassie flipped through her file and noted that the statement was indeed dated the day after the assault.

She said, "So the uncle and mother brought Franny here instead of asking you or your officers to go out to the ranch."

"That's what I said."

Cassie jotted it down and looked up. "Were you working late that night and you just happened to be here?"

Wagy narrowed his eyes. "Dispatch called me at home to meet the reporting parties here so I came in. I don't sit on my ass in this office twenty-four-seven, but when a serious allegation is made I drop everything and show up. That's my job. Are you suggesting something here?"

"Not at all," Cassie said. "I'm just trying to get the time line straight in my notes."

Wagy didn't comment. She could tell she was losing him as a cooperative subject.

"How would you describe Franny's state of mind when she came in?"

"I'm no shrink," Wagy said, "but I'd say she was pretty upset. Distraught, crying, that kind of thing. I did my best to make her comfortable. Sometimes sexual assault victims blame themselves so

I didn't want to add to that in any way. I called in one of my deputies who is a girl to do the test."

Girl.

"How would you describe the state of mind of Fanny's mother and uncle?" Cassie asked. She studied Wagy's face when he answered.

"How do you think?" he said. "Cheyenne was on the edge of hysterical. She's a strange bird, but I thought she might lose it any minute. Imagine having to go through that with your only daughter."

"I understand," Cassie said.

"John Wayne wanted to find Blake and blow his head off," Wagy said. "I was able to calm him down, but I had no doubt he'd do what he said he'd do. That's one reason we moved on Blake right away and found his car at the motel and arrested him in that room. It was for Blake's safety as much as anything."

"Did you contact the press to be there for the arrest?" Cassie asked. "I saw video clips of it on the internet."

Wagy bristled. "Are you accusing me of grandstanding?"

"Not at all," Cassie said again. Wagy was much more thin-skinned than she thought he'd be.

"No, somebody must have tipped them," Wagy said. "There's always a concerned citizen or two listening to their police scanner. That's probably why they were there. My guess is the word was out about the assault even though we were trying to keep it under wraps. This is a small town with lots of gossips in it, and, you know, the Kleinsasser name gets everyone's attention."

"I can imagine it does," Cassie said.

Wagy made a show of looking at his watch. It was a signal to Cassie that the interview was about to conclude.

"Another state of mind question," Cassie said. "What about Blake? How did he react when you arrested him?"

"Are you asking if he proclaimed his innocence?" Wagy asked with a cold grin.

"Yes."

"Of course he did. He said he didn't have any idea why we were there. And then he turned into the asshole that he is. He started throwing his weight around and said his lawyers would have him out of jail by the next morning and that he was going to sue me and the county. He blamed his brothers and his dad for everything."

Wagy said, "He was inebriated. Drunker than hell, and he smelled like he hadn't had a bath in a while. It was a real pleasure throwing him into our vintage slammer. I'm sure you've seen our jail."

"I have."

"It's a real jail," Wagy said. "Not like one of those cushy country club motel rooms some counties have. When you're in there and that steel door closes behind you you know you're actually in *jail*. That was the first time I think Blake actually took it seriously. He sobered up in record time. And he thought he could talk his way out of it all the way up to the preliminary hearing. You've met him, right?"

"Just yesterday," Cassie answered.

"He's a piece of work, isn't he?"

"How do you mean?"

"Such an arrogant prick," the sheriff said. "He thinks he's better than everybody around here—that he can talk his smooth New York bullshit and do whatever he wants. He's always been like that."

"So, you've known him a long time?" Cassie asked.

Wagy caught himself and sat back. He didn't want to respond. Cassie found that interesting.

"I think we're done," he said.

"I'd like to request a copy of the DNA report from Missoula," she said. "We've got the Christmas tree test but not the match. And I'll probably have additional questions. Can I meet with you again before I go back?"

"Set up an appointment," Wagy said.

"What about the DNA match?"

Wagy sighed theatrically and reached for his hat. He was in a hurry to get to his make-believe meeting.

"I'll authorize Linda to pull the documents and make copies," he said. "We do charge for them, though. I hope your employer will reimburse you twenty-five cents a copy."

"Thank you," Cassie said, standing up. "I'd also like to review the physical evidence. You know, so we can compare the items to the list submitted to the court."

Wagy squinted. "You want to handle the evidence? Sorry, no can do."

"Not *handle* it," Cassie said. "Sheriff, I know how this works. I'd never dream of contaminating evidence. I simply want to photograph the items with my cell phone camera so Rachel has a record of everything. I anticipate that she'll show the photos to Blake in an effort to persuade him the case against him is as solid as it appears."

Wagy glared at her, obviously suspicious of her request.

"You can view it," he said finally. "But only with my people standing right there with you. And if you reach for anything I swear I'll arrest you for tampering with evidence and you'll get to see our jail from the inside out. Just like Blake did."

"I understand," Cassie said.

"We've got nothing to hide from the defense," Wagy said. "My office is totally transparent. We're an open book."

"It was a pleasure to meet you and thank you for your cooperation and time," Cassie said, extending her hand.

"Wish I could say the same," Wagy said with a smile that could be taken either way. "I guess you'll be headed back to Bozeman later today."

"Not quite yet," Cassie said. "I've got to talk to a couple of people."

"And then you'll be gone." It was a statement more than a question. Cassie didn't respond.

Then he ushered Cassie out of his office and with a few words to Murdock en route he went down the hallway toward the parking lot jingling his keys.

That left Cassie and Linda Murdock together in the squad room.

Murdock said, "What he didn't want to tell you is that he has coffee with the city fathers every morning. He rarely misses it."

That accounted for the discrepancy, Cassie thought.

"The sheriff asked me to make some copies for you and escort you to the evidence room," Murdock said.

"Thank you."

"Follow me."

Cassie hoped that Murdock would turn out to be a potentially valuable asset within the Lochsa County Sheriff's Department. Not that she expected Murdock to turn on her boss, but the administrative assistant was a breed Cassie was familiar with from working in other law enforcement departments: the key civilian who knew how things worked and where the bodies were buried.

Murdock was the heart and brains of the organization, the staffer who quietly did her job and observed the goings-on around her while various deputies and sheriffs came and went. She had the institutional memory of the organization and was rarely given credit for it. Cassie had gleaned more inside knowledge and intelligence from stalwarts like Linda Murdock over the years than from elected sheriffs or assigned chiefs of police.

"Is the sheriff hostile to all women or just me?" Cassie asked Murdock as the administrative assistant fed the forensics documents through the copier.

Murdock said, "Oh, you noticed?"

"It was hard not to."

"I don't mind getting coffee for him once in a while. It makes him feel important."

"It rankled me."

"I honestly think he doesn't even realize it," Murdock said.

"That's kind of you," Cassie said with a smile.

"My husband's on disability. I need the job."

"I understand."

Cassie added the DNA reports to her folder. Murdock dutifully copied all of the photos and documents in the case file even though Cassie recognized many of them as items they already had. She was grateful for Murdock's thoroughness.

It was always better to have too much documentation, including duplicates, than not enough. Plus, from the standpoint of the defense, if exculpatory evidence was withheld *twice* it showed malice on behalf of the prosecution and not simply a procedural error.

"How much do I owe you?" Cassie asked when the task was complete.

Murdock waved her off. "Don't worry about it."

Cassie followed her down a hallway toward the evidence locker in the back of the building. Over her shoulder, Murdock asked, "Did he give you the line that he doesn't work for the Kleinsassers? That he works for the people of Lochsa County?"

"Yes, he did."

"Don't believe it," Murdock said. "Between you and me, he answers to them. All of the electeds around here do. The school board was independent for a few years but even that's back to the point where every board member owes their office to the family."

Cassie nodded that she understood. Rachel would no doubt find that information intriguing.

A large older man in a deputy uniform sat at a desk in front of the secured evidence locker. He had a sweeping white mustache and

jowls and he reminded Cassie of a walrus. He was in the process
of hanging up the phone.

"Just talked to the sheriff," he said as Murdock and Cassie approached. "He said you were here to look at the Blake Kleinsasser
box but only to photograph the items."

Cassie nodded.

The deputy turned to Murdock. "Are you going to sign it out?"

"Yes."

"Give me a minute," the deputy said as he pulled on a pair of
blue latex gloves. "I'll be right out."

Cassie watched as the deputy rose, turned, and used a set of
keys attached to his belt to unlock a pair of heavy locks on the
chain-link door behind him. He had a pronounced limp and his
movements were stiff. Cassie guessed that he was a longtime LEO
who'd been assigned to an easy desk job until retirement rolled
around. It was one of the remaining perks of every bureaucracy
that no longer existed in the private sector, where seniority counted
more than usefulness. She'd seen examples of it in every department she'd ever worked for.

The evidence room was crammed with metal shelving. On the
shelves were boxes marked with the names of the investigations
they corresponded with. Along the back wall was a large cabinet
filled with long guns and other weapons including a samurai sword
and a chain saw. Every item was tagged and marked.

The deputy emerged and placed a large white legal box on a
table beside his desk. It was marked KLEINSASSER, BLAKE.

Before he cut through the sealing tape with a box cutter, he
turned to Cassie. She knew that it would be resealed and marked
when they were done and the record of it being opened was to be
signed by Murdock and date-stamped by the deputy.

"Stand back."

Cassie took a step backwards. As she did she felt the vibration
of an incoming text from her phone in her pocket. She glanced at
it quickly. It was from Ben.

Call me when U can.

She pocketed the device.

The deputy sliced through the tape and removed the items one by one. He made it a point to make sure the evidence number on each tag was clearly visible. Cassie recognized all of the items from the evidence list as she photographed them, including:

- The largest item, a cast of tire tracks found on the dirt road outside the house on the ranch where the assault took place. It allegedly matched the tread from Blake's rental car.
- Individual fingerprint cards in glassine envelopes identifying both Blake's and Franny's prints.
- Empty and half-full liquor bottles that had been found in the rental car, the structure on the ranch, and Blake's motel room were placed in a row on the table.
- Two smudged glasses in Ziploc bags, which the deputy put on the table in front of the bottles. Cassie recognized them as the glasses from the ranch house with both Blake's and Franny's fingerprints and DNA on them. They were heavy cocktail glasses as opposed to drinking glasses.
- Thumb drives of closed-circuit video in clear plastic sleeves placing Blake at the Corvallis and Hayloft bars prior to the assault.

In all, Cassie thought, the accumulation of physical evidence was overwhelming. She took several shots of the entire table to emphasize that fact.

"Got it all?" the deputy asked her.

Cassie nodded but then paused. "Is this all the evidence?"

"How much more do you want?" the deputy said with a laugh.

"I was hoping her phone would be in there."

The deputy checked his sheet again and shrugged. "No phone," he said.

"Where is her underwear?"

Murdock looked up in alarm. The deputy shrugged. "I'm guessing they're still at the lab in Missoula. They probably haven't sent them back yet."

"But you don't know for sure?" Cassie asked.

The deputy reddened, but walked over to his desk to review the list of exhibits associated with the box. It took him minutes to check each item by pointing a stubby fingertip on the list and then visually checking each exhibit on the table.

Finally, he said without confidence, "That has to be what happened. The lab hasn't sent them back yet."

"Could you confirm that and let me know?" Cassie asked. She knew her tone was strident.

"I'll check with the sheriff," the deputy said without meeting her eyes.

When Cassie looked over to Murdock she noted that the woman seemed poised to add something. Instead, she remained silent.

"That might be a problem," Cassie said as she followed Murdock back toward the front of the department.

"It's probably nothing," Murdock said without conviction. "Mistakes happen. Things get misfiled or lost in the mail. I'm sure the evidence will be located. The sheriff is a stickler about that kind of thing."

Cassie nodded. Then asked, "It looked like you were about to say something back there. Is there anything else?"

"No," Murdock said. "Nothing else."

Cassie gave Murdock her card. "My cell phone number is on there and so is my email address. Feel free at any time to contact me."

"About what?"

"Whatever it is you think I should know," Cassie said.

She retrieved her phone to speed-dial her son while she walked toward her Jeep in the parking lot. It was 9:15 A.M. and she knew he had an open-study period from nine to ten and she assumed that he wasn't studying.

After she talked to him to find out what the problem was, she planned to touch base with Rachel and give her an update. It roiled her stomach to do so because she knew the missing underwear could be seized upon by the defense, DNA report or not.

While the prosecution had the awesome power and treasury of the state behind them at trial, the defense had the luxury of second-guessing and questioning every move made by law enforcement and spinning simple errors that occurred in every organization into diabolical conspiracies. Cassie had been on the stand on multiple occasions when defense attorneys questioned her motives, ethics, and competence. It was always demoralizing, and it bothered her to think that she could conceivably play a role in a similar effort.

She didn't want to be a party to that in this case, especially given the overwhelming evidence against Blake Kleinsasser.

ten

⊷═◉═⊶

Ben Dewell waited for Erin Reese on a cold concrete bench that had yet to warm from the morning sun outside Bozeman High. He kept a close eye on the double doors for her because he planned to spring up and greet her the moment she came outside.

It was pure fortune that Erin's free period occurred the same time as his. They'd started meeting outside and walking the two blocks to the Kum & Go convenience store for a morning snack. But it was more than that. He couldn't wait to see her.

Erin was a new kid to Bozeman and the school, like Ben. And like Ben, she'd arrived with no friends or connections or cliques that immediately welcomed her to join them. Ben had the wrestling team but it was almost as if having no group at all because he was a freshman and he was so lousy at the sport. He wasn't even sure he'd make the freshman team because his only value, it seemed, was to serve as prey for better wrestlers who needed their confidence built up. The coaches made sure of that. As a result, he was a mass of bruises and sore muscles, and the only other wrestlers he'd really bonded with were as inept as he was and most of them had already quit the team.

That Erin hadn't found her place yet was more of a puzzle for Ben because she was attractive, quirky, and exotic. She was also flighty and book-smart, and she seemed to be very comfortable in her own skin, unlike him. There was no doubt she was considered weird and seemed to care not at all about what other kids said about her with her odd clothing, floppy hats, and flowing scarves.

He expected to lose her friendship at any time when, inevitably, she fell in with the right crowd. He'd noticed some of the drama and theater nerds hanging together at lunch and he guessed she might fit right in with them.

But so far, it seemed, he was her only friend. And he thanked God for it twenty times a day.

They shared two classes, the study period, and late-night texting together. She seemed to like his company and she laughed at his attempts at humor. She lifted his spirits when he was down and playfully called him "Eeyore" after the gloomy donkey in the Winnie-the-Pooh books. When he complained to her about Isabel, which he often did, she laughed uncontrollably in person or replied with laughing emojis in her text responses.

When she appeared behind the heavy glass in the vestibule—her sheer lavender scarf flowing behind her and giving her away—he felt a trill that shot up both legs into his groin.

And, of course, at that second his mother called.

"Ben, is everything all right?"

"It's fine," he said quickly. He wanted to get off the phone before Erin saw him talking to his mom.

"But you texted me to call you right away." She sounded rushed and annoyed.

"Isabel went on strike this morning," he said.

"What do you mean, on strike?"

"That's what she said. She said I don't appreciate her and neither do you. She said she was on strike until further notice."

"Ben, what did you do?"

"Nothing."

"Ben?"

"Why do you automatically blame me? You know she's a crazy woman."

"That's no way to talk about your grandmother, Ben. She means well. So, what happened that she decided to go on strike?"

He sighed. "I wouldn't eat granola for breakfast. I told her I need protein, like bacon. I'm a *wrestler*, Mom."

"And she went on strike over that?"

"That's what she said. So, you need to come home."

"I can't right now," his mother said. "Look, I'll call her and try to straighten things out."

"She's not answering her phone. That's part of her strike."

The conversation was becoming time-consuming and it was getting complicated, he thought. Erin was pushing through the doors to come outside. That she seemed to be searching for him made his legs even weaker.

"I've got to go," he said, making eye contact with Erin and leaping up as planned.

"Ben, you need to try to get along with Isabel."

"Mom, I've got to go. I'm in *school*."

He said it as he approached Erin and rolled his eyes for her benefit.

"We'll talk tonight. In the meanwhile, I'll try to talk to your grandmother—"

He disconnected the call and slid his phone in his shirt pocket.

"Was that your mom?"

He tried for a dismissive tone. "Yeah. She's always checking up on me."

"That's nice."

"Not always."

"Believe me," Erin said with a flip of her strawberry blonde hair, "it's better than not caring at all."

Which made him realize he knew nothing at all about her family. Their conversations had been solely about school, other students, movies, music, and things like that. Ben made a mental note to ask her about her situation when the time was right. He'd heard that girls liked it when boys showed a genuine interest in their lives.

He was *so* new to this, he thought. This girl thing.

Erin smiled at him and gestured up the street in the direction of the Kum & Go. She said, "Ice cream for breakfast sounds awesome to me."

"Ice cream it is," he said, taking her backpack and throwing it over his shoulder. She was a few inches taller than him but he was stronger. She'd told him she really liked how polite he was. She'd called him a "true gentleman."

Ben casually reached into his pocket to make sure he had money. He knew at this rate he'd burn through all the cash his mother had given him in a couple of days. And he didn't care.

Ben listened as Erin told him about her English teacher from second period, how they'd gotten into an argument about *The Iliad*. They were side by side down the sidewalk and twice she grasped his hand for emphasis as she made a point. Her touch made his mouth go dry.

"I told him the poem would be much more interesting if it was told from Helen's point of view," she said. "As it is it's no better than a cheap sword-and-sandals B movie. He disagreed."

He loved the way she talked. It was lyrical and sophisticated and nothing ever seemed to bother her. And she had courage taking on a teacher like that.

Ben couldn't stop staring at her naked ankles as she walked. The hem of her pants was short and he didn't know if it was because her family couldn't afford clothes that fit her or if it was her style. He came down firmly on her style.

As she told him about the flaws she found in the narrative of the epic poem, how she thought it was a "cheap trick" to have Zeus suddenly appear and solve the problems of the Greeks versus the

Trojans, Ben realized that it was getting harder to hear her because of escalating street noise. A low rumbling filled the air.

Her spell over him temporarily broken, he looked up with annoyance.

It was a clear shot to the parking lot of the Kum & Go and the street ahead was empty. Then he turned around to see the grille of a huge tractor-trailer rumbling up the street behind them. It was black and dirty and massive, and he couldn't see the driver because the windows were tinted.

Ben couldn't believe it when the semi crossed the center line of the street into the other lane. It kept coming until the front tires were on the sidewalk right behind them.

Then it sped up.

He grasped Erin's arm and pulled her into an alleyway between the corner and the convenience store. As he did so her backpack slipped off of her shoulder and fell to the pavement. He felt a wave of hot exhaust on his back.

They both watched as the Peterbilt rolled over the top of the backpack. Two sets of front wheels and two more sets of dual tires under the trailer.

Thump-thump. Thump-thump.

Once the truck was gone, accelerating loudly as it passed in front of the Kum & Go and turned at the corner, they looked at each other as if to confirm what had just happened.

"That idiot almost ran us over!" she said. "What do you think he was doing?"

"I don't know," Ben said. "He wasn't looking where he was going. Maybe he was texting or something. I hear they do that when they drive."

"He could have squashed us." Then she said, "You saved my life."

Ben flushed red. No one had ever said anything like that to him before, something so dramatic yet clichéd.

"Thank you, Ben Dewell. You're my hero."

He didn't think he could turn any redder, but he was sure he did.

Ben was surprised by what Erin did next when she leaned into him and kissed him on the mouth. He was too surprised to respond.

Then she laughed as she retrieved her backpack from the sidewalk. She peeled it off the concrete and marveled at the fact that it was totally flattened, like the Road Runner in the cartoons.

Ben's heart raced, and not just from the unexpected kiss. The vehicle was just like the truck his mom had chased for years. He knew the description of it by heart. He also knew his mom had been there for the last breath of the Lizard King.

So, who had been behind the wheel? And why had the driver targeted him?

Should he tell Erin about the Lizard King? Would she think he was crazy or paranoid? Or would she really get into the story because it was so lurid and dramatic?

He thought he knew the answer to that question.

eleven

⫷━◉━⫸

Attorney Andrew Johnson was seated at the defense table in Lochsa County courtroom number one when Cassie entered the room. His back was to her.

She knew his location because she'd called Johnson's law office and asked for him. The secretary said he was in court.

Cassie slipped into an empty bench and placed her bag next to her. The security officer in the outside hallway had kept her phone and keys. She'd known better than to enter the chambers with her weapons or electronics and she'd left them in her Jeep.

The pretrial hearing had already begun, and Johnson sat next to his client. Across the aisle from him was a young woman prosecutor.

The courtroom was virtually empty except for two other defendants and their respective lawyers who sat on opposite sides of the aisle. Both defendants—an unkempt man in his sixties who noticed her and scowled and a stringy-haired thirtysomething with the toothless grin of a meth addict—seemed as if they'd been there before. There was also an older woman knitting a baby blanket. Cassie guessed she was the type who simply enjoyed sitting through courtroom procedures.

Johnson's client wore an orange jumpsuit with LOCHSA COUNTY DETENTION CENTER stenciled in black across the back of it. He had jet-black hair in a ponytail, and when he turned his head toward Johnson she could see he had Native American features.

The judge was a severe woman who had a grating voice. She seemed bored with the proceedings. Cassie assumed the morning was scheduled for multiple hearings and that it was the judge's intent to bang them out as quickly as possible.

"Mr. Johnson," the judge said, "your client"—she glanced down at her notes for a moment—"Mr. Leland Red Star Wolf, has been charged with driving while under the influence of alcohol and resisting arrest. How does he plead?"

Johnson gathered himself and stood up. "He pleads not guilty, Your Honor."

The judge snorted and rolled her eyes. "Lovely."

"Your Honor," Johnson said, "my client is a member of good standing of the Nez Perce nation. In addition to serving on the Salmon Recovery Board, he's a former vice-chairman of the Nez Perce Tribal Executive Committee. Therefore he's not a flight risk. We would ask the court to consider a reasonable bail so that he can resume his duties for the tribe while he awaits trial."

"That's touching," the judge said with sarcasm.

"This is Mr. Red Star Wolf's first offense in Lochsa County," Johnson continued.

The prosecutor stood up quickly. "Your Honor, what Mr. Johnson fails to note is that although this is Mr. Red Star Wolf's first offense in Lochsa County, he's been arrested two times for the same offense—DWUI—in Missoula County and another time in Idaho."

Johnson looked over at her with faux indignation. Cassie had seen it all before.

"Right," the judge said. She glared at the defendant and said, "Let's hope your client sees his way to a plea deal and doesn't take any more valuable time in my courtroom," before setting his bail at twenty-five thousand dollars.

She banged her gavel and said, "Next!"

Cassie found that amount unusually high considering the charges. She thought that they didn't mess around in Lochsa County.

★ ★ ★

After whispering briefly with his client, Johnson watched as the deputies led Red Star Wolf away. When the defendant was gone, the attorney abruptly loosened up and exchanged pleasantries with the prosecutor and both of them laughed at a shared joke Cassie couldn't hear.

As Johnson gathered papers to clear the table for the next case, Cassie approached the bar that separated the spectator gallery from the well where the lawyers' tables and bench were located.

"Mr. Andrew Johnson?"

He turned around as if startled. He was thin with close-cropped silver hair, a sharp nose, darting blue eyes, and a cautious manner. His suit seemed to be a size too big.

"Can I help you?" Johnson said.

"I'm Cassie Dewell with Dewell Investigations in Bozeman. I'm working on behalf of Mitchell-Estrella and I was hoping I could ask you a few questions in regard to the case against Blake Kleinsasser."

When she said Mitchell-Estrella she noticed a tightening of his jaw.

"As you can see, I'm busy," he said.

"I'm happy to make an appointment for later today."

"Not possible," Johnson said. "I'm on my way right now to do depos in another case. I'll be occupied for the rest of today and tomorrow."

"It won't take long," she said.

"I can't be late."

"Then we can walk and talk."

He sighed and turned his back on her so he could slide his files into his briefcase. When he turned back around she was still there.

"Walk and talk," he said without enthusiasm.

Cassie noted that the prosecutor watched the exchange with a small grin, as if Johnson's sudden predicament amused her.

"I want to get my facts straight," Cassie said as she trailed Johnson in the hallway. He was a fast walker, and he was determined to get to where he was going.

There were several small knots of people in the hallway; cops, prosecutors, defendants, lawyers, witnesses.

"What is it that you want to know?" he asked sotto voce over his shoulder. It was in the same manner, she noted, he had talked with his client before the defendant was led away.

"Our records show that you were Blake's initial criminal attorney. Is that correct?"

"Blake? He's Blake to you?" As if the accused was her close friend.

"Only because there are so many Kleinsassers in this valley that I want to be clear."

"Ah, got it."

"So that's correct? You were his defense counsel?"

"That's correct."

"You petitioned the court for a change in venue from Lochsa County. May I ask you why?"

"You can ask," Johnson said, his voice rising inexplicably. "But there's such a thing as attorney-client privilege. I can't tell you about our discussions and if you continue to ask about them I may need to notify the sheriff."

Cassie snorted. "Come on, this isn't my first rodeo. I'm not asking you to re-create your discussions with Blake and you don't even represent him anymore. I'm not asking that you be a witness in his defense, either. I'm just trying to verify the facts and the time line."

Johnson paused at the elevator and pushed the down button.

Loud enough for everyone milling in the hallway to hear including cops and court personnel, he said, "Ms. Dewell, I've said all I'm going to say about the Blake Kleinsasser case."

The doors opened and he stepped in and turned around to face her. He crossed his arms in a petulant fashion. Nevertheless, she joined him in the elevator car.

As soon as the doors closed, she said, "Our understanding is that you quit the case on account of your health but I have to say you looked pretty spry in the courtroom back there. How are you feeling?"

"I'm making a living," Johnson said softly as if he were concerned about microphones inside. "I do have prostate cancer."

"I'm sorry," she said. "Are you at a critical stage?"

He shrugged. "My urologist says every man either dies with it or dies from it. We're doing what's called 'watchful waiting' or 'active surveillance' to figure out what we're going to do next."

"So, it's really not that bad," Cassie said. "Thank goodness."

"I suppose," Johnson replied. "If there's such a thing as not bad cancer. Is there such a thing as not bad cancer?"

She knew she had a very short time before they reached the ground floor and the doors opened. He'd made it clear in his way that he was much more willing to talk to her when others couldn't overhear their conversation, so she cut to the chase.

"Was there anything about the case that led you to believe that he might not be guilty?" she asked.

"I never allow myself to think that way. My only concern is to provide the best defense possible."

"Well said. But I guess what I'm asking is whether or not you saw flaws in the prosecution's case at that early stage."

"It seemed airtight," Johnson said quickly.

"So is that the reason you stepped away?" she asked.

The car reached ground level. Cassie prepared to lose Johnson and the opportunity to ask any additional questions.

He surprised her by reaching out and pressing the button that prevented the doors from opening.

"Look," he said, again adopting the sotto voce manner. "I already told you. My only concern is to provide the *best defense possible* for my client. In this particular case, given the defendant and the unique situation here in this county, I did the only thing I could do."

Then she got it. "You're saying that he couldn't have received a fair trial in Lochsa County?"

He nodded. His face was animated while he did it.

"Is that because of the Kleinsasser name?"

Another quick nod. He didn't want his words on record.

"So it wasn't about your health?"

"Actually, it was," he said. "I've been married thirty-one years to the long-suffering Kendra Johnson. We have two daughters and five grandchildren. I'm the patriarch of our little clan."

He leaned so close to Cassie she could smell his Axe aftershave. "If I stayed on the case I would have had all kinds of problems in regard to my health and well-being. You have no idea what it's like if you ruffle the wrong feathers around here. Half my cases are as a public defender assigned by the court. That's done arbitrarily, and those cases can vanish if I'm poorly thought of by certain people. As I said earlier, I need to be able to make a living."

"You were threatened?"

"I didn't say that."

"But that's what you're telling me," she said. "If that's the situation it was pretty gutsy to go for a change of venue."

"It was the least I could do," he whispered as he pressed the button to open the doors. "And believe me, it didn't go over well in some quarters."

She wished he wasn't being so vague but he was a lawyer and for lawyers, she knew from experience, words were a kind of currency. And they were of greater value within the profession than outside the legal world.

The doors wheezed open to reveal two uniformed sheriff's deputies waiting to go upstairs to testify.

"That will be enough for today," Johnson said.

"Christ," one of them said to Johnson. "I thought you were going to take all day. I thought I was going to have to take the damned staircase."

"It's all yours," Johnson said, stepping out and ushering them in. Cassie noted that both men's eyes stayed on her a beat longer than necessary, and it wasn't because she was so obviously attractive that they couldn't help it.

"Have a good day, Ms. Dewell," Johnson said as he left her. "I hope you enjoy your stay."

He said it for the benefit of the deputies, she thought.

Then, as the elevator doors began to close, he said, "Those are the last words you and I will have together and if you quote me on anything I'll deny it."

She nodded that she understood.

Cassie stopped by her motel room to grab a jacket and she found that the room had already been cleaned for the day. Glen Steele was on his game.

Rachel answered on the second ring.

Cassie told her about her investigation thus far. She said Franny's phone wasn't among the items of evidence in the county jail, and Rachel replied with a curse. When she mentioned the missing underwear, it was like tossing a handful of white bark pine seeds to a grizzly bear. Rachel pounced, as Cassie feared she would.

"Honestly," Rachel said, "this is literally the first chink in their armor. Good work."

"They could show up anytime," Cassie cautioned. "And there's still the DNA analysis from the lab even if the actual article goes missing."

"Of course," Rachel said. "But if our experts can't analyze that particular item . . ."

"I know," Cassie said woodenly.

"It's not enough to derail the prosecution, but it's something," Rachel said.

Cassie sighed. "I thought my purpose here was to give you ammunition to convince Blake to take a plea deal. Now you're talking like you're preparing for trial."

"I have to prepare for every possibility," Rachel said defensively. "You know that."

Cassie let it go. She told Rachel about her brief conversation with Johnson in the elevator.

Rachel said, "He didn't give you names or specifics. Very cagey. But *really* interesting. I'm amazed that he felt such pressure.

"You're a bulldog, Cassie," she continued. "You can make people tell you things."

Cassie shrugged, but it was true.

She recalled the long looks the deputies had given her and she said, "I've been here less than twenty-four hours and it seems like more and more locals know why I'm here. I think I need to accelerate the pace of the investigation before everyone in Lochsa County knows me by name. I feel like I'm under a microscope and the Kleinsassers are watching me through it."

Rachel told her to be less paranoid, but then said, "There's another reason why that's a good idea," she said. "Blake sent me a message this morning. He's heard some rumblings and he thinks he's going to get jumped by some of the other inmates. He even thinks a couple of the guards are in on it."

"He is a child molester," Cassie said. "They don't do well in jail, you know."

"There's that," Rachel conceded, "but he seems to think the order to go after him comes from where you are. The inmates he suspects have Lochsa County connections."

"The Kleinsassers?"

"That's what he thinks. But who knows," Rachel said, "he might be as paranoid as you and there's nothing to it. Besides, I wouldn't put it past him to try and get transferred to a cushier facility. He's not exactly used to hardship.

"So, what's next?" Rachel asked.

Cassie told her.

"Be careful," Rachel said.

"I thought you just said I was paranoid."

"You can be both."

twelve

On her way north to Lolo, back on U.S. Highway 93, Cassie made several stops along the way. The first was at the Corvallis Tavern, then Hayloft Saloon in Darby, and finally the Corvallis Tavern in Hamilton. Blake had drunk at all three of the bars when he went on his bender.

All were dark and desperate and bleak the way saloons were in the daytime. The only customers had the wan and sallow faces of day drinkers. Although they turned on their stools to check her out when she walked in, they turned back once they saw that she was a stranger and not one of their drinking buddies. She felt like she was crashing exclusive club meetings.

Except for the crazy toothless woman at the Rainbow, who swore Cassie was her long-lost sister from Ekalaka.

"I've been to Ekalaka," Cassie told her firmly. "But I'm not your sister."

"You're *her*," the woman insisted. "I knew Daddy was lying when he said you got kicked in the head by a horse."

Cassie backed away.

None of the bartenders or servers knew who Hawk was or where to find him, but Cassie got the impression the afternoon staff encountered an entirely different breed of customer than the night crew who came in later.

★   ★   ★

The atmosphere on the highway was otherworldly. Rising after-noon temperatures and a stiff northwestern breeze fed the fires in the mountains and filled the valley with heavy smoke. It hung thick in the timber and tendrils of it flowed down the sharp draws like molten lava. Oncoming cars kept their headlights on. The bare summits of several mountains appeared to be snowcapped, but with white ash instead of snow.

To kill time before getting to the Hayloft Saloon in Lolo where Lindy, Blake's lover, allegedly worked, Cassie took Highway 12 west toward the Idaho border and Lolo Hot Springs. It was a thirty-one-mile detour each way, but distances were relative in Montana. She'd driven much farther to simply meet someone for lunch.

The highway wound up through a canyon that was torched by fires from several years before. Bright green grass bristled on the blackened meadows, but there were no flames on the mountainsides. There was nothing left to burn.

Lolo Hot Springs, a kind of resort within shouting distance of the Idaho border, was nearly unrecognizable to her when she arrived. What she remembered about it from a brief high school basketball trip to the area was how old, steamy, and decadent it was at the time.

Cassie drove into the parking lot and backed into a space in the very last row. She was virtually alone.

She recalled that on the school bus some of the girls had smuggled bottles of cheap white Zinfandel they'd been able to steal in Missoula. The team, most of them anyway, had passed the bottles from girl to girl in the back while the coaches huddled and gossiped unaware in the front.

By the time they reached Lolo Hot Springs for dinner and a "swim," Cassie was drunk, as were her friends. What she remembered—through fuzz—was that to her Lolo Hot Springs was a torrid combination of hot sulfur-smelling water, alcohol, and leering old cowboys who seemed to occupy every shadowed corner of the pool. She recalled one of them who reached out under the water and jammed his hand between her legs from behind.

When she wheeled on him to slap his face he'd laughed and ducked. She recalled that he was wearing a sweat-stained cowboy hat with a feather. She'd swung with her left hand and connected. The cigarette he'd been smoking fell from his mouth and hissed dead in the water.

The lewd cowboy had rubbed his jaw and he chuckled at the blow and he'd sidled away, leaving a wake.

"Watch out for that one," he'd laughed to his buddies. "She's a pistol."

At the time, the incident wasn't that unusual—or that shocking. She'd dealt with the unwanted grab by taking a swing at him.

The incident didn't scar her. In fact, she'd never mentioned it to her coaches and hadn't even thought about it until the moment she parked in the lot.

Cassie felt very old. Today, she knew, a high school girl being groped like that would result in arrests, outrage, and recriminations. Goofy old ranch hands would go to prison for what they did.

The place was different now. It had been modernized, revamped, and looked more like a family water park than the seedy place it had once been. She watched as tourist families led children in bathing suits toward the entrance. There were no leering cowboys with roaming hands.

How the world had changed.

It was important, she'd learned from her previous stops, to arrive at the Hayloft in Lolo when the night crew was working. It was the best chance she had of talking to Lindy.

Cassie didn't want to arrive early and stick out like a sore thumb while waiting for Lindy to go on duty. She'd been to enough Montana bars in her life to know that a single woman sitting by herself—unless she was crazy and looking for her long-lost Ekal-aka sister—was considered either desperate or suspicious. She wanted to arrive when the night was in full swing and she could move around and blend in with the crowd.

Which meant she had at least an hour more to kill before driving back to Lolo.

She thought about her conversation with Rachel, how they'd both agreed that speed was important. She checked her cell phone to make sure it had a good signal.

Then she placed a call to the headquarters of the Iron Cross Ranch.

Her call was answered on the second ring.

"This is John Wayne." His voice was gruff with a Southern twang.

"John Wayne Kleinsasser?" she asked, surprised that he'd answered the phone himself.

"Yep."

"My name is Cassie Dewell. I'm in the area verifying evidence in the case against your brother."

"Yeah, I heard something about that," he said but didn't elaborate further. Then added, "He's not my brother. A brother wouldn't do what he did."

"I understand—"

"I've got a real brother and his name is Rand," John Wayne interrupted. "That phony you're talking about is a bad apple that fell a long way from the tree. Landed in New York City, in fact. I don't know him any more than I know any cowardly low-life bum, and he don't know me. Do you get what I'm saying?"

She did. What surprised her was when she realized John Wayne was talking about Blake leaving the ranch and the state. Not about the assault of his niece.

So she brought it back to that.

"I spoke with Sheriff Wagy this morning. He said you and Franny's mother brought her in to the department the night and the day after she was assaulted."

"Yep. She was very upset and distraught by what Blake did to her."

"You were there when Franny gave her statement, correct?"

"Yep."

"It's a terrible thing for an uncle to hear," Cassie said.

"Yep."

"What I was wondering is if I could come out to your ranch tomorrow. I'd like to see the old building where the alleged assault took place. I'm not one to trespass."

"Good thing you aren't," John Wayne said with a harsh laugh. "Trespassers don't get far on our place, and some of 'em wind up injured."

"Will you be around tomorrow? I won't take too much of your time. You can just point the way to the building and I'll not bother you further."

"I'll be around in the morning," he said. "Follow the signs to the Iron Cross HQ."

"Thank you. I'll be there no later than nine."

He paused. He said suspiciously, "Are you trying to prove that Blake didn't do it?"

"Not at all," Cassie said. "I've seen the evidence."

"Then what are you hoping to accomplish on our place?"

"I just want to get it all clear in my mind where it happened."

"You said 'alleged assault,'" John Wayne said. "There was nothing *alleged* about it. He raped his damn niece."

"It was just an expression," she said. "I used to be a cop. That's how we talk."

"What are you now?" he asked.

She didn't like the turn in the conversation. He was getting more and more hostile.

"I'm a private investigator. I've been hired by Blake's attorneys to verify the evidence in the case. I'm not here to try to prove his innocence."

"Have you met the son of a bitch?"

"I have."

"He's an arrogant prick, isn't he? He thinks he's superior to everyone else. Always been that way, too."

"I see." She didn't know what else to say.

"He couldn't wait to get out of here," John Wayne said. "He just couldn't wait to hit the road and pretend he didn't like or know any of us. Then he shows back up and expects us all to say, 'Thank God you're here to solve all of our problems, Blake!' But it ain't like that. He can eat shit as far as I'm concerned. He's no damned brother to me."

Back to that, Cassie thought.

"I'll see you tomorrow then," she said.

"What are you driving so I'll know it's you?"

She described her Jeep.

"Come straight to the house," he said. "Don't take any joyrides. Not everyone on this place is as easygoing as me."

She was glad he couldn't see her roll her eyes at that.

Cassie disconnected the call and dropped the phone on her lap. She was shaken by John Wayne's strident tone and she didn't look forward to meeting him.

After checking the time, she placed a call to her mother. Cassie hoped she could talk things out with Isabel on Ben's behalf. Plus, there could very well be another side of the story.

When Isabel didn't answer, Cassie left a message. Then she started her car and headed for Lolo. Smoke undulated in the headlights.

thirteen

<del>◆━━◎━━◆</del>

The parking lot of the Hayloft Saloon was vast and unpaved, and Cassie pulled into a space between two four-wheel-drive pickups on the south side of the building. She slid her Glock into her handbag and slipped the strap over her shoulder so that it hung against her right hip.

She walked past the entrance door to the restaurant and glanced up at the façade before pushing through the saloon door. Flood-lights lit up the carved figure of a naked cowgirl sitting in a frothy beer mug kicking up her heels.

The lounge was cavernous and the jukebox was playing Hank Williams, Jr., when she stepped inside. It wasn't packed with cus-tomers but the room had the roughed-up and lived-in feel of a place that was often shoulder to shoulder on busy nights. A group of drunk fishermen whooped at one table, and a knot of baseball cap–wearing locals shook their heads at them. Glass-covered panels displayed old and new guns and even a small cannon. Fox News was on one television and bull riding on the other.

Cassie shouldered through a group of young men watching the rodeo toward the long bar that stretched the entire length of the southern wall. An old neon sign for Schlitz beer painted the bat-tered bar top with pink. Several geriatric bikers sat side by side on stools, their gray ponytails hanging down their backs over black leather vests.

An attractive redheaded woman about Cassie's age sat alone at the bar. She was looking at her phone and scrolling through the screen with one hand while holding a smoking cigarette aloft with the other. She wore a blue dress and tooled red cowboy boots. One leg was crossed over the other, revealing her slim calves and white skin.

Cassie was struck by how regal she looked in comparison with the other customers, most of whom were men. She seemed to be living in her own bubble and no one appeared to be bothering her.

"Is this seat taken?" Cassie asked before sitting down.

The woman looked up and noticed Cassie for the first time. "By you," she said. It was a neutral statement—not exactly welcoming but not off-putting, either.

"Thank you."

A platinum-haired server in a sparkly black tank top appeared and raised her eyebrows to Cassie.

"What can I get you?"

Cassie looked around. Most of the males were drinking draft beer and shots, and the attractive woman was sipping on what looked like bourbon on the rocks.

"A glass of wine, please."

"Red or white?"

"Red."

"Red we got," the server said.

Cassie watched as the server filled a wineglass to the top from a cardboard box with a spigot.

"I don't think they serve a lot of wine here," she said to the woman.

"Are you surprised?"

"I guess not."

The woman turned slightly away on her stool as if to signal that she found her phone more interesting than Cassie. Cassie got the message, but she couldn't help not doing a quick visual profile on the woman.

Her big diamond ring glinted in the overhead bar lights, and beneath a gold pendant necklace a dime-size ruby hung at the plunge of her breasts. The ruby matched the color of her lipstick and manicured nails.

Cassie felt dowdy sitting next to her. What didn't add up, though, was why an attractive woman in a place like the Hayloft would be sitting alone.

The question was answered a few seconds later when one of the drunk fishermen approached from behind them and leaned on the bar with both elbows and turned to her. "I was wondering if I could buy you a—"

"Fuck off," the woman said quickly and firmly before he could finish.

"Drink," the man finished.

"Maybe you didn't hear me?" the woman asked.

"I heard you loud and clear," the fisherman said.

"Then fuck off," she repeated.

"Okay, I got the message."

Rather than continue to glare at the exchange and watch the wounded fisherman skulk away, she studied the mirror and the backbar. Above the bar was a long row of ancient beer cans. Cassie recognized some of them from her youth: Great Falls, Schlitz, Hamm's, Grain Belt.

"Would you like to see a menu?" the server asked when she delivered Cassie's wine.

"Sure."

Cassie was careful when she raised the glass to take her first sip. It was so full she didn't want to spill it on her clothes. The wine was better than she would have guessed it would be.

She glanced around the bar. There were three female employees serving drinks and food. One was a severely thin blonde with huge breasts, the other a cowgirl with tight sequined jeans and a massive buckle, and the server who poured Cassie's wine. All wore the tight black tank tops and any of them could be Lindy, she thought.

It was a long menu but several items were highlighted as local favorites, including the patty melt, chicken-fried steak, and fried chicken gizzards. Cassie ordered the patty melt.

"It goes excellent with your wine," the server said unconvincingly.

"Thank you," Cassie said. "Can you tell me—is Lindy working tonight?"

She hoped the server would say, "I'm Lindy." Instead, she frowned at the mention of the name.

"Not tonight, I guess," the girl said.

"When will she be in?"

The server rolled her eyes. "Your guess is as good as mine." Then she left to put in Cassie's order.

An odd thing to say, Cassie thought. Didn't the employees have a schedule posted somewhere of their shifts?

"You're looking for Lindy Glode?" the woman next to Cassie asked.

"Yes."

"Let me guess," the woman said, leaning back to give Cassie the once-over. She did it in a way that was full-on, not in the furtive way Cassie had profiled *her*. "You're either a pissed-off wife out to tell Lindy off for flirting with your husband or you're a cop."

"More the latter," Cassie said. She was impressed but not flattered.

"I know all the cops in this neck of the woods so you're from out of town."

"Bozeman."

"So why is a cop looking for Lindy?"

"I want to ask her some questions. Her name came up in an investigation. She's not in any trouble."

"Ah," the woman said with a sly smile. "You don't want to tell me."

"Do you know her pretty well?" Cassie asked.

The woman continued to smile as if she was in on the conspiracy, whatever it was.

"I'm in here two or three nights a week, honey. I'd say I knew her pretty well."

"Do you know where I can find her?"

The woman turned and sipped the last of her drink. She signaled the server for another, and nodded toward Cassie's wineglass as well.

"Really, I'm okay," Cassie said.

"That's what you think."

Another odd statement, Cassie thought.

"Lindy kind of sets her own hours," the woman said. "I think she's using again. When she jumps back off that wagon her appearances here can be few and far between."

"Do you know where she lives?" Cassie asked.

"Now why do you think I'd know that?"

"Just asking."

The server delivered another full glass of wine to Cassie and a bourbon on the rocks to the woman. She said, "Do you want me to put both of these on your tab, Cheyenne?"

"Yes."

Cheyenne. Cassie tried not to let her mouth drop open in surprise.

"You're Cheyenne Kleinsasser?"

The woman nodded. "I was three husbands ago. Now I go by Cheyenne Kleinsasser Porché, or Cheyenne K. Porché, which I prefer because of the musical sound it makes. I've been told it sounds more like a brand of perfume or brandy."

She laughed huskily at that and it made Cassie smile.

Then it got quiet between them. It was Cassie's move.

"I'm a private investigator," she said. "I talked with your brother John Wayne just an hour ago."

Cheyenne took a long drag on her cigarette and squinted through the smoke at Cassie.

"You're Franny's mother," Cassie said. "I'm sorry for what happened to her."

"We all are," Cheyenne said. "So you're working for my big brother Blake?"

"His defense attorney," Cassie clarified. "As I told John Wayne, I'm simply here to verify all of the evidence in the case."

"And you're looking to talk to Lindy why?"

Cassie had nearly forgotten about Lindy now that she had Franny's mother sitting right beside her. Cheyenne was a much bigger fish in the pond as far as the investigation went.

Cassie said, "In the time line we're checking on Blake's movements before the assault"—she deliberately left out the word "alleged" this time—and Blake said he was with Lindy. He was unclear on the details and he couldn't even remember her last name. I got that from the sheriff's report. Anyway, I wanted to verify that her recollection matched his."

Cheyenne did the laugh again. "Blake couldn't remember the last name of the barmaid he was fucking? That's . . . so *Blake*."

Then she waved her hand as if erasing Cassie's explanation. "You're assuming that Lindy knows what month it is right now, which is quite the stretch. If she can remember details about her and Blake back in July I'd be astounded."

"She gave a statement back then," Cassie said.

"That's before she was using again, I'm sure."

Cassie nodded. She still wanted to talk with Lindy, but she now doubted it would be helpful.

Her patty melt arrived. Cassie was hungry but she didn't want to dive in and lose Cheyenne's attention or company.

"Do you remember when you and John Wayne took Franny to the sheriff's department?"

Cheyenne looked offended. "Of course I remember. She's my daughter."

"Why did John Wayne go with you?"

"He insisted on it," she said. "As soon as he found out Blake was involved, he was all over it. Before that he pretty much ignored Franny. And me, for that matter. See, if Blake is the black sheep in the eyes of the rest of my family, I'm the gray sheep. Or brown sheep. I don't know which. The only reason I'm tolerated is because of my two X chromosomes. Therefore, I'm no threat to them or the ranch. They haven't approved of me for quite some time. Because of my bloodline, they had no choice but to provide me a house to live in when I moved back here from France with Franny, but they weren't enthusiastic about it. They were pleased I left Mr. Porché behind, however."

She stubbed her cigarette out with more force than necessary.

"I was the only one who was kind of happy to see Blake when he came back," she said. "After all, I spent the most time with him growing up. John Wayne was a squirt when Blake left, and Rand didn't hardly know him at all. Rand knows the stories my father and John Wayne told him. They hated Blake and they despised the fact that he left the ranch. They thought he was the devil himself."

Which might have proved to be true, Cassie thought but didn't say.

Cheyenne finished her drink quickly and crooked her finger at the server for another. Since Cassie was still sipping her first glass she didn't order another for her, for which Cassie was grateful.

Let her drink, Cassie thought. Let her drink and keep her talking. The scenario playing out was a private investigator's dream.

Cheyenne slipped her phone into a bejeweled handbag on the bar. Cassie hoped that was an indication that she wanted to continue the conversation.

"Were you surprised when you heard Franny's story?" Cassie asked her.

"Fucking shocked is a better description," Cheyenne said. "I knew Blake was a hound dog, but this . . ." She shook her head in disgust. "And leaving her out there to find her way home. That was so low."

"Prior to the attack," Cassie asked, "what would you say Franny's relationship with Blake was?"

"Cordial," Cheyenne said. "Nothing special, but Blake was nice to her without being over-the-top. I got the impression he was looking for friendlies in hostile territory and he'd be happy with anyone who didn't hate his guts. Why do you ask?"

"I'm just tying up loose ends," Cassie said. "One of the things that kind of puzzles me was the fact that Blake picked her up at the church. That suggests a closer relationship than I would have guessed."

Cheyenne nodded. She said, "What you have to understand is that everything is a long way from everything else here. The ranch is twenty-five minutes from Horston, so nearly an hour round-trip. I was meeting with my lawyer at my house about some changes I wanted to make in my divorce settlement and I knew Blake was somewhere in town. I texted him and asked that he pick her up. Of course, I really regret that now."

Cassie sat back. "That you asked him to pick her up wasn't in any of my documents. Even Blake didn't tell us that."

Cheyenne rolled her eyes. "He probably doesn't remember. From what I understood later, he was in the midst of a blackout drunk at the time. He claims not to remember anything from that night."

"That's true." Cassie glanced at Cheyenne's bag on the bar. "Do you still have that text exchange with Blake on your phone?"

Something passed behind Cheyenne's eyes, and Cassie took it for a second of panic. Then it was gone just as quickly.

"I've replaced my phone since this summer," Cheyenne said. "Not all of the data got moved over to the new one, including my texts. Sorry about that."

"That's okay. Just asking."

"I dropped my old phone in the toilet and it didn't work after that," Cheyenne explained. Cassie wasn't sure why she'd provided the detail.

"Do you mind if I take some notes?" Cassie asked. She wanted to remind herself to do a check on Blake's phone to confirm the text. As far as she knew it hadn't been done.

"Please don't," Cheyenne replied. "If you start to take notes like this is some kind of interrogation I'll leave and you'll never see me again. People in here will notice that you're interviewing me. This is just talk as far as I'm concerned. Woman-to-woman."

"Woman-to-woman," Cassie repeated. She didn't dare reach for her notebook or the digital recorder in her bag.

"Along those same lines," Cassie asked, "did Franny ever get her phone back?"

"Her phone?"

"She said Blake took it and put it in the console of his rental car so she couldn't call for help."

Cheyenne nodded her head. "She's got her phone with her. I guess they gave it back to her. I didn't know it was an issue."

"It isn't. It's just one of the items I had on my list to account for."

Cheyenne looked at her suspiciously, and Cassie knew she needed to soften her line of questioning.

"If you don't mind," Cassie said while taking a sip of wine, "I think I understand the relationship between Blake and the rest of the family to some degree. There's a lot of hate and resentment toward him."

"Envy is a word you might throw in there as well," Cheyenne said. "But don't ever tell my younger brothers or my father I said it."

"They envy Blake?" Cassie asked, surprised.

"They'd never admit to it but they do. At least John Wayne does. He absolutely hates the fact that his brother went out into the world and made something of himself. It's an irrational hatred. John Wayne thinks anyone who leaves the ranch and the family is despicable. Especially if they do well."

She chuckled and said, "Unfortunately, I reinforce his view on that. Every time I leave I end up coming back with my tail between my legs."

"You said Franny and Blake's relationship was cordial," Cassie said. "What about Franny and her other uncles?"

"This is getting very personal," Cheyenne said.

"I'm sorry. I just want to understand the family better."

"You'll *never* understand this family," she said. "*I've* never understood this family. An army of psychologists would never understand this family. Suffice it to say that it's rotten to the core. Lawyers use a term called the fruit of the poisonous tree. Maybe that describes the Kleinsassers."

Blake said a similar thing, she recalled. But she didn't bring that up.

"Franny's relationship with Rand is the same as mine—nonexistent," Cheyenne offered. "I see him strut around town from time to time, but he's usually gone from the ranch. John Wayne uses him to deliver things around the state or pick them up. What Rand actually does is a mystery to me, and I don't ask."

"What about Franny and her grandparents?" Cassie asked.

"She's scared of them, especially my father. He has dementia and he's turning into a nasty, bitter old man. She stays as far away from them as she can get."

Cassie observed that Cheyenne's face tightened and her mouth turned down when she talked about her father.

Cheyenne said, "My parents didn't really raise us like normal parents do. They just sort of threw us out there and observed us for flaws. My father, especially. I think we all spent more time with ranch employees growing up than with our parents.

"We didn't do things together like families do," she said, looking away from Cassie toward something in the middle distance. "We never went on a vacation together, or got together for holidays. We still don't. My mother tried for a while, like insisting that we all go to church together. But that didn't last. My father used my bad behavior or Blake's moodiness as reasons why we couldn't do that anymore.

"I'm close to my mother but I resent that she never stood up to him. I know she saw that as her role. His role was to lecture us about upholding our good name so we wouldn't disappoint him or our legacy in this stupid fucking valley. He instructed us about the Kleinsasser Trust and all of the rules laid down by my creepy grandfather. I've always thought my father disliked Blake because his oldest son had absolutely no interest in the legacy, which is true."

"And John Wayne?" Cassie asked. This was the question she wanted answered most of all, especially since her exchange with him earlier in the evening.

"John Wayne ate that shit up," Cheyenne hissed.

"And you?"

"It doesn't matter," she said. "I'm a girl."

"What about Franny and John Wayne. How do they get on?"

"They're close, I'd say," Cheyenne said with a roll of her eyes. "He loves to school her on the importance of the family name and what goes with it. She eats that stuff up, or at least pretends to. I'm not sure she isn't just kind of shining him on because she's good at that. I've tried to talk to her about it, you know. I tell her not to necessarily treat everything John Wayne tells her as gospel. I think she gets it, but she's her own person. Young people of a certain age are suckers for family lore, I think. Not because they really care about history but because it maybe helps explain who they are, you know? It gives them an anchor as well as an excuse to act badly because they can say it's in their genes. I think she'll eventually figure him out," Cheyenne said. "I certainly hope so."

Me, too, Cassie thought. Little she'd heard about the Kleinsasser legacy thus far seemed like something to aspire to.

"I have to say this about John Wayne, though," Cheyenne said. "When Franny showed up that night saying Blake had attacked her,

John Wayne was right there. I know some of it was his animus toward Blake, maybe most of it. But he was there when both Franny and I were a mess. He took charge and thank God he did.

"Oh, my," Cheyenne said with a laugh. "Did I just say something kind about my brother?"

"You did," Cassie said, smiling.

"I need another drink," Cheyenne said. And she ordered one.

"Are you going to be okay to drive?"

Cheyenne turned on a full-force grin. It was dazzling. It was her way of saying, *I never have trouble getting a ride home.*

"What about Franny?" Cassie asked. "Is there any chance I could talk with her? I promise to be very gentle and you can be in the room—"

"Fuck off," Cheyenne said. It was just as harsh as the tone she'd used with the drunk fisherman. Her entire demeanor had changed.

"Look, I'm sorry if I—"

"I said *fuck off.* Can you even imagine what she's gone through? And you want to bring it all back up to her?"

"Really," Cassie said, "I just thought she might want to tell me her story."

"She's told it enough. What she needs is peace and normalcy. That's why you'll never find her."

What did that mean? Cassie wondered.

Cheyenne leaned into Cassie so closely Cassie could smell the bourbon on her breath.

"We're done here," she said. "Leave Franny and me alone."

fourteen

❖══◉══❖

Disturbed and shaken by how the conversation with Cheyenne had turned, Cassie walked out into the cool and smoke-filled night air. Her hands were trembling and she shook her head as if to confirm what had just happened.

She sat in her Jeep for a moment and replayed the entire exchange over in her head. She'd rarely encountered a woman who could shut down and lash out so suddenly. Maybe it was the cumulative effect of all of those glasses of bourbon, she thought. But Cheyenne's tone and demeanor absolutely changed when Cassie brought up the subject of her daughter.

Cassie would still need to try and find Lindy Glode although it sounded like Lindy's condition and credibility might be dicey. She wondered if Cheyenne would ever talk to her again. And she dismissed the possibility of meeting Franny.

Cassie checked her phone to see that Ben had tried to call her while she was talking with Cheyenne. As usual, he didn't leave a message. Isabel had not returned her call.

Cassie checked her mirrors and eased out of the parking lot onto Highway 93. There was no traffic.

When she reached cruising speed she punched the button on the steering wheel that activated the Bluetooth system.

"Hi, Mom." He sounded jaunty, which pleased her.

"I see that you called. Did you get things worked out with Isabel? I tried to talk with her earlier but she didn't pick up."

"She's still on strike," Ben said. "That's part of her strike, you know. She only takes calls from her weird hippie friends."

"Ben, please don't call your grandmother's friends 'weird hippies.'"

"That's what they are and you know it," he said. He still sounded happy.

"You seem to be in a good mood."

"I am. I can do what I want now. I cooked a cheeseburger for dinner and I liked it so much I cooked another one. I hope she stays on strike forever."

"Ben . . ."

"Oh, and something really wild happened today. It was *crazy.*"

Cassie braced herself for what would come next.

"I was walking to the Kum and Go . . ."

As she crossed the Lochsa County line, red and blue wigwag lights filled her vehicle and a siren whooped from behind.

"What was *that?*" Ben asked. "Was that a cop car? Are the cops after you?"

Cassie squinted into the rearview mirror to see the cruiser just a few feet from her bumper.

She glanced at her dashboard. Her lights were on and she was going four miles under the sixty-five-mile-an-hour speed limit.

"I'm being pulled over," Cassie said.

"By the cops? What did you do?"

"I have no idea but I need to call you back."

"Keep the phone on so I can hear," he said. Ben seemed to be enjoying the situation a bit too much, she thought.

"Ben, I said I'd call you back," she repeated.

"Don't get thrown in the slammer, Mom! But if you do I'll bring you a file in a cake so you can break out."

She disconnected the call.

★ ★ ★

Cassie eased over to the shoulder of the highway until her passenger-side tires sunk into the loam. The cruiser stayed just a few feet from her Jeep, which went against her training as a young deputy sheriff. She'd been taught that when pulling over a driver she should maintain at least a car length distance away from the citizen. That way, the officer could clearly see the plates and call them in to find out if the vehicle was stolen or if she had any outstanding warrants. Also, if the offender decided to reverse his vehicle and ram her unit she'd have enough warning to take evasive action.

This cop, however, had apparently not received the same training. Or he'd chosen to disregard it.

She'd never been on the wrong side of a roadside situation before. It was embarrassing and intimidating. She also hoped that the reason she'd been pulled over was innocuous, that the officer had noted that her taillight was out or he was simply warning her that the fire had jumped the road ahead on the highway.

Cassie placed both of her hands on top of the steering wheel so they'd be in plain view. She didn't want to give the cop any reason whatsoever to suspect her of anything.

So many things could go wrong, she knew. But she'd always experienced a situation like this from the viewpoint of the cop pulling someone over, not the other way around. Would the driver be belligerent? Would the subject pull a weapon or try to drive away? Was there a body in the trunk?

She could see the officer clearly in her rearview mirror. He was angular and young with a shaved head and eyes that were close together, which gave her the impression—likely undeserved—that he was petty and mean.

He was a sheriff's deputy, she could tell by the uniform. Not a state trooper, not a Lolo city cop. He raised a microphone to his mouth, spoke briefly to someone, and reached onto the passenger seat for his jacket and hat.

Then he walked out of the angle of her rearview mirror as he got out.

She shifted her eyes to her side mirror as he closed his car door and approached. When his belt buckle filled the glass, she turned her head toward him and slowly reached down for the button to lower her window.

Cassie was blinded by his Maglite beam aimed squarely into her face.

"That flashlight wasn't necessary, Officer," she said as she looked away.

"It was if I wanted to see your eyes," he said. "They look kind of glassy and unfocused to me."

"They aren't."

"Here's what you need to do for me," he said. "You need to keep your hands on the wheel where I can see them. Do not make any sudden moves unless I ask you to do so." She thought, *Uh-oh, one of those.* But she complied with his order. All she could see were two bright orange orbs from the beam. She tried to keep her anger in check.

"I saw you drift across the center line back there," he said. "Have you been drinking?"

"I think you might be mistaken, Officer. I've been driving very carefully." She kept her voice neutral and measured. "I had one glass of wine at the Hayloft. One."

"It's usually two," he said. "Most folks say they only had two. Two can equal two or it can equal ten."

"Well, I had one."

"Are you under the influence of any other substances?" the cop asked. "Maybe prescription meds?"

"No."

"Then why were you weaving all over the road, ma'am?"

"I don't believe I was, Officer."

"Then I'm sure you wouldn't object to a Breathalyzer test."

"Correct," she said. "I wouldn't object at all."

Cassie knew she had the right to refuse to take the test because taking it was implied consent. But she also knew that refusal could result in additional charges and consequences such as suspension of her driver's license or possible arrest. Plus, she *knew* she wasn't inebriated or driving recklessly.

Her vision had finally been restored and she took him in. He was from Lochsa County, all right. His name badge said BRYAN "ALF" GRZEGORCZYK.

She asked, "How do I pronounce your name, Officer?"

"Why is that important?" he asked. "Do you plan to contest this?"

"No, sir. It's just an unusual name."

He said, "*Greg-or-check*. My buddies in the service couldn't pronounce my name so they called me 'Alf' like in 'alphabet.' It's Czech."

"So I gathered."

"Now that we've cleared that up," he said, "I need you to stay there and don't move. Keep your hands on the wheel at all times where I can see them."

"Yes, *sir*." She knew that some of the sarcasm she'd tried to hold in check had leaked out.

He paused on his way to his car. "What was that?"

"I said, 'Yes, sir.' I don't object to a Breathalyzer test."

"In the meantime, I need you to get out of your car. Let's see you walk a straight line."

"Really?"

"Do I need to repeat myself? Are you having trouble responding to my requests?"

She knew the tactic. Claim the citizen pulled over didn't comply with official police instructions. Then build from there.

"I'm getting out," she said as she opened her door.

Deputy Grzegorczyk stood near his driver's-side door with his hands on his hips.

"Walk toward me."

She did. She placed one foot in front of the other and she fought the urge to look down at her shoes. A pickup coming from Lolo slowed on the highway as it passed and she saw the driver and his elderly wife looking at her with big eyes. It was humiliating.

As she neared him the officer suddenly shot out his hand. "*Stop.*"

She instinctively stepped back.

"Little wobbly there," he said.

"I didn't want your hand in my face."

"Right," he said with a mocking tone.

"Look, Deputy Grzegorczyk," Cassie said, "I used to be a cop myself. I know how these things work. You can claim I was weaving down the road and you can claim I couldn't walk a straight line, but neither is true. I can dispute it, but it's your word against mine. I'm trying to cooperate in every way. So, let's cut the crap and give me the test so I can be on my way."

"You used to be a cop, huh?"

"Yes."

"Then you should know you shouldn't drink and drive," he said with a smirk. "And you know you shouldn't mouth off to a peace officer."

She bit her tongue. As much as she had always despised fellow cops who used their badges to intimidate and harass citizens, she didn't need to tell him that. She'd wait until the morning and file a complaint with Sheriff Wagy.

He opened his door and leaned inside. She waited and seethed.

After less than a minute, he stepped back onto the asphalt. "Looks like I left my Breathalyzer tester back at the department."

She waited for more. Then asked, "What's that mean?"

"I thought you said you used to be a cop. You know exactly what that means. It means I need to take you in so we can do it there."

"Take me in?"

"Yes, ma'am. To that place with lots of desks and cells and prisoners and jail bars and stuff."

He was being clearly provocative and sarcastic. He was, she concluded, trying very hard to bait her into a reaction.

She didn't bite.

"Can I please follow you?" she asked. "I don't want to leave my Jeep out here on the highway."

"In your condition?" he said with a grin. "That's fucking nuts. No wonder the cop shop you worked for let you go."

"My name is Cassie Dewell," she said. "I'm a licensed private investigator with the State of Montana."

"Let's hope you can keep that license after this," he said.

"Believe me, I will. Look, I know Sheriff Wagy. I met with him just this morning. He knows I'm here on legitimate business."

Grzegorczyk rolled his eyes. "You're going to try and play that card on me? Act like you and my boss are best buds? Even if he knows you I doubt he'd approve of you driving drunk in Lochsa County, lady."

Then he opened his back door and signaled for her to get in.

"Now I need you to take a seat in the cruiser. Try not to bump your head getting in."

"Can I at least get my purse and lock up my car?" she asked.

"I'll get it," he said. The deputy placed his left hand on the Taser on his belt and his right hand on the grip of his service weapon.

His voice was chilling. "I need you to get into this car right now, ma'am.

"You'll love our jail," he said, stepping aside so she could crawl into his cruiser. "It's really historic."

Deputy Grzegorczyk turned back onto the highway and Cassie watched her Jeep slide by with its driver's-side window and door closed but unlocked.

"So you're a PI, huh?" he asked, eying her in the rearview mirror.

"Yes. License number seven, seven, seven, five."

"Do you make a good living at it? It's something I might be interested in doing some day is the reason I asked."

"I do okay." She sighed. His change in tone was curious to her.

"Good to know."

As they drove toward Horston, she recalled something John Wayne Kleinsasser had asked her.

What are you driving so I'll know it's you?

Or had Cheyenne called a friend in the sheriff's department known as Deputy Grzegorczyk?

fifteen

The truck driver chose a different place to park the second time he came to the high school building. There was no need to arouse suspicion, no need to create a situation where a resident could later recall that he or she saw the same vehicle idling in the middle of the night at the same location.

So instead of a side street, he chose a gravel two-track on the far east end of the campus near the football stadium. The driver would have preferred to get closer because of what he was about to do, but he was convinced his logic was solid in choosing another spot. Plus, with the exception of a single pole light on the west end of the stadium that illuminated a closed-up concession stand, he couldn't be seen from the side streets.

He powered down the driver's-side window, killed the engine, and pocketed the keys. He sat silently for ten minutes letting the cold night air envelop him. As he did so he waited and watched. The engine ticked as it cooled.

The stadium itself was no different than it used to be although there were some new guest boxes on the top level and artificial turf had been laid down to replace the old grass field. Unlike the landscape around him of brittle tufts of dried grass and cover, the new plastic field with its perfect white stripes looked phony and cheap to him. Just like the coaches and physical education teachers who used to give him such a hard time.

Being so close to the stadium dredged up uncomfortable

recollections of doing laps around the track or running up and down the stairs as punishment. He could recall how his leg muscles burned, and how his lungs ached.

Those sadists.

He slipped out of the cab and slung a heavy duffel bag over his right shoulder by the strap and walked toward the high school building. The chain-link fence gate wasn't locked—it never was during football season because players couldn't be expected to wait for someone to unlock it before running through.

He chose a route between the fence and the cavernous back of the stadium itself. He kept in the shadows and moved from pillar to pillar. As his eyes adjusted to the gloom he could read the crude hand-lettered posters that were hung on the interior walls:

Hawk Power!

Bag the Bengals!

Red and Black—On the Attack!

He snorted and rolled his eyes. The cheerleaders who made the signs hadn't come up with an original thought or slogan in the years since he'd been there. Obviously, they'd be hosting the Helena Bengals on Friday.

The smells from the stadium were still the same as well: stale popcorn, spilled soft drinks, sweat, athletic tape. It jerked him back to a place he didn't want to go.

He remembered being told once that the sense of a familiar smell—called olfaction—could trigger intense recollections. It was true. He felt as if he was being jerked back in time.

He cursed and picked up his pace. As far as he was concerned, he couldn't get away from the stadium fast enough.

There were two vehicles in the teacher's parking lot, but no lights on from inside the building. He puzzled over that for a moment, then thought: *Of course. The cars belonged to coaches or advisors who had accompanied a team or group out of town. They'd left their cars for when they got back.*

The truck driver paused behind a spruce and surveyed the exterior brick wall of the auto shop. The broken camera still hung by its wires above the closed garage door. They hadn't even removed it yet. Typical.

He lowered the bag to the ground and grasped the door handle and tugged hard to the side. He heard the *click* and the door released.

After raising it two feet, he got on his hands and knees and crawled under it, then pulled the duffel bag inside behind him. He stepped on a steel rail and pushed the bottom of the door down within an inch of the concrete floor.

He turned and took in the room. Again, he was assaulted with familiar odors. Oil, gasoline, diesel fuel. There was a masking antiseptic sheen of floor-cleaning agent over the top of it, but the basic gearhead smells were still there.

That, he liked. At least some of the students were still learning *something* practical. It would only be a matter of time before the auto shop was replaced with a meditation room or multicultural studies area or overall safe space, he reckoned.

The shop was dimly lit by a row of amber emergency lights just below the high ceiling. It wasn't enough light to throw shadows but it was enough to see where he was going. He had no need for the headlamp he'd brought along.

A half-ton Toyota pickup with its hood up was in one of the bays, and a tricked-out Dodge Challenger was in another. He walked between them toward the heavy metal door that led to the main building.

★ ★ ★

It wasn't like he even needed the emergency lights or his head-lamp. He could have found his way down the hallways and wings with his eyes closed. He impressed himself with his perfect recall of the layout of the building with its banks of lockers and closed classroom doors.

And it was all the same. These people never changed. The teachers who thought they were cool and edgy taped slogans and cartoons on the outside of their doors. The display cases were filled with forgotten trophies and team photos. On the brick walls were posters boasting of "Hawk Pride" and bulletin boards covered with politically correct bullshit about suicide prevention and how to prevent sexually transmitted diseases.

The central hub of the building was the library, and he could see it in the distance long before he got there. The windows glowed light blue from the monitors of a bank of computers within. There had been a few of them before, mostly clunky beige PCs, but now the interior looked like Mission Control at NASA.

Those students could really update their Facebook profiles now, he thought.

But it wasn't the new computers he was interested in. What he wondered was if the maintenance crew had ever fixed the loose ceiling panel above the entry door to the library. That's where he and his buddies used to stash their weed and alcohol so it wouldn't be found in their lockers.

The sound of a human grunt stopped him cold. He froze in place and reached back for the grip of his .22 pistol that he'd tucked into his belt.

Then he heard it again, along with rhythmic flesh-on-flesh slapping.

He turned his head toward the sound and realized he was standing outside the open door of the teacher's lounge. In the ambient glow of the emergency lights inside he saw a purse on a table and a pile of clothing on the floor. And two teachers, a man and a woman, going at it on a couch. They were naked and white and she was on top. Her long dark hair obscured her face.

He assumed they were both doughy and unattractive people. But if he could see them they could see *him*.

He took a breath and stepped back. She didn't look up.

He took another step back, then another until he could no longer see them.

The man groaned again, this time with relief, and he recognized its meaning. Then they were done and both breathing hard, probably clinging to each other.

The driver was grateful that his trucker's boots had soft, quiet soles. He turned and found a girl's bathroom door that was propped open with a wooden wedge on the floor and he stepped inside. The room was completely dark.

He found a stall and backed into it and closed the door.

Less than ten minutes later, he heard the two teachers talking softly and he could discern from the sounds of zippers that they were getting dressed. The woman came out of the lounge first, her heels clicking on the linoleum tiles like castanets. The man followed. He said something that made her laugh.

Then there was the wheezing sound of a heavy door being opened and shut.

They were gone.

He closed his eyes and waited long enough to make sure one of them hadn't forgotten something and decided to come back.

There was a brief sweep of headlights across the frosted outside window of the restroom as one of the two cars pulled away. Then another.

They weren't coaches or advisors after all. They were just common fornicaters.

He thought, *What sick fucks. Using the teacher's lounge! They were probably both married and they were the type who wouldn't hesitate to judge him or lecture him about his behavior.*

Fucking hypocrites is what they were.

Literally.

The ceiling tile gave way just as he'd anticipated it would. He slid it to the side.

The driver stood on an upturned metal trash can and felt around at the opening to make sure the space wasn't still being used to hide drugs and contraband. It wasn't. He wouldn't have been surprised to find a baggie of old dried-up weed that he'd left up there.

But there were only dust bunnies.

He climbed down and unzipped the duffel bag. Into the space went a 12-gauge combat shotgun with a pistol grip, a .40 Charter Arms Pitbull revolver, three boxes of shotgun shells filled with buckshot, a heavy mesh bag of smoke and tear gas grenades, and a military-grade tactical gas mask.

When the tile was seated back into place, he briefly turned his headlamp on and choked the beam down.

Satisfied that he'd left no fingerprints or telltale dust smudges on the edges of the tile, he killed the light and waited for his eyes to readjust to the darkness of the hallway.

Then he retraced his steps through the halls and back into the auto shop. The empty duffel bag was now no heavier than an afterthought.

The driver raised the door again and crawled under it, then rolled it back down until it was secure. He walked toward the stadium and his truck in the cold night air.

Red and Black—On the Attack!

It was set.

Part III

There are inevitably two kinds of slaves: the prisoners of addiction and the prisoners of envy.

—Ivan Illich, *Tools for Conviviality*

The Family! Home of all social evils, a charitable institution for Indolent women, a prison workhouse for family breadwinners, and a hell for children!

—August Strindberg, *The Son of a Servant*

sixteen

—→══◉═══←—

Rachel Mitchell didn't arrive at the Lochsa County Jail the
next morning until 11:30 A.M. Cassie could hear her voice—it was
loud and angry and it bounced off the walls—in the reception area
down the hallway from her cell.

"Is that your girl?" Cassie's cellmate Delores Attao asked.

"Sounds like her," Cassie replied.

"She sounds pissed off. I wish I had a lawyer like that. I've got
a public defender named Kendrick who can't pronounce my name.
Do you think she'd represent me?"

"You should ask her," Cassie said.

It had been a long night, and Cassie felt dirty, disheveled, and
oddly ashamed of herself. She'd never spent a night in jail before.
It was more dehumanizing than what she'd imagined it to be, and
she felt a pang of guilt for placing so many violators behind bars
and not considering how awful it must have been for some of them.

Although she wanted out as quickly as it could happen, she
didn't want anyone she knew to see her in there. And she didn't
want Ben to know.

Throughout the night, there had been crazed shouts from other
cells in a different wing where males were kept. Putrid odors wafted
through the vents and nearly made her retch. They'd barely dimmed
the cold fluorescent overhead lights and everything took on a dull
blue-gray hue. She'd had nothing to do and no way to communicate with anyone outside. They'd taken her phone, keys, purse, and
shoes.

The cell for females was the closest to the door that led to the lobby. Three or four other cells reserved for men were farther away down the hallway. Therefore, as drunks and other miscreants were brought in during the night they were led past Cassie. One of them looked in at her, smirked, and did a lizardlike sexual maneuver with his tongue. Another grabbed his crotch and crab-walked out of view while laughing to himself even though the cop that brought him in told him to "move it along."

It was humiliating. And the worst thing about being behind bars was exposure. There were no doors to close or curtains to pull. Even the stainless-steel toilet was in plain and open view from anyone passing down the hall.

The old stone cell was twelve feet by twelve feet and the walls were cold and damp. She'd taken the top bunk because Delores was already camped out in the bottom.

When Deputy Grzegorczyk had led her inside, Cassie had assumed it would be temporary—that she'd be held until he returned with the Breathalyzer. She hadn't seen a holding cell in the ancient frontier jail, after all. An hour passed, then another. It wasn't until then that she realized he wasn't coming back.

Delores Attao was a Nez Perce who'd been arrested for public intoxication and resisting arrest hours before Cassie showed up. Attao was short and round with close-cropped black hair and she wore a billowy tunic and yoga pants that looked spray-painted on. She didn't have the figure for yoga pants but that didn't seem to bother her.

What set off Delores was finding her husband, Arthur, with another woman at the Corvallis Tavern. Delores freely admitted she'd caused a scene and that she'd thrown a glass of beer in Arthur's face. When the bartender called the sheriff's department and they quickly arrested her she surrendered willingly, she claimed.

There was no resistance. But the bastards, she said, had charged her for resisting arrest anyway.

Despite her own situation, Cassie had enjoyed listening to Delores talk most of the night. She could focus on Delores instead of the chaos down the hall or her own dilemma. The county had recently slathered the interior of the cell with pale blue paint so thick Cassie couldn't even make out the scratchings or drawings from previous inmates.

Delores had a musical cadence to her speech that was familiar to Cassie from listening to other Native Americans. That was in addition to being precise with her words and nonchalant when it came to spending a night in jail. Delores didn't seem to care if Cassie was listening closely to her or not. Cassie's only responses were variations of "Hmmmm."

Cassie guessed Delores had been there before because she seemed to know her way around and she gave Cassie good bits of advice like not to eat the meat loaf under any circumstances and to insist on Crocs that fit because the cops enjoyed giving shoes that were either too small or large to their "overnight guests."

Sheriff Wagy had not been in even though Cassie had asked for him. Deputy Grzegorczyk had apparently gone off shift.

The only person Cassie had recognized was Linda Murdock from the front office. Murdock had stuck her head through the outside door and stared dumbstruck at Cassie in the cell. Then she shook her head sadly and vanished without saying a word. Cassie couldn't tell if Murdock was disappointed in her or ashamed of the department.

That same door blew open moments later and Rachel Mitchell appeared like a force of nature. She was red-faced and furious, and her heels clicked on the cold stone floor like muffled gunshots. The undersheriff, whom Cassie had not seen or met, trailed behind Rachel.

"There she is," Rachel said, pointing at Cassie. "Let her out. *Now.*"

"You are a sight for sore eyes," Cassie said to Rachel.

"And if she spends one more minute in there," Rachel said to the undersheriff, "I'll not only sue your department like I'm planning to do but I'll contact the FBI to charge you with kidnapping."

The undersheriff, who was portly, bald, and shorter than Rachel, mumbled something about the whole thing being a mix-up of some kind as he approached the cell door with his keycard.

"I didn't even get to make a call," Cassie said. "I was starting to think I'd be stuck in here."

Delores responded as if slapped and Cassie felt guilty.

"Sorry, I don't mean you," Cassie said to her. "You got me through the night."

"Tell Arthur," Delores said. "Tell him I'm good company."

Before her cellmate could make her case to Rachel that she should represent her as well, Rachel grasped Cassie's arm and ushered her through the door. The undersheriff had to step back so Rachel wouldn't run him over.

Rachel wheeled on him and waved a painted finger in his face.

"Am I correct that my investigator was held overnight without any charges being filed?"

The undersheriff stammered and looked away. He said, "I just started my shift. I don't know what happened last night, but obviously there was some kind of screwup in booking."

Rachel bent down until her face was inches from his. "You seem to have a lot of screwups in this department. What about the fact that my investigator wasn't given her constitutional right to a phone call?"

The man shrugged as if to say, *same answer.*

"What's your name, Officer?" Rachel asked him.

"I'm undersheriff Richard Hewes."

"Thank you. I'll add your name to the lawsuit I'm going to file against Sheriff Wagy, the arresting officer, and Lochsa County for violating my investigator's civil rights. Not to mention false imprisonment. I'm going to hit you like a hurricane," she said.

Hewes grimaced. "But we're a poor county. We're not like Missoula or someplace like that."

Rachel said, "You should have thought of that before you locked up my investigator for no reason. When will the sheriff be here?"

"I don't know," Hewes stammered. "I called his cell when you got here but he didn't pick up."

"He 'didn't pick up'?" Rachel mocked. "The sheriff didn't pick up?"

Hewes shrugged and looked away.

"Let's get the hell out of here, Cassie," Rachel said.

"Gladly."

Cassie was happy to let Rachel take charge. She was too numb and exhausted to do otherwise. Plus, there was no doubt Rachel thrived in these kinds of situations.

"Return her possessions," Rachel ordered the undersheriff.

"Linda has them," he said.

"Then tell Linda to get her ass in gear," Rachel said while pushing through the metal doors to the lobby.

An unmarked plastic grocery bag with Cassie's phone and other items was on Linda Murdock's desktop. Linda had already gathered them and she instinctively stepped back as Rachel strode toward her and snatched up the bag and handed it back to Cassie.

"Check and make sure everything is there," she said. "Sometimes these people have sticky fingers."

Cassie did a quick inventory. All of her stuff was inside the sack. The gear bag was nowhere to be seen and Cassie assumed it was still in her car.

When she looked up, Murdock mouthed the words, "I'm so sorry."

Cassie nodded. Murdock did indeed act like she was slightly horrified about the incident.

In Rachel's car on the way to retrieve Cassie's Jeep, Rachel said, "What a pathetic shitshow back there. Do you think that for one minute it wasn't all orchestrated? Or are they really that fucking incompetent?"

"I was set up," Cassie said. "My only question is who was responsible."

"What if they stuck you in there with some kind of psycho meth head instead of what's-her-name? What if your throat got cut during the night?"

"Delores," Cassie said. "Her name is Delores. She was a sweetheart, actually. And I'd appreciate it if you'd consider taking her on as a client. From what she told me, the department overcharged her as well."

"I'll talk with her," Rachel said.

"You were magnificent back there," Cassie said. "Thank you."

"*This* is why I do what I do," Rachel shouted. She smacked the top of the dashboard three times for emphasis while she said, "*This, this, this!* Picking up an innocent person and throwing them in that shithole for the night without filing charges or allowing a phone call to me. It's pure intimidation. Everybody despises defense lawyers," Rachel continued. "Especially you cops. But when something like this happens aren't you glad we exist?"

"Yes."

"Did you ever think you'd say that?"

"No."

"Keep it in mind when you hear your brothers in law enforcement bitch about us. That's all I ask."

"How did you know where to find me?" Cassie asked.

Rachel took a deep breath but she was still clearly angry. "I called your cell five times and left messages," she said. "You *always* call me back within a few minutes. When you didn't call I tracked down Ben."

"My son?"

"Of course your son. He said that you were on the phone with him last night when a cop pulled you over. Otherwise, I wouldn't have had a clue what happened to you. I left first thing this morning and sped all the way. They could have held you there for days or worse."

Cassie recalled that Ben had something he wanted to tell her about the previous day, but they hadn't gotten that far before she had to terminate the call.

"How much farther is it?" Rachel asked. Cassie noted that she was going eighty—fifteen miles an hour over the speed limit.

"A couple of miles. And you might want to slow down."

"Fuck it," Rachel said. "Let them try to arrest me now. Let them try."

Cassie smiled. It felt like her face was cracking because it had been so long since she'd done it.

"Why were you trying to reach me?" she asked.

Rachel's face got grim. "Blake Kleinsasser was attacked by at least four inmates in jail. They stove his head in and they pounded a footlong length of steel rebar into his ear. He's in intensive care in the Bozeman hospital. Even if he makes it he might have permanent brain damage."

Cassie sat back, stunned. "My God."

"I should have believed him about the threats," Rachel said. "But he's such an asshole."

"Do they know who did it?"

"Not yet. I'm waiting to hear. But I'd bet you five dollars the bad guys have connections to Lochsa County."

"No bet," Cassie said.

★ ★ ★

When Rachel shot around a shadowed corner in the wall of trees, Cassie gasped for the second time in five minutes.

Her Jeep was a smoldering black box of steel and melted tires. The windows had all been smashed in or blown out by the heat and force of the internal fire. A yellow tag was affixed to the front door handle by state troopers who had found the vehicle and marked it to be towed away.

"Oh, no," Rachel said. "Oh, *no*."

"The files and my notes on the case were on the front seat," Cassie said, closing her eyes tightly.

They circled the blackened Jeep. It was a cool morning and Cassie could feel the heat emanate from the still-hot metal. The seat cushions were burned through to the spring coils. She couldn't discern if the ash in the passenger seat was from her burned-up files or from the fabric itself. Her gear bag had either been taken by passersby or had burned so completely it no longer existed.

Cassie studied the pine trees on both sides of the highway. The tops of many of them had been recently blackened and several were still smoldering. She knew enough about unchecked forest fires (everybody in Montana did these days) to know what had happened was called a "crown fire"—when flames leaped from treetop to treetop in a strong wind. Often, the fire didn't drop down to lower branches.

Was it possible that a crown fire had passed through during the night and sparks or burning embers had somehow dropped through the air via the open windows of her Jeep and ignited the contents? It was possible if highly unlikely, she concluded. Yet a potential case could be made . . .

She fought a surge of emotion that brought tears to her eyes that she quickly turned and wiped away. Although Rachel would likely understand and empathize, Cassie didn't want to give her the opening.

It wasn't the loss of the Jeep or her possessions—both could eventually be replaced. There were hours and days ahead of filling out insurance forms and making phone calls to banks and other entities to replace her credit cards and other lost items.

What overwhelmed Cassie was her sense of sudden helplessness fueled by exhaustion from the lack of sleep the night before. If someone were to design a scenario to make her simply want to go home and forget she'd ever come—they'd succeeded.

While Rachel pulled out her cell phone to call the highway patrol, Cassie shed her jacket and wrapped her right hand in it and reached down through the passenger window. She fished around in what was left of the car seat until she grasped something solid. It was her Glock .40. The plastic grip had melted onto the frame itself.

"They're coming," Rachel said of the highway patrol. "I don't know what they can do except tow it away, but I don't want the filthy paws of the sheriff's department anywhere near it."

"My PI identification is in my purse," Cassie said. "But my notes and my credit cards . . . everything was in the car."

"Do you think it was the same cops?" Rachel asked. "Do you think they threw you in jail and drove back here to torch your Jeep?"

"I don't know," Cassie said. "This is unbelievable. I do know that the guy who arrested me named Grzegorczyk never came back last night after putting me in the cell. I can't swear he left the building but I never saw him again."

"I think we know where he went," Rachel said. "I doubt he did this on his own, though. They're sending you a message, Cassie."

Cassie agreed.

"This will all be part of the lawsuit," Rachel said. "I'll depose Sheriff Wagy, this deputy who followed you and pulled you

over—anyone who was involved. I'll make their lives a living hell
for what they did to you."

"That will take time we don't have," Cassie said.

"Everything takes time," Rachel replied. "Sometimes the time
it takes them to fight a lawsuit like this is almost winning in itself.
This is the kind of corrupt crap that makes sheriffs lose elections
and makes county commissioners question who actually runs this
place."

It took Cassie a moment to figure out where Rachel was going.
"The Kleinsassers?" she said.

"At least the ones who were aware of this," Rachel said. "Starting with good ole John Wayne."

Or maybe Cheyenne, Cassie thought but didn't say.

Rachel said, "After the troopers get here for your car, you and
I are driving back to Bozeman together. You need to be gone from
this county for your own safety, especially when they find out I'm
going to hit them with a ton of bricks. Besides, we've probably got
as much as we're going to get from this wretched hellhole."

Cassie dropped her chin to her chest and placed her hands on
her hips. She didn't like feeling so defeated.

Rachel continued, "Who even knows if there will be a trial
for Blake now? I wouldn't put odds on it. If my client is deceased
or mentally incapacitated, this will all be over.

"What these idiots don't realize," Rachel said, "is even if there's
no rape trial it doesn't end things for them. Nothing is tied up in
a neat little bow. Not when they find out I'm coming after them
for kidnapping, false imprisonment, civil rights violations, and the
destruction of your car."

Her eyes gleamed for a moment. Cassie realized Rachel was
not only outraged by what had happened, but almost thrilled at
the prospect of suing Lochsa County for a large settlement. Blake
Kleinsasser was almost an afterthought.

Rachel said, "Come on. Let's get the hell out of here while *we're*
still among the living."

Cassie looked up at Rachel. "No."

"What do you mean, no?"

"You gave me a job and I'm going to finish it. I won't let them chase me out of here before I complete the investigation."

Rachel shook her head, puzzled. "But I'm the one who gave you the assignment. I can take it away just as easily. They threw you in jail and burned up your car and all your property. You don't owe me a thing."

Cassie set her jaw. "I've never achieved a thing by giving up. I'm not going to start now."

"Don't be ridiculous," Rachel said. "Even if Blake somehow recovers, we're still working for a guilty, rich asshole. Why risk your life for him?"

"He's an asshole, all right," Cassie said, "But until all of this happened I was convinced he was guilty. Now I'm not so sure. Why would they go to the lengths they've gone if they thought the conviction was a slam dunk? Wouldn't they do everything they could to help me confirm the case against Blake instead of stone-walling me at every opportunity?"

She pointed at her ruined Jeep. "Why would they do *this* if they didn't think I was getting too close to something?"

"Too close to what?" Rachel asked.

"I don't know."

"And I don't, either. But whatever it is it isn't worth Blake Kleinsasser. It isn't worth your life. Think of Ben."

Cassie nodded. She said, "I always think of Ben. What's important here is what he thinks about me."

Rachel didn't have a quick response although she was still flustered.

Cassie said, "We had a discussion about responsibility just a couple of nights ago. His father was a soldier and even though Ben never even knew him he thinks of his dad as strong and brave. Ben thinks of Jim as someone who would never retreat from a fight, because that's what I've always told him. Ben *needs* to feel that way about his dad, even though his dad was flawed in ways Ben will never know. Ben looks up to a man who never was, but that doesn't matter. I need to fill that role instead. I need to be that person.

"Let's go back into Horston," Cassie said. "We'll rent a car with your credit card and I'll stroll through the hardware store and re-stock. Then I'll continue working."

Rachel said, "As your lawyer I strongly advise you to come back home with me."

"You're not my lawyer," Cassie said. "You're my client."

seventeen

✦━◉━✦

The afternoon was dark and overcast when Cassie drove her rented Ford Explorer out of town north on Highway 93. She, like every other local in the area and throughout the state, watched her windshield glass with anticipatory glances hoping to see droplets of moisture.

Although hundreds of firefighters and dozens of aircraft did their best, nothing stanched mountain fires like a long, soaking rain—a phenomenon that hadn't occurred in western Montana in thirty-one days.

Lower temperatures and the heavy clouds had pressed a godly open hand over the whole valley, tamping down the rage of the many fires as well as the rising smoke. It was as if the western wall of the Bitterroot Mountains didn't exist.

After she'd left the rental car company in Horston she saw a sign on the marquee of an ancient movie theater that read:

EVEN IF YOU'RE AN ATHEIST—PRAY FOR RAIN.

For eight miles she'd noted the stout buck-and-rail fence that ran parallel to the highway. It looked serious and impregnable, as if built not only to dissuade casual visitors but to retard the advance of an army column. She'd passed by the barrier the previous day but not given it much thought other than *Whoever owns this place isn't friendly.*

The fence eventually led to a high archway constructed of massive ponderosa pine poles and a sign that hung from black iron chains that indicated it was the entrance to the Iron Cross Ranch.

Although the Explorer was a full-sized SUV, it seemed tiny beneath the height and width of the entrance arch, which seemed to have been built for a caravan to pass through. As she did, she glimpsed a small closed-circuit camera mounted on the right-hand pole and a wire leading to a boxy solar panel.

The heavy steel gates had been swung inward. She was grateful that she could drive right through without seeking permission via a microphone and speaker attached to a vertical post.

This was the Kleinsassers' ranch, and they obviously cared about who went in and who drove out.

She'd been able to assemble a makeshift PI kit in Horston. With Rachel trailing her with a credit card and a worried expression, Cassie had purchased a secondhand .40 Glock 27 and a Smith & Wesson Ladysmith chambered in .22 long at a pawn shop. She didn't like or appreciate the pink rubber grip on the Ladysmith, but the five-shot revolver was slim and hammerless and it fit into the shaft of her cowboy boot.

At a sporting goods store she'd purchased two boxes of .40 cartridges and a plastic container of a hundred hollow-point .22 rounds. A large can of bear spray replaced the pepper spray that had burned up.

She'd found commercial wire cable ties at a hardware store that would serve as zip ties if she needed them. She also bought a heavy Maglite flashlight and a good pair of binoculars.

To replicate her lost Taser, Cassie bought a 10,000-volt hot shot at the feed store that was designed for cattle. It would do in a pinch, so to speak.

She doubted she would need any of the equipment. She never

had. But replacing her lost gear with serviceable replacements seemed to restore her confidence and make her almost whole again.

Ben hadn't picked up when she called, and she really hadn't expected him to. Cassie knew she'd called in the middle of wrestling practice when his clothes and phone were secured in a locker.

She'd left a voice mail, "Ben, call me the minute you can."

Not that he ever listened to messages, but he'd surely see that she had tried to reach him.

Her call to Isabel went straight to voice mail as well.

"Mom," Cassie had said after a long sigh, "Enough is enough with the strike. I need to check in with you about when I'm coming back."

The well-maintained gravel road to the Iron Cross Ranch headquarters passed through several treeless miles of close-cropped cattle pasture. She noted thousands of dark piles of manure on the flat but not a single cow.

That puzzled her until the answer became clear. A semi-tractor pulling a long aluminum livestock hauler emerged from the smoke and fog headed right toward her on the road. Then it made sense. It was fall, and time for cattle ranchers to gather up their herds to sell or move to better pasture.

She eased off the track to give the truck plenty of room. As it passed she glimpsed the panicked white eyes of bald-faced Angus peering out at her through portal-like openings in the trailer. Twenty to twenty-four cattle cried out from each of the double decks of the transport hauler. The bawling of the cows punctuated the afternoon stillness as they passed.

Cassie recalled her childhood on her uncles' much smaller ranch near Helena. After the shifty cattle buyers had arrived and made their deals, after her uncles always swore they got screwed, the big trucks and trailers lined up on the county road that led to their ranch and it was time to ship.

Shipping day was a loud, wild, and exhausting day with all hands on deck. In addition to the single hired hand and her father and uncles, neighbors pitched in as well. Isabel didn't participate.

Penned cattle were sorted and driven through chutes into the trailers. Dust and the screeching of air brakes filled the air. Cows didn't meekly walk into the long boxes single file, either. They bawled, they bolted, they panicked, and sometimes they backed up on the ramps when they were expected to proceed.

Following the last shipment of cattle would be a huge feast of elk roast, mashed potatoes, and gravy prepared by her aunts in the dining room of the main house. Cassie remembered digging in with a knot in her stomach, still bothered by the events of the day. She tried not to cry knowing all those creatures were headed to their deaths. The silence outside following the cacophony of bawls and sounds was nearly overwhelming. She wasn't sentimental about the fate of the cows, but she couldn't deny their plight, either.

The truck Cassie pulled over for was followed by another, and then another. The heavy vehicles rocked her Explorer each time. She didn't ease back onto the road until six cattle haulers had passed by.

As she turned the wheel she saw a seventh truck coming and she paused for it. It was much smaller than the cattle haulers. Rather than an eighteen-wheeler, the last vehicle was some kind of utility pickup with a boxy shape and instrumentation built into the bed walls. Two men were inside and they nodded to her as they passed. The muddy white new model GMC had a graphic on the passenger-side door that read:

REMR

Houston, Texas

The company was unfamiliar to her, although she doubted that the utility pickup was associated with the cattle haulers. The pickup, like the tractor-trailers, eventually vanished into the fog and smoke.

Cassie knew that if it was loading day she was likely to find every member of the family—perhaps with the exception of Cheyenne— at the ranch compound. The knot in her stomach had as much to do with the passing of the cattle haulers and the fate of the animals as it did with what was coming next.

She took in a long breath and slowly expelled it. The confidence she'd gained from replacing her equipment waned, and she felt very much alone.

Cassie topped a rise marked with a large sign that read:

TURN AROUND NOW IF YOU DON'T HAVE AN APPOINTMENT
—*Iron Cross Ranch*

and immediately took in the layout of the Kleinsasser ranch head-quarters below.

Beyond a vast and complicated labyrinth of outbuildings, pens, barns, corrals, and loafing sheds was a massive and foreboding three-story stone home with gables and high turrets on each flank. The roofs of several additional stone houses showed through the high fall-bronzed cottonwoods on either side.

The Bitterroots that rose to the west and served as the back-drop to the scene were obscured by layers of clouds and smoke halfway up, making the range look like truncated buttes instead of mountains.

To the north of the huge compound was an ancient traditional red barn as well as a series of metal buildings and Quonset huts housing vehicles, tractors, ATVs, and other farm equipment. Several ranch employees, she assumed, milled outside the outbuildings and turned toward her as she got closer.

She slowed down as the ground leveled and she maneuvered her rental car through the stockyards toward the stone house. The pungent smell of manure and panicked cattle hung thick in the air.

Cassie pulled up to a knee-high barrier fence in front of the house and turned off her engine. As she did so, a half-dozen long-legged dogs boiled out from beneath Russian olive trees on the side of the small yard and circled her car, barking with percussive fury.

She wasn't surprised by the sudden appearance of a pack of dogs. She was used to it. Cassie knew it was impossible to sneak up on a ranch house.

Then she waited. There was no reason to open her door and go outside to challenge the dogs, which were particularly sleek and rangy and of mottled color. One dog had placed its paws on the glass of the passenger window in order to stare at her inside. It had remarkable green eyes.

Finally, the heavy timber front door of the stone house opened and a compact man with a thick mustache came out and glared at her. He was in his stocking feet and there was a fine delineation between the reddish tan of his face and the bald white crown of his head where his cowboy hat usually was.

He shouted at the dogs and they melted away.

She knew it was John Wayne from photos she'd seen of him online. Cassie studied him carefully as he took in her car and then squinted to see her through the windshield. She realized that the reflection of the rolling clouds above on the glass partially obscured her face at first.

Then she saw it: a tell. He'd identified her. At the second he did his mouth twitched involuntarily and he almost rocked back on his heels. But he recovered quickly and the puzzled look on his face softened.

He motioned for her to get out and she did.

"Are those Catahoulas?" she asked, referring to the breed of dogs. "I hear they're good herd dogs."

"Some of 'em are," he said with a low Southern drawl that was unlike anything she'd heard from a native in Montana. "Some of 'em are just a pain in the ass.

"What can I do for you? I wasn't expecting any visitors."

He said it in a way that told Cassie he was misleading her, that he knew exactly who she was. And she recognized his odd drawl as inauthentic, a way of speaking sometimes adopted by western men to make them seem more like the character they wanted to be perceived as.

"I'm Cassie Dewell," she said. "I talked with you last night."

He made a show of shooting out his sleeve so he could look at his wristwatch. Unlike his flannel western shirt, prominent rodeo buckle, and Wranglers still dusty from moving cattle onto the haulers, his large gold Rolex stood out.

"I'm John Wayne Kleinsasser. I thought you were coming out this morning," he said.

"Are you surprised to see me now?" she asked.

He lowered his wrist and looked at her from the top of her head to her boots. It wasn't a kind assessment, she thought.

"Why would I be surprised, other than you're seven hours late?" he asked.

But she'd noted the tell and filed it away.

"We've been moving cows all day," he said. "Now we're getting something to eat. It's tradition for hauling day."

"I'm not hungry," she lied.

"I don't believe I asked you if you were."

She said, "I'm happy to sit in my car and wait. I don't want to rush you. But if you'll recall, I was hoping to walk through the building where your niece was assaulted, as I said. I'm sorry I'm so late but I was . . . detained. Is there still a chance I could do that?"

"*Today?*"

"Either that or I could come out tomorrow," she said. "Or the day after that, or the day after that," Cassie added. Her clear meaning, *I'm not going away.*

Again, he looked her over. She strained a smile.

He sighed, and said, "Come on in. I'll finish up and drive you out there. When you're through you can go back to Bozeman and leave us alone."

"Thank you," she said. "I appreciate it. I know what a busy time this must be."

"Making a living," he said. "How'd you get here, anyway?"

"The gate was open."

It took him a moment, then he nodded. "We opened them for the cattle haulers and you slipped right through," he said as much to himself as to her.

He stood aside as she mounted the steps to the porch, then took another step back when she shouldered past him to enter the house.

He hadn't asked about the new car, she thought. Even though he'd made a point of getting her vehicle description the night before.

John Wayne closed the door behind them and Cassie paused near a tangle of cowboy boots on a rug to the side. He padded up behind her in his socks.

"Take your shoes off. It's something we do," he said.

"Okay."

Cassie was grateful that he walked around her as she bent over to pull off her boots. She was able to slip the .22 from her boot shaft into her purse without him noticing.

Then she stood and beheld the great room. High ceilings, heavy beams, dark furniture, mounts of deer and elk heads on the walls. Shafts of light from narrow windows on two exterior walls and a single skylight high above crisscrossed in the gloom.

"An iron cross," she said to John Wayne.

"My grandfather's design," he replied.

Warm odors from the dining room filled the house, and she could hear low chatter and the clinking of silverware and glasses from somewhere down a hallway.

"Please," she said, stepping aside toward a dark floral ottoman, "go finish your meal. I'll sit here and wait."

There was an unworldly squawk from the direction of the dining room that sounded to Cassie like part falcon, part hog. The sound stopped and started again until it ended abruptly.

She looked to John Wayne for an explanation.

"My father would like to meet you," he said. Then he shrugged, as if that wouldn't have been his choice.

"Horst?" she asked, trying to recall the given names of the Kleinsasser clan.

"Horst the second," John Wayne corrected.

She followed him across the polished dark wood floor of the great room and into the hallway. Over his shoulder, in a soft voice, he said, "He had a stroke recently. A pretty bad one. He's slowly getting his speech back, but right now I'm the only one who can understand him. I'm kind of his translator."

She nodded as if she understood. "Really, I don't mind waiting."

"If the old man wants to meet you he wants to meet you," John Wayne said with a shrug.

They took a sharp turn to the right and entered a narrow dining room paneled with light pine. The walls featured old sporting paintings from nineteenth-century Europe.

The table was stocked with a huge platter of roast beef, a bowl of quartered potatoes, a tureen of brown gravy, and trays of green beans, carrots, and sauerkraut.

A square-faced woman in her fifties wearing a full apron hovered briefly at the back of the room. No doubt the cook, Cassie thought. The woman scuttled away through a door at the end of the dining room without looking back.

That left only the family and Cassie.

Seven pairs of eyes greeted her. It was absolutely silent. The absence of Cheyenne and Franny were glaring, and Cassie noted that no place settings had been set for them.

Horst II, John Wayne's father, slumped in a wheelchair at the head of the table. His head rested on his left shoulder and his mouth gaped. His large hands rested on the arms of his wheelchair. He was unshaven and wearing sloppy sweat clothes that looked two sizes too big. Someone had tied a bib around his neck. Horst II looked nothing like the photos Cassie had seen of him in the internet. Only his eyes seemed alive, and they were fixed on her face.

Next to Horst II on the far side of the table was Margaret, Cassie guessed. She had metal-framed glasses and her head was covered with tight curls. Margaret had a fork in her hand with a square of roast beef on it poised to feed to her husband. She had a fleshy porcine face and she wore an out-of-fashion dark dress of thick material that looked like it would rustle when she walked. The expression she aimed at Cassie was equal parts dislike and suspicion.

Cassie didn't blame her. What kind of person crashed a family get-together?

Rand, seated next to his mother, didn't even try to disguise his contempt for her. He tossed his silverware to the tablecloth and sat back and glared at her in disgust. While casually refreshing an ice-filled cocktail glass with more bourbon from a decanter, he arched his eyebrows at her as if to say, *Get the hell out.*

Next to Rand was a young female who looked like she didn't belong, Cassie thought. At least in *this* family. She was thin and wore too much makeup and a multicolored tattoo snaked up the side of her neck from her very tight top. Cassie knew Rand wasn't married and she surmised the girl was either his live-in or somebody he'd picked up and invited to the hauling day meal. The girl nervously drank from an oversized goblet of red wine.

On the near side of the table were two boys aged probably eight and ten. John Wayne's sons, she guessed. They were duded up in cowboy clothes and the roast beef and vegetables on their plates looked virtually untouched. They looked at her like they enjoyed the distraction she'd brought.

Rochelle, John Wayne's wife and the boys' mother, was a wispy and featureless woman with mousy brown hair and an inoffensive manner. She was the first in the room to look away when Cassie found her eyes.

"Everybody," John Wayne announced, "this is Cassie Dewell. She's working for Blake's lawyer to get him off. She wants to walk through the old crew shack to see if the police missed anything."

No one said hello. No one said anything.

"Not necessarily," Cassie said softly.

Rochelle turned her attention to her boys and urged them to eat or they wouldn't get apple pie for dessert. Reluctantly, both John Wayne Jr., and Tristan proceeded to push their vegetables around on their plates as if the activity alone would fool their mother.

Cassie watched as Horst II took in a big wet breath as if loading up, then squawked a staccato series of bursts. She couldn't make out a single word. Then he did it again.

"Dad wants to know why you picked this moment to interrupt our hauling day feast," John Wayne said to Cassie with a bit of a smirk. "He wonders if it's because you don't look like a woman who misses many meals."

Margaret shot her husband a reproachful look. Apparently, Cassie thought, she couldn't understand him, either.

Horst II squawked again.

"He said he was joking," John Wayne said.

Cassie tried to summon up confidence. Her mouth was suddenly dry. She said, "I remember the hauling day feast. We used to have them when I was a girl. Everybody who helped out was invited. . . ."

She trailed off when she realized that unlike her uncles and aunts, who invited in all of the neighbors and friends who assisted in the work no matter who they were, the Kleinsassers had sent all their employees elsewhere. This meal was only for the immediate family.

Rand said to Cassie, "It's a little hard to enjoy my meal with you standing there staring at us like we're fuckin' zoo animals."

"I'm sorry," Cassie replied. She looked to John Wayne for some kind of guidance to stay or go.

Horst II said something that sounded to Cassie like, "Don't shit."

"Pardon me?" Cassie asked. She was rattled.

"He said, 'Don't sit,'" John Wayne said with a grin.

Before Cassie could reply, Horst II rattled out a long string of invective. While he did, Margaret fixed her eyes on the side of his face as if trying to silence him without succeeding. It was not a kind or sympathetic look, Cassie thought.

Finally, John Wayne said, "He says Blake means nothing more to him than any hopeless loser he passes on the highway or cow shit on the bottom of his boot. He says Blake is no more part of his family than you are and if you're trying to get him off you're just as evil as he is."

Cassie didn't respond. She couldn't.

"He also said this might be his last hauling day feast on this earth with his loving family and he'd like you to leave."

"Gladly."

"Now, *git*," Rand said, using his hands to shoo her away as if she were a dog.

"I'll be outside," Cassie said over her shoulder to John Wayne as she turned on her heel. He took a beat to move aside so she could go.

Red-faced and humiliated, she strode down the hallway in her stocking feet. There was a peal of laughter from Rand as the tin-kling of silverware resumed.

She fought the urge to run.

Cassie felt the presence of someone approaching from the hallway while she pulled on her boots. Then she heard the rustle of clothing.

Margaret eyed her coolly. Her bearing was more serious than what Cassie had observed inside the dining room, as if Margaret had shed the costume she wore around her family. She carried the empty tureen as if she'd used it as an excuse to leave the table.

"You should really go home," Margaret warned. Cassie was un-clear if it was friendly advice or a threat.

"Everyone in this county seems to agree with you. And I will—just as soon as I can."

Margaret fixed her gray eyes on Cassie. "You have no idea what you've stepped into."

"Your son Blake said the same thing to me."

Cassie watched carefully for Margaret's reaction. But the woman didn't even flinch.

"You don't understand," Margaret said. "Blake no longer ex-ists on this ranch."

"I get that. But he's still your firstborn son. And you probably don't know this but he was attacked in jail. From what I under-stand he may not make it."

Again, not even a tic. Cassie couldn't discern if Margaret had heard about Blake before she brought it up. Or if she simply didn't care.

Margaret sighed and shook her head. "He's just as bad as the others."

Before Cassie could respond, Margaret turned and walked away, cradling the empty tureen in her slender hands.

eighteen

A long hour later, John Wayne emerged from the house at the same moment Cassie's phone lit up with a call from Ben. John Wayne pulled on a barn coat, clamped on a black cowboy hat, and chinned toward his pickup to indicate she should follow him. He looked annoyed.

Cassie nodded that she understood his instructions. The man swung into the cab of his truck and it leaped forward, the rear tires raining gravel on her rental car as it turned in the yard and shot over a cattle guard. She gave pursuit and raised the phone to her mouth because she hadn't synched it to the rental's Bluetooth system yet.

"Hello, Ben."

"Hey, Mom. I just got done with practice and I saw that you called."

"Thank you. Yes, we got cut off last night after you started telling me that something crazy happened. . . ."

"Did you really get *arrested?*" he asked.

"Not officially. But a cop pulled me over and took me into the station. I couldn't call you because they took my cell phone."

"Mom?"

"What, Ben?"

"You're breaking up."

Although she was following John Wayne's vehicle on the gravel road at bone-rattling speed, she glanced at her phone to see there was only a single bar of reception. The farther she got from the ranch headquarters, the poorer it got.

The screen indicator changed to NO SERVICE.

"Oh, crap," she said aloud. She cursed and tossed the phone aside where it landed on the passenger seat.

John Wayne either didn't care that she could barely keep up with him as he raced through his ranch or he wanted to humiliate her further when she lost him and had to find her own way out.

Cassie was fortunate, though, in that the few times he vanished over a hilltop or took a sharp turn he left a telltale cloud of dust hanging in the air to follow. And she did.

She hoped when they got to the crew shack that she'd have the opportunity to question him. The gloves were off as far as she was concerned. John Wayne was no more than a cheap bully, and she'd dealt over the years with plenty of those. He'd been minimally accommodating when they first met when it was just the two of them, but he'd shown his true colors when he tossed her to his family to be demeaned like that.

So many questions. And if he didn't answer them or lied again, that very fact would be an answer in itself that he was hiding something. She created a mental list of topics:

- Did he or Rand order the sheriff's department to pick her up and detain her?
- Did any of them at the table know that her car had been torched?
- Had the news of Blake's assault reached them prior to her arrival? And if so, how?
- Did any of them order the jailhouse attack? Did they have a connection to the perpetrators?
- Was Horst II capable of communicating with anyone in the

outside world, or did he require John Wayne's "translating" ability to convey his wishes?

- Where were Cheyenne and Franny? Why didn't they come to the vaunted family hauling day feast?

And most of all, why did the family and their proxies in the sheriff's department do everything they could to make her investigation difficult if they were confident the allegations against Blake would land him in Deer Lodge for a very long time?

The two-track road paralleled a dry creek bed choked with rust-colored willows. It wound around an old copse of river cottonwood trees with dry leaves quivering on the branches like so many baby rattles. Suddenly the old crew shack appeared.

Cassie glanced down at her odometer to note that the journey was four-point-two miles from the ranch headquarters. That was a long walk for Franny that night, she thought.

John Wayne pulled off the road and motioned for Cassie to proceed. Instead, she stopped next to him. He quickly got out.

"This is the place my brother raped my niece," he said. "Have at it."

"Are you going to show me around?"

"No. I'm going home to take a nap."

"Will you be available to answer some questions?"

"I already did that. Ask the sheriff. Now please step back. I wouldn't want to run over your cowboy boots with my tires."

"I have a lot of questions. Some things just don't add up to me."

He looked at her for half a minute before rolling his eyes and throwing the transmission into reverse.

"Be off the property by sundown, lady," he said. She stepped back toward her car so the open pickup door wouldn't knock her over as he backed up.

She watched as he did a three-point turn and accelerated so rapidly back down the old road that the velocity of the maneuver slammed shut the passenger door on its own.

Cassie turned slowly and observed the crew shack. It was grander than she thought it would be: two levels, peaked roof, old shutters on the windows on both floors. It had obviously been built by people with ambition who later, for whatever reason, abandoned it.

Montana was filled with such houses and they could be found in dying small towns and within vast landholdings. They'd been built when the world was larger, when transportation was poorer. And because Montana was settled late in comparison to other parts of the country, many of the old ghost houses were originals. They'd once been attractive, well-appointed homes but they'd been left to rot. The low humidity and lack of subsequent development were two contributors to why the old structures still existed. Trees and bushes the original inhabitants had planted were dead or wild and untrimmed.

Cassie was always curious about what happened that resulted in the families who lived there to find the need to just walk away. Housing ranch hands was *not* the original purpose for the faded old house. That had come later.

She wondered if this house had been on an adjoining ranch to the Kleinsassers' original holdings, and when Horst I bought it he forced the former inhabitants to flee. She would likely never know.

Although Franny's affidavit had been in the file that either vanished or was burned up in her car, Cassie could recall many of the passages with clarity.

He said he wanted to show me where he spent most of his time when he was growing up on the ranch. He said he wanted me

to know that even though my uncles told me different, Uncle
Blake had spent a lot of years there and he had a real connection
to the ranch that I probably wasn't aware of. . . .

　　We arrived at a two-story old house on the side of a meadow.
The house was kind of dumpy, I thought. Some of the windows were broken out and the cattle had been on the porch
and collapsed it. There was old cow manure everywhere. It
was outside the house and inside the front door. The place
smelled like cows. I'm not fond of cows. I'm a vegan, you
know. . . .

Now, though, the structure was probably beyond repair and
in the process of collapsing in on itself. The wide front porch
sagged and the rail on the hitching post was missing. Most of the
windows were broken out and the door hung open at an angle.
Old wood shake shingles were missing from the bowed roof and
they littered the grass of the hard ground near the cracking foundation. Cattle had obviously used it for shelter although she didn't
see any now. There were manure piles on the porch and in the
grass.

　　A warped picnic table in the front yard had been upended and
rubbed on by cows until the wooden slats had become fuzzy with
hair.

　　She didn't like the feeling she got from the old house, and she
wondered if it was somehow more welcoming to Franny during a
sultry summer evening than it was now. Cassie couldn't understand
why Franny would want to go inside, even if it was with an uncle
who she seemed to like. Unless Franny had a dark side Cassie wasn't
aware of.

　　She reached in and turned off her engine and pocketed the key
fob. Not that she was worried about someone stealing her rental
car, but she didn't want to run the risk of a "smart" feature locking the vehicle with the keys in it. Cassie didn't want to be stuck
on the Iron Cross Ranch at night by herself.

★   ★   ★

After photographing the structure from the front and sides, she climbed the steps to the front porch. Cassie was startled when several rabbits shot out from beneath the porch in different directions. Then she was embarrassed for being so jumpy.

Before entering, Cassie carefully observed the open front door. The top and middle hinges were broken off and it hung precariously open and to the side by the bottom one. It looked like it had been open for many months, maybe even years.

> We stopped the car in front of the porch and Uncle Blake got out and asked me to follow him. The door to the house was unlocked and he went in first . . .

That was a discrepancy in Franny's account, she thought. Franny indicated the door was closed but unlocked. She'd made a point of saying that.

But careful examination of the doorjamb indicated the hinges weren't recently pulled away from the wood. The indentations where the screws had been were the same barn wood gray as the rest of the frame.

She took several photographs of the open door and door frame, but she really didn't think the discrepancy would turn out to be significant. Franny was fifteen, a little confused by what her uncle had in mind, and her recollection of that night was following a very traumatic experience. If she got the door wrong it probably didn't mean much.

Cassie clicked on the Maglite and opened the beam up wide before stepping across the threshold. Although the scene had no doubt been photographed, dusted, and examined by local crime scene techs, she stayed close to the interior walls rather than to walk into the center of the room.

Although crime scene tape had been removed (if it had ever been there at all), the floor of the dining room told a story in itself. The thick carpet of dust mixed with manure was a maelstrom of footprints and drag marks from law enforcement. A thin layer of new dust since the summer added a veneer, but the prints were numerous. She thought that within the many tracks were prints that could be matched with Blake's and Franny's shoes.

She took dozens of shots of the floor from several angles, although she doubted they'd be of any value.

> Uncle Blake lit a candle thing called a kerosene lamp and put it on the table. He said he wanted me to see all the old rooms but I said I was kind of scared. . . .
>
> Then Uncle Blake came around to my side of the table and lifted me up. He was strong. He sat me on top of the table and started kissing me. He has really fast hands and he was touching me everywhere. He stood there between my legs and held me in place.

There was the table Fanny had described, right in the middle of the room. It was old and stout, and unlike the counters and furniture it wasn't covered in a quarter-inch of dust and grime. That's because, she reasoned, Franny's clothes had wiped it clean as Blake molested her. The thought made Cassie cringe.

The vintage kerosene lamp Franny had mentioned was on the kitchen counter next to a dented metal tin of kerosene fuel. Cassie didn't know if Blake had moved it before the assault or the investigators had put it aside. It didn't matter other than to further corroborate Franny's account.

The liquor bottle and drinking glasses Blake had used had been taken away and were now in the evidence locker of the sheriff's department. She'd seen them. But she'd also wondered if Blake had brought the glasses with him or found them in the structure. When she opened the dusty cupboard she found a slew of glassware— mismatched plates, fast-food cups, even several martini glasses. No doubt, she thought, the ranch hands acquired glasses from all over the place and brought them back. The cocktail glasses Blake had used could have easily come from the cupboard.

Long tongues of flocked wallpaper hung from the interior walls exposing wooden slats behind it. There was a cowboy cartoon cal-endar from 1968 and the last page displayed was December. Cast-iron cookware was in the sink as if the last ranch hand to leave the place had forgotten to wash it.

She took more photos of the interior with her phone, and re-membered to close her eyes prior to each shot so the flash wouldn't blind her.

He showed me a room with bunk beds in it where ranch hands used to stay together.

Franny hadn't mentioned following Blake up the rickety stair-case to the second floor so Cassie didn't go there. Besides, the stairs sagged away from the wall and looked dangerous to try to climb. So she worked her way around the main room and through a door-way at the back of the house past the kitchen.

Inside were four sets of old metal-framed bunk beds, as de-scribed. Mice and rats had eaten through the thin mattresses and left balls of the insides throughout the room and in each of the cor-ners. As Cassie moved the beam she caught glimpses of rodents before they scattered.

A *Playboy* pinup, circa-1960s because the blond model kept her legs together, hung above one of the bunk beds. A pair of cowboy boots, black with age, were under one of the box springs as if wait-ing for their owner to get up and pull them on.

She raised the beam to the rafters and was greeted by two dozen yellow eyes reflected in the light. *Bats.*

When they spooked and flew en masse she ducked down so they'd fly out the doorway and not get tangled in her hair or clothes.

Franny had been there, Cassie concluded. She'd actually described the old crew shack with remarkable accuracy, given the circumstances.

Cassie jumped when a blast of lightning lit up the room followed by a near instantaneous thunderclap. It had been very close.

She paused and waited for the patter of rain on the old roof that should have followed. But it didn't.

When she backed out of the old house and turned around she saw that a jacked-up ranch vehicle was now parked directly behind her Ford. With all of the noise in the house—the rats, the bats, her own beating heart—she hadn't heard it drive up. There was no one behind the wheel.

"Hey there," Rand said from where he sat on a bench at the righted picnic table, "I thought when them bats came pouring out of there you'd be right behind them."

"Bats don't scare me," Cassie said. "What do you want?"

There was a half-empty bottle of Wild Turkey on the table in front of him. Rand's face was flushed by alcohol. His smile was more of a leer.

He gasped the edges of the table and leaned way back as if to get a better view of her.

"Oh, Dad sent me out here to make sure you got what you needed. Did you?"

She nodded. She wished her Glock wasn't in her handbag in the Explorer. But she had the .22 in her boot top if necessary.

"I'm done. It all checks out."

"What were you looking for in there? What did you expect to find?"

She shrugged. "I don't know."

"And someone is actually paying you for your mad skills, Inspector Clouseau?"

He snorted at his joke. He said, "So you didn't believe the sheriff's department report?"

"It's not that. I'm just tailing up to make sure the investigation is solid."

"And is it?"

She thought, *He really doesn't want my opinion. He just wants to engage.*

"Pretty much."

"Good to hear, good to hear," Rand said with a smug nod, as if he knew her conclusion long before she did. "Did you see that old *Playboy* centerfold on the wall?"

"I did."

"The image is seared into my mind. I saw it as a kid and jerked off to it for years."

She thought his intention was to shock her. She didn't respond.

"Think about it," he said. "That girl is probably sixty-five years old now. Maybe older."

"So, you spent a lot of time here," Cassie said. "Like Blake."

That seemed to throw him for a minute. He started to answer but then reached for the bottle instead and took a long drink.

"I guess now you'll be headed back to Bozeman."

"Soon."

"That's one fucked-up place," he said. "Full of hipsters and goddam bark-beetles. I have to go there quite a bit on ranch business and once I get there I can't wait to get out. And don't think I haven't heard of you and your defense lawyer."

Again, she didn't respond.

He said, "I didn't spend three years of my life defending this country so the fuckin' green phonies and out-of-staters could move here from California to take over my state, you know? It just pisses me off."

She didn't think it was a good time to bring up his dishonorable discharge or his prison time later. She said, "Why is it that every member of the Kleinsasser family feels the need to give me a hard time? It's getting really old. And it isn't working."

Although deep in her mind she knew she was lying.

He looked up and squinted at her as if seeing her for the first time. Then he grinned.

"You're feisty," he said.

"And I need to get going. Your brother told me to get off the ranch by dark and I intend to do just that."

"Yes," he said, "you're feisty, aren't you?"

She wished at that moment that he would rise up to come after her or fumble for a weapon. She was ready for him.

But he just sat there with that goblinlike leer on his face.

She gave Rand a wide berth as she strode around him toward her car. She could feel his eyes on her the whole time.

"If you lost twenty you might be okay," he said.

"Isn't your girlfriend about due for her meth about now?" Cassie said. "She was looking a little strung out."

He laughed but it sounded false. She was past him now and it was a straight shot to her car.

"Where the *hell* are you going?" he called after her. "Don't you want to stay and chat? Tell me more about my girlfriend? Read me the riot act?"

She reached for the door handle.

"That guy you're trying to save is a fucking limp-dick monster. He ain't nobody. Why don't you come back here and explain why you want to save his sorry ass?"

Cassie threw herself in the car and started it up. She was furious.

When she turned on the headlights they bathed Rand in white light and he raised his hand in front of his eyes to block the beams.

Then she accelerated into a U-turn that spun the rear of the vehicle around and threw dirt from the rear tires all over him and drove away. Her last glimpse of Rand was in the rearview mirror.

He stood beside his truck with both middle fingers extended into the sky. He was laughing.

nineteen

Ben Dewell lay fully clothed on top of his bed with his phone in his lap and a Ziploc bag of ice cubes on the top of his head like a hat. He wiped the back of his hand across his face to stanch the dark red blood that oozed out of both nostrils from his swollen nose. Empty fry boxes and hamburger wrappers were at his feet. He was confused and depressed and had a headache and he didn't understand girls.

Especially Erin.

In fact, he'd been thinking about her and how she'd blown him off at break time during their usual foray to the Kum & Go instead of his challenge match against Jason Smithfield at practice. He'd been distracted at the moment when Jason shot across the mat toward Ben, wrapped his right arm around Ben's legs and pinned his left arm tight, then wrenched back with all of his strength to throw Ben face-first to the mat in a violent move known as a fireman's carry.

Ben had been so stunned that he'd lost control of his limbs for a few seconds as Jason rolled him over to his back and pinned him. Several wrestlers who'd seen the move whooped. The challenge match had lasted less than ten seconds, and Ben had what might turn out to be a broken nose, two black eyes, and a lump on the top of his head.

He looked so bad when he got home that Isabel suspended her strike and filled the bag with ice and sent him to bed. Most surprising, she asked Ben to place an order for what he wanted to eat.

She even agreed to go out and get it even though, she said, she would hold her own nose while doing so.

He'd jotted down:

Two Big Macs
Two Large Fries
Large Chocolate Milkshake

And he'd eaten it all. As long as Jason Smithfield ruled the 113-pound weight class, Ben had no choice but to either quit or move up to 120. So it was time to start gaining weight. There was a stud in that weight class named Philip Warden. Warden was just as unbeatable as Jason, but Warden was a dumb-ass who might have to leave the team because of his poor grades. Ben had that going for him, maybe.

But about Erin.

He'd waited for her on his usual bench. After ten minutes, he went inside the building. His insides were churning a little because she'd never not shown up before and he knew she was in school.

He found her near her locker. When she looked up and saw him—he was sure she did—she looked away quickly and walked in the other direction. But he caught up with her and something about her seemed different. She was more serious than usual and she was evasive. She said she "had to go."

Ben had tried to act like it didn't matter, that he had plenty of friends and plenty to do. But he knew his face betrayed his anxiety. They both knew he didn't. It was high school reality, and they'd talked about it before.

He didn't see her for the rest of the day, even though they had a kind of routine where they'd touch base in the halls during class breaks. Which meant to him that she was deliberately avoiding him.

Ben tried to figure out what he'd done to make her want to stay away from him. She wasn't a mean person or a cruel person—she wasn't one of those types. She didn't like those kinds of people. But there was definitely something he'd said—or worse, *not said*. Girls were like that, he thought. He could be in as much trouble for what he didn't do or say or think.

Had Erin met another boy? He thought she probably could have, she was certainly cute, although he couldn't imagine who the boy would be. Maybe she'd finally found her niche of thespians and dreamers who hovered around on the periphery of the rest of the student body and they'd invited her in. That invitation wouldn't include a ninth-grader like Ben. He wasn't sure if there was even a niche for him anywhere on the grounds of the school. He certainly wasn't one of the athletes yet, and especially after his performance against Jason in a challenge match that afternoon. But he wasn't yet ready to surrender himself to the pack of losers who hung around outside the auto shop smoking cigarettes and weed and hating on everyone else. Yet.

That's what he was thinking about when the assistant coach blew the whistle to start the challenge match against Jason Smithfield.

And that's what he was still contemplating while he lay on his bed with his nose swelling and twin drops of blood slowly creeping down his face.

It was a dilemma and he felt alone and lost. He couldn't ask his mom about it, and he certainly couldn't ask Isabel. In the past, it was the kind of thing he'd text with Erin about because she expressed so many of the same feelings of being new and somewhat lost.

Maybe, he thought, he'd interpreted the incident with the truck the day before completely wrong. He thought it had bonded them in a new and interesting way. After all, she said he'd saved her life. But it was possible she looked at it differently now. Maybe she was spooked.

He stared at the phone in his lap and came up with five or six opening texts to try out on Erin. Should he go nonchalant, like he hadn't noticed her change in behavior and was just checking in?

Or get right to the point? Ask her what was wrong and try to address it since it was likely something he'd done or said? Knowing Erin, he didn't think that would be the right approach. She might tell him he was beneath her or a creep. Or tell him to grow the hell up.

Or maybe, he thought, play it coy. Tell her she seemed to be troubled about something (not him). And was there anything he could do to help her through it?

In the end, after twenty minutes of deliberating, he sent a text to Erin Reese.

It said:

> Hey.

Then he stared at the screen, willing a response while at the same time fearing the wrong one. A small balloon appeared, meaning she was writing back. Then it went away. He imagined her somewhere trying to come up with the right words. He couldn't recall her ever taking so long to find them.

Finally:

> Hey back.

It wasn't hostile. It was sort of friendly, if resigned.

> Ben: How are you doing?

He immediately wished he'd written "How is it going?" instead. He sent her a curious face emoji.

> Erin: I've been better.

> Ben: Are you doing all right?

Erin: Not really. I feel weird. Everything is just weird right now.

Ben: Is there anything I can do?

Erin: The best thing you can do is stay away from me. I'm
toxic. It's for the best.

He sat back, his mind spinning in a dark swirl. He started to text "What did I do?" and deleted it before he sent it. Finally, he settled on:

Ben: I'm sorry you feel that way. I don't think you're toxic.

He fought the urge to say he found her wonderful and enchanting and really, really hot. But he didn't. He wasn't sure how she'd take it.

Erin: ♥

Ben: Really. Did something happen today?

There was a long pause. So long, he began to fear that she had moved on.
Then:

Erin: It's best for you if you keep your distance. There are
things going on that aren't good.

In the "things I should have asked her about" department, he realized he knew absolutely next to nothing about her family situation. Erin rarely spoke of her parents and he didn't even know if she had siblings. He assumed she didn't. He did remember her once referring to staying with relatives, but he didn't know if that was a temporary or permanent situation.

Ben: Is the situation bad at home?

Erin: Not really. Boring, but not bad.

Ben: Same here. Isabel is in the other room watching a doc
on a band called Jefferson Airplane.

Erin: ☺

Erin found Ben's stories about his grandmother hilarious, so
he kept her updated on things Isabel did and said. Erin said she
kind of admired Isabel's strike but wasn't sure why other than it
showed she wasn't a pushover.

Erin: I may have to go away for a while.

Ben was stunned.

Ben: Why? Where would you go?

Erin: I don't know.

He wasn't sure if she didn't know about why or didn't know
about where.

Ben: How long would you be gone?

Erin: Maybe a week. Maybe forever.

He tried a different tack.

Ben: My mom is a private investigator. She used to be a
cop. Do you want me to ask her to help?

Erin: God no. ☹

As if triggered by some psychic cue, Ben's phone lit up with an
incoming call. Mom.

He moaned. Her timing was horrible. He refused the call. He'd
call her back later.

Ben: Is there anything I can do?

Erin: Probably not.

Ben: Does this have something to do with that truck thing yesterday?

There was a very long pause, and several text balloons that appeared and were then cancelled by her.

Erin: It might.

Ben: What does that mean?

Erin: Please, dude. This doesn't have anything to do with you. It's my problem.

Ben: It doesn't have to be. Did you see that truck again?

Erin: Didn't see it. Heard it outside my house last night.

Ben: You're fucking kidding me.

Erin: Wish I was.

Ben: What time?

Erin: 2

Ben: Maybe we should call the cops.

Erin: And say what? Come on, dude. I've got to go.

Ben: Can I call you now?

Erin: No.

Ben: You're scaring me a little.

Erin: Don't worry. You're fine if you stay away from me. I
just want to be friends.

Ben: What does that mean?

Erin: Good night.

After thrashing around on his bed for a moment, he punched
Erin up on his phone and placed the call. It was the first time
they'd ever talked on the phone instead of texting.

It went straight to voice mail. Erin's dreamy voice said she
wasn't in and to leave a message.

He didn't.

twenty

⊷⇒◉⇐⊷

Cassie took the exit to Corvallis impulsively because she realized she was starving and she needed food. As she turned off the highway into the small town she checked her mirrors to make sure that her quick turn hadn't attracted the attention of Deputy Grzegorczyk or any other of Lochsa County's finest. Since she'd been to the Iron Cross Ranch in her new rental, she assumed the word was out on what kind of vehicle she was now driving.

Yes, she thought, she was getting paranoid. Justifiably so.

The Corvallis Tavern was an aged stand-alone structure lit up with neon beer and liquor signs in the window. Small floodlights lit the hand-painted outside sign that was lettered in orange and blue and mounted on a sheet of plywood above the overhung porch roof. It was the only business open on the short block but the parking places along the street were filled with four-by-fours and pickups. The plates were all from Montana. That was a good indication, she thought.

Before going in, she sat in her Ford and breathed deeply, trying to regain her bearings. Every interaction she'd had with a member of the Kleinsasser family had been unpleasant and vaguely threatening, even though it didn't seem they were in cahoots with one another. All indications were they hated one another with the exception of John Wayne and Rand. Rand, as Blake had indicated, seemed to revere John Wayne. But he was also a loose cannon and Cassie didn't want to encounter him again.

Cheyenne was a mystery wrapped in a riddle. Horst II was cruel, damaged, and vindictive. Margaret was either an enemy or a secret ally. Cassie couldn't decide.

And she wouldn't be able to sort it all out until she got some food and rest, she thought. She'd barely slept the night before in jail and she hadn't eaten anything the entire day. She was punchy and not at her best.

There was a text message from Rachel saying she'd arrived back in Bozeman.

Made it back. Blake is in IC and surgery is tomorrow.

Be careful and come home.

Cassie thanked her and left it at that. She didn't have the energy to fill Rachel in on her day at the Iron Cross Ranch.

She was frustrated that her call to Ben had gone to voice mail. She texted him that she was at dinner for thirty to forty minutes but she would call after that. She asked him to please pick up.

The tavern was much smaller than the Hayloft, and moderately busy. Local cowboys in hats and boots played eight-ball on the pool table and several locals swiveled on their stools to check her out as she slipped into a chair at a small table. The menu was hand-lettered on a board above the bar and she was grateful there weren't many choices.

She was pleased that the wine list had more options than "red or white" and ordered a glass of Pinot Noir, a CT burger, and a glass of water from a heavyset waitress with a thick helmet of black hair and a raccoon's mask of heavy mascara. None of the staff had been there the previous afternoon when she'd stopped by. Which meant, if she had the gumption, that she should ask them if they knew Hawk.

After some dinner, though.

The place was warm and intimate, and the customers seemed to be locals and they were comfortable with one another. University of Montana Grizzlies posters and paraphernalia were everywhere, and someone had stolen and mounted a street sign for BRETT FAVRE BOULEVARD.

As the waitress delivered her wine an older man with a full white beard and red suspenders over a long underwear top came in and asked her, "Has Jody been in?"

The waitress shook her head. "He usually comes in around eight for his nightly martini."

The man looked at his watch, then seemed to contemplate whether to wait a half hour or come back. He decided to wait. He took a stool at the bar and rotated it toward her.

"Beer and a shot," he said to the waitress.

"*Please,*" she corrected.

"May I please have a glass of beer and a shot of Jim Beam at your lovely establishment?" he asked. Cassie couldn't tell if he was grinning through the beard.

"That's better," the waitress said. Then to Cassie, "Never let 'em treat you like shit."

Cassie toasted her, and fought the urge to ask the waitress if she'd ever met any of the Kleinsassers. Because that's how they treated everyone.

Cassie wolfed down the burger and ordered a second glass of wine although she knew she probably shouldn't. The first glass had gone to her head because there was nothing on her stomach to absorb it. She could already feel warm tendrils of alcohol extending through her body.

The old man at the bar kept checking his watch. He was obviously waiting for eight o'clock to come around.

He gestured toward a poster board behind the bar. It was a hand-lettered weekly football pool where patrons could pay a few dollars and guess the sum of the scoring for the University of Montana game, the Montana State game, and either the Seattle Seahawks or Denver Broncos contests.

"Well, look who won," he said to the waitress.

Cassie followed his index finger to the pool results to see that "J. Haak" was circled in red. She guessed the "J" stood for Jody.

"I guess I know who will be buying a round for the house," the man said.

"Yeah," the waitress said. "I think that's two weeks in a row."

"Lucky bastard," the man grumbled.

"Oh, yeah," the waitress said with sarcasm. "Jody is really a lucky guy."

The old man snorted as they shared a joke Cassie wasn't privy to. She looked at the name on the football pool and formed an idea.

When the waitress delivered her second glass of wine and the bill, Cassie asked her, "I heard you two talking about Jody. How do you pronounce 'Haak,' his last name?" Cassie said it like *Hack.*"

The waitress looked at her skeptically. "Hawk. Like the bird. Why?"

Cassie tried not to react. "Just wondering. I've been trying to find a man called Hawk for a couple of days. I need to talk with him. Am I correct that he'll be here at eight?"

"Most nights," the waitress said. "Not all."

"Do you know where I can reach him if he doesn't come in?"

Something passed over the waitress's face, a kind of subtle mask.

"Who's asking?" She was obviously protective of Haak, which Cassie found interesting.

"My name is Cassie Dewell," she said, fishing in her purse for a card and handing it over. "I'm a private investigator."

"I've heard you were around asking questions."

"Really?"

"I work in a bar," the waitress said with a grin. "I hear everything."

"So, about reaching him," Cassie prompted.

"I'm not the one to ask. When he comes in for his martini I serve it to him. He doesn't talk to me a lot and I have no idea where he lives."

"Would the man at the bar know?"

The waitress looked over at the bearded man. "Yeah," she said. "Frank might know where he lives."

"Thank you."

"No problem," the waitress said. She'd been helpful, although Cassie always bristled when a service employee said "no problem" instead of "you're welcome." But it was a thing these days, she recognized.

"Hey, little lady," the bearded man said to her as Cassie took her wine and sat down next to him at the bar.

"I'm Frank," the old man said.

She introduced herself again. "I'm looking for Jody Haak. The waitress said you might know where I can find him."

Frank took a long time to draw a pocketwatch out of his jeans and look at it. "He's late. Maybe he's not coming in tonight to collect his winnings."

"But do you know where he lives?"

"Kind of. But I've never been to his place."

"Is it around here?"

Frank chinned vaguely toward the mountains to the southeast. "Jody lives off the grid," he said. "No phone, no internet, nothing like that. He makes a point of it. That's why I'm here trying to

run into him. I want to ask him if I can borrow his flatbed trailer
so I can take my ATV into the shop in town."

"Are you friends?"

Frank shrugged. "Not really. Jody is a hard guy to get to know.
He doesn't talk much. He's not like me—a guy who never knows
when to shut up."

She smiled.

"Hell," Frank said, "he left the state a while back. Never said
a word to anyone, he just up and vanished. It was when he got
kicked off the ranch where he worked, but he's obviously back now.
From what I understand, he's got a cabin up there somewhere."

"What's he hiding from?" Cassie asked.

"You'll have to ask Jody. But my guess is he wants to steer clear
of his old employers."

"Do you mean the ranch he worked on?"

Frank nodded.

"Let me guess," Cassie said. "He used to work for the Iron
Cross."

"For something like twenty years or more," Frank said. "He
knows where all the bodies are buried out there on that place, or
so I take it. When they run him off it wasn't a pleasant experience
for Jody from what I understand. Not that he told me outright. It's
just bar gossip. And here at the CT, there's plenty of that. You can
probably believe about half of it."

As Frank talked, he took several baleful looks at his empty beer
glass. Cassie understood the signal, and ordered him another.

"Thank you kindly," he said.

"Here," she said, giving Frank her card. "If you see him please
ask him to give me a call. If I'm not here in Lochsa County I'll be
at my office in Bozeman. I'd really like to talk with him."

Frank studied the card as if he's never seen one quite so interesting before.

"Are you working for Blake?" he asked.

"I'm working for his lawyer."

"Blake is a hard man to figure out. I can't say I like him."

"No one does."

"Except maybe Jody," Frank said.

"Did you see them together?"

Frank nodded. "Blake came in here on a toot last summer. The two of them spent a couple of hours having some kind of big discussion right in that booth over there," he said, pointing toward an empty booth near the back. "It was pretty animated and pretty unusual because Jody isn't usually much of a talker. I stopped by to say hello to Jody and he gave me a look like, 'please get the hell out of here,' so I got the message and left. Blake wasn't friendly at all, but I guess he's that way with everyone.

"A couple of days later I heard what happened to Blake's niece. So, I guess I saw them together the night before the, um, incident."

"Interesting," Cassie said. "Do you have any idea what they were talking about?"

"Some kind of secret ranch shit, I imagine. They both were on the outs with John Wayne and Horst, so I figure they had plenty in common."

"Was Blake drunk at the time?" Cassie asked. The story corroborated Blake's telling.

Frank shrugged. "I guess he was, but I couldn't tell at the time. He wasn't falling down or spilling drinks, but there was a real glassy look to his eyes. I've seen it on other big drinkers, where they don't even look like they're three sheets to the wind but they're actually blotto. Blake had that look, I'd say. Like he was there listening to you but he really wasn't there at all."

That also supported Blake's account.

"Was Blake by himself with Mr. Haak?"

"Nah," Frank said. "He came with that barmaid from up in Lolo. Now *she* was drunk as a skunk. She had her head down on the table sawing logs the whole time Blake and Jody were talking."

"Was it Lindy Glode?"

"That's her name," Frank said, snapping his fingers. "I'm pretty sure that's who it was. Cute and busty, but really out of it that night."

"I'm trying to find her, too," Cassie said as much to herself as to Frank. "Any idea where I could?"

Frank's eyes twinkled and she assumed he was smiling again. "Believe it or not, little lady, I don't really run with a crowd that includes cute and busty young women."

"Got it."

Frank's eyes slid from her face to over her shoulder. He said, "Well, speak of the devil."

"Lindy?" Cassie said. She could feel a breath of cool air from the open door on the back of her neck.

"The man himself," Frank said.

Cassie spun around on her stool. Jody Haak was short, solid, and stout. He had a long face with jowls and eyes that looked to have seen it all. He wore a stained cowboy hat with a short brim, a week's worth of silver whiskers, and scuffed cowboy boots.

His eyes shifted from Frank to Cassie and he seemed to know who she was by the tightening of his mouth.

Haak turned on his heel and walked straight out of the bar.

"Jody, can I borrow your trailer?" Frank called after him. Haak never looked back.

"Doesn't seem like he wants to talk with you," Frank said to Cassie.

She thanked Frank, quickly settled the bill, and strode across the Corvallis Tavern and out the door behind Jody Haak.

All she saw of him were the taillights of his pickup headed southeast.

★ ★ ★

She was exhausted when she got to her room at the Whispering Pines. Her plan was to talk with Ben, have a nightcap, and go to sleep early. She closed the door behind her and eyed the bed.

She'd not even kicked off her cowboy boots before there was a gentle knocking on the door. Cassie rose, fetched her handbag with the Glock in it, and peered out through the peephole.

Linda Sue Murdock stood a few feet away in a brown cloth coat. She was looking over her shoulder as if suspicious that someone had followed her.

Cassie slid the bolt and opened the door.

"I've been waiting for you to show up. May I come in?" Murdock asked.

"Of course," Cassie said, stepping aside.

Murdock entered quickly and waited for Cassie to close the door.

Cassie asked, "Is someone following you? You seem nervous."

"I *am* nervous. I shouldn't be here. I need a drink."

"All I have is wine."

"That's fine."

Cassie poured some into two thin plastic motel room glasses.

"Do you have any ice?" Murdock asked.

"It's red wine," Cassie explained.

"I like it with ice and a little Seven-Up. I'm a lightweight."

Cassie nodded. "I can get you both. There are a couple of machines near the lobby."

"Don't tell Glen I'm here."

"The manager?"

"Yes. He's one of them."

"You mean friends of the Kleinsassers?"

Her eyes said yes.

"Okay," Cassie said. "Sit down and get comfortable. I'll go get a Seven-Up and some ice."

Murdock sat down on one of the two plastic chairs at the small table near the window. She kept her coat on and hugged herself.

"I understand you're looking for Lindy Glode."

"I am."

Murdock nodded, then looked away. "I know where she might be. You see, she's my stepdaughter."

Cassie trudged to the alcove near the manager's office with an empty ice bucket and a handful of change for the soft drink dispenser. The lights were off in the manager's office but she saw the form of Glen Steele lurking behind the counter of the front desk. He retreated back to his quarters as she got close.

Had he seen Murdoch enter her room?

She filled the bucket and fed coins into the vending machine. There wasn't any 7-Up so she chose Mountain Dew. Cassie figured that if Murdock liked sweet drinks it was as good as any.

As she turned to walk back to her room she noticed that the always-present hum of traffic from the main highway seemed to be louder than usual. And it quickly increased in volume.

Something blacked out the illuminated Whispering Pines sign at the curbside and she felt the roar of a big engine as well as a heavy vibration through the soles of her boots.

It was a massive eighteen-wheel tractor-trailer barreling through the parking lot with its headlights and running lights quenched. And it picked up speed.

She screamed and dropped the ice and soft drink as the big truck drove head-on into the front of her corner unit. The crash of broken two-by-fours and imploded wood paneling was tremendous.

The truck never stopped. It rolled into and through the motel room and continued out the other side, leaving a wake of twisted material and furniture and sparking electric wires.

Linda Murdock never had a chance.

Cassie wouldn't have, either.

Part IV

Nothing on earth consumes a man more quickly than the passion of resentment.

—Nietzsche, *Ecce Homo*

If you hate a person, you hate something in him that is part of yourself. What isn't part of ourselves doesn't disturb us.

—Hermann Hesse, *Demian*

twenty-one

—◦═◦—

"It shouldn't be all that hard to find," Cassie said to Sheriff
Wagy, "just look for an eighteen-wheeler with a smashed-up front
end."

He said, "I don't really appreciate your sarcasm at the moment.
I lost a very valuable member of my team in your room. She's the
first fatality the sheriff's office has ever had."

"I'm glad to hear you're worried about your record," Cassie said
bitterly.

"You didn't even provide a description of the truck," he said.
"Do you know how many eighteen-wheelers are out there on the
road?"

They stood in the parking lot of the Whispering Pines. It was
still hours before the dawn sun would slide over the top ridges of
the eastern mountains. Every sheriff's department vehicle was either
parked on the lot to block the entrances or out on the street to turn
away gawkers. Word of the incident had apparently spread quickly
among the residents of Horston. A photographer from the *Horston
Express* had already been shooed away.

Missing was Deputy Grzegorczyk, whom Cassie had seen
drive by. When he recognized her in the parking lot he kept
going.

The wreckage of unit number eleven was cordoned off with
yellow plastic crime scene tape and lit up by a battery of portable
spotlights borrowed from a construction company by the sheriff's

department. Smoke from the fires in the mountains hung in the beams of light.

The ambulance containing Linda Murdock's mangled body had left the scene two hours before. Cassie had watched in dulled horror as the EMTs lifted beams and debris off her torso and rolled it into a black body bag before lifting it on a gurney. Her body seemed smaller and lighter than when she was alive, and the harsh lighting was cruel to her memory, Cassie thought.

She also watched as several deputies picked through the demolished room. They wore gloves and paper masks and they carried flashlights. Cassie had no idea what they expected to find that could be of any help at all. It's what the sheriff had ordered them to do. One of them found the red wine bottle and lifted it up and shined his beam on it so Wagy could see it.

"So, you two were having a little party?" he asked her.

"Not at all," Cassie said. "I told you exactly what happened."

"Hmm."

"What in the hell is that supposed to mean?"

He shrugged, but the implication was clear.

"The only time I met her was in your office," Cassie said.

"But she was comfortable enough with you to visit you in your hotel room?"

Cassie closed her eyes and tried to keep her anger in check. Her world seemed to be spinning out of control.

She'd told him the sequence of events leading up to the truck taking out the room. He'd listened, but the skeptical look on his face annoyed her.

She told him everything *except* for something she held back. She hadn't told Wagy or any of the deputies that Murdock was there to tell Cassie about Lindy Glode, her stepdaughter. Cassie didn't trust them any more than she trusted Glen Steele, who was on the telephone in his office with his insurance agent.

"We'll find this guy," Wagy said to Cassie. "When we do I wouldn't be surprised to find out he fell asleep at the wheel or was under the influence of drugs and alcohol to cause this accident. He might have taken a wrong turn off the highway and just panicked. Hit the accelerator instead of the brakes—something like that. Once he woke up and realized what he'd done he just kept going."

Wagy had been talking this way since he arrived at the scene, and Cassie was beside herself with rage born of both experience and adrenaline.

Although she fought it, tears filled her eyes.

"It wasn't an accident, I told you that," she said to him. "I watched that truck speed up, not slow down."

"But you didn't see it closely enough to give me a vehicle description," Wagy said.

"He had all of his lights off. I told you that. Look, I was the target. Linda Murdock was just a very unlucky citizen who happened to be in the wrong place at the wrong time."

"A target, huh?" he said. He raised his eyebrows when he said it.

"There's history here," she said. "I once spent several years of my life going after a long-haul trucker who was a serial killer. I know you know the story."

He nodded skeptically. "I've heard," he said. "So, you think this guy came back to life and drove all the way here to target you?"

"I'm not saying it was him. But this was deliberate. It wasn't an accident."

"Then who would do this?" Wagy asked. "Who did you piss off? I mean, besides *everyone* around here?"

"Why won't you do your job?" she asked him. "You don't need every deputy in the department standing around here with nothing to do. Send them out on the road to find that truck. Have you even issued an APB?"

Wagy didn't respond.

She said, "Go talk to your buddy Glen in there. He was spying on my room last night. I saw him. Go ask him why and who he might have talked to about it."

"Glen called it in," Wagy said while he shook his head. "He

was very upset. Are you suggesting he knew that somebody would drive into his hotel and wreck it?"

"I don't know. Maybe you should ask him."

"And maybe you should step aside and let us sort this out," Wagy said. "Just because you worked in law enforcement once doesn't mean you have all the answers when it comes to me doing my job."

He reached into the pocket of his uniform trousers and came out with a Kleenex. He offered it to her.

Cassie slapped it out of his hand.

"Easy there," Wagy cooed. "Calm down."

One of the deputies in the debris held up Cassie's gear bag and displayed it for Sheriff Wagy.

"That's mine," she said. "I need that."

She started striding toward what was left of unit number eleven.

"Hold your horses," Wagy warned. "You've got no business entering a crime scene."

"I thought you said it was an accident," she hissed over her shoulder as she lifted the tape and ducked under it.

She stepped through a tangle of wood, broken ceiling tiles, and wires to retrieve her bag. It was covered with drywall dust but it hadn't been crushed. She looked around for her luggage but she didn't see it. The cheapness of the construction of the room was now exposed to all, she thought. It was as if a matchstick house had been kicked apart. No wonder the truck could blow through it and keep going.

"I'll need to ask you to leave," the deputy said. He wasn't as strident as Wagy had been.

"I want what's mine," she said while moving a piece of interior paneling with her boot toe.

"Sheriff?" the deputy asked. He wanted direction.

Wagy motioned for him to kick her out.

"You need to go now, ma'am," the deputy said.

"When I'm good and ready," she said.

"It's for your own safety," he said. She felt his hand grasp her arm.

She glared at him and she suspected that she looked a little insane. "Don't you dare touch me."

He relaxed his grip. She felt guilty for taking all of her anger and frustration out on him. He was simply following orders from Wagy.

"Okay," she said. "I'll leave. But if you find my suitcase and my overnight bag please return them. They aren't evidence of any kind and I'd like them back."

The deputy nodded.

As she carefully stepped around material to return to the parking lot her right boot was held back by a strand of wire. She bent over to remove it and she gave the wire a tug. A broken light fixture on the other end jumped out of the debris and she reeled it in.

The wire led to a small multidirectional microphone that had been embedded in the overhead light fixture. She studied it and her rage returned.

"See this?" she called to Wagy.

"What is it?"

"It's a fucking mic," she said. "Somebody bugged my room."

Which meant, she realized, that her conversations with Rachel about the case and who she planned to interview in the county had likely been overheard. Every move she'd made was known by someone in advance.

"I wonder how long it's been there?" she asked aloud. "I wonder if it was there when Blake Kleinsasser stayed here?"

Wagy gave no response. He appeared to be thinking of what to say.

"Now maybe you'll have your talk with Glen?" she said, nodding toward the manager's office. "And if you don't, I *will*."

★   ★   ★

Cassie had the microphone in her hand when she pushed through the office door. Sheriff Wagy was a few steps behind her.

Glen Steele was behind the counter and he looked up at her with alarm. He held a handset to his face.

Cassie reached over and pushed down the cradle of the telephone, killing the call.

"Hey," Steele said, "I was talking with my insurance guy."

She slapped the mic down on the counter so he could see it.

"You better have a damned good reason why this was in my room," she said. "Either you're a pervert or you've been keeping tabs on me for other reasons. Which is it?"

Cassie had experienced a similar situation when she was in pursuit of the Lizard King where a gas station owner had installed a secret camera in the women's restroom. She couldn't believe it had happened again.

Steele stepped back and slowly shook his head. He stared at the microphone. "I'm afraid I don't know what you're talking about," he said. She didn't believe him.

"Was there a camera in there, too?"

He continued to shake his head.

"Now I know why you put me in that room," she said.

"It's our best room," he said. Then he added, "It *was* our best room, I mean."

The bell above the door jangled as the sheriff came in behind her.

"Arrest this son of a bitch," Cassie said, pointing at Steele.

"She's a little worked up," Wagy said to Steele.

"I'd say," Steele replied.

"I was almost killed," Cassie said. She jabbed her finger toward the manager. "And this son of a bitch was listening in on my conversations."

"That's crazy," he said.

"Glen," Wagy asked, "Do you know anything about this device she found?" He asked the question in a very reasonable tone.

Steele quickly denied knowing anything about the mic. While he did Cassie noticed that he was looking over her shoulder to Wagy as if she weren't there. She had the suspicion that some kind of silent compact had passed between them, but when she looked over her shoulder at the sheriff he looked away.

"Hold it," Steele said, smacking his forehead with the heel of his hand. "I just remembered something. I know why it was there."

Cassie narrowed her eyes while waiting for the explanation.

Wagy said, "Sheriff, you'll remember a couple years back? The county attorney suspected that a guest in unit eleven was using it to sell meth?"

"I remember," Wagy said.

"They got a warrant to put a bug in there. They told me all about it and even though I pride myself on maintaining the privacy of my customers, I didn't see where I had much choice in the matter. The attorney's office sent a couple of men out here to install it when the guest was out of his room."

"They never got anything they could use in court," Wagy said helpfully to Steele. "I do know that."

"They must have forgotten it was still out there," Steele said. "It's been there the whole time. I'd completely forgotten about it or I would have asked them to come back and remove it."

"That's a lie," Cassie said. "You're lying."

"The sheriff here will confirm my story," Steele said.

Cassie wheeled on him.

Wagy shrugged and said, "He's telling the truth. We were trying to build a case against a drug guy and it didn't pan out. I plumb forgot about that bug in there."

Cassie's chest went cold with sudden realization. She looked at Wagy and back to Steele. They'd obviously settled on their story, and they were supporting each other while telling it.

"So it was *you* listening in," she said to Wagy. "It wasn't Steele.

You keep the mic there and Glen makes sure which guests get that room. First Blake Kleinsasser, and then me."

Wagy made a face suggesting she was out of her mind.

"Who else knew I was using that room?" she asked. "Somebody told the truck driver which one to aim for."

"That's a really dangerous accusation, Miss Dewell," Wagy said. "I think maybe you ought to just calm down and get some rest. You might want to see somebody at the clinic to help you deal with your trauma. I'm happy to make a call over there and let them know you're coming."

"I'm not going anywhere," Cassie replied. Then she asked, "Which one of the Kleinsassers is your boss? John Wayne? Horst himself? Do you answer to Cheyenne as well?"

"Actually," Wagy said, gripping her arm, "you *are* going somewhere. And if you stay here even a minute longer and continue to make accusations and impede the progress of this accident investigation, I'll arrest you and you can spend another night or two in our fine jail."

"Don't touch me," Cassie warned.

But Wagy was fast and he was strong. He spun her toward the counter and he pinned her arms back. She felt the cold metal of handcuffs tightened on her wrists. Wagy leaned into her until his weight held her in place. Then he bent her over until her face was mashed into the top of the counter.

His whisper in her ear was low and menacing. "You'll regret what you just said, you fucking nutjob. If you ever say anything like that again I'll find you and I'll take you out."

She didn't struggle or scream.

He said, "I'm going to take these cuffs off of you now and you're going to walk out there and get in your car and drive away. Go back to Bozeman and don't show your face ever again in my county. Do you understand?"

She nodded that she did.

The pressure of his full weight eased off. She heard the jangle of keys and the handcuffs were removed.

When she turned to face him, his face was once again a stoic mask. Glen Steele, meanwhile, was frozen to his spot behind the counter.

"I worked for years with good honest men in law enforcement," she said to Wagy as she shouldered around him toward the door and stepped outside. She leaned back in to say, "There's nothing worse than a corrupt cop."

She could feel his eyes burning holes in her back as she walked across the parking lot toward her Ford.

Cassie called Rachel on her home number and woke her up.

"You won't believe what just happened," she said.

She told her the whole story.

"You need to get out of there now," Rachel said.

twenty-two

Cassie awoke when her cell phone burred. She thrashed around in bed and for a moment she didn't know where she was. Morning light streamed through the curtains and pooled on the floor and she remembered checking into the Holiday Inn Express in Lolo and paying with cash the night before. She recalled the puzzled expression on the face of the night manager when she said the room needed to be on the top floor or she wouldn't take it.

She finally found her phone buried in the folds of the covers after it had stopped ringing. Ben had called and of course he hadn't left a message.

It was ten thirty in the morning and her head was foggy despite nine hours of sleep. As it cleared, the events of the night before came flooding back and she rubbed at her eyes. It was all still unbelievable and immensely depressing.

The foundation of the case against Blake Kleinsasser was crumbling all around her. The sheriff in charge of the investigation was crooked which meant everything he'd been involved in—the time line, the affidavits, the evidence—was suspect. Witnesses including Jody Haak and Lindy Glode were either avoiding her or hiding out. She'd been spied on by someone. Her car and possessions had been destroyed. The entire Kleinsasser family wanted her gone. The accused was in a coma and might not recover.

And a truck driver had tried to kill her but instead murdered an innocent woman.

You need to get out of there now rang in her ears.

★   ★   ★

"Why aren't you in school?" she asked Ben when he picked up.

"I'm not feeling good today. I'm sick."

He did sound very down and unlike himself, she thought.

"What's wrong?"

"Oh, my stomach. I might have eaten too much."

Despite herself, she smiled.

"Is Isabel okay with you staying home?" Cassie asked.

"I guess. She went to her hot yoga class."

"We've been really missing each other on these calls," Cassie said. "You were going to tell me something the other night and we got cut off."

"By the cops," Ben said.

"Yes, by the cops. So, what was it?"

"It seems like a million years ago now," he said with a sigh.

Cassie sat straight up when he told her about the eighteen-wheeler.

"Did you get a look at the driver?"

"No. He was too high up to see in the window."

"Did you get the license plate number?"

"No, Mom. I didn't even think about it."

"Did you call the police?" she asked.

"Nah. Erin said they'd think we were crazy."

"I don't," Cassie said. "I absolutely believe you."

She debated whether to tell him about the destruction of her motel room and decided against it. She'd tell him later when she returned and they were together. She didn't want to alarm him.

"Have you seen it again?" she asked.

"No."

"Has Erin?"

"She might have. That's what she told me last night."

"Ben," Cassie said, "I'm not really convinced that you're sick enough to stay home. But I'm glad you did."

"Why?"

"I'll explain it all later," she said. "I'm just glad we finally connected. It's been just as crazy here and it's nice to talk with you. It feels so normal."

"Are you coming home?"

"Yes. Probably tonight."

"Good."

She'd just made the decision during the phone call with her son. Cassie would make another attempt to find Lindy Glode and Jody Haak, then return to Bozeman even if she wasn't successful in locating them. It seemed almost pointless now to continue her investigation. All she was really doing was checking off boxes. She'd had enough. She was whipped.

"Is that all that's wrong—that your stomach hurts?" she asked. "I can tell by your voice that something's bothering you."

"You can?"

"I'm your mother. Are you doing all right besides?"

He paused for a long time. "I guess I just don't get girls very well."

"Are you talking about this Erin?"

"Yeah, I guess."

So now she knew who he'd been texting. And who had put him into such a giddy mood for the last week or two.

"Teenage girls are hard to figure out sometimes," she said. "Even mature women are sometimes hard to figure out. Except me, of course."

He laughed weakly at that.

"It's just hard to know what to say," Ben continued. "Or how to know what I should have said, I guess."

"Do you want to tell me about it?"

"Not really. Why would I want to tell my mother about it?"

"Because maybe I can help a little," she said.

He seemed to think about it, then said, "Nah. That's okay."

"You know you can always talk to me," she said.

"Yeah."

"So, rest your stomach and plan to go to school tomorrow. Okay?"

"Okay."

"Don't fight with Isabel."

"That's a little harder to do," he said. She could tell he was smiling.

"And don't worry about Erin," Cassie said. "Girls that age can turn on a dime. You never know why they act a certain way. It may even not have anything at all to do with you."

"Yeah."

She disconnected the call and hugged herself. It was nice to have a hopeful feeling. She loved that boy.

Cassie dressed in the same clothes she'd worn the previous day since her bag was still somewhere under the wreckage of her motel room. Then she made bad coffee in the hotel coffeemaker and opened her laptop on the small table.

She rarely looked at Facebook and never posted anything. Her account was under Dewell Investigations, not her own name. Occasionally, someone would try to contact her there and she had received a couple of pieces of business that way.

Since Jody Haak didn't have a phone or internet, he likely didn't have an account. He didn't look like the type. And he didn't, at least under his own name.

But Lindy Glode of Lolo, Montana, did. She was of the right age. Cassie sent her a friend request. Maybe she'd respond.

Then Cassie checked out Ben's account. She always felt a little guilty when she did so, but not guilty enough to stay away.

She was curious about Erin Reese. She wanted to see a photo of the girl who had broken Ben's heart. She scrolled through Ben's friends and Cassie gasped when she found her.

Erin Reese looked just like Franny Porché. Cassie had seen

photos of Franny in the case file. And she recalled Ben saying his new friend had just moved to Bozeman and was new at the school as well.

Erin Reese *was* Franny Porché.

Cassie shared the profile picture to her phone and attached it to an email to Rachel.

Cheyenne had created a new identity for her daughter and moved her to Bozeman. Whether it was to protect Franny by getting her away from Lochsa County and what had happened there, or away from the Kleinsasser family snake pit, Cassie didn't know.

Perhaps, Cassie thought, the reason might be to hide Franny away from people like Cassie and Rachel.

Rachel called before Cassie left the room. "Is this photo who I think it is?" she asked.

Cassie explained where she'd found it.

"She's been right under our noses the whole time," Rachel said with astonishment. "It does make some sense, though. Cheyenne's stashing Franny away where she can go to school and live a normal life until she's called to testify at trial. Either that, or she's hiding Franny so no one can talk with her about her story."

"My thoughts exactly," Cassie said.

"Does Ben have any idea who she really is?"

"No, and I don't look forward to telling him. He's smitten with her, although he's worried about her right now. He doesn't understand how she's acting or why. It's possible she feels threatened and she's trying to keep him out of it."

Cassie relayed to Rachel what Ben had told her about nearly being mowed down by the semi-truck.

"Do you think it was the same one that went after you?" Rachel asked.

"Who else could it be? It's too hard to conceive of more than one driver doing all this. I think Ben is a target because of *me*. He doesn't know it yet. And Franny might think, given her situation, that the near miss was about her instead of him."

Rachel didn't disagree.

"Where are you now?"

"I'm at the Holiday Inn Express in Lolo."

"Does anyone know you're there?"

"No."

"What about your rental car?"

"I parked it in a safe place and walked," Cassie said. "That's not to say that it hasn't been located by Sheriff Wagy's thugs, but I wouldn't bet on it."

"Good," Rachel said. "Get packed up. Then go get in it and come back."

"There's really nothing to pack. All I've got are the clothes on my back."

"Will you drive straight here?"

"Later today. I promised Ben."

"Thank God you've finally come to your senses," Rachel said. "Look, our firm has good connections with the administration of the school district. Jessica used to represent them and she's personal friends with the superintendent and the principal of the high school. I think we can work through them to make Franny available for an interview."

"Really?"

"I'll take Jessica along to be in the room with me when we talk with her," Rachel said. "You should be there as well."

Cassie said, "That might be a little awkward. Ben's mom interviewing Franny, after all."

"Good point. We don't want to spook her."

"Won't you need permission from Cheyenne?" Cassie asked.

"Who knows? We don't even know Franny's situation here. She might be staying with relatives or friends of the Kleinsassers until she testifies at the trial. I'll try to find out and I'll keep you posted."

★　★　★

Things were moving fast now. Cassie felt a sense of exhilaration that the end of the investigation was in sight. She also hoped that she could make it out of Lochsa County before they closed in on her.

She stepped out of the elevator and walked past the front desk on the way out. It felt odd not having a clothes bag of any kind.

A young woman behind the desk said, "Ma'am, were you in Room 827?"

Cassie looked at her key card because she couldn't remember. The number 827 was written on the sleeve.

"Yes."

"I'm sorry, but the night clerk didn't check you in properly."

"I paid cash."

"Yes, but he didn't get an ID."

"That's okay," Cassie said as she walked out through the double glass doors.

The morning was warm and it was even smokier than it had been. It felt more like dusk than mid-morning as Cassie looked for oncoming cars before crossing the highway. She didn't see any, and she was grateful. Cassie had the feeling there were lots of people looking for her, which is why she hadn't presented her driver's license at the front desk the night before. The extra twenty she'd given the night clerk helped him forget about that step.

There wasn't a sidewalk on the other side of the highway and she followed a trail two blocks south to the used car lot where she'd parked her rental Ford. There had been an opening between two pickups for sale and she'd left it there, thinking that local law enforcement wouldn't cruise a used car lot to look for her rental.

As she passed through a stand of pine trees toward the lot something crashed from within the brush. Cassie jumped back and dug into her handbag for her Glock, her heart whumping in her chest.

Something big and dark pushed through the tangle and she trained her weapon on it.

It was a lone cow elk and the creature's left side was blackened by fire, the hide burned down to cracked black skin. The elk saw Cassie at the same time and froze, her nostrils enlarging and her eyes widening.

"Poor girl," Cassie said, lowering her handgun.

The elk snorted and pivoted on her hind feet and smashed through the cover. Cassie could hear its hooves pounding through the timber until she could no longer see it.

The elk was singed, but still alive. Cassie felt a kinship with her.

Cassie walked through two rows of vehicles and used her key fob to unlock the Explorer from twenty feet away. A salesman in a short-sleeved dress shirt and tie appeared from a low-slung office.

"Is that your car?" he asked her.

"Yes."

"You left it here?"

"I did."

"Well, that solves the mystery of the morning," he said.

"Thanks for not selling it to anyone." She smiled as she climbed in and drove away.

From her car, she called the Lochsa County Assessor's office.

Since her arrival, Cassie had played fair and followed the rules. That was over. Rules no longer applied when the people she was up against were venal and corrupt. She could hear the words of her mentor Cody Hoyt in her mind.

You'll find, Cassie, that it's us against the world. . . .

"Hi," she said. "I'm Sandra with UPS. We're trying to deliver a package to a rural resident named Jody Haak. That's spelled H-A-A-K. Unfortunately, the address has only a post office box and we need his physical address for delivery. I've tried to reach Mr. Haak with no luck. Is there any way you can help me since he sends his property tax check to you?"

"Well, this is kind of an unusual request," the woman on the other end said. She sounded matronly, Cassie thought.

"The problem is," Cassie said, "I think it's a food delivery of some kind and there's an expiration date on it. We'd hate for it to spoil."

There was a long pause, then a sigh. The woman said, "Just a second and I'll look it up."

"Thank you so much."

Cassie wrote down the address on the back of her rental car folder.

Then she called the Lochsa County Sheriff's Department. A man answered, and Cassie recalled the large jowly deputy she'd met running the evidence room and she thought the voice sounded like his.

She made her own tone high and breathy and she hoped he wouldn't recognize her.

"I just heard that my friend Linda Murdock was involved in a horrible accident last night. I've called around and no one seems to know where her body was taken. Can you please help me out?"

"Hold on," the man said.

He came back in less than a minute. "Ma'am, her body was taken to Hamilton Mortuary and Chapel."

"That's in Hamilton, then?"

"Yes, ma'am. We don't have a funeral home here in Horston or anywhere in the county."

"Thank you. That's very good to know."

She disconnected before he could ask her name.

Hamilton was twenty miles south, just beyond Corvallis on the highway. After trading her rental in for another make and model that wasn't yet known to law enforcement, she'd drive straight through Lochsa County and out the other side.

Hamilton Mortuary and Chapel was a few miles farther south. Jody Haak lived somewhere farther up a mountain road. She had the address.

With luck, she could be on the road back home by late afternoon.

twenty-three

Cassie drove through Horston in her new car, a Honda
CRV with Nevada plates, wearing sunglasses and a complimentary ball cap from the rental agency. She didn't see any sheriff's department vehicles and no one pulled her over. She didn't begin to breathe easily until she drove past the Lochsa County line. She kept an eye out for the injured cow elk but didn't see her again. The heavy smoke hung in the trees as if being pushed down from above by a giant hand. Her throat was raw from breathing it.

The Hamilton Mortuary was on Main Street a block west of the small downtown. It had a façade made of logs and a sign beneath that read, CARING FOR YOUR LOVED ONES SINCE 1978.

She turned off the engine and checked her face in the rearview mirror. The bags under her eyes were annoying but she no longer had her makeup kit so there was nothing she could do to fix her look. She sighed and climbed out. There were four other cars in the parking lot, all with Montana plates.

The reception area was somber and hushed. Gentle Muzak played at very low volume, although she recognized the song as "Every Breath You Take" by the Police. She thought it was an inappropriate choice for a funeral home, but it was such an anodyne version that it probably didn't draw much notice.

A plump woman in her sixties sat behind a desk. She had glasses with faux tortoiseshell frames and tight curls of silver hair. A kindly smile was part of her ensemble.

"May I help you?" she asked gently.

"I'm here to pay my respects to Linda Murdock. I understand she's here."

The woman nodded that she was. "Are you with the family?"

Cassie couldn't make herself lie or come up with a ruse. The seriousness of the situation almost overwhelmed her, and she felt guilty for being there. After all, she'd thought that if there was any chance to finally meet face-to-face with Lindy Glode, her step-mother's death might smoke her out. But Linda Murdock was a real human being and she deserved respect. She was a wife to a disabled husband and the stepmother of a likely grieving stepdaugh-ter. And she'd died because she came to Cassie to offer informa-tion and help.

Cassie was exploiting the situation.

"I'm not with the family," Cassie said. "I was with Linda when she was . . . killed."

"It was a horrible accident," the woman said. "It was a real trag-edy what happened."

It wasn't an accident, Cassie wanted to say but didn't.

"Have they found the driver?" the woman asked.

They aren't even looking for him.

Instead, Cassie asked, "Is the family here?"

The woman nodded. "We have a grieving room. It's a place for the family to gather and mourn the deceased before funeral ar-rangements are made."

"Is it in the back?"

At that point Cassie envisioned entering a room as a stranger while Murdock's loving family sought comfort from each other. It was as inappropriate as the song being piped through the facility. If the woman behind the desk asked Cassie to leave the premises, Cassie was okay with it.

"Lyle is back there with them in case they need anything," the woman said. "Maybe you can check with him."

"Lyle?"

"Lyle is my husband. We own and manage Hamilton Mortuary and Chapel."

"Thank you."

The hallway was dark and her footfalls were cushioned by thick pile carpeting that, she guessed, had not been updated since the building had opened.

A man approximately the age of the woman at the receptionist desk sat in a high-backed wooden chair outside of a closed door. He wore a suit and his trouser cuffs were hiked up to reveal bands of white ankle. He quickly pocketed the smartphone he was looking at when Cassie appeared.

"Lyle?" she asked.

"Yes. May I help you?"

His voice was low and preternaturally soothing. It was well-practiced and likely beneficial for his line of work, and Cassie fought the urge to ask him questions that would require long answers just to hear his voice.

"Is the Murdock family inside?" she asked, gesturing toward the door.

"Yes."

"Is Lindy Glode with them?"

"I'm sorry," he said, "but Lindy is quite bereaved and she asked me to screen any visitors with a couple of questions."

"Go ahead."

"Are you with law enforcement?" he asked.

The question surprised her and it must have showed.

"No."

"Are you here representing the Kleinsasser family?"

"Absolutely not."

She stepped forward and handed Lyle one of her cards.

He read it and asked, "Couldn't this be done at a later time?"

"I wish it could," Cassie said. "If she doesn't want to talk to me there's nothing I can do about it. I'll leave quietly. I know this must be a very difficult time for her.

"But when you give her the card please tell her something for me. I was there last night. Her stepmother came to see me to tell me something important. I was the only eyewitness to what happened and Lindy might have questions about the . . . incident. Her stepmother seemed like a very nice person who was trying to do the right thing. I might be able to provide some answers to questions she might have."

She deliberately refrained from using the word "closure." She hated that word for a reason. When the military liaison showed up at her door to break the news about the death of Jim overseas, they said they were there to provide "closure." It was a word they'd been taught to say, she guessed. But Jim's death brought no closure at all. Instead, for a pregnant woman without a job at the time, it opened up a terrifying new world for her.

Lyle looked back at the card, then again at Cassie. Then he gathered himself up without a word and slipped into the grieving room and closed the door.

Cassie had been right about finding Lindy Glode. But she didn't feel good about doing it.

She leaned back against the wall and waited. She couldn't hear the words but Lyle's soothing tone filtered through the paneling.

Cassie expected Lyle to emerge from the room, hand her back her card, and tell her that Lindy was too upset to consent to a meeting. Instead, the door opened and Lindy emerged with Lyle.

Lindy Glode was exactly what Cassie had imagined her to be: blond, thin, and curvy with blue eyes and a hard set to her mouth. She looked like she'd fit right in at the Hayloft. She also seemed frail; either hungover or truly overcome with emotion.

She said to Lyle, "Give us a minute, will you?"

★ ★ ★

"Thank you for seeing me and I'm very sorry about the timing. I'll try to keep this short." Cassie said.

Glode nodded. "I appreciate that. Lyle said you claimed you were there last night."

"I was. I saw it."

Glode looked up and her eyes flashed. "What the fuck happened? It doesn't make sense to me that a big truck just drove off the highway and plowed through a motel and kept going." As she talked Cassie noticed how Glode pounded her right fist into her left palm with pure frustration.

"No, it doesn't make sense if you think of it as an accident. I know that's what the sheriff is claiming, but—"

"I don't trust anything that man says," Glode cut in. "He's bought and paid for."

"So I gather. I'd classify what happened as a homicide. What I can't determine at this point is if the driver was aiming for me or your stepmother or both."

Lindy Glode stopped pounding her fist. The implication of what Cassie just said took her aback.

"Why would someone want to kill Linda?"

"I don't know."

"Why would they want to kill you?"

"I've turned over a lot of rocks since I've been here. No one seems to like that."

"What happened last night?"

Cassie told Lindy Glode the story as briefly as she could, from meeting her stepmother at the sheriff's department to the incident the night before.

Glode listened closely and sadly shook her head while doing so. At the conclusion, she said, "It sounds just like them."

"Them?" Cassie asked.

"You know who I'm talking about."

"The Kleinsassers?"

Glode nodded her head. Then she smiled slightly. "You know that detail about you going to get soda and ice? That sounds just like her. The sweeter the drink the better as far as she was concerned. I used to tell her to learn to drink like a real woman, and she'd just laugh at me. Who knew it would be the death of her?"

Or what saved my life, Cassie thought but didn't say.

"She wanted to quit that job she had," Glode said. "I hope that wasn't the reason they went after her. But it was hard for her to give up the benefits. My dad is disabled."

"I understand. I know it's not much consolation but she died quickly. She didn't suffer."

"That happens when a truck tire rolls over your head," Glode said bitterly.

"Do you have any idea what she wanted to tell me?" Cassie asked. "She led off by saying you two were related."

"Yeah. I think she heard you were looking for me. I heard the same thing. She was worried about me."

"Why was she worried?"

"I think she heard something at her job to make her worried. Maybe she wanted you to find me before the sheriff did. You know, because of that thing I had with Blake."

"They might have found out that I wanted to talk with you because the room was bugged," Cassie said. "I found the device."

"That doesn't surprise me at all. It sounds like something they'd do."

"Did your mom know where you were living?"

"No," Glode said. "I move around a lot. I stay with friends. She didn't know exactly where I was but she knew who to ask. We kept in contact through text messages."

"I do that with my own son," Cassie said. She wasn't sure why she said it.

"Yeah, well. It looks like they got to her before they got to me."

"And all of this was because of Blake?"

"No doubt in my mind."

Cassie studied Glode's face and tried to put things together. She was having trouble understanding what Lindy was telling her.

"What is it they wanted?" Cassie asked. "Do you have information that would benefit Blake's case? Is that why you were hiding?"

Glode shrugged. "They seem to think so. Or at least, that's what I was told by someone who was in the position to know."

"Who would that be?"

"Cheyenne Porché," Glode said. "She was a customer at the bar. She told me her brothers were worried about me and she said I should disappear for a while."

This was information Cheyenne hadn't shared.

"That makes no sense," Cassie said. "Cheyenne should want Blake prosecuted more than anyone else. Do you know why she told you that?"

"No. But I believed her. Especially when Rand and Sheriff Wagy came by the Hayloft the next night and asked about me. Lucky for me, I'd taken the night off. And I haven't been back since."

"And you don't know why they were trying to find you?"

"No," she said. "I don't. I told the prosecutor and Blake's old lawyer everything I remembered. I wasn't with Blake the night it happened. Half of the time we were together I really can't even remember, to be honest. I don't think Blake does, either."

"He doesn't," Cassie said. "He said he was mostly blacked out the time you two were together."

Glode snorted. "That's not exactly what a girl wants to hear— that the man she was with for forty-eight hours straight can't remember a damned thing about it. But Blake is Blake, I guess. I know he's an asshole, but I got along with him. I guess I like assholes. My track record is filled with them."

"I've got a few in my past," Cassie conceded. "So you don't

recall anything Blake said or did that would be relevant to the charges?"

"Not that I can remember," Glode said. "Like I said, it's all kind of hazy. We drank, we fucked, then we drank some more."

Cassie tried not to react to the bluntness of her statement.

She asked, "Did he ever come across to you as someone capable of raping his niece?"

Glode shrugged again. "He didn't seem like that kind of guy, but who knows? I know sometimes I have blind spots. Like, why was I hanging out with the guy in the first place? We both knew it wasn't going to go anywhere. As for Franny, I don't remember him talking about her very much except to say that he liked her more than the others."

"In what way?" Cassie asked while narrowing her eyes.

"Not in that way," Glode said with a shake of her head. "Blake said he liked Franny because she didn't seem to have what he called the Kleinsasser gene."

"What does that mean? The Kleinsasser gene?"

"I think he meant she wasn't toxic."

"Ah."

Glode said, "I do remember getting kind of paranoid when I was with Blake. I'd see a sheriff car parked down the street from the bar, or I'd see John Wayne or Rand out of the corner of my eye. Blake just laughed about it because he said his family suspected he was back to do them some kind of harm, which he said he wasn't. He all but convinced me I was paranoid and losing it."

Cassie urged her to continue.

"I know all about the bad blood between Blake and his family. Everybody does around here. Maybe I was just sort of imagining things. But at the time I had the feeling they were shadowing us as we went from bar to bar and back to the motel."

"Did you tell the prosecutor or lawyer about that feeling?"

"No," she said. "I knew how nuts it sounded. Plus, they weren't asking me about my feelings. They just wanted me to confirm I was with Blake for two full days leading up to the arrest, which I was."

"Obviously," Cassie said, "those feelings you had were strong enough that you listened to Cheyenne when she told you to run and hide."

"Obviously," Glode repeated. "I mean, they must have figured Blake told me something they didn't want me to repeat. I've beaten my head against the wall trying to figure out what that might be but for the life of me I can't come up with anything. We just talked about life and drinking and fucking, like I said."

"Got it," Cassie said. "When you say you knew they were probably following Blake around, what exactly do you mean?"

"I know they were," she said. "I caught them."

Cassie didn't understand.

"After the second night we were together," she said, "I left his room that morning and realized I'd left my cell phone there. I was *really* hungover. I went back to the Whispering Pines in my car because obviously I couldn't call Blake to ask him if he'd found it. But when I got there he'd already left for the day and they were searching his room."

Cassie felt hair prick up on the back of her neck. "Who was searching his room?"

"There was a deputy there inside the room. The manager was standing outside. He must have let the cop in, is what I thought at the time."

"Can you identify the deputy?"

"He has an unpronounceable name," she said. "Gregor-something. I've seen him around. He still works for the sheriff, which means he works for the Kleinsassers."

"The manager was Glen Steele?"

"I guess. I really didn't meet him. Oh, and I saw John Wayne and Rand there, too. They were sitting together in a pickup. They left when I showed up."

"What happened next?" Cassie asked.

"I told the manager I'd left my phone in the room and he told the cop I was coming in."

"Did they say why they were searching the room?"

"No, and I didn't ask. Like I said, I was so hungover. And after spending all that time with Blake, I'd had my fill of Kleinsasser drama. I just wanted to go home and sleep it off."

"Lindy, did you see anything unusual in the room? What was Deputy Grzegorczyk doing?"

"He was on his hands and knees looking under the bed. In fact, he was the one who found my phone. It was on the floor. He handed it to me and I went on my way."

"And this was the morning of the assault, correct?"

"Yeah, but of course I didn't know it at the time," she said.

Cassie observed that Glode was tired and running out of steam. She understood. The girl had been through a lot.

"This is all really interesting," Cassie said. "Thank you. Is there anything else you can recall?"

"Not really. I'm exhausted."

"You have my card," Cassie said. "If you think of anything please give me a call."

Glode sighed. She said, "Honestly, I probably won't. I think I'm hitting the bricks as soon as the funeral is over. I really don't want to stay here anymore. I need a fresh start somewhere—maybe Seattle. I hear it's cool. Don't tell the Kleinsassers."

Cassie grinned and hugged her. "I won't," she said.

Cassie was nearly to the lobby when she stopped. She turned back around slowly. Lindy Glode had returned to the grieving room and Lyle was making his way back to his chair.

Cassie suddenly recalled the condition of unit eleven immediately after she'd checked in. Before Glen did a thorough cleaning.

She returned to the alcove in front of the grieving room.

"I need to ask Lindy one more thing," she said to Lyle.

Lyle sighed. "Haven't you taken up enough of her time?"

"Please."

Lyle sighed and stuck his head in the room. Without being asked, he trudged away as Lindy Glode came out.

"I need to ask you a very personal question," Cassie said.

Glode screwed up her face as if expecting anything.

"When you and Blake had sex in the room at the Whispering Pines, did he use a condom?"

Glode's shoulders relaxed and she smiled. Cassie could only guess what the girl had been anticipating.

"Of course he did," she said. "I always insist on it. None of them like to, of course. But it's a deal-breaker for me. I don't want STDs and I sure as hell don't want a baby. Can you imagine me as a mother?"

Cassie ignored the question. "Do you have any idea what Blake did with the condom when you were done?"

"Which time?" she asked with a devilish grin.

"Anytime."

"He got rid of it, I guess."

Cassie said, "Did he go to the bathroom and flush it away? Did he toss it in the waste can? Please try to remember. This is important,"

She shook her head. "I really can't remember. I was probably mixing up a new cocktail at the time."

"Is it possible he dropped one on the floor?" Cassie asked.

"Anything's possible, I guess. He was pretty sloppy by that point as well. Why are you asking me these questions?"

"Because when I checked into that same room there was an old condom wrapper on the floor. Under the bed. Maybe at one point there was a used condom there as well."

Glode winced. "That's kind of gross."

"It is," Cassie agreed, "But it would be a really efficient way of collecting Blake's semen."

Lindy Glode furrowed her brow. She didn't understand what Cassie was getting at.

"Plus," Cassie said, "They'd know what took place in that room between you and Blake. They'd know what to look for because they'd listened to you when you were in there."

"That's really sick," Glode said.

"It's likely even more than that."

twenty-four

⊷══◉══⊷

Still reeling from her conversation with Lindy Glode, Cassie drove south from Hamilton on US-93 into a bank of smoke so thick it triggered the automatic headlights on her rental car. She'd plugged Jody Haak's address—2952 County Road 38—into her phone to find out that it didn't officially exist. The graphic on the screen suggested the closest address to the one she keyed in for Haak was 2800 CR-38. Nevertheless, she planned to follow the route where it took her and hope she'd somehow find his place. It wasn't the first time for Cassie that an obscure rural address didn't produce a satisfactory exact destination from her GPS in Montana.

Because of the smoke, Cassie drove well under the speed limit. She checked her side and rearview mirrors obsessively, hoping not to see a Lochsa County sheriff's department vehicle or a Kleinsasser ranch truck. If either were following her she couldn't see them due to the poor visibility.

She connected with Rachel as she neared her turnoff for the county road that would take her deep into the mountains and over the top of Skalkhano Pass. Cassie glanced at a notice stapled to a wooden sign ordering residents along the road to evacuate due to the fire ahead.

When Rachel answered on the first ring, Cassie said, "The case against Blake might be falling apart. That's not to say he didn't do it, but the prosecution's case isn't the slam dunk we thought it was."

She relayed what she'd learned from Lindy Glode. Rachel's silence on the other end spoke volumes—she was hanging on to Cassie's every word.

When she was through, Rachel said, "Do you think Lindy would testify to what she told you?"

"I'm not sure. She seems ready to get out of this county as soon as her stepmother's funeral is over. I got the impression she wants to wash her hands of all things Kleinsasser."

"I don't blame her," Rachel said. "But we need to get her someplace safe where no one can get to her. Do you think you could convince her to ride with you here? We can put her up in a nice place."

"I can try."

"Please do," Rachel said. "Her testimony could be dynamite."

"Agreed. Now think about it," Cassie said to Rachel. "There are four foundational pieces of evidence they have to convict him: the semen on her clothes, the whiskey glass in the line shack with his fingerprints on it, the tire tracks from his rental car, and Franny's affidavit.

"So far, we've found out that Franny's clothing is missing but that DNA result is still pretty strong evidence on its own. But if the DNA came from a discarded condom found in the motel room, well, that's a big problem for them. We probably can't prove it unless somebody confesses, but it's big."

"It's unbelievable, is what it is," Rachel said. "I could drive a truck through that hole in their case."

"Then there's the glass," Cassie said. "I have no doubt at all that Blake's fingerprints are all over it. But how many glasses did he use when he went barhopping with Lindy Glode during his blackout drunk period? If he was being followed like Lindy thinks they were, anyone could have collected a glass or two from his table after he left the place.

"Three," Cassie said, "Blake didn't deny ever going to that line

264 C. J. BOX

shack this summer. In fact, he mentioned to us that he drove to it to see if it was still there after all these years. There wasn't any rain here this summer, which is one of the reasons we have all the fires. His tracks could have been made days or even weeks before the assault accusation.

"What I'm saying," Cassie continued, "is that the whole case looks different if you consider that Blake might have been set up the whole time. And if the Lochsa County sheriff and his thugs were working with the Kleinsassers, which appears to be what happened, the whole scenario the prosecution has laid out falls apart.

"The enmity the family has for Blake is well-documented. That goes to motivation."

"I can see it," Rachel said. "You're sounding more and more like a defense lawyer all the time. This has reasonable doubt written all over it."

Cassie responded as if slapped. The last thing she ever wanted to hear was that she was sounding like a defense lawyer.

Then Rachel said, "This is all important, except for one big fat problem."

"Franny's statement," Cassie replied.

"Exactly."

"Have you set up an interview with her yet?"

"I've run into complications with that, but now they seem to make a little more sense," Rachel said.

Cassie waited for the explanation and she hoped Rachel would get on with it. The county road she was on wound up through the eastern mountains into the teeth of the fire. She wasn't sure how much longer she'd have a strong cell signal.

"Cheyenne didn't hide Franny away like we assumed," Rachel said. "Apparently, according to the school, Franny was taken from her mom by the Montana Child and Family Services Division for her own safety and placed in a foster home. I don't know the circumstances because it's under seal, but she was assigned a guardian ad litem in Bozeman."

"*What?* Why didn't we know about this?"

"It was kept confidential because she's fifteen," Rachel said. "I had to pry that information out of my friends at the school district, and they probably shouldn't have even told me. But in order to talk to Franny, I need permission from the guardian ad litem and I don't have a name yet."

Cassie was puzzled. "For her own safety?" she repeated. "Who did she fear?"

"I don't know."

"My money would be on her uncles or grandfather," Cassie said. This, she thought, might explain Cheyenne's odd reaction to Cassie's request to speak to Franny. But why would Cheyenne want to protect the siblings she despised, especially if they threatened her daughter?

Cassie put her thinking into words to Rachel.

"Again, I don't know," Rachel said. "It doesn't make sense to me, either, except that there is a lot more going on here than we realized. We seem to be witnessing the Olympics of family dysfunction, right here in Montana."

Rachel went on to say that prior to Cassie's call, she'd had a conversation with the neurosurgeon in the hospital who was overseeing Blake Kleinsasser's injuries.

"They're going to put him into a drug-induced coma until the swelling on his brain goes down," Rachel said. "It may or may not work. The doctor said he gave it a five percent chance that Blake will ever recover."

Cassie shook her head, not sure of what to say or think.

"Are we still working for him?" she asked.

"Unclear at this point," Rachel answered. "I'd say yes, we proceed. Think of it this way: we're working for truth and justice, whether or not Blake comes out of this."

"I like that," Cassie said. "It's better than saying I sound like a defense lawyer."

"I thought you would," Rachel said with a sigh. Cassie could imagine her rolling her eyes as she said it.

"Oh," Rachel said, "I almost forgot. After we talked this morning I called the DCI and made a formal request for an investigation of law enforcement in Lochsa County. I got the strong impression they might have been waiting for someone like me to get the ball rolling."

The Division of Criminal Investigation for the State of Montana was the agency that not only certified law enforcement officers, but it was the one entity that had the mandate and authority to look into malfeasance at a local or county level.

"Good call," Cassie said.

"Which is one more reason why you need to get out of there as fast as you can," Rachel said. "My guess is that Sheriff Wagy is not going to like it when DCI agents show up."

Then Rachel asked, "What turned it for you? What happened that made you start thinking of this whole case a hundred and eighty degrees differently than when you started?"

"I just followed the evidence," Cassie said. "There's a big difference working with law enforcement when they want to help you and when they want to obstruct what you're doing. Then when that truck drove through my room and killed that poor woman, I knew they thought I was getting too close to the truth—whatever it is.

"The thing is," Cassie said, "they overplayed their hand. If they all would have just cooperated and stepped aside, I think I would have proceeded and concluded that the case was a little sloppy but it was as solid as it looked at first. There were red flags like the missing underwear, but there are *always* red flags. But they had to keep overdoing it, like destroying my car and putting me in jail for the night. They thought they'd chase me off."

"They were messing with the wrong woman," Rachel said.

Cassie blushed and changed the subject. "I still don't know where the truck driver fits, though. I don't know if he's somehow involved or on an entirely separate track."

"I only heard half of that," Rachel said through popping static.

Cassie pulled over to the shoulder of the road and checked her phone. She had only one bar of cell reception.

"Can you hear me?" she asked.

There was no response, followed by a prompt that said NO SERVICE.

"Shit," she cursed.

Cassie realized she'd been in such intense discussion with Rachel that she hadn't paid enough attention to her surroundings. The paved two-track road had given way to gravel, and it climbed and wound up into the mountains following the curves of a nearly dry creek. The canyon walls on both sides were nearly vertical. Smoke poured down through the canyon from fires on both sides like a current of water through a chute.

The fire was close although she couldn't see it clearly because of the smoke. It produced an eerie orange glow ahead, and ash fell on the hood of her car and the windshield.

She checked her GPS to see that the address she'd settled on was less than two miles farther up the road. She assumed Haak's property would be near it—if it was even his property at all. And if he had remained in his house despite the posted fire evacuation orders.

When her rearview mirror suddenly filled with the headlights of a massive truck coming up the road behind her Cassie's heart pounded with panic. She felt the power and weight of the vehicle vibrating through her rental and she gripped the steering wheel and held her breath. She braced for a violent rear-end collision.

But instead of the eighteen-wheeler she feared, it was a heavy mountain fire truck. It shot past and she got a glimpse of a fire-fighter in the passenger seat gesturing for her to turn around.

She gave a "will do," wave to him and waited for the truck to vanish into the smoke. When it did, she eased back onto the road with her phone on her lap and continued on.

twenty-five

∘══◦══∘

Cassie drove past a turn-in for 2800 that was marked only by a dented rural mailbox. She couldn't see a home on the end of the road because of the thick trees and hanging smoke. She decided to go another mile in search of an additional road that might lead to 2952.

The conditions were getting worse the farther she drove up into the canyon. Not only ash but live embers floated through the air.

She nearly drove past it—an unmarked path off the right side of the road that led into a thick wall of trees. There was not even a mailbox, but she noted fresh tire tracks in the ruts. Cassie backed up, dropped the transmission into drive, and took the road.

It curved through two walls of pines on either side of the road and when she saw that the crowns of the trees she was driving under were actively inflamed she accelerated. A short burning branch fell across the hood of her rental and landed with a shower of sparks. She pushed through because she sensed a clearing ahead of her where she hoped she could turn around. The acceleration of the car caused the burning branch to roll off the hood and to the side of the road.

Paint blistered on the hood of her car from the heat of the fire and smoke filled the interior. Taking the two-track had been a mistake, she concluded.

A smudge appeared ahead that became a small log home as she neared it. There were a pair of pickup trucks parked near the front and a flatbed trailer was on the side of the home. She recalled that Frank in the Corvallis Tavern had been there because he wanted to borrow a flatbed from Jody Haak.

And there he was in the flesh: Jody Haak standing in the front lawn of the structure wearing a battered straw cowboy hat and bib overalls. He was arcing a stream of water from a hose at the roof of the house to wet it down. His back was to Cassie as she drove up although she'd seen his profile as he glanced to the side.

She parked and got out. She could hear the roar of the fire up in the canyon. It sounded like a jet engine. Embers floated through the air and landed on the moistened shake shingles of Haak's house, where they extinguished with sharp hissing sounds.

A yellow piece of heavy equipment roared around the side of the house. It was a skid-steer loader and it was plowing up a ditch in the dark loam. She couldn't see who was driving it.

"Jody Haak?" she called out.

The man froze. The stream of water from his hose wavered for a moment. Then he turned and shook his head.

"You found me," he said. "How in the hell did you do that?"

She didn't explain.

"Is there anything I can do to help you save your house?" she asked.

"I appreciate the offer. I could use some help. But for right now, just stay out of the way of that skid steer," Haak said. "We're building a firebreak."

Cassie stepped back and watched as the loader passed between them. The blade churned up dark soil and exposed rocks and lengths of white tree roots that looked like bony fingers. As it went by she got a full look at the driver.

Alf Grzegorczyk, out of uniform and wearing soot-covered jeans and a cowboy shirt, tipped the brim of a ball cap to her as he went by. He had a sly smile on his face and he seemed to enjoy her look of befuddlement.

★　★　★

Cassie assisted, as directed, by moving heavy plastic containers of fuel from a shed alongside the house and placing them in a creek that snaked through the property. She noted that the water in the creek was warm and murky with ash, but at least the fuel wouldn't ignite and take out the shed and the home. Her clothes and hands were filthy with dirt and soot.

The fire seemed to pass right over them from the top, igniting the crowns of the pines but largely not burning to the lower branches or to the floor of the valley. It created its own environment as it moved, heating up channels of rushing hot air and swirling through the timber. One line of flame did drop to the dry pine needles and yellow grass, and it flew along the surface toward the house until it met with the freshly upturned soil of the firebreak, where it stopped and went out.

Next, she found another spigot and hose behind the home and wetted down a four-foot-high stack of split firewood. The light pine turned dark as she soaked it. But it didn't catch on fire from the floating embers.

In the distance, she could hear the rumble of mountain fire trucks on the road. They were racing down the canyon to try and head off the flames, she guessed.

The worst of it was over for now.

Cassie found Jody Haak and Alf Grzegorczyk sitting on opposite sides of a splintered picnic table in Haak's front yard. They were drinking cans of Coors beer and there was a small plastic cooler on the tabletop between them.

She approached tentatively. "Why didn't you evacuate?" she asked. "I saw the orders on the way up."

Haak shrugged. "Where would I go? If you didn't already figure it out, I prefer to keep a real low profile since I got back. Showing up at the high school gym with a bunch of locals who know me didn't seem like a very smart move. Word gets around here pretty fast, you know."

"I've learned," she said. "Who are you hiding from?"

"I think we saved the place," Haak said, ignoring her question. "Thank you for pitching in like that."

She nodded. Her eyes were on Grzegorczyk. He didn't seem hostile.

"Join us and have a beer," Haak said. "You deserve it."

"I think I'll pass on the beer."

"That's right," Haak said. "If you're a wine gal. I might have a bottle or two in the house."

He started to get up but Cassie said, "Really, I'm fine."

"Suit yourself." He settled back down.

"I was hoping I could ask you a few questions," she said.

"I figured as much."

Haak and Grzegorczyk exchanged a look. Whatever was conveyed resulted in Grzegorczyk rising from the table and turning back toward the skid steer.

"Guess I'll churn up some more ground," he said while snatching another beer from the cooler.

She waited for him to go, then took his place at the table.

"We have a little history," she said.

"I'm aware of it," Haak said with a slight smile. "But Alf's a good guy. You may have him all wrong."

"Maybe not."

Haak shrugged. Oddly enough, she thought, the man looked more bemused and relaxed—even with the forest fire all around him—than she remembered from seeing him at the bar. It was as if he was resigned to her being there. She thought that she might be able to use his resignation to her benefit.

"He quit, you know," Haak said as he nodded toward Grzegorczyk's back.

"The sheriff's department?"

"Yes."

"Because of what he did to me?" she asked.

Haak looked long and hard at her. "No," he said, "because of what he didn't do to you."

She narrowed his eyes at him, not understanding.

"You spent the night in jail," Haak said. "You weren't supposed to ever get there."

"What does that mean?"

"You were supposed to disappear, never to be heard from again. Alf couldn't go through with it. He's the reason you're here today."

"What do you mean—disappear?"

Haak took a long drink from his can of beer, then opened another. "Lochsa County has more than its share of missing persons. If you did a deep dive in the records over the years you'd find that out. I'd guess that more people go missing per capita in Lochsa County than anyplace else in Montana, including the reservations. It's been happening for years."

"My God," Cassie said. "It's the Kleinsassers?"

"They run everything," Haak said. "It would be hard to prove, but that's the way things work around here. That's the way they've *always* worked."

"How can you be so sure?"

"Because I used to be one of 'em," Jody Haak said.

"Tell me about it," Cassie said. "And I just might have a beer."

He nodded his approval.

Jody Haak worked for the Iron Cross Ranch as the foreman for twenty-six years, he said. He was hired by Horst II when he returned to the valley after serving in the U.S. Navy, and for most of those years he was the only permanent employee on the ranch. Horst II preferred that Haak use transients when he needed manpower rather than full-time employees for tax reasons—they were paid in cash—and because transients could be cut loose quickly and without process if they got too familiar with the operation or started asking too many questions. It was the standard operating procedure on the ranch since it had been founded.

"That's something you might find a little hard to believe," Haak said, "but the Iron Cross has never been a prosperous ranch. They're land-rich but cash-poor. The only way they could stay in operation was to shoestring it and do everything they could to have their fingers in everything that happened in the county. Jakob learned early on that if it was a level playing field his whole ranch would go under in a hurry. So, they had to control things: the county government, the school system, the adjuster's office—everything."

"The sheriff's department," Cassie added.

"Oh, yes," he said. "There hasn't been a sheriff in that county that wasn't handpicked by the family in years. Same goes with the county attorney, Horston's mayor, the bankers, and most of the business owners. People who don't like it move out or they disappear. It's just the way it goes around here. Jakob and Horst would rather control everything than let the free market work. That's why this whole valley is booming except for Lochsa. You can see it as you drive from south to north."

Cassie nodded for him to go on.

"When I got married to Cindy Lou we moved out on the ranch to a damned fine house," he said. "Horst made sure I was happy and we had a hell of a deal. I had a free house, free beef, free transportation, and enough cash to live pretty good. I kind of felt privileged. I'll admit that I liked it when I was younger. Everybody in Horston knew I was the man from the Iron Cross, and they treated me with the same kind of respect they treated Horst or Margaret or the kids. I kind of let it go to my head, which is something I feel like shit about now."

"Why you?" Cassie asked.

Haak nodded. "I sometimes wondered the same thing myself.

Cindy Lou, too. I mean, I *was* a good ranch manager. I was a tough negotiator when the cattle buyers showed up, and I maximized profits on every sale. I learned to hire folks who wouldn't stir up the family, and I cut them loose fast if they screwed up. I protected the interests of the Kleinsassers in every way, and I was rewarded for it."

As he spoke, Cassie could see that his thoughts were wandering off a little. She wondered if there was something he was trying to say but steering clear of it.

"I'd do stuff for 'em I really regret," Haak said, shaking his head. "It's too late now, but I wish I could take many of the things I did back."

"Like what?" Cassie asked.

He broke eye contact with her and stared over the top of her head. He said, "I'm going to miss that view of the mountain. Now all I can see is a bunch of burned trees."

She waited.

Finally, he said, "I'm not going to tell you everything but I'll give you one example."

"Okay."

"Cheyenne was a beauty growing up. If you met her you'd see what I mean. The boys buzzed around her like she was honey. And she didn't exactly discourage them."

Cassie saw no need to interject that she'd met Cheyenne and her effect on men was still the same.

Haak said, "There was a local kid named Steve Bishop. He was a big handsome kid, quarterback on the high school team. Anyone would tell you he was destined for great things. Montana State was looking at him for a football scholarship. His dad was a Lutheran pastor and they moved here from Oregon. The Bishops hadn't been here long enough to learn about the Kleinsassers and the hold they have on everything. Either that or Steve just didn't care. He liked Cheyenne and she liked him. Too much.

"Horst didn't like the way things were going. He didn't want anyone encroaching on his family, especially some dumb preacher's kid who'd likely want to get married. Horst didn't like Lutherans, either, which was some old German Hutterite thing. He didn't want them polluting his line, you know?

"Well," Haak said, still refusing to look at Cassie, "it turns out that Steve picks up a little extra money babysitting in town. I know it sounds crazy that a high school athlete babysits, but it was a different time and that's what was going on. And I find out he's babysitting the kids of one of the guys I'd hired temporarily out on the ranch. This guy was deep in debt and hurting for money. So I had a little talk with him."

Haak shifted uncomfortably and turned his head. He spoke softly and Cassie watched his lips carefully so she could pick up every word.

"So this nine-year-old girl says Steve Bishop exposed himself to her and asked her to put it in her mouth. Then the sheriff finds her panties in Steve's old car. It was a hell of a scandal. The pastor and his family picked up and moved."

He turned to Cassie. His face was haunted. "Situation resolved."

"Horst paid off the father of the girl?"

Haak nodded.

"They've been at this kind of thing a long time," she said.

"That they have. It's the main reason Cindy Lou left me. She didn't like the man I'd become. I don't blame her for it."

"Why are you telling me all of this?" Cassie asked.

"Because I see in you an instrument to bring them down even quicker," he said.

"Which brings us to Blake."

"I figured that's where this was headed," Haak said.

Although Blake was bright and accomplished, Haak told Cassie that he was a major disappointment to his father because his oldest son had little interest in the family's history, legacy, or staying on the ranch.

"I've never seen anything quite like it," Haak said. "Most parents I know would be proud as hell that their boy got all kinds of honors and awards. But not Horst. It just made him angry that Blake was able to accomplish all these things on his own. Horst thought Blake made him and the rest of the family look like second-class citizens, and I heard him say it more than once. Of course, Blake heard it, too, and it drove him even further away from the Kleinsasser clan.

"I remember Cindy Lou telling me she thought the Kleinsassers reminded her more of a cult than a family. She was right about that, and Blake wanted out."

Haak sighed. "I really did like that kid and he stayed over at our bunk shack with my guys quite a bit when he was growing up. I think he preferred the company of stinky hired cowboys to being with his own family. Horst knew it, too, and he was always asking me to tell him what Blake said about him and his mom. He wanted dirt on his own son."

"Did you tell him?"

"I probably would have because I wasn't a good man back then," Haak said. "But the fact is Blake kept that kind of thing to himself. Even then, he kept his own counsel. He knew he was headed out of here the first chance he got, so he didn't try to stir things up to make that more difficult than it had to be, you know?"

Haak shook his head. "Horst is just like his dad. He's mean and vindictive as hell. And the way he treated his kids—all those years, I looked the other way. I wish now I would have stepped in or called social services or something."

"He treated the other kids poorly?" Cassie asked.

"He turned them into dependents instead of independent people. Horst was so pissed off at his oldest son for going his own way that he drilled Cheyenne, John Wayne, and Rand on what he called the Kleinsasser way. Those kids grew up thinking they were some kind of entitled royalty in this valley and they would always be like that as long as their dad favored them. He made them hate Blake as much as he did. It's what bonded them all together: envy, resentment, and hate. No wonder that they all turned out to be monsters."

"Do you include Blake in that description?"

Haak hesitated. "No," he said. "Blake got out in time. But he's still screwed up. I spent some time with him this summer. I'll admit I told him some things I probably shouldn't have about his dad and the rest of them. None of it surprised him, though."

"Like what?"

"Blake didn't realize what a hold he has on the rest of them," Haak said. "He thought by going his own way they'd forget about him. But it was just the opposite. The more he did, the more he accomplished on his own, the more they resented him for it. So when he showed up here it was like lighting a fuse on a stick of dynamite. He never really got that."

"Do you think he was set up?" Cassie asked.

"No doubt in my mind," Haak said. "It was the same MO as what we did to Steve Bishop. Only this time, I think John Wayne and Rand were behind it all, along with the sheriff. They learned plenty from Horst before he had his stroke."

Cassie simply nodded.

"I can't prove any of that," Haak said.

"That's my job," Cassie said. Then she asked, "Where do Cheyenne and Margaret play in all of this? Do you think they bought into the Kleinsasser way to the same degree John Wayne and Rand did?"

"I could never really tell about Margaret," Haak said. "She didn't say much and I don't think she holds any sway over Horst or her sons. They just ignore her and I don't think they respect her at all. As for Cheyenne—who knows? She tried to make it on her own when she moved overseas and married that French guy. But she came back with her tail between her legs, so to speak. She's

headstrong, for sure, but I don't think the rest of them pay any attention to her."

"Even though she's the second oldest in the litter?" Cassie asked.

Haak shook his head. "It doesn't matter to them. After all, she
tried to get away. In the mind of the males, that revealed her weakness. She'll never get back in even though they let her live there."

"You've thought a lot about the Kleinsassers," Cassie said.

"I have. I spent years watching that slow-motion car wreck."

"So why did you leave the Iron Cross?"

Haak flinched. "John Wayne fired me after Horst became incapacitated. Twenty-six years and boom—I'm out the door."

"Did he say why?"

"He didn't need to. John Wayne never liked the fact that I got
along with his brother. As long as I was around I would remind
him of Blake. Plus, he wanted to clear the deck and consolidate
his power. Cheyenne's too flaky to be a threat to him and Rand
worships the ground he walks on. He really believes that Kleinsasser way shit. Especially now that Blake's out of the way.

"But there's another reason he fired me," Haak said.

Cassie urged him to go on.

"Have you ever heard of rare earth minerals?"

"No, I don't think so."

"I didn't know much about them until recently, either, but John
Wayne is convinced that the Iron Cross is sitting on tons of 'em.
He thinks he's going to get rich real soon."

"*What?*"

Haak labored to his feet and chinned toward his house. "Let
me show you something inside," he said.

Part V

Mother died today. Or maybe yesterday, I don't know.

—Albert Camus, *The Stranger*

Three generations of imbeciles are enough.

—Oliver Wendell Holmes, *Buck v. Bell*

twenty-six

⊷══◉══⊶

"It's called neodymium," Jody Haak told Cassie as he spread a sheaf of papers across his rough-hewn table. "It's a chemical element that's widely distributed across the globe but really rare to find in concentrated form."

Cassie looked at photos and graphics of the mineral on several printouts Haak had gathered. Neodymium was silver-white in color and displayed on the sheets in either powder or crystalline form.

"I'm no expert at all," he said, "But I've read a lot about it. Most of it in the world today is mined in China and it's used in the manufacture of all sorts of high-tech gadgets like lasers, computer hard disks, glass for high-tech lightbulbs—all sorts of things. Its big selling point is that it's used to make really powerful magnets for hybrid motors for cars—so it's increasing in price every year. It's gone as high as five hundred bucks per kilogram recently."

Cassie made the leap. "Horst and John Wayne think there are supplies of it on the Iron Cross Ranch."

"John Wayne does," Haak corrected. "I don't think Horst has any idea. Maybe Rand knows, but I doubt anyone else has a clue."

"Hold it," Cassie said. "I remember seeing a utility pickup coming out of the Iron Cross when I went there. It didn't quite fit because it was in a line of cattle haulers. But I remember it said 'REMR, Houston, Texas' on the door of the truck."

Haak nodded. "Real Earth Mineral Recovery. I looked them

up. John Wayne hired them to do survey work after Horst had his stroke, and I'd seen them sniffing around well before that. John Wayne has spent every nickel the ranch has on retaining REMR. They've already started filing environmental impact statements, from what I understand. And he's gotten a bunch of loans from his friendly bankers in town to do the preliminary work. He's deep into debt to them. I don't think the old man is even aware of what's going on."

Cassie sat back. If what Jody Haak told her was true, things were starting to fall into place.

"The Iron Cross Ranch has always just kind of limped along financially," Haak said. "I know that for a fact. It's damned hard to make money off of cows, and there is too much timber for growing much of anything. There were years when it all looked so bleak I thought Horst might have to sell pieces of it off or even get rid of the whole operation. The Kleinsassers have always gotten by by the skin of their teeth. But John Wayne thinks he's figured out a way to make himself a multimillionaire. He's banking everything on a neodymium mine located in the foothills of the mountains."

"What do you think?" Cassie asked. "Is he right?"

Haak nodded his head yes. "The mineral is there. It may not be in the quantities John Wayne is hoping for, but there's enough of it to create the biggest mine in North America. I know it to be true because I talked to an REMR employee about it one night in the Corvallis Tavern. He confirmed everything I've told you. Those guys are supposed to keep everything confidential, but it's surprising what a man will tell you if you're buying."

Cassie felt electrified. "Talk about motivation for getting Blake out of the picture," she said. "Did you tell Blake about it?"

"I didn't." Haak said. "I probably should have. That would have really made things interesting, wouldn't it? But you can see now why John Wayne and Rand didn't want to talk about selling or diversifying the ranch and all the other ideas Blake had. They just wanted him to go away."

"I know about the Kleinsasser Trust," Cassie said. "They wanted him not only to go away but to be ineligible to make decisions or share in the windfall. So, they settled on a plan that would trigger the moral turpitude clause."

"They were successful," Haak said. "But what John Wayne doesn't know is that he's basing everything on air."

Cassie cocked her head, not sure what Haak meant.

"That's why I came back," he said. "That's why I've been hanging around in the background. I want to be here when the Kleinsassers go down once and for all. I want to see it happen. That'll be the sweetest thing I've ever witnessed when it happens, and one of the best things that ever happened to Lochsa County."

"What are you talking about?" Cassie asked.

Haak sat down. His eyes were animated, as were his gestures. "I was with Horst twenty years ago in his office when he signed away his mineral rights."

"*What?*"

"It was a really bad year," Haak said. "Beef prices were in the toilet, and Horst had overextended himself paying bribes and payoffs to keep afloat. He couldn't see any way out of it so he took a meeting with some land men representing an energy company. Horst knew there was no coal or oil on the Iron Cross because he's had several surveys done. But the land men didn't know that and Horst didn't disclose the information. He signed away his surface and subsurface mineral rights for cash. I saw him sign the contract."

"*John Wayne doesn't know,*" Cassie whispered.

"No one does except me," Haak said. "Horst made me promise to keep my mouth shut. But he really gloated about that deal—how he'd duped the land men into paying him for nothing. He always thought it was one of the best deals he ever did."

"Who has the mineral rights?" Cassie asked.

"Some conglomerate," Haak said. "That energy company sold out to a bigger outfit, and that one sold to an international conglomerate. It's hard to keep track. But I do know that they'll show up to claim their rights as soon as the word gets out about the neodymium deposits. And there's nothing John Wayne can do about it. With the debt he's racked up on his bet, they'll probably take the ranch away from him as well."

"My God," Cassie said.

"I've got a ringside seat to watch the fall of the Kleinsasser way," Haak said. "Would you like to pull up a chair and watch it with me?"

"This is a lot to take in," Cassie said to Haak, pushing away from the table. "But it works in a sick way. John Wayne had his scheme going when Blake just showed up out of the blue. John Wayne *had* to take Blake off the table in a way that would remove him from the trust."

Haak agreed.

"But what I don't yet understand is why Cheyenne cooperated with the fake assault and why she brought her daughter along with her? Why would Cheyenne suddenly decide to help out John Wayne and Rand when she obviously despises them?"

Haak said, "I don't have a theory on that. It doesn't make sense. Maybe the brothers had something on the two of them?"

Cassie shook her head. "Cheyenne doesn't seem like the type to meekly go along. I don't know her daughter, but this just doesn't make sense to me."

"Here," Haak said, sliding the information on neodymium across the table to her. "Take this with you. I've got copies. Maybe you can speed things along when you show this to the lawyer you work for."

Cassie gathered up the paperwork. Her head was pounding. Her mouth was dry.

"Thank you for all of this," she said.

"My pleasure," he grinned. He gave Cassie the number to a

cell phone he rarely used. "Call me when it all goes down," he said. "I want to be there for it. I want to see the look on John Wayne's face."

"This *family* . . ." she said. She couldn't finish her thought.

"They need to go away for good," Haak said. "Are you going back to the ranch at some point?"

"I don't know," Cassie said. "I'm not sure I can get through the gate. It just happened to be open the last time."

Haak scratched out a series of numbers on a scrap of paper he'd torn from the documents. "Here," he said, handing her the scrap. "It's the key code for the front gate. They never changed it after I left."

"Remind me to never fire someone after twenty-six years of dedicated service," she said to Haak.

He laughed and slapped his knee.

As she stepped over the firebreak on the way to her car, the skid steer zoomed up behind her. Cassie paused and turned around.

Alf Grzegorczyk leaned out of the metal cage. "Sorry about what happened to your car," he said. "That wasn't me."

She acknowledged him with a curt nod.

"I don't know who did it for sure," he said. "But I think we both have our suspicions."

He seemed to be waiting for her to thank him, she thought. But thanking a man for arresting her for no reason and not driving her into the timber and putting a bullet into her head didn't sit well with her.

She turned and strode to her car.

Two miles down the road, her phone chimed with a series of texts and messages once she was back in cell phone range. They were all from Rachel.

When she had a strong signal Cassie speed-dialed Rachel's cell phone.

"You're alive!" Rachel answered. "I was starting to get really worried again."

"I'm more than alive," Cassie said. "I think the case has broken wide open."

"It absolutely has," Rachel said breathlessly. "How did you know?"

Cassie frowned. "How did I know what?"

"Franny recanted. I wasn't in the room with her two minutes before she said it was all a lie about the assault. She said her uncles put her up to it and she couldn't wait to tell someone."

"You're kidding," Cassie said.

"No. She agreed to give a new affidavit spelling it all out. She's coming into the office with her guardian ad litem tomorrow after school to do it."

Rachel went on to detail how the meeting had gone, how Franny had broken into hysterical tears and said how sorry she was for getting her uncle Blake into trouble.

"Why did she do it, then?" Cassie asked, suddenly filled with anger.

"She said John Wayne threatened to throw her and her mother out on the street if she didn't cooperate," Rachel said. "Franny said she did it to help out her mom."

"Do you believe her?"

"I don't know what to believe," Rachel said. "Franny does come across as quite the drama queen. But it's not my job to believe her or not. Let a judge or jury make that decision."

That grated on Cassie. "I thought you said we were doing this to discover the truth."

"We are," Rachel said, "but sometimes the truth is really complicated. We can only go on what we've got, and as of tomorrow we'll have a recantation of the assault taking place. Since you've got information to knock down the rest of their evidence, I think we're looking at an acquittal."

Cassie thought for a moment, then asked, "Who besides you knows about Franny's new statement?"

"Well, Jessica. Jessica was there with me. Oh, and Franny's guardian here in Bozeman."

"What do you know about the guardian?"

Rachel hesitated. "I don't know anything about her, really. Her name is Deb Rangold."

"Do a deep dive on her," Cassie said. "I can't do it myself at the moment. Find out everything you can about Deb Rangold and call me back."

"Why? I don't get it."

"Nothing in this investigation has turned out to be what it seems," Cassie said. "This whole social services thing seems fishy to me."

"I'll find out what I can," Rachel said. "Are you headed back now?"

"Not yet."

"*Cassie . . .*"

"I need to pay a visit to Cheyenne first."

twenty-seven

Cassie was within a half mile of the headquarters to the
Iron Cross Ranch when she realized she didn't know where Cheyenne's house was located. She'd never been there before, and no
one had pointed it out. The smoke was hanging so thick on the
valley floor she couldn't clearly see the layout of the grounds. She
wondered if the flames moving down from the mountains would
destroy the ranch before she could find Cheyenne.

As Haak had indicated, the key code he'd written out opened
up the entrance gates and she drove right through.

She parked out front and knocked on the heavy front door.
When there was no response, she tried the latch. It was unlocked.
She opened it a few inches and called inside. Silence.

This time, she didn't take off her boots. As she passed by an
ancient mirror she was shocked at her appearance: sunken, red-
rimmed eyes, dirt and soot-covered clothes, a tangle of hair,
muddy boots from traipsing around Jody Haak's property.

"Margaret?"

Cassie thought she heard a chair leg scrape linoleum down the
hallway in the direction of the dining room. She called out again.

"What do you want?" Margaret responded. Her voice was soft.

Cassie went down the hallway to find Margaret sitting at the
table with a cup of coffee in front of her. To her right, two spots
away, Horst slumped to the side in his wheelchair with his mouth
gaped and a string of saliva that strung from his bottom lip to his

left forearm. His eyes were open but opaque. He was gasping for air.

"Oh, dear. Do you want me to call 9-1-1?" Cassie asked.

"No need," Margaret said. "There's nothing they can do."

Cassie studied Margaret. She seemed oddly passive, even relieved. She seemed to be enjoying her coffee and the serenity of the silent room. She seemed younger than before, and lighter than air. Was she in shock?

"I think we forgot his medication this morning," Margaret said. Horst seemed to hear it and he emitted a low moan.

"It's his time," Margaret said. "We'll bury him up on the hill next to his father and his grandfather. They all like to be together. Other family members are buried farther down the hill."

Cassie wasn't sure what to make of that but the horror of the situation started to fill her up. She said, "We should probably call somebody. We can't just leave him here to suffer like this."

Margaret shrugged and sipped her coffee. "He's fairly quiet right now," she said. "No more of that horrible moaning. Can't you at least let me savor the moment?"

Cassie could hear a hundred-year-old clock tick in the next room. She asked, "Has it always been bad for you, or just since he had a stroke?"

"The stroke was a godsend," Margaret said calmly. She glanced over at Horst but he couldn't turn his head toward her. She was speaking for his benefit, and Cassie shuddered.

Margaret said, "It was like all of the pressure lifted off of my shoulders. I could just move him around the house to where I wanted him. I could feed him what *I* wanted to eat. I could leave him in the bathroom for hours with the door closed until he stopped bellowing, and he had no choice but to watch the television programs I favor. I could dress him in clothes he didn't like. For the last few months he's found out what it's like to be controlled by someone else."

Cassie shook her head. She had no words. Margaret's demeanor was absolutely calm.

Finally, Cassie was able to ask: "Can you please tell me where I can find Cheyenne?"

"Oh," Margaret said, "She's not here today. She went into town."

"Do you know where?"

"I never know where." She sighed.

"Thank you, Margaret. I'm leaving now. Are you sure you don't want me to call the sheriff or the ambulance?"

"Not now," she said. "Not yet."

Margaret turned to her husband and addressed him. "Horst, just sit there and be still. And don't give me that look, or I'll turn you toward the wall."

Horst's eyes widened and his lungs rattled out his last breath.

"There," Margaret said. "It's finally over."

Margaret closed her eyes and let out a deep sigh. A smile tugged at the corners of her mouth.

Cassie backed out of the room. She'd never seen anyone as cold-blooded.

The REMR pickup emerged from the bank of smoke as Cassie reached for the door latch of her rental car. It pulled into the ranch yard and parked next to her. She didn't know the driver, who was obviously an employee of the company, but she nodded at John Wayne in the passenger seat.

The windows of the pickup powered down but neither man got out.

"What are you doing back here?" John Wayne asked her. His face was dark with anger, but he seemed to be trying to keep his emotions in check from the REMR man.

"You need to go inside," Cassie said. "Your mother needs you right now."

John Wayne cocked his head, then dismissed Cassie's suggestion. "I asked you what you were doing here."

"I'm here to pay my respects to the Kleinsasser family," Cassie said after a beat. "It's over, John Wayne. I know everything."

His face twitched. The color drained out of it.

"What in the hell are you talking about?" he asked.

"I know about your mine," she said. "I know how you framed Blake. I know enough to put you into Deer Lodge prison for a very long time."

"You're crazy," he said. He forced a laugh for the sake of the REMR man who was now looking back and forth from John Wayne to Cassie as if watching a tennis match.

"You don't own the mineral rights," she said. "Somebody else is going to make all the money."

John Wayne reacted as if he'd been slapped. The REMR man looked over at him accusingly.

"I knew you were crazy," John Wayne said to Cassie. Then to the REMR man, "She's crazy. Don't listen to a word she says."

Cassie said, "We'll see. What did you have on Cheyenne and Franny to convince the girl to make up that story?"

"It wasn't a story," he said. "It was the truth. My brother did it."

Cassie shrugged. "I'm sick of talking to Kleinsassers."

"You don't know anything," John Wayne hissed.

"Where's Rand?" she asked before opening her car door. She gestured toward the house. "He might want to be here for this."

"He's on a run," John Wayne said. Then: "Be here for *what*?"

"Go inside."

With that, she swung into her Honda and backed out of the ranch yard. She hoped it was for the last time ever.

She drove to Lolo as darkness overtook the valley and the fires in the mountains zigzagged across the slopes.

★   ★   ★

Cheyenne was on the same stool in the Hayloft she'd been on when Cassie first met her. She sat alone within a cloud of cigarette smoke that was lit up pink from the neon beer signs behind the bar. When Cheyenne saw Cassie, she narrowed her eyes and raised her chin and blew out a long stream of smoke.

Cassie sat down next to her and ordered a cup of coffee from the bartender. Cheyenne ordered another bourbon on the rocks. Cassie could tell by the deliberate way Cheyenne spoke that she'd been drinking for hours.

Cheyenne lifted her glass. "To my lovely father," she said. "May he rest in peace."

"So you know."

Cheyenne nodded.

"Who told you?"

"Mother called."

Cassie was surprised. "When I left I told her I thought she should call someone."

"*Moi*," Cheyenne said.

"You seem okay with the news."

"I'm more than okay. I'm ecstatic, can't you tell?"

Cassie looked Cheyenne over. She looked put-together and dangerous at the same time.

"I'm leaving now," Cassie said.

"It's about time."

"But before I do, tell me about Franny," Cassie said. "And this time try to stay cool."

A whisper of a smile floated across Cheyenne's mouth. "Give me your phone."

"Why?"

"I don't want a record of what I'm about to tell you."

Cassie had not activated the recording app on her phone so she passed it over. Cheyenne powered it off and placed it facedown on the counter. She asked, "What do you want to know?"

"Why is she in Bozeman under another name?"

"We thought it best. She might have wilted under the pressure around here. It was best for everyone that she try to live a normal life."

"Until she had to testify," Cassie said.

Cheyenne turned to Cassie and bent close to her. "She was never going to testify. She was always going to recant when the time was right."

Cassie froze for a moment. "You knew it was a false accusation."

"Of course I did. Anything John Wayne came up with was bound to be idiotic. He's really not very smart, you know."

"Why go along with it, then? I thought you got along with Blake."

"I do," Cheyenne said. "Or I should say I did. But getting him out of the trust wasn't personal. It was a business decision I made for me and my daughter. Blake has all the money in the world as it is."

That took Cassie a moment to process. Then she said, "You knew Horst didn't have long to live, so you set them all up: Blake, John Wayne, and Rand. You let it happen so all of them would be kicked out of the trust by a judge. But how can you expect to be the last one standing?"

She shrugged. "I have John Wayne on tape laying out the whole scheme to me. I have him making Franny repeat the story over and over until she had it right. I even have that idiot Wagy telling me not to worry—that he was fully on board and he could make it happen the way John Wayne dreamed it up. I recorded everything on my cell phone and I never said a word the whole time. There's nothing in those recordings that would implicate me, and it certainly *sounds* like those dumb-asses are threatening us to do what they want."

Cassie felt blindsided. She tried to get her bearings. "So, it was for control of the ranch? For the money?"

"Partly," Cheyenne said. "Not all."

"Then why?"

Cheyenne drained her drink and lifted a painted finger to signal for another. The bartender scrambled to accommodate her.

"You have no idea what it's like to be a female in that family," Cheyenne said. "It's been going on for over a hundred years and it wasn't going to change. My grandmother was abused. My mother was abused. *I* was abused. It was a matter of time before one of her uncles cornered Franny. It was a family tradition."

Cassie recoiled.

"We figured it was time to blast the men out."

"We?"

"Mom, me, and Franny."

"Your mother was in on it?"

"Not that it could ever be proven. But when Franny agreed, I knew we were set."

Cassie leaned back. She didn't want to be any closer to Cheyenne than she had to be.

"You're more depraved than I thought possible," she said.

Cheyenne smiled. "I came from toxic stock. It's in my blood."

Before Cassie could reply, Cheyenne said, "I didn't know they'd hurt Blake so badly in prison. They were just supposed to rough him up a little and help convince him to go back to New York when he could. I thought I could cut a deal with Blake when he was acquitted. He could go back east and I'd stay just long enough to sell the ranch to the mineral people or whoever wanted it. That would be enough for Mom, Franny, and me. The men would be blasted out for good."

"My God," Cassie said.

"Not everything worked to perfection," Cheyenne said. "John Wayne is stupid but he's conniving. He didn't fully trust Franny so he had a friend of his in Bozeman serve as her guardian. They went to high school together. When I found out I warned Franny to just keep playing her role so the guardian wouldn't get wise to it. From what Franny told me today it worked perfectly. Deb Rangold didn't know that Franny was going to recant until it happened."

Cassie said, "Is Franny in danger? Are you worried that Deb Rangold might harm her?"

"No, not at all. Deb is a snitch but she isn't a criminal. She's probably snitched to John Wayne already, and I can only imagine what kind of state he must be in right now. But he wouldn't harm Franny directly. John Wayne is at his core a coward. He manipulates others to do his dirty work. He'd never do it himself."

"You've got it all figured out," Cassie said with sarcasm.

"Yes, I do. But I didn't know everything. I didn't know what role you would play in all of this," she said, clinking her bourbon glass against Cassie's coffee cup. "You really moved things along. I could just sit here and watch it all unravel all around me. It happened much faster than I thought it would."

Cheyenne took a long pull from her fresh drink. "I wish I could see John Wayne right now. His entire twisted world is falling apart, and he can't even get advice from his daddy."

"Do you know about the mineral rights?" Cassie asked.

Cheyenne nodded. "I met a man from REMR who sat where you're sitting now. It might not surprise you to find out that he told me all kinds of things that night."

"I'm not surprised."

Cheyenne made a "what are you going to do" gesture with her hands.

She said, "REMR isn't loyal to John Wayne. They're loyal to rare earth mineral deposits. They don't care who owns them."

"You and Franny may not walk," Cassie said. "I may not have a recording of your confession, but I'm duty bound to report it."

"We'll walk," Cheyenne said. "There's not enough there. No one is going to prosecute a fifteen-year-old girl who was pressured and threatened by her uncle."

Cassie knew she was probably right. "I need my phone back."

Cheyenne handed it to her.

"It was a pleasure to meet you, Cassie Dewell."

"I can't say the same."

Cheyenne tilted her head back and laughed at that. "I'll bet you can't wait to get out of Lochsa County."

"You're right about that."

Two DCI agents from Helena were waiting in their sedan next to Cassie's Honda. They got out, badged her, and asked if she had time to tell her story.

Cassie sighed and asked if they had all night.

It was dawn by the time she signed her statement and drove out of Lolo. She had a tremendous headache from talking all night. The sense of relief she felt when she crossed the Lochsa County line again was palpable.

The DCI agents had asked if she wanted to be there when they picked up Sheriff Wagy and John Wayne for questioning. She'd replied that she never wanted to see either one of them again although she knew she'd have to when she testified against them in court.

She couldn't wait to see Ben. And she couldn't wait to see her mother. Cassie craved some kind of normalcy.

The things she'd learned and conveyed within the last twenty-four hours were a jumble in her head, although she was proud of herself for being able to communicate a coherent time line of what she'd learned and what she'd been through to the DCI agents.

Still, though, something was missing. She wished she could define what was bothering her.

Then she remembered what John Wayne had said when she asked about Rand. He'd said, "He's making a run."

Making a run?

Then it hit her.

Cassie was grateful and very surprised when Jody Haak answered his cell phone. She knew he must be somewhere other than at his place since she knew he didn't have service up the county road.

"It's happening," he said as a greeting. His tone was giddy. "My sources in town say the state cops are on their way to talk to John Wayne as we speak. They've already informed our sheriff that they've opened an investigation on him and his office."

"I know about that," Cassie said. "I have another question for you."

"Shoot."

"What does Rand do for a living?"

"You mean besides harassing tourists and laying around the Iron Cross?"

"Yes."

"He works freelance as a truck driver," Haak said. "He makes a couple of runs a week between Horston and Billings."

Cassie sat up straight and nearly drove off the road.

"He drives an eighteen-wheeler?"

"Yes, he does."

"Have you seen it?"

"If he still has the same rig I've seen it dozens of times," Haak said.

"Is it a black Peterbilt cab? Smoked windows? No chrome?"

"That sounds like it," Haak said.

"Anyone driving from Horston to Billings would go through Bozeman four times a week," Cassie said.

"I guess," Haak said.

She disconnected before saying goodbye. Then she woke up Rachel.

twenty-eight

---◆══◎══◆---

The driver, Rand Kleinsasser, sat high in his cab while the diesel engine idled. He'd parked once again on a residential street where he could have a good view of the grounds of Bozeman High School through his windshield. He watched as students entered the school that morning for their first period classes.

He narrowed his eyes when he saw Franny. She was within a knot of students but she was not of them. There seemed to be an invisible bubble around her that she floated in despite the other students streaming the same direction. There was no interaction with any of the other kids and she clutched her books to her chest as if wielding a shield. For a very brief moment, he felt for her. He understood what it was like to be an other. But that quickly passed.

He noted that she'd changed her look, all right. Her hair was shorter and darker, she wore more conservative clothing than he recalled, and she'd affected an awkward gait to her walk.

But it was her.

And it had been Franny on the street that day and now he was sure of it. Unfortunately, that damned boy she was with had pulled her out of the way at the last moment. But it was her.

Rand knew that she'd be going to her AP English class to start the day. Deb Rangold had outlined her schedule to John Wayne months before. The classroom was located less than seventy-five yards from the library and his cache of weapons.

★ ★ ★

Watching the students enter the building brought back unhappy memories for Rand. It all came rushing back once again, and he squirmed.

After he'd been expelled from Horston High for fighting, and despite his father's anger and threats to the Lochsa County school board, Rand had ended up in Bozeman all those years ago, where he attended Bozeman High his senior year. God, how he'd hated it.

They didn't know him there, and they didn't know that his name meant something. He'd been bullied and beaten when he tried to stand up for himself, and the girls looked down their noses at him when he tried to explain that back home he was somebody special.

He could remember the day outside the auto shop when he'd told a couple of his friends that someday he'd come back.

That someday they'd all know his name.

That day had come.

Rand had never trusted Franny. She was too precious and too clever, too much like her mother. Even though John Wayne assured him that he had everything under control—that Blake would go down with Cheyenne's and Franny's participation—Rand had his doubts.

Wouldn't it be better, he'd said to John Wayne, if something just happened to her before the trial? Something completely unrelated to the assault?

That way, he'd explained to his brother, her affidavit would stand there forever and be used to convict Blake. Franny couldn't screw up her story on the stand or change it.

Cheyenne might be a problem, but Cheyenne was always a

problem. She was born a problem. But Franny's last statement—
before she was gone—would stand like a monument.

Rand had reminded John Wayne about his suspicions—and his
solution—when his brother had called him hours before in a panic.
Rand was leaving Billings in his rig, bound for Horston with a load
of drywall for the lumber store. He'd just delivered pallets of rough-
cut logs from the Lochsa Valley, like they did twice a week.

Deb Rangold, John Wayne said, told him Franny planned to
recant later that day at a lawyer's office.

"I fucking told you this would happen," Rand had said.

"What good does that do now?" John Wayne asked.

"Don't worry about it," Rand had said. "I've got it handled."

And he did. He was just waiting for the bell to go off to begin
the school day.

Rand watched as a few stragglers ran across the lawn toward
the front doors. Most of them made it inside before the bell went
off. A couple didn't.

He wondered how many of the individual students he'd seen
would come out of the building feet first.

There was a moment of panic before Rand traded his cowboy hat
for a black balaclava and got out of his cab. Out of the corner of
his eye he saw a Bozeman police department cruiser flash through
an opening in some tree trunks headed toward the west side of the
high school. It was moving fast, he thought.

But then he lost sight of the cruiser, and he didn't see additional cops. The morning was quiet, and there were no sirens.

He figured the cop had chased down a speeding student trying to get to school on time. It was out of view on the opposite
side of the big brick building.

Rand left the truck running. He climbed down and stuffed the
balaclava in his front jeans pocket. There was no reason to put it

on his head and risk drawing attention to himself. People were jumpy around schools these days.

He planned to leave his .22 pistol in the console of his truck, but at the last minute he snatched it out and slid it muzzle-down into his back waistband.

He crossed the lawn and didn't rush it. Like that night, he moved from tree to tree toward the back of the school. Rand could be a maintenance worker or a cafeteria employee out on his break.

At one point he glanced back at his rig. He wished it didn't look so beaten up. The black steel cowcatcher on the front of the grille was mangled, and the grille itself was smashed in. Both head-lights needed to be replaced. He thought that if someone saw his truck sitting there they'd reason that it was out of commission and waiting for repair.

That's what happened, he thought, when you drove your truck through a motel.

As he worked his way down the side of the building toward the auto shop, Rand envisioned once again how it would go when he got inside. He'd gone over it in his mind a dozen times, but now that it was here he needed to concentrate. Which was hard. He'd always had a problem with that.

It was highly unlikely that a class would be in session in the auto shop. He recalled that vocational classes didn't start until later in the day. He assumed they maintained the same schedule. But if there were students in the auto shop for first-period class he was going to walk right past them with the mask over his face. He wouldn't threaten them or say a word. He'd just walk right by them as if he owned the place and leave them guessing. High school stu-dents weren't all that sharp first thing in the morning, especially auto shop losers like he'd been.

Then Rand would stride down the hallway toward the library without looking right or left. He'd pull down his cache of weapons and go straight to the AP English classroom and close the door behind him.

Franny wouldn't be the first to go. That would be too obvious. He'd start with the teacher and whatever targets made themselves available. Franny would be in the middle or toward the end. That way, no one would ever suspect that he was there specifically for her.

Because he wasn't. He was back for revenge. Franny was simply the vehicle to get him there.

Rand was crazy, but he wasn't stupid. He knew the in-school cops might come after him. In a perfect world, they would. They'd take him out before he ran out an emergency door and drove away in his truck.

But it wasn't a perfect world. He'd read about other school shootings. He knew that there was just as much chance that the school security officers would cower outside waiting for backup, or hide in a closet once the shooting started.

Rand paused at the corner of the building and poked his head around it. As he'd surmised, the security camera he'd disabled was still hanging limp from its mount. They hadn't even removed it yet.

Did he know how things worked in a state-run system, or what?

He fished the mask out of his pocket and pulled it over his head. He looked over his shoulder and out on the street. A car passed by but the woman driving it didn't even turn her head toward him.

The garage door shivered when he yanked on it and he could feel the latches give way. He took a deep breath and pulled up on the door and it sounded like thunder as it rolled up.

There were no students in the class, as he'd thought. Unfortu-

nately, there were four black-clad SWAT cops wearing helmets and
tactical gear and leveling automatic weapons at him. They took
cover between two older-model cars inside and aimed at him over
the hoods and trunks.

One of them screamed at him to get down on his belly.

To hell with that, Rand thought. Instead, he reached behind his
back for his pistol. Who were they to tell *him* what to do?

It was the last thought Rand Kleinsasser ever had.

twenty-nine

❖━━◦◦━━❖

Six weeks later, Cassie Dewell and Rachel Mitchell sat next to each other at the funeral of Blake Kleinsasser at Jenkins Funeral and Cremation Service in Bozeman. The ceremony took place in the smallest room in the facility because there were fewer than ten people in attendance. Blake's urn had been placed on a faux-granite column at the front of the room.

He'd died of his injuries five days before without ever regaining consciousness.

The funeral director had given a generic eulogy and no one had volunteered to say anything afterward.

The front row of seats was empty, but in the second row sat Jody Haak and Lindy Glode on opposite ends of the aisle. They'd arrived separately. Cassie and Rachel sat in the third row behind them.

Three of Blake's New York business associates were across the aisle. They'd introduced themselves but they spoke so quickly in their East Coast cadence that Cassie couldn't recall their names.

Margaret, Cheyenne, and Franny sat in the last row. They'd arrived late and Cassie noticed that Margaret looked vibrant and ten years younger than when she'd last seen her. She nodded at Cassie as if sharing a secret and then looked away.

Cassie was startled by Franny's appearance. She was dressed in funky clothing and she had a sexy, sophisticated haircut. She didn't look Cassie's way.

Cheyenne saw Cassie's obvious puzzlement and winked at her. "My God," Cassie shuddered.

Cassie couldn't help noticing that the girl looked like a wholly different person than she had that day at the school, when Cassie arrived to find Rand's dead body sprawled out near the open auto shop garage door. At that time, Franny appeared frail and shaken. She knew what had almost happened to her, and she knew why.

Cassie had explained to her at the time that through Rachel the Bozeman PD had been on the lookout for Rand and his damaged tractor-trailer. When it was spotted on a side street near Bozeman High School, the SWAT team was dispatched inside. Their plan, until Rand decided to get out and walk into the building itself, was to lock down the school and then isolate and arrest him outside. Rand had literally walked into them as they were assembling.

"It was death by cop," Cassie had said to Franny. "Rand made the choice himself."

"That sounds like him," Franny had said.

Cassie had taken Franny in her arms and comforted her. She'd sat with her when Franny gave her statement to the police identifying her uncle and confirming that she'd lied under pressure. The authorities had treated her with kid gloves, and so had Cassie.

John Wayne Kleinsasser was in the Missoula County Jail awaiting his criminal trial. The judge had agreed with state prosecutors that he shouldn't be housed in Lochsa County because of the very real chance that an associate might *accidentally* release him.

Sheriff Ben Wagy was suspended without pay from the Lochsa County Commissioners awaiting the conclusion of the DCI investigation into his department.

Both had been implicated by recordings that appeared on social media of them discussing how to frame Blake for rape and kidnapping. No one had claimed credit for posting the dialogue, but experts had determined that the recordings were authentic.

Prosecutors had dropped the charges against Blake Kleinsasser but he never knew it. Rachel was delicately attempting to receive legal fees for her work defending him from his estate once it was settled in probate court in New York State.

The Iron Cross Ranch was in the process of being sold to a Canadian land development company who'd already made an agreement with REMR and the conglomerate that owned the mineral rights to build a rare earth mine on the property.

Cheyenne was the sole beneficiary of the ranch sale, and rumors were circulating about the massive nine-bedroom home she was building at the confluence of the Lochsa and Bitterroot rivers.

The funeral ceremony didn't so much end as fade away, and Cassie looked up to find it was over. She turned her head to see Cheyenne ushering Franny and Margaret toward the back door.

"They're leaving," Cassie said to Rachel. "I'll catch up with you in a minute."

"Cassie," Rachel said, reaching out for her hand, "let it go."

"I can't."

The Kleinsasser women were almost to their new black SUV when Cassie caught up with them.

"Excuse me," she said.

Cheyenne turned and looked at her and her eyes narrowed. She proceeded to help Margaret into the passenger seat and then closed her door and turned around.

Franny stood off to the side. She seemed cold and detached although slightly taller than Cassie recalled. That was because she was no longer slouching. She looked at Cassie as if Cassie was some-one she'd long ago left behind in another world.

"Yes?" Cheyenne said impatiently.

"They'll eventually catch you both," Cassie said. "I just want you to know that."

"We'll see," Cheyenne said with a smile. "But I wouldn't bet on it."

"I told the DCI agents everything. They know about you."

"I know you did," Cheyenne said. "I sat down with them for an interview. They didn't have much except your version of events and they never will. I'm quite good in those kinds of situations," she said, slyly batting her eyes and faux-fanning herself with her fingers.

Cassie said to Franny, "You broke Ben's heart. You do know that, right?"

Franny shrugged. "He's a nice boy, I guess. You should be proud of the way you raised him."

"I am. He saved your life."

Franny nodded her agreement. "He did, and so did you. I'll keep you both in my thoughts."

Cassie felt her anger rise. "You say that as if being in your thoughts is reward enough."

"What do you want?" Cheyenne interrupted. "Money?"

"No. I'm not like you. I'm just trying to figure out what Ben saw in her."

Franny chuckled. She said, "That wasn't me. That was Erin Reese. Erin was," Franny hesitated, "fun to play. She was a lot more fun than 'traumatized Franny Porché'"

Franny lifted her chin. "This is the real me."

Cassie stared at Cheyenne and Franny and shook her head in disgust. An acid taste filled her mouth.

"Don't mind her," Cheyenne said, placing her hand on Cassie's shoulder. "We move on and adapt."

"It's the Kleinsasser way," Cassie said bitterly.

"That it is," Cheyenne said. She nodded for Franny to get in, then left Cassie and walked around the front of the car to get behind the wheel.

"Take care," she said. "If I were you I'd stay out of Lochsa County."

Acknowledgments

The author would like to sincerely thank those who helped in the research and narrative of this book, including Butch and Dana Preston of Montana, two wonderful long-haul truck drivers, for technical assistance and the staff of Chapter One Bookstore in Hamilton for area support in Montana.

My invaluable first readers were Laurie Box, Becky Reif, Molly Box, and Roxanne Woods. Thanks again.

Kudos to Molly and Prairie Sage Creative for cjbox.net for social media expertise and Becky Reif for legal advice and terminology.

It's a sincere pleasure to work with the professionals at St. Martin's Minotaur, including the fantastic Jennifer Enderlin, Andy Martin, and Hector DeJean.

Ann Rittenberg—thanks for always being in our corner.

C. J. Box is the author of thirty books, including the Joe Pickett series and the Cassie Dewell series, and a story collection. His books have been translated into twenty-seven languages. He has won the Edgar, Anthony, Macavity, Gumshoe, and Barry Awards, as well as the French Prix Calibre .38, and has been a Los Angeles Times Book Prize finalist. A Wyoming native, Box has also worked on a ranch and as a small-town newspaper reporter and editor. He's an executive producer of ABC TV's *Big Sky,* which is based on his Cody Hoyt/Cassie Dewell novels, as well as executive producer of the Joe Pickett television series for Spectrum Originals. He lives with his wife on their ranch in Wyoming.